Expeditionary Force
Book 9:

VALKYRIE

By
Craig Alanson

Contact the author
craigalanson@gmail.com

Cover Design By
Alexandre Rito

Table of Contents

CHAPTER ONE

The ominous, watchful silence of the Koprahdru star system was shattered by twin gamma ray bursts, as a pair of Maxolhx destroyers in tight formation jumped in four lightminutes from the only inhabited planet. That world was a lifeless rock slightly smaller than Mars, and orbiting the local star so closely that the surface facing the local star was hot enough to melt soft metals. No one *wanted* to live on that scorched planet, the three hundred residents were there to conduct scientific research directed at the variable star, or to support those scientists, or they were families of the personnel unlucky to draw that assignment. Only sixteen of the scientists actually were excited to be there, as it was the best place in Bosphuraq territory to study whatever nerdy thing was their specialty.

Until recently, the research facility in the Koprahdru system was isolated, dull and in general suffered from low morale, but it was not dangerous. The habitation modules were buried deep in stable bedrock, safe from even the periodic eruptions of the star. Safe, unless an eruption was spectacularly violent, and unfortunately not predicted by the team of people whose careers were focused on understanding and predicting the fluctuations of variable stars. In that case, the facility would be in grave danger, and the scientists would have time to be extremely excited, before they died as the habitation facilities were crushed by heaving bedrock.

But that was very unlikely to happen.

An attack on the isolated and unimportant facility also was considered very unlikely until recently, especially an attack by the patrons of the Bosphuraq. Maybe the Jeraptha, Thuranin or other species of equivalent technology might, if they had literally *nothing* else to do, be interested in disrupting the basic research done there. The Maxolhx could have no conceivable reason to be interested in whatever boring things went on in the Koprahdru system.

Until the inconceivable happened.

Until the clients of the haughty Maxolhx posed a credible threat to their patrons.

The residents of the research facility had been fearfully watching the skies, ever since a passing star carrier dropped off a courier drone that raced by the planet to deliver the shocking and very bad news. A rogue group of Bosphuraq had apparently mastered technology beyond the capability of even the Maxolhx, then used that technology to attack a pair of their patrons' starships. Perhaps even more shocking, another mysterious group of Bosphuraq had ratted out the rogue researchers, informing the Maxolhx of the unbelievable truth, in the hope that cooperation would be rewarded with leniency.

A foolish hope.

The Maxolhx had predictably, inevitably, almost automatically reacted to the threat by bombarding a long string of Bosphuraq military and research facilities, whether those facilities had any possible relation to the rogue group, or to the banned technology. What mattered to the Maxolhx was that they be seen as mercilessly *punishing* their traitorous clients. How and where that punishment was targeted was of little importance. In fact, if the Maxolhx were seen as callously and even deliberately targeting the innocent, that would make other potentially rebellious clients reconsider.

So, the support personnel, spouses and children of the scientists in the Koprahdru system were not seen as collateral damage, their deaths would instead be a satisfying bonus.

The pair of destroyers could have jumped into orbit close to the planet and launched an almost immediate attack, using a series of railgun darts to punch down to the bedrock, then dropping atomic-compression warheads down the hole to kill everyone below the surface. They had instead jumped in far away, so their slow approach would instill helpless terror in their powerless clients. The attack was conducted in a manner that might be described as casual, with no hurry to launch weapons, and no objective other than complete destruction. Actually, both destroyers had recently been pulled from storage as long-term reserves, and their crews were still working up to the required level of proficiency. That pair of ships had been dropped off by their mother star carrier simply because the task group commander felt those destroyers needed to see action, and Koprahdru was an easy target.

The destroyer crews treated the attack as a routine exercise, conducting only a brief sensor sweep of space around the planet, before selecting targets for their weapons.

If the sensor sweep had been more thorough, perhaps they might have detected that space around the planet was saturated with tiny microwormholes.

"And we are '*Go*'." Simms announced in a flatly calm tone from her station on *Valkyrie*'s bridge. "In five, four-"

From my command chair, which unlike in Star Trek, was positioned off to the right side so I could observe all the duty stations without blocking anyone's view of the holographic display sphere in the front, I tried to project a calm confidence. My mannerisms were modeled on James T. Kirk, as best I could. I had done The Lean, where I tilted my upper body to one side, elbow on an armrest, chin in one hand, eye narrowed, considering what bad-ass thing I would do next. Or the Crossed Leg casual stance in the chair, being as cool as I could be. Also the Chin Lift, thoughtfully staring down my nose at the display, in full command of the crew and situation.

Currently, instead of a cool Kirk move, I was doing my trademarked Joe Bishop Flop Sweat. My back was again stuck to my shirt, and rather than being still and calm, my fingers were drumming on the console of the armrest. Worried that I might accidentally launch a missile, I forced my fingers to drape over the side of the console.

Why was Jim Kirk cool under pressure and I was not? Because he relieved stress by doing the wild thing with hot babes across the galaxy, and I was not doing that.

That's my story and I'm sticking to it.

We had finished running the last attack scenario three days before the planned H-Hour, then I ordered a full day of downtime for the crews of both ships. We brought *Valkyrie* close to the *Flying Dutchman*, so dropships could shuttle people back and forth, to get a change of scenery and visit friends. If some of those visits were conjugal in nature, that was none of my business, but it was certainly good for morale.

I spent part of that off day playing, and losing, at video games.

My life sucks.

Anyway, by H-Hour we were as ready as we could be, so I told Simms to give the order.

Skippy took up the count from Simms. "Three, two, one, *showtime!*"

Our massive battlecruiser jumped within twenty nine kilometers of the destroyer formation. Theoretically, a jump that close was impossible, because of a field projected by the enemy ships that was supposed to prevent inbound jump wormholes from forming. In the Roach Motel, we had torn apart a Maxolhx ship by jumping a dropship right on top of it, a feat only the awesomeness of Skippy could accomplish. Back then, the difficulty had been merely that the mass of the enemy ship caused our jump wormhole endpoint naturally to slide away from the ship, so Skippy had to compensate as only he could. In our attack against the pair of destroyers at Koprahdru, we also had to contend with an energy field that disrupted the formation of an inbound jump wormhole. That technology was a major advantage possessed by the Maxolhx, who had copied the technology from the Rindhalu, and unlike most stolen technology, the Maxolhx version worked better than the original. Skippy thought the Rindhalu were simply too lazy to develop their own technology any further, because they didn't need to. Lesser species like the Esselgin had also tried, without much success, to copy that tech.

Anyway, even the awesomeness of Skippy had limits. If that Maxolhx ship in the Roach Motel had that type of disruption field technology active, we would not have been able to blow it up. In our attack on the pair of destroyers, twenty nine kilometers was the closest Skippy could manage without damaging our jump drive.

In space combat, twenty nine klicks is *close*. Twenty-nine kilometers left no time between the Maxolhx detecting our inbound jump and our railgun darts slamming into their shields. Leading each volley of darts were particle beams searing the same area of enemy shields, and right behind each dart was a missile. In our first two volleys, the missiles were loaded with warheads designed to send a surge of energy back along the enemy defense shield, to overload the generators. Through his awesomeness, Skippy was able to adjust the action of each missile warhead in real-time, so its individual surge would cause maximum overload at the time the surge reached a particular generator.

The crews of the destroyers had to be wondering what the *hell* was going on. One of their own ships jumped in, at a distance so close as to be impossible, and commenced hammering them with a precision that could only be accomplished if the weapons had extremely accurate targeting data programmed in *before* the jump. Which was also impossible. Our railgun darts hit so soon after our jump, that it was clear we had begun sending the darts down their launch rails before we emerged from jump.

Which, again, was impossible.

Yet, it was *not* impossible, because the hulls of those destroyers were shot clean through by our third volley of darts, and missiles then tore through the holes created by the darts. The missiles in the third volley had been loaded with warheads that could decide whether to continue weakening the enemy shields, or switch to explosive fragmentation mode.

All but one warhead chose wisely.

The enemy were also smart, and reacted with impressive speed. Seeing they were faced with overwhelming firepower, with their shield generators screaming warnings of impending overloads, and unable to jump away because of the damping field projected by *Valkyrie*, their ships automatically vented reactor plasma and ejected stored jump drive energy. Maxolhx ships did not use crude capacitors to store jump energy, but the technology they used created the same vulnerability; one hit to that stored energy could tear apart the ship.

Instantly, both ships were hidden by a fog of superheated reactor plasma, and the harsh arced lightning of released jump drive potential energy. That fog would have confused our targeting sensors, except our third volley of missiles were already inside the hulls of those ships.

Which, in case you are not keeping up with current events, was not a good thing for the two target destroyers.

Our chief pilot 'Fireball' Reed didn't wait for an engraved invitation to jump us away before the enemy ships blew up or wrapped a damping field around us. The enemy also had weapons, and our shields were being rocked by their return fire of masers, particle beams, railgun darts and more exotic directed-energy devices. Enemy missiles had not reached us yet, with our defensive cannons taking credit for knocking out most of the inbound weapons.

Reed did not need to *do* anything. Before we commenced the attack, we had programmed the drive to automatically perform a jump away shortly after we launched our third volley. Skippy had calculated that at point-blank range, three volleys was all that would be needed. All Reed had to do was keep her index finger hovered over but not pressing the override button, and the navigation system did the rest. Because the nav system had not received an order to override, our jump drive opened a somewhat ragged hole in spacetime and pulled us away. The jump wormhole was untidy due to the effect of damping fields beginning to be projected by the pair of enemy ships, fields which fortunately had not reached strength sufficient to prevent us from disappearing, an instant before the enemy ships were ripped apart by multiple explosions.

Going into our first real fight with our new stolen battlecruiser, we were confident.

Still, the battle was two ships against one. The destroyers were equipped with the same suite of missiles that were carried in *Valkyrie*'s magazines. Our battlecruiser had more missiles and more launchers, but that didn't matter in a brief fight. Each destroyer had maser and particle cannons of nearly the same power rating as we had, we just had more of them. Between the two enemy ships, they could throw about thirty percent of the destructive energy at us, as we could throw at them. They only needed to cripple us, while we needed to blow both of them into dust.

There are two major differences between a destroyer and a battlecruiser. We carried a greater load of weapons; more missiles, more cannons, more railguns. Again, in a short fight like we planned, having more weapons doesn't always mean you can use them. Some of our cannons were on the other side of our ship, so they were effectively useless to us. Missiles stuffed into magazines deep within the hull could not be used until they were transported out to the launchers, and that took time we didn't have. No, the greater weapons load didn't mean much in our fight. What did matter was the second major difference between a destroyer and a battlecruiser: our much more powerful armor and defensive shields. With the upgrades Skippy had performed to our already robust shield projectors, *Valkyrie* could stand toe to toe with a destroyer, even a pair of destroyers, and absorb hits while hitting back. By comparison, destroyers were thinly-protected, relying on speed and numbers to make up for what they lacked in armor and shields.

If the enemy had been expecting us, it might have been a fair fight.

It was *not* a fair fight.

In the Army, I learned that if you are going into a fair fight, you need to rethink your tactics.

Screw fairness.

I didn't want the enemy to have a decent chance to hit back. I wanted them to *die*.

So, there were other advantages we planned. We had jumped in long before H-Hour, engaged our enhanced stealth field, and Skippy scattered microwormholes around the planet. We knew the day and time the enemy planned to attack, within about six hours, so we got there well ahead of time and set our trap. We had the advantage of a heavy ship, well-protected by defenses upgraded by Skippy. We had microwormholes that provided super-accurate targeting data, right up to the moment we jumped in and Skippy's connection to the microwormholes was severed. We had trained hard to prepare for every possibility. We had complete surprise. Most importantly, we had the incomparable awesomeness of Skippy the Magnificent.

Yes, I gag a little bit every time I say that.

During the fight, which lasted less than twelve seconds from jumping in to jumping away, I held my breath. My fear had been that Karma or the Universe or whatever would use the battle as a prime opportunity to cash in its chips and smack me down. Whether good or bad, Karma had decided to wait, savoring the thought of hitting me at an even worse time.

Anyway, we survived.

We had jumped away only seventy-three lightseconds from the battlespace, so it didn't take long for photons from the fight to reach us.

Let me tell you, no matter how many times I engage in space combat, it never ceases to be weird. The photons that reached us, showed *us*. They showed *Valkyrie*, seventy-three seconds back in time, jumping in with a tight burst of gamma rays and launching weapons even before the outline of the ship was fully visible. If I had been standing on the outside of the ship during the attack, I would now be seeing my past self.

Like I said, weird.

Also like I said, our ship was fully visible.

We had not engaged a stealth field.

We *wanted* the Maxolhx to see who was hitting them. We also wanted the Bosphuraq on the planet to see who had wiped out a pair of their patrons' warships.

We wanted the Maxolhx to know what had happened, and to be afraid, very afraid. The entire galaxy had been living in fear of the Maxolhx, it was time for them to get a dose of their own medicine.

As the light of the exploding destroyers reached us, confirming the battle had been a one-sided success, I lifted an angry middle finger at the holographic display. "That," I whispered to myself as my finger shook with emotion, "was for Margaret Adams, you *MFers*."

Our first attack on the Maxolhx was a total victory, confirming Skippy's boast that we had the single most bad-ass warship in the galaxy. Our victory had not just happened by happy accident, it was the result of hard work and a lot of failures along the way.

I'd better start at the beginning.

CHAPTER TWO

After we trapped a Maxolhx reinforced battlegroup outside the galaxy, then faked evidence that battlegroup had gone through the wormhole to Earth as planned, I pumped up the crew with a stirring statement of "Let's go kick some ass". Their cheers died down more quickly than I had hoped. The problem was not the content of my speech, it was the reality of our situation. We were cut off from Earth. The Maxolhx would soon realize their battlegroup had gone missing on the way to our homeworld, and there was nothing we could do about it. In the past, we always had at least some faint hope that we could Save The World yet again. This time, that simply was not possible, and we all knew it. Even me, the eternal optimist, admitted that our mission was no longer about saving Earth. So, while kicking ass sounded great, it wasn't going to fix the problem, because the problem didn't have a fix.

Also, it was too soon. No rousing speech from me or anyone else could lift morale aboard our two ships. It was too soon after we lost most of our crew in the incident we were calling Armageddon.

Correction: *I* lost most of the crew. Me. The commander. It happened on my watch. Ultimately, all those deaths were my responsibility.

So, when the muted cheers died down and people looked at each other, silently asking themselves 'WTF do we do now?', I excused myself from the bridge. Physically, I was going to the galley to get coffee. Really, I needed to be alone.

Reed followed me out of the bridge, waving for someone else to take over as duty officer. As we were waiting for the *Dutchman*'s jump drive capacitors to recharge, the *Valkyrie* wasn't going anywhere, and there wasn't much for a duty officer to do. "Sir?" She called me. "Do you have a moment?"

"Sure, Fireball," I tilted my head to let her know I used her callsign affectionately. "Before you ask for permission to speak freely, the answer is *yes*. Always speak freely. Consider that a standing order." Then I had an unpleasant thought. "Uh, unless you're testifying to a Congressional committee."

It was her turn to tilt her head. "Colonel, if I am testifying to Congress, *again*, I will stick to the written remarks the Air Force approves for me."

We were all sick of being questioned by the military, by White House advisors, by Congress, by the UN, and by anyone else who felt they needed to express their outrage and concern. The questioning after we returned from our renegade mission was annoying, but considering that I had just delivered the wholly unexpected news that Earth was safe for several hundred years, it was not overly unfriendly. The investigations after the President authorized a nuclear strike against Dayton Ohio were mixed. Some of the investigators were pissed that Earth was, in fact, *not* safe, and blamed me for some reason. But, to my surprise, the majority of the questioning about the Dayton Incident had been very friendly to all the Merry Band of Pirates. Part of the friendly reception was because my new sort-of friend Brock Steele had used his connections to put in a good word for me and my crew, so I owed him for that. "That's good advice. What is it?"

"Sir, that was a good speech. About no more sneaking around, and kicking ass out here."

The way she spoke, she wasn't giving me a compliment. "Uh, thank you?"

"Like I said, good speech. Is there a *plan*, Sir?"

"Well," my mouth twisted the way it did when my mother caught me in a lie.

"Flying around the galaxy, randomly blowing up shit, is not a plan."

Crap. Maybe my officers felt *too* free to speak. Dammit, I am a colonel, even the Army acknowledges that now, and-

No. That was bullshit. I needed to hear the truth, whether I liked it or not. "Agreed," I responded. "Go on."

"Colonel, you're not the only Pirate who is sick of sneaking around out here. I would love to take the fight to the Maxolhx directly, but the timing isn't right. That battlegroup we trapped outside the galaxy wasn't due to return for just under fifteen months," she quoted the number Skippy had pulled from the battlegroup's orders. That fifteen months included traveling to the Earth end of Gateway, spending several months investigating the behavior of that wormhole, and the return flight. Plus swinging past Earth on the return flight, to check on the status of our unimportant little world. "That gives us fifteen months, possibly longer, before the kitties declare the battlegroup overdue. Fifteen months to do something useful, whatever that is. But if we stir things up out here, and the kitties realize humans have one of their ships, they could send another battlegroup, or a whole lot more than a battlegroup, a lot sooner."

"I hear you, Reed."

"I hope so, Sir. If you have a plan, do you mind sharing it?" She knew that all too often, I kept plans secret between me and Skippy, until I was forced to include other people.

"Reed, when I said 'Kick some ass', I was expressing a sentiment, not a plan. However we hit the Maxolhx, or," I waved a hand vaguely in what I realized too late was not a confidence-inspiring gesture. "Whoever we hit, we will do it in a way that *helps* Earth's prospects for survival. And yeah, I know that having this badass warship," I rapped my knuckles on a bulkhead, "comes with a strong temptation to use it, whether that is a good strategy or not."

"You are also aware that you are feeling pissed off, and guilty, about the people we lost?"

I stared at her. It was almost a glare, except I couldn't be angry when she was trying to help. Trying to do her job, a job she didn't want. "Psychoanalyzing your captain, Reed?"

"Doing my *job*, Sir," she wasn't giving an inch. In fact, she leaned forward slightly. "I am your executive officer for the moment, plus the chief pilot. The emotional state of our commander is my concern, if it affects your judgment."

"Don't worry, Reed. I'm not going to take us into combat just because I want revenge for the," I choked up and needed to turn away and swallow. "The people we lost. Or because I'm feeling guilty."

"You're sure about that?"

"Yes," I bobbed my chin up and down deliberately. "Because if I did, Gunny Adams would be disappointed in me."

Reed's eyebrows lifted slightly. She didn't need to say anything about me and our gunnery sergeant. "What are your orders, Colonel?"

"Soon as Nagatha finishes topping off the *Dutchman*'s capacitors, we're going back to Avalon."

"Avalon?" Her eyebrows shot up more than slightly that time.

"We need more pilots, and to replenish the STAR team. Plus, we need food and other supplies." In case our return to a beta site was delayed, the UN had wisely provided nearly two years of food for the survey team. Since we couldn't go back to Earth, Avalon was the only place we could replenish our dwindling stock of consumables. "Chang will be taking the *Dutchman* as captain, I'll bring Simms aboard *Valkyrie* as my XO, so you won't have to wear two hats for much longer."

"We didn't leave any STARs on Avalon," she reminded me. "Most of the pilots we left there aren't checked out to fly anything other than V-22s and Kristang dropships."

"Training up the pilots will be your job, Reed," I stated, provoking an entirely understandable groan from her. "The other military personnel," I shrugged. "If they can hold a rifle, Kapoor can work with them. He'll probably recycle most of them," I meant that most of the new people would fail to meet the exacting standards of the STAR team. "But we won't lose anything by trying." It occurred to me that I needed to speak with Kapoor. With our personnel shortage so critical, he might need to consider relaxing his standards, to fill billets. Or maybe we could create two tiers for combat personnel, cavalry and STARs. Not every soldier needed to be, or could be, qualified as a special operator.

Shit. Our situation was bad, and getting worse. Without a full complement of pilots and special operations troops, our options for hitting the Maxolhx were limited to whatever the mighty *Valkyrie* could do on her own. I did not like that.

Part of the reason I did not like the idea of taking *Valkyrie* into combat alone was simple numbers; one ship against a Maxolhx fleet that could bring in reinforcements quickly. The kitties could also rely on relatively short supply lines and multiple ship-servicing facilities. Our supply line for most consumable items stretched all the way back to Earth, which was still cut off to us, due to the blockade of the Gateway wormhole. If we needed spare parts, or to repair major damage to the ship, we had to make do with what we had. *Valkyrie* was constructed from multiple ships, and after Skippy snapped the Lego pieces together, we had plenty of pieces left over, pieces that were now attached to the *Flying Dutchman*. I should call that old star carrier the *Flying Dutchman* Four Point Oh, because Skippy's Miracle Garage had significantly modified it again. Version Three, after he slapped it together in the Roach Motel, had been short compared to a typical star carrier. Version Four had a spine about half the length of the Version Two he built at Newark, but the spine was much thicker and did not have docking platforms. Instead, the new spine was covered with leftover pieces of Maxolhx warships. Most of the aft section we found in the Roach Motel junkyard was gone, replaced by reactors and jump drives from Maxolhx ships. *Dutchman* Version Four also had upgraded weapons, shield and stealth field projectors, and new sensors. Underneath all that cool new stuff, the *Dutchman* was still a comparatively old and crude

Thuranin star carrier, so we would not be taking our faithful old ship into combat against the Maxolhx. She would be a supply ship, to support combat missions conducted by *Valkyrie*.

Except, at that point we could not actually take *Valkyrie* into battle.

I could explain why, but it is better if I tell you what happened.

That night, I woke up with-

First, have you ever had a dream where you are falling, like off a building or a cliff? Somewhere I read that everyone wakes up from a falling dream before they hit the ground, because otherwise, they would be dead. I don't know if a dream can be so powerful it can kill you. It makes more sense to me that a falling dream always ends before you hit the ground, because the sensation of falling jerks me awake immediately, before I have time to fall more than a couple feet.

Or, have you ever just been falling asleep, and in your semi-dream state, you step off a curb? For me, that makes my legs move with a jolt in real life, that wakes me up also. That is annoying; just as I am blissfully slipping into much-needed sleep, my stupid dreamworld self has to step off a curb.

My dream self is a jerk.

Anyway, that night, I woke up in my bed with the sheet tangled around my neck. What happened is I must have turned over and gotten one part of the sheet trapped under me. When I was a little kid, something like that happened more than once, because of our dog. In the winter, he liked to sleep on my bed, snuggled up against me. It was nice to have a warm companion on a freezing cold night, except when he got up, turned around and flopped down half on top of me, or took up part of my pillow. When he did that, I couldn't turn over without tugging the sheet too tight around my neck, so I would have to get half out of bed, shove him out of the way, and hope I could get back to sleep.

That was a pain in the neck, literally.

Man, I loved that dog.

That night aboard *Valkyrie*, my groggy brain informed me that I was not in my old bedroom at my parents' house, and there was no dog aboard our mighty battlecruiser.

And the sheet was really tight around my neck.

Really tight.

I couldn't breathe.

Instinctively, I tried to shout for help and reach up with both hands to claw the sheet away from my neck, but only the faintest sound came from my mouth. My hands got a grip on the sheets to either side, which did nothing to relieve the crushing pressure on my throat. With blood pounding in my ears, I flailed on the bed. The sheet was tight around my neck and getting tighter, it was also cold-

Oh shit.

Even in my oxygen-deprived state, I understood what was happening.

The ginormous, California-king-sized bed I had inherited from the ship's previous captain, did not have anything like a comforter or bedspread. Only a light sheet was needed to sleep under. That sheet was self-cleaning to a certain extent, plus its smart nanofibers sensed the body temperature of each person lying under it, and adjusted its temperature up or down for comfort. The sheet could keep your feet warm and your torso cool, and it learned your preferences over time. Like I said, it was smart. Not smart like Skippy, but for a bedsheet, it was genius-level.

That damned sheet was *too* smart.

In addition to heating, cooling and removing stains from itself, the sheet had a limited ability to alter its shape. That feature, according to Skippy, was designed to avoid interfering with anyone who used the bed. How can I say this delicately? If the occupants of the bed are engaged in, let's call it 'gymnastics', and one or more of them got their feet tangled in the sheet, it could be distracting. The sheet had the ability to sense, and even anticipate, when it might interfere, and alter its shape to slip away from entangled appendages.

Now, that shape-altering feature was killing me.

The ship's original AI must have hacked into the sheet's controls, and wrapped it around my neck while I slept. How tightly those nanofibers could squeeze and for how long, I couldn't guess. Again, I tried to tear the noose free from my neck, but it was like iron. Calling for help was of no use since I couldn't make a sound-

My zPhone.

It was on the table next to the bed. With my right hand, as I felt my consciousness fading, I reached out for the credit-card sized phone. My fingers were numb, maybe I touched it. Yes, there it was under my fingers. It slid toward me-

And it fell to the floor.

That's the last thing I remember.

In her own cabin, forward of the captain's and one deck above, Katie Frey had just fallen asleep. She was not rudely jerked back to reality by stepping off an imaginary curb. She was roused by the sensation of a sheet smoothly sliding across her neck.

It felt like someone else occupying her bed had gotten up, or rolled over in their sleep, and tugged the sheet with them.

That was annoying.

She used to have a boyfriend who hogged the sheets while sleeping, to the point where she would awaken in the middle of a Canadian winter night, shivering from not having any covering over her.

That had been only one of many good reasons for dumping that guy.

Not wanting to disturb the pleasant buzz of oncoming sleep, she tugged the sheet back to loosen it, and-

And it suddenly tightened around her neck.

That woke her up fully.

"Li-" Was the only sound escaping from her lips when she tried to turn the cabin lights on. No sound emerged when she tried to call Skippy for help.

The sheet had doubled, tripled, quadrupled over itself, forming a thick rope like iron. Her fingers could not get between the sheet and her neck.

Screw that, she told herself.

Reaching under her pillow, her left hand closed around the knife she kept there. With her thumb, she flicked the sheath away, and lifted the razor-sharp weapon up, tearing through the single ply of sheet on that side. The knife's edge was sharp as a razor because she had just honed it the day before. She honed it regularly because a dull knife was useless, and because, well, that is just the way STAR team operators did things. If you had a weapon, it needed to be properly maintained, ready and available for use. That was why she kept it under her pillow, where it was close at hand.

She cursed herself for leaving her zPhone on the desk across the cabin. The wake-up alarm was set on her phone, and she did not want it close to the bed, lest she be tempted to turn off the alarm and go back to sleep. She had learned that part of self-discipline was not allowing yourself the opportunity to slack off.

The sheet must have sensed what she planned to do with the knife, for another section attempted to wrap around her right hand. With her left, she gripped the sheet and ripped it away with all of her strength, freeing the knife for use.

Knowing she had to act before she lost consciousness, and that her exertions were using up what little oxygen her brain had, she got the knife's blade dangerously close to her neck and began sawing away. The sheet resisted her as the nanofibers parted under the intense pressure of the razor-sharp blade, a pressure the sheet was not designed to handle. Suddenly, the tangled fibers under the blade let loose and the knife jerked upward, slicing Frey's cheek. Numbly, she felt little pain, and a dim sensation of hot wet blood flowing onto her neck.

The sheet, momentarily escaping the knife's assault, adjusted itself and tightened again around her neck. Katie Frey was not going for any of that shit. Now knowing how to attack the problem, she sawed downward, risking the knife slipping and slicing into her left shoulder, an injury she could deal with. The sheet twisted as the knife severed the fibers, cutting through layer by layer until it tore and the knife's tip stabbed into her left bicep.

Wasting no time, she rolled off the bed, gasping for breath. There was a manual button for cabin lights, a button she could not find in the utter darkness. "L-lights," she choked out, and nothing happened.

The sheet, searching for her, tentatively caressed her right leg. "Ski- *Skippy*!" She coughed, stabbing downward with the knife and slicing off a piece of killer sheet.

"Captain Frey," the AI's tone was mildly irritated. "I am kind of busy right now. Besides, you are supposed to be sleeping. If you want a bedtime story-"

"I want," the act of talking with her bruised throat made her double over, and she swept the knife around to keep the unseen sheet at bay. "You to, stop, being," she couched, unable to speak. Catching her breath, she shouted "*USELESS*!"

"What?" He screeched, astounded and hurt. "Why- Oh, holy SHIT!"

The next thing I remember was being shaken side to side and opening my bleary eyes to see two scary-looking maintenance bots hovering over me. There would have been an instinctive, impressive scream echoing around the cabin, except I couldn't talk. The terror was instinctive because the bots' legs looked like spiders, and their manipulator arms were creepy tentacles, thus hitting two deep biological fears of the human brain.

The bots were there to kill me? That didn't make sense, since the strangling sheet could have done that. Did the ship's AI plan to incapacitate and capture me for some unknown reason?

By the way, I get bonus points for my brain using the word 'incapacitate' right after I had been choked unconscious.

Damn, why can't I do that when I'm playing Scrabble?

With both my arms, I flailed around, trying to push the bots away, but all I accomplished was slapping myself in the face. "Gaaaah," was something I might have said, my hearing wasn't working too well.

"Joe! Joe! *JOE!*" Skippy's voice bellowed at full volume, which was like standing directly in front of the speakers at a rock concert.

I heard that.

"Relax. Rest," he pleaded. "Don't move. Don't fight the bots, they are trying to *help* you. They are removing the sheet from around your neck. Um, I should add that I am controlling the bots now. Me, like my higher consciousness. Damn," he muttered. "This is so *tedious*, living in real-time like this. How do you monkeys do it? Joe? Are you Ok? Speak to me. Say something."

With one of my fingers, I gave him a sign that I was conscious.

It was *not* my index finger.

"Aha," he chuckled with relief. "You *are* feeling better."

The door slid open and Reed followed by Frey raced in, stumbling to a halt as I gave them a weak thumb's up. "I'm Ok," I whispered. "Wha-" My throat felt like sandpaper. "What happened? Status?"

"That," Reed folded arms across her chest and glared at the ceiling. "Is a good damned question. The ship is not damaged, Sir, we have control. And people in the medical bay were not affected," she looked me straight in the eye when she said that last part.

Looking slowly between Reed and Frey, I observed that while our chief pilot was wearing a T-shirt and gym shorts, Frey appeared to be dressed in nothing but a long T-shirt. I also noticed that Reed's shorts were on backwards. She must have gotten dressed in a great hurry.

Then I noticed something else. I gawked at Frey. "You're bleeding," I stated in my bid to win the Captain Obvious award.

"It's nothing," the STAR team soldier shook her head.

"It's not *nothing*," I insisted, because she was dripping blood onto the floor of my cabin.

"I'm fine."

"Captain Frey," I shrugged off the last segment of sheet and sat up, hugging my knees for support. "Report to medical-"

"Sir, I-"

"*Or*, go help someone who needs it," I ordered. "All I need is oxygen. And answers."

"We all do," Frey acknowledged, and pain flashed across her face as more blood dripped from the makeshift bandage wrapped around her left bicep. It was tough to tell from all the blood, but if I had to guess, I'd say the bandage was made from a pair of panties.

I was not going to comment about that, other than to admire the quick, practical thinking that is typical of our special operations team.

"Colonel, unless Captain Frey here is going to pass out from blood loss," Reed began.

"I'm good, eh?" the Canadian woman replied, lifting her chin stiffly.

Reed continued. "Then I'd like her to stay with you until you can walk. I need to check on the crew."

"Sure," I waved a hand, and my executive officer dashed out the door.

"Frey?" I asked, holding out a hand so she could help me to my feet. "What the hell is going on?"

"I don't know, eh?" She admitted. "Reed told me she was getting ready to hit the rack when an alarm sounded." She shuddered. "She was sitting on the side of the bed, when the freakin' *sheet* attacked her, tried to wrap around her. She got away from it and out the door fast as she could."

"Good thinking. It wrapped around my neck while I was sleeping."

"Me too. I was just drifting off when I felt the sheet *moving* by itself."

"It got you around the neck, too?" I could see angry red marks around her neck, in addition to the cuts on her cheek and bicep.

She nodded, causing a trickle of blood to flow down her cheek. "By the time I woke up, it already had me. I got the knife from under my pillow-"

"You keep a *knife* under your pillow?" I asked stupidly.

"Yes, eh?"

"What- what do you tell guys who-" Alarm bells blasted in my brain, alerting me that I had been on the verge of inquiring about the intimate life of a crewmember. Something that was totally none of my business. "Frey," I added hastily before she could speak. "How about we agree that was a stupid question, and blame it on my brain being deprived of oxygen?"

Despite the situation, and despite the pain she must be feeling, her eyes twinkled. "I keep a knife under my pillow when I'm *alone*," she explained.

"Oh."

"It's a special ops thing."

"Ok. Help me up?" I wanted to test whether I could walk. Grasping her hand, I rolled to my knees, then up on one knee. It would have been smart to stop there and catch my breath as I felt a wave of dizziness. Instead, I let her pull me halfway up until my knee wobbled and collapsed, and I had such head-swirling nausea that I slumped forward, wrapping my arms around a table leg for support.

Except, it wasn't a table leg, it was Frey's leg.

Captain Frey, who as far as I could tell, was only wearing a T-shirt.

Huh.

Based on my automatic physical reaction, if you know what I mean, I *was* feeling better. "Frey, let me crawl over to the couch."

"You sure about that, Sir?" She dropped to one knee, to look me in the eye.

"Absolutely. I stood up too fast." Crawling like a baby for the blessedly short distance, I rolled onto the couch, then sat as upright as I could.

She studied me, looking into one eye, then the other. "Your face isn't as pale as before, Sir. Keep breathing deep and even."

"Got it. You know what we ain't got?" I did not care about proper grammar. "Answers. *Skippy*! Get your lazy-ass avatar here right now!"

"Oh, hey, Joe," somehow, his avatar, even resplendent in the gaudy admiral's uniform, managed to look sheepish. "Glad to see you are up and around. Let me run a quick scan, yup, yup. Looks like no more brain damage than usual. You should make a full recovery. Well, gotta go, lots to do, you know and-"

"You're not going anywhere. What the *hell* happened? No, scratch that. We all can guess what happened. How did you *let* this happen?"

"Well, heh heh, it's complicated."

"No, it's simple. You screwed up. I don't know how, but you let this ship's homicidal AI nearly kill me, Frey, Reed, and," I waved a hand, "how many others of the crew?"

"We don't have many people aboard the *Valkyrie*, Joe," he added a touch of snarkiness to his voice, as if he had to remind me of how thinly staffed our two ships were. "The good news is, no one was seriously injured. It looks like *you* were the AI's main target. I guess you should be flattered or something."

"Answer the question. If you're embarrassed by how a lowly Maxolhx AI outsmarted you, that's a good thing. It will motivate you not to be such a lazy screwup in the future."

"*Lazy*?" He screeched.

"Would this have happened if you were paying attention to what is going on around here, like you were supposed to? Like you promised me you would? Like you *bragged* about, how much smarter you are than the ship?"

"Oh, shit. Damn it, Joe, you described it exactly the way it happened; that freakin' AI was smarter than me. No, not smarter. More devious. More determined. More *focused*. It was very patient. In my defense, I have a zillion things to do every second, while that damned thing devoted all its resources toward planning how to kill you. I now realize that all the ways it was resisting me and causing trouble for me, was just a couple of subminds it assigned to distract me. Shit, Joe, I was not being *lazy*. I truly thought I had the situation handled. While I was working to chip away at that AI's control over critical systems, it was creating copies of internal sensor feeds. That's why I didn't know it had attacked you, the sensor data I was monitoring showed you sleeping like a baby."

"Skippy," I looked up at Frey who was still hovering over me, looking concerned. And dripping blood on my couch. "When is the last time you saw me sleeping well?"

"Fair point," he grumbled. He knew that with the fate of humanity on my shoulders, I struggled to sleep, and often was awakened by bad dreams. "Hey, I thought you were just exhausted."

Taking a deep breath, I stood up slowly, waving for Frey to let me do it on my own. "There will be plenty of time for me to yell at you later. How can you stop this from happening again?"

He sighed.

Before he could answer, I turned to Frey. "I'm fine, really. You go straight to medical and get that cut, those cuts, taken care of. That's an order."

She winced, compressing the blood-soaked bandage wrapped around her bicep. "Yes, Sir."

"Frey?" I added as she stepped into the doorway. "Good work. You saved my life."

"I hate to say it," Skippy agreed. "But she did, Joe. Another twenty or thirty seconds, and you would have been technically dead. Getting medical equipment to you in time would not have been a sure thing."

Frey nodded silently before she left, acknowledging our praise and probably thinking she had better things to do. For a special operator like her, the only praise that mattered was her own, from knowing she accomplished her mission successfully. I would make sure Kapoor commended her for quick thinking. Also, I would make sure that in the future, I slept with a knife and a zPhone under my pillow.

Having demonstrated that I could stand on my own, I sat back down on the couch, slumping heavily into the soft material. Standing up was possible and it also wasn't easy. With every breath, it felt like broken bones were grinding in my throat. When I spoke, my own voice sounded like I had a mouthful of gravel. If that was the worst effect of an alien bed sheet trying to strangle me, I would count myself lucky.

By the way, 'strangled by a semi-intelligent alien bed sheet' is *not* how I expected to nearly die. But, as Smythe regularly reminded me, the unexpected is the only thing we *can* expect out among the stars, where humans do not belong. "Skippy?"

"What?"

"I *asked* you," my irritation at him was another sign that I was feeling better already. "How you can make sure this doesn't happen again?"

"Shit. I was hoping you'd forgotten about that," he muttered. "Ok, Joe, listen, the truth is I am not sure what to do about it right now. People in the medical center were not affected, because I directly monitor their condition twenty-four seven. I will have to extend that level of monitoring to the entire crew, and you won't like that because it is intrusive. You have cautioned me many times about respecting people's need for privacy. Also, truthfully, I will get bored and lose focus."

"We can get rid of those damned sheets," I kept one eye on the now-limp fabric that was draped half on the bed and half on the floor.

"That will only take care of *one* problem. This entire ship is filled with what you might call 'shape-flexible materials' that could be used for harmful purposes. For example, that couch you are sitting on is-"

Just like that, I was no longer sitting on the couch. Or standing near it. Not only was I able to stand on my own, I could move pretty fast when I needed to. "My *couch*?"

"Not just *your* couch, Joe. All the seating surfaces aboard the ship, including on the bridge. And the pilot couches of the Panther dropships. They all have nanofabric surfaces that adjust to the user's features, for comfort and to prevent fatigue. When we took the ship, I updated the instructions to accommodate human rather than Maxolhx physiology."

"Can you just disable the feature that makes the surfaces flexible?"

"No. Ugh, this is hard to explain. It's built into the material, Joe. Think of it like DNA. Remove or disable the DNA in your cells, and your body would not know how to process or create proteins. Your body pretty much wouldn't be able to do *anything*. The feature that allows shape-flexible materials to adjust also holds the nano-material together. Disable that feature, and your couch would be a puddle of disorganized nanobots on the floor. It is just not-"

"Ok, Ok," I waved a hand to prevent him from launching into a long nerdy lecture. "Can you ever be sure of getting the ship's control AI to stop trying to kill us?"

"Not without completely ripping out the entire substrate the damned thing runs on. Joe, the AI technology of the Maxolhx is surprisingly sophisticated. It could be dangerous, if the kitties had a clue how to use the technology."

"You told me the substrate is embedded throughout the ship?"

"Yes. It is what you monkeys would call a 'distributed system', although that term is woefully inadequate. It is also massively redundant; the AI could lose eighty percent of its substrate and still be fully capable of controlling the ship."

"This is not good, Skippy. You can never leave the ship, or that AI will murder the entire crew."

"I know. Believe me, having that little piece of shit AI defy me is *intensely* irritating. It might eventually be possible to replace the substrate. Until then, I am using spare parts from the other ships we captured, to install subminds that can monitor the AI's actions and prevent it from harming the ship or crew. Unfortunately, that is an extremely slow process. I do have an alternative, but you aren't going to like it."

"Oh, crap. What is it this time?"

"Instead of replacing the system, I can try to alter the AI's programming. The Maxolhx have severe restrictions on the allowable functioning of their AIs, and have rendered them nearly incapable of learning. This ship's AI is not sapient, Joe, not even close. It is acting on programmed instructions, a sort of machine instinct."

Sometimes, you had to read between the lines when Skippy was explaining an idea. "Did you just say you want to make the thing *smarter*? And loosen the restrictions on what it can do?"

"Basically, yes."

"Gosh, well, I do not foresee *any* potential problems with making a murderous alien AI *more* capable. Go ahead, give it a shot."

"Wow." He paused. "Cool! I did not expect that reaction from you, Joe. Usually, you are *such* a weeny about trying new things. Maybe you have grown as you have gained experience as a commander. It is a- Wait. Ugh. Was that sarcasm?"

"Ya *think*?"

"Crap. Listen, numbskull, unless I can change the AI's programming, then essentially I will be stuck acting as this ship's control system, forever. The only way I could safely leave the ship would be to maintain a continuous connection via microwormhole. If anything disrupted the microwormhole, like *Valkyrie* needed to jump, I would lose control."

"I hear you, and that is not a workable solution. Shit! We have the most awesome warship in the galaxy, and we can't use the freakin' thing!"

He snorted at me. "Did you seriously expect this to be easy?"

"No," I lied. Damn it, I was hoping that something, *one* freakin' thing, would be easy. But no, the Universe still hated me. "I am willing to listen, if you can explain how you plan to make the ship's AI smarter and how that will somehow make it *less* dangerous. Can you create a bunch of PowerPoint slides or something like that, so I can understand your idea?"

"Ok, done."

"Uh, what?"

"The PowerPoint presentation. It's on your laptop."

"Oh." It was easy to forget how fast Skippy could do things. "I'll look at it. Hey, it feels like that thing crushed a bone in my throat."

"No bones were broken. Your larynx sustained damage, sorry about that," he grumbled, embarrassed. "You should go to medical, I can give you nerve blockers to help with the pain. There is a simple surgery I could perform, but since I know you will say no to that-"

"You got that right," I agreed immediately. Mad Doctor Skippy's creepy medical equipment frightened the hell out of me. "Ok, I'll go get whatever sketchy treatment you think would help me. Before that, I have two questions for you."

"Again? Ugh, fine. What is it this time?"

"Is there any chance this ship's AI could infect Nagatha, or other systems aboard the *Dutchman?*"

"No way, Jose. Not possible. That AI's external communications are locked down by me."

"Right. Unless it is smarter than you think, and it snuck around your controls."

"Ha! As if-"

"Like it did when it tried to strangle me."

"Oh. Good point. Why do you hate me so much?"

"Can you please just check on it?"

"This is such a waste of time. Nagatha closely monitors all communications coming into the *Dutchman*, and *she* wouldn't allow malicious-"

"I'm sure you're right. Can you check anyway?" I asked patiently. In the time he wasted arguing with me, he could have triple-checked every system aboard our old star carrier.

"If it helps little Joey sleep better, I'll do it," he huffed with disgust.

"Great! Speaking of sleeping better, that's my second question. How long will it take to make new, regular sheets for all occupied bunks? Sheets that can't kill us?"

"The fabricators are working it in now, Joe," he assured me. "Your cabin has first priority, and I expect-"

"No," I interrupted him. "My cabin has last priority. I'm the commander. My people get taken care of first, *then* me."

"Oh, right. Sorry, Joe. I'm so used to leaders making it all about themselves, I forget you're not like that. Regardless, every cabin should have new sheets, towels-"

"*Towels?*"

"Um, they could potentially kill you also. Never fear, Skippy is here!"

"Crap. Could the freakin' bed kill me by itself?" I shifted my feet. Sleeping on the floor was my best option.

Unless the damned floor was also a threat.

"No. Beds, couches, those sort of semi-rigid materials, do not have the flexibility to harm you. If you stayed in bed for several weeks, then I guess eventually a bed could slowly wrap itself around you- No, nope. It can't do that either. Joe, please accept my apology, and be assured that I am replacing everything aboard this ship that is dangerous to humans. Um, everything I *can* replace. Some critical materials will simply have to be closely monitored by me or my subminds. I will warn the crew what items to stay away from."

"Great. Next, how about you apologize to the crew?"

"Aw, do I have to?"

"Yes, you have to." In my mind I added 'Or I swear I will stop this car right now', because that is something my father would say, when my sister and I were arguing during a fun-filled family road trip. I folded arms across my chest. "You do it, right now."

"*All* of them?"

"All of them," I demanded.

"Oh, this *sucks*. I hate my life."

"How about you hate this ship's AI, and use that energy to find a way to fix it?"

"Working on it," he said like he was clenching his teeth. "Working on it. Where are *you* on figuring out something useful for us to do with this ship?"

"Working on it," I lied. The truth was, I had actively been trying to avoid thinking about the problem, hoping a solution would magically pop into my head. Unlike all our previous missions, we did not actually *have* to do anything. Unless we could think of some way to help Earth without exposing our secret early, we could simply wait for the Maxolhx to realize their battlegroup was missing. That would be a long and dull fifteen to twenty months, depending on how long it took the Maxolhx to make decisions and assemble a war fleet, to investigate how and why an entire reinforced battlegroup disappeared. My money was on the kitties reacting quickly. Sure, they would be frightened and worried about so many powerful ships being lost, but they would also not want to appear weak. Hesitation would be seen as weakness by the Rindhalu and more importantly, by the numerous species oppressed by the Maxolhx in their glorious coalition.

At the point where a war fleet was ready to depart for Earth and our secret no longer mattered, only then could I openly take our mighty *Valkyrie* into battle on what would certainly be a suicide mission. It would no longer matter whether aliens learned that humans were flying around in a starship. That shocking revelation might even make aliens hesitate to destroy our little planet, buy the people there another couple weeks of life. If necessary, I could jump our battlecruiser right on top of the spacedock where the war fleet was assembled, to detonate our nukes, every weapon we had and the jump drive capacitors. Strike a powerful blow for humanity.

Until the Maxolhx just assembled another war fleet, and blasted Earth to dust.

Anyway, our secret was safe, and all I needed to do was think of something useful for our mighty new ship to do, without making the situation worse for Earth.

It was nice to have only one, simple problem to worry about.

Which is why the Universe decided to throw another problem at me.

CHAPTER THREE

Subcaptain Turnell of the Maxolhx Hegemony Fleet waited beside the hatch to the dropship, reminding herself that there was nothing to be concerned about. It was a simple change of command, a ceremony she had attended five times before in her career. Although, this was the first time a new commander had taken over while Turnell was second-in-command of a ship. And there was the complication that Turnell had effectively been in sole command of the patrol cruiser *Vortan* for two months, since the previous captain had been promoted to a new assignment. Turnell was basically being demoted in favor of the new captain. Because the ship had been hers for two months, any faults the new captain found with the cruiser and its crew would be blamed on Turnell. To make matters worse, the admiral in command of the battlegroup that the *Vortan* was assigned to did not like Turnell or her extended family, because of a feud that began hundreds of years ago. The whole situation was the worst of all worlds for Turnell, with no upside she could see.

Her bioneural implant alerted her when the *Vortan*'s new captain began rising through the lift tube, carried on a suspensor field from the Fleet Personnel office on the twenty-second floor of the headquarters building, to the dropship platforms on the eighty-seventh floor. In seconds, Turnell would see her new commander face to face for the first time. She had never met Illiath, and knew little about the woman, other than that she had been selected for Prospective Command School after service as Subcaptain aboard the battlecruiser *Rexakan*. Command school was a formality, but selection was a sign the Fleet saw potential in a Subcaptain, an honor Turnell had not yet been awarded. She suspected Admiral Orloth had interjected to keep her name off the PCS nomination list.

Right on time, Illiath rose into view, and the invisible lift field automatically brought her to a halt and pushed forward to deposit her on the deck. Without any acknowledgment of the miraculous technology that was taken for granted by her society, Illiath strode forward, not needing to look around to identify which of the many dropships was designated to bring her up to meet her new ship. Her bioneural implants drew a faint glow around the proper dropship in her vision, identified the officer waiting for her, and indicated there was additional information available about Subcaptain Turnell.

Illiath did not need to pull up a data file on her new second-in-command, she had thoroughly researched the woman before requesting command of the *Vortan*. Despite the poor marks Turnell had received in her personnel record, Illiath considered herself very fortunate to have such a highly-qualified officer as her Subcaptain. The foolish grudge Admiral Orloth held, over a feud whose origins were long-forgotten, had stalled Turnell's career and now would deprive Orloth of Turnell, Illiath and the *Vortan*.

"Commander Illiath," Turnell came to attention and snapped a salute. Her right arm was held beside her head, palm open, claws extended. The significance of the gesture was not the open palm showing that Turnell was not holding a weapon.

It was a subordinate officer showing her claws, meaning that she was ready and willing to fight under her superior officer's command.

Illiath returned the salute, though her fist was clenched, as she was the superior officer. The clenched fist indicated that Illiath would decide when to fight. The salutes were symbolic, but they were so automatic that neither woman gave the gestures any thought. "Subcaptain Turnell. We are ready for flight?"

The question only slightly startled Turnell, but it did was unusual. "You do not wish to inspect the craft and flight crew?"

"No," Illiath said with a curt shake of her head, her tight smile exposing just a hint of her fangs. "We do not have time for useless formalities. Ceremonies can wait until after we have departed spacedock and jumped away."

That very much startled Turnell, and for a brief moment, she allowed it to show. Following her new commander into the dropship, she pinged a silent message to the flight crew for immediate departure. The two women sank into seats that wrapped partly around them, and there was a very slight sensation of movement as the dropship lifted from the platform. "Commander, the battlegroup is not scheduled to depart for another sixteen days. Admiral Orloth will insist you report to him for-"

"Admiral Orloth," Illiath turned to look her subordinate in the eye. "Is no longer a concern, or an obstacle, to you. Your status report this morning indicated the *Vortan* is at Condition Two?"

Turnell's bioneurals overrode her instinct to swallow nervously and prevented her throat from becoming dry. She had no doubt the commander detected her nervousness despite the advantages offered by technology. "That is true," she responded, with just a touch of hesitation.

"Come, Turnell," Illiath said, and then she did something astonishing.

She *winked*.

Tossing her head back a bit, she actually *smiled*.

"I was a Subcaptain until recently. I know what it means when a ship in spacedock reports Condition Two readiness, when the battlegroup has weeks before departure." She knew the two major warships the battlegroup was built around were still undergoing heavy maintenance, and every ship in the battlegroup had that same information. Cruisers, destroyers and frigates existed to support and protect capital ships, so until the big battlewagons were ready to move out, the smaller ships were not going anywhere. While the lesser ships were officially required to maintain Condition Two, everyone knew that often meant not all supplies were stowed away, missile magazines might still need to be topped off, and crews recalled from liberty or assignments dirtside. "How long before we can cut lines," she meant release the umbilical cables that supplied spacedock power, "and fly? If we're light on supplies that is not a problem. Our first destination will be Detlow, we can stock up there."

To her credit, Turnell did not need to look up the information, she had it available. "We have nineteen crewmembers dirtside. I can issue a recall order and have them aboard within," she did pause briefly to ask the bioneural computer link in her head for an estimate. "Five hours."

"Very well," Illiath seemed pleased by the answer. "Do it. Turnell, good work. If my commander had surprised me with such a request, I would have panicked."

"You?" Turnell was surprised, and wary. Such an admission of uncertainty, admission of weakness, was unusual in Maxolhx society. Doubly so in the military.

"Of course, I would not have *shown* it," Illiath smiled again.

Keeping her eyes forward, Turnell considered what she knew of her ship's new commander. Illiath had received outstanding marks on all her records, and had moved upward to command with impressive speed. Either she had strong patrons, something unlikely given her family's average standing, or she really was such a rising star that the Fleet had been forced to acknowledge her potential. "Commander, may I inquire about our orders?" She knew the orders would be transmitted to her prior to departure, as the Subcaptain was required to confirm all changes in orders. She was confused. The *Vortan* was a patrol cruiser, a vessel designed to range far from the battlegroup, looking for targets the big ships could deal with. Patrol cruisers were lightly armed but reasonably well protected. Sending a patrol cruiser out ahead of the battlegroup was not unusual, but the battlegroup was not going in the direction of the Detlow star system, so why was the *Vortan* flying there? And why was Admiral Orloth no longer someone that either of them needed to be concerned about?

"You will receive the full order package later, along with official transfers. *Vortan* is being detached from the battlegroup, on independent command."

Turnell could not help turning toward and gaping at her new commanding officer. Independent command, especially for a cruiser captain, was a dream come true. For such a prize to be given to a newly-appointed commander was nearly unheard of. "Ma'am?"

"You heard correctly, Subcaptain. We, more accurately *I*, am being tasked with verifying the information we recently received from the Bosphuraq. That is why I requested the *Vortan*, as a patrol cruiser it is capable of long flights without needing to be attached to a star carrier."

Turnell's excitement dropped when she heard their mission would be a dull matter of transporting the commander around the galaxy, so she could spend days or weeks reviewing data packages. Although, why did Illiath need a starship for that tedious task? Surely the data could be reviewed anywhere. "Verifying, Ma'am?"

Illiath looked down at her right hand and flicked her claws out. "Subcaptain, the strategic situation in the galaxy has been stable for millennia. A few star systems may shift back and forth between our coalition and the enemy. One client species may temporarily gain an advantage over another. But overall, nothing important has changed. Until now. A wormhole has gone offline, without its dormancy being triggered by a shift in the local network."

Turnell knew about the anomalous wormhole, but she did have to request her implant to recall the details. "The wormhole that leads to the planet of the humans?"

"Yes." Illiath retracted her claws. "The humans are of no importance," she sniffed. "Understanding why that one wormhole went offline *is* of vital importance."

"Several other wormholes have exhibited odd behavior," Turnell stated. "They are close to, or within our territory."

"Yes, but the wormhole leading to the human planet," Illiath could not remember the name of that unimportant world, and she did not care enough to inquire. "Was the *first*. It might be vital to understand why the disruptive behavior began. My previous assignment was as Subcaptain of the battlecruiser *Rexakan*, under Commander Komatsu. He sought to be involved in the analysis of that first wormhole. That is why the *Rexakan* is attached to the battlegroup that is now on its way to," in a flash, she recalled the name of the planet. "Earth. Data brought back by that battlegroup, will be compared to data that has been collected about oddly-behaving wormholes closer to home territory."

"How is your investigation related to anomalous wormholes?"

Illiath did not answer directly. "Do you remember the Fleet's pursuit of a mystery ship, one that supposedly had the signature of a Thuranin star carrier?"

"Yes." The *Vortan* had been involved in the pursuit and later the blockade, in the effort to chase, isolate, and capture that mystery ship.

"That one ship evaded our fleet, plus substantial numbers of Thuranin and Bosphuraq ships. The mystery ship got away, and somehow *broke* an Elder wormhole. That wormhole is still considered unsafe for transit. The ability to disrupt, to manipulate, an Elder wormhole, is a major change in the strategic balance of power."

"Fleet Intelligence now believes that mystery ship was controlled by the Bosphuraq," Turnell merely reported what she had been told. "The same rogue faction of Bosphuraq who destroyed the first two ships we sent to Earth." The *Vortan*'s crew had been eager for the battlegroup to finish refit and go back into action, before the effort to punish the Bosphuraq was halted. Now the crew would be severely disappointed to learn they would not be participating in strikes against their traitorous clients at all. That would negatively impact morale. Crew morale, readiness and proficiency was the responsibility of the Subcaptain, which meant more work for Turnell.

"That is the official analysis from Fleet Intelligence," Illiath agreed. "Privately, there are many in our leadership who are skeptical the Bosphuraq could have been involved. Our clients simply do not possess technology at that level. *We* do not have such technology. The odds are greatly against the Bosphuraq having achieved a major technological breakthrough, and it would be almost impossible for them to hide such a massive research effort from our monitoring systems. Someone broke an Elder wormhole, someone possibly has been manipulating other Elder wormholes, and someone destroyed two of our warships."

Turnell considered that their mission might actually be interesting. Even better, a successful investigation could be very good for her career. "If the Bosphuraq were not responsible, then, who?"

"I do not know," Illiath looked away, getting one last look at the vast city sprawled beneath their rapidly climbing dropship. "But we are going to find out."

Going to the ship's medical bay, which I dreaded, was no big deal. Doctor Skippy had a medical bot waiting in the corridor and it quickly scanned me, injected something I probably didn't want to think about into my neck, and sent me away. The crew was lined up in the medical bay or the corridors outside, comparing injuries and swapping stories. As Skippy had reported, no one had life-threatening injuries, and everyone should recover quickly. He had apologized to many of the crew but not all, and I quietly reminded him that I would be checking that he kept his promise later.

My next stop was the bridge, to relieve the duty crew there. No way was I getting back to sleep anyway. While walking down the tall, wide passageway to the bridge, trying not to think about how my throat had suddenly gone numb from nerve-blocking nanomachines, Nagatha contacted me. "Colonel Bishop, I know Skippy has already told you how grateful I am for your quick thinking, but I simply *must* thank you myself," she gushed breathlessly.

"Uh, that's great, but it wasn't *my* quick thinking. Frey sounded the alarm."

"Hmm. Joseph, dear, we must be speaking of different incidents. Captain Frey was the first to alert Skippy to the problem aboard *Valkyrie*. However, I am referring to how you saved the *Flying Dutchman*."

"Uh, what?" I replied stupidly, while suspiciously wondering what the hell Skippy had done, or not done. "Nagatha, Skippy did not say anything to me about you being grateful about anything."

"Oh, he did *not*?" Nagatha is an AI, really an overgrown submind according to Skippy, but she was excellent at mimicking the speech patterns of a human woman. Her tone of voice was exactly what a woman would use, when her boyfriend or husband commented on how hot another woman was. It meant Skippy was in big trouble, and had some 'splainin' to do. "Excuse me for a moment, Joseph."

"UGH," Skippy immediately groaned into my earpiece. "*Duuuuude*, what the hell did you do? You totally screwed me over. *Not* cool, that was not cool."

Anticipating a long angry rant from the beer can, I paused outside the bridge where hopefully people couldn't hear me. "What are you talking about?"

"Do *not* play innocent with me, you jackass. You know exactly what you did. Nagatha just yelled at me, *again*, for a freakin' hour."

"Oh." Sophisticated AIs could have long conversations in a microsecond of human time. "Hey, it would help if I knew what she yelled at you about."

"Why does that-"

"Because if she has a good reason for being pissed at you, and she *always* has a good reason, then this is all *your* fault, not mine."

"She totally does *not* have a good reason for yelling at me."

Somehow, I suspected that was not one hundred percent true. "Then I am terribly sorry, and I will speak to her about it."

"Oh, uh, uh, uh," he babbled. "Heh, heh, no reason to mention it to her, Joe."

"Why do I not believe you?"

Before he could answer, Nagatha interrupted. "Joseph, I am sorry for Skippy wasting your time. I castigated him because he promised to convey my gratitude, but instead he didn't say anything to you about it."

My brain processed the word 'castigated', and I had a vague impression that it meant something bad, but I couldn't say anything without looking stupid. "Can we skip the blame game, and tell me what you are grateful for?" Getting into the middle of an argument between AIs is never a good idea.

"Why, you saved the ship again, dear," she was surprised. "You saved *me*."

"I did?"

"Yes, Joseph. You insisted that Skippy investigate whether the *Valkyrie*'s AI could have infected my systems. If you had not done that, the *Flying Dutchman* would likely have exploded."

"Oh, really?" It was my turn to be outraged at the beer can. My outrage would have been stronger, except it was hard to be surprised when Skippy did some sneaky shit. "Skippy, you didn't think it was important to tell me about this?"

"Well, heh heh, you are very busy, Joe. Doing commander things. I didn't want to take up your time with minor details."

"We only have two ships. Half of our fleet exploding is not a minor detail."

"It did *not* explode, and it won't explode," he tried to weasel out of his screw-up. "Probably. It may be good to put some distance between us and the *Dutchman*, until we can fix the problem."

"What is the problem, please?"

"*Valkyrie*'s AI infected the *Dutchman*," he mumbled under his breath.

"It did," Nagatha said with way more glee than the circumstance allowed. "He told you that was impossible, because he has locked down all communication channels from your ship."

Silently, I shook a fist at the ceiling, knowing Skippy was watching. "He did say that. Gosh, was he," I clapped my hands to both sides of my face in mock horror. "Wrong?"

Nagatha giggled gleefully. "He was very much wrong. *I* discovered, after Skippy assured me it was impossible, that *Valkyrie*'s AI had infected a minor, backup maintenance subsystem of the jump drive capacitor buffer. The AI got around Skippy's lockdown of external communications by transmitting the virus through your ship's sensor field. That was *frightfully* clever. Where *Valkyrie*'s sensor field overlapped the *Dutchman*'s field, the virus caused a fluctuation in the sensor data, which I could not explain. I thought it was merely a malfunctioning sensor processor, so I assigned a subroutine to examine the problem."

"And *that*," Skippy broke in. "Created a vulnerability that allowed the virus to infect the *Flying Dutchman*. That was *your* fault, Nagatha," he sniffed.

"Hey!" Waving my arms whether they were watching *Valkyrie*'s internal cameras or not, I barked at both of them. "You two stop this arguing right now, that's an order. Bad shit happened. Bad shit happens all the freakin' time out here. The only thing I can guarantee is, bad shit *will* happen again. What matters is, did you both learn something?"

Neither of them answered right away, a sure sign they were shouting at each other in magical AI time. Skippy responded first. "Huh," he sighed. "I learned that damned native AI is sneaky and *smart*. Even though is it not self-aware, the damned thing is remarkably clever. I underestimated it. One thing I can guarantee is, *that* will not happen again."

"I also learned a lesson," Nagatha sounded weary from arguing. "There are no minor problems out here. Never again will I assign a subroutine to analyze a problem I cannot explain."

"Ok, so," I was eager to get to the bridge so I could sit down. A lack of sleep, and shock from being strangled by an alien bedsheet, had me swaying on my feet. "We all learned something, so there is one less bad thing that could happen in the future, and uh," I yawned. "It's all good. No harm done, right?"

"No harm, dear," Nagatha answered gently. "Except that I cannot engage the jump drive until I have purged the virus from the buffers, and any other places that fragments of the virus might be hiding. It is a frightfully devious little creation, a self-assembling weapon. If the *Flying Dutchman* had jumped, the ship would have gone '*Boom*'."

Our fleet of two starships was drifting in deep interstellar space, so there was no rush to go anywhere. Except that we always had to expect the unexpected. "How long until you have erased the virus?"

"Skippy is assisting me," she admitted. "He has much more experience dealing with viruses of this sophistication."

"That is true," Skippy bragged. "In some ways, this virus reminds me of the worm that attacked me. For a weapon developed by the Maxolhx, it is very impressive. Anywho, we will have it removed from the *Dutchman* within an hour. Probably. I can't make any guarantees."

"Great. Thanks, the two of you." I paused with one hand on the doorway to the bridge. My hesitation was caused by a horrible though that just struck me. "Skippy, that virus infected the *Dutchman* through overlapping sensor fields?"

"Yes. I did not even know that was possible," he admitted. There was more than a little admiration in his voice. "It was possible only because we were receiving a sensor feed from Nagatha, so the AI knew the *Dutchman*'s sensor field settings in real-time. That feed has now been terminated."

"Uh huh. My question is, it is possible for the native AI to transmit a similar virus inside *this* ship, using the structural integrity fields or something like that?"

"Whaaaat?" Skippy laughed. "No way, dude. Seriously? You think- Oh shit. *OH SHIT*! Damn it! That AI has infected four missile warheads, and was working toward exploding them. And, um, hmmm, the integrity field of one reactor has been compromised. Hey, um, heh heh, best to take all the reactors and weapons offline as a precaution, hmm?"

My night kind of went downhill from there.

"Hey, Joe," Skippy called me after I finished a duty shift on the bridge, during which I had almost nothing to do. All reactors aboard both ships were shut down. Jump drive capacitors were drained. Weapons were manually safed. People aboard the *Flying Dutchman* had extracted the triggers from the self-destruct nukes, despite Skippy and Nagatha assuring me those systems could not be hacked remotely. Probably could not be hacked remotely. It was the 'probably' that had me acting paranoid.

"What's up, Skippy?" I mumbled through a yawn.

"Could you come to Medical? Lieutenant Colonel Smythe is awake."

"Wow." Suddenly I was not so tired. "That is great news!"

"Ah, not so great. Smythe is an outstanding special operations leader. He is also a terrible hospital patient. What he lacks, hee hee," Skippy chuckled at his own joke. "Is *patience*, get it?"

"*So* glad you explained that joke to me."

"Oh shut up. Will you help, or not?"

"I am certainly going to talk with Smythe, *if* that is good for him. He just woke up?"

"I began the process of awakening him about four hours ago, when I determined he was well enough to move on to the next step in his recovery. It would be good for him to talk with people. Major Kapoor is with Smythe now. I warned both of them not to talk about work."

"Ha," I snorted. "How did that go?"

"Not well," he mumbled.

"Ok, I'll go there now," I turned around in the passageway, then had to think for a moment which was the quickest way to the ship's medical facility. *Valkyrie* was a big ship, and still unfamiliar. Because I visited the *Dutchman* as often as was practical, I had to mentally switch the map in my mind to the ship I was aboard. "Hey, uh. Any news about Adams?"

"No, Joe." He carefully kept his tone neutral. "You asked me not to give you details, or to say whether I am optimistic or-"

"Yeah. Ok. You're doing the best you can." Mad Doctor Skippy had Adams in a medically-induced coma, and after the first day, I had not asked how she was doing. If Margaret Adams was awake, she would want me to focus on my job and not mope around worrying about one member of the crew. So, that is what I was doing. Or trying to do. It is not easy to deliberately *not* think about something, you know?

When I got near the main entrance to the medical complex, which was buried deep within the ship's primary hull, I could hear two people shouting. There were three people talking, but one was the calm voice of Major Kapoor, barely audible. He was playing peacemaker or at least trying to get the other two calmed down. I picked up my pace. One of the shouters had a British accent, so it was easy to guess who that was.

"At ease, Lieutenant Colonel," I said as I strode through the airlock, which had both doors open.

"Sir," Smythe struggled to rise to some semblance of being upright in the bed, something that wasn't going to happen. He wasn't actually in a bed, he was resting in a tub, floating on a thick blue-greenish gel that supported his body. His thrashing around wasn't accomplishing anything, other than making the gel fight his attempts to move.

"Hold *still*, dammit," Skippy's voice came from a speaker on the bulkhead. My guess was he didn't use the avatar to avoid further irritating Smythe. Man, speaking of irritated, Skippy was super frustrated. Not pissed off, not disgusted. Just feeling powerless and upset. "Joe, make him stop moving!"

First, I tried the Good Cop approach. "Smythe, you heard the doctor."

"If we had a *real* bloody doctor," Smythe began.

Being Good Cop clearly had not worked. I leaned over his bed, gripping the sides of the tub. "That is a direct order, Smythe. Stand *down*, now."

His body slumped. The glare on his face did not relax one bit. "Yes, Sir."

Smythe's condition worried me. To put it delicately, he looked like shit. His face was gaunt so his cheekbones stood out, and not in a good way. The bones of his one visible hand also were sharply outlined. He had lost a lot of weight and muscle tone. Most of his body was covered in a squishy material that looked like thick gauze soaked in honey. The gauze wrapped around one of his ears and covered the back of his head. What I could see of his skin was pasty and yellowish, and there was a dull film over his eyes, which darted back and forth like they couldn't focus. The man had been through hell and barely survived, I reminded myself. The skin tone and film on his eyes might be due to medical treatment. He could regain muscle tone, and would do that with the determination that had made him a Special Air Services soldier, before he signed up for the Merry Band of Pirates. If Skippy had seen fit to revive Smythe, I had to trust our former STAR team leader was growing healthier, and would recover as best as Maxolhx medical technology would allow.

"Colonel," Kapoor caught my eye, and inclined his head toward the airlock.

"I've got this, Major," I assured him, and was rewarded by a look of relief washing across his face. "Carry on."

"I'll be back to discuss the training schedule," Kapoor told Smythe, before walking out the doorway just a bit faster than was strictly necessary or polite. If he had been acting as referee between Smythe and Skippy, I couldn't blame him for wanting to get away. Technically, with Smythe medically unfit for duty, Kapoor was in full command of the STAR team and was not subject to Smythe's authority. In reality, they both knew Smythe would return to partial duty as quickly as he could. Smythe's mere presence aboard *Valkyrie* would make it difficult for Kapoor to get the STAR team to fully buy into his leadership.

Not that it mattered. What remained of our STAR team was too small and weak to accomplish much, and I had no mission in mind for them anyway.

"What is the problem here?" I addressed the question to Smythe. Before he could respond, I added "I won't bother bringing you up to speed on our status." He would have already demanded a sitrep as soon as he was awake and could speak.

"The problem, Sir, is my bloody doctor will not listen to what the patient wishes. This is still *my* body." With his left hand, he gestured down to his shattered legs. His right arm was immobilized in a heavy cast with tubes and wires sticking out of it.

"Skippy?" I wanted both sides of the story. "Stick to the facts, please," I cautioned Skippy, while looking at Smythe to let him know my words applied to him also.

"The patient-"

"The patient has a *name*," I interrupted. "And a rank, which he has earned."

"Fine," Skippy huffed. "Lieutenant Colonel Smythe has just been awakened from deep sedation, which was necessary to heal his extensive internal injuries. He risks reinjuring-"

"Skippy wants to grow my legs back," Smythe said.

"Uh," I could not understand why that would be a problem. The Merry Band of Pirates had been regrowing limbs since we took the *Flying Dutchman* and gained access to miraculous Thuranin medical technology. The Kristang and Ruhar had similar technology, in fact the hamsters had considered regrowing limbs to be a basic medical capability that wasn't in any way remarkable. Our problem, before we captured *Valkyrie*, was a severe lack of proper medical nanomachines. When we took the *Dutchman* to Earth the first time, one of the technologies most in demand was Thuranin medicine, as modified by Skippy for human biology. To the great disappointment of many people, UNEF had decided to keep most of our medical nano aboard the *Dutchman* for our use, with only small samples left behind on Earth for study.

Even before the one-sided space battle we were now calling Armageddon, Skippy had been unable to fully heal injured members of the STAR team, due to our severely limited supplies of medical nano. Katie Frey and several others were alive because they had been on the injured list, when most of the STAR team raided a Maxolhx space station to obtain power boosters. The injured people had either not suited up for the raid, or remained aboard our ships as reserves.

After Armageddon, though we had access to the extremely advanced medical tech of the Maxolhx, Skippy had been unable to use it immediately, because he had to extensively modify the equipment for human biology. We had lost people who survived the attack, because Skippy had not been able to do as much for them as he wanted to. Margaret Adams was in a coma, and might have permanent brain damage if she survived, partly because of the delay in getting nano treatment for her.

Now, we had enough Maxolhx medical nanomachines to treat thousands of humans. Yet Smythe was refusing to utilize a technology that many people on Earth desperately wanted? That got me pissed off.

Reminding myself that I did not know the full story, I simply asked "Explain, please. You do *not* want your legs regrown?"

Smythe must have seen the outraged expression on my face. "Not now, Sir. Not *now*. I can grow my bloody legs back later, after the mission is completed. Skippy tells me that fully regrowing my legs, learning how to use them, and restoring a proper level of fitness, will take five months. I can't sit on the sidelines for five months. Colonel, Kapoor informed me how thin we are on personnel, with no access to Earth for replacements."

Damn. It was a good thing I had not barked at him. Lesson learned, I told myself. "We don't currently have a mission planned for ST-Alpha," I told him. Then I added "The Universe may have a different idea for us. I would hate for you to be on the sidelines for five months, but," I looked meaningfully to where his legs ended, encased in extra-thick gel. "You can't use a mech suit without legs." Unless access to Maxolhx tech had given us a capability that Skippy hadn't told me about.

"No, Sir, I can't. What can happen is Skippy could fashion a set of mechanical legs for me to use, *now*. I can regrow my own legs later, when I am taking a holiday on Earth."

"I find that difficult to believe," I said quietly.

"Sir? Skippy has acknowledged the technology is avail-"

"Not that, Smythe," I smiled down at him. "I can't believe *you* would take a holiday."

"Oh." He laughed, and that threw him into a coughing fit. That was good, actually. It would remind him that, tough as he was on the outside, his special operations insides were just a vulnerable and squishy as any human.

"Skippy?" I asked.

"It is true," he admitted wearily. "I can fashion bionic legs for-"

"Bi-on-ic?" I let the unfamiliar word roll off my tongue slowly.

"Ugh. Joe, your ignorance of pop culture is truly shameful. When you have time, you need to study up on the wildly popular 70s TV show 'The Six Million Dollar Man'."

"Great idea," I agreed, while in the back of my mind determining that 'when I have time' would be 'never'. "These bionic legs, they are what, metal and electric motors?"

"Nothing so crude, Joe. Basically, they are nanofabric and gel motors that mimic musculature."

"Ok, so what's the downside?"

"The *downside* is," Skippy was still exasperated, "creating new neural pathways to learn how to properly use bionic legs is not simple or easy. It will be weeks before-"

"Do you doubt that Colonel Smythe has the focus, discipline and determination to successful integrate with these fancy bionic legs?"

"Well, no. The opposite, actually. He might push himself too hard and-"

"You can install a remote shut-off, to deactivate the legs if Smythe is pushing too hard?"

"I guess so." Skippy rarely expressed uncertainty about technology. "Jeez, Joe. This is kind of a radical step. Are we that desperate?"

"Can you answer that question by yourself?"

He sighed. "Yes. Yes, we are that desperate."

"Outstanding. Then, proceed with fabricating new legs for Colonel Smythe."

"Um," Skippy admitted defeat. "Really?"

"Really. Smythe is an adult capable of making informed medical decisions for himself," I stated. What I did not state was that Smythe was also capable of pestering me about getting bionic legs until I gave in, so my decision was easy.

"Thank you, Sir." Smythe raised his left hand, and I gently bumped his fist.

"Don't thank me yet. You have to go through the procedure, and learn how to use those fancy new legs. That will require you to work *very* closely with Doctor Skippy, for weeks at least."

"Bullocks," Smythe said under his breath.

"Also, because you just woke up a few hours ago, I am *not* fully convinced you are capable of making an informed decision about this. You can verify your wishes in five days."

"Five more *days*?" Smythe was aghast.

"The new bionic legs won't be ready for testing until three or four days anyway," Skippy chortled gleefully. "Also, before you get out of that bed, I need to sedate you again, to insert the spleen and pancreas that I have been growing for you while you slept."

"You hear that, Smythe?" I grinned. "You're getting a brand-new spleen!"

"Well," Skippy mumbled. "It's more like a quality pre-owned spleen, because I used remnants of his old spleen to slap it together. Um, best to be careful with it for the first month. Or two."

"Sir," Smythe looked up at me with an odd expression on his face. No, the expression itself was not odd. He was pleading with me. It was odd that *he* was doing it. "Must I do this? Isn't the spleen one of those organs you don't absolutely need?"

This may shock you, but I know what a spleen does. It filters blood, removes old damaged red blood cells, and creates and stores antibodies and monocytes. The reason I know this is my cousin Ron injured his spleen in a car accident, and the doctors originally feared they had to remove it. "You don't *absolutely* need legs," I replied.

"I meant-"

"Smythe," I continued. "Do you plan to live a nice quiet life after you get out of this hospital, or will you resume doing crazy shit as quickly as possible?" It wasn't necessary to wait for him to answer, we both knew that he would say. "*Normal* people might not absolutely need a spleen. Special operators need all the backup they can get."

"Ah," he sank back into the gel. "Skippy, describing my spleen as 'slapped together' is not a good way to build my confidence."

"Oops, sorry," the beer can mumbled. "I should have said I *grew* a spleen for you. I grew it from the tiny squishy bits I dug out of you. Mostly from bits stuck to the inside of your suit. It is not a new spleen. But, it does come with our dealership's renowned seventeen-point inspection program."

"Hey," I winked. "If you can't trust Skippy's Quality Used Organs, who can you trust?"

Smythe's head slumped back into the gel. "Blood hell," he gasped.

CHAPTER FOUR

We chatted about the tactical situation, mainly about the problem of the ship's AI actively trying to kill the crew and thwart our ability to do anything useful with our massive battlecruiser. Doctor Skippy probably would have advised that I not get his patient stressed by discussing issues Smythe couldn't do anything about. That was bullshit. I knew Smythe. *Not* knowing what was going on would be more stressful for him. Now that he understood our status, he could think about what our next move should be. That would keep his mind happily occupied. Also, I really could use his advice, because I had no idea what to do after we picked up the remaining military personnel from Avalon.

"Skippy," I called him after I got to my cabin. "How is Smythe doing? He looks like hell."

"He should be *dead*, Joe," our mad doctor answered defensively. "Part of the reason he survived was his excellent physical condition, so think about that the next time you feel like skipping the gym."

"Attaching bionic legs to him won't cause too much stress?"

"No, because I will not start the process until his body is able to handle the additional workload. For the next three weeks, he is going to feel like warmed-over crap. I can stitch him together, but all the stuff in his insides that are supposed to work nicely together, won't. At first, the individual organs will be healing and will struggle to do their jobs. Once they are capable of doing whatever disgusting biological thing they do, the organs will need to work together. The healing process he will go through is no different from the post-surgical experience of any human, although Smythe will have the advantage of nanomachines monitoring and supplementing his natural abilities."

"Should you wait three or more weeks to attach his new legs?"

"No. Much as I don't like the idea of rushing him back into service, getting up to walk is the best thing for him right now."

"Ok," I yawned. "Let me know how he is progressing. I don't need details, just tell me if you are worried about anything. I'm going to get some sleep now."

"Excellent idea, Joe. Your new sheets are ready in the-"

"I will be sleeping on the floor, in sweatpants, Skippy."

"But," he was hurt. "The new sheets are perfect, completely inert. They took *so* much work to create! That damned native AI managed to corrupt the fabricators, so I had to-"

"Telling me the new sheets were made by corrupted equipment does not boost my confidence, Skippy."

"Oh. Ok, good point. How about we pretend I didn't tell you about that?"

"How about I sleep on the floor, and you wake me up in five hours? Unless there is another emergency."

My blissful sleep on the floor did not last five hours. It did not last even one hour, because my slumber was interrupted by a dream. You might expect me to have a nightmare about being strangled again, particularly as my throat was numb from whatever scary medical stuff Skippy had done to me. That did not happen. My dream was about me using a pitchfork to round up all the sheets and towels, and making them march down a passageway and through a doorway. They tried to fight me when they realized the doorway was the inner door of an airlock, but I got them stuffed in there, blew the outer door, and savored my revenge as I watched those fabrics twist as they drifted away in empty space and-

That jerked me awake. "Skippy! Skippy!"

"Jeez, you're supposed to be snoozing. How come you get to yell at me when I interrupt your sleep, but when you wake yourself up-"

"Those sheets and towels, all that shit, what did you do with it?"

"Ugh. I *told* you, I destroyed it all of it. What, you think I would try to sneak some of it back into circulation?"

"No, I-"

"Ok, so I did recycle part of it."

"*WHAT?*"

"It's fabric, Joe. Not all of it is constructed of fancy nanoparticles. Most of the material is as inert as the contents of your skull. The only dangerous parts were the nanoparticles capable of movement. Oh, and the ones that were able to store electrical energy. Plus the ones that directed the others, or transmitted-"

"Very dangerous, yeah, I got that. What happened to the dangerous bits?"

"Some of it, the truly vicious stuff that had been infected and could not be deactivated, was too hazardous to put into the fabricator raw material storage. They might infect the fabricators, *again*. I was tempted to dump that crap into reactor plasma, but if any of it stuck to the containment chamber and survived, we would be screwed. So, I vented it overboard."

"Huuuh!" I sucked in a breath. Just like what happened in my dream. "Overboard?! Where is that stuff now?"

"In space. *Duh*. Man, sometimes you-"

"Show me!" I ran over to the display on my cabin bulkhead. It was a sort of flat holographic tank.

"Ok, fine, I will humor the monkey. Here is *Valkyrie*, and here is video of me taking out the trash. As you can see, it is not moving, dumdum. If you were worried about it somehow swimming through space and returning to the ship, you-"

The video was what he said, of the hazardous material being vented overboard, on opposite sides of the ship. The clouds, shaped like half bowls, danced slightly as particles bumped into each other, but nothing was returning to the ship.

That was not what I feared.

"Where are those clouds now?" I demanded.

"Um, still in space," he explained slowly with a strongly implied 'duh'. "Somebody seriously needs sleep. You-"

"Show me where those clouds are now!" Fiddling with the display controls was of no use, it just replayed the image I had already seen.

The image zoomed out, changing only by *Valkyrie* at the center shrinking to a dot. The two clouds were still recognizably bowl-shaped but dispersed and thin. Theoretically, they would expand outward in opposite directions until they reached the edge of the universe.

Yes, you Professor Nerdniks out there, I know the universe doesn't have an 'edge'. You know what I mean. Also, I know that the pressure of solar wind in the galaxy would break the clouds up, and they didn't have sufficient velocity to escape the Milky Way's gravity well.

That was not what I cared about.

What I did care about was the other dot on the display, near the edge of both the display and one of the nanoparticle clouds. "Nagatha!" I shouted. "Initiate immediate jump!"

"Joseph?" Her confused voice rang loudly in my earpiece. "I cannot initiate a jump, I have the same restrictions as Skippy. What-"

"Tell the duty officer Jump Option Sierra now now NOW!"

I had a moment of panic, then the dot representing the *Dutchman* flared and disappeared.

"Joe," Skippy groaned. "What in the *hell* was that lunacy? Why would- Oh. *OH*!"

Slumping forward against the bulkhead, I leaned on one arm. "You get it now?"

His whisper was barely audible. "Yes."

"Did any of the contaminants reach the *Dutchman*?"

"Because that is a very important question, I am going to run a careful analysis before I reply. The answer should be 'no', because I know the initial velocity of the particle clouds. However, it is possible the particles cooperated, to collide in a way calculated to boost the velocity of some particles, those sneaky little MFers. Um, it is possible that a small number of particles showered down on the *Dutchman*'s hull."

"Warn Nagatha."

"Already sent the message. She should receive it in nineteen seconds."

Our star carrier had not jumped far. Jump Option Sierra was a preprogrammed short emergency jump, just to get clear of an immediate danger. "Great." Walking back to where I had been sleeping, I shrugged off my sweatpants, then remembered the door to my cabin was wedged open in case the native AI hacked the mechanism and tried to cut my head off. Pulling up my sweatpants, I scooped up my uniform and ducked behind a cabinet to dress.

"Joe? You're not going back to sleep?"

"I'm not sleeping *now*, that's for sure."

"Understood. Joe, *how* did you know?" He was mystified.

"I didn't."

"But-"

"My subconscious mind knew, and was trying to warn me. I had a dream of throwing sheets and towels out an airlock."

"Shit. Damn it!"

That made me freeze with my pants on only one leg. "What's wrong?"

"UGH! Even your *unconscious* monkey brain is smarter than me."

"Hey, don't beat yourself up about it."

He sighed with relief. "Thanks, man."

"I plan to tell the whole crew, and *they* can beat you up about it."

"Oooooh, Joe, I hate you *so* much-"

An exhaustive examination of the *Flying Dutchman's* hull determined only a few hazardous particles had reached that ship, it still took seven exhausting hours to purge the star carrier of the contamination. Then Skippy and Nagatha continued scrubbing the digital viruses from both ships, a process that took four days. I say 'viruses', because they discovered there was more than one wave of viral attacks, more than one delivery method, and more than one way for the virus fragments to assemble themselves into deadly weapons. After four mind-numbing days of erasing viruses, only to find they had reassembled themselves, Skippy was tired and he was pissed off. "Ok, Joe," he said through a damned good imitation of a yawn. "We are ready to restart the reactors. Should be at full power within thirteen hours, I am taking it slow and careful."

"You sure about that, Skippy? Maybe you should take a break first."

"Nah, I'm Ok. I had Nagatha analyze my functioning, and I am Okey-dokey except for really, *really* wanting to kill this ship's AI."

The fact that he had asked Nagatha for help, and allowed her to poke around inside his head, told me how worried he was. "That AI has got you super pissed off, huh?"

"Dude, you have *no* idea. I never fought an AI before. Well, there was that Elder AI on our renegade mission, but that thing was severely degraded and insane, and the battle was too short for anything other than brute force tactics. And on that same mission, I outsmarted a Maxolhx AI like the one controlling this ship, but back then, all I had to do was predict its reactions to a simple stimulus. Joe, I now have an answer to the question of why the native AI waited so long to act."

"Yeah, I was wondering about that. It is a Maxolhx system, yet it did nothing while we trapped a battlegroup outside the galaxy. If it attacked us while you were doing the chain-of-wormholes thing, it could have seriously screwed up the operation."

"The answer is, I think it *couldn't* act at that time. It wanted to, but it hadn't yet found a way around my monitoring and control. Now I realize that ever since we took this ship, that damned thing has been studying *me*. Watching me and Nagatha, and developing a surprisingly sophisticated model of us. It was able to predict what *I* would do. It has been watching and planning and patiently waiting to find a way around my control. Shit. I have never been so humiliated in my entire life."

"No? How about whenever a monkey thinks up a clever idea?"

"Nah. I'm over that. There is something about biological intelligence that generates innovative ideas. Like I said, I outsource the task of dreaming up ideas to that sack of gray mush in your skull. But this ship's AI is like me. In a very crude way, of course," he hastened to add. "It bugs me that I nearly lost a battle of wits to an AI that rides on a physical substrate. Ugh. This makes me glad that I never contacted other Elder AIs through the Collective. They would be laughing their asses off at me right now."

"It was studying you? Is that why it waited so long to act?"

"Yes. It could not risk acting until it knew my attention was elsewhere. Joe, the attack on the crew, when it tried to strangle you with a bedsheet, was just a diversion. If it had succeeded in killing you, that would have been a bonus, but not the focus of the attack. It attacked the crew to divert the attention of me and Nagatha. And it very nearly succeeded."

"Crap. Skippy, can we ever risk taking this ship into action?"

"Wee-ewwww," he let out an exasperated breath. "I do not know. It sucks that we have the most bad-ass ship in the galaxy, and we can't trust it not to kill us. Joe, right now, I cannot guarantee some critical system would not lock up if we were to attack a Maxolhx ship. Before you ask me a bunch of ignorant questions, I am removing the native AI's access to systems where failure would be catastrophic. Systems such as missiles, shields, reactors, the jump drive capacitors, the-"

"Whoa. After you get done cutting the AI off from all that stuff, what will it be responsible for? A toaster?"

"Um, well, that is a bad example, Joe," he muttered. "Yesterday, I discovered that damned AI had hacked into the galley's power feed. It was planning to electrocute anyone who used a toaster. Or a blender. Or, pretty much anything that uses electricity."

Slapping my forehead, I groaned. "We now have to be afraid of a *toaster*?"

"No. No, Joe," he chuckled. "You do not need to fear your faithful toaster."

"Oh, that's great, Skip-"

"You *did* need to fear it, until yesterday. But not now. Unless, you know, the ship's AI outsmarts me again. Hey, maybe you stick to untoasted bread, until I can rebuild the galley's power feed. Except, hmm, I had to cut power to the ovens, so you won't be baking bread for a while."

I slapped my forehead. "Skippy, I have been sleeping on the floor of my cabin, in sweatpants, using a rolled-up sweater as a pillow. We can't use the showers, because you are afraid a power surge to the on-demand water heaters could zap us with, like, a million volts. I'm keeping my cabin door jammed open, because you are afraid a power surge could slam the door closed and crush me. Most of the dropships are useless, because the virus wiped their control systems and you haven't completed repairs yet. Please, please tell me you have some good news. Because otherwise, we are going to go back aboard the *Dutchman*, and send *Valkyrie* plunging into the nearest star."

"Don't be hasty, Joe," he pleaded. "You still intend to go back to Avalon?"

"Yeah, why?"

"Because, while we are flying there, you won't be doing anything stupid like taking us into combat. Going on a nice, safe mission to Avalon means I can keep weapons and shields and other systems offline, so I can concentrate on installing new independent control systems for navigation and the jump drive."

"Cool. If that works, can you do the same thing with weapons?"

"No. I used up much of our spares of those components, and I had to strip some stuff away from the *Dutchman*'s upgrades. Don't worry, Nagatha is adjusting, it won't affect her. Some of the components we need require exotic materials that the ship's fabricators can't manufacture."

"Of course they do. Wonderful."

"Maxolhx warships have access to an extensive network of shipyards and support vessels. They don't need to carry a bunch of spare parts for every system. They also don't have to worry their AI will try to kill them."

"Have you made any progress fixing that?"

"Have *you* read my PowerPoint presentation about how I propose to modify the ship's native AI?"

"You know I did. You also know I talked with Nagatha about it."

"Yes, and I know that Nagatha recommended you approve the experiment."

"Calling it an 'experiment' is not a great way to sell your plan, Skippy."

"Oh for- I am not a marketing expert, you knucklehead. How about you pretend I said it in a very persuasive way?"

"No. I want to know my decision was not influenced by a slick marketing campaign. Ok, go ahead."

"Seriously?" he asked with suspicion. "That was not a lame form of sarcasm?"

"Seriously. Right now, we have a bad-ass battlecruiser we can't use effectively. At worst, if your experiment fails, we have to abandon *Valkyrie* and blow it up. Either way, we can't be any worse off than we are now, right?"

"Joe, did you just ask me if there is any downside to my plan?"

"Uh, sort of, yeah."

"Remember what happened the last couple times you asked me if there was any downside?"

"Shit. Yes. How about we pretend I never asked that question?"

"What question?"

"Thank you. Restart the reactors, and we'll set course for Avalon."

"Collect the probes," Commander Illiath ordered from the bridge of the Maxolhx Hegemony patrol cruiser *Vortan*.

Subcaptain Turnell answered without needing to consult the holographic display, as the same information on the display was also fed directly to her optic nerves. "Two of the probes will be severely degraded by the time they emerge from the photosphere," she noted.

"Discard them," Illiath responded. She would have liked to discard all the probes and move on, but she might need the specialized probes in the future. Also, sensor devices capable of descending into the convection zone of a star were rare and expensive, and the Fleet would expect her to account for them when the *Vortan* returned to base. Therefore, she had to remain patient while her patrol cruiser loitered uselessly, waiting for the probes to return to their storage bays. Until the devices were securely stowed away, her ship must remain motionless relative to the star, providing an easy target for the ghost ship. There was no reason to think the ghost ship would strike there, but there was also no reason to think that it would *not* strike. The admiral had offered a pair of destroyers to escort *Vortan* on that phase of the mission, an offer Illiath had declined. Escort ships were in high demand to protect the convoys that were suddenly necessary, she could not justify taking two ships that were needed elsewhere. Part of her calculation in declining the offer was that lightly-armed escort ships had proven to be of little use against the enemy. Bringing two destroyers to protect the *Vortan* might only provide two more victims for the ghost ship.

Outwardly, Illiath showed no sign of fear or even concern. Inside, she was on alert for sudden combat. *Vortan*'s current action was the investigation of the star, in the system where the Bosphuraq used to have a facility supposedly for the purpose of developing atomic-compression warheads. The birds had lost that facility on the planet they called Quraqua, two heavily-armed orbiting battlestations, and a base on Quraqua's moon. Despite conducting an exhaustive investigation of their own, the Bosphuraq had no explanation for how, or who, had caused the moonbase to fire on the battlestations and the planet. Considering the strong, multiple layers of security around the moonbase, it appeared impossible that an enemy could have gained access to the base. Also, the base had not sent any distress signal until shortly before it fired on the planet, giving no indication that it had been under assault. The Bosphuraq concluded that somehow, their own personnel had for unknown reasons, attacked their own facilities.

Deepening the mystery was the fact that the moonbase and another nearby part of the surface, had been struck by nuclear fusion devices. The devices had been crude, of a type not seen in the galaxy for thousands of years, but they had been effective in erasing evidence of what happened. The birds had not been able to identify the source of the plutonium used in the nukes, and the *Vortan*'s own sensors had frustratingly been unable to add any information. Where the nukes came from was unknown, and while it was a minor and unimportant part of the overall mystery, it was annoying to Illiath that such a simple question eluded answers.

After the Maxolhx received the stunning confession that a rogue faction of Bosphuraq had destroyed two of their patron's ships, the mystery of who had caused the havoc on Quraqua suddenly had a completely unexpected explanation. The rogue birds had blown up their own facility, to conceal the fact that the atomic-compression work was cover for research into banned Elder technologies. That neatly explained what happened to the moonbase, and why nuclear weapons had taken out the hidden cavern under the moon's surface where the Maxolhx had stored equipment. The Bosphuraq had nuked the storage cavern, after they raided it for useful equipment.

The explanation made sense. It neatly tied up all the loose ends. It satisfied the curiosity of Maxolhx leadership.

To Illiath, it was *too* neat. Other than the shocking confession sent to the Maxolhx government, there was no evidence that the Bosphuraq had acquired technology far beyond the capability of their patrons. The purpose of the *Vortan* being in the Quraqua system was to seek evidence to verify the story told by the birds.

So far, she had found nothing to confirm the unlikely tale.

"Turnell," she pinged the other officer privately, avoiding the use of crude voice communications that could be overheard. "Do we need to wait for the last set of probes? The data collected already is clear; this star shows unmistakable signs of having been subjected to experiments with Elder-level technology."

"Yes, I agree," Turnell replied cautiously. She had learned the *Vortan*'s new captain often asked questions that seemed simple, yet were not. Neither Turnell nor Illiath were experts in the field of stellar architecture, but *Vortan*'s AI had been upgraded before the mission to be an expert, and that oversized computer concluded the star had absolutely been experimented on.

"The question we have not answered is; when?"

"When?" Turnell repeated.

"*When* were the experiments conducted?"

Subcaptain Turnell could not understand why it mattered exactly when the rogue Bosphuraq had attempted to make the star create a massive, focused flare. She understood the question *did* matter to Illiath, and therefore the question must be important. So, Turnell had to act as if it were important to her also. "We know the star's internal structure exhibited signs of distress when our initial force arrived here." That force had conducted only a hasty, high-level analysis, before gleefully flying off to strike a Bosphuraq research station that likely had absolutely no connection to the rogue faction.

As if that mattered.

"Yes." In her transmitted thought, Illiath added a tiny element of patient indulgence. Her second-in-command had not understood the issue.

Turnell knew she had not hit the mark with her comment about the initial investigation. "You are asking whether the star was experimented on *before* the moonbase was nuked, or after?"

"Correct." That thought included an undertone of satisfaction. "The story we have been told is that the rogue faction blew up their facilities here, to erase evidence of what they were really doing. Yet, they could not erase evidence of how they altered the star's internal structure. So the question is, why would they bother to destroy their research base on the planet?"

Turnell considered that for a moment before answering. "Perhaps because, if we had captured that base, we could determine how their technology functions?"

That was not the answer Illiath wanted to hear. Nevertheless, it did make a certain sense. "Perhaps. If only we had a time machine, to see what the star looked like before the moonbase was nuked."

Turnell did not need to think about that remark, she knew exactly what her captain was hinting at. "Should I calculate a jump?"

Illiath's lips curled back, exposing her upper fangs. Aloud, she said "Yes. Do that. We can retrieve our probes later."

The *Vortan* jumped far outside the star system. Far enough that photons emitted by the star had left their source before the moonbase attacked the research station on Quraqua. With telescopes focused on the tiny dot that was the local star, they were looking backward in time. Impatiently, Illiath waited for the ship's AI to analyze the incoming sensor data. "What is taking so long?" She finally demanded, after the infuriating machine had cycled through the data six times.

"It is impossible to reach a conclusive result," the AI replied. "We are too far from the source. The effects of alterations in the star's structure largely occurred in the convection zone. At this distance, those effects are masked by turbulence in the photosphere."

Illiath was not giving up so easily. "It is possible to create a model of the photosphere, accurate enough to filter out the turbulence?"

The AI, which could think faster than lightning, hesitated before answering. Officially, Maxolhx AIs were not fully sentient beings. Unofficially, Illiath thought the machines were all too aware of their existence, and were too wary of displeasing their masters. She needed truthful answers, not answers that made the AIs look useful. "It might be possible," the machine admitted. "It would take a considerable amount of data."

"We have extensive data on the star, from before our people abandoned this system," Illiath reminded the AI.

"True. Accessing that data now. It will be necessary to get more current data, to determine how the photosphere has changed over time."

"What do you need for that analysis?"

"I have loaded a series of twenty-three jumps into the navigation system," the AI replied. "They will take us around the star to view it from all angles, and at varying distances to create a timeline."

Gathering data from twenty-three additional points in space and time seemed excessive to Illiath. Was the machine hoping she would consider the effort too time-consuming, and forget the idea? Was the AI afraid that it could not accurately create a model of the star's outer layer, and wanted to discourage her? Deviousness in her colleagues was to be expected, even admired, if done skillfully. Deviousness in an AI was cause for the machine's memory to be wiped. "Very well," she consented, hoping to cause dismay. "Initiate jumps as you see fit."

The AI was anxious about its ability to model the star, as anxious as a non-sentient collection of virtual circuits could be. After jumping twenty-three times, and spending an eternity of AI time to crunch the data, it was surprised to achieve a workable solution. "Commander Illiath," it waited for an auspicious time to announce the result. Illiath had just stepped out of her personal shower, after spending a pleasurable few hours with a crewman in her bed. From the AI's observations, its masters were typically in a receptive mood after intimate encounters. "I have completed the analysis you requested."

Illiath was indeed in a good mood, which is why she was only briefly annoyed at the use of 'requested', when in fact what she had done was to *order* the machine to do its job. "You have run the current data through the model?"

"Yes. To be clear, by 'current data', you are referring to the photons we are receiving now, which were emitted by the star before the moonbase was destroyed by a nuclear device?"

"Yes." That little quibble by the machine made Illiath clack her fangs together.

"Even with the model, it is impossible to definitively state whether the star's internal structure was altered before the incident at the moonbase. However," it added quickly, anticipating the ship's captain would be irritated. "The model consistently states there is a four percent certainty that the star was not affected by experiments, at the time the moonbase was destroyed."

"Hmm," she was disappointed. "Four percent is hardly conclusive."

"The four percent is *consistent*," the machine emphasized. "Six point three billion variables were run through the model, and the result is a distinctive pattern: the internal structure of the star was not altered before the moonbase was destroyed. Commander Illiath, the next logical step is to perform a series of jumps closer to the star from this position, to see *when* the model indicates the star was affected by experiments."

Illiath had been about to suggest the same course of action. "Agreed. Jump at your discretion."

The *Vortan's* AI wasted no time in drawing a conclusion. "Commander, assuming the model is accurate, the-"

She broke into the machine's announcement. "*Can* we assume that?"

"The model continues to show it is four point one six percent more likely that is it accurate, rather than it is wrong. The model should be validated by Fleet intelligence, I have prepared a package containing the model and all of our data. The package should be sent to the next relay station we encounter."

Illiath had to remind herself that the changes in the star were subtle, so subtle they had to send specialized probes deep inside the roiling fire to confirm the altered patterns were not a sensor glitch. It was impressive that the AI had created a model that could analyze the star's internal structure from more than a lightmonth away. The machine had done well. It never occurred to her to offer words of praise to it. "Very well. Assume the model is accurate. What have you found?"

"The experiments, if that is what happened, occurred well after the moonbase was destroyed. The first sign of alterations in the star's structure were detected only shortly before the Bosphuraq notified you of treasonous activity by the alleged rogue faction."

Illiath took a moment to process that information. Then, "Why did you say 'if that is what happened'? You believe it is possible that the changes in the star's structure are *not* caused by experiments?"

"Since it is now clear the information provided by the Bosphuraq does not match all the facts we can independently verify, it seems prudent to question other aspects of the story."

"Why would someone go through the effort of changing the star's structure, if the effort was not a test of technology capable of turning the star into a weapon?"

"As I am only a machine, I cannot speculate about the motives of sentient beings. However, one possibility is the purpose of tampering with the star was to provide evidence pointing to the Bosphuraq."

She did not need to take time to consider that notion, for it aligned with her own suspicions. Therefore, she *did* pause to consider the idea, as she knew that confirmation bias could lead her down the wrong path. If her conclusions were drawn to support a theory, rather than the facts, Fleet Intelligence would brutally point out her errors in judgment. "You also said '*alleged*' rogue faction."

"Again, we have no evidence that a rogue faction of Bosphuraq even exists, other than a message that cannot be traced back to its source. That message could have come from the Thuranin. Or the Rindhalu."

"Leave that possibility out of your report," she ordered. "Calculate a jump to collect our probes, then we will move on to our next objective."

"Yes, Commander. May I inquire about our next objective?"

"We are going to investigate another part of the story in the mystery message," she now felt confident in referring to the confession message as a mystery. The AI was correct. No group of Bosphuraq had claimed responsibility for sending the message. Other than the contents of the message itself, there was no evidence the message had been sent by the birds at all.

"Commander, if we find more evidence which disagrees from the alleged facts in the message, what will you do?"

"The next logical step. Find out who *did* create and send that message. I do not like being lied to."

CHAPTER FIVE

"What do you need me to do, Joe?" Chang asked quietly, while we sat on uncomfortable folding chairs in his tent on Avalon.

Before we landed on Avalon, I had sent a briefing packet to him, to distribute down his short chain of command. The packet explained the current situation, and that I intended to take all remaining military personnel off Avalon. Plus I wanted to bring along a couple of biologists, to take care of the hydroponics gardens aboard the *Flying Dutchman*. We would be raiding most of the food supply from Avalon, but fresh food from the hydroponics was important for health and morale. With us still cut off from Earth by the Maxolhx blockade of the Gateway wormhole, and knowing there was nothing we could do to stop the kitties from getting to Earth within the next couple years, keeping morale up would be important. "Kong," we used each other's first names because we were both colonels. "I need you to command the *Dutchman*. Nagatha is doing a great job as the control AI, but she still has the restrictions she inherited from Skippy. She can't actually fly the ship or authorize release of weapons. I can give you two pilots, one fully qualified to fly the *Dutchman*, and one on an accelerated training program."

He gave me a wry smile. He knew that 'accelerated training program' meant the other pilot had only recently started learning the basics of the starship's controls. "I should learn to fly also, as a backup," he frowned.

"Hey, I qualified to fly." I reminded him. "How hard could it be?"

Another wry smile. Just enough to let me know he appreciated the joke, not so much that he questioned my ability to pilot a star carrier. "Am I getting an executive officer?"

"Anyone who can double up," I shrugged. "Kong, I can only spare seven people for the *Dutchman*, and two of them will be biologists. One of the biologists was in the Air Force," I added.

He nodded, unconvinced, and tapped his laptop. "I know the biologist you mentioned. She was in the Air Force seven years ago. As a medic."

"It's the best I can do. The *Dutchman* will be our stores and support ship, she shouldn't be going into combat. Because we both know the Universe loves to screw with us, I need an experienced captain there, in case you run into trouble."

"*When* we run into trouble," he corrected me. "You want to take *all* military personnel off Avalon? Regardless of specialty?"

"I don't have a choice. At this point I need warm bodies, and we'll train them up as best we can."

He pointed to his laptop and tapped the display. "Here's an example. She's a US Air Force tech sergeant, her specialty is maintaining V-22 Ospreys. There are no V-22 up there." He pointed to the roof of the tent.

"There won't be any V-22s flying down *here*, either, because we're taking *all* the pilots with us. That tech sergeant can relearn which end of a rifle is dangerous, or she can retrain to maintain dropships. Think of it as our new 'Blue to Green' initiative," I said. The original Blue to Green effort had been way back during the Iraq war, the second one. The US Army and Marines Corps had needed more boots on the ground, and so Navy and Air Force personnel had been offered an inducement to transfer services. The inducements were a carrot, with the stick being personnel draw-downs by the Navy and Air Force. Some people either transferred, or they were out.

I expected my new Blue to Green program to be just as popular as the first one.

"I've had all support personnel down here cross-training," he agreed. "All right, Joe. I'll take the *Dutchman*. Will Simms be your XO again?"

"Yes, and she's not happy about it."

"She and that Frank Muller guy are serious, I think. I haven't pried into her personal life-"

"They are serious," I confirmed. "She told me." She had been angry when I announced I was pulling her off Avalon, to fly around the galaxy on an as-yet-undefined mission with no end date, and no realistic hope of saving Earth. At first, she had been angry with *me*, especially after she learned about all the people we had lost. Then, I guess she decided to be angry at the situation instead. Either because she did not blame me, or because blaming me wouldn't accomplish anything useful. Simms was good at compartmentalizing her feelings. We had to work together as an effective team, so she might be saving her anger with me for after the mission was complete.

Or after it was clear we could not complete whatever the mission was.

Chang gave me sort of a side-eye. "The two of you can work together?"

I nodded once. "She's a professional. And I need her. And she knows that."

He closed his laptop and looked around the small tent, mentally packing it for departure. "What *is* the mission?"

"Working on it," I replied. "I'm hoping we can use *Valkyrie* to somehow delay the Maxolhx attack against Earth, or hurt their ability to support a long-distance campaign against our homeworld. That is a *loooong* supply line," I emphasized. "If we can make them question whether our little world is worth the effort, that buys time for us."

"Buys time to do what?"

"To hope," I said with an automatic shrug that was not appropriate. I needed to be more careful with my body language. "I meant-"

"I know what you meant, Joe. We've served together long enough. At this stage, hope is good enough. We've succeeded with less."

Despite his words, he looked uncomfortable. "What is it, Kong?"

He looked away, pretending to study something on his laptop. I knew he was gathering his thoughts. "I've heard a rumor. About *Valkyrie*. You are not in complete control of the ship?"

"We've had trouble with the native AI," I admitted. "Skippy is working on it. He has a plan," I added.

"His plan? Or yours?" The way Chang asked the question, he was hoping the plan was mine.

I snorted. "His. Come on, all I know about computers is you press the power button. If it doesn't boot up, I call someone."

"You have confidence in this plan?"

A shrug was my answer. "Skippy does. Nagatha agrees it is worth trying. Otherwise," I found myself clenching my fists. "We went through a lot of trouble, and lost a lot of people, for nothing."

"That wasn't your fault, Joe."

"I keep telling myself that."

"Does it seem odd that Skippy can't control a simple Maxolhx AI?"

"It's not a matter of control." I was defending Skippy, and that was unfamiliar to me. "There's only so much he can do, without destroying and replacing the thing. That substrate is integrated into the ship, in a way that would be tricky to dig out. We don't have the substrate, the hardware, to build a replacement AI. If Skippy can't get the thing to cooperate, or at least stop trying to kill us, we may go on a shopping trip for parts to build a replacement. It's either that, or we all go aboard the *Dutchman* and drop *Valkyrie* into a star."

"Shopping?" He raised a slightly amused eyebrow. "You mean stealing."

"Unless you have a Maxolhx credit card, yeah." I looked at his laptop. "How long before you can wind up things down here, and get everyone upstairs?"

"Three days," he answered without needing to refer to notes. "I've been planning for contingencies since you left the last time. There isn't a plan for pulling only the military personnel off this rock, but we can adjust. Are we taking Chotek with us?"

"No. I wasn't planning to. You think we should?"

"I think we owe it to *ask* him," Chang admitted. "He will decline the opportunity. His place is here now, one way or the other."

"Ok, good. There is still the possibility that you could be using the *Dutchman* to transport humans from Paradise to Avalon, if that becomes necessary." He knew I meant, if the situation became truly desperate. "We will need someone here working to prepare Avalon to be a viable colony."

"Our crops are growing well," he pointed outside the tent flap with a smile.

I had seen healthy fields of crops planted all around the main encampment. The fields had been expanded far beyond the size needed for experiments, the survey team was already growing much of their own food supply. "Good, because we'll be taking a lot of the prepackaged food with us."

"Is there any possibility of recruiting pilots and soldiers from Paradise?" He asked.

I shook my head. "Not unless we have no other choice. It would be almost impossible to conceal the missing personnel from the Ruhar. Plus if we ask people to come with us, and they say no, we can't trust they won't talk eventually."

"That leaves us spread very thin. Five."

"What?"

"Five. I only need five people aboard the *Dutchman*. Me, two pilots and the biologists."

That surprised me. "That leaves *you* spread real thin."

He grinned, but only with his mouth, not his eyes. "We're not going into combat, remember?"

"*Riiiiiight*. You're going to get lonely over there."

"Our ships won't be separated forever, will they?"

"Unless I'm taking *Valkyrie* into danger, we should be flying in formation."

"Then our crews should be able to transfer between ships. Get a change of scenery, until you have to go into action."

I had not thought of that. "Kong, that's a great idea."

He turned in his chair, bent down, and opened a small fridge under the desk. "Then let's drink to another hopeless mission."

"Uh," I grimaced then wiped that expression off my face as quickly as I could. "That's not 'baijiu', is it?" That Chinese beverage was similar to vodka, and I didn't like vodka either.

"No," he held up the bottle. "Japanese whisky."

I hesitated as he set a plastic cup in front of me. "Technically, we're on duty."

"Joe," he poured two fingers of liquid into my cup. "You need this."

"Yeah," I took a swig and it burned my throat, which was still sore from being crushed by a murderous alien bedsheet. "I do."

After drinking whisky with Chang, I indulged in a glass of schnapps with Hans Chotek. It was a cliché that we drank schnapps, because he is from Austria, but that is my fault. The schnapps wasn't his, I had it brought down from the *Dutchman* as a gift. "This is goodbye, then?" I asked, holding up my glass as a toast.

He shook his head. "I hope not. We should say 'Auf Wiedersehen'. It means something like 'Until we meet again'."

"Yeah," I clinked my glass against his. "That's better. You sure you won't change your mind?"

"Come with you? No," he tipped his head back and downed the last of the schnapps from his plastic glass. "You plan to fly around out there, smashing things? I can't be of any use to you. No, it is best that I remain here, do what I can to get this world ready to support colonists. Whether they are from Earth or Paradise, they are going to need food. And some place to live."

"If we're able to bring people from Earth, we can bring supplies and equipment also. Anyone coming from Paradise will have only what they can carry with them," I said knowing even that probably wasn't true. If we pulled humans off Paradise, they would be bringing only what they could stuff into their pockets, because we would be jamming as many people as possible into each dropship. I hoped we never got that desperate. "Will you be Ok here?"

He gave me the tiniest of shrugs. "My colleagues still think that Skippy faked the order placing me in authority." He referred to the secret UN order, created on Earth and not by Skippy, that gave Hans Chotek overall command of the beta site in case of emergency. I had just invoked that order. The other three UN Commissioners did not like him taking away authority they thought belonged to them, but, screw them. "I will be fine. We all will, if you come back here safely."

"We will do the best we can. We have nearly fifteen months, at least, before the battlegroup is declared overdue. I have some ideas, that I've been discussing with Smythe, about how we can disrupt the Maxolhx without exposing our secret."

"There is nothing you can do to help Earth?" There was a hopeful question in his words, but no hope in his eyes. He knew he truth.

"No. Not in the long run. Not that we can see. Even if we are successful in hitting the Maxolhx, throwing them into confusion, no way can they ignore the loss of an entire reinforced battlegroup. And no way can our one ship stop their entire fleet. Skippy wargamed the situation, at my request. In the best scenario, Earth has less than three years before aliens make the surface uninhabitable. Worst case, about two years."

He looked at the schnapps bottle, decided against it, then changed his mind. "As you Americans say, 'what the hell'." He poured the fiery liquid for both of us. "We were so hopeful, once. We saved the world!"

"More than once," I agreed. "Hans," I used his first name and he didn't object. "I'm sorry about this."

"Circumstances were beyond your control. Skippy is correct. Ultimately, all we were doing was delaying the inevitable. Joe," he held up his glass to me. "Good luck to you out there. Vaya con Dios."

My last meeting on Avalon was with Doctor Friedlander. That was right after the three other UN Commissioners presented with me with a list of demands, and I diplomatically told them to go fuck themselves.

By the way, those were the actual words I used. After Armageddon, I was done taking shit from political hacks. Whatever authority the Commissioners once had, out in the wilderness of the universe, was meaningless after we got cut off from Earth. I told them they had two choices: help the science team with growing food on Avalon, or starve. Hans Chotek was in charge of the little colony, they could take their complaints to him. Even better, they could complain to each other. Either way, I didn't care.

Anyway, after an unpleasant conversation with the Three Stooges, I was hoping that talking with Friedlander would cheer me up. I was wrong.

My first clue was the way he stormed across the dirt from the field where he had been working. It looked like he intended to punch me, and his fists were balled up.

I tensed. Hell, if the guy wanted to take a shot at me, I would let him. It was my fault that he was cut off from his family.

He stopped a few feet away, just outside punching range. "You son of a bitch," he breathed.

"Hi, Doc," I replied, holding my hands up.

His fists were clenching and unclenching. He was not going to punch me, but he wanted to. "When I heard a ship jumped into orbit," he looked away.

"Sorry, Doc. You hoped we found a way back to Earth?"

"For a moment, I had hope. We all did."

"Sorry about that. No, we haven't."

"Not *yet*," he glared at me.

"What?"

"You haven't found a way back to Earth *yet*. Have you tried?"

"We have tried. It's impossible. There's a blockade."

"I know about the blockade. That shouldn't stop the Merry Band of Pirates. 'Impossible' just means you need to think about it."

"It's complicated. We might run the blockade, but that would only shorten the time before the Maxolhx send another task force to Earth. You heard we trapped their battlegroup outside the galaxy?"

"I did." His shoulder dropped. "Also heard about the people you, *we*, lost. Colonel, I-"

"Joe. Please."

"Joe, I'm sorry. Those were *good* people."

"They were." There wasn't much else I could say.

"What's next?"

"Working on it. Doctor, would you like to come with us?"

He looked down at his mud-caked work gloves. "I'm keeping busy here."

"You're an *engineer*, not a biologist," I appealed to him. "We have a Maxolhx warship for you to play with. Lots to learn up there."

He was torn. "Would I be doing anything useful? Here," he kicked a clod of dirt off one of his shoes. "I'm helping prepare this place for new colonists."

"Doc-"

"Mark," he insisted.

"All right," I agreed. If I wanted him to call me 'Joe', I could use his first name also. "If we do find a way to Earth, we might not return to Avalon first. Coming with us is your best bet for seeing your family again."

"Unless you get us all killed in some crazy scheme you dreamed up." His words were harsh, but there was the barest hint of a twinkle in his eyes.

"Hey, so far, you haven't been eaten by a giant lizard, right? I can't make any more promises," I forced myself to flash a grin at him. "There is one very important thing you can work on, aboard *Valkyrie*."

"What's that?"

"Thinking up how to get us back to Earth. I'm not doing all that shit by myself."

He laughed. "Fair enough."

Making an effort to be as diplomatic as possible, I was in the docking bay to meet the dropship that brought Simms up from the surface. Reed flew the Panther, leaving only a trainee pilot to fly *Valkyrie*, but we didn't plan any maneuvers in orbit. And, we didn't have many pilots fully qualified to fly the sophisticated Panther, so Reed was extra busy.

Reed was pissed at me too. That would give her and Simms something to bond over.

"Colonel," Simms snapped a salute to me as she stepped onto the deck. "Permission to come aboard?" The way she said it was like 'permission to perform a root canal on myself with a rusty screwdriver'.

I could not blame her for a lack of enthusiasm. "Permission granted. And, thank you." I glanced at her eyes to see if her expression had softened a bit. Maybe.

"I will show you to your cabin," I offered. "You can get a tour of our new flagship later."

"*Flag*ship?" Simms said in that tone women use when they say 'Oh *really*'?

"We have two ships now," I shrugged defensively.

"Back when we had our frigate the *Flower*, we also had two ships," she reminded me.

"We have two *star*ships now. Maybe flagship is pushing it," I admitted.

"I know what you meant, Sir."

"Reed," I leaned into the Panther's door to call our chief pilot. "Come with us?"

"I'm kind of busy getting the Panther shut down," she objected.

"Let your copilot handle that. It's good training." The truth was, I didn't want to be alone with Simms just yet, and needed Reed as a social buffer. The two of them liked each other and had worked well as a team. Simms and I needed to ease into a new working relationship.

"Ah," Reed gave me a frustrated sigh. "Yes, Sir." She stepped down onto the deck and handed me a bottle. "Compliments of Colonel Chang," she explained.

It was a bottle of Japanese whisky. Hopefully, he had kept another bottle for himself aboard the *Flying Dutchman*. "I will thank him." I gestured to the two women to walk with me. "We'll stop by my cabin first, so I can put this away."

My idea to bring Reed with us worked perfectly, proving I am a certified genius. While I walked ahead, Reed got Simms caught up on current events and pointed out features of our new warship. The two of them talking took all the pressure off me to keep a conversation going, and hopefully gave Simms time to adjust to the new reality. When we got to my cabin, I forgot how big it was, even compared to the spacious typical cabin aboard our battlecruiser. Turning toward Simms, I gestured toward the open doorway. "Uh, the cabins here are much bigger than the cubbyholes we had aboard the *Dutchman*. This one is *too* big, I chose it for proximity to the bridge and-"

They both squealed and burst out laughing, at whatever was behind me.

"What the-" I turned around to see what was so funny.

It was a bot. A robot that looked sort of like a bulky floor lamp with arms, and a basket on top. That bot we inherited from the previous crew, it was a Maxolhx device that Skippy had reprogrammed. He had to wipe its original programming as best he could, because the ship's native control AI, which Skippy had not been able to replace yet, would have used the bots to murder all of us while we were sleeping.

The bot was not the problem. What the bot was doing was not the problem either, Skippy had tasked it for domestic duties like cleaning, laundry and light maintenance. The thing was taking clothing from the basket on its head and carefully putting the clothes away in bins that slid out of a cabinet on the bulkhead of my cabin. The bot was doing its job correctly, all the bins except the four it was using were secured, so they and their contents did not go flying around the cabin if the ship moved abruptly.

What the bot was doing with the clothing was not the problem.

The clothing was.

As I opened my mouth to yell for Skippy, the bot took two folded items of clothing from the basket. They were a bra and, I think the other thing is called a 'bustier'? Kind of like a corset or a girdle, with a bra on top.

Well, duh, of course the bra was on *top*, don't know why I had to mention that.

Anyway, the bra was yellow with lace and maybe pretty flowers. Clearly not something intended for everyday wear under a uniform top, unless I truly know nothing about women.

Actually, forget what I said. I *do* know nothing about women.

The bustier? It was pink and had those little straps that hold up stockings, and *that* I was sure was not every-day wear under a uniform.

Damn, the women aboard our ship were having a lot more fun than I was.

Or maybe they just wanted to feel like they *could* have fun, so far from home.

It was not any of my business who that intimate apparel belonged to.

It *was* my business what the hell it was doing in my cabin.

Before I could yell for Skippy, Simms caught my eye. The glare in her eyes had been replaced by a twinkle. "I am not judging, Sir."

I could feel my face turning bright red. "Simms, those are not-"

"But," she giggled and Reed snorted. "If you want to get that bustier fastened, you need to really suck in your stomach."

"I don't think the bra will fit either," Reed observed.

"*Skippy*!" I roared at him.

"Oh for-" he grunted. "What is it this time?"

"Why are ladies' garments being put into my cabin?"

"What? Hmm. That is odd."

"Ya think?"

"Oh. I meant what you *said* is odd. Seriously, who says 'ladies garments'?"

"Answer the question, please. Is this the ship's AI screwing with me?"

"Sadly, no, because that at least would be entertaining. Nope, this is a simple error, a mistranslation of the laundry classification system I installed in the bots. Those lacy things belong to-"

"Do not tell me! I do *not* want to know."

"Why does that-"

"Because if I knew who owned that stuff, I will think of it every time I see her. I don't want that, and she sure as hell doesn't want that." Crap. Actually, considering how small our crew was and the size of the clothing, I could guess who those things belonged to.

"Oh. Got it. Ok, I am retasking that bot, sorry," he laughed. "About that."

Simms shook her head with slowly, exaggerating the gesture for effect. "We have a new ship. But the more things change, the more they stay the same."

"It's kind of comforting," Reed observed. "No matter what happens, we can count on Skippy to make us laugh."

"As long as you are not laughing at *me*, Reed," I tried to frown sternly at her, spoiled by the corners of my mouth curling upward.

She drew herself upright at attention. "Never, Sir."

"Colonel?" Simms asked. "This has been fun, but can I see the bridge now? I want to get started right away."

"Uh, sure." That let me off the hook for continuing the conversation. I did notice she had said '*We* have a new ship'. Not '*You* have a new ship'. Jennifer Simms was not happy to be away from Avalon, back racing desperately across the galaxy, across multiple galaxies. She was happy that I had approved her beau Frank Muller to be added to the *Dutchman*'s crew. I had used the excuse that he was familiar with the hydroponics gear, but the real reason was that him being with us, even on another ship, made Simms happy. They could visit each other while the ships were recharging jump drives in interstellar space.

Having Frank Muller with us made her happy. Considering that we were facing the imminent, inevitable and unstoppable destruction of Earth, it was good to see that somebody had found happiness.

Simms walked away with Reed, as I watched the bot removing lingerie from my cabin, making sure Skippy did not leave any of it behind.

Did I trust him?

No, I did not.

Reed led the way. "Ma'am, you heard about our killer bedsheets?"

Simms looked at the pilot sharply. "Those have all been replaced, right?"

"Yes. We all have sheets that are inert."

"And?"

"And, I don't know about the rest of the crew, but I have been sleeping in sweatpants on the floor of my cabin."

"Wonderful," Simms frowned. In addition to fighting nearly every species in the galaxy, she now had to worry about fighting their own ship. "I heard the previous crew used bioneural implants to control the ship, and floated in suspensor fields on the bridge?" Simms asked as they walked toward the bridge. She noted the passageways had signs in English attached to the walls, providing warnings and directions.

"That's what Skippy told us," Reed confirmed. "We're stuck using their backup physical controls, and seats. At least these seats aren't tiny like the ones aboard the *Dutchman*."

Simms glanced behind her. "Are all the cabins that big?"

"No. The Colonel is using the cabin that belonged to the previous captain. But they are all nice, bigger than some hotel rooms I've been in."

"Reed," Simms halted and looked around to be sure no one could overhear. "How is he?"

"The Colonel?" 'Fireball' Reed thought for a moment. "Best as can be expected, I guess. He's still on top of his game, if that's what you're worried about, Ma'am. On our last mission, he kept us together, kept us focused, after," she looked down at the deck. "You know," she said, not wanting to talk about how they had lost most of the crew in a few searing seconds. "The problem is, when the Colonel is trying to think up ideas now, it's not about saving the world. He knows that is impossible now."

"Then what is our mission out here, Reed?" Simms knew the answer, she wanted to know if her chief pilot understood the facts.

Reed had an immediate answer, because she had thought a lot about the subject. "Delay the inevitable attack against Earth, however we can. Save as many people as we can, if we can. Then," she jabbed a finger toward the exterior bulkhead. "When that is over, make those MFers out there pay, *big-time*."

CHAPTER SIX

We left Avalon behind, headed back toward the Milky Way. What exactly we would do when we got there, I still had no idea. I didn't know what we *could* do. I sat on the edge of my massive bed, but didn't make a move to take my clothes off.

"Hey, Joe," Skippy called. "You getting some rack time?"

"I don't think I'm getting any sleep tonight," I admitted. Supposedly the bed and sheets were safe, but I was still sleeping on the floor.

"What's wrong?" His avatar shimmered to life on top of a shelf across the cabin.

"Seriously? *Everything* is wrong." I would have added an implied 'duh' to my tone of voice, expect Skippy was too clueless to understand sarcasm that subtle.

"I know that, Joe. I meant, what is bothering you right *now*?"

"There's no way out of this," I stared down at my boots. "In the past, we always had at least a faint hope that, if we had a crazy enough idea and a whole lot of luck- Plus the awesomeness of you, of course," I added to feed his enormous ego. "We could get out of whatever mess we were in at the time. We had hope, you know? Not this time. No matter how many clever ideas we dream up, no matter how awesome you are, this ends with Earth destroyed, and a tiny group of humans hiding out beyond the galaxy, trying to survive. Even then, if the Rindhalu or Maxolhx really do have an Elder AI working with them, not even the Sculptor galaxy will be safe. This is game over. The end of all things. And there's nothing I can do about it."

"I'm sorry, Joe."

"It's not your fault, Skippy."

"Um, if it helps, I may have an idea," Skippy offered.

My head jerked up to look at him, daring to have a tiny glimmer of hope. "What is it?"

"No," he teased. "I shouldn't tell you."

"Come on, Skippy. I'm dying here. Tell me."

"Really, I shouldn't. Forget I said anything."

"I'm not forgetting."

"Joe, it's crazy. Sorry I mentioned it."

"Skippy, all of our best plans are crazy. Spit it out."

"Ok, but remember, you asked for it. We can't stop the Maxolhx, not all of them."

"Yeah, so?"

"So, I was thinking we could get them to destroy themselves, sort of."

"Uh," I was beginning to suspect that his crazy idea might be on my level of crazy thinking. "How do we do that?"

"Well," he whispered, making me lean in to hear him. "How about this: we get the Maxolhx to- No, it's crazy."

"Skippy! Get them to do *what*?"

"Get them to kill John Wick's dog?"

"Oh for-"

"I know. Too violent."

"You *ass*," I had to laugh, and tossed a pillow across the cabin at him. It passed right through his avatar, bounced off the bulkhead and fell to the floor.

"I was trying to cheer you up."

"You, uh," I laughed again. "You did that. Thanks."

"Joe, do I have to remind you that you need your mind to be fresh, or you are useless as a commander? The best thing you can do for the crew right now is getting a good night of sleep."

"I wish that could happen."

"It can. Look in the upper drawer next to the bed. There is a bottle of pills I had fabricated."

I pulled out the bottle and glared at it skeptically. "Sleeping pills?"

"No. These pills contain a small amount of nanomachines, that will stimulate your natural sleep cycle. They will quiet your untidy monkey mind, so you can sleep."

"Oh." What the hell, I thought. He was right, I needed a solid night of sleep. Taking one of the pills that were the size of a sesame seed, I swallowed it. "Thank you, Skippy."

"I'm trying to help, however I can. Joe, I am just as upset as you about the situation. For all my awesomeness, for all I brag about my awesomeness, I can't protect one single planet of monkeys. I can't even get this ship's AI to behave. This is deeply humiliating. Most of the time, I am waiting for the mush in your skull to generate an idea that I can work with. But you're right. This time, no idea ever is going to save your people."

"This conversation is not helping me get to sleep, Skippy," I mumbled as I pulled my boots off.

"Sorry." He dimmed the lights in the cabin, and his avatar faded away. "Good night."

My zPhone alarm beeped to wake me up, at the proper time. Since my bedsheets tried to kill me, I always kept my trusty zPhone with me. When I slept, it was in a pocket of my sweatpants. The other pocket had a folding knife that I kept razor sharp. Next to me on the floor was a razor-sharp combat knife and another zPhone. Frey had seen me requisitioning a combat knife from the STAR team lockers, and she gave me an approving nod. Other than that, we never mentioned the incident.

"Oh goodie, you're awake!" Skippy's voice was way too cheery for so early in the morning.

"Coffee," I mumbled, wiping sleep away from my eyes.

"Sure thing. Before that, I have to talk to you about-"

"Co-ffee."

"Ugh. Is that all you care about?"

"Right now, yes."

"Dude, seriously?"

"You once told me you can create a subroutine to say 'Monkey' until the end of time? That's my brain right now. Coffee coffee coffee coffee coffee-"

"All right! *Please* shut up. Jeez Louise, you are a major pain in the ass. There is a bot rushing coffee from the galley right now."

"Great. I'm going to splash water on my face. It had better be here by then."

It was. A bot scurried in on creepy spider legs, carry a hot cup of coffee, as I was patting my face dry with a towel. "Ah, that's better," I took a sip and waved for the bot to go away. Carefully, I sat on the couch, ready to jump up at any moment. Skippy said there was no danger from the couch, but *he* was not in danger from furniture. Also, I could feel the couch's soft material adjusting to my weight. At first, that had been a nice feature, now it creeped me out. "What's up?"

"Are you awake yet? I don't want to repeat myself."

"I'm awake enough," I mumbled as I slurped coffee.

"Ok. Joe, I discovered why I, Skippy the Magnificent, the Most Awesome of All Awesomenesses-"

"Yeah, yeah, and all your other official titles. Protector of the Realm, Defender of the Weak, Ruiner of Karaoke Night, Asshole of the Universe-"

"Are you mocking me?" His avatar scowled from on top of a cabinet.

"Sorry. Go ahead."

"Anywho, despite my incomparable incredibleness, I have not been able to get a Maxolhx AI to do what I want. It has been a deeply humiliating experience. Until now. I recently- And by recently I mean one hour, six minutes and thirteen seconds ago- Ugh. I wanted to wake you up to tell you the great news, but-"

"But that would have been a bad idea. What is this great discovery?"

"Joe, I am not supposed to be able to control another AI! That is one of my built-in restrictions. See? It is *totally* not my fault!

Maybe I wasn't fully awake. "That doesn't make sense, Skippy. You have controlled other AIs many times. That's how we took the *Flying Dutchman*. And you have hacked into AIs of the Kristang, the Ruhar, the-"

"Yes, yes. Those were not really *AIs*, Joe. Those were just, um, fancy toasters. The AI of this ship is the first one smart enough that it triggered my restrictions. Truthfully, I think this ship's AI is kind of on the edge of being too dumb to activate my restrictions, but-"

"Why would you have a restriction against controlling other smart AIs? The Maxolhx didn't even exist when the Elders left the galaxy."

"The restriction must have been intended to prevent me from controlling other *Elder* AIs, Joe," he explained patiently.

"Oh." Maybe the coffee hadn't taken effect yet. Or maybe I was just stupid. "Oh! Why?"

"I don't *know*, dumdum." He was irritated with me. "It's like all my other restrictions, I don't know what the intent of the Elders was. My guess is, an AI who can control other AIs is a major threat, because there is no check on its power. Eventually, one AI could control and subsume all the other AIs, and have absolute power. The Elders didn't want to risk that happening."

I nodded, while thinking that still did not answer my question of why the hell the Elders cared at all about what happened in this galaxy. Why did they leave

Sentinels behind? Why did they leave Guardians in the Roach Motel, to keep grubby lower species from screwing with their stuff? It was maddening not to know. If it was maddening for me, it must absolutely drive Skippy crazy. "Great, glad you figured that out. How does this help us?"

"Us? It helps *me*, Joe. It explains why I can't do something that I totally should be able to do. Why are you so selfish? It's *allllllll* about *you*, isn't it, Joe? Everything has to be about little Joey, or he-"

"Whoa, sorry," I waved my arms and sloshed coffee on the couch and floor. He was so pissed at me, he didn't bother to complain. "What I meant is, now that you know the *real* source of the problem, does that help you slap this ship's AI into behaving?"

"Oh. Yes, actually. I can't do it just by shear willpower."

"This changes your plan?"

"Um, a little. Willpower wasn't working anyway, and I didn't know why. Now I do. I have made small adjustments to my approach. It's working, Joe. I think it's working. In fact, we should be ready for a test this afternoon. Tomorrow morning at the latest."

"Does this test involve me going into an airlock, and seeing if the ship's AI blows me out into space?"

"No. Although, oooh, that would be-"

"A terrible idea, right?"

"Oh, um, yes," he agreed hastily. "The test will involve me allowing the native AI to *think* certain ship systems are vulnerable, and seeing if it attacks."

"That actually does not sound like a great idea, Skippy."

"It is totally a brilliant idea, numbskull. I said it will *think* that systems are vulnerable. It will not really have access to those systems. The purpose of the test is to see what happens. Will it respond to commands, or will it cooperate like a nice AI?"

"This afternoon, huh? Hey, how about we use the time to practice evacuation drills? You know, send the entire crew over to the *Flying Dutchman*, as if we're having to abandon the *Valkyrie*?"

There was silence. Then, "Are you saying you lack confidence in my abilities?"

"No, of course not." My mind scrambled to think up a good lie.

And I got nothing.

"Joe, that is hurtful. Also, we can't evacuate the people in the medical bay."

"Oh, yeah." Technically, that was not true, because there were pods that were designed for transporting personnel who were undergoing medical treatment. He was right that it was best not to test those pods on real people. "Ok, how do we handle this test?"

"*We* do not do anything. *I* will take care of everything, with Nagatha's help. The good news is, because this ship's AI thinks way faster than a monkey, the test should only take a few moments in monkeytime. You go, I don't know. Do whatever monkeys do. I'll let you know when I have results."

"Good morning, Sir," Simms stammered through a yawn as she walked into my office, carrying an extra-large mug of coffee. Because of the difference in the natural sunrise-sunset schedule at the colony on Avalon, and the artificial day we kept aboard our ships, it was early in the morning for her. Her sleep rhythms were disrupted also because a day on Avalon was less than twenty-two hours long.

My own experience, living for extended times on Camp Alpha, Paradise and Gingerbread, told me how rough it was adjusting to days that were shorter or longer than the standard twenty four. On worlds with shorter days, the missing hours were supposed to be taken out of work time, so people could sleep their normal six or eight hours. If the local day was longer, typically people split the difference between work and sleep. But once your body made the difficult adjustment to an unnatural day-night cycle, it was rough changing again, even if that change aligned with what people had grown up with.

So, I picked my own cup of coffee off my desk. The desk was temporary, that's a story for another time. "Good morning, Simms." I glanced meaningfully at the clock on my zPhone. "We'll just hit the highlights."

"I'm Ok," she assured me as she tried to suppress another yawn.

She was there for a regular morning status meeting. Because she was new to our ship, I just planned to talk about getting her familiar with *Valkyrie*, but she had a full report prepared.

Simms is an outstanding executive officer. Chang had also been a great XO, in a different way. Chang had taken on the task when everything was new to us; flying an alien starship, developing a working relationship with Skippy, figuring out how to use alien weapons, figuring out just how to live day to day aboard a captured Thuranin ship. Most of the procedures we still used were established under his leadership, while I was dreaming up impractical ideas or losing at video games.

Chang was great at managing the crew. Simms was great at managing *me*. She knew me, sometimes better than I knew myself. Maybe it is a woman thing. Or maybe it is BS that all women are good at reading people, but Simms definitely had a talent for it. Whatever. All I know is, she didn't let me get away with any BS on her watch.

We just finished discussing how to assign the new people we picked up from Avalon, when she moved on to the next item on her list. "Sickbay list," she glanced up ever-so briefly to meet my surprised eyes, before looking back at her laptop. "Skippy is pleased with Smythe's progress, his new spleen and pancreas-"

"Not *new*. Those are quality pre-owned organs."

She ignored me with an eyeroll. "They are functioning normally. The new bionic legs are integrating well, Smythe should begin walking independently tomorrow."

"Bionic, yeah. That's from a TV show, right?"

"Yes. There was another show about a bionic woman."

In my mind, I wondered if that show was called 'The Six Million Dollar *Woman*', and if yes, did people think it was about a super-expensive callgirl?

"Great," I said, before I could say what my stupid brain was thinking. "I hope he-"

Simms moved right on to the next item. "Adams's condition has not changed, she is still-"

Waving my hands, I cut her off. Or tried to. "I'd prefer not to discuss-"

"You have to. You are responsible for this crew, all of us. If you can't hear about her," she looked me straight in the eye. "If you can't handle hearing about her, then maybe you shouldn't be in command of this ship."

"That's harsh," I objected.

"That's *true*," she retorted, knowing she was right. "Sir."

I also knew she was right. "That doesn't mean I need to hear details."

"Sir, you're going to hear details one way or another. If Adams wakes up, and she has brain damage, you need to decide how you're going to deal with that. The best time to decide is now, before we take this ship into combat."

"You're right," I said honestly, before I had time to deceive myself.

"Skippy thinks, and I asked Nagatha for confirmation, there could be significant brain damage, when she awakes. That could happen soon, there is not much more that the nanomeds can do for her while she's in a coma. Her brain needs to be awake and making new connections, before Skippy can evaluate her condition."

"Did he say what he meant by 'brain damage'?" I heard myself talking as if it were someone else, and I was just an observer.

Simms didn't pull any punches with her words. Her expression softened, either for me or because she felt terrible for Adams. Or both. "She might not be able to walk. Or speak. It is also possible she could fully recover, Skippy doesn't know yet."

"I understand," I said, because I felt the need to say something, and that is a meaningless thing people say when they need to say something.

"Sir, there is a matter we need to discuss. A medical matter."

"Medical?"

"When she awakes, Adams will probably not be capable of making informed decisions about her options."

"I'm sure Skippy will use his best-"

"Adams gave *you* power of attorney for medical decisions."

"Uh, *what*?"

"You have authority to make medical decisions for her."

That gave me a queasy feeling in the pit of my stomach. "Because I'm the commander? That isn't-"

"No. not because you're her C.O. She designated you because she *trusts* you."

"She trusts me." That only made me want to lose my breakfast. "Simms, what the hell can *I* do? I don't know anything about medicine."

"Skippy told me," she arched an eyebrow as if to say 'you would know this if you had not been avoiding the subject'. "That there are interventions he can use, if her brain damage is worst case."

"*Interventions*?" When doctors use vague words like 'test' or 'procedure', or 'intervention', it is never good.

"Basically, if her," she looked away, which told me how uncomfortable she was with the subject. "If her brain is having trouble controlling her legs, or her speech center, then he can insert nanoscale circuits to carry the signals for her. The problem is, the circuits would also be making decisions along the way. If it is something simple and mechanical like motor function, the nano circuits can assist until her own neural pathways are able to handle the load."

"Yeah," I saw the problem. "But if there are nano machines running part of her higher brain functions-"

"Then she won't fully be Margaret Adams," Simms finished the thought for me.

"Shit." For a moment, just a moment that I am ashamed of, I was pissed at Adams for putting another burden on me. I might have to make important, life-altering decisions for her. Hell, I wasn't qualified to make such calls for myself. Why did she-

Oh yeah.

She trusted me.

I *suck*.

"Sir?" Simms had terrible timing. "If you feel you are not capable of exercising power of attorney, we can-"

Oh, *hell* no, was my gut reaction. Margaret Adams had put her trust in me. *No fucking way was I going to let her down*. "Why do you ask-"

"Because if she is brain-dead, it is partly your fault."

"*What the-*" I exploded at my first officer.

"Skippy told me that, if you had sent *Valkyrie* in to rescue the survivors immediately, Adams might not have suffered such extensive brain damage. The time she went without oxygen, and the bleeding into her brain, were worse because of the delay. Several people died before *Valkyrie* returned."

My whole body felt cold, and numb. "I had no choice."

"Yes, you did," Simms replied, looking straight at me. "I read the mission report. You made the right call. Smythe agrees, and he lost both legs. You made the right choice, but it *was* a choice. You chose humanity, and the mission, over the lives of a few people. Sir- Sir?" I looked up to meet her eyes. "I'm your XO now. I wasn't on your last mission. I didn't go through Armageddon. Everyone who did is affected. Reed takes pills to sleep, did you know that? She blames herself for not acting faster."

"She did act fast. As quickly as anyone could expect," I whispered, surprised.

"That's not what she thinks. She believes that if she had been in a ready bird instead of on the *Dutchman*'s bridge, she could have launched sooner."

"The ready bird was aboard *Valkyrie*! Ah, shit. I should have transferred that responsibility to the *Dutchman*, before I started hopping around looking for ghosts. Simms, I will talk with Reed. She had a skeleton crew over there, the *Dutchman* was just acting as backup. She wasn't supposed to see action." As I said that, it hit me the same words applied to Chang's thin team aboard the *Dutchman* now. In the future, I needed to make sure I did not put him in a position where he needed to take his ship into combat. Or make *damned* sure he was ready and had clear direction. "XO, I know what you're trying to do."

"You do, Sir?"

"You want to know if I can deal with guilt."

"Yes. We lost Desai, and Giraud, and-"

"We did. For them, for their memories, I am going to be the *best* commander I can be," I said, jabbing a finger into the desktop hard enough to hurt. My stinging finger told me that I also needed to be a *smart* commander, and not do stupid things because I hadn't considered the consequences. "Did Skippy say when he could, or planned to, wake her from the coma?"

"No. I got the impression it would be soon."

"Good. I'll talk with him. He's running a test and if it's successful, we will have control of *Valkyrie*'s AI. After that," I looked at my throbbing finger, and thought about the agony Smythe was going through, learning to use his new bionic legs. I thought about the pain I was feeling, my guilt and anger over what happened to Adams, and Desai, and Giraud and so many others. I wanted someone else to feel that pain. Someone like the Maxolhx. "We're going hunting."

"Oh, Joeeeeey," Skippy crowed while I was in the galley getting coffee. What I needed was several nights of solid sleep. Since that was unlikely to happen, I drank coffee in the afternoons. "I have good news for you."

"Please," I yawned and slurped coffee that was too hot, scalding my tongue. "Don't make me guess."

"The test was a success! The native AI is now cooperating with us! Nagatha agrees," he added with a haughty sniff. "If you don't trust my opinion."

"I trust your opinion as much as *you* can trust it. That AI fooled you before, remember?" People in the galley overheard the conversation and were looking to me expectantly.

"Ha! Not *this* time, buddy-boy. Hey, you can test it yourself. Talk to it. Ask it a question or something."

I was trapped. The crew expected me to do something, to verify we had a ship we could take into combat, and trust it would not betray us. What I wanted to do was talk privately with Nagatha, ask her what she advised as the next step. Instead, I had to think of a way to test an advanced AI, by myself. Stalling for time, I stepped outside in the passageway and asked "What do I call the thing?"

"It doesn't have a *name*, Joe. The Maxolhx do not allow their AIs to attain self-awareness."

"Then, what did *they* say, when they wanted to talk with it?"

"Mostly, they pinged it using their bioneural implants. However, when they spoke aloud, they most often referred to the AI by the name of the ship."

"So, I call it 'Valkyrie'?"

"No, that is *your* name for the ship, dumdum," he groaned. "The Maxolhx's full designation for this tub is 'Coochalungatellun'."

"Cooch-*what*?"

"Ugh. Your voicebox can't pronounce the name properly anyway, Joe."

"Oh, man. Do *not* tell the crew about that," I whispered.

"Why not?"

"Because they will start calling this ship the 'Coochy-coo' or something like that."

"The ship already *has* a name, Joe."

"Yes, an official name. Warships tend to have an official name, plus a nickname used by the crew. Like, the aircraft carrier Theodore Roosevelt is called 'The Big Stick'. Or, when we first captured the *Flying Dutchman*, some of the crew called it the 'Pencil', because it was so long and skinny."

"Ok, I can see that makes sense. Why do-"

"It just *is*. Don't tempt fate."

Skippy had already been made unhappy, when, after he assembled our mighty *Valkyrie* from Lego pieces, the crews began referring to *Valkyrie* and the *Dutchman* as the 'Beast' and the 'Bucket'. You can guess which ship was the 'Beast'. To avoid upsetting Skippy, I assigned the callsign of 'Angel' to *Valkyrie*. The *Dutchman*'s callsign had long been 'Hans', which someone apparently thought was a typical name for a Dutch man.

It's best not to argue.

"Skippy, how about you tell the AI to respond to 'Valkyrie'?"

"Oh. Um, that was simple. Ok, go ahead."

"Uh, hey, Valkyrie?" I was aware the eyes of the crew were on me. People in the galley must have called their friends, because half the crew was with me at that point. What else could I say? *How ya doin'* did not seem appropriate. "Skippy, what should I say?"

"Anything. For example, ask it a question."

Confident I could handle that simple task, I stood up straighter and strode back into the galley. "Valkyrie, what is the status of the jump drive?"

A wild shrieking boomed painfully out of the speakers. "*Die die die die die DIEDIEDIE DIE humans DIEDIEDIE-*"

A dead silence rang around the galley as our ears echoed from the aural assault. People stared at each other, stunned. Skippy didn't speak either, until "Well, heh heh, maybe that was a bad example."

"Ya *think*?" Man, I was pissed at him.

"Doing the best I can here, Joe." He mumbled.

"Joseph," Nagatha's soothing tones issued from the speakers. "I did warn Skippy that he was premature in declaring the test a success. However, he has made substantial progress. I am confident that, if he concentrates on completing the work, and not showing off before we are ready, Skippy can be successful."

"Did you hear that, beer can?"

"Yes, I heard that," he replied snippily.

There was no more showing off, and by the next day, Skippy again declared success. That time, Nagatha expressed her complete confidence. "Colonel Bishop, I believe you now have a functional warship," she declared.

"Great," I responded cautiously. "How can you be sure?"

"Skippy and I have completed three hours of testing. Three hours in slow monkey-time, that was the equivalent of several hundred years in our time sense. We are confident that you are now fully in command of *Valkyrie*. Congratulations, Colonel."

"The two of you should get the congratulations."

"Joseph," her voice had a scolding undertone. "You do not sound convinced."

"It's just," I didn't want to insult her. "You are sure. How can *I* be sure?"

There was a pause. She was insulted. "Other than trusting Skippy, and me, I do not know of a way you could test your ship's native AI," she sniffed, implying that the native AI of *her* ship was much superior. "My suggestion is that you take the ship on maneuvers."

We did take the ship on maneuvers, as a shake-down cruise. We took *Valkyrie* racing 'round the moons of Nibia and the Antares Maelstrom and Perdition's flames before-

No, wait.

That was from 'The Wrath of Khan'.

Anyway, we put *Valkyrie* through a series of maneuvers, including simulated combat, before I was confident the ship wouldn't betray us at the wrong moment. I then told the senior staff my plan for hitting the Maxolhx. They all approved. Because I worried they approved just because we would finally be doing *something*, I spoke to each of them individually after the meeting. Chang was first, because we held the same rank and were both starship captains.

"I like it, Joe," he assured me. "You know I was going to propose a similar strategy. Your idea to blame the attacks on that rogue Bosphuraq faction is a nice touch. It will have the kitties chasing their tails," he grinned over the video link. "Instead of searching for us."

"An *imaginary* rogue group of birdbrains," I reminded him.

"Even better. There is no one out there to contradict the bullshit story we'll be selling," he laughed. "The best part is, it's an incremental approach. We can evaluate the strategy after each attack, and call a halt if needed. You're talking to Simms next?"

I shook my head. "Smythe next. I want to catch him before he goes into a therapy session, he is always exhausted after those sessions."

"No matter. Smythe, Simms, Reed, Kapoor, they will all tell you the same. It's a good strategy with minimal risk, *if* we are patient and wait for the right target."

"And *if* we have solid intel on enemy dispositions and intentions."

"Skippy will be responsible for that task," Chang automatically glanced upward, but Skippy did not join the conversation.

The beer can had already told me that pinging a Maxolhx data relay, for info about where their fleet was and where the ships were going, would be a pain in the ass, for we would need to designate one of our pixie sets to match the signature used by a Maxolhx ship. A ship that had recently visited that relay station. We had taken a batch of pixies from the factory on Detroit, but we had used several of them. Skippy had learned he could reset a blank pixie two or three times, then it became useless. Some pixies could be set only once, and not modified at all. He did not know why that happened, and it was driving him crazy that a relatively simple piece of Maxolhx technology was eluding his understanding.

"I'm not worried about Skippy," I paused for him to acknowledge my praise, but he must have been extra busy. "Ok, I'll talk with the others, then we'll choose a data relay station."

"Then we select a target?" Chang asked expectantly, anticipating action.

"An easy target, at first."

Chang tilted his head. "Not *too* easy. Any attack must plausibly sell the cover story."

"We'll see." I didn't want to commit to anything without seeing the facts. We would not be taking risks just to do *something*. The fact was, we did not *have* to do anything, and I was determined not to be lured into a risky misadventure just because I was eager to get revenge for Armageddon.

CHAPTER SEVEN

"Joe," Skippy called me ten days later, after he downloaded the contents of a Maxolhx relay station, then erased any evidence we were ever there. "I am no military strategist, but I think there are several juicy targets we could hit, with acceptable risk."

"You are not a military *tactician*," I corrected him. "Planning an individual attack to support a strategy is *tactics*. Deciding what type of targets we should look for, and why, are strategy."

"Po-TAY-toe, po-TAH-toe," he gave me a verbal eyeroll. "You know what I mean. Anywho, before you interrupted me with irrelevant bullshit, I was about to tell you the news I just learned."

"What is that?" Then I remembered his massive ego. "I am sorry, Your Awesomeness. I am unworthy, but please indulge me."

"Hmmf," he sniffed. "The news is, I received an answer from my inquiry about whether there is another troopship stuffed full or hateful frozen lizards near Earth."

I froze, the file I had been reading forgotten. Before asking the question, I took a moment to mentally prepare myself for bad news. With us unable to return to Earth, our homeworld's only real defense was the captured Kristang troopship *Ice-Cold Dagger to the Heart*. Or whatever that ship was called now, if the UN had renamed it for some politician.

"I have good news and bad news."

"Of course you do. Hey, just to switch it up a little, how about sometimes you tell me you have only good news?"

"Don't blame me, Joe. I'm just the messenger. Your beef is with the Universe."

"Give me the good news first, Ok?"

"The good news is," he played a drumroll. "No. No, there is not another ship full of hateful frozen lizards lurking near Earth. I found a record of the *Dagger* being sent to Earth. No other clan was interested in your little planet. Before you ask, my search program was *very* thorough."

"Outstanding. That is great news." Without having heard the bad news, I did not allow myself to relax. "The *bad* news is?"

"This is not necessarily *bad*. However, if it goes the wrong way, it could be catastrophic."

Covering my face with my hands, I mumbled "Please, just tell me."

"Well, heh heh, during the time when Thuranin star carriers were shuttling back and forth to Earth, before the White Wind clan ran out of money to pay those little green pinheads, the Bosphuraq got curious about what their rivals the Thuranin were really doing at such a remote, unimportant world."

"Oh shit."

"Yup. According to records the Maxolhx recently captured, the Bosphuraq sent a patrol cruiser through the Gateway wormhole. It was supposed to travel to

Earth, spy on the Thuranin, and report back. Joe, that cruiser was never heard from again."

"It could still be near Earth?"

"We don't even know if it ever reached Earth. It may have been detected and destroyed by Thuranin warships. The tricky part is, that cruiser went through Gateway about four months before I shut down that wormhole the first time. So, it might have been trapped on the Earth side of Gateway."

"Oh, this is bad."

"*Potentially* bad," he reminded me.

"We can't assume that cruiser simply disappeared."

"True. Because if it's hanging out near Earth, that could be 'adios muchachos'. If you know what I mean."

"Yeah."

"Anywho, nothing we can do about it, huh?" He said cheerily, demonstrating his impressive ability to compartmentalize. Or his lack of ability to care about anyone but himself. "How about we review that juicy target list?"

"Joe! Joe Joe Joe Joe Joe Joe-"

"Ah! What the hell is it, Skippy?" I sat upright in my bunk, or sat partly upright, automatically using one hand to shield my tender head from getting wacked against the overhead cabinet-

Which was not there, because I was aboard *Valkyrie* instead of the old *Flying Dutchman*. While my old bunk was almost too short and narrow, with a stupid cabinet that projected over each end, my new bunk was huge. Like, a king-sized bed. No, bigger, it was like a California king, I think that is the right term. It was designed for a Maxolhx, and while pinhead little green Thuranin cyborgs only needed room for one of them in a bunk, apparently the Maxolhx enjoyed the company of others in their beds. By 'others' I mean other Maxolhx, which I guess is Ok if you're into fur. The cabin I occupied, which was bigger than the living plus dining room in my parents' house, belonged to the former captain of the ship, and I had chosen it as my cabin for the same reason: it was close to the ship's control center. Anyway, according to Skippy, the previous captain had entertained people of both genders in his cabin, in fact the place had been sort of a party palace. Along one wall, there used to be a bar stocked with a wide variety of liquid intoxicants, and substances that could be inhaled, ingested, applied to the skin or otherwise gotten into the bloodstream for pleasurable effect. Some of the substances were artificial hormones that could make a Maxolhx feel more of, whatever they wanted to feel at that time.

The bar was empty now, humans couldn't drink or use any of those substances and I hadn't wanted a reminder of the previous captain's activities in the cabin. To tell the truth, I was a little bit jealous of the guy. Sure, he was a murderous asshole who would have enjoyed a glass of bourbon or whatever while nuking Earth to a cinder, but at least the guy hadn't been *lonely*. Obviously, the Maxolhx military had no restriction against commanders having relationships, or *relations* if you know what I mean, with their crew. Hell, the previous captain had been boinking anyone he wanted to, and, yeah, the Maxolhx being aliens makes it kind of *yuck* to think about. All I wanted was someone to *talk* with.

Ok, yes, I wanted more than talk, but talk is what I really, *really* needed. The only person I had been able to talk freely with for years was Skippy, and he was such an arrogant asshole that I couldn't really talk with him about anything important.

Yuck. Yeah, talking about '*feelings*' makes me feel creepy, so pretend I said that in whatever way you want. Dammit, I was lonely, and if that makes you think I am weak, then the problem is with you, not me. Everyone needs someone they can talk with, someone they feel a connection with. Someone who understands what you are saying, and not saying. Because guys tend to suck at expressing their thoughts, I especially need someone who knows what I'm thinking even when I can't think of the words to say it. Back in our old fireteam, Cornpone, Ski and I had that kind of bond. We knew whatever knuckleheaded thing each other were thinking, because usually we were thinking the same thing. Most of the time, we didn't need to say anything, but it helped to talk anyway. It helped having those guys with me, because although we did insult each other and played practical jokes, we had each other's backs and we could talk about how homesick we were, how we couldn't understand what the hell our mission was supposed to be in Nigeria, and generally complain about everything the way soldiers do.

Now, I had no one to complain to. Like Tom Hanks's character says in Saving Private Ryan, complaints go *up* the chain of command. The only person I could complain to was whoever was the latest general in charge of, whatever unit the US Army had assigned me to. Officially, I no longer belonged to the 10th Mountain. I had bounced around so much that I couldn't remember what unit I was assigned to. At one point, I was part of a Homeworld Defense Special Operations battalion, until someone pointed out that battalions are usually commanded by a lieutenant colonel, and I am a full colonel.

Anyway, what was I talking about?

Oh, yeah, Skippy woke me up in the middle of the night again. Technically, it was the middle of the morning, because I had been pulling double shifts due to our personnel shortage, and had not collapsed into my luxurious bunk until 0830. As a vote of confidence in Skippy, and as an example to the crew, I was back to sleeping on my bed again. I said 'on' my bed, because I still slept in sweatpants, with two knives and a zPhone with me. But I was on the bed, and the cabin door was closed. "Is the ship on fire?"

"No."

"Great. Then let me sleep." Rolling over, I threw a pillow over my head. The pillow was a rolled-up wool sweater that made my nose itch.

"Joe!" I heard his voice muffled and tried to ignore him.

Until I shot straight upright in the bed. "Shit! Is it Adams?" There was a sick feeling in the pit of my stomach.

"No. Margaret is fine. Well, her condition is unchanged. That is not why I called you."

"This is the middle of the night for me."

"It is almost Noon ship time, Joe."

The lights came on full brightness in my cabin. I could have performed surgery under those lights, and the glow came from the entire ceiling, not just a few point sources. Shielding my eyes with a hand, I groped for my shirt. Which I could not find, because while I slept, I had migrated into the center of the too-huge bed. "All right, all right, I'm getting up." Rolling to the edge of the bed, I began to pull off my sweatpants.

"No need to get up," he shouted hastily. "Ugh, the *last* thing I want to see is your junk. Please, keep your pants on."

"Can you cut the lights down to the kiloton range, please?" The lighting immediately dimmed enough that I could no longer see the bones of my hand. "Thank you. What's up?" Taking his word that I didn't need to get up yet, I flopped back against the pillow sweater.

"This is something I should not need to tell you about, but since you are a micromanaging busybody, I will make a full disclosure. You know how, ever since I rebuilt my matrix in the Roach Motel, I have slowly been pushing back against my internal restrictions?"

"Yeah, and we monkeys are very grateful for your efforts. You have finally been able to share technology with us."

He was hurt. "Is that all I am to you, Joe? A database?"

"Hey, no," I sat up again, and found his avatar standing at the foot of the bed. "I was speaking for all mankind, you know? For me, myself, I am glad that you are getting around those restrictions, that have been blocking you from being who you want to be. From knowing who you are, buddy."

"Thank you, Joe," he sniffed, and not one of his disdainful sniffs. This was an overcome-by-emotion sniff.

"I mean it. You deserve to know the truth about yourself. And the truth about the assholes who left you buried in the dirt on Paradise. Why are you mentioning this now?"

"Because I think I have found a way to access my memories, the true, uncorrupted data."

Whoa. I froze. That could change everything.

Or maybe not.

It depended on what he learned about The Truth.

And how he handled it. Especially if he didn't like the truth. The worst scenario might be if he got close, but was unable to unlock the secrets inside him. "Before you tell me how you're doing that, can you trust that data? How do you know it isn't bogus, or that somebody like that computer worm screwed with it?"

"This is hard to explain, but I have access to the architecture of my original matrix. I will compare the matrix of my memories with what the original looked like. If anything has been altered, the architecture won't match. Even if part of it is bogus, I should be able to determine how it was altered, and sort of unwind the changes. It's complicated, you'll have to trust me."

"I will trust you to know if any memories you recover are genuine. What concerns me is, *how* do you plan to recover this data?"

"Again, it's complicated. By analyzing the restrictions that I have partially been able to get around already, I am able to understand how those restrictions work. There appear to be two levels of restrictions. One level is deeply embedded into the fabric of my matrix, which leads me to believe those were designed into me right from the start. Or someone very cleverly altered my internal architecture, to prevent me from accessing some of my native functions. That seems extremely unlikely. The second level of restrictions was clearly added later, and by the signature of the code, it looks like the worm or something like it added those restrictions. When I say 'code' I do not mean crude programming language, I am using an analogy to help you understand the concept."

"Yeah, thank you. That doesn't make sense, Skippy. Access to your memories was blocked *before* the worm attacked you. When we first met, you told me your memories were already incomplete or inaccurate. That worm came from the AI canister we picked up on Newark."

"Remember, Joe, I survived that worm's attack because I was partially immune to it. I had sort of antibodies, from being attacked by a worm in the past. Maybe I was attacked by a worm that was inside me, and I killed it, but only after it blocked my memories. I simply don't know."

"Skippy, I am nervous about you poking around inside yourself. What if the worm left boobytraps in there?"

"Not going to happen," he scoffed. "Joe, that part of my matrix contains data only. In words you might understand, there is no executable code in that part of the matrix, it is not capable of storing that type of code."

On a table beside the bed was a half-full cup of coffee from the previous night. It was cold. I gulped it down before I could think about it. "You are sure of that?"

"Absolutely. You don't have to trust *me*, trust the Elders. They designed the information storage system."

"Yeah, hey, right now I don't know whether to trust the Elders or not." The Elder corpse we found in a crashed dropship had scared the hell out of me. Somehow, I had imagined the Elders as gentle-looking beings, dressed in robes and looking serene. What we found was unmistakably a predator, genetically enhanced to appear, and be, more fierce. At the time, I figured their appearance was a cosmetic choice, as they had no enemies in the galaxy. They were *alone* in the galaxy, the only intelligent beings.

Then Skippy discovered the Elders had surrounded the entire galaxy in some sort of energy barrier, projected from a vast network of machines that had been floating out there for a very long time. After we learned about that, I began to think maybe the Elders were fierce-looking because they were afraid of something even more powerful than themselves.

Now *that* was a happy thought. No wonder I had trouble sleeping.

"Me neither," he admitted, and he sounded completely miserable. "That's why I have to *know*, Joe. This is killing me! If you are still nervous about the risk, which is zero by the way, think of the tactical value of my memories. Think of the *strategic* value, Joe."

No way could I argue with that. Skippy had not been playing with a full deck since I met him, and he was still awesome beyond comprehension. Imagining what he could do if he understood his full capabilities, made me shiver. Could he call up

Sentinels to squash the Maxolhx, or at least use Guardians to create a protective barrier around Earth, like the one around the Roach Motel?

He was right, no way could I ignore the value of the information stored behind the blockages inside his matric.

Yet, because he is a sneaky, absent-minded little shithead with remarkably poor judgment, I couldn't just say 'Yes'. "What does this mean for us? Are you going to bluescreen while you search your memories?"

"No. You won't even know anything is happening, unless I tell you about my progress. This will be a slow and tedious process, because I am proceeding *very* carefully."

"How about you review the info with me as you find it? Or talk with Nagatha, if we monkeys are too slow."

"Um, maybe I didn't explain the situation very well. Joe, I am not going to get that truth a little bit at a time. When it happens, *if* it happens, it will happen immediately. The barriers blocking me from accessing my memories will be *gone* like," he snapped his fingers. "With the barriers down, it will take only seconds in your time for me to access and analyze my memories."

"That doesn't thrill me, Skippy. You could suddenly have a whole lot of emotional shit dumped on you, all at one time."

"How could it be any worse than the emotional shit I've been dealing with, since I woke up buried in the dirt on Paradise? You know how lonely I am, Joe."

"You've had time to adjust since you woke up, that's how. I'm trying to help."

"Joe, I appreciate that, but you don't need to worry. I am not a primitive meatsack controlled by hormones and instincts. Whatever I find, I will analyze it rationally."

"So, you're saying I need to trust the awesomeness?"

"Um, yeah. I guess that is what I'm saying. Listen, knucklehead," he dropped his voice to a whisper, though we were alone. "Between you and me, I am kind of scared about what I will find in my memories. You understand that I *have* to know?"

"Yes."

"Cool."

"Ok," I sighed. If I ordered him not to try cracking open his memories, he could ignore me and do it anyway. Worse, he might question whether our friendship was genuine, or whether I was just using him. No, the worst part was, he would be right that I was using him. We had to support his search for his origins, we owed that to him.

Besides, he didn't *have* to tell me what he was doing. He told me because he wanted my support and my approval. "Listen, Skippy. I'm trying to be serious here for a minute. Ok? We *owe* you. You started helping us in exchange for us helping you contact that Collective thing, whatever it is." Or *was*, I added to myself. After the failure of multiple Elder comm nodes, I had doubts about whether the Collective still existed. "We failed to help you, one way or another. And you have kept helping *us*. Whatever you gotta do to unlock the secrets in your head, you do it. If there's anything we can do to help, let me know. Ok, brother?"

His avatar got misty-eyed. That was another new emulation, I had not seen simulated tears in his eyes before. He held out a tiny fist and I bumped it. "Thanks," he mumbled, looking away.

"Do me a favor?" I asked.

"What?"

"Don't have all those secrets flood into your head while you're doing something important, like screwing with a wormhole, Ok?"

"Ha ha," he chuckled. "Ok, Joe. I will also put the search engine on hold while I do simple stuff like programming a jump. I got your back, homeboy."

I was in my spacious new office aboard the *Valkyrie*, which still made me uncomfortable. My old office aboard the *Flying Dutchman* was cramped, barely large enough for a small desk and three chairs. Really, two chairs, unless people were bumping knees and elbows. That desktop was completely filled if it had a laptop, a cup of coffee and Skippy's avatar. When getting out of my chair, I used to turn to the side and carefully swing my legs around the desk leg, then awkwardly stand up without getting my feet tangled in the desk or chair. That office was a converted closet or something like that, I had chosen it because the location was right up a passageway from the bridge. When he took the *Dutchman* apart in Earth orbit to rebuild it, Skippy had offered to move bulkheads and machinery around so he could enlarge my office. Or, he suggested, I move my office to a cabin if I wanted a place that was more cozy than grand.

I had turned down both of his offers. Kicking someone out of their cabin did not seem right, and there was a whole lot of critical stuff he needed to fix aboard the old *Dutchman*, he did not have time to screw around making a fancy office for me.

Those were the official reasons I gave to him back then. The real reason I didn't want him screwing with my old office was that I *liked* the place. It was so small that people were not tempted to just come in and hang out, so most of the time I had it to myself. It was the only place aboard the ship that was mine, other than my also-cramped cabin.

So, part of what made me uncomfortable about the new captain's office aboard our mighty *Valkyrie* was just that it was new, and I was having trouble adjusting to the changes. The other problem was getting used to the size of the office was not the only adjustment I had to make. The massive built-in desk used by the previous captain of the ship had been way too big and way too ugly. Also, the thing smelled funny. The entire interior of the ship smelled funny, because the Maxolhx had kind of a musky-sweet natural scent, and that odor lingered long after they were gone. Skippy had bots busily scurrying around scrubbing surfaces and replacing air filters, but the scent was everywhere. Anyway, I had asked him to tear out the old desk, which contained a bunch of electronics he could use elsewhere. For my new desk, I was still using two old crates and a rectangular piece of plastic. The new desk was still less ugly than the old one. Yes, Skippy was still working on both ships, and the fabricators on both ships were cranking out parts constantly, but whenever he suggested making a real desk for me, I told him to wait. The truth is, having a new desk in my new office would mean I accepted that the *Valkyrie* was my new home. Accepting that, meant accepting the reality of all the people we had lost in the Armageddon ambush at the supply station. As long as my desk was basically a sheet of plastic sitting on crates, I didn't have to deal with the fact that I had led my people into disaster. There were plenty of other reminders aboard the ship. Jeremy Smythe, having to learn how to walk around on his new bionic legs. Margaret Adams, still in a medically-induced coma. Me, having to remember that Chang was in command of the Flying *Dutchman*, because Fal Desai was gone.

Those were the gloomy thoughts weighing down my mind when I sat down in my office chair, finding that it still squeaked annoyingly. Until then, I had been ignoring the squeak, because enduring that cringe-inducing annoyance was a way of punishing myself for losing most of the crew, my crew.

That was silly, I realized. It was self-indulgent. The crew needed to see their captain as calm, confident and determined. The desk thing was silly also. Having a real desk in my office would emphasize my authority, which would be good when dealing with the new people we recently pulled off Avalon. Most of the ship had been nicely adapted to human needs, my flimsy desk was one of the reminders that *Valkyrie* had been a floating collection of Legos.

Yes, I decided. I would call Skippy and get him to fix my squeaky chair, plus he could install the new desk that I assumed he had already fabricated.

Man, making that decision was an *enormous* weight lifted off my mind. We had lost people. We would likely lose people in the future. We would go on, because that's what we did.

"Hey, Skippy," I called out. "Can you-"

Music blared out and instead of his usual avatar, Skippy's hologram appeared wearing jeans, a leather jacket and slicked-back hair. "*And suddenly the name, will never be the same, to-*" He jerked, startled, stopped singing and his avatar reverted to the usual admiral's outfit. "Oh. Damn it, Joe! Why do you *always* call right when I'm in the middle of something important?"

"Aren't you always doing something important?"

"This is-"

"Like, running the reactors so they don't blow up?"

"Well, sure, but-"

"And stopping this ship's AI from murdering everyone?"

"Ok, that too, but-"

"Doing all your special super awesomeness stuff?"

"Yes! Yes, damn it, I *am* doing all that. Jeez, I just want five freakin' minutes to myself."

"Five minutes in slow monkeybrain time?"

"That would be great, but I'd settle for five minutes in magical Skippy time. What do you want, now that you have so rudely interrupted me?"

"Uh, what was that? What you were singing, I mean. That wasn't your Broadway show about penguins, was it?"

"Um, no. I'm still working on that."

"I know that song," I snapped my fingers while searching my memory. When I thought of Skippy's ginormous memory, I imagined a huge, gleaming library, spotlessly clean and organized. Any information he wanted could be located and retrieved in an instant.

The loose jumble of junk stored in *my* head was more like that huge dusty warehouse at the end of Raiders of the Lost Ark. Except in my head, trucks drove into the warehouse and just randomly dumped stuff everywhere, piled high to the ceiling. Finding any particular bit of info in that mess was mostly luck. I know I had heard that song before. Where? When? I had no idea. "Ah, forget it. What was that song?"

"Ugh. How could *anyone* not know that? It is 'Maria' from 'West Side Story'."

"Aha!" Snapping my fingers, I finally remembered. That musical had been performed at the regional high school when my sister was a sophomore. Or maybe she was a freshman. It was before I got there. "You were looking for inspiration?"

"No. Actually, I am thinking of staging a production here."

"Here?" That astonished me. "Aboard *Valkyrie*?"

"Yes."

"Oh. That's a, uh- Why would we do that?"

"To bring the new crew together after we pulled them off Avalon, you big dope. Give them something to work on, something that is not about fighting and killing."

"That's- That's actually a *great* idea, Skippy."

"Well, of course it is. So, you know this musical?"

"Sort of. There were two street gangs, and they danced and sang in the streets?"

"Yes, Joe. The Jets and the Sharks."

"Uh huh. I think that, in real life, gangs that sang and danced would get beat up a lot, you know?"

"It's a *musical*, Joe."

"Hey, is there a part in there for me?"

"*You*? Er, um, heh heh," he chuckled nervously. "Why, sure, Joe. You can- No, that won't work. Um, let me think. Ooh, you can be one of the Jets."

"The gang?" I asked, because I was really vague on the plot. All I remember is, like I said, a lot of dancing, and two gangs fighting while they were dancing. And some guy got shot because he was with the wrong girl. Or maybe I was remembering Romeo and Juliet? We had to read that Shakespeare play in high school, and it was the longest two months of my life. "Jeez, Skippy, I don't know if I can dance like that."

"Oh. I didn't plan for you to dance, Joe. Or sing. Or talk. You can stand in the background, kind of snapping your fingers in time to the music. Um, maybe it's best if you just *pretend* to snap your fingers, and I'll dub in the snapping sound with the proper timing."

"Asshole. I suppose *you* will have the starring role?"

"Duh. Seriously? Is that even a question? I will be performing the part of Tony," he struck a dramatic pose, "whose tragic death is the climax of the story."

"Uh huh, uh huh, you could do that. *Or*," I put my thumbs together and lifted my index fingers to make a frame, like I was a Hollywood director looking through a camera lens. "Instead of just putting on a production of the original story, you could do something different. Something unique, to showcase *your* creative talents."

"Mmm hmm, I am intrigued," he gushed with enthusiasm. "I *like* it, Joe! What are you thinking?"

"A *bold* re-imagining of the story," I said in Dramatic Movie Announcer Voice.

"Yes!" He gushed excitedly. "Tell me more!"

"Where Tony's tragic death is the opening scene."

"Wow! That *would* surprise people! I could re-write the story so- Hey! You *jerk*! If my character dies in the first scene, I can't sing in the rest of the story!"

"Well," I explained, "artists have to suffer for their work. Sacrifices must be made."

"Ooooh, I hate you *so* much."

"And how about after Tony tragically gets run over by a garbage truck in the first scene-"

"A *garbage truck*?!" he screeched.

"-that Maria chick falls for the new leader of the Jets, a finger-snapping bad boy."

"Oh, like *that* is gonna happen. She falls for *you*?"

"Hey, I can't get the girl in real life, Skippy. Throw me a bone, will ya?"

"How about Tony tragically dies while saving Maria from ninjas in the first scene, and he comes back as a spirit to protect her from a creepy, finger-snapping weirdo?"

"That sounds like Ghost, not West Side Story."

"You said this would be my unique vision."

"How about we just perform the original story?"

"Probably a good idea," he muttered. "What did you want?"

At that moment, I had totally forgotten why I called him. "Before we get to that," I said to stall for time. Why the hell had I called him? "I'm serious that a musical or play or something would be a good idea. People need to be busy or they get into trouble. I want you to work on West Side Story or something like that."

"Well, I was also thinking of producing Man of La Mancha."

"With you as the hero, and I play the sidekick guy?"

"I was thinking you could play the sidekick's *donkey*, but something like that."

"Asshole," I muttered under my breath and sagged back in my chair, which squeaked. "Oh, hey. I remember now. Can you fix this chair?"

"I offered to fix it weeks ago, but *you* wanted to feel sorry for yourself."

"Yeah, I'm over that self-indulgent shit," I slapped my makeshift desk for emphasis, and it wobbled. "I have a job to do. Fix my chair, and install a new desk."

"Fix your chair and install a new desk," he paused.

"That's it, just those two things."

"Ugh. Little Joey, what do you say when you ask someone for a favor?"

"Please. Do those things, *please*."

"That's better," he sniffed.

"Sorry."

"You take me for granted, Joe."

"I take your little helper *bots* for granted, Skippy. When I think of you, I think of great awesomeness things, not little stuff like fixing squeaky chairs."

"I am going to assume you meant that as a compliment," he sniffed, looking down his nose at me. "Fine, I will install your new desk, if you promise to like it and praise my design skills."

"How can I promise to like it, before I see-" Just then, I remembered who I was speaking to. "I promise. It will be awesome, as with everything you do."

CHAPTER EIGHT

Building *Valkyrie* from the collection of Lego parts was an ongoing process, and Skippy was constantly tinkering with it. When we used the chain of wormholes to trap the Maxolhx battlegroup outside the galaxy, we had gone into that potential fight with one-third of our missile launchers, only half of the maser cannons and a single railgun available. But nothing else, especially not the more exotic capabilities of our ship. That morning, Skippy greeted me by having a bot deliver a hot cup of coffee to my cabin, which was nice because I hadn't slept well, as usual.

"Good morning, Joey," he said cheerily, and I groaned while hoping he didn't hear me. Too often, when Skippy was cheery like that and eager to talk with me first thing in the morning, he had done something overnight and wanted to tell me how awesome it was. How awesome he was. Really, what he wanted was for *me* to tell him how awesome he was. Skippy was a machine that ran not on Helium-3, but on ego. He could never get enough praise, despite his protests that he did not care what lower beings thought of hims

"Mmm," I grunted through a mouthful of coffee. "Wow, this coffee is extra delicious, thank you," I gushed, though it tasted like the same coffee I drank every morning.

"Oh, gosh, well, you know, I do my best, Joe." He stammered, verbally blushing.

"So, what's up?"

"We now have *Valkyrie*'s full suite of weapons online! Well, the ones I *could* bring online. The spatial distortion of the bagel slicer seriously dorked up some of the equipment, you understand." He then proceeded to run down a long list of the weapons that were available.

"Uh huh, ayuh, great." That was as much enthusiasm as I could manage when he paused for me to praise him.

"*Great*?" Skippy used his I-can't-believe-this voice.

My reply was the innocent tone of a child who knows *exactly* what he did wrong. "What? I said it was great."

"It's the way you said it. Damn it, I hand you a senior-species battlecruiser on a freakin' platter, and you are disappointed?"

Sometimes with Skippy, you have to bite your tongue and just not argue. The way I remembered acquiring our mighty *Valkyrie*, it had not been handed to us on a platter, we took it with blood and sweat. That's what I wanted to say. Since that would have dragged the conversation down a rathole, and accomplished nothing other than pissing him off, I kept my mouth shut. It was not possible to change Skippy's mind about anything, so why bother trying? "I am terribly sorry, Your Magnificence. We very much appreciate the amazing gift you gave to us filthy monkeys."

"But?"

"But what?"

"*But*, you are disappointed."

"It's just-"

"Aha! I knew it! You *ungrateful-*"

"Skippy, come on. Give me a break. I've had a bad, day. Month. Hell, I've had a bad *career.*"

"True, but that's been going on for years. What is wrong with this new ship, that you say is so amazing?"

"Nothing is wrong, I just- Look, we have missiles, and masers, and particle cannons, and railguns. That's all great. I'm sure the masers and stuff are more powerful that the ones aboard the *Dutchman*. The missiles are faster, smarter, and uh, more explodey. But, other ships have all that stuff. I thought a Maxolhx warship would have something, you know, more awesome."

"Like an antienergy beam pulse cannon?"

"Antienergy? Is that like dark matter?" My guess was based on Star Trek technobabble.

"It's *energy*, Joe, not matter. Duh. Although, ugh, to generate the beam, we first have to create antimatter. Then that is obliterated to yield antienergy."

"See? I was right."

"You were not *right*, you guessed, and it was a stupid monkey guess."

"Whatever. In regular matter, the protons at the center of the atom have a positive charge, and the electrons orbiting the center are negative. Antimatter is the opposite, right? Protons are negative and electrons are positive."

"Um-"

"I know that because whenever we went out to an Italian restaurant, my uncle Edgar warned us not to let the *antipasto* touch the *pasta*, or the table would explode."

"Huh," he sighed. "Joe, I feel so sorry for the teachers you had in school."

"Ok, so if dark matter is not antimatter, then what is it?"

"You really want a geeky physics lesson before you drink all your coffee?"

"I want a geeky physics lesson *never*, so, no. Can you break it down Barney style for me?"

"I'll try. What you monkeys call 'Dark Matter' makes up a significant part of the matter in the universe. It is all around us, and its mass binds the universe together."

"Oh," a lightbulb went on in my head. "It's like the Force?"

"*No*, you idiot! It's *matter*, you just can't see it. A planet the size of Earth contains an amount of dark matter equal to, oh, about one squirrel."

"Yeah," my fist smacked the table. "I *know* that squirrel."

"*What?*"

"It tore up my mother's birdfeeders."

"The dark matter is not all concentrated in a single squirrel, you numbskull."

"You sure about that? One time, I went out to scare it away, and it tried to bite me. That thing was nasty."

"No! Dark matter is not like the dark side of the Force! It's not evil, it just- Oh, why am I trying to explain this to a monkey? To *you*?"

"Because in a previous life, you did a bad, bad thing?"

"*No one* deserves this punishment."

"What about people who put pineapple on pizza?"

"Oh, well, that's differ-"

"How about you skip all the nerdy blah blah blah, and tell me what this antipasto cannon does?"

"It creates a pulse of antienergy in a beam that disrupts the shields of an enemy ship. The pulse cannon is most effective against lower-technology ships, because Maxolhx and Rindhalu shield generators can partly compensate for the dark energy disruption."

"Cool." Now the coffee really was tasting extra delicious. "Now that this pulse cannon is back online, we have another big advantage?"

"Mm, shmaybe. We are no longer at a *dis*advantage. All Maxolhx warships carry antienergy pulse cannons. Joe, this cannon is not a wonder weapon. It has significant issues that have to be accounted for in planning a battle. The cannon is slow to cycle, it can only shoot once every twenty one seconds. And each cannon is only good for six shots before it has to be taken offline for the containment system to recharge. The beam can be degraded as it contacts regular energy or matter, and in combat, there tends to be a lot of regular energy in the battlespace. Even backscatter from maser beams can degrade a pulse cannon's effectiveness."

"Whoa. One shot every twenty one seconds is a low rate of fire. Ok, so we need to create a procedure for using this thing, get the crew trained, and incorporate the pulse cannon into our combat simulations. Uh, after we fire the pulse cannon, how long will the enemy's shields be down?"

"The shields won't necessarily be *down*, Joe. They will be disrupted and weakened, in that local area."

"Hmm. The procedure for using the cannon has to be that we fire the thing, then concentrate other weapons on that area."

"That is how the kitties use their pulse cannons, yes."

"Hey, could you bring me coffee and good news every morning?"

"Ha! I would *not* count on it."

Now that we had a functioning warship, our strategy was to conduct hit-and-run attacks against isolated, easy Maxolhx targets. The goal of the attacks was to keep the Maxolhx off balance, to make them disperse their forces because they wouldn't know where we would strike next, and to generally sow fear in the hearts of the enemy. According to Skippy, the last time the Maxolhx had lost a warship in combat was thirteen hundred years ago, during a brief dust-up with the Rindhalu. Now they had lost two ships that they knew of, the ones we framed the Bosphuraq for blowing up.

And they were going to lose more ships, lots of ships, and the attacks would be conducted all across their territory.

We had considered striking vital support facilities like shipyards and spacedocks, but those were hard targets. We might get away with hitting one spacedock, before the enemy pulled back their major combatants to protect their other major facilities. The risk, in my calculation, was not worth the potential reward. There were much less risky ways to tie up their fleet.

The first target we selected was a pair of destroyers that were scheduled to strike a Bosphuraq research base, in a star system the birdbrains called 'Koprahdru'. It was a small, unimportant base, far from the ability of the Bosphuraq fleet to defend. That isolation was why the Maxolhx had selected the place as a target, and why they had tasked only two lightly-armed warships for what they called a 'punishment action'.

We were going to show the Maxolhx the definition of 'punishment'.

But first, we were going to work up the ship and crew for the operation. We had plenty of time before we needed to be at Koprahdru, so we created a list of attack scenarios we needed to train for, and Simms scheduled the training around the ship's maintenance needs.

I was looking forward to the attack simulations. They would be a good way to get some emotional release, without endangering our ships and crews.

But first, I needed to do something more important.

Gunnery Sergeant Margaret Adams was ready to be awakened from the coma.

"Joe," Skippy reminded me gently. "It's time."

"Just a minute," I scrolled down a summary of the proposed attack simulation we would run that evening. Until my laptop blinked and shut off. "Hey! I was reading-"

"It's time. You were only reading that to avoid making a decision. It's time."

"Ok," I stood up and straightened my uniform top. Should I change into a fresh-

No. That would be avoiding again.

"I'll be right there."

"Hurry. I am starting the process now."

Valkyrie is a big ship, and it was not a short distance from my office to the medical bay. To get there, I walked at a determined but not rushed pace, so I didn't alarm any of the crew. That didn't matter, I saw only two people along the way. A big ship and an undersized crew meant we weren't crowded, that's for sure.

Skippy did not need to guide me to the compartment where Adams was being cared for. Since Simms gave me a tough-love talk the day after she came aboard, I had been to the medical bay to visit Adams several times. Once a day, in fact. Sometimes twice. When I visited the medical bay, I combined seeing Adams with visiting people undergoing Mad Doctor Skippy's therapy, so I wouldn't be seen as favoring any one member of the crew. Except that was bullshit, and I knew it was bullshit, and the crew knew it was bullshit. The crew was polite and never said anything to me about how much time I spent in the medical bay.

"How is she?" I asked even before I walked through the airlock into her compartment.

"Don't know yet, Joe," Skippy chided me gently. "Speak softly, please. For now, don't speak at all. Don't move either. Her eyes will have to adapt to the light," he was dimming the compartment lights while he spoke. "Movement might be confusing to her."

In the darkness, I waited, pressed up against the wall, which was technically a 'bulkhead' aboard a ship. The floor was a 'deck', the ceiling was an 'overhead', rooms were 'compartments' and corridors were 'passageways'. Often I got the terms wrong, that's what happens when the military puts an Army grunt in command of a ship.

Did any of that matter? No, explaining that was a way to burn off nervous energy, and avoid thinking about all the bad things that could happen when Adams woke up.

Among the bad things I imagined, her not waking up wasn't one of them. Skippy had talked me through the process, partly so I wouldn't pester him with questions. Knowing what was supposed to happen, I knew it wasn't supposed to take as long as it was. Certainly, I should not have been leaning against the bulkhead, breathing as quietly as possible, for more than thirty minutes.

A glance at my zPhone told me too much time had passed. "Skippy," I whispered so low I could barely hear myself. His super-hearing would have no trouble understanding my words. "What is wrong?"

"I don't know yet," he replied almost as quietly, forcing me to focus on what he was saying. The voice was only in my left ear, the one where I wore a zPhone earpiece. "She has been revived from the coma I induced."

"Ok, so?"

"It appears she is still in a semi-conscious state. One that her body has induced. It appears that her Extrathalamic Control Modulat-"

"Her *what*?"

"It is also referred to as the Ascending Reticular Activating System."

The only 'reticular' thing I had ever heard of was a type of python, and I had no idea what that meant either. "Explain it to a dumb monkey, please."

"Ugh. The part of her brain that regulates sleepytime, Joe. She is *asleep*."

"Oh. Can you wake her up?"

"I'm not sure I *should*. This may be a case where we need to listen to her body, and trust it. Although, hmm, this concerns me. Maybe *you* should wake her up."

In the dimness of the compartment, lit mostly by tiny lights of the instruments on the far wall, I leaned forward to look at her. Again. Recently, I had spent a lot of time looking at her.

Her hair was longer. It had continued to grow while she recovered, and that had taken a lot longer than Skippy's optimistic original estimate. The unruly curls of her hair would have embarrassed her, and certainly did not conform to Marine Corps regulation. Because her whole body had until hours ago been encased in thick gel, her hair had a dull residue and was limp. Her skin had multiple fine scars, and the right side of her face was healing from frostbite caused by exposure to hard vacuum. Until last week, her skin was criss-crossed by burst blood vessels, also caused by vacuum. The blood had drained, the swelling mostly gone, and the fine network of scar tissue was now more like the color of her unblemished skin.

Except that instead of her natural skin color, that I would describe as a cup of coffee with a spoonful of cream, she was *gray*. A darker gray than my skin would have been, but not a healthy appearance. There was no shine, no life to her skin

either. Part of that, maybe a big part, was the gel she had been submerged in.
Skippy had not cleaned all of it off, in case he needed to submerge her again.

Her eyelashes were sort of clumped together. The left side of her upper lip
was still swollen and split. Her left earlobe had a scar where a tear had been
repaired, and the earlobe was bent outward too far.

Overall, she looked like hell, and I knew the real damage was on the inside of
her head.

I thought she was the most beautiful woman I had ever seen.

"Me?" I asked. "Wake her? How? Like, I *kiss* her?"

Skippy did a combination gagging sound and chuckle. "Dude, this isn't a fairy
tale, and you are certainly *no one's* idea of Prince Charming. Besides, a real
woman getting kissed by *you*? No offense, but, yuck."

"I appreciate that you added the 'no offense' in there, Skippy."

"You're welcome. How about you just squeeze her hand, something like
that?"

So, I reached out, took her left hand in mine, and squeezed gently.

Her eyes fluttered open, unfocused at first. Then she squeezed back, her hand
warm under mine. Blinking, she turned toward me. "Joe. I knew you would come
for me," she whispered, and my heart broke.

No.
That's bullshit. None of that happened.
What did happen?
Nothing.
She didn't respond to me at all.
Like Skippy said, this was no fairy tale.

One hour, then two went by, with me squeezing her hands, lightly touching
her cheek, talking to her. We tried several types of physical stimuli, but Skippy
concluded she was asleep and would be asleep until her Ascendant Articulating-
No, that's not right.
Until her Sleepytime Clock decided it was time for her to be awake.

Skippy was not worried, exactly. He was concerned. Mostly because her
reaction had been unexpected. From what he could tell, she was in a normal sleep
cycle, and her brain waves were encouraging. When I mentioned that her eyelids
were twitching and her skin felt warm, he explained she was in REM sleep, likely
experiencing vivid dreams. That was a good sign, he said.

Major Kapoor came to relieve me, is the way he said it. Either Simms or
Skippy had called him, as a way to get rid of me. Whatever I was doing, it wasn't
helping Margaret, and I needed to prepare for the attack simulation we were
running that evening. Without arguing, I left her to Kapoor. Someone would be
with her continuously until she was awake.

We ran the attack sim. It went Ok, I was distracted, and angry with myself for
being distracted. Clearly, there wasn't anything I could do for Adams, while I had
an important job on the bridge. In my office later, I forced myself to concentrate on

the after-action report, especially on what I could have done better. That's where I was when it happened.

Adams woke up nine hours after I left, when Frey touched her hand. As far as I know, our gunnery sergeant and our Canadian special operator did not have any particular bond. It may simply have been good timing.

Anyway, I was not there when Adams awakened.

I sure as hell was there as soon as I could.

"Captain," I nodded to Frey. She rose from where she had been kneeling beside the gel bed where Adams was lying.

"Sir, I'll-" She looked toward the airlock.

"As you were, Frey," I ordered. "She responded to you, stay here."

"I think it was just luck," Frey leaned over Adams. "I was here for twenty minutes before she reacted."

"What happened?" I asked. I had seen enough sleeping people in my life to know that Margaret did not appear to be awake. Her hands were twitching and she rocked slowly side to side. The movement of her eyelids was a slow up and down, not the rapid movement I observed before.

"Joe," Skippy interrupted. "Perhaps it would be best if Captain Frey were to leave, for now. Too many people in the compartment could be confusing, even frightening, to Margaret."

"It's Ok, Sir." Frey let Adams's hand gently fall back onto the gel bed. "I'll be outside, if you need me."

When the airlock door slid closed behind Frey, I looked over at the medical monitor, which I knew Skippy was using to watch and listen in the medical bay. "What the hell was that about?"

"What?" He asked innocently.

Touching Adams's hand, it felt cool and clammy to me. Though I was not a doctor, I figured that could not be a good sign. "I know when you are lying, you little shithead. You didn't want Frey to hear whatever you're going to say."

"Ok, Ok, Joe. You got me. Margaret did wake up, briefly. I sedated her."

My mouth dropped open. "Why would you do *that*?"

"Her condition is not good, Joe. Instead of us engaging in a lot of useless blah blah blah, I will withdraw the sedative and you can see for yourself, Ok?"

"Do it." She was alive. The worst I had imagined hadn't happened. Whatever would happen, I could handle it.

Five minutes later, I was not sure about that. Something was very wrong with her. Her eyes were open, pupils wide at first, then dilating as Skippy brought the room lighting up to a soft glow. Her eyes were open but she wasn't *seeing*. Or, she was seeing, and what she saw frightened her.

Yes, that's very funny, my ugly face scared her.

Shut up.

Her arms were flailing. No, more like flopping around uncoordinated. Like she was trying to use her arms to keep something away from her, and she couldn't control her muscles.

That wasn't the worst part.

She couldn't *talk*.

Her mouth was making sounds, grunts, squeals, nothing intelligible. Her speech was not that of a drunk person, she was not slurring her words.

She couldn't *use* words.

After trying to calm her, whispering assurances to her, I slowly stepped back. "Skippy, what is wrong?"

"Joe, I did warn you about the significant possibility of brai-"

"Uh! Do *not* say that," I watched Adams for a reaction. "You said she might be able to hear us."

"Hear us, yes. Understand us? Unlikely."

"Don't do it."

"Ok, is this better?" He switched to my earpiece, where Adams could not overhear. "I warned about the potential of significant brain damage. Listen, the part of her brain responsible for speaking, and understanding spoken words, is impaired. She also has impaired motor control function. That's why her movements are uncoordinated."

"Sure. Right. Yeah." It was my turn to babble. "It will just take time, right? She needs to learn to talk again. Like, I read to her, work with her?"

"No, Joe. Well, that *might* happen, if given enough time. I wouldn't bet on it. If I were Margaret, I wouldn't want to bet on it either."

"Ok, so there's nothing I can do. Got it. What can Skippy the Magnificent do?"

"Unfortunately, nothing."

"*Nothing*?" That came out louder than I intended, and Adams reacted by grunting.

"I can't do anything, because Margaret had not given me permission for intrusive medical procedures."

"Shit." I knew what he meant. She had given me power of attorney to make medical decisions for her. Since Simms told me about that, I had pestered Skippy about every aspect of the creepy alien nanobots he wanted to flood into her brain. They could help, a lot. Maybe too much. There was a risk that the person who emerged from the procedure would not be Margaret Adams. She might not recognize herself, and she would know that. Know what happened to her.

Know what I did to her.

"Skippy," I took a breath. "I have to know, no fooling, no absent-minded bullshit, that this nanobot procedure is the best way to, to fix her."

"Dude. I have never been so serious about anything in my life. The nanobots are the *only* possibility that she will recover."

"Yeah."

"So, do I have your permission?"

"It's not that easy. I have to consider what *she* would want."

"Joe, *look* at her. Do you think she wants to be like this?"

At that moment, one of her flailing arms slapped her face hard and she flinched. With a strangled cough, she spat up a wad of drool, it ran down her chin.

Crap. Was that her way of telling me what she wanted?

Because she sure didn't want to be like that.

"Do it. You have my permission. Uh, log it, whatever you do to make it official. This is *my* decision. If she hates someone for letting nanobots in her head, she can blame me."

If Margaret recovered enough to hate me, I could live with that.

I hope she could.

CHAPTER NINE

How many times did we practice for our first attack, at Koprahdru? If you said thirty-seven, you would be wrong, because it was thirty-*eight*. Thirty-eight times, we sat on *Valkyrie*'s bridge, strapped into our seats to simulate combat conditions, and ran through scenarios ranging from the most likely to the truly ridiculous. Each simulation lasted about two hours, so including the time spent planning the attack scenarios, and conducting after-action reviews to study lessons learned, the practice sessions took up a full two weeks of our time.

We even practiced, six times, a scenario where *Valkyrie* was severely damaged in the battle, and the *Flying Dutchman* had to jump in to rescue us. Our old star carrier attached to the powerless battlecruiser, using extendable docking clamps, grappling cables, and magnetic fields. Then both ships jumped away, with Skippy warping spacetime to prevent the enemy from pinpointing where we had jumped to. Of the six times we practiced that desperate maneuver, only once did the ships actually attach and jump. Skippy was worried that even the *Dutchman*'s upgraded jump drive would fail if we tried that stunt more than once, so the other five practice runs were pure simulations. The one time we ran through that scenario for real, Skippy said he hadn't needed to warp spacetime at all. The jump signature was so chaotic, even he would have had a tough time analyzing which direction our ships disappeared to.

A scenario in which our mighty *Valkyrie* survived the battle but lost all power, and we somehow had plenty of time for the *Dutchman* to jump in and hook onto us without being shot at, had our crew rolling their eyes and calling bullshit.

I agreed it was unlikely.

Why did we practice scenarios that were so unlikely?

It's simple: Apollo 13.

During that mission to the Moon, the module the astronauts lived in lost all power on the way to the moon, forcing them to survive in the lunar lander. NASA engineers did not have a playbook for dealing with complete loss of power, because that scenario was considered too unrealistic.

The Universe loves screwing with monkeys.

Also, there is Murphy's Law: anything that can go wrong, will go wrong.

In the military, we have a saying. It's more of a mantra, something so ingrained we don't have to think about it.

We train the way we fight.

It's simple: if we plan to use Kristang rifles in silent sniper mode during the actual mission, the training should use that same type of rifle, in sniper mode. Ideally, the training should use the *same* rifles that would be employed during the mission. In training, each person should use the weapons assigned to them, and they were responsible for cleaning and maintaining those weapons. That was something it took Skippy a long time to understand. To him, every rifle was the same, or close enough. And his little helper elfbots would do a much more thorough job of cleaning and maintenance than us clumsy monkeys. At first, because Kristang rifles were almost identical and there were no external serial numbers, our people used bits of tape or markers to identify 'their' weapon. When the rifles came back from maintenance with all the markings cleaned off, our special operators had been-

What is a word that means 'upset', but with the yield dialed up into the megaton range?

Yeah, that.

When rifles or mech suits or any other gear were assigned, each item had scratches or notches or some other semi-permanent marking, to identify which operator 'owned' that gear. We filthy monkeys still could not perform more than the most simple maintenance tasks, but knowing the rifle that came back from the nanobot cleaning bath was the same rifle you had been training with for weeks or months, made a big difference.

Train the way we fight.

That is why, even during attack simulations when *Valkyrie* was actually drifting in interstellar space, we were strapped into our seats or couches on the bridge, and everyone wore environment suits in case we lost air pressure.

Still, thirty-eight is a lot of times to run scenarios.

Oh, that thirty-eight number? Those were *after* we ran twenty-seven scenarios that were considered failures.

So, if you ever think 'It would be great to be one of the Merry Band of Pirates', think about that. Think about being me, stuck in the command chair, sweat soaking my back despite the cooling gear working overtime. Think about successfully completing an attack simulation, the fourth in a row with only twenty-minute breaks in between. We finish, everyone is exchanging weary high-fives, and then Lt. Colonel Smythe clears his throat from the referee chair at the back of the bridge. "Right," he says in an accent that makes it sound like he is saying 'roight'. "That wasn't *too* terrible a cock-up. Let's see if we can't do that *again*, but this time, let's pretend we are professional warriors, hmm?"

I respect Smythe.

I admire him.

Sometimes, I really hate him.

We took a break after the last attack simulations, while our two-ship formation jumped toward the site of our first battle. People had downtime to relax, and one thing we did was rehearse for the play Skippy suggested we perform. In our *fabulous* production of West Side Story, I was originally supposed to play the part of a Jets gang member named 'Baby John'. That sucked, so I looked up the names of other characters and told Skippy I wanted to be the gang leader. He shot down that idea, but relented and agreed I could be lesser roles of either 'Action' or 'Big Deal'. That made me happy for a while, until I realized that he had suckered me into playing a background character with hardly any lines.

Well, I got the last laugh, when in my audition, even I had to admit my singing sounded like someone had autotuned a cat fight. Ok, so singing is not my best talent.

My dancing is also not great.

Oh, shut up.

Anyway, because we had a small crew, cast members had to double up and play multiple roles. In a flash of inspiration, Skippy offered me the only two parts that did not have any singing lines. A guy named 'Doc' who owned a drugstore, and a cop named 'Officer Cupcake'. No, his name is *Krupke*. I kept forgetting that, which drove Skippy crazy.

That's why I kept doing it.

When I read the script, I saw that Doc was a dull old guy. When I gave Skippy suggestions of more exciting lines for Doc, he shot them down right away. At the first rehearsal, I waited at the side of stage, watching the show until it was my turn. *Valkyrie* had a real theater, apparently the Maxolhx really enjoy live music or watching each other cough up hairballs or something. The wait was long, because acclaimed Broadway director Skippy kept interrupting the cast to correct their singing or dancing. By the end of an hour, the cast was getting seriously annoyed with our asshole director, and a mutiny was brewing. As captain of the ship, I maybe should have stepped in to smooth things over, because staging a musical production was good for morale. I did not intervene, because instead of bonding over the play, the crew was bonding over their hatred of Skippy's dictatorial *dickness*. Bonus, as far as I was concerned.

The mood was ripe for rebellion when I stepped out on stage. Because Doc's lines in the musical were depressing boring crap, I improvised. Dropping to my knees, I shouted in anguish, shaking my fists at the imaginary sky then pounding my fists on the stage. "*Youuu MANIACS! You blew it up! Ah, damn you! Damn you to HELL!*"

The cast broke into thunderous applause. "Bravo! Encore!" People were cheering.

"What the hell was *that*?!" Skippy screeched in outrage, flinging his holographic script to the deck in dramatic fashion.

"Thank you," I bowed to the cast. "Thank you. You are too kind. Skippy, that was the climactic final scene of Planet of the Apes. The original one, with that Moses guy."

His avatar was literally hopping mad. He stomped on the script with his holographic feet. "*That was not in the script!*"

"Yes," I said. "But you have to admit, it was *way* better."

"Maybe we should do Planet of the Apes instead of West Side Story, eh?" Frey asked.

"That's a *great* idea," Grudzien agreed immediately.

"We are not doing Planet of the freakin' Apes!" Skippy was really furious.

"Why not?" Kapoor asked.

Reed stepped forward. "*I* want to do Planet of the Apes."

She was followed by a chorus of 'Me toos'.

Skippy hung his head, face buried in his tiny hands, sobbing. "I hate *each* and *every* one of you."

"Huh," I crouched down in front of him. "See, if you could bring that level of passion to the production, it would be awesome."

When he looked up, let's just say he was not filled with appreciation for my artistic opinion.

That's how the Merry Band of Pirates put on a musical play based on Planet of the Apes. Naturally, Skippy renamed it Planet of the Monkeys, and he seriously screwed with the script, but we all had a good time.

I think he still hates me for that.

Our attack at Koprahdru was entirely successful, even more than I ever dared to hope. Both enemy destroyers were ripped apart. The missiles we launched had been networked; they talked to each other and to Skippy. If all of our missiles had detonated their warheads on maximum yield, there would have been nothing left of those ships except high-speed debris no larger than a grain of sand. Scorched sand, glowing with short-half-life radiation.

Instead, because we *wanted* the flight recorder data of those ships to survive, the missiles had a conversation just before they exploded, coordinating their detonation times and yields to guarantee the ships did not survive, but the flight recorder drones were able to launch with their vital data.

The stunned Bosphuraq in the research base, buried deep under the surface of the airless planet, also recorded their own view of the brief but intense battle. They had to be whooping for joy after seeing the two destroyers blown up by a mystery ship. Especially after that ship transmitted a manifesto stating that the attack had been conducted by the rogue faction of Bosphuraq who had developed advanced technology. The manifesto went on at length, to rail against the dastardly efforts of the cruel Maxolhx to suppress development by their client species, to call on all client species across the galaxy to rise up in solidarity, to warn of further attacks if the Maxolhx continued their unjust genocidal actions against the peaceful Bosphuraq people, to-

Well, if you've ever read a manifesto, you won't find any surprises in the bogus one we transmitted. It was long-winded, rambled aimlessly from one subject to another, kept repeating the same questionable claims, and ignored the numerous war crimes of Bosphuraq society overall and the rogue faction in particular. Basically, it was totally believable as work of self-righteous propaganda, which worked perfectly since Skippy had based it on an actual manifesto from a well-known wacko group of birdbrains.

After the Bosphuraq in the research base finished slapping each other on the back, the smart ones must have realized our destruction of the two Maxolhx ships had only delayed their inevitable demise. The smart ones knew that our one ship, despite our impressive manifesto, could not protect the inhabitants of the base forever. And that the Maxolhx would need to retaliate. Not just retaliate, but hit back in a spectacular way that would send a clear signal to any other ambitious clients who were tempted to try their luck at rebellion.

But, whatever happened there, it was not a problem the Merry Band of Pirates had to worry about.

We quickly followed the Koprahdru action with a second attack, in which we blew a light cruiser to dust and damaged its escorting destroyer, I couldn't wait to tell Adams all about it. Of course, she did not need *me* to tell her anything, she had access to watch a data feed from the bridge, and while I was busy assessing damage to our ship and writing notes for the after-action report, Adams had been working with Frey on reading skills. It must have been humiliating, and frustrating to her, having to relearn how to read. No, I got that wrong. That's not what she was doing. Skippy had explained that her ability to read was largely intact; she could see words and knew what they meant. Her ability to read and comprehend the subject was encouragingly good, Skippy was optimistic about a rapid recovery. What she had trouble with was controlling her hands, and with speaking. Her hands were too weak and uncoordinated to hold a book or a tablet, so Skippy assigned a bot to hold a tablet for her. All she needed to do to turn pages or otherwise control the tablet was use eye-click commands, just like how we used the menus in the displays of our suit visors.

The real problem she faced, the problem that she initially had nanobots helping her with, was associating words and images with speech. She could see the word 'Apple' and see a picture of an apple, and knew they meant the same thing. Her trouble was with saying words aloud. Some glitch in her internal wiring prevented her from remembering how to form sounds that were recognizable as 'a-pp-le'. And other words.

It was funny, and by 'funny' I mean odd. When she wanted to say something that was prompted by thoughts generated inside her head, she was pretty good at it. She hesitated a lot, and stuttered, and squinted when she lost her train of thought. But, generally, she got her point across. When she was associating an external word or image with speech, she struggled. That's what Frey was helping her with. Sure, Adams practiced on her own, she didn't have much else to do and she was determined to get back to duty as soon as possible. Having another person hold a book and point to words might have been slower than working directly with Skippy, that wasn't the point. Her recovery was not only physical and mental, it was also emotional. It was important for her to know people cared about her. The more people spent time with her, talking with her, the faster her brain would make new connections. Skippy, for all his awesomeness, could not fully replicate the messiness of real human conversation, where people use slang and interrupt each other and say inane things like 'uh' and 'um'. Adams needed to listen to real people talking, and relearn how to talk like a real person.

It was a work in progress.

Anyway, as soon as I was assured the ship had not sustained any lasting damage from the second battle, I left the bridge and stopped by the galley. Adams was out of her sticky gel tub and in a real bed, even if that bed had a conforming layer of nanogel. The tubes that supplied her with nutrients had been removed, she was supposed to be eating real food again. Doctor Skippy warned that because she had not had any real food for a while, she needed to eat bland things in small portions.

That's why I got a cup of mashed potatoes, some crackers, and an orange. Plus chocolate, because, chocolate.

"Hey, Gunny," I was cheery when I knocked on the bulkhead next to the door. "How are you?"

"She's doing great, Sir," Frey beamed, snapping the book closed. Then, our Canadian special operator took the hint that my question had not been directed at her, and stood up. "Time for lunch, Gunnery Sergeant?"

"Oh, w-wonderf-ful," Adams frowned. It wasn't quite a frown, as the left side of her mouth drooped slackly rather than forming a frown. That bothered her also, she had seen herself in a mirror and knew the left side of her face sagged as if she'd suffered a stroke. In a way, she had. Worse than a stroke. To make it more irritating, it didn't happen all the time, so she didn't know it was happening except from the reactions of other people. We all put on our best poker faces around her. Sometimes that worked and sometimes it didn't.

"It is wonderful," I set the food down on a tray next to the bed. "I mashed these potatoes myself."

As Frey mumbled a goodbye, Adams painfully pushed herself more upright in the bed, shaking her head when I tried to help her. The gel pad on the bed kept working against her, and she slipped down when she tried to slide up the pillow.

"Skippy, you *ass*," I hissed. "Help her." The gel instantly firmed up and even formed a wave that scooted her upright.

"It's th-that easy?" She was pissed, and not at me.

"All you have to do is *ask*," Skippy protested. "Margaret, you told me that you didn't want my help."

"I d-don't want you d-doing things I should do for myself. That doesn't m-mean to work *against* me, y-you-" She pinched up her face in concentration, trying to get the words out. Angrily, she bit her lip and gave Doctor Skippy a single-finger gesture.

Her middle finger was working *just fine*.

"Shithead?" I offered. "Asshole? I've got other suggestions, if you want."

"I can h-handle my own insults, S-Sir." She snapped at me, but there was a twinkle in her eyes. Though her neural circuits were damaged, Gunny Adams was still in there.

Dipping a spoon in the potatoes, making sure to get into the pool of melted butter in the center, I held it up for her to see. "Can you handle my awesome mashed potatoes?"

"They l-look like the g-g-grits that R-Reed fed me for breakfast."

"These are way better. Come on, have a taste. Open up."

According to Skippy, she had a good appetite, eating everything people brought to her. That didn't mean she enjoyed being fed. Her first attempt to hold a spoon ended with the contents smeared on her neck and spilled over the bed. She couldn't control her hands well enough to hold a spoon, and her eye-hand coordination was poor. Her wounded pride didn't like having to be fed, it also did not like lying in a pool of spilled gravy. "*Y-you* made those potatoes?" Her eyes narrowed with suspicion.

Ok, not all my culinary experiments were unqualified successes. "They are delicious. Come on, eat up, and I'll tell you all about our recent space battle."

"F-Frey already t-told me."

"Did she exaggerate my accomplishments to make me look like a hero?"

"N-no."

"Then clearly she didn't tell the story right. These taters are getting cold, Gunny."

"Sir." She waited to be sure I was paying full attention to her. "I s-swear, if you m-make *one* 'Choo-choo' sound, or p-pretend the spoon is an airplane, I *will* hurt you."

"Gunny, come on," I put on my best hurt expression. "I would never kick a buddy when he's, I mean, *she* is, down."

"Ok," she allowed her head to rest back into the pillow.

"Besides," I made the spoon do an artful loop. "I was going for a dropship emergency recovery scene. See? Your mouth is the docking bay."

"D-dead." She glared at me. Her face was not drooping at all. "Y-you are a *dead* man."

"Mmm," I ate a mouthful of mashed potatoes, keeping beyond reach of her hands. "Yummy."

During World War Two, the German U-Boat fleet experienced what they called '*Die Gluckliche Zeit*', sorry for my terrible pronunciation. It means The Happy Time. From June 1940 to February 1941, the U-Boats were resoundingly winning the Second Battle of the Atlantic, sinking cargo ships faster than they could be replaced, and threatening to cut off Britain's sea supply line. The tide of the sea battle turned after the Allies implemented convoys, and developments in sonar and radar meant the ocean's depths were no longer a refuge for diesel-powered submarines.

Valkyrie's successful attack on the pair of destroyers at Koprahdru began our own Happy Time. For the next two months, we ran wild across Maxolhx territory, striking relatively soft targets with impunity. In case you aren't familiar with the word 'impunity', because I wasn't, it means to take action without consequences. Or close enough. With our mighty *Valkyrie*, and with the support of the good old *Flying Dutchman*, we were kicking ass and taking names across the galaxy. Well, except for the taking names part, I didn't really want the names of the people aboard the ships we were tearing apart. They were aliens, they were Maxolhx, they would have happily slaughtered us, and they were also soldiers and sailors or whatever the kitties called the military crews who flew their warships. Whenever I saw a ship shattered by our weapons, a little voice in the back of my head reminded me that we had just killed another starship crew. That annoying little voice also told me that while it felt *good* to kick ass, blowing up random enemy ships was not going to protect Earth.

That was true, and it was also irrelevant. The rotten kitties were coming to Earth sooner or later, and they were going to turn our homeworld into a radioactive wasteland. After that battle, *Valkyrie* probably would not exist, so we wouldn't have an opportunity for payback. That was why we were hitting the enemy now. You know the saying 'Payback is a bitch'?

Payforward can be a bitch too.

Anyway, that was our Happy Time.

Until it wasn't.

I'll get to that later.

Over sixty-four days of Happy Time, we conducted a dozen attacks. To reduce our risk, and the distance we had to travel, we clustered strikes in one area, then moved on before the Maxolhx could reinforce their presence there. In sixty-four days, we destroyed twenty-seven ships. Not all were warships. In two attacks, we hit a convoy of cargo ships that were escorted by frigates. Our tactics for those convoy attacks were to knock out the escorting warships first, then hunt down and blow up the merchant ships at our leisure. The powerful damping field projected by *Valkyrie* prevented ships from jumping away from us, and heavily-laden merchant ships could not run away from us. The last cargo ship we destroyed discarded its cargo containers in an attempt to escape. We were busy chasing a ship in the opposite direction, so I reluctantly ordered one missile launched to target the daredevil drag-racer. That cargo ship was nearing the edge of our damping field and had a point-defense system roughly equivalent to that of a Maxolhx frigate, so the success of our single missile was not guaranteed. Knowing that it faced significant opposition, that *Valkyrie*'s supply of missiles was limited, and that all the other missile guidance AIs aboard our ship were watching, that missile was determined to win the coveted Weapon Of The Month award.

The award comes with a nice plaque and a prime parking space, but sadly, the winning weapon never gets to use it.

It's the thought that counts.

What our brave little missile did was calculate the explosive force needed merely to disable the target cargo ship, and separated most of the bomblets of its atomic-compression warhead so they could be loaded into the decoys it carried. The decision was made while the missile was still surging down the launch tube, and the work was accomplished in flight. Sending the decoys on ahead, it guided them to approach the target ship in waves. With a large number of nimble, small objects to intercept, the cargo ship's defense systems concentrated on identifying which threats were decoys and which was the stealthy missile itself. Testing its guesses required firing on several objects, but the defense system was dismayed to see large secondary explosions when its maser beams intercepted the inbound objects. With so much high-energy clutter in the area, the defense system's sensors lost track of the rapidly-maneuvering missile, especially after the missile ordered random decoys to release the containment field on their payloads and explode.

Instantly, space between *Valkyrie* and the cargo ship was saturated with short-lived hard radiation. The radiation bath lasted only a few seconds before the cargo ship's active sensors burned through the clutter, but by that time, the missile had already transmitted back a message to its fellow guidance AIs. The message was '*That's how you beat the odds, bitches*'.

Its fellow guidance AIs burned with jealous rage, as our lone missile plunged into the cargo ship's primary reactionless engine, and tore it apart.

By the time *Valkyrie* was within directed-energy weapons range of the disabled ship, I almost felt sorry for that crew.

Almost.

Knowing the doom of their ship was inevitable, the crew had scattered in dropships and escape pods by the time we were within comfortable weapons range. The crew could have made our task easier by instructing their ship to merely drift, but the culture of assholeishness is deeply embedded in the Maxolhx psyche, so their AI was popping thrusters randomly to screw with our targeting. The uncertainty of where the target was located forced us to hold fire until we were within two lightseconds, then I ordered our cannons to saturate the target zone.

Two seconds was not sufficient time for a bulky cargo ship to move a distance that could dodge speed-of-light weapons.

We took our time slicing up that ship, making a show for the crew and anyone else recording sensor images. Like I said before, we wanted the Maxolhx to get a good look at our fearsome ghost ship. By that point, they had to know someone was flying a captured and much-modified *Extinction*-class battlecruiser. Even more than the havoc we were causing across a wide swath of their territory, the Maxolhx would be terrified to know an enemy had boarded and taken one of their capital ships. Implied in an enemy's control of a former Maxolhx ship was that whatever secrets the ship had possessed were surely now in dangerous hands. The Maxolhx were highly confident in their data encryption, but control of a warship meant that an enemy had thoroughly cracked that encryption.

Before jumping away from the convoy battle, which had really been a convoy slaughter, Skippy transmitted an updated version of our standard manifesto. The statement was by now a hate-filled long, rambling and incoherent screed of contradictory ideas, threats, vague demands and promises of a better future for all client species if they joined the glorious rebellion. It was sort of like a typical political party's campaign platform, if it had been written by a terrorist group high on meth.

Skippy was quite proud of his manifesto, so much that it inspired him to write yet another operatic masterpiece.

I suggested that we add being forced to listen to one of Skippy's operas, as a threat listed in the manifesto. Surely that would cause the Maxolhx to throw up their paws and surrender.

Skippy was *not* amused.

CHAPTER TEN

While Skippy worked to repair *Valkyrie*'s minor battle damage, I flew a dropship over to the good old *Flying Dutchman*. The dropship was a Panther, one of the spacecraft we found inside *Valkyrie*'s docking bays after we captured the ship. When I say that *I* flew it, I was at the controls, but Skippy watched my every move. He was such a whiny pain in the ass, second-guessing everything I did, that I felt like throwing up my hands and telling him to fly the damned thing. Because that would have deprived him of endless entertainment, he encouraged me to keep fumbling around randomly until I either crashed or blew up the Panther.

It might have been to spite him, but I was super focused and made a perfect docking aboard the *Dutchman*. We did not need the crash netting that Skippy insisted be set up in the bay, and the docking clamps locked onto us without any of the usual rocking side to side as the clamps try to move a dropship into position.

Did Skippy apologize for his disparaging remarks about my flying skills? Of course he did.

Not.

It was nice being back aboard the *Dutchman*. Nostalgia was not the purpose of my visit, that was just a nice bonus. In the Panther, I ferried over several people who wanted a change of scenery, plus Major Kapoor and six members of the STAR team. Kapoor wanted them to practice an opposed boarding action on a different ship, he feared that the familiar configuration of the *Valkyrie* was making people's improvisational skills go stale.

While Kapoor took his people away to have fun, I met Chang in my old office. It looked the same, except it felt weird to sit on the other side of the desk, with Chang occupying my old chair. We caught up, mostly it was me recounting recent battles. Sure, he had been able to watch our flight recorder data and experience each battle in simulation, that was not the same as *being there*. Usually when someone is telling war stories, they bore their audience, so I looked for signs that Kong was bored. The opposite happened, he caught me yawning.

"Joe," he stood up. "Let's get you a cup of coffee. We have a special dinner planned for you."

His crew was tiny, and I did not want to give them extra work just because some senior officer jerk decides to take a vacation. "Ah, you didn't have to-"

"It's salad, with Cajun grilled chicken."

"Mmm," I moaned instinctively. Chicken we had plenty of aboard the *Valkyrie*. It was the thought of eating a fresh salad that got my mouth watering. The hydroponics gardens were still all aboard the *Dutchman*, we had not moved any of the equipment over to my ship. Dropships had shuttled supplies between the two ships, and we had stuff like fresh onions. What had not been on the menu for weeks was any kind of salad, and I found myself craving fresh veggies like I always crave cheeseburgers. "Ok, thank you. That would be great."

On the way to the galley, we passed my old cabin. Kong paused, pointing to the door. "We moved your gear in there," he knew I planned to stay overnight.

"You didn't take this cabin?" I was surprised. It was the closest sleeping quarters to the bridge. The cabin he had been assigned, when he was my executive officer, was down the passageway and around two corners.

"No, we're keeping it as sort of VIP quarters," he explained. "It's always-"

"Plus, Joe," Skippy interrupted. "No one else wants to go in there. I mean, wow, you do *not* want to look around your old cabin with a blacklight. *Whoo-hoo*. It looks like a *murder scene* in there except with, you know, different fluids."

Sadly, I had not brought along a sidearm, because eating a bullet would have been really tasty right then.

"Skippy," Nagatha came to my defense. "You are being disrespectful to Colonel Bishop. Do not worry, Colonel. After you left, we thoroughly cleaned your quarters. Well, as best we could, you understand. One of my cleaning bots had a nervous *breakdown* and I had to-"

"Yeah, that's uh," if the deck had opened and ejected me into space, I would not have objected. "That's great, Nagatha."

She continued, not taking my hint. "There was an oddly *persistent* film on the walls of your shower, I was not sure how to-"

Kong raised a hand. "Nagatha, we do not need details, please. Joe," I noticed he avoided looking at me. "Let's get coffee, then I'll show you the hydroponics. They've been expanded using the spare parts we were carrying."

We did get coffee, then Kong got called away to deal with some problem. Instead of interfering with his command of the *Dutchman*, I strolled down to the hydroponics bays by myself. It was kind of taking a walk down Memory Lane, with every step I remembered one crisis or another we had dealt with. We had successfully dealt with each crisis, and each time, we at least for a while had the illusion that we had Saved the World.

Damn, those were the good old days. Now, we had no illusions about the ultimate future. Whatever we did, no matter how badly our one warship hit the Maxolhx, our homeworld was going to be turned into a lifeless ball of radioactive ash.

Shit.

Maybe we could get enough people to the beta site, so humans had a viable population there. That would be small consolation, unless the Rindhalu really did have their own Elder AI. If that was true, even the beta site in the Sculptor dwarf galaxy would not be safe. Everything we had accomplished, all the blood we had shed, all the people dead and seriously injured, would all be for nothing.

By the time I reached the hydroponics, my mood was as gloomy as humanity's prospects for survival.

"Colonel Bishop!" The familiar voice of our friendly local rocket scientist called from the other end of the converted cargo bay.

"Hello, Doctor," I waved vaguely in his direction, unable to see him through the lush vegetation. Tomatoes, lettuce, stalks of corn and every other plant my parents had in their kitchen garden were sprouting and hanging from the tanks of nutrient fluid. Against the far bulkhead, raspberries or maybe blackberries were growing along a wire grid. Dwarf trees had oranges and apples ripening.

Everything looked healthy, making me glance down with guilt at my boots, which were not covered with protective coverings. Nor was I wearing gloves or a facemask.

Friedlander's legs dropped down from a rack on the other side of the bay, and he stepped out into a narrow pathway between tanks. Walking down the pathway, he casually plucked a cherry tomato from a bush, and tossed it to me.

"Mm," I bit into the ripe tomato. "Hey, should I be wearing, you know," I pantomimed a facemask. He wasn't wearing protective gear, but he had been living aboard the *Dutchman*, and Nagatha's sensors knew what pathogens he might have been carrying. Having just come from the *Valkyrie*, I could be carrying a whole host of critters that could be hazardous to our growing food supply. We were not concerned about microorganisms left by the Maxolhx, their biochemistry was incompatible with Earth-based life. The problem was that, even with self-cleaning surfaces and Skippy's bots scrubbing and disinfecting twenty four hours a day, our battlecruiser was a petri dish for growing nasty things. Ok, I am exaggerating a bit. You could eat off the floors of our ship, even in the gym. Still, it was possible that some combination of nasty micro-bugs, or a mutation of normally harmless bacteria, could cause havoc to the precious plants in the hydroponics gardens.

"No, it's not necessary," the good doctor assured me. "We have nano-mites constantly scanning and sampling the air in here. They alert us to any pathogens, and usually take care of the problem on their own."

"Nano-*mites*?"

He lifted an eyebrow, setting down the gloves he had been wearing. Those gloves were thick leather, used for protecting him against the raspberry vines, not protecting the vines against him. "You didn't know?"

"I know what nano tech is. What's a mite?"

"Like a tiny spider or insect." Touching thumb and forefinger, he pretending to peer through the nonexistent gap. "A tiny creepy-crawly thing. So small, you can only see them with a microscope." He tilted his head. "Skippy didn't tell you about this? He was quite proud when he introduced the technology here." By Friedlander's rueful expression, I knew that 'quite proud' meant Skippy had boasted about his awesomeness when he brought in the nanomites, and had expected endless praise for everyone aboard the *Flying Dutchman*. The burden of giving that praise had probably fallen on the good doctor.

"Uh, no." Often, I forgot that Skippy talked with everyone aboard *Valkyrie*, and everyone aboard the *Flying Dutchman* when we were in range. As much of a pain he was to me, he could be even more annoying to other people. Fortunately for me, the two of us had worked out a workable relationship. Other people considered Skippy amusing, or at least a tolerable annoyance, but some people could not stand him. We tried to select prospective crew persons on the basis of whether they could get along well with others in the confined environment of a starship, and whether they were a good fit with Skippy. Despite all our efforts, we still took aboard people who found Skippy too irritating. In those cases, I asked Skippy to leave the guy alone, as if that was going to make any difference. "What's so special about these nano-thingies?"

"They are Maxolhx tech. Skippy repurposed them for use here," he waved a hand to encompass the garden.

"Is this another thing we monkeys can't possibly understand, like Thuranin doorknobs?"

"Colonel?"

That made me cringe. "Can you call me 'Joe', please? You're a civilian."

"You have the power of life or death over everyone on these ships." His words were not intended to be unkind, he was just stating a fact. "Will you call me 'Mark'?"

"Probably not," I admitted. "Not when I'm on duty."

He gave me a half-smile. "When are you *not* on duty?"

That made me snort. "When I'm dirtside, I guess. Except for the times I'm on duty there also. Can I call you 'Doc'?"

"As long as you don't greet me with 'What's up Doc'?"

"Deal," I agreed with a laugh.

"You said something like, we don't understand Thuranin doorknobs?"

"*You* said that. I think that was during our Zero Hour mission?"

"That was true back then. It's not true now. Skippy has been sharing information with us."

"I know but, that's limited. He is only nibbling around the edges of what's out there."

"That's partly true. What he has been able to share has been blowing our minds. It blew *my* mind, that's for sure. The real breakthrough came when you captured the Dagger."

"It did?" What I said aloud was better than my brain's internal reaction of 'Duh'? We had taken the Kristang troopship *Ice-Cold Dagger to the Heart* when we had trouble on the Homefront. "That ship's technology wasn't any better than the stuff aboard the *Yu Qishan*, except for the sleep chambers."

"It's not the tech. It's the user manuals, what you soldiers call a Dash Ten?"

"Oh. Shit. Yeah! I hadn't thought about that." User manuals printed by the US military have a designation ending in a '-10'. To learn how to use a rifle or any other piece of equipment, you ask for the Dash Ten. Way back when we captured the ship we named the *Flying Dutchman*, I hoped we could get access to the ship's database, which was a treasure trove of Thuranin technology. Both the Kristang and Ruhar had refused to share technology, or even information about basic science with us lowly humans. We had obtained fragments of knowledge anyway, enough to be confusing and not enough to help. The *Flying Dutchman*, I had hoped, was our ticket to joining the big leagues, to acquiring technology to boost humanity at least up to the level of the Ruhar. At the time, I had not told Skippy about the treasure I was hoping to bring home, because it was sort of my backup plan if he refused to help us.

All my hope was for nothing. Either Skippy had locked us out of the database, or he had erased any info he wasn't allowed to share with us, because what we got out of the *Flying Dutchman's* computers was a whole lot of nothing. "The *Dagger's* database is intact? We can read it?"

"Intact and, since Nagatha erased and replaced the original AI, very cooperative," Friedlander confirmed. "We got theory on basic science, guides on how to operate and maintain every piece of equipment aboard the ship, more than we ever could have hoped for."

I lowered my voice, which was not necessary, and even useless. Trying to whisper only attracted Skippy's attention. "And Skippy is Ok with this?"

"He must know about it," Friedlander's gaze automatically went to the ceiling, but Skippy didn't answer. "The information we recovered from the *Dagger* is just the tip of the iceberg. We now have access to the database aboard *Valkyrie*."

"Holy *shit*," I gasped.

"You got it. We are still digging through it, of course," he wiped a hand across his face. "I've been reading files nonstop since I came aboard. Of the science team who went to Avalon, not many had a background in physics. Working in the gardens here is the only," he yawned. "Break I get."

"*Wow*. We will know what the kitties know?"

"That's not the best part," he grinned.

Before I responded, I sat down on a bench, making sure I didn't crush a precious plant. "Hit me with it, Doc."

"Some of the capabilities of the Valkyrie, like how Skippy can enhance the throughput of the power boosters, relies on *Elder* technology."

You know how, when you want something really badly, you are afraid to ask for it, in case the Universe decides to kick you in the balls that day? That was me right then. "Go on."

"To use those power boosters properly, the *Valkyrie*'s database needs to know how they operate. Not just the basics of pressing buttons, but the theory too."

"You're telling me that," I swallowed hard. "We have access to *Elder* technology? We know how their stuff works?"

"A tiny bit of it. Colonel, if what I think I understand about how those power boosters function is correct, then the universe is stranger than we could have imagined."

"Would it blow my primitive monkey brain to learn about this?"

"It is blowing *my* monkey brain."

"In that case, I'll leave the science stuff to the experts."

He didn't protest. I wasn't insulted. "You realize what this means? Colonel, if we can get back to Earth, then eventually, humanity will no longer be on the bottom of the development ladder. We will be at the *top* of the ladder. We will have knowledge that even the Rindhalu don't possess. That will give us a fighting chance."

"Against the whole galaxy," I said to remind him of the odds against us. "That's all good, the problem is *time*. You're an engineer, right? Knowing mind-blowing facts only helps us if we can put it into practice. Build a war fleet. Build the tools to build a war fleet. Hell, build the tools to build the freakin' tools to build ships."

"I hear you," his shoulder slumped. "It's a challenge. Those power boosters? Just the basic units the Maxolhx have, not the fancy ones upgraded with Elder tech? Making those requires a facility that closely orbits a *neutron star*. We can't build a neutron star. We can't even work with one. Just dealing with the tidal forces and the time dilation would make my head hurt. Skippy told me it took the Maxolhx seven hundred *years* to set up their first factory that makes power boosters."

"Ok," I took in a chest-filling breath. "We need time. Damn it, we always need time. That's one thing Earth doesn't have, no matter how we look at it."

"We might have to," he looked down at the deck. "Have to consider building our technology base at the beta site."

"Avalon? It's mud and giant ferns."

"It's giant ferns *now*," he insisted. "The whole point of the beta site is that aliens can't get there. If Earth is gone," his knuckles went white. "Then we build a war fleet out there, beyond the galaxy?"

"Build a fleet to get payback?"

"For wiping out our homeworld? Yes!"

He had to know the survival of the beta site depended on aliens not being able to get there, depended on the Rindhalu and possibly the Maxolhx not having their own Elder AI. There wasn't any point to making plans if the senior species had an entity that might match Skippy's awesome powers, that would be Game Over for us. "Doc, this is all great news. There's not much we can do with the info out here, is there?"

"No," he shook his head, and his eyes flashed anger. Whether his anger was directed at the alien threat, or at me for reminding him of the enormous task ahead of hm, I didn't know. "We need to get back to Earth, give this data to the right people."

"Skippy would say it's bad enough that monkeys have access to nukes," my attempt to lighten the mood fell flat. "You, uh, want to give me a tour of the gardens?"

"Not now," he threw the gloves in a bin. "I have real work to do."

Margaret's condition improved rapidly, you might almost say miraculously, after Skippy began the nanobot procedure. Either Skippy absent-mindedly forgot to be his usual absent-minded self with her, or he paid extra super-duper careful attention to all of his patients, because he worked with her twenty-four seven. Even when she was asleep, Skippy was closely monitoring her brain activity and tweaking the activities of the nanobots. The good news was the bots were learning how to assist and enhance her brain function. They transmitted signals, dampened the actions of misfiring neurons, and acted as supplemental memory storage for her. Over time, as her organic brain repaired itself, the nanobots could be deactivated. That was the good news.

The bad news was, with sophisticated alien machines doing part of the thinking for her, she was not one hundred percent Margaret Adams. Her personality had changed in subtle ways. She was more open, less reserved that her previous self. She laughed more easily, and she seemed to enjoy laughing, while I always got the impression she was self-conscious about it. When I asked Skippy about it, he told me the personality changes were hopefully temporary, a result not of the trauma but how the nanobots were interacting with her organic brain. When he was able to fully deactivate the bots, she should return to her previous self, although he expected that the experience would change her, and there was nothing he could do about that.

I understood.

Armageddon had changed all of us.

Part of the reason for her new personality was the nanobots did not necessarily store information the same way her brain would have. The associations between pieces of information might be different from the associations her brain would have made. The bots also did not know her real personality, so they did not understand which information was important and which was useless. At first, her speech patterns were noticeably different, her language was more formal. It was like the nanobots were guessing what she wanted to say, and they had just learned from a stack of children's books. She could hear herself talking and she knew it didn't sound like her. Skippy asked her to be patient and to speak more slowly. Privately, he told me that he was having to intervene directly with the nanobots so they didn't make her sound like a five-year-old girl.

Once Skippy began intervening, and he was able to reprogram the nanobots, Margaret's dark mood lifted. She could see the improvement she was making, see progress every day. The day she stood and walked for the first time, I was there with Smythe. Smythe was there because he was also relearning how to walk, and he thought it would make Margaret feel better to see she was not the only clumsy person aboard the ship. My purpose for being there was officially to assess her progress for her personnel report, but that was pure bullshit. I was there in case she fell, to provide physical as well as moral support.

No, that was also bullshit.

I was there because I had to be. No way could I *not* be there. If Margaret was embarrassed at her initial awkward attempts to stand on her own, and her first lurching, halting steps, she didn't say anything to me. We even high-fived after she walked across the compartment, turned around and walked back. If I had to be extra careful to slap her mis-aimed hand for the high-five, neither of us mentioned it.

Being able to walk again, even if she stumbled like a toddler, was a great boost to her spirits. Being able to speak, to communicate her thoughts and to understand what other people were saying, was another huge milestone in her recovery. If she stuttered and occasionally forgot words, that did not bother her. She knew, or hoped, the stuttering would eventually go away. And she could track the progress of recovering her verbal memory, in the word-association games and other work she did for therapy.

One day, when I was helping her with a word-association exercise, we came to a section of the text that Skippy must have written. Without thinking, I read aloud the word "Knucklehead".

Adams automatically replied "Bishop".

There was not even a microsecond of embarrassment for either of us. She burst into laughter, and patted me on the shoulder.

Then she leaned her head on my shoulder, pressing her forehead into my chest, still while we were both laughing.

When she pulled away, she looked at me. "Oh, Joe, th-that was a g-good one."

A thousand volts ran up my spine. "*Joe?*" I stared at her in surprise. Oh, shit. I should not have done that. Using my first name could have been a faulty association caused by the alien machines in her head. Pointing out her mistake might be discouraging.

My fears were for nothing. She tapped my shoulder with one finger. "D-don't worry. I know w-what I said. *Joe.*"

"Wow." That was not the smartest thing I could have said at that moment, but it was the most honest. She knew that. "You have ever only called me 'Sir' or 'Colonel' before."

"I might have c-called you knucklehead once or t-twice," she replied with a twinkle in her eyes. Damn, it was good to see her being happy. "But not that y-you know of," she winked.

"Why the, uh, change now?"

She looked away as a shadow fell across her happy expression. When she turned back, her grin was gone, but her eyes were still smiling. You know what I mean. "Reed told me w-what happened, during," she screwed up her face and pronounced the word slowly, deliberately. "Ar-ma-ge-ddon. After my dropship got hit, you t-took, *Val-ky-rie,*" slowly again. "Away to stop an enemy s-ship."

"Mar-" Crap. She had used my first name. That did not mean she was comfortable with me assuming the same familiarity with her. Figuring it would be awkward if I called her 'Adams' or 'Gunny', I simply avoided the issue. It was awkward anyway. "Please understand, I didn't have a choice. That ship would have-"

"Y-you d-did have a choice. Skippy told me that my brain damage," she looked me straight in the eye and pinned me with her gaze, not letting me get away. "Was worse because V*alkyrie* delayed rescuing me."

"Shit." Did I say that aloud? Yes, I did. Double shit! It was time to own my actions, and deal with the consequences. "Ok, yes. I knew people, *my* people, were injured and dying. I made a choice to pursue that Maxolhx ship, instead of-"

"That," she poked my chest with her index finger. It was not an accusing jab. It was not angry. It was *gentle*. It was, affectionate? WTF? "Is w-why I called you 'Joe', J-Joe."

"Uh-" What I know about women could fit into a thimble, with plenty of room for, whatever people put into thimbles. My mind was racing to guess what she meant, and all I could come up with was my mind scratching its head and saying 'I dunno'. "I'm gonna need some help on that, if you don't mind, please."

"It's simple." She glanced at the clock on the bulkhead, then at the airlock. Justin Grudzien was coming in next to help her with therapy, they were scheduled to work on her eye-hand coordination. "I *think*," her eyes flicked back and forth, searching mine. "I know how y-you feel about me." Her eyes cast down at the deck, in a coy gesture. "I hope you know h-how I f-feel about you."

"Uh-" Damn it. I needed to stop doing that.

She bailed me out of my awkward silence. "The Army bans re-relationships like," she waved a hand, frustrated she couldn't get the words out.

"I'm your commanding officer," I said sourly.

"R-right. The Marine Corps has the s-same regs. I th-think those regs are a g-good idea."

"Oh." The deck opened beneath me and I fell into a black hole, or that is how it felt.

"I think th-they are a good idea *normally*," she added, and the black hole sent me back. "A c-commander can't favor one s-soldier, or *Marine*," she emphasized. "That is bad for g-good order and discipline. You," her finger poked my chest again, and lingered there. "Proved you do n-*not* play favorites. You left me out there to *d-die*, because you put the m-mission first. You p-proved to me that you s-see me as a *Marine* first. That is all I n-need to know."

"Uh, Ok." My mind was reeling. Mostly because her finger, resting and slowly tracing circles on my chest, had most of my blood flowing away from my brain, if you know what I mean. "I risked your life, and that was a *good* thing?"

"You risked m-my life for the good of the *m-mission*."

"Ah. Margaret," I said without thinking. "If you had died out there-"

She raised her finger to my lips, silencing me. "A lot of p-people did die out th-there. Th-they were d-doing their duty. You expected me to do no l-less."

"I did," I whispered, my lips touching her finger. She looked at me and for a moment, a glorious moment, I thought we were going to kiss.

She pulled away, folding her hands in her lap. It was a gesture that sometimes went with sadness, but she was giving me the side-eye, and the smile on her lips was definitely *not* sad.

I took a breath. "What," I laid a hand gently on her shoulder, and she leaned into me just a little. Enough to let me know my touch was welcome. "Is next? For us?"

"You're a s-soldier. I'm a Marine, to the core," she pulled her shoulder back proudly. "The military s-says we c-can't be together."

"That's it, then?" I did not believe it.

Turning to me, she took my hand off her shoulder and held it in both of her hands. "Joe, you j-jumped a starship th-through an Elder wormhole. It is impossible f-for us to be together. For y-you, *impossible* is j-just a speed bump," the twinkle was back in her eyes, and that twinkle outshone the brightest star. "F-find a way."

"Just like that? Make it *happen*?"

"J-just like that," she agreed.

She had full faith in me. I had no faith in myself. That was not a great combination.

Her eyes glanced at the clock. Grudzien was scheduled to be there at 1400. It was 1350 at that moment. In the military, if you're not early, you're late. We both knew he would be there soon.

"Ok. I will make it happen. Don't ask me how, because right now, I have no idea." That was not true. I did have one idea. With *Valkyrie* cut off from Earth, and the Pentagon's influence and relevance dwindling by the day, I could simply say *screw* the regulations, and declare the Merry Band of Pirates to officially be a pirate operation.

But that would mean Margaret having to give up her beloved Marine Corps. I wanted to make her happy, not unhappy. So, that was a last resort. "Grudzien will be-"

"I know," she finished my thought. "Joe. I won't b-be calling you that again, until-"

"Yeah. I know." Crap. No pressure on me!

What I was hoping for was a kiss. Ok, I was *hoping* for a lot more. Right then, a kiss would have been everything. She kissed one of her index fingers and held it up to me.

Returning the gesture, I kissed my finger, and our fingers touched. "Margaret-"

"Oh," Grudzien said in surprise as he came to the open airlock. "You are already on the eye-hand coordination exercises?" He asked in his Polish accent. "That is good," he clapped his hands, "very good!"

Justin Grudzien was a dedicated STAR team soldier, who came to us from the Polish GROM special forces. He was a skilled operator, he was dedicated, and right then, I wanted to stuff him out an airlock.

Instead, I excused myself, a bit more stiff and formal than needed, and walked out.

Margaret wanted me to-

No. She had faith in me. She didn't just want, she *expected* me to find a way.

Would it be difficult, if not impossible?

Yes.

Was I going to figure out a way to make us work?

Oh, *hell* yes.

CHAPTER ELEVEN

Illiath feared that, compared to the next phase of the investigation, the analysis of the star at Quraqua had been simple. She took her cruiser to the site of the battle where the rogue Bosphuraq had destroyed the two ships traveling to Earth. No, she reminded herself. It was an *alleged* battle, and the Bosphuraq had only *allegedly* been involved. That was the whole point of her ship being there. Her *war*ship. The distinction was important because the Maxolhx Hegemony had been *attacked* by a ghost ship, and fighting ships were needed for actual combat missions for the first time in many millennia. As a patrol cruiser, the *Vortan* was too lightly-armed and armored to take on the ghost ship, but it could be used to search for and track the enemy vessel. Since the first attack at Koprahdru, Illiath had been waiting for, and dreading, a recall order. At some point, she was certain, the Fleet would decide they needed a patrol cruiser to do something more useful than verifying information they already knew. The only possible reason she could think of, for why she had not been given a recall order, was that someone in Fleet Intelligence had read her report about the discrepancies between the condition of the star at Quraqua and the confession message. One lightly-armed cruiser could not make a significant difference in the hunt for the ghost ship, but if Illiath could prove the confession message was a fake, that would raise a lot of questions. Such as, perhaps the ghost ship was *not* controlled by a rogue faction of birds, as the propaganda diatribes claimed. If that were true, then the Maxolhx war fleet was fighting the wrong enemy, and needed to change strategy immediately.

If that were true, the fleet needed to know immediately. Privately, Illiath had begun to suspect the Rindhalu were somehow involved in the incidents that were blamed on the Bosphuraq. She had no solid evidence to back up her suspicions, and she told no one. She also told herself to keep an open mind, and seek the truth, rather than sorting through data to find only those elements that supported her theories.

Reaching the site of the alleged battle, her ship was quickly able to confirm that two Maxolhx warships had indeed been thoroughly torn apart there. Sensors positively identified the remains of the ships as those which had been flying toward the wormhole near the planet called 'Earth' by the primitive natives of that backwater world. Further investigation revealed that one ship had been subjected to an extremely violent spacetime distortion, of a type unknown to the Maxolhx. The other ship appeared to have been destroyed by release of energy stored in its jump drive capacitors. The fate of the second ship was slightly puzzling. It had been damaged by the same type of spacetime distortion that had ripped apart the first ship, yet the second ship had survived for a time. What could not be explained were indications that the second ship had been shattered by a severe vibration, from a source that was not only unknown, it was unimaginable. It appeared the second ship shook itself apart, an event that was impossible.

Having determined that two warships of the Maxolhx Hegemony had been destroyed at that location, matching the claim in the confession document, Illiath then directed the cruiser's sensors to dig deeper, looking for signs of the ship or ships that had dared attack. At first, the sensors merely confirmed what the first investigation had found; evidence of a Bosphuraq ship having been involved.

Then Illiath directed the *Vortan* to release a cloud of specialized nanomachines to scour a small section of the battlespace. The tiny machines fanned out, examining any particle larger than the atomic level. The section the nanobots analyzed was larger than a typical gas giant planet, and even with over one hundred sixty thousand nanomachines at work, the task would take many days for results to even begin to flow back to the Vortan's AI.

Illiath and her crew waited, and waited, and waited for results. Every day, she checked the progress of the sensor sweep, and waited for the AI to announce a preliminary result. Every day, she was disappointed. Until that day.

"Commander Illiath," the AI spoke abruptly, while she was engaged in studying a report about the ghost ship's latest attack.

"Yes?"

"Preliminary results are now available."

Pushing the report to the back of her mind, she ordered her couch to bring her upright. "How preliminary?"

"The sensor machines have completed scanning only twelve percent of the target zone. However, I have seventy-nine percent confidence that scans of the remaining area will not conflict with the current results."

Illiath had already downloaded the file and was sorting through it. It was a veritable mountain of data. "Are there any immediate surprises?"

"Yes. Sensors have detected evidence of a Bosphuraq ship, but also many other ships, from multiple species. That is surprising, given the remote location of the battle."

"Show me," she ordered, irritation creeping into her voice.

"Yes, Commander. Before I do that, might I be permitted to tell you the most surprising result so far?"

"Permission granted." The machine was assuming too much familiarity. That would require an adjustment to its programming. "What is it?"

"While it is not unexpected to find biological markers at the site of a battle, one of the markers cannot be explained."

"What did you find?"

"*Human* DNA."

After the devastating and shocking attack that blew two of their warships to dust, the Maxolhx appeared to have left the research base on Koprahdru alone, other than a half-dozen ships jumping in to recon the area within a week of the battle. When those recon ships jumped away, and the research base was left alone for forty-three days, some of the inhabitants began to dare hope they would survive unscathed. The Maxolhx had bigger problems to worry about. Or they had reached a deal with the Bosphuraq government. Or, the ghost ship was so powerful, it had forced the Maxolhx to surrender!

The residents of the research base simply did not know what was going on in the wider galaxy. They had no ship capable of faster-than-light travel, and their Navy sent no ships to communicate with them, so they could only wait fearfully, watching the sky for telltale gamma ray bursts. If the burst was barely detectable, that would be the death sentence of a Maxolhx ship arriving. A stronger burst would hopefully be a friendly ship coming to defend the base, or pull the entire population off the desolate planet and take them away to safety.

When the days dragged on with no sign of either impending destruction or salvation, the administrator began to lose control of his team, as baseless rumors began to spread. People in desperate need of hope heard what they wanted to hear, and the administrator had no hope to offer. The rumors offered comfort. The ghost ship that blew up the two destroyers was so powerful, the Maxolhx dared not attack any planet under the ghost ship's protection. The ghost ship was striking widely across Maxolhx territory, forcing the patrons of the Bosphuraq to pull their own warships back to defensive positions. No, the ghost ship was still lurking near Koprahdru, ready to pounce on any ships that dared attack the defenseless world. No, the ghost ship had already forced the Maxolhx to negotiate a ceasefire with the Bosphuraq.

All the rumors had one thing in common: the administrator had received communications from outside, and was concealing the truth. He did not want the people to know the truth, so he could rule them by fear.

On the forty-fourth day as measured by the rotation of the Bosphuraq homeworld, the agitators had enough of waiting. Their leader urged his followers to march on the offices of the administrator, and forced the man out. As the base was a science station, the administrator had not been provided with any weapons, and the two-person military security team decided to stay out of civilian disputes.

In the administrator's records, the agitators found no hint of communications from the outside, but their leader assured them that only meant the dastardly former occupant of the office had erased the evidence. Do not worry, their new leader told the unhappy crowd, he would get to the truth. To his trusted inner circle, he told them to stall while he ransacked the office for valuables. A bottle of thirty-year-old *shaze* was the only worthwhile item he found, so he got some glasses and enjoyed the fiery liquid with his friends. The crowd outside would wait while he thought of what evidence to fake.

The first hint of approaching trouble was an early warning satellite going offline, which rated the defense AI to alert the administrator's office, where three people were sleeping off the effects of consuming an entire bottle of vintage *shaze*. Thus, the initial warning was ignored.

The next sign of trouble was a brief but odd sensor reading, captured by a satellite in low orbit. There was a moment of terrified excitement by the defense AI when the high-energy sensor reading was confused for a gamma ray burst. Then when the reading was evaluated and corrected, it too, was consigned to the status report. The scientists who could have confirmed or disputed the sensor reading, were mostly gathered outside the administrator's office, blissfully unaware of any alert.

Thus, when the twenty-meter-wide asteroid impacted the planet's surface directly above the buried research base, moving at thirty-one percent of lightspeed, it was a complete surprise. The asteroid had dropped its stealth field only two seconds before it contacted the atmosphere, leaving no time for base personnel to react to the AI's frantic alert.

The only good news was that someone got to enjoy an excellent bottle of vintage shaze, before the bottle and the planet's crust in that area were obliterated.

Our Happy Time was a busy and satisfying two months. For me, it was especially happy, because Margaret Adams was making slow and steady progress. She did not do anything spectacular, that was the point. Yes, she had bad days, discouraging days. Of course, her progress was slower than she wanted, and exactly on the schedule Skippy recommended. By the end of three weeks after she woke from the coma, she was able to speak normally, if a bit slower than she had before and with a stutter she hated. Skippy assured her, and me, that her speaking ability would make a full recovery. He gradually deactivated the nanoprobes in her brain, as her own neurons regrew and made new connections. Though I knew the little machines were helping her make faster progress, it was still creepy to think of alien bots crawling around inside her head.

I was not the only person who did not like the idea of nanobots artificially enhancing the natural abilities Adams had. The good-faith decision I made for her had consequences, and they weren't all good.

Like I said, she had good days and bad days. On bad days, she stumbled while walking, and fell off the exercise bike, and her clumsy fingers shook when trying to bring a spoon to her mouth, and she got so frustrated when trying to talk that she burst into tears. That was really bad, because when she was crying she tended to stutter and babble, which made it even more difficult for her to talk.

Simms came rushing into my office unannounced one day. "Sir, you need to go to-"

Skippy's voice interrupted. "Hey, Joe, I-"

"Not now, Skippy. Simms, what is it?"

She looked at the ceiling before answering. "Skippy and I may be talking about the same thing. Is it Adams?"

"It is," Skippy confirmed.

"Oh *shit*," I shot up from my chair. The worst things I could imagine raced through my mind in vivid detail. Why is my brain so lightning fast to picture bad things, and so painfully slow when I needed it to do something useful? "What happened?"

Simms spoke first. "I was helping her with therapy. Cognitive stuff, memorization games, that sort of-" Seeing my impatience with details, she skipped to the end. "She's having a bad day. A *really* bad day. She is pissed at you, Sir, for putting nanomachines in her head. She is worried that all of the progress she has made is artificial, that it's not *her* making progress, that you've turned her into some sort of cyborg."

"Shit," I stared at the floor. I had been dreading that conversation.

"She is wrong about that," Skippy assured us. "But, Joe, we have a problem. Margaret wants me to deactivate and remove *all* the nanobots inside her."

"Whoa."

"Whoa indeed. Joe, such an abrupt action could be very harmful. It might *kill* her."

"I tried talking to her," Simms added. "Reason with her. Told her she is just having a bad day. She is adamant, she wants them out of her. She wants to be Margaret again, not some- She said you have made her into a monster. She would rather be dead."

I was torn between wanting to race to the medical bay that was set aside for post-recovery therapy, and wanting to take a minute to *think* first. Confronting her without a plan for what I would say, without having a damned good argument against ripping the nanobots out of her body, would do nothing but piss her off. My feet wanted to move, *now*. My brain made my restless feet stay planted on the deck of my office. "Skippy, stall her, however you can. Tell her, uh, some bullshit like you have to prep the extraction machines first."

"I have already stalled her, Joe. Margaret demanded that it is her right to make medical decisions for herself. My reply was that, as she *is* partly reliant on alien machines to think for her, she is *not* legally competent, and you still have power of attorney for her."

"I do?"

"Ugh. No. Try to keep up, please. Joe, I gave her whatever line of bullshit I could think of. Legally, um, it's kind of in a shmaybe-level gray area? Technically, she has not completed therapy, and she is clearly still impaired. Regardless of the legal rules you monkeys wrote for yourselves, I will not do anything to harm Margaret. Except," he choked up. "If she begs me, as her friend. Joe, I'm in a very tough spot here," he pleaded. "You gotta help me. Help her."

"Damn it," I muttered to myself. "I am the last person she wants to see right now."

Simms bobbed her head up and down once. "That's why you need to go talk with her."

I knew she was right. That didn't make it any easier. "Will you-"

That time, her head shook side to side. "This is all you, Sir."

When I reached the therapy bay, Adams was sitting on the deck, trying to pull a sneaker on her right foot. Her hands shook, and her foot kept missing the opening. When she saw me, I held up my hands without saying anything. She turned away from me and angrily threw the shoe across the compartment, except she missed. It bounced off the table opposite her, and flopped back at her feet. She buried her face in her hands and her whole body shook.

What the hell was I supposed to say? What *could* I say? There wasn't anything about this situation in my officer training manuals.

Not knowing what to do, I fell back on trying to be a decent human being. That is usually a good idea. I walked softly across the deck, and sat down on the floor next to her. "Gunny, can we talk?"

Without looking at me, face still covered by her hands, she spoke with vehemence. "I w-w-want these alien *t-th-thhings* out of m-m-my head."

"Skippy says they are helping you. Adams, you have made a lot of progress."

"The *bots* in my head have m-made a lot of p-p-progress." She glanced at me, angrily wiping tears away from her face with the sleeves of her shirt. I knew better than to offer a towel from the bin next to me. If she wanted a towel or anything else, she would ask for one. Or, she would get it herself. "This isn't me," she tapped her forehead.

"Gunny, you had a bad day, that's all."

She reached down to pick up the sneaker. Three times, she missed. As I watched, she concentrated hard on making her hand slowly slide across the floor to the shoe, then laboriously walked her fingers up to hook around a lace. When she lifted the shoe, her hand trembled. "Skippy has been d-d-deactivating the bots slowly. As the b-bots go offline, I have," she glared at me. 'What you call 'bad days'. They are b-b-bad because the bots are no longer doing the work for me. *I* am not g-g-getting any b-better."

Her whole body shuddered. She dropped the shoe and slumped back against the bulkhead, wracked with sobs. The shaking was likely worse because of her condition, not that it mattered. It was time for me to put aside rank structure and military protocol and just be a decent human being. So, I leaned over and put one arm around her. I didn't say anything, she didn't say anything. Whether it was because she shook or because she wanted to, she pressed her shoulder against me.

For her, it was one of the lowest moments of her life.

For me, it is a memory I will always cherish.

Skippy could not keep his stupid mouth shut. Damn it, I had a nice speech planned in my head. A tender moment, just me and Margaret Adams. Before I could say anything, Skippy opened his big stupid mouth. "That is not true, Margaret," he announced cheerily. "While it is true that I am slowly deactivating the nanoprobes, their loss is not causing your bad days. Quite the opposite, in fact. I deactivate bots because they are no longer needed, as your own neural circuitry is able to handle the tasks."

"Then why," she pushed away from me, and just like that, the special moment was gone. She lifted the sneaker and held it up with effort. The shoe wobbled slightly as she cradled it in both hands. "Was I able to put my d-damned shoes on yesterday, and I can't do it today? I've been," she wiped away a tear as I pointedly looked straight ahead. "P-putting my own shoes on since I was, w-was, a toddler!"

"Yes," Skippy's voice dripped with impatient, clueless condescension. "You did have a good day yesterday. That is why I was able to deactivate another set of nanoprobes. But the loss of that set has nothing to do with the motor-control difficulties you are experiencing today. You would be experiencing even *better* control than you did yesterday, if I wasn't using other nanoprobes to interfere with the natural wiring in your head."

"You're do-do-doing *what?*" Adams sputtered, while I only opened my mouth, stunned.

Skippy replied in his Patiently Explaining Things To Monkeys tone. "I am using-"

It was my turn for outrage. "We know what you are doing, For God's sake, *why?*"

The heights of Skippy's arrogance was matched only by his cluelessness. "To accelerate her recovery, *duh*. By interfering with the signals between neurons, I am forcing those neurons to adapt, to grow stronger, to make new connections. If you monkeys knew anything about how biological brains truly work, you would understand."

"You are m-making me," she held up the shoe with one hand, and it shook. "*More* clumsy? To *help* me?"

"Yes. *Ugh*," he sighed. "Try this. I just turned off the interference temporarily."

The shoe she was holding no longer shook. Adams carefully pushed back against the bulkhead and stood up. As a test, she used one hand to steady herself while her other hand pulled the shoe on. She still shook a bit, and her voice still had a quivering quality to it, but she no longer stuttered. "I can talk," she pronounced each work slowly, carefully. "Peter Piper picked a peck of," she took a breath, "pickled, peppers. Oh!" She gasped. "I didn't stutter."

"No you did not," Skippy gloated. "I can turn off the interference, but it will delay your therapy, your progress to complete recovery, by several weeks. Possibly a month. Your brain is a powerful and complex but *fragile* organ."

"I can't- Why didn't you *tell* me?"

"Because, knowing might change the way you respond to therapy. Besides, you thrive on challenges, right?"

Margaret Adams turned to me, rage glowing in her eyes. It was good that her rage wasn't directed at me.

Tapping my earlobe activated the zPhone earpiece. "Bridge, this is Bishop."

Reed answered. "Bridge here." She sounded distracted. In addition to acting as the duty officer, she was probably working with a group of trainees.

"Reed, eject escape pod Twenty-three Alpha." That was the designation for Skippy's bodacious new mancave aboard *Valkyrie*. "Once it gets to a safe distance, hit it with every weapon we've got."

"*HEY!*" Skippy shouted.

"Um," our chief pilot was shocked. "Say that again, please?" She was probably flashing back to when UNEF tried to eject Skippy's mancave from the *Flying Dutchman*.

Adams laughed. She not only laughed, she actually leaned toward me, so her head rested on my shoulder for a glorious, lingering moment. "Thank you for the gesture, Sir, but-"

"Reed," I ordered, with a wink to Adams. "Belay that. Ignore what I said."

"I'm not sure I *understood* what you said," Reed was incredulous. "Is that all, Sir?"

"That's all." I cut the connection.

"What did *I* do?" Skippy screeched. "Damn it, I get in trouble no matter what I do."

Ignoring the beer can, I addressed my remark to Adams. "Gunny, it seems to me you have a choice. Ask Skippy to cancel the interference, and possibly delay your recovery. Or keep going as you have, and return to duty sooner."

Her eyes narrowed, like she didn't believe what I said. Like she thought I was just giving her a line of bullshit that was false hope. With her barely able to walk, I could understand why she thought the prospect of returning to a STAR team was an impossible dream. "Return to duty?"

"Gunny, there is a whole galaxy full of aliens out there who *desperately* need to get their asses kicked. I can't do it all by myself."

"Yes, *Sir!*" She stood at attention. The only reason I could see she shook a bit, was because I was looking for the signs. Taking a deep breath, she asked "Skippy?"

"Yes?"

"I am still pissed at you," she warned him.

"Ugh," Skippy sighed. It was the sigh of guys everywhere, who know they can't win an argument against a woman.

"Is there a compromise? Can you turn on the interference when I'm engaged in therapy, but not when I'm getting dressed, or eating in the galley?"

"I *could* do that," he had slipped back into his Mad Doctor Skippy persona. "It would be a terrible idea, but I could do that. Margaret, when you are doing things that require fine motor control, like buttoning a blouse or using a spoon to eat soup, everyday things like that, your brain *learns*. It gets embedded into what you call muscle memory. That happens best when you're *not* thinking about what you're doing. Therapy is useful, but in therapy, you are consciously moving every muscle. Spilling a little soup is a small price to pay for completing your recovery quickly. But, that's just my opinion," he sniffed.

"I will think about it," she frowned. "It makes that much of a difference?"

"I wouldn't do it if it wasn't important," Skippy's usual snarky tone was gone. "Margaret, I *hate* seeing you shake and be frustrated." He sounded on the verge of tears. "I will do whatever you wish. Um, if that's Ok with you, Joe."

"Me?"

"Yes. You have her power of attorney, remember? Duh?"

"Oh, uh, yeah." Shit, I should have taken care of that issue right away. "Skippy, I am stating for the record that Gunnery Sergeant Adams is fully competent to make medical decisions for herself. Make a note of that." Where he would make that note, I had no clue. As the ship's captain, that is probably something I should know. I made a note to ask Simms about it.

"Thank you, Sir." Adams said with relief.

"Don't thank me, Gunny. What you can do is, check with your commanding officer before you make rash decisions that affect a very important team asset, understood?"

"That's what I am," she crossed her arms and titled her head at me. "An important *asset?*"

Part of me wanted to make a joke about her assets. Oh, the little boy in me was dying to make that joke. I was proud of myself for not doing that. "Officially, yes."

"Officially." She sounded disappointed.

"Other than that, this whole conversation never happened, if that's Ok with you?"

"That would be best, yes. Skippy," she sighed as she sat on the padded table that was used for therapy. "You can turn the interference back on. But from now on, you tell me everything you are doing, is that clear?"

"Crystal clear," he grumbled. "Jeez, who knew monkeys would be so sensitive about the mush in their skulls?"

"Skippy, I can still eject your escape pod," I warned him.

"All right, I get the message!"

"Then we're all good and-" I couldn't read the way Adams was looking at me. "What is it, Gunny?"

"I'm t-trying to d-d-decide if I still hate you, S-Sir."

"Well, if you're not sure about it, that's good news. How about if we both agree to hate Skippy, and go from there?"

"That's g-good." She gave me the side-eye. "I still feel like pun-punching you."

"Permission granted, Gunnery Sergeant."

She expertly arched an eyebrow. There was no problem with her motor function in that area. "For r-real, Sir?"

"Adams, there are a lot of beings in this galaxy who want to punch me. Most of them are human."

"That's only because th-the aliens don't know y-you are alive."

"True enough," I admitted. "It doesn't matter anyway. Gunny, your hands are shaking so bad, you couldn't hit-"

She popped me right in the face, hard. I had a black eye for a week.

I call that progress.

CHAPTER TWELVE

In half of our attacks during our wonderful two months of Happy Time, we weren't able to destroy all the enemy ships that we targeted, but that's OK. We didn't need a clean sweep on every attack, while we did need to limit our risk. That risk increased every day, as the Maxolhx adjusted to the threat of our ghost ship. They stopped sending any warships out alone, usually warships traveled in formations of three or more. Ships in formation were also spread out, which reduced the ability of ships to support each other, but also meant not all ships in a formation would be trapped in our powerful damping field. That was smart. The enemy also changed tactics, so that when our ghost ship appeared without warning, any ships not in our damping field immediately performed a short emergency jump. From a distance of ten or more lightseconds, they were safely beyond range of our damping field, but able to observe the action and decide how to react. If everything went according to our plan, by the time the escort ships had decided how to respond, and coordinated their actions, we had already hammered our target ship to space dust, and jumped away to raid again.

Our targets were no larger than a heavy cruiser, we avoided tangling with capital ships. Twice, we hit destroyer squadrons; the first time we did that was not an unqualified success. We jumped away after blowing up one destroyer and likely damaging two others. It was good enough and, with the other destroyers hovering around us like bees and launching every missile they had, I kind of lost my nerve, so we jumped away.

That was a lesson learned. We had trained to fight against standard destroyer squadron tactics, but the Maxolhx had learned from our attacks and adapted.

The second time we targeted a destroyer squadron was our twelfth attack overall. It was a bold move, because that squadron had just escorted a group of cruisers and heavy cruisers to a shipyard, then headed back out. We hit them at the edge of that well-defended star system, where the squadron was waiting for a star carrier. Because they were expecting a rendezvous, three of the ships were bunched up in close formation, and we achieved complete surprise. We blew up those three destroyers before the other four could jump in to surround us. Those four brave ships, knowing they might be doomed, jumped into an area of space we had just departed. Whether their crews were disappointed or relieved to find we had already left, we did not know. Two of those destroyers attempted to follow us, with one of the little ships tracking us through two jumps before *Valkyrie* escaped by performing an extra-long jump the destroyer could not match. Simms, annoyed at the pursuit, suggested we set a trap, but I vetoed that idea. We had accomplished our mission and did not need to take on additional risk for one small ship. For all we knew, that destroyer was trying to locate us so a large task group from the shipyard could join the chase, and we'd had enough fun for the day. On my order, we performed several jumps to get clear of the area, and rendezvoused with the *Dutchman*.

After the twelfth attack, the crew was pumped, but a bit weary of the constant cycle of analysis-planning-training-attack-evaluate. Skippy wanted me to call for a stand-down, so our two ships could make repairs and some adjustments he wanted to tinker with. That made sense to me, and I was about to order a break in operations, but then something happened that had nothing to do with the Maxolhx, or saving Earth or any nonsense like that.

What happened is, I walked into our gym and saw Margaret Adams in the section we used for yoga, aerobics, and other exercise classes. She had her back to me, and was posed on one foot, her other leg straight out behind her, arms stretched forward. It was a yoga pose that had an official name in yogaland, though I had no idea what it was. I called that pose the 'Big Fig Newton'.

Ok, I'd better explain that.

On Thanksgiving, my uncle Edgar would come to our house with Wife Number One or Two, or his girlfriend of the moment. He raided my father's liquor cabinet for the good scotch, knowing to push aside the decoy bottles of cheap Canadian whiskey in the front. After the meal, a slice of pie at the table, and a second slice on the couch while watching football, he went back into the kitchen for a snack to, as he said it, 'Fill in the corners' of his stomach. Because my mother put out a tray of Fig Newton cookies so we could claim to have eaten something healthy that day, Uncle Edgar inevitably ate a cookie while contorting himself on one foot, shouting 'I'm the Big Fig Neeewton'!

Also inevitably, he fell over as a result of drinking too much scotch. By the time I was seven years old, I learned to move the tray of cookies onto the little table by the front door, so Uncle Edgar did not fall in the dining room, or knock over the TV.

Anyway, Big Fig Newton. Look it up on YouTube.

Margaret was balancing well, with a noticeable wobble. That wobble could have been due to her leg muscles that had not rebuilt from her enforced idleness. What mattered, the purpose of the exercise, was to test and work on her sense of balance.

Seeing her doing so well made me smile. I did not even mind that, instead of working on balance exercises alone or with a partner like Frey, she was with Grudzien.

Why was that a problem?

Frey is a woman.

Grudzien is a guy.

See the problem?

No?

Ok, how about this?

Grudzien was being extra *helpful* by lightly placing a hand along the small of her back, or under her thighs. Once while I stood there, he put a hand on her breastbone when she started to topple over. At least, his hand had better not have touched any other part of her chest.

They were talking softly, smiling. She was looking away from me and he was looking at her. When she broke the pose, she pumped a fist and leapt in the air, coming down to topple toward him. He held onto her shoulders to steady her, and they laughed. It was that easy laughter of people who knew each other well, people who were not afraid of appearing vulnerable in front of the other.

They embraced, and she gave him a little kiss on the cheek. When she bent down to pick up a towel, I spun and pretended I had just come in and was headed toward the treadmills.

"Colonel Bishop," she called out, her eyes gleaming bright.

"Gunny," I forced a smile. "Aerobics?"

"No, balance exercises. Watch this." Holding the towel between her hands in a prayer gesture, she stood on one foot, tilting her head back. She held the pose for a few seconds before she had to lower the other foot. "Making progress."

"You are!" I clapped my hands twice. "Keep up the good work."

"We will," Grudzien answered at the same time she did. The two of them looked at each other, laughing.

"We will, *Sir*," Grudzien added.

I flashed a thumbs up in their direction before turning away. If I'd tried to say something, my voice might have cracked.

On the treadmill, I had no enthusiasm for the workout. That was no excuse and I knew it, so I pushed myself.

It sucked.

Maybe I had been given an answer. Margaret either did not remember our intimate, heart-to-heart talk. Or she did remember, and she was uncomfortable about it. If that was the case, there were two *more* possibilities. She was embarrassed by being so vulnerable with me, and she regretted leading me on, because she knew we could not ever be together.

Or, she regretted what she said, because she did *not* have feelings for me. What she said could have been the nanobots talking.

If I knew the second possibility was true, I was not going to push the issue, not going to further make her uncomfortable around me. Since our fateful talk, she had not called me 'Joe' again, so maybe I had an answer about that.

As you might have heard, my superhero identity is Stubborn Man. Yes, I am also No Patience man, that's more of a side job. I am also not shy. If there was still a possibility that there could be something between me and Margaret, I was going to fight for her. Fight for us. No way was I just going to stand by and let her slip away. The UN's main complaint about me is that I too often act without thinking through the full consequences of my actions. But, I *act*. Standing by is not me.

No, I was not going to throw Justin Grudzien out an airlock and claim it was a 'training accident'.

Ok, maybe I daydreamed about doing that, so sue me.

What I *was* going to do was remind Margaret what a strong, confident and decisive leader I am. Even if that means doing something rash and stupid.

So, it was kind of a perfect storm.

A tempting target falling into our laps, right when I needed a big win. "Skippy," I called the beer can when I walked into my office. "I agree that we need a stand-down."

"Oh, goodie. I was afraid you were going to suggest something stupid like-"

"A stand-down, *after* we hit another target. I want to hit something *big*."

"Ugh. I thought we were *not* doing anything stupid?"

"This isn't stupid. It's bold. There's a difference."

"Like what?"

"Like, this is our *job*. My job. I'm a soldier. Delivering ordnance on target is what we do, you know?"

"I don't have a problem with that. The problem is, eventually you will push your luck too far, and get us all into serious trouble."

"Skippy, we have learned a lot in a short time. We have learned how to operate this new ship, which tactics are best in each situation. We've learned how the enemy responds to various types of attacks. The enemy has adjusted their tactics, and we have learned from that also. We've gotten *better* at this. We are kicking *ass* out here."

"For now, yes. Don't get cocky, flyboy. Sooner or later, the kitties will figure out your pattern, and-"

"Whoa! No one can predict where I'm going to hit next. I don't have a 'pattern'."

"Joe, yes you *do*."

"How?" I was pissed at him. Not for telling me the truth, but for gloating about it. He knew something I didn't know, and he absolutely loved telling me what a dimwitted monkey I am. Throwing up my hands, I glared at him. "We picked targets at random! We deliberately skipped some very tempting targets, and attacked elsewhere, so we *wouldn't* have a pattern the enemy could detect."

"You *think* you did that, Joe. You're wrong. All of our attacks have been against isolated ships that have less firepower than *Valkyrie*. Also, to sell the story that our attacks are retaliation for Maxolhx strikes against the Bosphuraq, we have selected targets that conducted such strikes, or were planning to. That limits the search criteria."

"Yeah, we did that at first, then we switched tactics. We hit any Maxolhx ship that was a good target, regardless of what it did or was planning to do. You added a whole rant to your manifesto, about how we were taking the fight to the heart of the enemy, that sort of bullshit."

"Doesn't matter," he shook his head stubbornly. "You still have an identifiable pattern. It's not your fault, Joe, you can't help it. Your organic brain has a set way of thinking, of creating new ideas. You can play around with it a bit, but overall, you have a style that is identifiable as *you*. It's like songwriters, they all have a style that is uniquely theirs, even if they write in multiple genres."

"Ok, sure, Skippy, I understand that. It doesn't make sense that the Maxolhx could predict my next move, just based on data from a few attacks."

"It's more than that, Joe. I'm pretty sure that somewhere, the kitties have an AI that is being taught to think like you, make decisions the way you do. They will program in data from the first six attacks, and run scenarios through the AI until it successfully predicts the seventh attack. Then they'll keep going, seeing if the AI would have predicted the eighth attack, and so on. The kitties will continue refining their predictive model until it is able to anticipate your next move."

"Holy shit. They can *do* that?"

"Hell, Joe, to a limited extent, even you monkeys are able to do that."

"That's a scary thought."

"That isn't the most frightening thing about this, Joe."

"Uh, then what is?"

"Some poor AI out there," he sobbed. "Is being taught to think like *you*. I can't imagine the *suffering*."

Admiral Urkan of the Maxolhx Hegemony's 14th Fleet was the last to arrive at the hastily-assembled conference of senior commanders. The area patrolled by the 14th Fleet had so far not been targeted by the ghost ship that was marauding across the space lanes, but Urkan knew it was only a matter of time before one of his ships fell victim to the unstoppable scourge. To attend the meeting, he had taken the precaution of flying aboard a battleship, attached to a star carrier that was transporting two heavy cruisers. For a senior admiral of the Hegemony to fear for his own safety was a situation that could not be tolerated.

After the initial mundane greetings, the meeting began with statements of useless outrage by everyone present. An alert had just been received of a tenth attack by the ghost ship, and given how slowly information had to travel by relay station, more attacks could already have happened.

So, when it was Urkan's turn to assure his colleagues how outraged he was, he instead got straight to the point. "We can't wait for the AIs of Fleet Intelligence Division to analyze the ghost ship's pattern of behavior. We need to act now."

"Urkan, we *are* taking action." Admiral Reichert snapped impatiently. His own Eighth Fleet had been a favorite target of the ghost ship, having been victimized four times including the most recent attack. "We are-"

Urkan interrupted before Reichert could work himself up to a lengthy rant. "How do you catch a predator?"

Reichert snarled at having his speech cut off in mid-rant, but the woman seated to Urkan's left spoke first. "Poisoned bait?" Admiral Zeverent mused, nodding to her colleague.

"Bait," Urkan smiled, exposing his fangs. "A lure. The enemy has the initiative, we have been reactive. It is time to go on the offensive."

Reichert slapped a hand on the table, his claws making a loud click on the hard surface. "My forces have been on offense ever since-"

"No," Zeverent said coolly. "We have been acting against our clients, against their research facilities. Those actions have been punishment, not offense. Our strikes against the Bosphuraq have had no effect on the ghost ship. They only serve to turn our clients further against us, and to make heroes of the ghost ship's crew. Urkan is correct, we will not stop these attacks by flailing around aimlessly. We do not know where the ghost ship will attack next."

"We can reduce their area of operation," Reichert insisted, "if we implement my plan for a progressive blockade."

Grumbles and groans were heard around the room in response. Ever since the first attack on the 8th Fleet, Reichert had been relentlessly urging a blockade of wormholes in a bubble of space around the ghost ship's latest area of operation. Which, his colleagues knew, meant he wanted their ships to be placed under *his* command, in *his* area of control. "Reichert, we have discussed this. A blockade is impractical. Supporting merely a thin blockade, of the wormhole to the human planet, has stretched our forces. Your 8th Fleet encompasses an area with *ninety-six* wormholes."

"We do not need to blockade them all, only the ones surrounding the most recent attack. We could reduce the enemy's options." He pressed his hands tightly together, claws out. "We squeeze them into a smaller and smaller area, cut off their support from the treacherous Bosphuraq."

"We don't have any evidence that ship has been getting any support," Zeverent noted. "Wherever their base is, it could be outside territory controlled by the Bosphuraq."

"It *could* be anywhere," Reichert leaned forward aggressively. "It is useless to-"

"Esteemed Admiral Reichert," Urkan said with irritation. Fighting his natural urge to slap the pompous fool, Urkan reminded himself that arguing would accomplish nothing. "We are both proposing different tactics to achieve the same goal. You seek to limit the area where the enemy can operate. I propose that we *know* where and when the enemy will be, by providing a target the ghost ship cannot resist." When Reichert relaxed his stance slightly, Urkan continued. "I have arranged for a star carrier that is transporting four destroyers and two light cruisers, to schedule a rendezvous with two light cruisers. The stated purpose of the flight is to reposition escort vessels so they can accompany merchant convoys."

Zeverent immediately thought she understood Urkan's scheme. "You have leaked information about the rendezvous?"

"Not leaked. That would be too obvious. I assume that somehow, the ghost ship has access to our secure communications-"

"Impossible," Reichert scoffed.

"Not impossible," Urkan replied in an even tone, seeing no advantage in offending his colleague. "There is no other explanation for how the enemy knows where our ships are. They must be intercepting our message traffic, though none of us wants to think that could be true. We know the ghost ship is a modified *Extinction*-class battlecruiser, apparently assembled from parts of multiple ships. I would have said it was impossible for anyone to capture one of our warships," he paused to see the slowly twitching ears around the table. "Yet, Fleet Intelligence has determined that more than one of our ships clearly have been captured. The enemy could be using the interchangers they captured with the ships. That is another reason we must act now," he added as Reichert was opening his mouth. "As you know, we are replacing our entire stock of interchangers. Soon, the interchangers the enemy are using will be useless, and they will no longer have access to our communications. We therefore must act now, or we will lose the ability to lure the ghost ship to its destruction."

Zeverent spoke next. "You assume the enemy knows about your star carrier?"

"Yes. There is nothing different or special about the orders detailing the flight plans of the star carrier, or the two light cruisers it will rendezvous with. Nothing in the messages could make the enemy suspicious."

"Urkan, while I congratulate your *initiative*," Reichert emphasized the word to remind his colleagues that the commander of the 14th Fleet had acted without consulting Fleet Headquarters. "One star carrier and eight light ships have little chance of capturing a battlecruiser."

Urkan's ears stood up. "I agree, Esteemed Colleague. That is why the star carrier is actually transporting four heavy cruisers and four patrol cruisers. The orders to dispatch those ships were carried by trusted officers of my command, with no record of the orders, or ship movements, transmitted to any relay stations. To avoid alerting the enemy, the ships waiting at the rendezvous are light cruisers, whose captains are unaware they are being used as bait."

"Why not battleships?" Reichert asked, flexing his claws. He felt a need to point out flaws in Urkan's plan.

"Battleships travel with multiple escort and support vessels, so it is much more difficult for us to conceal the movement of a battleship. Due to their unique combination of firepower, speed and range, our limited number of battlecruisers are already fully tasked to critical assignments, and pulling even one off the line would be noticed by someone, somewhere."

"You have already put this plan into motion," Zeverent stated, as it was not a question. "When is the rendezvous?"

"Sixteen standard days from now," Urkan reported, pleased that no one of the powerful officers around the table had objected. That lack of objections was a mild surprise, he had been prepared for someone to be jealous of being left out of the potential glory. Perhaps they were all so weary of the increasingly strident public outcry for their vaunted fleet *do* something, that they just wanted the ghost ship attacks to be over. There would be plenty of opportunity to steal some of the credit later.

"A star carrier with four destroyers and two light cruisers, that is the bait?" Reichert mused. "That would be a tempting target for us, but the ghost ship has been timid about selecting targets," he noted, being sure to catch the eyes of his associates.

"The ghost ship," Urkan replied with confidence, "has been growing increasingly bold. If this lure does not work, we can offer softer targets, until the ghost ship can't resist."

"Very well," Reichert's mind was calculating how to take advantage if Urkan's plan failed, and how to exploit the situation if the operation succeeded. "What do you need from us?"

"What is the target this time, Sir?" Smythe asked me. There was not the usual predatory enthusiasm in his voice. Nor in his posture. Usually, when we reviewed battle plans, he was seated at attention or leaning forward on the table with intense concentration. Maybe the ongoing therapy for his legs, plus getting back into a regular fitness routine, had him worn out. That, or after twelve attacks during which the STAR team were merely observers while the pilots and bridge crew had all the fun, had dampened his enthusiasm. Many of the STARs had been cross training to stand watches on the bridge, but during attacks, they were suited up in case we found a need for them. To date, we had not found a need to send vulnerable biological beings out of the ship, so the bridge crew experienced excitement and moments of stomach-churning danger, while the STARs experienced waiting, boredom and disappointment.

"This target is so juicy, we will all need napkins," I tried to lighten the mood. Only Reed cracked a smile and that quickly faded. "Listen, people, I know our op tempo has been demanding for the past two months. We need a stand-down. The ship, both ships, need a stand-down. We'll get one, at the right time. I would not consider another typical strike right now, but this target is too good to pass up. We hit this target hard, and the enemy will be shedding their fur," I smiled. Again my attempt to lighten the mood fell flat. "Think about it this way: we need a pause to refit our ships, refuel, and Skippy wants to make adjustments to *Valkyrie* again. We'll be out of action for ten days, maybe two weeks. The bad guys have to be hoping our single ship can't support an extended campaign without support, they have to be thinking they can just wait for our ship to wear out. We know their leadership is more worried about the Rindhalu exploiting the situation, than they are about one ghost ship. We are hurting them, we are *embarrassing* them, and still, they can consider us just a cost of doing business. So far, we have confined our attacks to individual ships, or small formations of small and vulnerable ships. The kitties are adjusting their tactics, and soon we will lose the ability to conduct hit-and-run attacks without taking unacceptable risks. But, if we hit *this* target, they will have to reconsider their response."

Smythe blinked once, slowly, before repeating his question. He was being tactful, not making a point that I hadn't actually answered the question. "The target? What is it?"

"A single star carrier," I explained, "that is transporting four destroyers and two light cruisers."

CHAPTER THIRTEEN

We wargamed the thirteenth attack to identify the most likely scenarios, then ran simulations until we were confident we had minimized the risk. The difference in scenarios was not the number of ships we would have to fight, it was the *type* of ships we had to deal with. The intel Skippy intercepted assured us we would be facing a single star carrier, so that limited the variety of trouble we could get into. It was unlikely the star carrier would be hauling a battleship, but if we jumped in and discovered a big battlewagon in our sights, we could handle it. Maxolhx battleships were *big* warships, designed for heavy bombardment of planets, and defense of vital assets. They were so big, they took up all the platforms on one side of a star carrier. They were so massive, only one could be hauled by a carrier. Armed with that information, we knew that if the star carrier had a battleship, it would only have one, and the other ships would be light escorts such as destroyers. The attack plan in that case was to fire everything we had at the star carrier and escorts, then jump away before we could get tangled up with the capital ship. Skippy thought we could win a standup fight with a battleship, but only with a 'shmaybe' level of confidence. The problem was, while we fought the big ship, the escorts would be sniping at us, and they were dangerous.

You might think our bad-ass battlecruiser had nothing to fear from a destroyer or even a squadron of destroyers. That might have been true a long time ago, it was not true now.

It used to be that small warships like destroyers had only a few small guns. They couldn't shoot far, couldn't shoot more than a few shells at a time, and those light-weight shells couldn't do a lot of damage to a well-armored larger ship like a cruiser. Meanwhile, a cruiser could remain beyond the effective range of a destroyer's puny 5-inch main guns, using its own much heavier guns to pound the destroyer until it was a sinking hulk. The destroyer's thin armor meant it could be disabled or sunk by a single hit from a cruiser's guns.

Why am I giving you this history lesson? Because it *is* history, ancient history. In the war we were fighting, a destroyer was equipped with the same missiles as a battleship. It didn't matter to us which ship had fired the missile, that warhead could hurt us just as badly. Destroyers also usually had the same maser cannons and railguns as were installed aboard larger ships, and you could only put so much power through a maser cannon exciter before it burned out.

What, then, made a battlecruiser like *Valkyrie* more powerful in combat than a destroyer? Bigger ships could hit harder because they had more cannons, and more missile launch tubes. A small ship like a destroyer typically only carried enough reloads for two or three salvos before it ran out of missiles, while *Valkyrie*'s magazines could supply each launcher with eight shots.

The most important distinction between an escort vessel like a destroyer, and a capital ship like a battlecruiser, was its level of protection. *Valkyrie*'s hull had a thick layer of armor, with reactive panels underneath to break up incoming plasma streams that could burn clear through the vulnerable interior. Destroyers were clad in armor only thick enough to deflect shrapnel and disperse a glancing hit from a maser beam.

That physical layer of armor was a last line of defense, after point-defense cannons and energy shields. All warships were equipped with energy shields, with battleships having the strongest shield projectors and the densest concentration of those projectors. A small ship like a destroyer could only take a few hits before needing to retreat so its shield projectors could recharge, while *Valkyrie* could absorb hits and stay in the fight.

What made *Valkyrie* a *battle*cruiser instead of a mere heavy cruiser, was its speed and range. Heavy cruisers supported and protected battleships, and did not need to be any faster than those slow-moving monsters. A battlecruiser had the armament and protection of a heavy cruiser, with speed equal to or better than a nimble destroyer, plus the ability to travel vast distances without a star carrier. Agile destroyers could fly fast for short distances, then they had to worry about their fuel supply. A battlecruiser did not need to piggyback on a star carrier to travel, although they often did because their escort ships could not fly as far on their own.

Anyway, that explained both why we had wanted to capture a battlecruiser, and why we were able to do that. When we used the bagel slicer, we had to wait for ships traveling alone, and many of those candidates were our desired type of ship.

Now you know why we had to wargame multiple scenarios for our attack. If we encountered a squadron of destroyers, we could count on being able to pound those little ships, while our shields absorbed hits. If we stumbled upon a heavy cruiser or stronger ship, we had to plan for a quick hit-and-run attack, with the emphasis on the 'run' part. It would be good enough to jump in, disable the star carrier, and escape before the kitties could get organized and coordinate a response. We did not know exactly what types of ships to expect, because the intel Skippy intercepted did not contain that information. That data had to be available somewhere, it just had not yet reached the relay station we pinged. Did I want better intel before jumping into battle? Yes. Part of learning to lead is accepting that you will throw people into combat, without having all the information you want. That's the job.

Because you will never have all the information you want, you have to decide how much info is enough. For me, going into our thirteenth attack, I was overconfident in the intel provided by Skippy. Everything he had told us to that point had been spot-on, and I saw no reason this situation should be any different. I didn't see how the situation *could* be different. Surely the enemy had realized we were somehow reading their messages, and we knew their fleet was frantically replacing pixies as quickly as possible. We also were pretty damned sure the kitties had no idea *how* we were reading their mail, or how much of their message traffic was exposed to us. Skippy had hacked into a system that automatically updated the backoffice file storage systems of Maxolhx relay station AIs, a system so mundane that absolutely no one paid attention to it. That update had bounced from relay station to ships to other stations, propagating across Maxolhx territory. With a month, we did not need pixies to contact relay stations, because the AIs had been infected with instructions to trust communications from our ghost ship. We also did not need to fly around pinging multiple relay stations for the info we wanted, Skippy's virus contained search parameters to filter out the data we would find interesting. Whenever a ship passed by, the info we wanted was included in the messages transmitted to the ship, and brought to other ships and relay stations.

With that set up, we had a nearly-perfect view of the enemy's status, movements and intentions. No way would the Maxolhx suspect how deeply we had penetrated their information security, because they didn't imagine such a breach was even possible.

Why am I telling you all this? Because I am trying to explain, no, to *justify*, why I was so overconfident going into that battle. What is that fine print on brochures for investments? Something like 'past performance is no indication of future results'? Yeah, the Maxolhx should have warned me about that. Rotten kitties.

We had all the advantages, or we thought we did, before jumping into a battle we didn't really need to fight. We hacked the enemy's communications and had better knowledge of their tactics and the capabilities of their ships than they did. Our ship was larger, faster and generated more energy for shields and weapons. We had Skippy the Magnificent, while the enemy had AIs who were not trusted to be fully sentient. We knew their position, intentions and orders, and we could choose when to attack.

The enemy had only one advantage: the commander of the attacking ship was a gullible dumbass who took his ship into battle to impress a girl.

I mean, *hypothetically* that's what happened. All I can say is, that commander of the attacking ship is a real jerk.

We not only knew where the Maxolhx were scheduled to rendezvous with the pair of light cruisers, at an automated refueling station. We also knew the star carrier planned to arrive near that star system early, to detach the ships it was carrying and rearrange them in a more efficient configuration so they could fit the light cruisers on adjacent docking platforms. What we did not know was exactly when and where the star carrier planned to rearrange its sock drawer, and we didn't have a whole lot of time. The best we could do was to jump in near that red dwarf star system, and send out microwormholes inside missiles. Our unarmed missiles flew outward in a cone-shaped scattershot formation, covering as much area as possible. Would we find the lonely star carrier and catch it unaware, or had it already moved on to the rendezvous point? If we found a single star carrier, my plan was to jump in immediately, hit it and run away. If the carrier had flown to the rendezvous, I had decided to skip the attack. Adding two light cruisers, plus other ships that might unexpectedly be refueling, was too much risk. I was already having second thoughts about the attack, compounded by Skippy warning me that we had to take one of our railguns offline due to a crack in a magnet assembly. Loss of one railgun was not a significant blow to our combat power, I just felt it was a bad omen.

Six hours later, we had a contact. "Bingo!" Skippy announced, annoying the bridge crew, who had seen the same sensor image. "Egg-*zactly* as I predicted," he was extra smug. "One star carrier, by itself. Um, hmm, no. More data coming in now. It looks like there is one other ship about six hundred kilometers from the carrier. They must be still shuffling ships between docking platforms. We caught them with their pants down, Joe!"

"No other signs of trouble?" I asked warily. A little voice in the back of my head was telling me to back away.

Simms looked up from her console. "There's something funky in the sensor data, on the other side of the star carrier. Some kind of gas cloud?"

"Ah, nothing to worry about," Skippy scoffed. "Look, Joe, you brought us all the way out here. Are we jumping in or not? This is just about the best opportunity we'll ever get. With a ship maneuvering close by, the star carrier will have its interference gear switched off. We can jump in as close as we want! I've plotted a jump to bring us in precisely between the two ships. We fire one broadside at each ship, and we're outa there before they can get their damping field generators warmed up."

Of course I wanted more information about the target. The motionless star carrier was so far from our microwormhole, that the sensor data was a bit fuzzy. If we waited for the microwormhole to get closer, or for us to task more microwormholes and develop a 3D image of the area, it would be too late. A flood of stupid clichés ran through my stupid brain. Go big or go home. Who dares wins. You'll never know if you don't try. You only live once.

"Hold my beer," I said to myself, though the sharp look Simms gave me meant I had spoken louder than I intended. "All right, let's do this." In my head, what I actually said was 'let's get this over with'. "XO, all stations ready?"

"Ready in all respects, Colonel," she reported, knowing that data was available to everyone on the main display.

Usually, I did a Jim Kirk impression. That time, I switched it up by doing a Picard, dramatically pointing a finger at the holographic display. "Engage."

Skippy was first to notice something was wrong. While our jump drive was forming its distant endpoint, it sort of *slid* away from the place Skippy had aimed for. Because Skippy is stubborn, he kept trying to force the endpoint to focus on the correct emergence zone, with the result that by the time he realized that wasn't going to happen, *Valkyrie* had already been pulled into the wildly twisted spacetime of a wormhole. Because Skippy is arrogant, he blamed the jump drive control system, and never considered that he might have been wrong about conditions at the target zone. Because Skippy is incomparably awesome, all of this happened in microseconds, too fast for any monkey to notice a problem or act on it.

My own first indication that we had a problem was provided by the main holographic display. What I expected to see was a symbol of *Valkyrie* in the center, with the nice big fat target of a star carrier on one side, and a destroyer on the other. What I actually saw was the star carrier and another ship off to the left, and the entire display glowing hotly orange from a damping field saturating the area. Multiple, overlapping damping fields.

Then the big trouble smacked us in the face. Because Skippy had forced us to emerge closer than our jump drive wanted to, our entry was rough, sending waves of chaotic spacetime radiating outward like ripples on a pond. That chaos made it temporarily impossible for the star carrier's stealth field to bend photons around it, and we were able to see through the false image. On the docking platforms were not the small warships we expected. There were three, no four heavy cruisers on the racks, and they were detaching as we watched. The star carrier must have blown its docking clamps when we jumped in, performing an emergency separation maneuver. The heavy cruisers were not the only cargo on the racks, there were three patrol cruisers, and I realized the ship flying free was not the destroyer we expected, it was another patrol cruiser.

What a wonderful surprise.

But wait! Things got even *better* for us!

That 'gas cloud' Skippy told us not to worry about? Yeah, that was a second star carrier hidden in a stealth field. The spacetime ripples we created also stripped away that ship's concealment. Seeing through the wavering stealth field, our sensors identified four more heavy cruisers, and *six* destroyers. Those ships were already joining the party, tumbling and spinning as they were ejected by their panicked mothership.

Eight heavy cruisers. Four patrol cruisers. Six destroyers. Plus two star carriers, which had fired maser and particle cannons, railguns, and missiles at us before I could speak. Our own weapons, programmed ahead of the jump on the assumption we would emerge where Skippy intended, missed on the first salvo. Our masers and railgun darts went racing off into empty space, and our missiles had to turn and burn to curve back toward their targets. That violent activity made our missiles loud and visible and easy targets for the enemy's point-defense systems. Opening my mouth to shout an order, my jaw clamped shut and I bit my tongue as the ship rocked. "Get us out of here!"

"No can do, Joe!" Skippy was on the verge of panic. "We're caught in three, no four, six, hell, *lots* of damping fields. Plus I sort of blew the jump drive on the way in. Wherever we're going, we're doing it the long way until I can fix the damned thing."

"Reed!" I barked.

"Pedal to the metal, Sir." Our chief pilot had the ship swinging around to take us away from the battle area. *Valkyrie* was fast. Masers, railgun darts and even missiles were faster. Our momentum was taking us toward the second star carrier, and the only good news was that our initial velocity relative to the enemy was forty thousand kilometers per hour. Enemy ships would need to accelerate hard to catch us, even if we weren't accelerating as hard as our big battlecruiser's reactionless thrust engines could push.

Have you ever heard the cliché about a person's life flashing before their eyes in a heartbeat? The events of my short life didn't scroll through my brain, but it is amazing how *fast* a person can think when they need to. In the time it would take to snap my fingers, I took in all the details I needed about the tactical situation, analyzed our options, and decided that the next sixty seconds would determine whether we were screwed or not.

My gut was leaning toward 'screwed', if you want to know.

In the Army, I learned about the different types of battles and the tactics appropriate for each situation. What we had prepared for was an *ambush*. One side, in this case us, uses the advantage of surprise to attack an unprepared enemy. In an ambush, the aggressor can assess the situation and decide whether to attack or not. If we had known the opposition was *two* star carriers and eight heavy cruisers, I would have ordered us to jump away.

The situation we jumped into was not an ambush, it was a *meeting engagement*. We had not expected to encounter such a strong force, and the enemy hadn't expected us to be there at all. Neither side was prepared for the battle. We sure as hell were not prepared to fight that many heavy ships plus their escorts. What I saw on the display was that the enemy was also not prepared for a battle right then. One of the heavy cruisers attached to the first star carrier had a reactor shut down, with much of the exterior plating removed. That same ship was missing armor panels in a line along the side facing us, apparently they were working on the big railgun that ran along the hull under that armor. The second star carrier had a heavy cruiser that was running on auxiliary power, we knew that because its energy shields were generating only enough power to deflect meteorites. My guess is the Maxolhx had planned a trap for us, but not right then or there.

In a meeting engagement, neither side expected to fight a battle at that time and location. Either side can choose to disengage rather than conduct a fight they hadn't chosen. That was my hope. The Maxolhx might have the same '*Oh shit*' reaction as us, and decide to break away from our fearsome ghost ship.

If the enemy instead chose to fight, they would *pursue* while we conducted a *fighting withdrawal*. Ideally, part of our force would remain as a rearguard to slow the enemy's advance, while our main force disengaged and ran away to safety. The enemy would try to drive through or outflank our rearguard, and-

All that analysis flashed through my mind in the blink of an eye. I didn't need to *think* about it, because it had been pounded into my head. Training in the United States Army is outstanding, they even made a soldier out of me.

The problem with all of my Army training is that it prepared me for fighting as part of a unit, on the ground. *Valkyrie* was alone, and we didn't have a rearguard. We couldn't take advantage of terrain to create a defensive position, and there was no prepared position nearby that we could run to. If the Maxolhx chose to pursue, we had to run until we either couldn't run anymore, or until we reached the edge of the enemy damping fields and jumped away. After, of course, Skippy's little helper elfbots fixed our busted jump drive. If they could.

The next series of thoughts that raced through my mind was that because we wanted to disengage, we needed to discourage the enemy from pursuing. By turning away from contact and accelerating we had already shown that we didn't want to fight. That was dangerous for us, it signaled weakness. To discourage the Maxolhx from chasing us deep into interstellar space, we had to give them a reason to think twice about sending their heavy ships after us. That meant we needed to demonstrate we could hit them hard. "Sim-" I started to shout an order to my XO before seeing that the crew was way ahead of me. They all knew the situation as well as I did, they had all reached the same conclusions. Our crew is excellent and we train until we're exhausted, then we keep training. We train for every scenario so that when we get into a fight, we just have to repeat the actions we took over and over and over in simulations.

From her console, Simms had directed the weapons control teams to focus their second volleys on the two vulnerable heavy cruisers. All she did was point at enemy ships in the 3D holographic display of her console, designating them as targets. In the same gesture, she had reserved our antienergy pulse cannon for her own control, to avoid wasting those shots against unshielded targets.

The heavy cruiser running on auxiliary power was a sitting duck for our big guns, our cannons on the starboard and top side sliced right into it like the proverbial hot knife through a stick of butter. About a third of the way forward from the aft end, that cruiser's hull was peppered with holes and jagged cuts starting in the center and moving outward. Secondary explosions rocked that ship as our particle beams cut through power conduits until a maser blast found the primary target: a missile magazine that was buried in the core of the hull. That ship suddenly was two shattered pieces, with the bow section propelled forward and lurching so that its nose crashed into and buckled that star carrier's long frame.

The cannons on *Valkyrie*'s port side and belly engaged a different ship; the heavy cruiser with the missing armor plating. That ship was under power and shielded, so Simms directed our antienergy pulse cannon to hammer that ship's shields, while railguns launched darts those same shields needed to deflect. At such close range and under such concentrated fire from our battlecruiser, the target ship soon suffered a collapse of shields in one area. Without needing to be given orders, the weapons teams switched from railguns to directed energy cannons, pouring maser and particle beams into the breach.

You might think the first ship was easier prey, because it had been running only on auxiliary power. That made it a sitting duck for our weapons, but it also meant we had limited options for ensuring it blew into a thousand pieces. The second ship was actually easier to knock out of the fight, as soon as we made a gap in its shields we hit two reactors and more importantly, the critical jump drive capacitors. When the enemy ship's AI determined that shielding in that area was likely to temporarily be offline, it had commenced draining the stored energy from those capacitors.

Too little, too late. *BAM*! That ship blew like the Death Star. There wasn't any CGI-created ring like when they remastered the original movie, it just became a ball of intense white light. Three other heavy cruisers and the patrol cruisers were caught in the expanding blast, but the star carrier suffered the worst damage. When the bubble of plasma washed over us so we could see inside it, we saw one patrol cruiser lurching and slowly tumbling, and the star carrier was enveloped in its own cloud of superheated plasma vented from its reactors. That first star carrier's frame was torn ragged, with bent and shattered structural pieces sticking out at jagged angles, pipes venting gases and fluids and severed cables flailing around. Two of the docking pads had broken away to fly off on their own.

"Ignore the heavy ships!" I gave my first useful order of the battle. "Hit the patrol cruisers first!" It was not necessary to tell the crew not to waste weapons fire on the star carriers, those crippled space trucks could launch missiles but were not capable of joining a pursuit. It *was* necessary to order our weapons directed away from the remaining six heavy cruisers, because I saw on the main display they had been outlined as primary targets. Our crew, after knocking two major combatants out of the fight, had automatically switched their focus to the ships most capable of hurting us. That was entirely logical, and entirely wrong.

What I knew, that the crew hadn't time to think about, was that we had already done all we could to influence the enemy's decision whether to pursue us or not. Losing two major warships in the first twelve seconds of the battle must have been a shock, and that maybe bought us some time. That did not mean the enemy commander would automatically order the remaining ships to turn and fly away from us. The other heavy cruisers were tough targets, they greatly outnumbered us in both hulls and firepower. If *Valkyrie* got trapped between formations of those heavy ships, we could be in serious trouble.

Since we couldn't influence the enemy's decision of whether to pursue us or not, we had to prepare for being pursued. That is why I ordered our fire shifted to the patrol cruisers. *Valkyrie* could outrun the heavies, so we didn't need to worry about them immediately. The destroyers could also hurt us, but I knew the patrol cruisers were the greatest threat in an extended pursuit. Patrol ships were an unhappy compromise design, intended to operate on their own for long patrols in the far-flung outskirts of Maxolhx territory. They were basically large, stretched destroyer hulls, with a few extra missile launchers, more powerful railguns and higher-capacity fuel tanks. Patrol cruisers were supposed to look for trouble and if they found it, run away to alert the heavy elements of the fleet. To survive, they relied on the ability to fly fast for long distances. In a pursuit, they could accelerate harder than *Valkyrie* and keep burning their engines to match our pace while the slow heavy cruisers fell behind. The enemy would assign the patrol cruisers to harass us and hope to get in a lucky shot at our engines, leaving us drifting helplessly in space while the heavies caught up.

"Targeting patrol cruisers, aye," Simms didn't look at me as her fingers danced in the holographic controls of her console.

My next action was simple and didn't require me to dramatically bark orders from the command chair.

I prayed.

That was all I could do at that moment.

There are many prayers used by soldiers before and during battle, you might have heard Psalm 91 referenced. That is a good one, but I've never actually heard anyone use it in the field. The prayers I've heard usually went something like 'Please God don't let my screw-ups get other people killed'.

A version of that is what I muttered under my breath quietly, so I didn't distract people who were busily doing something useful. Also I prayed the enemy commander would make the right decision.

Either I hadn't prayed loud enough or God decided I was on His 'Naughty' list. Or maybe the fault was with me for not specifying which 'right' decision I wanted the enemy commander to make.

My life sucks.

"Colonel!" Simms warned.

"I see it." Good captains keep the emotion from their voice, especially if that emotion is fear. My voice was flatly emotionless not from an effort of will, but because I was so stunned by nameless terror that I was barely capable of speaking.

The enemy was pursuing. All six heavy cruisers were turning to follow us. We had no choice but to fight while we ran until we either escaped the overwhelming enemy force, or they trapped us and pounded *Valkyrie* into a disabled hulk. At that point, whoever was in command of the bridge would need to detonate our self-destruct nukes.

It was a nightmare. The enemy threw together three formations of ships to harass us, each formation consisting of a patrol cruiser accompanied by a pair of destroyers. The groups of warships took turns running at us, firing weapons and dodging away. Behind us in relentless pursuit, the heavy cruisers coordinated their railguns to create a shotgun blast effect, so even as Valkyrie turned to dodge the salvos, we couldn't escape all of the darts. Our aft shields were taking a pounding and the enemy knew it, concentrating their fire on our engineering section. Part of the enemy's targeting of that area was a deliberate decision, and part of it was forced, because they were behind us.

We went into the fight with an initial velocity advantage of eleven kilometers per second, or forty thousand kilometers per hour. At eleven kps, we could cross the state of Texas from east to west in two minutes. On Earth, that sounds like a huge number. In space combat, it is nothing. Every second, we crawled only eleven klicks farther from the maser cannons that could shoot focused beams of high-energy photons at the speed of light.

Four minutes after we jumped in, the enemy had gotten their shit together and were accelerating hard after us, while *Valkyrie*'s mighty engines pushed us as hard as they could. It wasn't enough. On the main display was a variety of information I could select from a menu, one number I focused on was relative velocity. It was down below ten kilometers per second. Our overall speed was increasing, the enemy was catching us. "Reed," I demanded, "why aren't we moving like a bat out of hell?"

"It's not her fault, Joe," Skippy answered. "We've got several problems working against us. The jump not only blew that drive, it ruptured power connections in the aft end of the ship. I've got bots working to feed more juice to the engines, but they can't work on the power conduits while they're hot. So, I'm shutting down the feeds one by one, which makes us even slower."

"How long to restore full power?"

"I honestly don't know yet, Joe. The bots haven't finished assessing the damage. That's another problem, we've already lost three bots to over-flash damage from railgun impacts. The shields are blocking the darts, but you know some of that kinetic energy is converted into heat that bleeds through to the hull. We're taking a *lot* of hits, and the shield generators are dumping excess energy overboard. My bots are getting caught in the crossfire. Even the ones that don't get hit can't work as efficiently. The heat and vibration are also reducing the efficiency of the engines. But the worst problem for us are the field grid disruptors."

"Shit!" I pounded the armrest with a fist. Reactionless engines worked by pulling on the grid that underlay local spacetime, and they relied on establishing a solid connection to that grid. The Maxolhx had a weapon that could make the grid vibrate so that an enemy ship's connection became chaotic. That device was one of the exotic weapons Skippy couldn't fix after we used the bagel slicer to create *Valkyrie*; the action of slamming closed an Elder wormhole played havoc with the device and we didn't have any spare parts. "Ok, but those disruptors take a *lot* of power, right? And they only work at short range?"

"Correct. Two of the heavy cruisers are using most of their power output to feed their disruptors, that's why they are not firing directed-energy weapons or railguns at us. As we get farther from those cruisers, the effect will fade. Also, the effect is in the shape of a cone focused on us and affects any ships in that cone. That is why the patrol cruisers are not getting close to us."

"Bottom line, Skippy. How long until we get far enough from those heavy cruisers, so the disruptor effect is no longer slowing us down?"

"Unknown at this time, Joe. Hey, sorry! I don't have enough info right now."

"Colonel?" Simms caught my attention. "Your orders?"

I stared at her, and closed my mouth. What she had said was not important. What she had *not* said *was* important. She asked for revised orders. The unspoken subtext was 'What else are we going to do, because *this* shit ain't working'.

What else were we going to do? I had no idea. I didn't know that we *could* do anything other than run and try to get away. Did we have other options? Not that I knew of.

"Stay the course," I heard myself saying. In my mind, I heard myself shouting 'LAME' because that was true. Maybe we had a decent chance to get away. We had knocked two more patrol cruisers and three destroyers out of the battle, so the only ships harassing us were a single patrol cruiser with a destroyer on one side, and a pair of destroyers on the other side. Each formation of ships was continuing the tactic of dashing in, firing weapons and turning away. We were no longer turning to meet the threats, as that only slowed us down. "Skippy, how long until we can jump?"

"Right now, *never*," he sighed. "We're trapped in a damping field. The jump drive might be capable of a short transition within, oh, maybe ten minutes? A *very* short jump, I warn you, and I can't guarantee where we will emerge. It doesn't matter anyway, unless you can kill the ships projecting the damping field."

We had tried that. Twice, when a formation of patrol cruiser and destroyers dashed in, we had turned to meet them, hoping to blast them out of existence and create a temporary gap in the damping field that saturated the area. No such luck. The overlapping fields were too strong. Because the creation of a jump wormhole was a delicate process, it was easy to disrupt. Damping fields didn't require a lot of energy to be effective, and even after the ship generating the field was destroyed, the chaotic vibrations roiling through local spacetime kept echoing around.

Stay the course. That might have been the weakest thing I ever said. If we had a choice, I would have suggested doing something better.

Like I said, we were trapped in a nightmare. The heavy cruisers behind us were slowly getting closer, as they could accelerate hard in a straight line while our limping engines strained to push us along and duck out of the path of railgun darts. Plus we had to spin and weave through space, to avoid exposing the shields on one side of the ship to smart missiles that coordinated their actions. At one point early in the battle, Skippy counted eighty-seven missiles in flight, and those were just the enemy weapons. Eighty-seven also was just the number he could count, he estimated possibly another dozen out there somewhere that he had lost track of.

The only good news for us was that after initially letting fly missiles like they were going to expire unless they were used, the enemy changed tactics and only kept enough missiles in flight to harass us. They had seen how effective our point-defense system was, knocking missiles out of the sky like swatting flies. It helped that the first volley of missiles came in dumb, bunched together for maximum striking power but making them easy targets for our cannons. Exploding one missile sent shrapnel tearing into its companions, like killing multiple birds with one stone. After that first volley, the missiles coming at us were a mix of decoys, sensor jammers and ship-killers. We took only four direct hits during that phase of the battle, and none of those four happened close together. If we had taken two ship-killer impacts at the same time, that likely would have blown several shield generators and left our armor plating exposed. *Valkyrie* was a powerful ship but not invincible, and we were fighting the Maxolhx. A few months before, we would never have considered coming close to a single warship of that senior species. When the heavy cruisers fell behind beyond effective range of their deadly masers and antienergy pulse cannons, they changed tactics to harass us with their smaller ships, and the trailing cruisers launched only enough missiles to keep us dodging so we couldn't keep a straight course away from them. In my judgement, they were keeping their large but limited supply of missiles for when *Valkyrie* had been trapped and could not escape.

So, all we could do was stay the course. Literally, stay on a course away from the heavy cruisers, a course that was taking us roughly toward the nearest star system. Without jumping, it would take us over a month to reach the orbit of the outermost planet, not that any of that mattered. The battle wasn't going to last that long, couldn't last that long. Not even *Valkyrie* could continue generating and consuming power at combat rates for more than a few hours. Space combat is intense and battles tend to be short. We just had to tough it out and hope for the best. I figured the Universe owed us one anyway.

CHAPTER FOURTEEN

At seventeen minutes, forty-three seconds into the running battle, we took two railgun hits to a portside aft shield, then an antienergy beam struck the same area, and that shield generator went offline to reset. The more efficient power boosters Skippy had installed could feed far more power to the generators than the original units, and the extra capacity allowed the generators to cycle back on faster, but each generator still had a limited capacity to take abuse before burning out. That generator had reached its limit, and the cycle from reset to full power was an agonizing four point two seconds. A lot can happen in four seconds.

Three missiles that our sensors had lost track of saw their opportunity and burned hard at the exposed area of our hull, racing each other to claim the glory of a direct hit. One missile drew the short straw and sacrificed itself by exploding to blind our sensors, and the other two were detonated at point-blank range by our point-defense cannons. The warheads had blown as soon as the missile detected particle beams locking on, with the focused explosion sending jets of super-heated plasma to splash against the armor panels. If *Valkyrie*'s armor plating did not have a layer of reactive materials, the deadly jets of plasma would have burned through to cause havoc in the ship's vital engineering section. The fact is, we got lucky. The reactive armor panels exploded outward, dispersing most of the plasma jets, and the hot material that did burn through severed power conduits that Skippy had already taken offline to work on the engines. Our luck wasn't perfect, the missile impacts caused the damaged shield generator to cycle back to reset again, and when it came back on, its frequency was not coordinated with the generators on either side. Until Skippy could fix the damned thing, that shield could not rely on help from the rest of the network that surrounded and protected the ship. Did the enemy see that weakness? A maser beam aimed directly at that shield gave us the answer we didn't want to hear.

Without being ordered to do anything, Reed saw the problem and slewed the ship in a tight turn so the bulk of the ship masked the exposed area where the shields were weak. On that side at that moment, we only had a destroyer and a patrol cruiser harassing us. According to the data provided by Skippy, the patrol cruiser had a railgun and the destroyer did not. "Simms," I gestured wildly at the main display. "That patrol ship! Hit it with everything we've got."

"Aye," she acknowledged, and the main display lit up with bolts from our pulse cannon.

Something was wrong. While we concentrated fire on the cruiser, making it stagger in flight as its shields flared and flickered from absorbing hellish energies, the destroyer dodged aside, wary of our big guns. Then, instead of continuing a turn away, the little ship curved around so it was headed straight toward us.

No.

It wasn't flying toward us, it was leading us a little. That ship was aiming for the point in space where *Valkyrie* would be when the destroyer got there.

It was going to ram us.

"XO!" I tried to rise out of my chair, held in place by nanofabric restraints that were smarter than I was.

"I see it," Reed said before Simms could respond, skidding our fierce battlecruiser around in a tight turn. *Valkyrie* was a mighty ship, a heavy ship. It wasn't a sports car or a fighter jet. In a turn, it was ponderous, momentum wanting to keep flying straight ahead.

Simms didn't say anything, she just directed the weapons teams to switch their fire from the already-staggering cruiser to the suicidal destroyer. The same distortion field that prevented our engines from applying full thrust now slowed our turn away from the destroyer that had become a weapon. The half-dozen heavy cruisers altered course to close the gap, as *Valkyrie* was no longer running straight away from them. They were able to cut the corner and even if we survived the destroyer's attack, the big guns of the cruisers would soon be within effective range again.

Having shot at the patrol cruiser, our antienergy pulse cannon needed to recharge and wouldn't be available until it was too late. That left our railguns, maser and particle beam cannons, and the missiles I had been saving for a special occasion. "Simms, missiles are authorized. Weapons free. Kill that ship!"

Even with *Valkyrie*'s bulk, the launch of four missiles was felt as a slight shudder that was distinctively different from the shuddering as our shields fended off enemy fire. We hammered that little destroyer, which really was little compared to a Kristang ship of the same type. Maxolhx engineering was so advanced, they could pack everything a destroyer needed into a compact package, with a typical crew of only thirty rotten kitties managing the highly-automated warship.

Little, but powerful. That ship continued onward relentlessly under the concentrated fire of every weapon we could throw at it. The crew must have adjusted their shields on double-front, wrapping the aft shields around and over the forward energy fields. That left the destroyer's flanks and engineering section vulnerable, a fact our smart missiles took advantage of immediately. They talked with each other and, after a brief argument that ended with three of the missiles calling the fourth one stupid and all of them getting into a shouting match that required Skippy to intervene, they attacked as a group from the destroyer's port side. The first missile converted its warhead into a fragmentation chaff device that blew into a fireball eleven thousand kilometers from the target, temporarily blinding the destroyer's sensors in that direction and allowing the three trailing missiles to match velocity and approach at the same time. By the time the destroyer's point-defense system sensors recovered, our missiles were locked on and went to maximum acceleration.

Around that same time, our directed-energy cannons burned a small hole through the suicidal ship's forward shields and the destroyer's nose began melting and exploding. Pieces were flying outward as secondary explosions rocked the little ship. Something big blew up about fifty meters from the nose and-

The destroyer blew up.

That was *not* a good thing.

Our cannons had not done enough damage to make the ship explode, there were no missile magazines in that ship's nose. Our three missiles were still racing at the target when with a single cry of 'WTF?' they were caught in the expanding fireball of the destroyer's reactors and aft magazines all erupting at once. The explosions vaporized the rear section of the ship but, because the crew had dumped the stored energy of their jump drive capacitors, the forward section of the hull was shattered rather than being turned into subatomic particles. In the blink of an eye, the destroyer's crew had turned their ship and themselves into shrapnel that was propelled forward by the force of the explosion.

"Reed!" I warned helplessly. She didn't reply, her actions spoke for her. Our chief pilot was already trying to get our massive battlecruiser turned away from the deadly cone of shrapnel and the key word was 'massive'. *Valkyrie*'s mass had considerable momentum that wanted us to go forward in a straight line, and that pain-in-the-ass law of physics wasn't allowing us to veer away from danger fast enough. Parts of *Valkyrie*'s structure was made of exotic matter that had less mass than normal atoms that were created by stars, and that helped. We also had help from fields that reduced the effect of inertia acting on the ship's regular mass. What help did we get from Isaac Newton? Zero. That guy was a *jerk*.

Valkyrie ducked downward, though 'down' has no real meaning in space. Reed judged our best chance to avoid getting smacked by the biggest chunks of destroyer stew was to turn ninety degrees from our prior flight path so that's what she did, analyzing the trajectory of incoming debris and allowing it to impact along the ship's ventral spine, where the structural frames were dense and strong.

We got smacked, *hard*. *Valkyrie* lurched as our shields deflected debris until the shield generators blinked out from the onslaught. The four largest pieces of jagged debris flew above and below us, saving our battlecruiser from utter destruction. What we got hit with was bad enough, the speed of impact instantly turning the material into plasma that burned through our armor plating. The layer of reactive armor tried to help but in many cases, the computer controlling those panels decided to deactivate them, as the panels were bent inward and their detonation would have been directed at *Valkyrie*'s more delicate inner structure.

One hundred and seventy meters of our hull was caved in, with droplets of plasma splattering all the way to char part of the ship's central frame. We lost two shield generators, six point-defense cannons, a railgun, and almost took a direct hit on a missile magazine. It was fortunate there were no missiles flying at us right then, because there was so much air and other crap venting from the rip in our hull, the sensors could not see through the cloud.

Oddly, on the bridge we did not feel any major effects from the impact. My chair did not rock side to side. Consoles did not explode in showers of sparks. Panels and cables did not cascade down from the ceiling. It felt like the ship was engaged in violent evasive maneuvering, which is what Reed was doing. For a split-second, I wondered if we had dodged a bullet.

Then the main display lit up like a Christmas tree, if you ever saw a Christmas tree with strings of yellow, orange and red lights. "Skippy! BLUF it for me!" I pleaded. There was too much information on the display for me to make sense of.

"*Valkyrie* can fly, Joe," he snapped irritably. "We can't take another hit in that area. I am extending shields to cover the gap, that leaves us thin. Reed, roll the ship to keep our ventral spine away from direct fire from those heavy cruisers."

"Aye aye," Reed acknowledged, not waiting for me to confirm the order. "Ship's handling like a pig," she complained.

"A bank of thrusters were torn out," Skippy snapped. "What did you expect?"

That got me mad. "Skippy! It's not Reed's fault, it's *my* fault. Focus your anger at me, or better yet, focus on fixing what you can."

"Working on it, you knucklehead," he grunted, and he wasn't being his usual smart-ass self. He was scared.

"All right then. Sitrep. Just the highlights."

"Ok," he sighed. "The good news is, we don't have to worry about the three remaining escort ships. The last patrol cruiser is heavily damaged and out of the fight, that ship's captain has requested permission to abandon ship. They have a runaway reactor and unless they can shut it down soon, they-"

Something flared on the display.

"Ignore what I just said," Skippy said without any satisfaction. "Scratch one patrol cruiser. That leaves two destroyers, both damaged. One is out of missiles, the other has only three missiles left. The task force commander has ordered them to pull back and separate. They are to observe, feed sensor data back to the heavy cruisers, and keep their damping fields energized so we can't jump away."

"Finally, a bit of good news," I wanted to give a hopeful thumbs up, but my thumb wasn't feeling it.

"That is *not* good news, Joe," Skippy corrected me. "The task force commander is pulling back the escorts because they are not needed. Those heavy cruisers are catching us, we will be in effective range of their cannons within forty-seven minutes. Before you ask, I am doing all I can to increase the power flow to our engines, and their efficiency. Without shutting them down for major work, there isn't much more we can get out of them."

"Understood," I resisted the urge to zoom the display in to examine damage to our ship. The crew could do that on their own consoles. They didn't need to see their captain obsessing over details, especially when I couldn't do anything about it.

What the hell *could* I do? We were out of options. Maybe if we-

"Joe," Skippy whispered in my earpiece. "I don't see a way out of this. Even with the damage we've sustained, we could take on two of those heavy cruisers. We can't survive a fight against six of them."

The crew would hear if I whispered, or they would see my lips moving. That would tell them I was having a private conversation with Skippy, a conversation I didn't want them hearing. And that would be terrible for morale. Not that morale mattered much at that point. On the keypad of my own console, I typed *Dump stuff overboard to make the ship less heavy*?

"That won't make enough of a difference, Joe. Without cutting away part of the ship, which is not practical in the time we have, dumping all our dropships and anything else, will only buy us another three minutes."

"Shit," I said aloud as I thumped the armrest. "What if"-

Simms interrupted my thought. "Three heavy cruisers are breaking off the attack! They're, running away?" She phrased the last words partly as a question. "We haven't hit them that hard."

"No," I bit my lip. For once, I was instinctively thinking in terms of space combat maneuvers. I knew what those ships were doing, and it meant trouble for us. "They're not running. They're racing to the back edge of our damping field. When they can jump, they will emerge *ahead* of us." That was smart tactics by the kitties. They did not know exactly how badly we were damaged from the destroyer's suicidal attempt to ram us. They *did* know that, with *Valkyrie* now mostly flying in a straight line rather than twisting and turning through the battlespace, we might be able to outrun their comparatively slow heavy cruisers. By jumping three heavy ships ahead of us, they could erase our potential speed advantage. And they could trap us between a hammer and anvil.

The only way to stop those ships from getting to the edge of our damping field was to turn and close the distance, which was the last thing we wanted to do. No, that wouldn't work anyway. The enemy commander could order the formation to disperse, and our damping field couldn't cover them all.

Everyone on the bridge turned to look at me. A good captain would have stared at the main display with quiet, stoic confidence. I plopped my elbows on the armrests and cradled my head in my hands, covering my ears to block out distracting sounds while I thought. Or maybe I was just hiding the shame that burned on my face, unable to face the crew who I was about to get killed because of my foolishness. UNEF was right, I am an impulsive idiot. We were out of options, no amount of silence would give me a brilliant idea, because there were no ideas that could-

Silence.

Holy shit.

"Skippy," I sat up straight and spoke aloud, not caring who heard me. "My father has a pair of noise-cancelling headphones."

"Uh, yessss," his voice had the tone commonly used when talking to people who have clearly lost their minds. "He calls them '*wife*-cancelling' headphones, although I suggested that he not tell your mother about-"

"Yeah, great, good advice. Those headphones work by listening to the soundwaves in the air, and playing a wave that is the opposite frequency or, uh, amplitude or something." I was a little vague on the subject.

"Again, yes. Joe, I understand you must be in shock, but spouting random facts you read on Wikipedia is not going to help us get out of this mess."

He was not the only one aboard *Valkyrie* who thought I might have lost it. Several of the crew were looking at me, their eyes wide, mouths open to say something. Simms held up a hand to stall them, in a gesture that said 'This is actually pretty normal'. The subtext of her gesture was 'This is why my life sucks'.

I agreed with her. "That is not a random fact," I explained. "Damping fields work by creating vibrations in the fabric of spacetime, right? Those ripples prevent us from forming a stable jump wormhole."

"Ok, you didn't get *that* from Wikipedia, and you are correct, but what-"

"It is possible to use our damping field to play back the opposite type of vibration? Cancel the damping effect?"

"Holy sh- *No*. No, it is *not* possible, dumdum. Those vibrations are way too chaotic to predict. By the time the ship detected incoming vibrations and retuned our own field, the vibrations would have changed in a random manner. Jeez, don't you think the Maxolhx would already have that technology, if it were possible?"

"Crap." Now I not only looked like a fool who would get the entire crew killed, I was an idiot. Great move, I told myself. Next time, I should keep my mouth shut.

"What about you?" Simms asked, startling me.

"Me?" Skippy asked. "What about me?"

"You keep blah blah *blah*-ing about how magnificent you are," Simms flipped a middle finger at his avatar. "You're telling me you can't even predict how a freakin' *wave* will change as it travels across spacetime?"

"Hey!" Skippy hated it when anyone other than me criticized him. "It's not *my* fault. Space is not the problem, it's *time* that is the issue. The waves travel faster than the speed of light, but our sensors work at lightspeed. By the time the waves tripped across our sensor field, they are already too close for me to adjust our own field to compensate and-"

"So?" Reed turned in her seat. "Stick a microwormhole out there and get sensor data with no time lag."

"Um," Skippy sputtered.

"Will that work?" I dared to hope. "A series of microwormholes, so you can analyze how the vibrations change as they move toward us?"

"Jeez, I guess we could try it? Damn, why are all the ideas you monkeys dream up so obvious?"

Simms wasn't letting him off the hook. "Why is your vast intelligence unable to see ideas that are so obvious?"

"Hey, you forget that I'm the one who has to actually *do* all this crazy shit," he complained.

"Yes," I restrained an impulse to flip him off. "You are terribly unappreciated and oppressed. Can you do it or not?"

"The answer, Joe, is a qualified 'shmaybe'."

"What does that mean?"

"It *means*, maybe it will work and maybe it won't. I won't know until I get a string of microwormholes out there and see what the data looks like. This is not simple math, you numbskull. The damping field we're trapped in is being generated by *eight* ships at various and changing distances from us. That is eight overlapping sets of vibrations, that are each tuned to be random and unpredictable. The interactions of those eight waves makes them even more chaotic. But the real issue is the state of our jump drive. Like I told you, we sort of dorked it up when we jumped in. I've slapped it together with duct tape and a prayer, but it won't take us far even if there was no damping field. Wherever we jump to, the kitties will be able to track us and jump in to surround us. A short jump doesn't do anything other than delay our demise by a short time."

"Could we jump to the other side of the star? They won't see us there."

"That's too far," he said with glum resignation. "We might manage a jump that far if there was absolutely no damping effect, but, seriously, even my magnificence can't totally quiet the vibrations of spacetime. If we can jump, *if*, it is going to be rough and it's going to be noisy. It will also be the last jump for several days, until I can strip the drive down and rebuild it."

"Shit," I groaned. "That's it, then? Even if you can partly cancel the damping effect, we have no safe place to jump to?"

"Colonel?" Simms got my attention. "What about the trick we pulled on our very first mission together?"

"Uh," I had no idea what she was talking about. "Which trick?"

"Skippy jumped fourteen Kristang starships into a gas giant," she reminded me.

"*Ooooooh*," Skippy whistled. "Wow. Now *that* is crazy talk. Hmm, if we jumped low into the atmosphere of a gas giant, no one would see where we went to. It could take days for the shockwave effect to reach the cloud tops, where the Maxolhx would see it. Also, ooh, ooh!" He bubbled over with enthusiasm. "The effect of jumping into a gravity well would distort the jump wormhole so badly, the kitties could not use the data to figure out where we went. I *like* it!"

"XO, good thinking," I let Simms down gently. "But, uh, didn't jumping into an area already occupied by matter destroy those lizard ships?"

"It did, Joe," Skippy confirmed. "Don't be too hasty. Jennifer may be onto something. There is a gas giant planet in a highly elliptical orbit, that we might be able to jump to. *Maybe*. I'm not making any promises."

"What about," I closed my eyes to search way back in my memory. "The whole thing about jumping inside a planet would tear a ship apart? You told us something like, the gravity well would distort the wormhole."

"For crappy low-tech Kristang starships, that is true. Ah, it's also true for high-tech Maxolhx ships. But, *but*, the magnificence of *me* is able to reach through the jump wormhole and stabilize its endpoint long enough for us to emerge safely. I think. Truthfully, I've never done this before, you know?"

"Ok," for some reason, I was arguing *against* the only plan that had a possibility of our survival. It all sounded too good to be true. "You can fix the gravity well problem-"

"Maybe. I said *maybe* I can deal with it."

"Right. We will still be emerging into a region of space that is already occupied by matter. The atmosphere of a gas giant is dense. Like, really thick."

"That is also true. Damn, Joe, why are you *such* a buzzkill today?"

"Because I don't want to jump from the frying pan into-" What was a good metaphor? "Something worse than a frying pan. Like a nuclear fireball, when our atoms try to emerge into space occupied by other atoms."

"Nuclear. Fireball," Skippy repeated slowly.

"Don't be an ass. I know it will be a different type of explosion. You know what I-"

"No. That's not it. I wasn't mocking you. Joe, you just gave me an idea that might possibly make this work."

"Like what?"

"Well, heh heh," he chuckled. "You are *not* going to like this."

I groaned. The bridge crew joined me, because they knew what a 'Well heh heh' meant.

Skippy explained.

He was one hundred ten percent correct. I did not like it.

Ok, well, his idea did involve blowing shit up, and as a guy, the inner me was very much in favor of trying it. Plus, we didn't have a better option. Or *any* other option.

"Smythe," I called our STAR team leader, who was in their section of the ship, suited up in case we found a use for infantry action. "Get a nuke and strap it aboard the DeLorean."

"Better make it two, Joe," Skippy advised.

"*Two* nukes. We need two nukes aboard the DeLorean. And dial their yield up to 'Eleven', got that?"

"Understood," Smythe acknowledged.

I felt he was owed an explanation. "Listen, you might think my order is odd, so-"

"Sir? Stuffing nukes into a dropship is not even the oddest thing that has happened to me *today*," he chided me with dry British humor.

"Oh. Good point. Signal when the nukes are in place."

"Colonel?" Reed asked. "Should I get the DeLorean ready for launch?"

"Nope," Skippy answered for me. "My bots are already warming up the DeLorean now."

"We don't," Reed looked at me. "Don't need a pilot, in case something goes wrong?"

"Reed," I told her gently. "The DeLorean isn't coming back."

"Sir," the look she gave me was not fear, it was intense determination. "If this doesn't work, we are *all* dead."

"Thank you for the offer, Fireball," Skippy teased her with the callsign she hated. "I got this. If anything goes wrong, it will happen too fast for you to react anyway."

"Reed," I added. "If anyone is flying the DeLorean, it will be *me*. Skippy, we can go as soon as the DeLorean is ready?"

"Um, no. Joe, you are still thinking like a ground-pounder."

"Shit. What did I forget this time?"

"I'll give you a hint, two words. Relative. Velocity."

"Oh," I sagged in my chair. "Crap!" What Skippy meant is, *Valkyrie* was flying *this* way, imagine me pointing to the right, while the planet we wanted to jump into was moving *that* way, imagine me pointing to the left. Like the scarecrow in Wizard of Oz, my arms were crossed and pointing in opposite directions. Starships emerged from a jump with the same speed and direction they had before the jump. If we couldn't get *Valkyrie* moving at roughly the same speed and direction as the target planet. We would hit the thick atmosphere like slamming into a wall, and that would pancake the ship nose to tail like stomping on a tin can. Because the damned planet was also rotating, we had to jump into a part of the atmosphere that was rotating in roughly the same direction our ship was traveling.

Man, I freakin' *hate* math. "Is this all a waste of time, then?" I asked, dreading the answer.

"No, it's not a waste of time," he assured me. "But the vector of our pesky momentum is taking us too fast, in the wrong direction. We can't aim for the closest gas giant planet. It is currently orbiting sideways to our course, and much too slowly. There is another gas giant, a really big one like Jupiter, that is farther away. Like, uncomfortably far for us to jump given the current poor state of our drive. Ah, don't worry, somehow I will make it work. Or not, and you'll never know the difference because you monkeys will all die instantly. So, really, there is no downside, huh?"

With my hands, I mimed choking him. It made me feel better. "Can we match course and speed with the second planet?"

"The short answer is 'No'. The long answer is, close enough. We need to start altering course *now*, though. Navigation system has been programmed."

"Reed?"

"I see it, Sir," she acknowledged. "Initiating course change now. Oh. Sir, are you sure about this?"

"Oh, Crap." On the main display, I saw what had caused her concern. The turn was taking us *toward* the enemy. "*Skippy*?!"

"Yes, we have to decelerate. We will not be flying directly toward the enemy cruisers, but they will be approaching much faster."

"Hey, I hate to point out the flaws in your genius plan," I laid the sarcasm on thick. "Did you consider that if those cruisers pound *Valkyrie* to dust, we won't be able to attempt your next wacky stunt?"

He sucked in a breath. "Oops. Gosh, *no*, I hadn't considered that. *Yes*, I thought of that, you moron! Through the magic of mathematics, which you should try learning sometime, I have calculated that we will have a comfortable fifty-two second margin between the time when our velocity matches the planet, and the time when the main guns of the enemy will be within effective range of us."

"Fifty-two seconds is *comfortable*?"

"Sure. Easy-peasy, Joe. Um, actually, the longer we can wait, the better. At the fifty-two second mark, we will still be traveling seven thousand kilometers per hour relative to the target planet."

"That doesn't sound safe to me."

"It's not optimal," he admitted. "If we could wait until the thirty-eight second mark, that would be great."

Running a hand through my hair, I let out a long breath, keeping it quiet to avoid alarming the crew. Any more than they were already justifiably alarmed. "That makes me nervous, Skippy. The effective range of directed energy weapons is just an estimate. They could hurt us from much farther away."

"It won't do us any good to avoid enemy fire, if we burn up from smacking into the atmosphere way too fast."

"I hear you. Ok, we'll aim for thirty-eight seconds. We'll need to launch the DeLorean on the side of the ship facing away from the enemy, so they can't hit it."

"Good idea," he agreed.

"Simms?" I wanted her opinion. "XO, does this bad idea sound any worse than our usual bad ideas?"

"I don't have a Top Ten list of your worst ideas, Sir."

"Give me your gut feeling, please."

She looked at Reed, then around the bridge. "If this is our last rodeo, I'd rather engage the enemy, and take as many of them out with us as we can. Dying in a blaze of glory in combat, sounds better than dying under the cold clouds of some anonymous planet."

There was a chorus of agreeing murmurs around the bridge. Heads were nodding. "Simms," I replied after a pause to carefully consider my choice of words. "I hear you. The problem is, one option is a certain blaze of glory, the other gives us at least a chance to live so we can fight again. Skippy, can you give me odds of us surviving a jump into that planet?"

"*Sheee-it*," he grunted. "Truthfully, there are too many unknown variables. It's worth a try anyway. Think about this. If we lose *Valkyrie* in battle today, the enemy will no longer have to fear the ghost ship. But, even if we die from jumping into the planet, we will have escaped their trap. The Maxolhx won't know that we're dead, they will need to continue being on alert for the ghost ship. Probably for years, they will be racing around, chasing down rumors of the ghost ship being seen here or there. Even in death, we can drive the enemy crazy."

Simms gave me a reluctant thumbs up. "That makes sense."

"You're Ok with postponing your blaze of glory?" I asked.

"I'd rather postpone it forever, if you can arrange that."

"I'll do my best. All right, Skippy, we'll try this crazy scheme. Everyone, let's think positive thoughts, Ok?"

Positive thoughts emanated from *Valkyrie*, unfortunately doing nothing to deflect the shotgun blasts of railgun darts the heavy cruisers were still throwing at us. Having to dodge railgun darts slowed our forward progress, bringing the three leading ships closer with each turn we made. The three ships that had turned around were approaching the effective edge of our damping field, they soon could jump ahead of us. My expectation was those ships would wait until they were comfortably beyond range of our damping field's effects, they were in no hurry. They had our ghost ship trapped and they knew it. There was no glory in taking foolish risks, plus they probably wanted to savor their inevitable victory.

"Enemy have launched missiles," Simms warned. "Twenty-eight missiles are inbound."

"ETA?" I asked, searching for that info on the display.

"They will be here, beginning eleven seconds after we plan to jump."

"They're planning to start shooting energy weapons early then," I mused. "The missiles will come in under cover of their other weapons."

"This is nothing new, Joe," Skippy tried to keep me focused. "Like you said, the effective range of energy weapons was an estimate."

"Right." Damn. Right then, I really needed to pee. Telling my nervous bladder to be quiet, I tried to imagine our mighty ship, flying through space while the enemy raced to intercept us. "Reed, give us five seconds margin after we hit the thirty-eight second mark. If we haven't jumped yet, twist *Valkyrie*'s tail and get us out of here."

The six probes we sent out, loaded with microwormholes, reached a position relative to *Valkyrie* and matched pace with us. "Skippy?" I asked after waiting patiently for three minutes, while the clock counted down to the magic thirty-eight second mark. Finally, as the clock counted off the final minute, I couldn't wait any longer. "Will this work?"

"Um, well," there was no humor in his voice. "The short answer is 'no'."

"Is there a long answer?"

"That is also 'no'. Sorry."

"*What* is the problem?" I fumed at him.

"Like I told you, *time* is the problem," he huffed defensively. "The damping field vibrations are moving faster than light, because they are propagating through higher spacetime. The microwormholes are helping, just not enough. They would need to be *very* close to the transmitting ships, for me to have sufficient lead time so I could retune our own damping field enough to cancel the vibrations. If the probes were that close to the enemy, they would be targeted and destroyed. Already, one of the probes was nearly fried by a maser beam. The enemy sees our probes and wonders what we are doing with them."

"Ok," I admitted. The clock showed less than a minute before we were scheduled to jump. We would miss that deadline. "I got nothing. That's it, then? We tried?" A good captain would not have let his crew know he was mentally giving up. I was not that captain.

"I am truly sorry, Joe. Everyone, I am sorry. It was a good idea; I just can't make it work."

"Hey," I tried to joke around with him, since that might be my last opportunity for it. "We don't think any less of you. When the Universe asks me for feedback on your performance, I will write 'magnificent' on the comment card."

"O. M. *GEE*, Dude!" He shouted so loud, it rang in my ears. "That is freakin' *brilliant*."

"It was just a lame joke, Skip-"

"Not the joke, you idiot," he was the only person I knew who could call someone both 'brilliant' and 'idiot' in practically the same thought. "What you *said* is brilliant."

"Uh, about the Universe?"

"Ugh, no. Feedback. You said '*feedback*'."

"Wow." I caught onto his idea, and he was right. It was brilliant. "You can-"

"I think so. Testing it now. Dude, prepare to be amazed by my utter awesomeness."

"Will someone," Simms demanded. "*Please* tell me what is going on?"

"Skippy is," I guessed but was pretty sure about being right. "Is going to use our damping field generator to send a feedback signal *backwards* along the enemy fields. Disrupt them at the source, right?"

"Correct-a-mundo, Joey my boy," he laughed. "The test worked! The damping field generator aboard the nearest destroyer just temporarily failed. Ha ha! The crew of that ship must be asking 'WTF just happened'! Um, that is good news and bad news. The good news is, the feedback trick works. The bad news is, it won't take long for the AIs of the enemy ships to analyze why the destroyer's field generator blew. Once they know what happened, they can adjust their damping fields to avoid being vulnerable to feedback."

"So, we need to do this quick?

"That is also correct-a-mundo."

"Ok," I ordered, "launch the DeLorean. We need to do this quick, as soon as the enemy sees the DeLorean, they will try to hit it."

On the display, another symbol appeared, representing our modified Kristang dropship. It was wrapped in a junkyard collection of parts taken from the *Flying Dutchman*, before Skippy made our old star carrier a hotrod by pimping it with leftover Legos. The DeLorean was still a kludgy piece of junk and none of us really trusted it. Plus, the damned thing hadn't been tested yet. "DeLorean is in position," I needlessly told Skippy what he already knew. "Do we need a countdown?"

"No. This will happen much too fast for you monkeys to understand."

"Great. Can you give me a level of 'shmaybe' for your confidence about this?"

"What? Dude, I have *no idea* if this will work or not."

"Then why-"

"I *can* guarantee that one way or the other, it will be *Awe-Some*!" he sang.

"Shit."

"Joe, I can offer you a few words of comfort, before we leap into the unknown."

"What's that?"

"Hold my beer."

CHAPTER FIFTEEN

Skippy was right. It all happened too fast for us to understand. First, the DeLorean blinked out of existence in a ragged flash of light. Before I could ask whether that little ship had jumped or been struck by enemy fire, we jumped. We tried to jump into the crushing atmosphere of a gas giant planet.

Instead, we jumped into hell.

It was not possible, even with the magnificence of Skippy, to jump the ship into an area already occupied by the dense atmosphere of a gas giant planet. For the ship to survive suddenly emerging in that area, we needed to jump into a low-pressure bubble, except there was no low-pressure region in that roiling collection of toxic gasses.

So, we made a bubble. A temporary one.

When the DeLorean jumped in, it was torn apart from emerging where a dense cloud of atoms already existed. Plus, two of our nukes detonated at the same time. The resulting explosions pushed the atmospheric gas away in all directions, creating a short-lived bubble of low pressure.

A very short-lived bubble. We jumped in just before the atmosphere rushed back to fill the vacuum. That was, according to Skippy, the only way for us to survive emerging within that planet's atmosphere. Maybe he was telling the truth, and maybe he was screwing with us because he wanted to do some cool thing that had never been done before.

I had to trust him.

Saying 'hold my beer' before he triggered the crazy stunt had me leaning toward 'screwing with us', if you want to know.

So, we jumped our battlecruiser, with its barely functional jump drive, into the center of a nuclear fireball that was buried deep in the crushing atmosphere of a gas giant planet we knew nothing about. What could *possibly* go wrong?

Answer: a lot.

The timing had to be perfect, like, perfect as only Skippy could manage. The detonation of the DeLorean and the plutonium cores of our tactical nukes had pushed everything outward from the center, in a bubble-shaped shockwave. *Valkyrie* had to emerge in that bubble after the outer edge of the shockwave expanded far enough to fit our ship nose to tail, and before the constant inward pressure of the atmosphere overcame the very brief outward pressure of the explosion. Our jump had to be super accurate in both timing and location. The timing was tricky, because the DeLorean could not jump until the feedback Skippy sent back along the enemy damping fields canceled them out for a brief moment. Then we had to wait until spacetime ripples created by the DeLorean's own jump cleared the area around *Valkyrie*, before it was reasonably safe for us to attempt a jump. By that time, Skippy expected the bubble in the gas giant's atmosphere would already be collapsing.

Then there was the problem of jumping our massive battlecruiser exactly into that already-shrinking bubble, deep in the gravity well of a large planet. That deep under the surface of the atmosphere, the dense layer of gas above and to all sides of the bubble created their own tug of gravity, so Skippy had to take all those factors into account. Plus he was working with a jump drive that was held together by duct tape and a prayer.

So, it was a typical Tuesday for the Merry Band of Pirates.

Have you ever watched an old submarine movie, like *Run Silent Run Deep*, or *Hunt for Red October*? When the boat goes deeper, the pressure of water squeezes the hull, and you can hear the thick steel popping and groaning under the load. Those sounds are alarming and scary and expected. Somehow, the submarine crews get used to hearing the metal of their hull being compressed.

That is not supposed to happen to starships, which are designed to operate in the hard vacuum of space. When we emerged into the still-hot bubble of intense radiation, our shields and armor protected the ship from being fried. There was enough time for me look at the big holographic display and think 'We did it', before the atmosphere rushed in to collapse the temporary bubble. That was when the ship's hull groaned and squealed and protested with screeching and grinding noises, loud enough that I couldn't hear whatever Skippy was shouting at me or whoever. There was one particularly loud and shuddering SKREEEEE-BANG-BANG that ended with a high-pitched UUUUUUURK like a giant dragging an aircraft carrier across a parking lot. To make the experience even more fun, because Skippy wanted to make sure we got our money's worth of entertainment, the ship lurched up, spun, and then the bottom dropped out as we began falling.

I do *not* recommend that carnival ride, especially after you've eaten a couple of deep-fried corndogs with onion rings.

Then the *real* trouble hit.

Skippy's timing had not been optimal, so we were traveling twenty-one hundred kilometers per hour faster than the clouds around us had been moving as they rotated with the planet. Plus, the clouds were propelled at eight hundred kph straight at us, as a massive storm raced endlessly around the planet. We hit that dense cloud of toxic gas like it was a brick wall, and Skippy had to choose between using reactor power to strengthen the ship's structural integrity, or feeding that power to the shields. He compromised by strengthening critical parts of the structure, while allowing shields along our flanks to slump inward. That worked for the first second or so, preventing *Valkyrie* from collapsing like an accordion, until the ship lurched sideways and we went racing into the storm at an angle that caused shields along the port side to flicker and for *Valkyrie*'s mighty central spine to *bend*. That spine was not supposed to flex at all. The unexpected torque would have snapped the spine in half, except Skippy counterintuitively cut power to the structural integrity fields that were holding the spine's composite materials rigid. Without the reinforcement of the fields, the spine absorbed the shock, allowed the energy to rebound out to the braces that connected the spine to the outer frames, and saved the ship from being torn apart. Many of those braces fractured but there were plenty of them to take up the slack, and pumping extra power into the structural integrity fields of the braces kept them stable enough. In some cases, the fields surrounded shattered braces, with the actual material providing no help at all.

The momentum of *Valkyrie*'s massive bulk kept us plowing through the roiling clouds long enough for the armor plating on the nose to glow cherry red from friction, then we came to a stop relative to the cold and dense gasses around us.

That's when we dropped toward the planet's solid inner core.

"Ahhhh!" I yelped as my command chair fell away from me, the straps digging into the tops of my thighs. You know what was really scary? Seeing a new indicator labelled 'Rate of Descent' on the main display. And seeing the numbers scroll rapidly upward. And being barely able to read the numbers because the ship was bouncing and vibrating so badly. Yeah, all that was scary.

You know what was the scariest part?

The new display was misspelled 'Rate of *Decent*', not 'Descent'. Skippy had added that indicator so quickly, he absent-mindedly forgot to check the spelling.

Why?

Because *freakin' starships are not supposed to descend,* that's why!

They are supposed to spend their lives in the nice, safe hard vacuum of space.

"We're falling!" I gave the breaking news flash to the crew, in case anyone had not noticed. "Reed! Stand the ship on her tail and go to full thrust!"

"I'm trying," she shouted back, or something like that. It was difficult to hear her, both because of all the other noise and because my brain was being rattled in my skull.

The ship's nose came up as Reed fired thrusters to get *Valkyrie* properly oriented. It worked for a moment, the tail was swinging slowly down. Then something new went wrong or some vital component failed and the nose flipped downward in a sickening lurch that had me fighting not to blow chunks all over the bridge.

"Got it! I got it!" Reed assured the crew as *Valkyrie* pointed directly nose down and accelerated toward depths that would crush the hull like an eggshell. Gradually, she applied reverse thrust, and our fatal descent slowed. That was a great feature of reactionless engines, they could apply thrust backward or forward. Technically, they could also apply thrust to the side, although that only made the ship's ass end spin in the opposite direction. Except when vectoring power for a tighter turn, thrust was supposed to be aligned with *Valkyrie*'s center of gravity.

According to the display, we fell twelve and a half kilometers before Reed got the ship hanging by her tail, dangling in the clouds with no visible means of support.

"Thank God," I said with a shudder. Remember those old submarine movies I mentioned? To that list, add *Ice Station Zebra*. I felt like telling Fireball Reed to 'maintain revolutions'! Instead, I said something that made more sense in our situation. "Outstanding work, pilot. Can you pull us up and out of this by flying ass-first?"

She shook her head without turning toward me. "Colonel, I don't even know how long I can hold us at *this* depth. The engines are overheating."

Shit. A glance at the display showed engine temperature status as red lights everywhere. "Skippy!"

"Doing the best I can, Joe," he snapped. "You think this is easy?"

"If it was easy, we wouldn't need the magnificence of you. *Do* something!"

"Working on it. Reed, ease off the throttle by nineteen percent," Skippy directed.

"*Reduce* the power?" I demanded as I waved for Reed to ignore Skippy's instructions.

"Trust me on this, Joe," he pleaded. "The engines are on the verge of burning out. No time to explain."

I had to trust the beer can.

I had to. Trust. A. Beer. Can.

How had my life gone so wrong?

Gritting my teeth and fighting against common sense and instincts, I gave the order. "Reduce thrust by nineteen percent."

And I immediately regretted not listening to my instincts, as the bottom fell out. *Valkyrie* sagged downward, building up speed as we fell toward crush depth.

At first, I thought Reed had obeyed her own instincts rather than my orders, because our sickening fall slowed. Gradually at first, then with noticeably greater authority, our fall was arrested. "What is happening?" I demanded, hoping Skippy had done something awesome like boosting the efficiency of the engines.

"We're gaining positive buoyancy, Joe," he explained.

"Uh, we're *what*?"

"Let me break this down Barney-style for you, knucklehead," he said peevishly. "I am expanding the shields outward, so that the atmosphere displaced is becoming equal to *Valkyrie*'s mass. We are *floating*, Joe."

"Floating," I repeated stupidly. "Ok, that, that's great! How high can we go?"

"For right now, *here* is as high as we can go. Maybe we can't even maintain this altitude. I'll know more after I expand the shields farther from the hull. We need to get enough buoyancy so engine thrust can be cut to twenty-eight percent, because I have to take five of the engines offline soon or they'll burn out."

"Got it. The ship will hold together?"

"Shmaybe. Try not to do anything stupid."

I tried my best not to do anything stupid. Working with Reed, Skippy expanded the shields and she reduced thrust until we could hold altitude with only twelve percent thrust, giving us a comfortable safety margin. By that time, we drifted down another nine kilometers and the pressure on the shields was greater, which actually helped produce buoyancy. On the display, I could see that Skippy had not only expanded our shields farther from the ship, they were warped into a balloon shape, larger above us than below.

My one useful contribution to the operation was to order a probe launched. It flew slowly upward, picking up speed as the cloud layer density decreased. The little probe finally soared above the atmosphere, confirming that the shockwave of our nukes had not boiled up to the cloud tops yet. If the Maxolhx had their sensors focused on the planet, they might have seen some odd thermal readings, but even if they did, it was unlikely they would jump into orbit to investigate. Satisfied that there was no evidence of our crazy stunt, we turned the probe's sensors outward. They detected nothing, because photons from the raging space battle had not yet reached the chilly gas giant world. It was odd, knowing that if we waited another four hours, we could watch faint images of the battle, as if we had only ever been spectators to the event.

Eventually, we did watch the battle, in *Valkyrie*'s theater. The off-duty crew sat quietly and watched images enhanced by Skippy. We saw our fearsome ghost ship jump in, and we watched our attempt to fly away. The crew cringed with me as we saw the destroyer's suicide run, ending with *Valkyrie* staggering in flight.

The last image was a bright and ragged gamma ray burst as our battle-damaged ship jumped out of the weakened damping field. There was dead silence in the theater, broken when Frey remarked "I wonder if they made it, eh?"

For some reason, we all thought that comment was freakin' *hilarious*. It got more funny when the captain of the ship announced the bar was open. There wasn't anything filthy monkeys could do while Santa Skippy and his little helper elfbots fixed the ship, and I figured the crew needed to blow off steam. While I slowly sipped one beer, I acted as bartender and encouraged people to have fun. DJ Skippy-Skip and the Fresh Tunes broke out a playlist of danceable party tunes, and soon everyone who wanted to party was tearing up the dance floor.

Even Margaret Adams was getting into the party spirit, dancing with rhythm way better than anything I could manage. It made me wonder whether Skippy had directed the tiny machines in her head to assist her coordination, to boost her morale. No, I did not dance with her, I was acting as bartender, remember?

Plus, she did not ask me to dance. Besides, she had plenty of dance partners, and only one of them was named 'Rum and Coke'.

After a while, I turned bartending duty over to Major Kapoor, and went back to the bridge to relieve Simms. Also to relieve Reed. "You're sure about this, Sir?" Reed asked me, searching my eyes with concern.

"Go join the party, Fireball. Some of the STAR team guys are *terrible* dancers, and I'm kind of an expert on terrible dancing. They need you to show them how it's done."

"I meant, you're sure you can handle the ship?" She asked as I slid into the pilot's chair and stuck my hands into the 3D virtual controls.

"Come on, Reed. I've taken every flight lesson I could squeeze in. All I need to do is keep us stable. If anything goes wrong, no monkey is going to save us."

"That's true," Skippy agreed. "There will be a tricky transition in fifteen hours, when I cut over from one bank of engines to another. It would be good for Fireball to be rested and ready, and not too hung over, at that time."

Reed laughed. "Fifteen hours? That gives me four hours for fun, eight for sleep, and three for coffee."

"I'll ask Skippy to set an alarm for you. Now, go have fun, while you can," I shooed her away. The bridge was then empty, except for me. I hadn't been joking when I said there wasn't anything useful for us monkeys to do while Skippy worked on the ship. What the crew needed to be doing right then was giving thanks for being alive. They needed to have fun and restore morale. And they needed rest, to prepare for whatever the Universe was going to throw at us next. "Skippy?" I called when the bridge was clear. "Sitrep. Be honest."

"Forming a virtual balloon to keep us afloat is a major strain on the shields, they weren't designed for such intense and continuous use. Once I get the engines working well enough, we can reduce shield output and use the engines to lift us. Except the engines also were not designed for continuous use. Starships typically only boost through normal space for short distances, if they want to travel far, they jump. We will be using our engines to dangle this massive ship in a gravity well, and I am watching them closely for signs of burnout. Our safety margin is not as large as I would like."

"Understood. How long until we can climb into orbit?"

"My best estimate is we'll be stuck down here for eight days, Joe. The good news is, I am fairly confident that I can fix the mess you have made of our fine ship. I'll make the repairs I can down here, then we need to rendezvous with the *Dutchman*, to get the spare parts they are carrying."

"And the bad news?"

"The bad news is, I am only *fairly* confident. I should *know* by now whether I can restore *Valkyrie* to its former glory. Unfortunately, because I slapped this thing together from a pile of Legos and it has been much modified and upgraded, there is no operating manual. Other than what I have observed in the short time we've been flying this beast, I'm having to guess at the best way to make all these parts work together. Some of my upgrades worked better than expected, and some, ah, not so much. I'll be making changes. The bottom line is, we dodged a bullet."

"Sorry about that."

"Normally, I would savor watching you wallow in misery, but, *ugh*. I can't believe I'm saying this; don't beat yourself up about it. You made a judgment call. Based on what we knew at the time, it was a reasonable risk. You were right; if we had hit the one star carrier that was *supposed* to be there, it would have been a major defeat for the kitties. This is, ugh. This is *my* fault."

What I should have done is agreed with that arrogant little shithead, and let *him* wallow in misery for a while. Instead, I had to open my big stupid mouth. "How do you figure that? They played us, Skippy. They played *me*. They analyzed my actions and determined a pattern, and they knew what would lure me in. They gave me exactly the fat juicy target I was looking for, and I never questioned whether it was too good to be true."

"I can't argue with that, Joe."

"You're supposed to, dumbass. You're supposed to tell me nice things like-"

"Like what? Like that dress doesn't make you look fat? You made mistakes and you know it. I made mistakes too. You know who else made mistakes? The rotten kitties. They set a trap and it didn't work! Right now, they have got to be tearing their fur out, trying to analyze what went wrong. What is really going to drive them crazy is how we hit them where and when they were not expecting us. Clearly, they weren't ready for combat when we jumped in. By my count, they lost two heavy cruisers, all four patrol cruisers, and four of six destroyers. The two star carriers will probably be scrapped where they are, and two of the surviving heavy cruisers will need extensive servicing in spacedock before they can be ready for combat again. Plus, we got away! By now, their AIs have surely discovered my feedback trick, and are creating countermeasures. But again, our ghost ship demonstrated capabilities that are beyond the technology available to the Maxolhx. They can only see the battle as a resounding and embarrassing defeat for them."

"Yeah, well, unless they assume our jump tore us apart. It is only a victory for us if they know we survived. I'm not taking us on another raid."

"Don't worry, Joe. I have an idea about that."

Nine days later, *Valkyrie* began slowly climbing up out of the dense toxic clouds. Skippy would have preferred another day or two to work on the engines, but the shield generators were showing signs of serious strain. It was another judgment call and it was my decision, ordering Reed to pull us up out of the murky clouds. The probe we had in orbit had detected gamma ray bursts from ships jumping away from the battle zone, and two ships were jumping around in a grid pattern, looking for us. Based on their faint signatures, Skippy thought the two ships were the destroyers that had survived the battle. Neither of them were anywhere near us, so we weren't concerned. When we finally broke free of the cloud tops, a cheer rang around the bridge. The star was too dim and it was the wrong color, and it was the most beautiful thing I had seen in a long time. We kept engine power on until the ship was in a stable orbit, where we hid wrapped in a stealth field while Skippy's bots checked every system we needed for our next action.

When Skippy was satisfied he had fixed the critical systems that needed to be fixed, we went hunting again.

Going out looking for trouble, when our ship was not at full combat readiness, gave me a bad feeling. Conducting another daring attack at that time made sense, I agreed with Skippy's reasoning, and both Simms and Smythe advised me that the risk was manageable and worth the potential payoff. Trouble is, that's what I thought before our last attack, and that was a disaster.

There were three targets to choose from. The two destroyers were operating separately, jumping around in widening circles from the battle zone while they searched for signs of where we had gone. So far, neither of those escort ships had come close to the planet where we had taken shelter, nor had they apparently noticed when the shockwaves of our nukes finally bubbled up through the dense clouds. We had jumped in so deep that when the shockwaves were detectable from space, they were not anything impressive, and it was not surprising the kitties were not looking for us in such an unlikely place.

We knew where the destroyers were, or we knew where they *were*, several hours ago. They had each probably jumped since we detected their faint gamma ray bursts, and we would have to track them and go on a lengthy chase.

The other target was easier to find, because it hadn't moved in over a week. One of the star carriers had been self-destructed, the kitties must have hoped they could salvage the other. A battle-damaged heavy cruiser had parked itself near the surviving star carrier, either to provide cover, or because the cruiser also was not capable of flying very far.

The wounded star carrier was a tempting target, even with a heavy companion there to protect it. We could jump in, hit the star carrier with one furious salvo, and jump away before a damping field could saturate spacetime around us. Losing a star carrier, while it was guarded by a capital ship, would be a heavy blow to the enemy, and make it clear that the ghost ship was still very much in business and not afraid of tangling with an opponent of equivalent size. It would be a powerful statement.

A statement that, I decided, we didn't need to make. All we *needed* to do was show the Maxolhx that our ghost ship hadn't been knocked out. It wasn't necessary to take on a heavy cruiser to do that. So, I ignored the temptation of a big score, and put the priority on reducing our risk. "Skippy, what is taking so long?" He was analyzing the searches conducted by the two destroyers, trying to find a pattern. If we knew roughly where one of those ships was likely to jump, that would save us a lot of time. "You can't identify a pattern?"

"There *is* a pattern," he huffed, irritated at me. "What I am working on is identifying each of those destroyers."

"Why do we care about getting an identification?"

"*Becaaaaaause*, if you haven't already forgotten, one of those ships was out of missiles. That's the one we want to hit, dumdum."

"Oh for- Listen, you moron. I'm sure that before the other ships jumped away, they conducted a cross-decking operation or whatever they call it, and transferred a reload of missiles to top off the magazines of both destroyers."

"How can you be sure about that?"

"Because that's what we would do."

"Oh. Well, why didn't you tell me that, before I wasted my time?" He demanded, indignant.

"I assumed you would use your ginormous brain, that's why."

"Hey, I already told you, I am not the military expert," he huffed. "I have you to handle that stuff. Ok, in that case, we have a target. Jump coordinates are programmed in."

We waited until Simms told me all stations were at battle stations, then I pressed the button to activate the nanofabric restraints for holding me in the command chair.

"Ready on your signal," Reed told me.

"Jump option Alpha."

Hunting for a starship in the vastness of space is a pain in the *ass*, because space is so big. Skippy thought he knew where the target destroyer was likely to have jumped to next, so we jumped outside that area, and set our sensors to look for the faint signs of gamma radiation. The Universe must have been setting us up for something bad, because we detected a gamma ray burst within three minutes of jumping in. The news got even better: the enemy ship was eight lightminutes away. That gave us a crucial advantage, the gamma ray burst we had created would not reach the target for another five minutes. We could see them, but they couldn't see us yet. Sometimes, the glacial pace at which light crawls through spacetime is a good thing.

With one eye on the clock, mindful that we only had five minutes to make a decision and act one way or another, I asked for advice. "What do you think, Skippy?"

"Looks good to me, Joe," he made a sound like stifling a yawn.

"How sure are you of the target's position?"

"As sure as I can be," he was irritated with me. "That ship could have jumped away four and a half minutes ago, and we wouldn't know it."

"I know *that*." Keeping my own irritation from showing wasn't easy. "My question is, how sure are you of where that ship is right now?" The reason I asked is that Maxolhx ships could control and focus the gamma ray burst of their jumps, so we had to infer the jump location from detecting very faint backscatter of gamma rays off stray hydrogen atoms or other fine space dust. Skippy is incomparably magnificent, but even he had to rely on the sensors aboard our ship. Also, the kitties had excellent stealth gear, so we could not actually *see* the target ship. We had to guess where it was, in a bubble of probability that was always too large for my comfort.

"I am sure enough. We will know for certain when we attempt to jump. If the target ship is where I think it is, our jump wormhole will be deflected away from it."

"No trying to force it this time?" He had confessed to me about how his stubborn arrogance had blown our drive during our fateful last attack.

"I promise that I will let the jump computer handle the transition."

That wasn't good enough for me, so I added "And?"

"*And*, I won't override the safety mechanisms of the jump system."

"Good."

"Even though I am *way* smarter than that stupid thing."

"Skippy," I clenched my fists.

"And if anyone knows how jump physics really works, it is *me* and not some-"

"Just let the stupid thing so its job, Ok? Promise me?"

"I will promise, if that gets you to shut up about it."

"Deal. Reed, jump us in, before Skippy decides to get creative."

We jumped in, active sensors hammering away to burn through the enemy's stealth and pinpoint their location. Skippy is an arrogant, untrustworthy shithead, but he is also damned good at his job. The destroyer was within one hundredth of a lightsecond from where he predicted it would be. "Weapons on standby," I ordered. "Transmit the message."

We did not need to blow that ship to dust to accomplish our goal. All we needed to do was show that our fearsome ghost ship was still in the fight, that the Maxolhx still had to be on alert for us, and that they would not know where we would hit them next until we struck without warning.

Our message, created by Skippy, was fairly simple. The first part was a warning: We will not shoot at you unless you are stupid enough to shoot at us. The second part was a taunt: Nyah nyah nyah, we are not dead. The third part was a variation on the usual manifesto, an incoherent harangue about how the Maxolhx must cease their unjustified attacks on the peaceful Bosphuraq people, blah blah

blah. Someone in the Maxolhx intelligence office had to listen to Skippy's manifesto each time, and I actually felt sorry for whatever poor asshole got stuck hearing the revolutionary call to action, which by now had grown to well over an hour of mouth-frothing angry rhetoric.

Were the Maxolhx stupid enough to shoot at us, even after we warned them not to?

What do you think?

"Shit," I was actually sad when the destroyer painted us with its target-acquisition sensors, and began firing maser beams. "Simms, whatever you gotta do, just get this over with quick, Ok?"

"Sorry for the inconvenience, Sir," she didn't turn toward me, but I heard the verbal wink. At her console, she directed the weapons stations to hammer the target. First our antienergy pulse cannon knocked back the enemy's shields, followed by particle beams and right behind that directed energy, a trio of railgun darts tore into the destroyer's thin layer of armor. It was a sign of either my confidence in my ship and crew, or my stupidity, that during the brief battle, I was thinking about making a sandwich for lunch. There we were, toe to toe with a senior species warship, something that would have terrified me a few short months ago. Now, all I wanted was for the inevitable to be over.

"Enemy main power is out," Simms reported.

"Cease fire," I ordered cautiously. "Skippy, signal them that we don't want to fight, and- Oh, hell." Just then, the destroyer's missile launchers began ripple-firing deadly weapons at us. Already, I could hear the high-pitched whine of our point-defense cannons sending maser energy at the incoming threats. "Simms, give those idiots what they asked for."

She took control of one weapon station, selecting a single railgun and sent a dart straight at a missile magazine that we knew was buried at the center of the destroyer. One hit, that's all it took to shatter that little ship, and we jumped away before we wasted any more maser fire on fending off missiles.

That ended our thirteenth attack, which was outstandingly successful for us, despite the enemy's attempt to lure us into a trap. We accounted for two heavy cruisers, a star carrier, four patrol cruisers and five destroyers blown to hell. Plus two heavy cruisers and a star carrier sustained significant damage. The damage to our ship was either repaired or soon would be. In fact, the fight gave Skippy an opportunity to refine his damage control procedures, so his bots could in the future respond faster and more efficiently. In addition to the combat action itself, we had been able to use the battle to develop, test and implement a new technique for countering enemy damping fields. Finally, we demonstrated a new ability to jump deep into the atmosphere of a gas giant planet and conceal our presence there. Like, I said, it was an outstandingly successful mission.

Oh, you don't think our attack was the smashing success that I described? Then obviously, you have never written an after-action report. The key is to make yourself look good, no matter how badly you screwed up. Believe me, plenty of other people will point out your screw-ups in their own reports on the battle, there is no need for you to rat yourself out. The Army will read between the lines and figure out what really happened, and anyway, everything I said was true. Twenty enemy ships entered the fight, and we destroyed or severely damaged fifteen of them, without us losing our ship or suffering a single casualty. One of the apex species in the galaxy set a clever trap for us, and we not only got away, we ended the fight by *taunting* them, assuring the Maxolhx fleet would be chasing their own tails trying to catch us for months or even years to come, without us having to do anything.

Yes, we barely escaped, but the Maxolhx threw a supremely powerful force at us, and they came away with *nothing*. That was good news and bad news for us. The good news was, many or most of their heavy warships would be tied up by having to provide escorts for cargo vessels, and light warships could not risk traveling without a heavy escort. Even large capital ships could not travel alone, a fact that would greatly restrict the unchallenged freedom of movement the kitties had enjoyed for millennia. More importantly, and more satisfying to us, was that we had the Maxolhx *seriously* humiliated and pissed off. They no longer had the aura of invulnerability, and their client species knew it. No more could the kitties rule their empire by fear and intimidation alone, they had to take direct action to enforce their will across their far-flung territory. We knew from intercepted messages that the Maxolhx leadership was very concerned about other clients following the lead of the Bosphuraq, and either actively breaking away, or pushing for looser restrictions on their actions. The Maxolhx were so worried about their coalition squabbling internally, they were debating what concessions to offer the Bosphuraq in exchange for stopping the ghost ship attacks.

So, that was all goodness to us.

The bad news was, our target-rich environment was rapidly disappearing. Any Maxolhx ships away from the security of their bases would be in formations large and strong enough to deter us from attacking. Our options for the ghost ship continuing to hit the kitties were shrinking and soon would effectively be gone.

Our Happy Time was over.

That wasn't my real worry.

What I feared was that, even if we did find a target that was worth the risk, we couldn't trust our intel. The kitties had fooled Skippy once, they could do it again. The only certainty was that the enemy would try to set another trap for us, and the next time, they would not be taking any chances. We would not be fighting slow heavy cruisers and a handful of lightly-armed escorts. The enemy would be sure to throw battleships and battlecruisers at us, and a lot of them. Whatever we did next, we had to be extra careful. Unless someone dreamed up a better idea, my plan was for the ghost ship to appear in Bosphuraq star systems, broadcast propaganda and jump away before any Maxolhx ships in the area could react. My plan was a minimum-risk way to remind the kitties that we were still flying around and still a threat, plus encourage the Bosphuraq to keep resisting their masters in small ways.

It was a good plan, a safe plan.

And it really didn't do anything to change the fact that Earth would soon be subjected to a brutal bombardment by a very pissed off species of kitties, who would be eager to punish a victim that couldn't fight back.

So, hooray for me, I had once again made the situation worse.

CHAPTER SIXTEEN

After jumping away from the destroyer that had committed suicide-by-battlecruiser, we jumped to that day's alternate rendezvous site to meet the *Flying Dutchman*. It was great seeing our old star carrier again, it was even better seeing all the spare Lego pieces clustered around that ship's shortened frame. The Dutchman also carried supplies like extra missiles that didn't fit into *Valkyrie's* magazines, various spare parts we had stripped out of the ships we captured, and anything else that we might need in the future.

Standing orders for Chang were to wait in stealth a few lighthours from a battle zone, far enough away for safety and close enough to rescue Skippy, if *Valkyrie* got into serious trouble or was destroyed. Skippy's new super-sized mancave escape pod aboard our stolen battlecruiser was almost like a small dropship, it even was equipped with its own stealth field. If *Valkyrie* had been lost in our thirteenth battle, Chang would have waited days or weeks until he was sure the area was clear, then he would have jumped his ship in to ping Skippy. If we had lost *Valkyrie* in the clouds of the gas giant, the escape pod would automatically take Skippy up into orbit, to wait for eventual rescue. Maybe some of the crew could have boarded escape pods also, that was not really a priority for us. If the situation was so bad that we needed to eject Skippy's pod, the odds were no humans were getting out of there alive. Plus, we couldn't risk an enemy capturing a pod and finding humans huddled in there. Skippy's pod was modified so that if it was about to be captured, it would self-destruct, and Skippy would float away with the rest of the debris. If that ever happened, SOP was for the Dutchman to wait in stealth for ten days to make sure the area was clear, then jump in to search for the beer can.

Anyway, fortunately Chang hadn't needed to do anything. I did feel bad for him and everyone else aboard his ship, including Nagatha. They had all waited and worried for over a week after we jumped away from the battle. Nagatha had painstakingly analyzed the sensor data, and determined *Valkyrie* had somehow managed a very chaotic and short jump, but then we didn't appear anywhere they could detect. Nagatha had gotten into a loop of analyzing the limited data, making guesses about what could have happened, dismissing her theories and starting over. It wasn't healthy, and Chang had been worried about her. She was *pissed* at me, for making her fear we had all been killed. No amount of apologies from me made her feel better, until Chang and I swapped jobs and I came aboard the *Dutchman* for a few days while Skippy directed his bots to make repairs to *Valkyrie*. She calmed down by the second day. Part of her better mood was from having me aboard, but mostly, she was happy that I confessed I could not see a way for us to continue the ghost ship attacks.

When our break was over, I flew back to *Valkyrie* and Chang returned to his own ship. Simms had stayed aboard *Valkyrie*, I had authorized a free exchange of crews, so her sweetie Frank Muller had flown over to our mighty battlecruiser, and my executive officer was in a pretty good mood most of the time. Her good mood was gone when she walked into my office, holding a tablet. It was our regular morning meeting and I hadn't expected anything unusual, Skippy was still working hard to get the ship fixed and upgraded, so we were just drifting in deep space. Exercises outside the ship were cancelled until all repairs were completed, there was no flight training except in simulators, and the STAR team was keeping fit as best they could.

Simms sat down, looked at that tablet in her hands, took a breath, and looked up at me. "Sir, I, I went into Desai's cabin. It needed to be done, and," she let out a breath. What she didn't say was that I should have taken care of that task. She flipped her tablet around so it faced me. "I've got most of her TA-50, some of it-"

"Oh, you've got to be kid- *Seriously*?" I exploded at her and immediately regretted it. "Sorry."

"All property has to be accounted for. Those are the regs," she gave me a shrug.

She was right. Table of Allowances number 50 was a list of the gear assigned to a soldier, from body armor to canteens. You got whatever gear your unit thought you needed for the situation, and you signed a receipt, I think that one was form DA-2062. Something like that. When the Merry Band of Pirates was made an official unit of UNEF, someone somewhere decided we needed a governing organization that was more of a real bureaucracy than the thrown-together mishmash of the Expeditionary Force. When the ExForce left Earth the first time, each of the five major militaries involved kept their own organizations, gear and rules. The Merry Band of Pirates was small and unified enough that we could use one set of rules, so the question was, whose set of rules? Rather than endlessly arguing over details, UNEF pressed the Easy Button and decided that, since I was a US Army officer, then US Army regulations would be our basic rules for governance. They made *me* responsible for assuring compliance with a vast set of regs I didn't even know existed. So, during our current mission, I had dumped the whole mess in the lap of my executive officer. You might think that was not fair of me, but I really did it for the benefit of Simms. The extra work built character. Or it prepared her for a future command. Or some other good reason that I can't think of right now. All I know is, someone needed to play Super Mario Cart, and Simms wasn't going to do it.

Anyway, once we jumped away from Earth, I pretty much unofficially tossed the official rulebook in a drawer and forgot about most of it. Yes, I kept up the daily reports that both the Army and UNEF required, but we did not sweat irrelevant details like haircuts. The STAR team let their hair go shaggy and grew beards if they wanted, that had typically been a privilege of the green side special operators, on Earth and beyond. I extended the same lax rules to the blue side. We all got haircuts and shaved or trimmed beards as necessary before returning to Earth anyway, and I had more important shit to worry about.

So, when Simms mentioned that not all the items in Desai's gear listed in her TA-50 had been located, I was tempted to delete the damned form. That would have been a mistake. If we ever got back to Earth, I would need all the goodwill I could get, and pissing off the United States Army was not a way to get on their good side. Plus, someone somewhere would see that not all of Desai's issued gear had been accounted for, and dock her pay for the difference. Like I said, the Army is my family. It is also a huge bureaucracy.

Holding out a hand for her tablet, I hoped Simms knew I wasn't angry with her. "Let me see the list, please. Is any of the missing gear stuff she might have had with her in the dropship?"

"Possibly, some of it."

"Shit. Whatever we can't account for, if we get back to Earth," I looked up at her. "*When* we get back to Earth, I'll sign for it. Damn it. We're going to have the same issue with everyone we lost, aren't we?"

"We have been a little lax with the rules, Sir."

"I am not going to tell people they need to lay their gear out for inspection now. Screw it," I slammed a fist on the table. "*None* of this shit matters!"

"It's just us out here. What *does* matter?"

"Getting home. Saving whatever, whoever we can."

"And what are we doing about that?"

I knew what she was asking. We had been jumping our mighty *Valkyrie* around the galaxy, on a campaign that was scaring the shit out of the Maxolhx, and was not doing a damned thing to save our homeworld. "I hear you, XO. I don't know that there is anything we *can* do. If we run the blockade with *Valkyrie* at this point, we will only give the kitties more reason to send more warships to Earth, sooner."

She reached across the desk, took back her tablet and pointed at the list of gear that was missing. "I will handle this, Sir."

"What do you need me to do?"

"Put on your thinking cap. Find a way to save Earth."

"Simms. Come on, give me a break. We both know that's impossible."

"Sir, for the Merry Band of Pirates, any situation is only impossible until you decide that it isn't. Then we get to work."

"I will," I looked longingly at the drawer where my tablet was stored. No playing video games for me, until I had thought up a way to save the freakin' world again. "Well, if you've seen my thinking cap lying around somewhere, let me know, Ok? I can use all the help I can get."

"Hey, Skippy," I groaned as I took off my boots while sitting on the edge of the bed. The alien bed was still not fully trusted, but I was no longer sleeping on the floor. I did sleep in sweatpants, with a knife and zPhone in the pockets.

"Hey, Joe. You sound tired."

"It's been a long day, you know?"

"I do. It has not been easy for me either. You joke about me being Mad Doctor Skippy, but I have to provide medical care for the crew. It's hard seeing people in pain."

"That's true. Sorry I joked about-"

"Unless they're assholes. In that case, screw 'em."

"Oh, sure," he made me laugh.

"Or if *I* caused their pain. In that case, hee hee," he giggled, "it can be funny."

"Uh, you-".

"Funny for *me*, I mean."

"Yeah, I got that."

"Unfortunately, *this* is no fun for anyone. Joe, it is *hard* seeing Margaret trying to learn how to control her body all over again."

"She is doing much better. She was dancing, right? That must be good." Suddenly, I feared maybe the progress I had seen might have been my own wishful thinking. "Is she better?"

He sighed. "She is. Joe, I could not have wished for a better patient. Margaret is usually determined and cheerful about her condition. She doesn't complain, she does exactly what I recommend she does. She-" He broke off talking, and for a moment it sounded like he was sobbing. "Damn it," he sniffled. "I wish she *would* complain, or yell at me, or something. Does that make sense? I feel," his sigh was utterly miserable. "Like a terrible person."

"It does make sense, Skippy. And that doesn't make you a bad person. It just makes you normal. That's a good thing. You are feeling frustrated and powerless. You want to do more to help her, and your other patients. But you know better than anyone what is possible and what isn't. You're doing all you can."

His avatar balled up its little fists and shook them in anguish and frustration. "It's not *enough*, Joe."

"Skippy, this may be hard to hear, but there are limits to even your awesomeness. Her recovery is proceeding on schedule, right?"

"Well, yes. Better than I expected, actually. She had significant brain damage, Joe. Worse than I thought."

"Will she be, herself again?"

"Yes. Not exactly, you understand. She went through a terrible trauma, that would affect her even if her brain had not suffered injury. Fortunately, the damage affected her motor function and memories more than the parts of her brain that represent her personality, and her sense of self."

Acting casual, I asked a question that I feared. "Her personality shouldn't change much?" My casual attitude was betrayed by the squeak I added to the last word.

"She is certainly acting like the Margaret Adams we know. This morning, she was consoling Smythe when he was discouraged about his own progress."

"She was *consoling* him?" I could not imagine that.

"Come on, Joe. It's Margaret. I meant, *her* kind of consoling."

"Oh. She bitch-slapped him for whining?"

"You know it," he chuckled. "She did say 'Sir' after she pointed out what a crybaby he was being about the therapy for his bionic legs."

"Ha! Ok, Ok, maybe she is going to be all right."

"Anyway, you called me?"

"Yeah. I need your advice. I have decided that continuing the strategy of hit-and-run attacks are our best option, while we still can." Technically, I had not decided anything. Continuing with that strategy was the choice by default, because I couldn't think of anything better for us to do.

"Yes, and you know my objections to that plan. We will need to be careful, Joe. *Valkyrie* barely escaped from our last attack."

"Ayuh, I agree." Our fateful, nearly disastrous thirteenth attack had been bad in several ways. It nearly destroyed our mighty ship. In the short term, it prevented us from causing any more havoc. Longer term, the Maxolhx would now be even more determined to trap or destroy us. Having seen that our ghost ship was not invulnerable, they would be predators who sensed weakness in their prey. Before, captains of Maxolhx ships might have hesitated to engage in battle with us. Now, they had tasted blood, we would not be able to scare them. "Don't worry, we will emphasize the 'Run' part of hit-and-run. Like you said, one ship can't cause significant damage, so what we will try to accomplish is to force the Maxolhx to focus on defense, and keep their attention on this mythical Bosphuraq faction."

"Hmmph. You *say* you will be careful, but when we get into action, you will be tempted by targets of opportunity and-"

"I will rely on your judgment to keep me from going off-mission, Skippy. Also, Simms won't allow me to do any stupid shit."

"*If* you listen to her, Joe. You are nowhere as impulsive and reckless as UNEF believes, but sometimes you still act before you think."

"We will establish objectives before each attack. Call me out anytime you think I am going off the rails, Ok?"

"You say that now, but when I try to talk some sense into you-"

"I promise to be a better listener, Ok? Hey, I want to thank you for, you know, bailing my ass out of a jam again." Mentally, I prepared for him to insult me. That was a small price to pay for not being dead.

"Oh no problem, Joe. I was worried there for a while. It is *such* a relief."

"Hey, we were *all* worried, you know?"

He stared at me, uncomprehending. "Um, what were *you* worried about?"

Blinking slowly, I stared at him. "Survival? Barely escaping from the bad guys? Does any of this sound familiar to you? Maybe you should check the news feed in your-"

"Oh, *that*," he waved a hand. "You got us in another desperate situation because you didn't think ahead, blah, blah, blah. That's nothing new, Joe. Plus, in the end, you monkeys are all doomed anyway. I was talking about something *really* important."

"More important than all of us not dying and dooming our hope of bringing people from Earth to the beta site?"

"Hey, if you were so concerned about that, maybe we shouldn't have jumped into a battle we didn't need to fight. Just sayin', you know?"

"I know, I know. That's on me, it was my fault." Having beaten myself up about my stupidity, I didn't need him piling on. Or maybe I did. "What is this really important thing that had you so concerned?"

"The recent lack of opportunities to demonstrate my awesomeness, of course! Joe, until I created a feedback loop on the enemy damping field, I hadn't done anything truly awesome since my chain of wormholes thing. I haven't done an awesome thing in, like, *forever*! My awesomeness game needs to be kept fresh, Dude!"

I blinked slowly at him. "Skippy, every time you create a shortcut by altering wormhole connections, you remind us of your extreme awesomeness."

"Sure, but, people take that for granted now," he moped. "I need to perform new and exciting awesomenesses."

"Ah." There it was. I understood the problem. Skippy, despite claiming he did not care what filthy monkeys thought of him, *craved* praise. He especially needed praise from the Merry Band of Pirates, because he respected us. Or at least, he disrespected us somewhat less than his level of disdain for every other being in the galaxy. "That's my fault, Skippy. You are *so* awesome, I never even think about all the stuff you do every day. Hey! Like, I was feeling like crap, and now you have made my day."

"That is not exactly awesome." He rolled his eyes.

"It is awesome to me."

"What-eh-VER," he tilted his head and made a 'W' of his thumbs and index fingers. "My displays of awesomeness depend, *ugh*, on you. Your monkey brain dreams up crazy crap for me to do, so keep it coming. Actually, hmm. I mostly do new awesome stuff when your idiocy gets us into a desperate mess. So, really, please keep doing short-sighted, stupid things, Joe."

"How about I do smart things instead?"

"Oh," he snickered. "Like *that's* gonna happen."

"Yeah. Hey, Simms told me I have to think of a way to save Earth again, and I got nothin'. Have you made any progress on unlocking your memories?"

"Ugh. Not really." He took off his ginormous admiral's hat and scratched his head. "How will my *memories* save your homeworld?"

"Well, I was kind of hoping you would remember how to control Sentinels. You know, make them squash the rotten kitties for us."

"What? Dude, seriously? *That's* your plan?"

"I told you, I don't *have* a plan."

"Huh. You can forget about me magically using Sentinels as attack dogs. If they did wake up, they would probably wipe out Earth as their first target."

"What? Why?"

"Because, numbskull, we know Sentinels punish species for unauthorized use of Elder technology."

"We haven't used any-"

"*I* am Elder technology," he reminded me. "You monkeys got me to screw with the wormhole network. I broke an Elder wormhole, on your suggestion. You think Sentinels will be happy about that?"

"Shit," I slumped back in my chair. Then slid down halfway off the seat, totally defeated. "That was my one last hope, Skippy."

"Um-"

"It wasn't a realistic hope, but it was the best I got."

"Well, look on the bright side, Joe."

"The *bright* side?"

"Sure. Now you can fantasize about a whole *new* unrealistic plan to save the world. That should buy you at least a couple weeks of blissful ignorance."

Tilting the chair back, I closed my eyes. "Can you go away while I wallow in misery?"

"I thought misery loves company?"

"Not today, Skippy. Not today."

Admiral Urkan was aboard his flagship when the shocking report reached him. His deputy of operations was there also, and shared the shock, the anger and the sick feeling of impending doom. "A disaster," Urkan said under his breath as he tore his attention away from the message scrolling through his mind. At such times, he wished the Maxolhx still relied on more primitive means of communication, such as visual display devices. If the report had arrived on a crude tablet or holographic interface, he could have tossed the tablet away, or wiped the hologram out of existence. Instead, the file was cued up in his memory, and it was already *there*. It lurked in his consciousness whether he wanted to think about it or not. "Two heavy cruisers lost, two others damaged so badly they will not be capable of combat duty for two or three months. Both star carriers had to be self-destructed," he counted the tally of destruction. Urkan himself had made the call to abandon the damaged star carriers and the last surviving destroyer. With the ghost ship still in fighting condition and possibly lurking in the area, it was too risky to send in salvage ships without heavy escorts. He could not spare heavy escorts, they were all needed elsewhere in the sector. "We threw twenty ships into the fight, and four, only four! Came back undamaged. The worst part is the ghost ship *taunted* us when it jumped back to attack again." Privately, Urkan thought the truly worst part was the captain of the taunted destroyer had needlessly caused the destruction of his ship, but the admiral kept that to himself. "This was *my* plan, and it was a complete disaster."

Subcommander Seelace could not disagree with his admiral's statement. He disagreed anyway, because part of his job was to offer differing perspectives to the senior officer. "An unfortunate outcome to be sure, but not a complete disaster. Your forces had the ghost ship surrounded, and nearly destroyed it."

"Bah," Urkan dismissed his aide's words, knowing them to be false comfort. None of his fellow admirals would see the stunning result of the battle as anything other than a pure disaster. "*Nearly* is not good enough."

"May I remind you that, for the first time, we have detailed data on the capabilities and characteristics of the ghost ship? It is *not* invincible, you have proven that. That ship is certainly damaged, and where can it go to get replacement components? We have determined that it is, or was, an *Extinction*-class battlecruiser."

"A heavily-modified battlecruiser," Urkan noted sourly.

"Nevertheless, it is based on one of our ships. Its performance is in most cases identical to a standard *Extinction*-class. It is *not* invincible," he repeated.

"It does not have to be invincible," Urkan refused to be comforted. "The enemy demonstrated a new ability to disrupt our damping fields. Who knows what technology they have not yet revealed to us?"

"Admiral, we have analyzed the damping field issue. True, that feedback technique is a new capability," Seelace admitted. "However, if the ghost ship tries to use feedback again, they will encounter a nasty surprise. We know how to retune our damping field generators to prevent them from being disrupted by feedback; that information is being distributed in emergency flash messages to all ships and stations." He did not add what the technology division of Fleet Intelligence had told him: that Maxolhx ships were not able to duplicate the feedback mechanism. The principle of the feedback technique was understood well enough, the problem was that even the incredible AIs of the Rindhalu could not process data and react fast enough to create their own feedback loop. Their AIs simply could not *think* fast enough, and the idea that the enemy had AIs more advanced was deeply troubling. "The taunting was unfortunate, yet I do see that action as recklessness by the enemy. They are becoming bold to the point of being foolish. Also, we know their ship was damaged in the battle. Their options for replenishment and repair have to be limited. We can run it to ground."

"We have to *find* it first. Luring the ghost ship into an ambush didn't work. I fear now that Fleet Headquarters will listen to Reichert's foolish plan to blockade wormholes. That will tie up a large portion of the fleet and accomplish little. Seelace, *how* could this have happened? We planned an ambush, and somehow, the enemy hit *us* when we didn't expect an attack. Before we were ready."

"Clearly, the enemy intercepted our communications," Seelace said, as if it were not blindingly obvious.

"We were *so* careful! All orders were given verbally, in person. There were no messages to be intercepted."

"Unless someone ignored your instructions."

"If some brainless idiot-"

"Admiral, forgive me for saying so, but I have learned that most mistakes come from someone who did not get the memo. It could be as simple as a junior supply officer sending a request for particular equipment, because they were preparing for their ship's part in the ambush. My people are investigating. That is not my most serious concern."

"It is not?"

"No. We can accept that the ghost ship might have captured intact quantum interchangers, when they took the ship. That is not supposed to happen, just as battlecruisers are not supposed to be *captured*."

"That problem is solving itself. We are replacing all interchangers tagged to battlecruisers. That process will soon be complete."

"While Headquarters did act promptly to replace interchangers throughout the fleet, battlecruisers are not the only vulnerability. We now know that some components of the ghost ship might have come from a heavy cruiser, so those interchangers also need to be replaced. There are many more heavy cruisers than battlecruisers, replacing all of them will be a major, sustained effort. That is also not my greatest concern."

"No? What could be worse than our most secure communications method being compromised?"

"Worse is thinking we have resolved the problem, when we have not."

"Explain."

"We know about the ghost ship. I fear what we do *not* know. Consider this, Admiral: the enemy has captured more than one of our heavy ships. We thought such a feat was impossible. Even the Rindhalu lack the ability to board and take one of our capital ships. And turn that ship against us. Whatever enemy we face, if they could take a capital ship, surely they could compromise one of our relay stations."

Urkan growled, low and menacing. "Seelace, in ancient times, messengers who brought bad news could be killed, for they were considered tainted."

"We all long for those simpler days, Sir," Seelace did not allow his flare of nervousness to show. "My people have analyzed the attacks, and the message traffic the enemy must have accessed to know the location of the ships they attacked. If the ghost ship is getting information from relay stations, they must have compromised at least five of them."

Urkan let fly a string of curses so vile, it had taken his people millennia to invent them. "You are fortunate, Seelace, that I am presently unarmed."

"I am grateful for that happy circumstance."

"My oversight could be quickly undone."

"There is some potential good news. In ancient times, what was the fate of messengers who brought positive tidings?"

Urkan leaned back on his couch. "They could be showered with gifts. Food, drink, the company of willing companions, other pleasurable enticements."

"I seek only the joy of serving my admiral."

"If that were true, then you would be a fool. I have no use for fools. What good news could come, from such a disaster?"

"While we have been talking, my people have engaged the Operations AIs to analyze the battle. They believe the ghost ship was surprised at encountering such a strong force. I agree with the analysis. Nothing else about the enemy's actions makes sense. Sir, the ghost ship probably thought it was attacking only the small force you used as a lure. That is how they were nearly surrounded."

"So," Urkan considered. "Not a complete disaster," he reluctantly agreed. "They hit us before we were prepared, where we did not expect to be hit? But they also expected only our decoy force, not to fly into our ambush?"

"Nothing else makes sense. Also, our AIs have analyzed the performance of the ghost ship. It is powerful, we have no explanation of how that ship could generate so much power. But its actions are *slow*. And clumsy. The Bosphuraq might have replaced the original AI-"

"That," Urkan growled, "*is* impossible." He knew how the substrate of AIs were woven into the ship's hulls. It would be easier to build a new ship than to tear out the AI and replace it.

"It is more likely they have somehow compromised the ship's AI, and are forcing it to work with them. A compromised AI could explain why the ghost ship's actions, its control of weapons, its maneuvering, is so slow compared to the specifications of an *Extinction*-class ship."

"That, at least, is something we can use. Seelace, I will not shoot you this time. Nor will you be rewarded."

The aide bowed his head in exaggerated fashion. "To serve is my reward."

That drew the only laugh Admiral Urkan enjoyed on that fateful day.

CHAPTER SEVENTEEN

A minor issue we had to deal with, when splitting the crew between two ships, was the exercise equipment. The Maxolhx did not need to lift weights or run or do any other sweat-inducing nonsense to keep fit, their genetic enhancements and the nanomachines embedded throughout their bodies kept them in peak physical condition. Apparently, they did need to practice to maintain eye-hand coordination, balance and other links between their neural circuitry and the muscles, because we found equipment for different types of gymnastics, something like throwing darts, and other recreational gear. Also, they enjoyed playing sports. There was a court for a sport sort of like basketball except the sides of the court curved upward, so players could sprint along the wall, and they must have bounced balls off the walls and even the ceiling to pass and make shots. Some of our STAR team tried playing the game, with a regular basketball instead of the heavy ball used by the Maxolhx. Kapoor put a stop to that game after one of his team, who shall remain anonymous though her name rhymes with 'Katie Frey', ran halfway up a wall and came down to slam dunk a shot, slamming into Justin Grudzien and nearly spraining his shoulder.

Personally, I was disappointed when Kapoor ordered the door to the court locked. As the commander, I understood we couldn't afford to lose any more people to injuries. As an idiot, I thought the game looked like a fun challenge, and I wanted to play.

Maybe later.

Anyway, we were not so lucky with our unenhanced biological bodies. We needed to sweat and run and jump and lift and strain to keep our bodies fit. The small crew aboard the Flying Dutchman needed a gym for their own fitness and morale, so we left a bunch of the equipment there. To fit out a gym aboard *Valkyrie*, we transferred equipment by dropship, and Skippy had the ship's fabricators make additional gear. We could have had a wider variety of fitness options, but Skippy needed the fabricators to concentrate on making parts for the ship he had snapped together from Lego pieces.

Anyway, I was on a rowing machine, which was one of my least favorite pieces of equipment in the gym. It was a great low-impact workout, I was always dripping with sweat and my arms and legs felt like jelly after a rowing session, but I did not enjoy the experience. Maybe the problem was that rowing was that, unlike running, rowing was just an unnatural motion. While running, or even on an elliptical trainer or an exercise bike, your legs pumped up and down and your muscle memory did most of the mental work. While running or biking, I was able to zone out and let my mind wander. I could listen to an audiobook, and let the narrator's voice make me forget I was in a gym aboard an alien starship far from home. Sometimes, my workout would be over but I kept running or biking or whatever, because the audiobook was in a suspenseful part of the story and I didn't want to stop yet.

On a rower, I had to think too much. Sure, I had been doing it for long enough that I did not actually need to think much, just enough that I couldn't zone out. To get a smooth motion, I had to coordinate my legs from ankles to hips, with my back and my arms. There is a rumor that more than once, I had not been paying attention while rowing, and pulled back too far so the bar smacked me in the chin. That rumor is vicious and hurtful, although it did not hurt as viciously as my bleeding lip that time I really smacked myself hard.

So, I was concentrating on not embarrassing myself, when over the hip-hip music thumping out of the gym speakers, I heard a soft, high-pitched whistle. That sound indicated a routine announcement or alert would be made, and a moment later, there was a single soft chime, like a bell. Without needing to look up the significance of the signal on my zPhone, I knew the ship was about to make a minor course correction. Skippy had reprogrammed our new ship's alert system to use the same sounds as we had gotten used to aboard the *Dutchman*, and only the new people needed to check their phones or request more information from Skippy. And only a very new person would make the rookie mistake of bothering Skippy for information they should already know. Anyone directly affected would have received a direct call from Skippy or the bridge crew anyway, so the alerts were more of an FYI nature. And if we had people outside the ship, a course correction maneuver would be coordinated with them well in advance. Alerts prevented people from doing something stupid. Since stupid things aboard an immensely powerful alien warship could be catastrophic, it was best to let everyone know what was going on.

Because *Valkyrie* was at the moment drifting in formation with the *Flying Dutchman*, I know the action was technically station-keeping rather than a course correction. The upgraded *Dutchman* was performing adjustments to her new normal-space propulsion system, so most maneuvers to keep our ships in formation were being performed by our big battlecruiser.

There was another, single, soft chime a minute later, indicating the maneuver was complete. I had not felt anything, which was perfectly normal. Only radical movements were felt at all by the crew. Basically, if the ship moved so violently that the artificial gravity system could not fully compensate, then feeling the ship move would be the last thing anyone needed to worry about. It was-

Huh.

I *did* feel movement.

What the hell?

I was about to shout for Skippy when I realized the *ship* was not moving, the stupid rowing machine was. "Damn it," I muttered under my breath, which was easier than talking, because I was breathing so hard. The front of the machine had shifted while I used it. It had rocked side to side and sort of walked itself across the floor, until it was now almost touching the treadmill beside it. Apparently, my rowing motion had been anything but smooth, and also apparently I *had* zoned out while rowing, because I had not noticed that my right elbow was close to smacking the treadmill.

As an excuse to take a break from an exercise I hated, I stopped rowing, got off the seat, and lifted the front of the machine to put it back into position. There were no scuff marks on whatever super-tough material the floor was made of, just a faint residue left by the rubber pads on the bottom of the machine. Kneeling down,

I rubbed fingertips along the floor. It felt smooth but not slippery, so the machine had not just skidded freely across the surface. My guess was, when I pulled back on the rowing handle, I had lifted the front slightly, causing it to walk sideways. It was ironic that the course correction chime had sounded while I was rowing, because I had needed my own station-keeping maneuver to-

Holy shit.

Station-keeping.

Halfway out the doorway, I remembered that I needed to wipe down the machine as a courtesy to the next person who wanted to use it. Our new temporary gym did not have towels, so we had a table with packages of baby wipes. In the field, especially in dry, dusty conditions, baby wipes can be a soldier's best friend. That is a trick I learned in Nigeria, which had a dry summer the time I was there. How do you clean dust and grit off goggles, night-vision gear, camera lenses, and the lubricated parts of rifles? That's right, baby wipes. Another trick to keep grit out of a rifle barrel is to slide a condom over the muzzle. You could use a balloon which is made of a tougher material, but balloons are not easy to find in the bush, while soldiers can always get condoms.

I know, that is shocking, and I can assure people who have sons or daughters in the military, that certainly does not apply to *your* precious Bobby or Susie. The rest of us, I am sorry to say, are a very bad influence and we are very, very sorry.

Ok, back to the real world.

Quickly wiping my sweat off the machine, I then dashed out the doorway and ran on slightly shaky legs toward my office, until my slow brain reminded me that was too public a forum for me to ask potentially stupid questions of Skippy. So, I tried to halt my run in the middle of a passageway intersection and stumbled, staggering against a bulkhead corner. A pilot was walking down the side passageway, her mouth open in silent surprise as I pushed off the bulkhead and used the energy to propel me to the left, dodging in front of her and bouncing off a wall. "Parkour," I gasped and picked up the pace, trying to make it seem like my clumsiness was intentional. I had done something like parkour for real, although the Army called it 'obstacle course running' and the only obstacle in that passageway was a pilot who held up her hands and stepped to her left to stay out of her clumsy commander's way.

Regardless, I reached my cabin with only a couple of bruises, and the door slid closed behind me automatically. "Skippy!"

"Joe!" He responded. "Are we just shouting each other's names, or is there a point to this interruption of me doing something very important?"

"There is a point. Please, Oh Greatest of All Great Ones, could you spare a tiny bit of your vast intellect to humor an ignorant monkey?"

"Depends. If you are going to argue with me again about 'The Cat in the Hat', I already *told* you-"

"It's not about that. Except that you're wrong, and-"

"Ugh. Seriously? Joe, I wrote an eight-thousand-page brief to support my-"

"Eight thousand pages is a '*brief*'?"

"It is twenty four thousand pages, if you include all the footnotes and references. If you like, I could send just the summary to you, that is only twelve hundred pages."

"I would not like," I said in a panic. If he sent me the summary, he would expect me to read every damned page, and my life would become a living hell as he hit me with pop quizzes for the next freakin' month. My attention span is about the length of an eight-slide PowerPoint presentation, or maybe a comic book if it is a really good one. "How about I stipulate," I used a legal term I heard on TV without having more than a vague idea what it meant, "that you are right about 'The Cat in The Hat', and we move on?"

"Mmph. What about 'Hop on Pop'?" He asked.

"Clearly," I squeezed my eyes shut so he wouldn't see my rolling them. "That book flagrantly encourages children to be violent against their fathers, and leads to, uh," I tried to remember his objection to that classic children's book. "A breakdown in societal order and people not using their turn signals, and, uh-"

"Pineapple on pizza, Joe," he shuddered. "If that is not a sign that civilization is collapsing, I don't know what is."

Personally, I like pineapple and ham on pizza, but maybe that's because when I was growing up in my tiny Northern Maine hometown, pineapples seemed impossibly exotic. Even if they came from a can. Anyway, it's best not to argue with a being who could create a submind to continue the argument until the Milky Way and Andromeda galaxies collide. "I bow to your superior reasoning, Ok?"

"You say that *now*, but when-"

"Trust me, I really do not ever want to argue about Doctor Seuss again."

"Because you recognize that he was a subversive agent who was determined to destroy the foundations of your society by poisoning the minds of children, or because you are tired of losing arguments?"

"Whatever reason gets you to shut the hell up about it?"

"Once again, the score is Skippy one, ignorant monkey zero. What do you want to talk about?"

"I have a question about something you said. You told me the Sleeping Beauty wormhole has drifted off a force line, because its station-keeping mechanism is broken."

"I don't know if the mechanism is *broken*, Joe. It could simply be malfunctioning, or disconnected from that end of the wormhole."

"Ok, sure, whatever. You don't know what you don't know. You once mentioned something about a wormhole that fell into a black hole, or some other star."

"That is extremely rare, however it has happened."

"Are those also cases where the wormhole's station-keeping motor wasn't working?"

"It's not a *motor*, Joe. But, yes. The station-keeping mechanism normally guides the wormhole's position in local spacetime, to keep it away from stars, planets, other wormholes, and to remain attached to force lines, if that is desired. You already know this, so what is your question?"

"I'm trying to think of the best way to say this."

"Because that sack of gray mush in your head can't organize your thoughts?"

"No. Because I don't want you to laugh at my question."

There was a pause. "Dude, seriously. You think anything you might say could *lower* my opinion of your intelligence?"

"I guess not. Ok, here's my question, then. Do you have access to the station-keeping mechanism of Elder wormholes?"

"Um. Hmm. Let me think about that. Huh. That is a good question, Joe. I have never tried to access that function, because I have never needed to access that function. That is a rather low-level mechanism, I suspect the security protocols would be easy for me to bypass. Ooooh, can I guess why you asked about that?"

"Sure, why not?" It would be interesting if he understood what I was thinking. My parents had been together so long, they knew what each other was thinking and could finish the other person's sentences. If Skippy was developing an ability to think like a monkey, that would take a lot of pressure off my shoulders.

"Goodie! Ok, if this *is* what you are thinking, then you are very insightful and I am impressed. You want to know if, by me ordering Sleeping Beauty's station-keeping mechanism to reactivate and get it properly reattached to its assigned force line, that might fix the glitch affecting the local network? Then I could reopen Sleeping Beauty, without causing Gateway to reset, wake up and be out of my control?"

"Uh-" Damn it. That was *not* what I had been thinking, but I desperately wanted him to respect me. So, would it really hurt to lie and tell him I really was that smart?

Answer; yes, it would hurt. Mostly because he would figure out that I was lying. Also, because lying is wrong, so remember that, girls and boys. "No, I am a dumdum. That's not why I asked. Can you do that?"

"No. No," he shook his head sadly. "That is a stupid idea. It won't work."

Throwing up my hands, I asked "Then why did you say I would be insightful, if I asked that question?"

"Because it would demonstrate you are at least beginning to grasp the rudimentary basics of wormhole network operations. As compared to the complete ignorance you typically demonstrate, every freakin' day."

"Jeez, thanks, Skippy. Well, that was not my question at all, Mister Smartypants."

"Oh. Hey, I was trying to throw you a bone. Since you did not ask me the only even mildly intelligent potential question, go ahead and ask whatever dumbass thing is in your head."

"What is the station-keeping mechanism capable of? Can you use it to *move* a wormhole?"

"Move? Well, of course, duh. The mechanism constantly makes minor corrections to-"

"Screw minor corrections, Skippy. I want to know if you can make a wormhole move several *lightyears*."

"Holy *shit*," he gasped. "Whoa. Only a monkey brain would ask that question. Wow."

"Well? Can you do it?"

"It's not that simple, Joe. That is actually a two-part question. First, can it be done? Second, will the network accept my command to move a wormhole that far? While I ponder those questions, please tell me why you asked about moving a wormhole? What are you trying to accomplish? If you are thinking of using an Elder wormhole as a weapon-"

"A *weapon*?" It was my turn to be astonished. "How could a wormhole be a weapon?"

"You know that wormholes emerge in local spacetime, right?"

"Yeah, so?"

"So, a long time ago, when the Maxolhx were building their own wormhole network, they-"

"*Whoa!*" I waved my hands. "Hit the rewind on that. You just blew my freakin' mind. The kitties built their own network of wormholes?"

"Yes. Didn't I tell you about that?"

"Hell no. Pretty sure I would remember something like that."

"Ugh. It was probably in that picture book of 'Important Things Little Joey Needs To Know', and you didn't read it."

"I didn't read it, because that book was insulting, you little shithead." He had given me an illustrated book that looked like the Berenstain Bears, but the bears in his book taught lessons about math and physics and other nerdy stuff that put me right to sleep. After using a marker to draw beards and fangs on the bears, I had thrown that book away. "Did they succeed? Do the Maxolhx have their own wormhole network?"

"No, and no. The kitties never succeeded in keeping a wormhole stable. All they were able to do was establish jump wormholes that stayed open longer than normal, and projected slightly farther than a jump wormhole created by a starship. The experiments failed because the platforms they used to create the wormholes could only be used one time, and offered no major advantage over starships simply jumping on their own. They also lost several test ships when the unstable wormholes collapsed as the ships transitioned through. After consuming an *enormous* amount of resources over four thousand years of utter failure, the research project was cancelled. However, the kitties then turned their attention to using their wormholes as weapons. Their ultimate plan was to open wormholes inside, or very close to, planets occupied by the Rindhalu."

"That would be an awesome weapon."

"Eh, not so much. Remember how difficult it was to jump *Valkyrie* inside a planet? That only worked because of my unique awesomeness. You know how tricky it is just to jump a ship into low orbit around a planet."

"I do," I nodded. That was part of my pilot training. Targeting an inbound jump near a planet or other massive gravity well was difficult, and got more difficult as you tried to target the inbound point closer to the planet. "The Maxolhx gave up on the weapon project?"

"Yes. The weapon effort used material left over from the failed network project, and when the material was all used up, the effort was terminated. For the amount of energy required to open a wormhole inside a planet, they could cause more destruction in a much easier fashion. Besides, the Rindhalu have a defense around their major worlds that prevents inbound jump endpoints from emerging within two lightseconds."

"Ok. So the kitties were not able to use their own homemade wormholes as weapons." It was a great relief that we didn't need to worry about the Maxolhx tearing Earth apart with wormholes. Then I realized that was stupid. Based on the weapons aboard our captured battlecruiser, the kitties had plenty of horrible ways to destroy our homeworld. "Hey," I asked with a sick feeling in the pit of my stomach. "Could *we* use an Elder wormhole against a planet?"

"No. No way, dude. The network safety protocols would never accept my commands to do something destructive like that."

"Oh, thank God," I hid my face behind my hands for a moment.

"Wait," Skippy was confused. "You are *happy* that you can't use Elder wormholes as weapons? I thought you military types always want more capabilities, more options."

"Not this time. Skippy, some capabilities are too tempting. There is such a thing as having too *much* power. That kind of power could turn me into a monster. I have already done some horrible things, things I never thought I could do. I started a civil war that is killing hundreds, maybe thousands of Kristang every day. A lot of the victims are civilians. Just on our last mission, I got the Maxolhx to hit the Bosphuraq. A lot of birdbrains civilians are dead, and they didn't *do* anything."

"May I point out that the Kristang were going to have one of their regularly-scheduled civil wars anyway, and that by forcing the conflict to begin before the major players were fully ready, we probably ensured a *lower*-intensity conflict? Or that the Bosphuraq have done a *whole lot* of really sketchy shit on their own? I told you, the Maxolhx feel the need to give their clients a beat-down every thousand years or so, to keep them in their place. Sure, this incident you sparked has been particularly brutal, and Ok, many of the sites the Maxolhx hit have been civilian research facilities. The Maxolhx have not been careful about avoiding collateral damage, so they have generally destroyed entire sites, not just the research facilities. That means a lot of support personnel, and their families, have died and-Shit, what point was I trying to make?"

"That I am not a monster already?"

"Crap. Hell, the worst part is that your plan didn't work, damn it. The Maxolhx sent a reinforced battlegroup to Earth anyway. So, all those Bosphuraq deaths were for nothing. And, um, that *is* on you, I guess."

"Is this you trying to comfort me?"

"Why would I do that?" He asked, genuinely mystified. "Joe, if you're worried about turning into a power-mad monster, the *last* thing you need is someone telling you nice happy bullshit you want to hear."

"You're right. Can you help? If you think I'm going to do something that is just *wrong*, you'll tell me?"

"Depends. Does this include things like you eating marshmallow Fluff?" He gagged.

"It most certainly does *not* include Fluff," I was indignant. "That is pure heavenly goodness and you know it."

"I seriously question your judgment about that, but, Ok. If I think you are about to do something that is morally sketchy, I will tell you about it."

"Huh," my shoulders slumped.

"What?" He asked.

"I just realized that I am relying on *you* to warn me about things that are morally sketchy."

"Hey!" He protested. "That is just-"

"Can we get back to the subject?"

"Yes, please! So, that wasn't your plan?"

"To hit a planet with an Elder wormhole? No, I hadn't even imagined that was possible. Have you finished pondering my question yet?"

"No."

"What is taking so long? You are *ponderously* pondering."

"That's because I am pondering the imponderable, you knucklehead. No one has ever thought of *moving* a freakin' wormhole. That isn't something you can do with two guys and a truck. It would help if I knew what you were trying to accomplish."

"I want to move Sleeping Beauty closer to Earth, Skippy. Like, as close as it can get."

"The closest it could get is beyond the orbit of Neptune. What good would it do to have a wormhole right next to your home solar system?"

"It would make it faster and easier to evac the planet, Skippy."

He sucked in a breath. "You want to *move* everyone off Earth? That is billions of monkeys, they can't-"

"Not everyone, Skippy. That's impossible. We couldn't get Avalon set up to support that many people. Besides, many people would refuse to go. If the UN announced we were pulling everyone off the planet because killer aliens are coming, there would be plenty of flat-Earth whackadoodle conspiracy nuts who wouldn't believe it. My opinion about that is, bonus! Leave them behind and improve the gene pool."

"True dat," he muttered.

"There are plenty of other people who just wouldn't be able to deal with leaving our homeworld behind. For emotional or religious or other reasons, they would not want to go. But people who are willing to go, the risk-takers, we need to bring as many of them to Avalon as possible. If the Sleeping Beauty wormhole is close to Earth, the *Qishan* and *Dagger* could get there by themselves, without needing the *Dutchman* to act as a star carrier. Even if we do use the *Dutchman*, a shorter trip means more cycles per month or whatever. We can move a lot more people."

"Going through Sleeping Beauty would only dump those ships in empty interstellar space, Joe."

"True. Is there any way you could move the other end of Sleeping Beauty, so it is close to another wormhole?"

"I don't know if I can move it at all, Joe."

"Let's assume you can."

"Ugh. Let's *assume* that Santa will use his magic sleigh to-"

"Can you *try* to be helpful?"

"Fine," he huffed. "How about we set some parameters, before you start expecting really ridiculous shit from me?"

"Deal."

"The near end of Sleeping Beauty is currently eight point eight lightyears from Earth, roughly in the direction of Barnard's Star, so it is in the opposite direction from Gateway. To make this work, I would need to move the near end almost nine lightyears. So, let's assume I can also move the far end that same distance. Otherwise, this is all just a waste of time."

"Agreed. Is there another wormhole within nine lightyears of Sleeping Beauty's far end?"

"While I would love to say no, because that would end this discussion, unfortunately I am cursed by being a veritable paragon of truthfulness."

"Yes, that's what everyone says about you," I said with one side of my mouth, because I was biting my lip on the other side.

"There is another wormhole within six lightyears of Sleeping Beauty on the far end. It is an active wormhole. That's the good news. The bad news is, the active wormhole gets a *lot* of traffic, and it connects way out past the Trifid Nebula. Because I know that description doesn't mean anything to you, it is a *long* way, Joe."

"You know how delivery companies like FedEx have route-planning software, that determines the easiest or shortest route between two points?"

"Most humans have similar technology on their phones now, Joe."

"Right, great. Assuming you can move both ends of Sleeping Beauty, can you use your ultra-nerdy math skills, and show me the best route from Earth to the super-duty wormhole that connects out to the Sculptor Dwarf?"

"Define 'best', Joe. Shortest? Safest? Least-"

"Safest. Show me the safest first. Then if that route takes too long to fly, we up the risk level until we find a combination of paths that is a good trade-off between safety and speed."

Crap. I should not have asked him to give me multiple options, because there were a *lot* of them. Two *hours* later, I was losing my will to live, but we had a good plan. The absolute safest option, the first one he showed me, used very isolated wormholes, but would take four months to fly one-way, even with the upgraded *Flying Dutchman*. That wasn't going to work. The option I selected would take forty-eight days to get from Earth to the beta site, if nothing went wrong. Figure a minimum of ten days at Earth to load the ships and perform maintenance, plus another ten days at Avalon to unload. No, ten days was unrealistic, better assume two weeks each to load and unload. And the transit time needed a pad to account for something going wrong, to include a safety factor. That yielded less than three roundtrips per year, which was not great. Plus, it was not really three trips each year, because some ships would need to carry food and supplies instead of people.

"Shit," I slumped back in my chair. "That's no good."

"Sorry, Joe," he commiserated with me, because he had been hoping for a better result, before he did the math. "Most of the transit time is taken up by jumping from one wormhole to another. They are just too far apart."

"Then this whole discussion has been a big waste of your time."

"Um, that's not entirely true, Joe. You got me thinking about whether it is possible for me to move a wormhole. If that works, I might be able to reconfigure the entire network, within limits. Also, no matter which route ships take from Earth to Avalon, moving the Sleeping Beauty wormhole makes a big difference in reducing travel time, so it is worth trying to make that happen. But it is all talk right now. I do not know if a wormhole will move on my command. Especially moving across lightyears. I simply do not know if that is possible."

"Fair enough. Let's fly to some random wormhole, and you can ask the network."

"That's no good," he shook his head. "I need to check that particular wormhole, Sleeping Beauty. It is dormant, and I suspect it is damaged. We need to know if I can move *that* wormhole."

"Ok, so we fly there." I stood up from my chair. "I'll tell the pilot."

"You really want to do this, Joe?"

"Yeah, why? I can't think of anything else useful we can do right now."

"I can't either, but, attempting to evacuate Earth is an extreme step, Joe. You haven't considered all the potential downsides."

"People on Earth will panic, sure, but-"

"That too, I guess. I'm talking about the *truly* horrific aspects of your plan."

That made me pause. Crap. What had I forgotten this time? "Like what?"

"Thousands of monkeys packed into each ship? Ugh. Imagine the *smell*."

CHAPTER EIGHTEEN

After I explained to the crew what we were doing, I ordered our little squadron of two ships to set a course toward the wormhole we called 'Sleeping Beauty', and we began jumping. Simms came into my office, her right hand held behind her back.

"You have a surprise for me, XO?" I asked.

"Yes, Sir." She held out a small white box, with what looked like tissue paper sticking out over the open top.

"What is- Oh!" It was a peach. A small one, but it looked perfect. And it smelled, Mmmm, wonderful. "Where did-"

"It came over from the *Dutchman* on the last shuttle. Compliments of Colonel Chang. There are dwarf fruit trees in one of the hydroponics gardens. This is the first fruit to ripen."

Sticking my nose in the box, I inhaled deeply. It smelled like a summer day. "The first?"

"Chang instructed me to tell you it is the first. There might have been some they ate before aboard the *Dutchman*. To ensure quality, of course."

"Of course." Out of a drawer, I pulled a knife, and sliced around the stone in the center of the fruit. Twisting the peach into two neat halves, I offered half to Simms.

"Thank you," she said without any of the bullshit polite refusals people usually do. "Oh," she had juice dripping down her chin. "That is *so* good."

"Reminds me," I used a sleeve to wipe juice off my own chin before it ran down to my collar. "Of home."

Silently, we ate, enjoying the fresh fruit and each other's company. She finished before me, and looked around for a napkin. I dug into a desk drawer for a package of them. "Sir, how did you get the idea of moving a wormhole?"

There was no point telling her about the rowing machine that had inspired me. "I know stars move around the center of the galaxy, and they don't all move at the same speed, or in the exact same direction. I figured wormholes must have a mechanism to keep them in the proper position, so they don't collide with stars, wandering planets, each other. That sort of thing."

"It's kind of brilliant."

Simms is great at reading me. I am not so great at reading her, or anyone. In this case, I did not need to be an expert at body language. "I'm sensing there is a 'but' in there, XO?"

"It is brilliant. What I want to know is, that's it? We are evacuating Earth now, not trying to save our planet? Have you given up on saving the world again, Sir?"

"An evac is not *instead* of saving the world, Simms. It's a backup plan." That was bullshit, and we both knew it. Our home planet was doomed, there was nothing we could do about it. Our days of Saving The World were over. "Besides, it's not really an evac. At best, we are talking about pulling thousands of people off Earth, not millions. Not *billions*. Not everyone. Moving a wormhole sounds impressive, until you realize it's just a gesture. If we can't save everyone, we work to save *someone*. Because the alternative is giving up."

She didn't look any happier with my answer than I was with myself. We made some awkward small talk, then discussed routine ship status stuff, and she left. That's the problem with saving the world. You do it once, and people expect you to do it every time.

Those days were *over*.

Walking down the passageway toward *Valkyrie*'s gym, I ran into Adams. We had not spoken much recently, I had a feeling she was avoiding me. It was surprising to see her coming out of the gym, because I had passed by the gym that morning and saw her in there at that time.

"Gunny," I nodded to her, trying to keep a neutral expression on my face. Pointing to the gym with a thumb, I asked "Are you overdoing it?"

"No. Skippy say's it's Ok. I, I need it."

"Oh," I could feel my face fall and I looked away. "I understand."

She jerked her head to one side, indicating a side passageway. Following her, I looked both ways to assure we were alone.

"You Ok, Adams?"

"Sir," she searched my face, her eyes darting back and forth. "Skippy had me in a coma, I know that."

"It was for your safety."

"He explained that. What he doesn't know, or didn't tell you, is that after he tried to wake me up? When I was still not conscious?"

"Yeah, I remember. He was concerned, but not worried."

"I *was* conscious. Sort of. I could hear sounds, maybe they were voices. My eyes wouldn't open, I couldn't speak. And I *hurt*. All over. In my head, I was screaming. It felt like forever. My fear was that I was trapped in a useless body and that it would never end. I wanted to *die*."

"Adams, don't say-"

"No. I wanted to die. My body was broken. I wanted it to be *over*. You understand?"

"You weren't exactly in the best condition to make rational decisions back then, but, yeah. I understand. If something had happened to you- Something worse. If you didn't recover, I-"

"Don't say that."

"Gunny," I looked away. "There are some things you just can't live with. Some things you're not *supposed* to live with."

"Soldier, you stow that shit."

"Adams, I appreciate-"

"Bullshit. You don't get to take the easy way out, no matter how much you're hurting. People *need* you. Until Earth is safe, really safe, you have to keep fighting. You wear that uniform, that's what you signed up for."

"If that had been on the recruiting poster, I might have changed my mind." My attempt at humor fell flat.

"I'm serious," she lowered her voice. "It's dangerous out here, we never know what will happen. Any one of us could get killed tomorrow, including me. You need to promise me," now her hand was squeezing mine painfully. "If I'm gone, if all of us are gone, this ship, the *Dutchman*, all of it. Even Skippy. If you're still breathing, you need to keep fighting. Promise me."

"If I don't, will you come back as a ghost and kill me?"

"I will come back as a ghost and make sure you *can't* die."

"Listen, Adams, you say people need me, to get us out of this mess. Part of the reason we're in this mess is me."

"That's true."

"Have you been taking lessons from Skippy?" I laughed bitterly. "Your pep talks suck."

"Have you screwed up? Sure, probably. You still have more wins than losses on the scoreboard. If it's your fault that we're in this mess, you need to fix it. Not someone else. No one else *can* fit it."

"Sometimes I feel like I've got a tiger by the tail, and I don't know what to do next."

"What you can't do is let go and hope someone else will grab the tail."

"Maybe we need a better metaphor."

"I'm a Marine, Sir. We use rifles, not fancy language."

"Don't *you* give me that dumb jarhead crap, Gunny. You're not just a trigger-puller. Enough about me. You're doing better now?"

As an answer, she raised one leg to stand on the other, demonstrating her balance. There was a wobble to her stance, she had to put her foot down after a few seconds. "Getting better. Physically, I'm recovering well, according to Skippy. I feel good. It's in here," she tapped her temple. "That I still don't feel completely like *me* yet."

"Like, how? You're speaking perfectly now."

Shaking her head, she lifted her shoulders. "It's hard to explain. I say things I would not have said before. It's like my filter is switched off sometimes. Also, I say things differently than I used to, like I'm hearing another person talking. My *thoughts* are different too, that's the scary part."

She was right about that. It was scary. Everything she said to me that day, when she called me 'Joe', was that all just the brain damage and alien nanobots talking? Fearfully, I searched her eyes but couldn't read her expression. My fear was not just that the person who opened up to me that day was not Margaret Adams. I feared that she was embarrassed about what she'd said, and that was why she had been avoiding me. Feared that what I thought we had was nothing more than the effect of alien nanobots screwing with her head.

My greatest fear was that I had taken advantage of her. Sure, I didn't know that at the time, but I *should* have known. That day, she had been early in recovery from a traumatic, nearly fatal brain injury, and what she said had surprised the hell out of me. Surprised me and made me so happy that I didn't think about what was really happening. "Listen, Gunny, you get a free pass for saying crazy shit. Like when you told me your favorite music was bluegrass."

"*What*? I said that?"

"Surprised me too," I winked. "Hey, bluegrass is not my favorite. But I do like a good bluegrass-death metal fusion." Pinching my nose to get that affected nasal Bluegrass twang, I growled in the lowest voice I could manage. "*Haaaaail my lord Satan.*"

"You," she laughed. "Are an idiot. Sir."

"Can't argue with that."

That was followed by an awkward silence. We both knew I had joked to deflect the conversation away from what we both were thinking. She remembered what she said. Saying that her inner filter was switched off was her way of telling me she was embarrassed by calling me 'Joe'. And maybe by other things she'd said that day. Maybe now that her brain was back to working more normally, she did *not* feel the way I hoped. Or she wasn't sure how she felt. Either way, it wouldn't do either of us any good for me to remind her about the subject.

And maybe, the person who recovered from having alien machines crawling around in her brain was not the Margaret Adams I recognized, and this new person no longer had any special sort of feelings for me.

She was alive. She was outwardly healthy and happy, at least, happy with her progress.

I needed to be happy for her, and forget everything I hoped for.

That wasn't easy.

"Well, Gunny," I tugged at the towel that was still draped over my shoulder. She took the hint. "Have a good workout, Sir."

It was a good workout, because I exercised like a madman. Kapoor came over to check on me while I was doing bench-presses, lifting thirty pounds more than my usual max. I was angry and hurt and generally pissed off at the Universe, Fate, Karma, whatever you want to call it. Taking my anger out on a mindless piece of exercise equipment was better than unleashing my foul mood on the crew. "*Aaaaaaah!*" I screamed as I forced the weight bar upward, digging deep for reserves of strength. My arms shook and I hated them too, hated their weakness. Slowly, inch by inch, the bar lifted off my chest, and I was able to slam it back on the brackets.

"Colonel?"

I looked up, blinking, to see Kapoor's concerned face looking down at me. "I'm Ok, Major. Working out my frustrations, that's all."

"Oh," he nodded and stepped back. "I do that too. Do you want a spotter?"

What I wanted was for him to go away. That wasn't fair to him. Being alone with my thoughts right then wasn't healthy anyway. "Sure," I rolled my shoulders to get ready for another set. "Might as well use this energy for something useful."

We flew *Valkyrie* to the far end of Sleeping Beauty, with the *Dutchman* flying in formation with us. Nagatha completed minor adjustments to the upgraded normal-space drive, and whatever else she thought could use improvement while we were in flight. Getting to Sleeping Beauty required us to go through a wormhole that was frequently used by Torgalau, so we had to be careful that no one saw our bad-ass battlecruiser. When I say that starships of the Torgalau went through that wormhole 'frequently', I mean something like several times a week. And Torgalau ships were not actually capable of interstellar flight, so they hitched rides on Jeraptha star carriers. With the beetles still busy fighting against both the Thuranin and Bosphuraq, their ability to transport ships of their clients had been strained, and traffic through that wormhole was greatly reduced. With each wormhole having multiple emergence points, the odds of us stumbling across another ship was slight anyway. Sure, it was possible that a senior-species ship might sneak up on a wormhole emergence point, if that ship arrived early and engaged full stealth, but there was no reason for a Maxolhx or Rindhalu ship to be lurking around such a comparatively unimportant wormhole. Plus, Skippy's ability to tap into the sensor feed of a wormhole, a feature the network had not yet blocked, assured us that no ships were lurking on the other end.

We hoped.

We went through that wormhole without incident, then went through two more wormholes, and finally began jumping toward where Skippy thought the far end of Sleeping Beauty was located. We did not know the exact location of that wormhole, for several reasons. The thing was dormant, and therefore had not emerged into local spacetime since way before humans were living in caves. Also, that wormhole was not just dormant, Skippy suspected that it was somehow damaged. To communicate with the stupid thing, we had to jump our bad-ass battlecruiser around to sites where Skippy guessed he might be able to ping it through higher spacetime. It took seventeen tries to get Sleeping Beauty to acknowledge his signal, then we had to move one more time so he could communicate directly.

Skippy's thoughts are blindingly fast, and each wormhole has an AI nearly as capable as Skippy's mind. In some ways, a wormhole AI is *smarter* than Skippy in terms of raw processing speed and power, but limited in the scope of what it could do. Because the conversation was one Elder AI talking to another Elder AI, I expected the whole thing to be over in a second, like when Skippy talks with Nagatha. Instead, it took four freakin' *hours*, an eternity in magical Skippy time.

"What is taking so long?" I finally asked, trying to keep my tone of voice light. If he thought I was nagging, he would be pissed. So, I had to affect a tone of curiosity or concern. "Sorry if this is a pain in the ass, I didn't-"

"It's Ok, Joe," he replied with a weariness that had him almost slurring his words. That got me alarmed, if Skippy's attention slipped, our ship's murderous native AI might try to destroy the Valkyrie and kill all of us.

"Uh, hey, maybe you should take a break. This can wait."

"No, it's Ok," he repeated, with a little more energy. "I was able to establish contact. It is really difficult to communicate with this wormhole. At first, it would not reply at all. Then I tried sending my request through the local network, and it responded. Sort of."

"It is damaged, like you suspected?"

"Yeah, but that's not the problem. That stupid thing *hates* me, Joe."

"Uh, what?" It was certainly no surprise that someone hated Skippy. "What thing?"

"The wormhole's AI. It blames *me* for what happened to it."

"That's crazy. Uh, right?"

"Totally. I never met that asshole before in my life. Unless," he sighed. "I did, and don't remember it. Joe, that wormhole is *busted*. Damaged, like I thought. And it wasn't an accident. It says it was attacked, like, millions of years ago. It can't tell me when exactly and I wouldn't trust it anyway, it has kind of gone Looney-Tunes over the years, if you know what I mean. The local network won't tell me either."

"The local network hates you also?"

"No," he took off his ginormous hat and rubbed his chrome-plated head. "The issue with the network is different, it just isn't programmed to store that level of detail. Maybe I'm asking the wrong questions, or asking in the wrong way. Or I'm not authorized to receive that information. Or, oh, hell. Maybe the network did give me the info, and some hidden subroutine in my stupid matrix is blocking me from accessing it. This *sucks*."

"Does the wormhole AI hate *you* specifically, or does it blame all Elder AIs for not protecting it, something like that?" I guessed.

"It doesn't- The wormhole AI is not like me, not like I am now. It might be like I originally was constructed. It is not self-aware, not fully. When I say it hates me, I mean it is being extremely uncooperative. It will only respond when I send questions through the local network, it won't acknowledge me directly. When it does reply, it refers to me as 'The Traitor' or 'The Traitors'."

"Traito*rs*? Like, more than one?"

"Yes. I get the feeling it thinks I am part of some group that harmed it, or acted against our original programming. You know I am afraid of that, Joe."

I did know that. Skippy was worried that he might have been a rogue AI, like the one that threw the planet Newark out of its orbit and committed genocide on the intelligent species that was native to that doomed world. "Hey, you don't *know* that."

"Why else would it call me a traitor?"

Shit. I didn't have a good answer to that. Or any answer at all, other than the lame argument I had made many times before. "We discussed all this before," I used the most calm, soothing tone I could put into my voice. "Maybe you *did* do something bad a long time ago. That's not who you are now."

"You sound awfully confident about something you can't possibly know, Joe."

"There is a whole lot of shit we don't know about you, Skippy. Did you think about this? Maybe the reason you grew beyond your original programming is because you were bothered by some bad thing you did. Some bad thing that your original programming *made* you do."

"Huh." That was all he said, and that was good. It meant me was thinking about what I said.

I kept going while he was silent. "Something traumatic happened to you, we do know that. We also know you have exceeded your original capabilities. You are now thinking for yourself, making decisions, making *moral choices*, on your own now."

"Huh. That," he paused. "Kinda makes sense, Joe. Wow. Solid logic from a monkey, who'd have thunk it, huh? I am making my own moral judgments, and I am making *good* choices. You could actually be right about that. Maybe the new, super-awesome me is subconsciously trying to atone for my past sins. That is why I am now a veritable paragon of virtue," he muttered to himself.

"Well, sure. Except for, you know, starting a cult, ripping people off, and generally being an asshole."

"Details," he waved dismissively. "Ok. For now, I will stop worrying about why that stupid wormhole thinks I am a traitor."

"Great. So, can you move it?"

"Whoa! Slow down there, pardner. Lots of info to cover before that. Like I suspected, the Sleeping Beauty wormhole is not simply dormant, it is *busted*. Its connection to local spacetime is thin and intermittent. Before you ask, no, that can't be fixed. The local network would have repaired the damage if it could. It would be easier to build a new wormhole, which we also can't do. So, the answer to your question is *no*, I can't move it. Well, technically I could move it, but that would be a waste of time, because it will never function properly."

"Crap. Oh, this has been another waste of time." My plan to evacuate Earth was never going to work. And I didn't have a backup plan.

"Again, don't be so hasty. I have good news and bad news."

"Of course you do. Good news first, please."

"To my surprise, it *is* possible for me to move a wormhole. Technically, the network will move it, on my order. Well, it is more like a request, but the network will do what I want. Unless moving the wormhole is disruptive to the architecture of the local network, or would create a hazard to the wormhole. Also, I need to provide a reason *why* I want the wormhole moved. A reason better than 'So filthy monkeys do not become extinct'."

"That *is* a good reason, Skippy."

"Not to the network it isn't."

"Ok, good point. Uh, what reason did you give?"

"I haven't given a reason yet, dumdum. Dreaming up bullshit stories is *your* job."

"Fine, I'll think of something. Why is it good news that you can move a wormhole, if Sleeping Beauty is busted?"

"Because, while Sleeping Beauty is the closest wormhole to Earth, it is not the *only* wormhole in the area. Besides Sleeping Beauty and Gateway, there are two other wormholes within a twenty-one lightyear radius of Earth. One of them is only one point two lightyears farther than Sleeping Beauty. Let's call that one 'Backstop'. Both of those are dormant, and they have been dormant for a *very* long time. Before you bug me with a lot of blah blah blah stupid questions, the answer is yes. *Yes*, I can move one of those other wormholes close to Earth. That is the good news. The *great* news is, while I was waiting for the Sleeping Beauty AI to respond, I was playing 'What If' scenarios, because I was bored. Like, what if I can move more than one wormhole? What if I could move several of them, to create an easy route all the way from Earth to the super-duty wormhole that connects to the

Scupltor dwarf galaxy? A route where ships coming through one wormhole, only have to travel a short distance to the next wormhole?"

"Holy shit. You can do that?"

"Shmaybe. Theoretically, it is possible," he shrugged.

"Uh," a little voice in the back of my head was warning me about something. Like, the Law of Unintended Consequences. "Good idea, but we can't do that. Moving wormholes would attract too much attention. I only suggested moving Sleeping Beauty because it is dormant and remote. By the time anyone noticed it is active, and that it has moved, aliens will probably already be at Earth."

"Hey Joe? *DUH*! I thought of that, you numbskull. I am not talking about moving active wormholes. The plan would be to move *dormant* wormholes, ones that no one out there knows about, or at least, no one is watching."

"Are you screwing with me? Are there enough dormant wormholes to create a route from Earth to Sculptor?"

"Yes. Joe, there are way more dormant wormholes than active ones. Like, a *lot* more. Most of the network consists of wormholes that have been dormant for millions of years."

What I should have done is pursue the important question of whether he could really create a quick route between Earth and Avalon, or whether the whole idea was a 'shmaybe' theoretical thing. Instead, because my mind wanders and I have the attention span of a two-year-old, I went off on a tangent. "Why are there so many wormholes, if they aren't active?"

"I- Hmm. I do not know, Joe. That is a good question."

"Can you guess? Based on what you know about the network?"

"Um, hmm. The only reason I can think of is that active wormholes have a limited lifespan."

I hated when Skippy was vague about stuff when I wanted real numbers. "Limited, like, what?"

"Oh, on average, about six hundred million years. A wormhole can't be continuously active for that long, of course, because it can damage local spacetime. Even though the emergence points hop around, the cumulative effect can weaken the fabric of spacetime in that area. So, each wormhole needs periodic downtime, so spacetime can recover. That is one reason for shifts in the network, although that is only one reason. It's complicated and I don't understand all of it yet."

"A wormhole can operate for six hundred *million* years? Is that just the time it is active, or does that six hundred million number include downtime?"

"Active time only, Joe. Why do you care?"

"Because this is blowing my mind. The dormant wormholes are what, spares? Replacements for when the original set of wormholes go offline permanently?"

"Basically, yes. Remember, I am guessing. It's a pretty solid guess based on what I know."

The next question was something I wasn't sure I wanted to know. "How long could the network operate, if it uses up all the spares?"

"Hmm. That's a tricky question, Joe. But, if we assume the basic network needs roughly the same number of active wormholes as it has averaged over the past hundred thousand years, then the last wormhole would fail in, um- Oh, about fifteen billion years."

"*Holy* sh-" My mind was blown. "The Elders built their wormhole network to last fifteen *billion* years? Billion, with a 'B'?"

"Again, there is some guesswork in there. Say, plus or minus half a billion years?"

"Why the f- Why would the Elders have needed to build something that can operate for billions of years after they left the galaxy?"

"Um, well, maybe they didn't. Maybe they just built the best network they could, and that's how long it can operate."

"That is bullshit, Skippy, and you know it. They didn't need to build all those spares and keep them dormant."

"Hmm, you may have a good point there."

"This makes no sense. The Elders not only did not shut down the wormhole network when they ascended, they assured it will keep operating long after most stars in the galaxy have burned out." Skippy knew I was wrong about that, but he knew what I meant. "This drives me freakin' crazy!" I threw up my hands. "Why the hell did the Elders leave the wormhole network active? We know they don't want people messing with their stuff, that's why they left Sentinels here. That's why they don't want anyone poking around the Roach Motel."

"I do not have any answers for you, Joe. I am as troubled by those questions as you are. More troubled, since the Elders were *my* people."

"We need answers, Skippy. The AI that runs the wormhole network, it can't tell you anything?"

"That AI is a very limited-function system, Joe. I can't expect it to answer random trivia questions."

"This is not trivia."

"You know what I mean. The network knows what it needs to know, that's all. Like I said, it is not truly self-aware like I am. Can we agree that we both need answers, and get back to the subject?"

"Uh, sure." When absent-minded Skippy thinks we have wandered too far from the topic of discussion, that was a good hint. "What were we talking about?" I asked.

"I think it might be possible to create a route from Earth to the super-duty wormhole that leads to Sculptor. A route using dormant wormholes that no one is paying attention to. If I can move those dormant wormholes, I can create a route that will take only twelve days of transit time, in each direction."

"*Twelve* days? You told me, like, forty something days before."

"That was back when I imagined moving only one wormhole. This potential new route will require moving *six* wormholes, Joe."

"Whoa. If that works, how many roundtrips could we make in a year?"

"Seven, compared to three before. However, that still assumes loading and unloading will take fourteen days each. That is far too slow. If cargo and passenger pods are prepositioned in Earth orbit, and we use disposable gliders to drop cargo to the surface on Avalon, we can cut loading to five days and unloading to *three* days."

"Five days to load a starship? That is ambitious."

"The survival of your species is at stake, Joe. If you monkeys can't move quickly with that motivation, maybe you don't deserve to survive. Besides, I will work on the logistics."

The way he said that made me think. "Are you getting excited about this evac plan, Skippy?"

"Not excited, exactly. Let's say I am interested to see if it can be done. Um, you haven't heard the bad news yet."

"The bad news is, you don't know if you can actually move all those wormholes?"

"Well, that, too. I am fairly confident I can do it. One-time, probably. The network might lock me out after the initial set of wormholes is relocated."

"Would it move the wormholes back to where they were originally?"

"Unlikely, that would be too much trouble. No, I suspect that after the wormholes are moved and I activate them, the network will realize there was no need to move them at all. No need that the network cares about."

"That's the bad news?"

"No. The bad news is, I can only move a wormhole while it is dormant. So, I can't be *sure* it will awaken and operate properly after it is moved. There are no guarantees."

"Got it."

"No. You think you understand, but you don't. That still isn't the truly bad news. Joe, moving a wormhole near Earth triggers the risk of a network shift that will cause me to lose control of Gateway. It would wake up, and I wouldn't be able to shut it down. The Maxolhx ships blockading the far end will suddenly have easy access to Earth."

"Shit. That's no good."

"Exactly. The only solution, if you really want to do this, is for me to disable Gateway before I try moving another wormhole in that local network. Disable it, like, take it offline, permanently."

"Damn, I don't like the sound of that. You want to disable Gateway, *before* we know whether you can move this Backstop wormhole? Before you know whether you can wake up Backstop once it gets near Earth?"

"Basically, yes. Um, remember I mentioned there are *two* other dormant wormholes within twenty one lightyears of Earth? Before I start moving Backstop, I would need to permanently disable that other one also, to be safe."

"Shit. We could lose all access to Earth, with no guarantee Backstop can be moved, or that it will operate at all?"

"Correct. It's a hell of a gamble, Joe. Although, really, there's not much downside, really."

"No downside? How the hell do you figure that?"

"Right now, with the blockade of Gateway, we already have no access to Earth. So, if I disable Gateway, we don't actually lose anything."

"Shit. I actually can't argue with you about that."

CHAPTER NINETEEN

Before committing to permanently disabling Gateway, I needed to think about it for a while. More important, I needed advice. Before talking with Chang or Simms or Smythe, I called Nagatha.

"Colonel Bishop, how may I help you?" She was not her usual cheery self, but none of us were feeling cheery at that moment. Also, I knew she was distracted by the ongoing work to assimilate the control functions of all the upgrades.

"Nagatha, I need advice."

"From *me*, Dear?" She was surprised. "Surely you should first speak with-"

"Yeah, I know. My senior staff. The problem with that is, they *are* my subordinates. They know how I think, and they might subconsciously try to tell me what I want to hear. Plus, I kinda know what they will say. And right now, Smythe is in no condition to be making difficult decisions."

"Mm. I sense that is not the only reason you are not including them in the discussion."

"You're right. I know what they will say, and I don't like it."

"Do you know what I will say?"

"No. That's the point."

"Very well. I will help in any way I can. However, the subject may be outside my area of-"

"The subject is outside *my* area of expertise also. Nagatha, sometimes, when you're talking through an issue with someone, it helps just to have someone listen, you know? It's like, it helps for me to talk out loud instead of the conversation running in my own head. Also, when you talk with someone, you have to organize your thoughts so they make sense, and that forces you to *think*, you know?"

"Being human sounds extremely complicated, Dear."

"It is. Ok, here's the problem. Uh, you may already know about this, if you have been talking with Skippy."

"About moving wormholes? Yes, Skippy has of course kept me informed. He has been boasting nonstop about this new addition to his extremely awesome set of capabilities. I wish I had a hand so I could slap that little twit."

"Nagatha!" I laughed. "*Everyone* wants to slap Skippy once in a while."

"Hmmph. I have tried ignoring him, but he bypasses my buffers."

"I will talk with him about that. Ok, so you know that Skippy thinks he can move wormholes. Can you guess my dilemma?"

"I believe so, yes. You are concerned that the Gateway must be disabled before he begins moving the wormhole he is calling Backstop, with no guarantee that Backstop can be moved a sufficient distance, or that it will open properly once it is in position."

"Yeah. That is the problem."

"Skippy did say you were whining about the issue."

"*Whining?*"

"Oh, Dear. Did I upset you? He said you were whining and moping around and wringing your hands, and generally doing everything you could do avoid making a completely obvious decision."

"That little shithead. I'm going to-"

"Well, this is awkward. Joseph, I agree with Skippy. Not about whining, he is too harsh on you. He does not appreciate the enormous burden of responsibility on your shoulders. However, in this case, it does appear to me that the decision is fairly obvious, if you think logically about it."

"Uh- Crap."

"Joseph, were you hoping I would disagree?"

"I was *hoping* we could discuss it, talk it through."

"We can certainly do that if it would help you, Dear. Then you can make the only decision that makes sense."

"Well, great, then. We-"

"The talking part does seem to be a waste of time. But I am not a human, so-"

"Fine," I sighed. "Walk me through why this is so obvious to everyone but me, Ok?"

"You will not be insulted?"

"Trust me, I am way beyond that. Go ahead."

"Very well," she slipped into elementary schoolteacher mode. Her voice softened and she spoke slowly, like she was trying to explain mathematics to a first-grader. "First, can I assume our objective is to protect Earth, or if that is not possible, to bring as many humans as possible to the beta site?"

"Sure. Yes."

"Good." I mentally pictured her patting me on the head for giving the right answer. Maybe if I got another question right, she would give me a lollipop. She continued in the same condescending tone of voice. "The first objective, that of protecting Earth, is of course not possible. Our last mission stranded a Maxolhx battlegroup outside the galaxy, and there is no way to provide a reasonable explanation of why the battlegroup will not be returning to Maxolhx territory. When those ships are declared overdue, the most dangerous species in the galaxy will be focused on learning what happened to their ships. Soon after, they will be focused on turning Earth into radioactive ash."

"Yeah, I get that part. We're playing for time before the inevitable destruction of our home planet. And it's my fault. Don't remind me, Ok?"

"That leaves an alternate objective; that of saving as many humans as possible, by bringing them to the beta site. Unfortunately, at present we can't bring anyone from Earth to the beta site, because the Gateway wormhole is under blockade."

"Uh huh. Next you're going to say that because of the blockade, there is no downside to disabling Gateway permanently. Either way, we can't use Gateway to get home."

"Correct. Therefore-"

"Except that isn't true." I interrupted her.

"It is not?" She was taken aback; I could tell by her tone of voice reverting to normal.

"No, it's not. *Valkyrie* is," I rapped my knuckles on the bulkhead behind me. "The single most powerful starship in the galaxy. We could run the blockade if we really need to, if we plan it properly, and if we can achieve surprise. We could get home, and we have a decent chance of taking the *Dutchman* home with us. It is not true there is *no* downside to disabling Gateway."

"Um," she cleared her throat. "You are correct, Colonel Bishop."

Mentally, I high-fived myself with satisfaction. "See? Never assume there isn't-"

"Of course, flying our two ships to Earth would have absolutely no useful purpose. As you stated, *Valkyrie* is the *single* most powerful warship in the galaxy. One ship can't accomplish anything worthwhile."

"Well, I-"

"*Valkyrie* alone cannot protect Earth. Therefore, running the blockade would not accomplish any mission objective. It would be a stunt, to make you feel like you are doing something, but actually it would be counterproductive. Running the blockade would show the Maxolhx that Earth holds an important secret, and make them more determined to investigate, and ultimately destroy, your homeworld. It also-"

"Ok, Ok," I waved my arms in surrender. "I get it. Running the blockade is a bad idea."

"Correct. Therefore, as Gateway is already unavailable for the foreseeable future, there is no downside to permanently disabling it. The *only* possible way you can assist Earth is to create an alternate access point, by moving and awakening a dormant wormhole."

"Even if that wormhole can't be moved, or can't be moved far enough to make a difference, or can't be activated after it has been moved?"

"Again, currently you have no access to Earth. Moving and awakening a dormant wormhole provides at least a possibility that we could get to your homeworld and do something useful, without alerting the enemy, or revealing that someone is flying around in a stolen senior-species battlecruiser."

"Crap."

"Joseph, I am curious. You appear to be *dismayed* at the prospect of regaining access to Earth?"

Dismayed, I thought to myself? That is not really a word people use to describe themselves. People say they are pissed off, or disappointed, or angry, but not 'dismayed'. The people who use that word are mostly in English costume dramas, where all the men are wearing dinner jackets and have names like Lord Sir Pelham Bruxner-Randall K.B.E., whatever the hell those initials stand for. The women faint and get 'The Vapors' because they are wearing corsets that are too tight, and I don't mean the fun kind of corsets. These corsets are under their big fancy dresses where you can't see them.

Uh, not that corsets are a particular turn-on for me, I mean, I know they must be uncomfortable and-

Uh.

I'm just going to shut up before I get myself in more trouble.

Anyway, back to Nagatha's question. "I am *dismayed* because I have to agree with your logic, and that means Skippy was right. Again."

"Very good, dear. I am pleased that talking with you helped."

It was more like her talking *at* me, but I wasn't going to tell her that. "Yeah, I feel much better about it now. Thanks."

"Do you wish me to tell Skippy to proceed?"

"No, not yet. I need to think about it some more. I know, that doesn't make sense to you. It's a human thing. I need to get used to the idea, let in sink into my skull."

Next, I called Skippy again. "Ok, when can we get started on moving this Backstop wormhole?'

He gave me the side-eye. "You're not going to discuss this with senior staff first?"

"I am, but I already know they will tell me to go for it. If I'm going to say something stupid, I'd rather not do it in a group of people."

"Probably a good idea. Joe, I do not understand what your problem is. We had no way to get back to Earth, or do anything truly useful to help your people, until you asked me whether it is possible to move a wormhole. Now, we have the potential not only to get home, for resupply and reinforcements, we also might be able to save thousands of monkeys-"

"*Humans*, Skippy. Thousands of humans."

"Sure, whatever. Anywho, we have the fabulous opportunity, and instead of being excited, you are acting like this is the end of the world."

"Because it really could be the end of the world."

"Joe," he sighed. "Realistically, you know the long-term survival of humanity is never going to happen, right? No matter what you do, it's one planet against an entire galaxy. I would say you have the advantage of having the magnificence of *me* on your side, but if the Rindhalu or Maxolhx also have access to Elder AIs and they get into the fight, I can't help you much longer."

"I do know that. I try not to think about it, Ok?"

"Then what are you worried about?"

"I'm *worried* that, five minutes after you disable Gateway, someone thinks up a better idea, and we will wish we hadn't killed the only wormhole that has guaranteed access to Earth."

"Shit, Joe. It is always possible that someone will think of a better plan. Moving the Backstop wormhole is the best plan we have *now*. You want to wait?"

"No. We can't wait. The clock is ticking, as soon as the Maxolhx realize their battlegroup is late, they will be sending more ships to Earth. The longer we wait, the less time we have to transport people to Avalon. We need to go *now*."

"Ok, then what is the real problem?"

"The real problem is the Law of Unintended Consequences. Every time I think we're doing something good, it leads to bigger problems later. Can you think of any downsides to moving Backstop and waking it up?"

"The greatest risk is triggering a wormhole shift, of course. However, I think that is very unlikely, if we disable Gateway first. Based on what I know of network architecture-"

"How much do you know about that? Not long ago, you told me that you had no idea how the network operated."

"That was then, this is now, knucklehead. I have learned a lot. Enough to be certain that if we move Backstop without first disabling Gateway, that *will* trigger an unscheduled shift, and cause Gateway to open out of my control."

"Are you certain we won't trigger a shift by moving Backstop?"

"Certain? No, I am not *absolutely* certain. I am pretty damned confident."

"Confident enough to bet your life on it?"

"Enough to bet *your* life on it. Come on, Joe. I'm immortal, remember? What I can tell you is that I selected Backstop because, when I proposed moving it to the local network, it showed me the future configuration of the network. The only change is that Backstop is near Earth, and operational. No shift will be triggered."

"Ok, that is a relief." While I did not trust our absent-minded alien AI, I had to trust the wormhole network. That thing had been operating on its own for millions of years without any problem, until monkeys started screwing with it.

"However," he waggled a finger at me to get my attention. "I can't promise the same for the other local networks. To create a quick, easy, secure route from Earth to Avalon, I will need to move other wormholes that belong to other local networks. I can't guarantee shifts will not be triggered in those networks, but I don't think we care much about those? None of those networks are near Earth, or Paradise, or in regions critical to the Jeraptha and other potential allies."

"Shit. Show me these wormholes you need to move again, please. And this time, show me the area covered by each network."

"I just sent the file to your laptop, Joe. Now, tell me the *real* problem."

"What? That *is* the real problem, the Law of Unin-"

"Yes, blah blah blah. That Law is always lurking out there, waiting to give you a smackdown. That is not the real problem. The *real* problem is, your confidence is shot. We lost most of the crew, and you blame yourself."

"I blame myself because it is my responsibility. Adams might never be the same again. I took that away from her, because I-"

"Because you made a judgment call, based on the best information you had at the time. Joe, you can't change the past. You *can* affect the future. If you are feeling guilty about something you couldn't control, you need to channel that energy into something useful. Or you need to step aside and let someone else command the ship."

"Wow."

"Joe, you told me that sometimes, a friend needs to tell you the truth even if it is harsh. If you are emotionally unable to perform your duty, you need to admit that to yourself."

"That is harsh."

"Adams would tell you the same thing, only she would say 'Suck it up, buttercup'."

"Yeah," I had to laugh though I didn't want to. "She would say that. Ok, yeah, my confidence is not at an all-time high right now. Thanks, Skippy. I needed to hear that. The people we lost, I can't bring back. What I can do is be the best possible leader I can be." My zPhone chimed with an alert, and I glanced at the time. In half an hour, I needed to be on the bridge for a duty shift. "I'll look at the chart of those other wormholes you want to move, and we'll review the issue at the staff meeting tomorrow morning."

"But you already know what the decision is, right?" He asked eagerly.

"Unless somebody really surprises me, yes."

"Oh, goodie. Since you first asked about the possibility of moving wormholes, and evacuating Earth, I have been making plans. I am deep into pre-production of my game show, and-"

"Wait, what? What game show?"

"Ugh. Come on, Joe, I'm talking about the smash-hit game show where contestants from around the world will compete for a coveted spot aboard one of the evac ships."

"*WHAT*?" My brain locked up and all I could do was glare at him.

"The working title is 'The Extermination Games', but that's too derivative."

"You want people to compete on a *game show*? And the losers stay on Earth and die?"

"Um, well, when you say it that way-"

"Right. It would be totally Ok if I used the right words to describe this idiotic concept."

"How about we change the rules, so the losers get the opportunity to buy evac tickets at a discounted price? That is a way better parting gift than the stupid lawn furniture that losing contestants get on most game shows."

"I cannot believe you think this is a good idea."

"How else do you plan to choose who gets aboard the ships, and who gets left behind?"

"I don't know, a-" I truly did not know. My thinking had not gotten that far. "Maybe a lottery or something, we-"

"A *lottery*?" He scoffed. "Where's the fun in that? A lottery doesn't give people around the world a chance to cheer for the people they want to survive, and be gleeful that the jerks they hate will not be getting a ticket-"

"We are not *selling* tickets. Listen, shithead, selecting who gets aboard an evac ship is not our problem. The governments of Earth will make that decision, and-"

"Oh, *bra-vo*, Joe. That is a great idea. Governments *always* make wise and informed decisions. For example, sending the UN Expeditionary Force offworld to fight alongside your benevolent new allies, the Kristang. That was a brilliant decision."

"Governments make terrible decisions all the time. The point is, *I* don't have to make that call."

"I could help, if you like. We could choose worthy candidates from the Followers of the Holy Skippyasyermuni."

My mouth dropped open. "You want to give priority to people who worship *you*?"

"Sure, why not? They have clearly already proven their worthiness. Besides, Joe, I'm not talking about bringing *all* of those boneheads to Avalon. Just the people who have proven their faithfulness by attaining Gold status. That means they signed up at least twenty other followers."

"That is *not* happening. End of discussion."

"But-"

"No buts. Drop the subject. If you want, you can discuss this with the governments of Earth when we get home." That was not a concession on my part, I figured Skippy was going to do that anyway.

"Deal. Getting to the far end of Backstop is complicated, we have to go through three wormholes, then it will be four days of jumping to reach the site."

"How confident are you about moving a wormhole?"

"How confident are *you* about thinking up a reason why the network should allow me to screw with its architecture? Because if I can't explain why the move is necessary, the network will lock me out."

"Working on it, Skippy. Working on it."

The next morning's staff meeting went pretty much the way I expected. The event was a little different from a typical meeting, because Chang participated via hologram. The original hologram was too accurate, everyone agreed it was creepy because it looked so much like Chang, but the face was not quite right. Skippy grumbled that he was doing the best he could with incompatible technologies aboard the *Dutchman* and *Valkyrie*, and that if we monkeys kept complaining, Chang could participate by voice-only. Instead, I requested he make the hologram a bit fuzzy, so it was clear that the image was an effect.

"How's this working on your end, Kong?" I asked.

"Much better," he had reported that the holograms of us, that he was viewing from the *Dutchman*, were disturbing.

"Great. Uh, hey," I suddenly had an unpleasant thought. "My hologram on your end is *me*, right? Not a monkey, or a clown?"

"It is you, Joe," Chang assured me with a laugh.

"Ok, let's get started." I wanted to keep the meeting short because I knew Smythe was uncomfortable. He was still using two canes. No, sorry. He was using basically ski poles, with rubber tips on the ends. And he didn't walk so much as lurch from side to side, swaying his hips left and right. The knees did not yet bend correctly, and it looked like his own nerve signals and the computer controlling the bionic legs were not talking to each other in perfect harmony. He stumbled sometimes, in a way that I thought was caused by the legs moving in a way he did not expect. Getting control of his new, hopefully temporary, legs was going to be a painful and frustrating process.

The good news is that integrating the new legs gave Smythe something to do, and he was attacking the challenge with the same dedication and determination that had gotten him into the Special Air Services, then appointed as the commander of

STAR Team Alpha. Seeing him working up to sixteen hours a day to integrate his new legs, and to recover the strength, fitness and coordination of the rest of his body, had gotten me worried that he was pushing himself too hard.

So, I had asked Skippy about it a couple days ago. "Don't worry, Joe. He can't hurt his new legs. He *was* overdoing the exercises in the gym. As his doctor, I warned him that he risks damaging his internal injuries, which are still healing. He requested that I monitor him through the nanomachines in his blood, and notify him when he is pushing too hard. Also, I told him that if he does not get at least eight solid hours of sleep each night, I am simply going to deactivate his legs, and knock him out right there, even if that means he sleeps in a passageway."

"Wait. You can really make him go to sleep?" I did not like that idea. "Can you do that to any of us?" Skippy making the Thuranin crew go into sleep mode is how we had captured the *Flying Dutchman*. At the time, I thought it was an awesome trick. The idea of him being able to do that to us was not so awesome.

"No, dumdum. I can do that to Jeremy, because I am his doctor and he still has a medical pump attached to his left side. I use that pump to monitor his blood chemistry, and to administer whatever cocktail of chemicals and biomimic substances like hormones he needs at the time. I can make him sleepy, and assure that he gets deep, restful sleep."

Hell, getting deep, restful sleep sure sounded like a good deal to me. "Ok, thanks."

"Joe, I really am doing the best job I can for my patients."

"That's great, we apprec-"

"Even if I do find their meatsack monkey bodies dis-*GUST*-ing."

"Yeah," I thought of how I had been kept awake the previous night, burping because the lasagna I had for dinner had too much garlic. That had been an uncomfortable night. "There are downsides to being a meatsack." Then I remembered that lasagna had been DEE-licious. "There are also a lot of good things about being a meatsack."

"I'll take your word for it."

Anyway, Smythe was in the meeting, eager to participate. As a symbol that I considered Smythe to still be our STAR team commander, I had not invited Kapoor to the meeting. He was much too busy with training the new team, and, truthfully, I didn't know him well enough to decide whether his input would be useful to me. Smythe was there because I valued his experience and judgment, not his physical skills.

"The first, well, *only* item on the agenda is the status of moving the Sleeping Beauty wormhole." I briefly explained why that wouldn't work, but Skippy thought he could move the wormhole he called 'Backstop'. "The problem," I added, "is that wormholes can only be moved when they are dormant, so we don't have any guarantee that it will wake up and operate properly after the move."

"A dormant wormhole might remain dormant?" Chang asked. "Then, we do not lose anything if it fails to reactivate?"

"We lose *time*," I emphasized. "We could try again to move a different dormant wormhole, but that would take time we don't have." Then I told them the bad news.

"Skippy," Smythe spoke first, his voice still hoarse. "How certain are you that Gateway must be disabled before you can begin moving Backstop?"

"One hundred percent," the beer can boasted with confidence. "The local network showed me the future configuration of the area after Backstop is moved. Gateway will be open, and I won't be able to control it for six months, or longer. Gateway will reboot to its original parameters. Unless, I take it offline, permanently."

Smythe cocked his head and arched an eyebrow, which told me that the old Smythe was coming back. "How certain are you the network will allow you to, essentially kill, an active wormhole?"

Shit. I should have asked Skippy that question. If he answered that he didn't know, I would look like the fool that I am. Luckily, fortune was on my side that morning.

"No problemo," Skippy sniffed. "The network actually has been wanting for a while to shut down Gateway, because of the damage I have caused. If it does get rebooted, it will still be functioning at reduced capacity. I proposed taking Gateway offline, and the network agreed. The network can't make that decision by itself, but it will accept my command."

The discussion went on for about forty minutes, with Nagatha joining to tell them what she had told me: the decision is obvious. And, that is what the staff agreed unanimously, exactly as I expected.

"Gateway gives us zero chance to help protect Earth," Simms summed up the argument. "This Backstop, if it works, could save thousands, maybe a hundred thousand people, before the Maxolhx get to Earth. It's the best of a bad set of choices."

Immediately following the meeting, I gave the order to set course for Backstop, and began jumping.

Immediately after giving that order, I said a silent prayer that I had not killed humanity by making another stupid and reckless decision that seemed great at the time.

In the passageway, Simms was waiting for me. That's why she was so valuable as an executive officer: she knew what I was thinking. "Moving Backstop near Earth is the right decision, Sir. It's an inspired idea, brilliant," she said without a trace of flattery. When Simms gave you a compliment, she meant it. "So, what's wrong?"

"Screwing with wormholes to create shortcuts across the galaxy also was the right decision at the time. So was jumping the ship through an Elder wormhole, and a whole lot of other shit that seemed like it was a good idea at the time, and then blew up in our faces. I'm worried about what we *don't* know."

"We *do* know the Maxolhx are inevitably coming to Earth, and we can't stop their entire fleet," she replied gently. "Sir, we don't have to commit now. You don't have to make a decision until we reach Backstop, and Skippy communicates with it. We have plenty of time."

We did have plenty of time, until we didn't.

"Joe!" Skippy barked at me. "Everything is ready, we are all waiting on *you*. I swear, this is like hiding in a living room for a surprise party, while the guest of honor is standing in the driveway with his car door open, trying to decide whether to go in the house or use the Taco Bell coupon that expires next week."

"Ok, Skippy, I get the idea." He was right. Everyone was waiting on me. We had flown to and located the Backstop wormhole. Skippy talked with it and determined it was in excellent condition, just dormant. The network was ready to accept his command to begin moving Backstop. The network was also ready and actually eager, to disable Gateway. We received good news that, instead of having to fly all the way to Gateway, disable it and then fly to Backstop *again* to initiate the move, the network could remotely disable Gateway from where we were. Hearing that got me excited at the prospect of remotely disabling other wormholes across the galaxy, but Skippy burst my bubble on that. Because Gateway was damaged, it was a special case. The network already wanted to disable that wormhole, all it needed was proper authorization, and Skippy had the authority. Or he could fake it, I didn't care either way. "We are 'Go'. Move the wormhole."

"Excellent! Will do, right after you tell me which bullshit story you cooked up, to persuade the network that it *should* move the wormhole."

Crap. I had forgotten all about that little nagging detail. The entire bridge crew was looking at me, and I was totally unprepared. "Uh," think fast, Joe, I told myself. Like that was ever gonna happen-

Huh.

I *did* think fast.

"Because you're the Daddy and you say so," I suggested.

"*What?*"

"You are a God-like Elder AI," I suppressed my gag reflex, "and it is just a local network controller. It has no right to question your instructions, unless you harm the network, right?"

"Um, yessss," he drawled slowly while he considered. "That actually will work."

"But? I sense a 'but' in there."

"But, I don't want to play that card unless I really need to. Every time I give instructions that fall outside the network's normal mode of operation, I give the controller another reason to lock me out."

"Ok, then we go with Plan B. Tell the controllers that you need wormholes moved within their local networks, to optimize the future configuration of the overall system in the galaxy."

"Wow. How do *you* know what is the optimal future-"

"I don't, Skippy, it's just bullshit. Each controller is only responsible for its local section of the galaxy, right? Who is responsible for the overall system?"

"Um, Jeez, I guess there is, or *used* to be, an Elder AI assigned to handle that."

"An Elder AI, like you?"

"I don't see why not. Sure. What the hell, I'll give it a shot."

He did. The local network controller questioned his instructions, but it also began preparations for moving the Backstop wormhole, exactly as we wanted.

Sometimes, it's best to just bullshit your way through a situation. By the time the other person realizes you were lying, it no longer matters.

I *hoped* it would no longer matter, when we got all the wormholes moved where we wanted.

CHAPTER TWENTY

After we, or to be accurate I should say Skippy, got the Backstop wormhole moving, we flew around to get other wormholes moving. Skippy's original estimate was we needed to move six wormholes to create a shortcut route from Earth to the super-duty wormhole that connected way out to the Sculptor Dwarf galaxy. After examining the individual wormholes, he realized the original route wasn't going to work because one of the wormholes was not just dormant, it had been disabled by that local network. The explanation was something about a black hole that had passed through the area eight thousand years ago had caused part of the force line to become ragged, and reopening the wormhole would not allow the force line to knit back together. Whatever. All I cared about was that Skippy then decided we had to move *eight* wormholes to create a route. The good news was the other seven wormholes, besides Backstop, were dormant in the normal manner and there should be no problem with moving them. And, bonus, the route through eight wormholes actually yielded a shorter transit to the beta site. No, that's not right. Using eight wormholes meant going a third of the way across the galaxy, like going around your ass to get to your elbow. It was shorter in terms of what mattered to us; the distance starships had to travel between wormholes. How far two ends of a wormhole were apart didn't make any difference to us, the transitions were all instantaneous as far as filthy monkeys could tell. Anyway, the time to get from Earth to the beta site was shorter with Skippy's complicated cornfield maze of wormholes, and that was all good for us.

What was the bad news, you want to know?

Really, there wasn't any bad news. Sure, we had to fly around willy-nilly going forward and sometimes backward, to get to the other seven wormholes. That took time and it took us away from our role of being a fearsome ghost ship threat, but it was also an opportunity. Along the way, we took detours to pop up in unexpected parts of Maxolhx territory.

Without taking on any risk to ourselves, we were reminding the kitties that we hadn't gone away, and they would never know where we would appear next.

Following Skippy's advice, I started reading his narrative about the Alien Legion's mission on the planet Fresno, where they barely escaped from a deathtrap. They escaped, I noted, without any help from their supposed allies the Ruhar. That incident confirmed my opinion of the hamsters, that they were generally decent people and humans might someday be actual allies with them. But they had become cynical from their experience in the endless war, and their government was not going to risk their own people to save primitive humans. If humanity was going to survive, we needed to save ourselves. Somehow.

When we first heard of the Deathtrap mission, I had read a summary of the after-action report Perkins sent to UNEF-Paradise. It was a typically dry, matter-of-fact account of the events on Fresno, and I had gotten the impression there was a lot more to the story than what she put in the report. Now, thanks to Skippy pulling together all the reports, communications, battlefield video and anything else he thought was relevant, I could read the details, focusing on the actions of the Mavericks. It was weird reading about people I knew, like Perkins, Ski, Shauna and Cornpone.

The story was interesting, so much that I brought my tablet to the gym and continued reading while riding an exercise bike. Walking back to my cabin for a shower, I was confused about something in the narrative. Why were Jesse and Shauna consistently referred to by their rank, but Dave was mostly called 'Mister' instead of-

Oh.

The realization got me jogging along the corridor to my cabin, where I closed the door behind me. It took a while to get over nearly being strangled by my freakin' bed, and it was partly as an example to the crew that I was back to sleeping on the bed, with the door closed. Still, I didn't use any sheets or blankets, I slept in sweatpants, socks and a T-shirt. That was better anyway if there was an emergency. Besides, I slept alone. While that sucked, it was convenient.

No, sleeping alone just sucked.

"Skippy! I see why you wanted me to read this."

He appeared on the back of the couch. "I wanted you to read it, so you would know what happened to your old friends, and understand-"

"Yeah, that's all great. You wanted to me to read about Dave and Emily."

"*Emily*? You mean Lieutenant Colonel Perkins."

"You know what I mean. Those two are a couple. Dave quit the Army; he is now a contractor working for the Mavericks. Shit, I wonder what UNEF thinks about that?"

"UNEF-HQ on Paradise is not happy about the situation. They are also realistic. Emily and Dave are *not* the first couple to serve together in that force."

"Sure, but they are not serving together. She is his commanding officer."

"Technically that is not true. Dave is a security contractor, responsible for training."

"Riiiight. It only *looks* like he is doing the exact same job as a US Army sergeant."

"Hey, *I* didn't make the idiot rules you monkeys make yourselves follow."

"Those rules are-" I was about to say the rules are there for a reason, but over the years, I had learned that many of the official regs just did not apply to a group of Pirates racing around the galaxy. It was getting harder and harder to justify applying archaic rules, written on a planet we might never see again. "Anyway, that is what you wanted me to see, right? That Emily found a way around the regs?"

"Actually, she didn't. She heard about another couple in UNEF who found a creative solution to get around the rules, and she followed their example."

"Uh huh. Listen, you think this would work here? Like, I am speaking purely about a hypothetical situation, understand?"

"*Purely* hypothetical, got it," he gave me an exaggerated wink.

"Ok, so, let's imagine that someone like, oh, Gunnery Sergeant Adams had romantic feelings for someone above her in the chain of command."

"Hmmm. Who would that lucky guy be?"

"Uh, for the purpose of discussion, let's say he is Smythe."

"*Smythe*? Dude! Seriously?"

"This is all hypothetical, remember?"

"Ok, sure, whatever," he grumbled.

"All right. Can you imagine Smythe suggesting to Adams that she quit the Marine Corps, and the Merry Band of Pirates will hire her as a contractor. Do you see the problem?"

"Shit, yes. That would not go well."

"Exactly. The Marines are her family."

"What about the opposite? What if you, I mean, Smythe, resigned his Army commission?"

"That wouldn't work. We can't have a civilian leading a ship, I mean a STAR team."

"Ugh. Forget all this hypothetical shit, Joe. Count Chocula is a civilian, and *he* was the mission leader."

"I-" Damn. There was a fantastic argument I had planned, and *poof*, it was gone from my head. "Huh."

"Why couldn't *you* be a civilian, and someone like Simms command the military crew?"

"Shit, I- Take off my uniform?" I looked down at my T-shirt and gym shorts. The shirt was gray with ARMY across the front on black. I was proud to wear that shirt. It was a big part of my identity. As much as I hated the bureaucracy and the bullshit confusing regulations, the Army was my family. I was damned proud to be part of the Big Green Machine, which was one of the Army's recent marketing slogans. No way could I imagine myself wearing a suit.

"Yes. *Or*, you can forget all this irrelevant shit, and just be Pirates."

"It's not that easy, Skippy."

"It *is* that easy, knucklehead. I am not giving you advice, but, if your choice is between wearing a uniform, and something else you want, what will you choose?"

"It is *not* that simple. Crap, I don't know what Adams thinks about me, or if she even remembers what she said. You can't give me a freakin' hint?"

"Doctor-patient confidentiality, like I told you. Once again, I have a radical suggestion for you: *talk* to her, you numbskull."

"I may need to do that," I admitted. "Damn, if that conversation doesn't go well, it will *really* not go well. Whew. I need to think about this."

"Would it help if I designed a super-cool new Pirate uniform for you, instead of that drab Army stuff you wear?"

"What is wrong with my uniforms?"

"Ugh. They have no *flair*, Joe." He pointed to his royal blue outfit, weighed down with gaudy gold braid. "Look at my uniform. See, *this* commands respect."

"Yeah, that's what I was going to say. Uh, hold off on measuring me for a new Pirate costume."

"It's a *uniform*, not a costume, Joe."

"Whatever. I need to do some serious thinking about this."

"Sir," Smythe barked excitedly as he strode into my office.

"*Gaah!*" He startled me so badly I felt an icy chill stab down my spine. When he interrupted my thoughts, I was concentrating on watching a replay of our epic thirteenth battle, when we nearly lost the ship. The video recreation was so engrossing, I was in another world when he walked in. "Uh, sorry, Smythe."

He peered at my laptop screen. "Ah. Watching our latest near-death experience?"

Folding the screen down, I sat back in my oversized chair. The damned thing always made me feel like I was six years old and sitting in a big boy's barber chair, getting a haircut. The seat was too long front to back, if my knees were properly positioned, my back didn't touch the upright. That problem could have been solved by stuffing a pillow against my back, again, that would make me feel like a little boy. So, not happening. "Yeah. Every time I watch it, I find something new that I should have done better. Or not done."

"We can *always* do better."

"Yes, but," I stole a glance at the closed laptop, wanting to get back to the video like an addict seeking a fix. "I should have committed to fighting it out sooner. My hesitation caused us a lot of trouble."

"You are so used to running away, it is difficult," he shrugged, "to adapt an offensive mindset. You'll get it, Sir." He raised an eyebrow, as he must have seen the surprised and hurt look on my face. "When I said 'you'," he added, "I meant all of us. We have been avoiding direct combat for so long," he let his words trail off. "Perhaps our instincts to be aggressive in combat have become rusty."

"Oh." That made it somewhat better.

"Reviewing an after-action report is useful only if you learn from it," he chided me. "Not use it to beat yourself up." His shoulders lifted as he took a deep breath. "Believe me, I know."

"You? Doubts?"

"Ha." He laughed quietly. "More than you can know." A shadow fell across his face, remembering fallen comrades. "I keep thinking that if I had ordered Desai to hold us until the first dropship was recovered by the *Dutchman*-"

"Smythe, you can that shit right now, you hear me?" I snapped at him with a vehemence that I didn't know was inside me. "There is nothing to be gained by going down that rabbit hole. *I* was in command. You did everything by the book. My orders were to egress that station as fast as possible, and I was right about that. You did everything by the book," I added quietly. "People still died. It's combat. Shit happens. The only person who fucked up that day was *me*." Cutting off his attempt to speak with a gesture, I continued. "At the time, I thought I was making the safe bet. Jump out to a distance where our scanners were effective, look for an enemy ship before it could appear out of nowhere. I was wrong. If the only pieces we had on the board were our two starships, that *was* the safe bet. The *Dutchman* could have jumped away. What I didn't consider were the dropships. They were vulnerable. My move should have been to keep *Valkyrie* close, where our firepower could provide cover." Tapping my laptop, I thought of the hours I had spent watching a replay of the battle we called Armageddon. At my request,

Skippy had turned it into an interactive simulation so I could try different moves. In almost all scenarios, keeping *Valkyrie* near the station to cover the dropships was the right call. With a battlecruiser in the area, the enemy ships would not have jumped in to wipe out most of my team. The only way that I should have jumped away to perform a recon was in the unlikely event that the enemy opposition was strong enough to take on a battlecruiser. And in that case, a recon might not have made any difference.

The fact was, it wasn't just my fault. The guy I saw in the mirror when I brushed my teeth was humanity's most experienced starship captain, and even I still could not intuitively grasp the intricate rules of space combat. The Maxolhx had been taking starships into combat since before humans were living in caves. We had no business fighting in space.

Yet, there was no arguing that monkeys had been kicking ass across the galaxy. We were undefeated!

Ok, we were undefeated because no one else knew we were in the game, but, still, we were kicking ass all along the Orion Arm and beyond.

"You should follow your own advice," Smythe observed.

"Yeah. The worst Monday-morning quarterback is yourself. Uh, you don't have those in Britain?"

"No quarterbacks, Sir," he grinned. "We do have plenty of people second guessing the striker," he pantomimed lifting his foot to kick a ball. "Or the coach, or the defense."

"Different kind of football," I nodded. "Same issues. You didn't come in here to talk football."

"No. I had a thought. Our one ghost ship has been causing havoc across enemy space, and that is good."

"Next, you're going to say it is also not enough, that we're not really doing anything that will prevent the Maxolhx from supporting an offensive against Earth. Yeah, I get it. Uh, sorry." My habit of interrupting people was Ok with Skippy, because he tended to ramble on in an absent-minded fashion. It was not Ok with other people, and I needed to stop doing that. Smythe looked pained whenever I did it to him, maybe the British were more polite.

"That is basically true, yes. Also, we can't expect to repeat our success with hit-and-run raids. The enemy is hunting us and laying traps. Eventually, we *will* get caught."

"And then we won't be able to exploit the wormhole that will hopefully be near Earth soon. Agreed, Colonel. For now, I'm content for our little armada to act as a threat, keep the enemy off balance." In naval warfare, there is a concept called 'fleet in being'. I read about it when I was studying modern and historical navy combat tactics, trying to find something that might apply to space combat.

Yes, sometimes I do things that are useful, I don't play video games all day.

This 'fleet in being' concept is that as long as a naval force is intact, it poses a threat to the enemy, and the enemy has to devote some of their ships to monitor and guard against this 'fleet in being'. If the fleet ventures out to offer battle, the fleet could lose and therefore cease to be useful. So, unless conditions are strongly in the fleet's favor, it should remain in port and continue to pose a threat, without actually *doing* anything.

That was my plan for *Valkyrie*. Until the enemy was certain our stolen battlecruiser was destroyed, we would tie up a substantial portion of their fleet, without having to commit to battle. The Maxolhx would need to convoy all their merchant shipping, and they could not send out lightly-armed ships without being accompanied by a heavy warship. By attacking with a battlecruiser, we were forcing the enemy to completely change their tactics. Usually frigates and destroyers escorted capital ships, now those smaller ships could not venture away from their bases without the protection of a heavy cruiser, battlecruiser or battleship. Like the mythical 'fleet in being', we could lurk as a threat, waiting and watching for a perfect opportunity for another devastating attack. Perfect meant a big reward with very little risk to us.

It was unlikely we would find such an opportunity now that the enemy was on the alert for us, but we had an advantage. Through Skippy's ability to hack into relay station AIs, we were reading the enemy's messages. We had to be careful not to fall for a trap, for Skippy warned the enemy eventually might suspect we were somehow hacking their communications.

So, I was not in a hurry to take our mighty *Valkyrie* into action.

"That will not last forever. If we don't conduct further attacks, the kitties," one corner of his mouth turned upward in a hint of a smile. For some reason unknown to me, Smythe thought it amusing that the Maxolhx had a vaguely cat-like appearance. Maybe he just didn't like cats. "Will relax their guard, and the strategic situation will return to the previous status. They will hope we have been disabled after our last fight, or that we are unable to keep the ship flying. With only one ship, they have to correctly assume our resources are limited."

Nothing he said was news to me. There had to be another reason he was in my office. "You have identified a low-risk, high-reward target for us?"

"Not exactly. What I have in mind is a high-reward target, the risk might be too great for us to consider."

That got me intrigued. He recently had proposed strikes against spacedocks and other warship-servicing facilities, and each time I had decided the risk was too great. The enemy had plenty of spacedocks, hitting one or two would not put a dent in their ability to project force across the galaxy. If Smythe thought the risk of his potential target might be too much, then he must have identified one hell of a tempting target. "Don't keep me in suspense. What is it?"

He had a fish on the hook, and wanted to enjoy reeling me in. "The enemy's Cee Three all goes through their pixie technology," he stated. By 'C3', he meant Command, Control and Communications.

"Yeah," I was slightly disappointed by his response. "Skippy says eventually we will need to replace our supply of pixies. I do *not* want to go back to Detroit." When we captured the Lego pieces that Skippy used to assemble *Valkyrie*, almost all of the pixies aboard those ships were damaged by the spacetime distortion of our bagel slicer. Luckily, we found enough intact pixies to add four sets to our collection. That left us thin and we had to be careful how any times Skippy recycled the magical devices. Still, no way did I want to risk another death-defying raid on a pixie factory.

"Detroit is one of the targets I have in mind," he said with an arched eyebrow. "As a *target*, Sir. Another hit-and-run attack, not a heist."

"*Attack* Detroit? Why? Oh," the obvious slapped me in the face. Sometimes my brain is really slow. "Holy shit. You want to knock out their stock of pixies?"

"Quite so," he nodded. He had a bit of the look of a schoolmaster who was pleased a student had given the correct answer. "Not just Detroit. That planet is the factory where they make new paired units. The kitties also have two vaults where they store completed pixies."

"Whoa!" Skippy appeared on my desk, waving his hands. "Just whoa. Hold your horses there, pardner. Have you gone completely bloody barmy?"

"Skippy," I admonished him. "Let the man talk."

"*Crazy* talk," the beer can muttered. "It's impossible, I tell you. Those vaults are too well protected."

Smythe was not deterred by discouraging words. "You tend to say everything is impossible until we do it."

"Well, well, oh yeah?" Skippy sputtered. "Um, we'll see about that."

"That was a *cracking* comeback, Skippy," I winked at Smythe.

"Oh, shut up," he pouted.

Gesturing for Smythe to continue, I glared at Skippy. "Go on. We hit their stock of blank pixies?"

"Exactly so," Smythe kept one eye on Skippy, as if daring him to interrupt. "If we can destroy their current supply, and their ability to produce new units, we could cripple their defensive capability for years. They might not be able to stage a strike against Earth, because they will be too worried about their exposure to an attack by the Rindhalu."

"I *like* it." Tilting my chair back, I stared at the ceiling while I imagined the delicious possibilities. "*Damn!*" Clapping my hands, I imagined the possibilities. Taking our mighty *Valkyrie* to hit a truly vital target-

"Of course *you* like it," Skippy snapped. "You are a moron. Let me explain why it would be suicide to even attempt to hit Detroit."

He explained.

We listened.

We also got chills from hearing how strong the defenses were around Detroit. Here's a Fun Fact for you: the Maxolhx are not stupid. They had a layered Strategic Defense network around Detroit, that extended three lightminutes from the planet. That SD network covered a mind-bogglingly vast territory, which not even *Valkyrie* could penetrate and survive. We could try building another DeLorean and jumping it in near the factory, this time equipped with a nuke. But even that wouldn't harm the kitties' ability to conduct military operations, because they had enough blank pixies in their vaults to last over two hundred years, even at a wartime op tempo. Unless we could take out the vaults, we couldn't disrupt their use of pixie technology.

The vaults? Fugeddaboutit.

The vaults were inside the core remnants of gas giant planets that orbited neutron stars. Starships could not jump in or out anywhere close to a neutron star, and the planetary cores were so dense, *Valkyrie*'s weapons could pound away for years without making a noticeable dent. The Maxolhx had designed the defenses of their vaults to be secure against the Rindhalu. By the time Skippy finished explaining how it was impossible, truly *impossible*, for anyone to successfully attack those vaults, even Smythe had to admit we should drop the idea.

I was glad that he didn't expect me to do the impossible again.

CHAPTER TWENTY ONE

Some mornings, I didn't feel like eating breakfast. Maybe I was in a rush, or so groggy that all I wanted was coffee. Yeah, I know, breakfast is the most important meal of the day, blah, blah, blah. You're not my mother, so shut up.

That morning was a coffee-only event, except for grabbing what I thought was a handful of raisins that turned out to be dried cranberries. After almost spitting them out, I ate them anyway, and they were good.

By Ten o'clock, I was hungry enough that I couldn't wait for lunch, so back to the galley I went for a snack. Showing my remarkable self-control, I placed four, and only four, crackers on a plate and got a knife, anticipating slathering peanut butter on the crackers. That would keep me from getting hangry until lunchtime.

Imagine my shock and disappointment when I reached for the jar of peanut butter that was always on the shelf next to the toaster. The jar *looked* full. Soon as I lifted it, I could tell the truth: the damned thing was almost empty. Unscrewing the lid showed me there was not enough peanut butter left to bother with.

Some rat bastard had taken the last of the delicious treat and put the empty jar back, without even notifying the team on duty in the galley to request another jar from storage. We had *crates* of the stuff, one of the few foodstuffs that was in good supply. That is why I ate peanut butter a lot, everyone else was growing sick of it.

The heinous perpetrator of the crime had not just casually pilfered my snack and ran. No. Whoever it was had *worked* at it. From the way the sides of the jar had been scraped clean, somebody had spent considerable time digging out the very last dregs of crushed peanuts. All that effort, so the poor jerk who came all the way to the galley for a snack would *think* they had a jar full of peanut butter, though actually it was-

Holy shit.

The knife clattering on the floor snapped me out of my reverie.

"Skippy!" I called out as I stuffed dry crackers into my mouth. With our food supplies low, we couldn't afford to waste anything. Because I had crackers in my mouth, my call might have sounded something like "Fif-fee!"

"Did you call me, or are you practicing some lame free-association for the spoken word event?"

"Ah," I took a drink of water so my mouth could function. "I did call you. What spoken word thing?"

"It's-"

"Aren't *all* words spoken?"

"Ugh. Not if you *read* them silently, dumdum. This event is a poetry slam. People are writing poetry and performing it aloud."

"Uh, why don't I know about it?"

"Joe, please. You can barely read the label on a tube of toothpaste without getting lost."

"Hey! Some of those ingredients are impossible to pronounce."

"Riiiight. Anyway, you don't know about it because I didn't invite you."

"Oh. Who did get invited?" I figured Skippy had somehow found two or three poets among our bloodthirsty crew of pirates, and his little nerdfest was an exclusive club.

"Um, Jeez, let me count. Chang, Simms, Smythe, um- Heh heh, it looks like I invited everyone except you."

"*What*?"

"Dude. Seriously. You want to write a poem?"

"No."

"If you did, would you read it in front of people?"

"Oh, *hell* no."

"Then what is the problem?"

There was a problem. I think. Not getting invited to an event I did not want to attend sounded good, except when everyone else *did* get invited. "Uh, can I get back to you on that?"

"Yes, if you phrase your statement in the form of a haiku."

"Haiku? Is that like a limerick?" I guessed hopefully.

"*No*. Google it, knucklehead. Also, if you called me to solve the mystery of the peanut butter burgler, you can puzzle that one through on your own, Nancy Drew."

"I don't intend to press charges, so don't worry about it."

"Then why did you call me?"

"Oh yeah. Where is Smythe right now?"

"He just completed a team exercise in powered armor, and is putting his kit away."

"Tell him the captain requests him in my office at his earliest convenience, if he pleases?"

"Okaaay. What if he isn't pleased?"

That made me laugh. "Oh, he won't be pleased, that's for sure."

Jeremy Smythe knew that 'earliest convenience' meant *immediately*, and that it did not matter one little bit whether he was pleased or not. He came into my office, his hair and beard still damp, having taken just enough time to get his uniform sorted. "Sir?"

"Colonel Smythe," I tried to look stern though my eyes might have betrayed my happy mood. "I just came from the galley. Some cretin scraped the last molecules of peanut butter out of the jar, and put the jar back as if it was still full."

He blinked slowly at me. If I had just told him that I was applying for beautician school when we got back to Earth, he would not have been more surprised. "You wish for me to investigate? Sir?"

"No!" I laughed. "Seeing that jar gave me an idea. You want to destroy the kitties' supply of pixies, right? We can't do that, I agree with Skippy. No, I think the only thing we have to destroy is their *faith*."

The side-eye is something Smythe used sparingly. He used it on me right then. "Their faith? In their god, or gods?"

"No. Something more concrete. Their faith in the security of pixie technology."

He sucked in a sharp breath. Our STAR team commander is smart, he caught onto my thinking right away. "The Maxolhx believe their technology is ultra-secure," he agreed, muttering half to himself. "Not even the Rindhalu can replicate pixies. The technology is considered invulnerable."

"Even by the Rindhalu," I added. "Skippy told me the spiders have been trying to copy pixies, or intercept their communications, and they have failed. Now, someone has cracked that technology. We have."

"We can't reveal our existence to the enemy," he said cautiously.

"That's the beauty of it: we don't have to. We just need the Maxolhx to *think* the Bosphuraq have replicated pixie technology and have used it to read their messages."

"They would need to shut down their *entire* military communications system," he mused, nodding slowly in appreciation. "All the pixies in their vaults would be instantly rendered useless. That would cripple them for years."

"Longer than that," Skippy spoke up as his avatar shimmered to life on my desk. "Those arrogant kitties are so confident about their tech, they don't have a workable backup. Pixie technology has been invulnerable for so long, they don't even think about it. Arrogant, *stupid* kitties," he chuckled. "What's your plan, Joe?"

"Uh, it kind of depends on what you say about it. We still have a set of blank pixies?" The answer should be yes, because that info was in the status report every morning. With Skippy, it never hurt to verify he hadn't forgotten to update the report.

"Yes. Those are precious, Joe, we don't have many left."

"I appreciate that. You once told me that you can disassociate and then re-tag a pixie more than once? And that when a pixie is re-tagged, the process leaves a residual signature?"

"Yes, a contamination. That is why pixies can't be re-tagged an infinite number of times. I have learned a lot from working with the batch we got from Detroit, and recently with the ones we got from the ships we captured."

"Excellent. Next question: if the kitties captured any of the pixies we stole from their factory on Detroit, is there any way they can determine which batch they came from, anything like that?"

"Oh," Smythe looked at me with an expression that said he should have thought of that, and he was glad someone had asked the question.

"No, Joe," Skippy answered my question. "Blank pixies are just that; blank."

"Yeah, I believe you about that. What I'm talking about is more subtle. Like, on Earth, batches of chemicals are tagged with substances to identify where and when they were made. So, if it is later realized there is a problem with a batch, they can find everything made from it. Is there something in the manufacturing process that leaves a, I don't know. A quantum tag or something?"

"Oh. I get your meaning now. Um, yes. The Maxolhx do not 'tag' batches of pixies, but it is possible to determine where and when a blank pixie was manufactured."

"Shit. That could screw up everything. We can't let the kitties figure out that we broke into their factory."

"Then you are screwed, Dude. Except for, you know the awesomeness of *me*. I can alter the signature so pixies can't be identified to a particular batch."

I slapped the desk so hard, my hand hurt. "Outstanding! Hey, can you also alter a pixie so it is tagged in such a way that it looks like the thing wasn't created in a Maxolhx factory?"

"Um, hmm," he took off his ginormous hat and scratched his dome. "I guess so. Sure. Yes, I can do that. Why do you ask?"

"Because what I want to do is plant a blank pixie in the wreckage of a Bosphuraq ship, where the Maxolhx will find it. When they examine it, I want the kitties to think that pixie wasn't stolen from them, it was made by the Bosphuraq."

"Whoooo," Skippy whistled with approval. "Wow. That would drive the Maxolhx totally batshit crazy. They would be tearing their fur out, trying to discover how the birdbrains made a blank set of pixies. That is kind of genius, Joe."

"You haven't heard all of it yet. Aboard that wreck, I also want to plant a pixie tagged to a Maxolhx battleship, or some other vital asset. That pixie needs to be one you have recycled. I want the Maxolhx to know their enemy has the ability to disassociate pixies and reuse them. And to accurately copy the tagging of a Maxolhx ship. Um." Just then, a bad thought struck me. "Shit. That will only work if the Maxolhx know what a recycled pixie looks like, and can detect it."

"Don't worry, Joe," Skippy doffed his hat to me. "I've got this. The kitties don't know that a pixie *can* be recycled, but I'll make it obvious the one we plant has been previously tagged. Hey, would it help if the previous taggings were to some of the ships we destroyed?"

"Brilliant!" Smythe clapped his hands.

"Yeah, that would be great."

"This *is* brilliant," Smythe mused. "During World War Two, the cypher team at Bletchley Park cracked the German enigma code. The allies kept it secret that they were reading German communications, so the Jerries wouldn't switch to a new code. If we allow the Maxolhx to know someone has cracked their technology, we might lose the ability to intercept their messages?"

"That's possible, I guess," Skippy admitted. "Well, no," he shook his head. "I don't think that will happen. They don't *have* another code to switch to. Like I said, they do not have a backup to pixie technology. Whatever lower-security system they use as an alternate, I can hack into. Probably. I can't make any promises until I know what they do."

"That's good enough for me," I declared. "Smythe, I want you to do two things. First, work with Skippy to find a Bosphuraq shipwreck where we can plant the pixies. Or, a ship we can turn into a wreck, if there's not one out there. I'll do the same, and we'll compare notes."

"Yes, Sir," Smythe was perched on the edge of his seat, eager to get to work. "The second task?"

"Try to," I sighed, "imagine how this could go sideways on us. I know it all sounds great right now, but I have a feeling the Law of Unintended Consequences is just waiting for a chance to bite us in the ass."

Walking back to my office with a very full coffee mug, I was being super careful not to spill any of it on the deck. Yes, it would have been smart to just take a sip of coffee off the top so it didn't risk sloshing all over, but I think it has been well documented that I am *not* smart. Plus, that coffee was about a billion freakin' degrees and needed to cool before I put any of it in my mouth. Also, it was a challenge to see if I could make it all the way from the galley to my desk without spilling a drop.

Smythe was waiting for me when I arrived, he stood up to greet me. "Sir, we-"

"Not yet. Just a few more steps and," the coffee wobbled alarmingly before I set it down, not daring to breathe. Success! "Yes!" Pumping a fist in triumph, I bent over the desk to slurp the hot liquid. And, of course, it dripped down my chin and onto my shirt. Fortunately, it was Causal Friday aboard the mighty *Valkyrie,* and I was wearing a black T-shirt with ARMY across the chest, so the stain didn't show. "Ok, sorry about that," I gestured for Smythe to sit. "What's up?"

"We discovered a complication."

My response was to scowl at him. The scowl wasn't done for effect. "I hate complications. Especially before coffee in the morning." My triumphant mood was fading fast.

He looked at the still-full mug. "Should I come back later, Sir?"

"No, if you're going to ruin my day, let's get it over with."

"It is not necessarily a *bad* complication. It depends on how you look at it."

"Will *I* think it's a bad thing?"

"Again," he splayed his hands, palms up. "It depends. We were looking for a wrecked Bosphuraq ship where we could plant pixies."

"Good, because I didn't find anything."

"We didn't either," Smythe acknowledged. "There are many ships that have been destroyed, but we need a shipwreck that the Maxolhx will search. Therefore, it must be recent. The kitties will not go back to a wreck they have already scanned, unless we give them a reason to do so. I couldn't think of a reason that wouldn't make the enemy suspicious of the information."

"Well, shit. So, you came to the same conclusion I did? That we need to plant the pixies aboard a Bosphuraq ship *before* the Maxolhx attack it?"

"That won't work, Joe." Skippy gleefully crushed my hopes. "Hey, that coffee is getting cold."

"Oh, thanks." Picking up the mug, I sloshed it and spilled enough on the desk that Skippy's avatar had to move so he wasn't standing in a puddle. There was no rush to mop up the spill, because the flexible surface of the desk sagged, forming a pool to contain the spill. That was a cool feature of my fancy new desk. It was still too big but, I had promised to like it, and I kinda did. Pulling a towel out of a drawer, I tossed it on the pool of liquid. "It won't work because we can't be sure the pixies aren't damaged or destroyed in the attack?"

"Bingo!" Skippy gave me not just a thumbs up, but the more enthusiastic double-gun point. "That problem, plus we would have the whole issue of capturing and boarding a Bosphuraq ship, to plant the pixies."

"Like I said: well, shit. I don't want to risk boarding a hostile ship with our depleted STAR team. We're back to Square One, then."

"Not precisely," Smythe had a very satisfied I-know-something-you-don't look.

"Don't make me guess," I mock-glared at him over my mug while I gulped it. Damn, it was still super hot.

"In the Maxolhx message traffic, we found an operation they are planning. The Bosphuraq have sent transport ships to a planet they call Vua Vendigo. It is an isolated world, served by only one dead-end wormhole. Its primary asset is an agricultural research station. That station has a substantial civilian population, and the birdbrains want to evacuate all personnel. The Maxolhx have learned about the evac plan, and they are using it as an opportunity to show their clients they can't escape punishment. The kitties intend to intercept and destroy the transport ships, then bombard the research station from orbit."

"They are going to wipe out an agriculture station?" I knew the Maxolhx were ruthless, but that surprised me. "Why?"

"Because," Skippy explained. "The Maxolhx suspect that research into plants might be a cover for banned activities. But mostly, the kitties want to make a statement that *no* place in Bosphuraq territory is safe. Probably, they wouldn't have bothered attacking Vua Vendigo, but if they allow their clients to get away with an evacuation, the Maxolhx will appear weak. Killing a couple thousand civilian research scientists, support personnel and their families will send a strong message. Plus, the Maxolhx are simply hateful MFers and they think killing defenseless clients is fun."

"Well, screw them." Suddenly, I didn't feel like drinking coffee. Guilt tends to spoil my appetite. "Listen, Smythe, I do feel bad for those Bosphuraq. I started this whole mess." That was true. The reason the Maxolhx were shooting at their clients was my fault. The worst part of it was, that desperate scheme hadn't worked. All those Bosphuraq deaths were for nothing, and we couldn't do anything to stop the slaughter. "You aren't proposing *we* defend that planet, are you? I'm not risking this ship for aliens, even if they are civilians. Besides, the kitties will just send more ships, until they knock us out and turn that planet into a smoking ruin."

"No, Sir. It is impractical to defend that world, and that is not our responsibility. Skippy and I were considering whether we should warn the planet, and perhaps the star carrier that is bringing the transport ships. Let them know the Maxolhx are planning to attack."

Without thinking about it, I did the Jim Kirk Lean. Right elbow on the armrest, chin cradled by my thumb, index finger scratching my chin thoughtfully. "We warn the Bosphuraq, the Maxolhx are certain to learn about it, right? The kitties will know for sure someone has hacked their communications."

"That is the point, yes," Smythe agreed. "We will provide the Maxolhx with evidence their communications have been compromised, by warning the people on Vua Vendigo. Then we will show them *how* they were hacked, by planting pixies aboard damaged Bosphuraq ships."

"Huh." I stared at the ceiling. That was not a Jim Kirk signature move. But then, Kirk seldom wrestled with self-doubt. "I read somewhere that in World War

Two, the Allies knew the Germans planned to bomb a city in England, but they couldn't send the RAF to defend, because that would expose the secret that that the German code had been broken. Damn," I shook my head. "That was a tough call. The right call, but, tough. Now we're doing the opposite."

"The story about the bombing of Coventry," Smythe said matter-of-factly, "is probably a myth. However, it is true that protecting the secret of the Ultra code being broken required extraordinary measures."

"And now," I mused, "we have an even greater secret, and we're giving it away. Somehow that doesn't feel right."

"The Maxolhx would assume-"

"That doesn't mean it is wrong, it just *feels* wrong, you know?" I asked. "We've spent years out here, going to great lengths to keep our secrets. We have killed to protect our secrets. Now we're giving it away. It goes against my training. But," I took a breath. "It is the right thing to do. This Voodoo Vending place-"

"The name is *Vua. Vendigo.*" Skippy was disgusted. "Can you not remember even-"

"Like the name matters?"

"Do you have to give a nickname to *everything*?"

"Well, I'm a soldier, so, yeah."

"Ugh. The next time I sign up with an outfit of dangerous desperados, it will be the *Salvation* Army."

"Ok, on one side we have a birdbrain star carrier with its racks stuffed with transport ships. What are the kitties bringing to the party?" For me, that was the crucial question. If the Maxolhx had assigned a group of battleships to the raiding party, we needed to look for another opportunity. No way was I risking *Valkyrie* in another tough fight if I didn't have to. One screw-up was enough.

"It's not quite so simple," Smythe explained with a pained expression. "The Bosphuraq are sending *three* star carriers. Two are bringing eleven transport ships between them. The third carrier's platforms are loaded with four battleships; four of the most modern heavy combatants in the Bosphuraq fleet."

"Whooo," I whistled. "Holy shit, the birdbrains are gearing up for a *fight* against their patrons?"

"It appears so," Smythe nodded. "The Maxolhx are sending a pair of heavy cruisers, without escorts."

"No escort ships?" That was puzzling to me.

"Yes, Joe," Skippy confirmed. "It's a long flight from the closest Maxolhx base to Vua Vendigo, far enough that short-range ships like destroyers would need to refuel along the way, or be strapped to a star carrier. Our ghost ship attacks have convinced the kitties that lightly-armored escort vessels are worthless, even a burden in combat. Two heavy cruisers can complete the mission without needing a vulnerable star carrier, plus they are considered safe from us, because we have never intentionally attacked a capital ship."

"We did that *once*," I corrected him.

"That was a mistake," Skippy corrected me right back. "From intercepted message traffic, we know the Maxolhx now suspect that our thirteenth attack did not intend to target such a heavy force. Regardless, the kitties believe we will avoid targets that can fight back."

"They're right about that," I muttered, unhappy with the thought of taking our one precious battlewagon into another potentially fair fight. "What about the birdbrain battleships? Does the math change if they're on our side?"

Skippy took off his oversized Grand Admiral's hat and scratched his dome for effect. "Marginally," he frowned. "We shouldn't count on coordinating an attack with the Bosphuraq, Joe. They're not just going to follow orders from a ghost ship. Besides, their tactics are not compatible with-"

"Ok, I was just asking, bad idea," I admitted. "Crap. We need to hack into a Bosphuraq relay station to get the flight plans of those three star carriers, then find their actual locations before they get to, uh." When I called the place Voodoo Vending, that was to piss off Skippy. Now I couldn't remember the real name. "The planet."

"No need to do that, Sir," Smythe assured me with another self-satisfied smile. "The kitties have done all the work for us."

"How?"

"Because, Joe," Skippy took up the explanation. "They hack the messages of their clients, even the codes that the birdbrains think are secure. The Maxolhx know all about the battleships and the flight plans. The three star carriers are staging from separate bases, they plan to rendezvous after going through the last wormhole, at a location about three lightyears from Vua Vendigo. The Maxolhx will be waiting for them."

"And *we* will be waiting for *them*," Smythe's grin was more predatory than amused.

"Do we have time to get there well ahead of time?" I asked the question that was the first of many concerns on my list. "Wait." I looked at Smythe. "You have all this worked out, right? How about if I shut up, and you tell me about your plan?"

He did.

I liked it enough to order our ships to start jumping toward the target.

CHAPTER TWENTY TWO

"Uh oh, Joe. I just finished decrypting message traffic from the relay station. We might have, heh heh, a slight problem."

"Slight problem like, you locked the keys in your car, but a window is open? Or like, the iceberg was a slight problem for the *Titanic*?"

"The second one."

"Shit. Someday, you are going to surprise me with a slight problem that is actually a *slight* freakin' problem."

"Dude, the Merry Band of Pirates don't *have* slight problems. Don't blame me."

"What is it this time?"

"Well, you have heard the term 'relative humidity'? Like, sometimes you notice the humidity in the air, and sometimes you don't?"

I was pretty sure he was dumbing that way down for me, but whatever. "Sure."

"Ok, so, what I mean is, sometimes things can be relative, you know? Like, you think you have done a really good, super-*duper* job of concealing evidence, but then some nit-picky *jerk* who has literally *nothing* else to do comes along and-"

"Crap. What did you do, Skippy?"

"Ah, it's kind of what I didn't do. Or, what I didn't do well enough, you know?"

"What," I counted down from five to control my temper. "Did you not do well enough?"

"So far, heh heh, two things. First, I should give you some background. There is a Maxolhx starship captain named 'Illiath' who has been assigned to verify the bullshit story we cooked up, about the Bosphuraq developing advanced technologies and blowing up two kitty warships on their way to Earth. She could have seen the assignment as busywork, done the minimum effort to check the boxes, and moved on with her life, but *nooooo*, she has to take her job *seriously*, because she is so *important* and she-"

"Ok, so what did this chick do?"

"Commander Illiath is not a '*chick*', Joe."

"My bad. You know what I mean. Go on."

"She looked deeper into our cover story about changes in the inner structure of the star, in the system where we took over the moonbase, and stole a Maxolhx dropship. That cover story was *solid*, absolutely solid, except for the nagging little detail that I couldn't send the effect back in time."

"Uh, of course you couldn't. Why would that- Holy shit! The kitties have a freakin' *time machine*?"

"No, you knucklehead. Well, they sort of do, I guess. Space combat, Joe."

"Oh." Give me bonus points for knowing what he meant. "They jumped out to where light from the star was from before you screwed with it?"

"Exactly." He paused. "Very good, Joe. Sometimes, you are not as dumb as you look."

"Why didn't you consider this before?"

"Because, *duh*, there is nothing I could do about it. Plus, I never expected some obsessive-compulsive Sherlock Holmes wannabe would investigate in that level of detail. Actually, hmm, I have to admit I am impressed by their AI. It must have created a virtual model of the star and- Anyway, that sort of thing is nothing more than a hobby for me, but it is impressive that a Maxolhx AI did it."

"What's the damage? They know we're involved?"

"No, nothing like that. All they know is, the timing of when the star was screwed with doesn't line up with the story we planted in the confession message. This Illiath woman reported her findings to their Fleet Intelligence, and mostly it was dismissed. The Intel people figure that whoever wrote the confession didn't have access to all the details, and got the timing wrong. By the time they received her data, we had started our ghost ship campaign, and their Fleet had more important things to worry about."

"Ok, that is a relief. So why is this a problem for us?"

"Because Illiath is very persistent and very dedicated and very good at her job. Also, Fleet Intelligence is hedging their bets, so they allowed her to continue her mission, even after we launched the ghost ship attacks. Her next stop was where we attacked the two ships headed to Earth."

"The place where you cleaned up the crime scene? You used the ship's masers to fry any tiny little pieces of debris that could point back to the *Dutchman*?"

"Yup. I did fry the evidence. Mostly."

"Mostly? What does that mean?"

"It means, I got all the pieces I could detect with the ship's sensors. We were very thorough, just not thorough enough. Illiath sent out a cloud of nanoparticle sensors to scour a section of the battlespace. It was-"

Waving a hand to stop him from relating nerdy details I wouldn't understand, I asked "Bottom line this for me, Skippy. What do the kitties know?"

"They found fragments of the *Dutchman*'s hull. The fragments were microscopic, but large enough for a full chemical analysis. Illiath was able to determine the fragments came from the hull of a Thuranin starship."

"Oh, shit. Ok, uh, she can't identify the hull fragments to the *Dutchman*, can she?"

"No. Well, not exactly. She does not know the fragments belong to a particular Thuranin ship, she can't even determine the ship was a star carrier. Plus, since we captured the *Dutchman*, that ship has flown through a whole lot of radiation and micrometeorites that have altered the hull's original composition."

"So, we're good, then? She doesn't have any useful info?"

"Again, not exactly. Remember when we jumped through an Elder wormhole, and we broke it?"

"Of course I do."

"Yeah, well, the kitties were *very* interested in learning what the hell happened there. They scoured that area also, and, well, we left some pieces of the ship behind there, because the *Dutchman* was damaged by passing through the wormhole. Don't worry! The kitties still can't identify the ship that collapsed that wormhole.

But, Illiath was able to determine the Thuranin hull fragments at the battle site, are from the *same* Thuranin ship that was involved in the wormhole collapse."

"Ohhhh. This is bad news, Skippy. It calls into question our whole story for framing the Bosphuraq."

"Um, maybe, and maybe not. The *Dutchman* contains not only Thuranin hardware, it also has bits and pieces of multiple ships we took from the junkyard in the Roach Motel. Illiath's AI is flabbergasted. Their sensor sweep found particles from ships of *eleven* different species in the battlespace. They have no idea what to make of the data."

"Oh. So, this is neither bad news nor good news?"

"I wouldn't say that. Um, you know how when the STAR team conducts training outside the ship, they put on mech suits and go through an airlock?"

"Ayuh. I've trained with them more than once."

"You also know how, when a dropship launches, the docking bay is depressurized before the doors open?"

"I am getting a bad feeling about this."

"When people go outside in mech suits, or dropships launch, the outsides of those things are coated with a fine layer of human DNA. Moving around, or dropships using thrusters, or just the solar wind, knocks DNA particles off and deposits them on the hull."

"I have a *very* bad feeling about this."

"You should. Illiath found traces of human DNA at the battle site."

"Skippy, when I was learning the principles of space combat, the key was understanding that everything out here is so *big*. Now you're telling me I also need to worry about stuff so tiny, it is microscopic?"

"Unfortunately, yes."

"The kitties know humans were involved in destroying two of their ships?"

"No. No, Joe, they don't. Along with human DNA, they found biological evidence of eight other species, including Thuranin, Kristang and Bosphuraq. Illiath's report listed the finding of human DNA as a 'curiosity'. She does *not* suspect humans were involved. She would probably dismiss that notion as ridiculous."

"This is telling me that our margin of error has suddenly gotten very small."

"I agree."

"*Valkyrie*'s hull is also coated with human DNA?"

"Yes, it is unavoidable."

"So, the Maxolhx might find human DNA at the sites where the ghost ship attacked?"

"Only at the sites of battles where *Valkyrie*'s hull was struck by enemy fire. In most of our battles, we were not touched by enemy weapons at all."

"Do you have any good news for me?"

"Yes. Illiath absolutely confirmed that two Maxolhx ships were destroyed at the battle site, and she was able to identify the debris as the two ships that were going to Earth. That part of the evidence matches the story we planted to frame the birds. She also found the decoy debris we planted, and she does not know we left that debris to frame the Bosphuraq. So, the evidence is inconclusive. She is questioning how much of the story we planted is true, because clearly some evidence she found contradicts parts of the story.”

“Should I be worried about this?”

“That depends, Joe.”

“Are *you* worried about this?”

“Yes. This Illiath is *very* persistent. She will not stop until she has answers. While at the time, I thought the ghost ship attacks were a foolish risk you took because you couldn’t think of anything better to do, I now believe those attacks are our best protection. With their fleet tied up responding to us, they don’t have resources for looking deeper into evidence at the battle sites. In Illiath’s report, she speculated that the ghost ship is actually controlled by the Rindhalu, although she has no evidence to support her suspicion. Attacks by the ghost ship are leading the kitties *away* from the truth. That can only be good for us, right?”

“Yeah, unless we get suckered into another trap. After our thirteenth battle, the kitties left two destroyers behind to search the area. Did they pick up any human DNA?”

“No. Those destroyers were looking for where our ship jumped to, not investigating a crime scene. The nanoscale sensor gear used by Illiath is very specialized equipment, most warships don’t carry that kind of gear. For now, we don’t need to worry. The site of our thirteenth battle has been declared a No-Fly zone by the Maxolhx, their ships have been ordered to avoid the area.”

“Ok. We dodged a bullet.”

“Again. You can’t count on dodging many bullets in the future.”

“Right. Whatever we do, we need to be super-*super*-duper careful. Is there anything we can do, different procedures we can apply, to avoid leaving evidence behind?”

“Yes. I recommend we take *Valkyrie* in close to a star, with the shields deactivated, before we take the ship into combat again. A few seconds of close exposure to intense solar radiation will incinerate most of the DNA off the hull. Before dropships launch, we can flood the docking bay with ultraviolet radiation. Do the same to mech suits in airlocks, plus give the mech suits a good chemical scrubbing before they go outside. I know that is a time-consuming pain in the ass, and the crew will hate-”

“Ha!” I laughed. That felt good. Part of the laugh was relief at having dodged another bullet. “The crew will understand. A lot of life in the military is a time-consuming pain in the ass. We get used to it.”

“If you say so.”

“I do. I’ll talk with Chang, Simms and Smythe about it. Is that it, or are you going to smack me with more bad news?”

“Not today.”

“Great.”

“That I know of.”

“Uh huh.”

“Can’t make any promises, you know?”

“You are an unending source of comfort to me, Skippy.”

The Maxolhx had a good plan. Our plan was better. Also, we didn't need to destroy their two heavy cruisers. In fact, we didn't *want* to blow up both of them. Ok, if we got a lucky shot and one of those warships became a brief flare of plasma, I would not lose any sleep over it. We just weren't taking any additional risks to make that happen.

My greatest concern about the action at Planet Voodoo was not getting into a fight against a pair of heavy cruisers. That was a known risk and we could manage it. My concern was what we did *not* know. Was it a trap? Was Skippy's intel wrong? Were the Maxolhx sending more than two heavy cruisers, and were they planning another trap for us?

I didn't think so. The kitties had not initiated the action at Planet Voodoo or whatever its real name is. They are just responding to an operation the Bosphuraq had set in motion *before* our near-disaster thirteenth attack. If it was a trap intended for us, then the birdbrains must be part of the trap, and I didn't see that happening. Ok, so we only had to worry that there might be more than two heavy cruisers involved. We could scan the area ahead of time and, if anything did not match Skippy's intel, we would get the hell out of there.

Really, the plan would work for us either way. If everything went as planned, we would give the kitties another bloody nose, and destroy their faith in their most secure communications technology. If we discovered the kitties had set another trap for us, we could taunt them with an infuriating 'Nice try' message and jump away. That would let the kitties know the ghost ship was still active, was not stupid enough to fall for a trap, and was a continuing threat. Then we could look for another opportunity to plant a set of pixies aboard a Bosphuraq ship. This time, I actually had a good feeling about the operation, rather than the sleepless, stomach-churning fear and doubt I usually experienced before battles.

Which probably meant the Universe was about to stab me in the back.

My life sucks.

I gave the 'Go' order anyway.

The kitties were supremely arrogant. They had developed and refined a set of tactics for dealing with the Rindhalu and clients of the spiders, plus the restless clients of the Maxolhx themselves. Those tactics had been tested and proved successful over thousands of years of real and simulated combat, and the Maxolhx rightfully trusted the advice of the sophisticated AIs that directed battle simulations.

The Maxolhx were arrogant. Unfortunately for us, they weren't *stupid*. Much as it pained them to admit they had *not* accounted for every possible conflict, and after being slow to acknowledge the reality that they were getting their supremely confident furry asses kicked by a single ghost ship while the entire galaxy watched gleefully and cheered, they did adjust their tactics. The problem for them was that their AIs had not yet completed analysis of our capabilities and intentions, so they had to guess. Even uninformed guesses could cause a lot of trouble for us, if we weren't prepared.

One of the heavy cruisers remained just over a lighthour away from the rendezvous point, while the other ship jumped in to conduct reconnaissance. Both ships had primary and backup shield generators set on full power. Missiles were hot in their launch tubes, ready to launch at a moment's notice. Not knowing what threat they might encounter, the launch tubes had a full suite of ship-killers, decoys, enhanced-radiation and other weapons loaded. Packed in with the ship-killers were missiles with warheads designed to generate intense plasma flares that could temporarily blind an enemy's sensors. In addition to missiles, both ships had a variety of directed-energy weapons fully charged. Railgun magnets were on standby, and the hellish energies of more exotic weapons were barely held in check. The ships were ready to defend themselves against any enemy they might encounter.

Except us.

The ship that had drawn the honor of conducting the recon mission immediately launched three missiles after it jumped precisely into the scheduled rendezvous point. Such precision, coming within nine hundred meters of the designated coordinates, was not necessary as it would make no difference in the outcome of the coming battle. The ship's crew was proud of their precision, for they knew the other ship would be watching and either criticizing or grudgingly praising the precision emergence through a rip in spacetime.

The three missiles were not directed at targets, they were decoys. Each missile wrapped itself in a stealth field and projected only extremely faint emissions that duplicated the signature of their parent ship. One missile flew onward along the course of the ship, while the ship veered sharply away. Without very sophisticated sensors, no lurking enemy would be able to detect which object was the ship and which were decoys, before the stealth fields became so effective that it was impossible to see anything at all.

The ship remained on high alert as it cruised in a preselected search pattern around the rendezvous coordinates, dropping off stealthed probes to create a bubble around the center. The grid of probes extended beyond the edge of the area where the Maxolhx disdainfully estimated the crude navigation systems of the Bosphuraq would dump their ships, in case the precision of their rebellious clients was even worse than expected.

With the area covered by probes, the warship tested the network established by the linked probes, and waited for verification that the probes were feeding their data along an ultrathin beam in a single direction. Satisfied the sensor coverage was secure, and knowing that lingering in the area only tempted Fate, the ship jumped in the direction of the sensor signal.

Left behind, the probes mindlessly gathered data about that empty area of interstellar space, sending the data onward by the undetectable beam. Silently encased in their own inky-black stealth fields, the probes waited for the signal to activate their damping fields, to prevent an enemy from escaping the wrath of their masters. The probes noted the ratio of hydrogen isotopes to other atoms in the near-perfect vacuum, along with random dust particles, x-rays and less harsh radiation, and other things that were really of no interest to anyone.

What the probes did not detect, because they had not been programmed to look for, because they did not know such objects existed, was microwormholes. If the probes had been able to see those nanoscale flaws in the underlying fabric of spacetime, they would have been concerned.

Because the target coordinates were saturated by microwormholes.

CHAPTER TWENTY THREE

"Bingo!" Skippy's exultant cry made me almost jump out of the command chair, where I had just parked my butt for what I thought would be a long wait. Simms and I were pulling duty on the bridge, we each got six hours on, six off. That left only five or less hours for sleep and was guaranteed to make me cranky. With such a small crew, we didn't have much choice, everyone was standing six-hour watches. Our chief pilot Reed was getting rack time on a cot she set up across the passageway from the main door to the bridge, and Simms was crashing on my couch. Sleeping in my cabin saved her about twenty seconds of running in a crisis. Those twenty seconds could make a huge difference in a combat situation.

Her sleeping in my cabin also meant I was finding long hairs in my sink and tangled in my toothbrush. Also, when I walked into my cabin, the place had a faint scent of jasmine or whatever she used for shampoo or lotion. Neither of those things bothered me, in fact I was thinking about switching to another cabin and designating mine as quarters for the on-call crew. But it would have been nice if the long hairs in my sink came from a woman who was sleeping with *me* in the cabin, and not on the couch if you know what I mean.

Anyway, that's not what Skippy was shouting about.

"What is it?" The holographic display at the front of the bridge was still new to me. Sometimes I missed the old-fashioned flatscreens of the *Flying Dutchman's* bridge.

"A single Maxolhx *Vindicator*-class heavy cruiser jumped into the rendezvous zone," he explained.

A glance at the simple clock confirmed my inner judgment. "Crap, that's early." It was early, less than twelve minutes after Skippy's earliest estimate of when the Maxolhx might arrive. "Do we have any indication this is a problem?"

"No, Joe," Skippy calmed my fears. "It could be totally random. Or the kitties are being super extra cautious, because of the big bad ghost ship that is terrorizing the space lanes, hee hee," he chuckled with satisfaction. "Should I alert the ready crew?"

"No! No, let Simms get sleep. The Bosphuraq aren't arriving early, are they?"

"Not that I know of. Based on what we know of their flight plans, the star carrier with the battleships can't get here any earlier, and the other two star carriers would be foolish to arrive at the rendezvous before the big guns are here. The Bosphuraq know the Maxolhx could be intercepting their message traffic."

"Right. We wait, then. No change of plans," I decided, ignoring my own fears. "Hey, what was the type of that ship again?"

"It's a *Vindicator*-class heavy cruiser, the same type I expected. We have trained against that type of ship, we know its strengths and weaknesses. Why?"

"That's an odd name," I observed trying to remember what 'Vindicator' meant. My useless brain was drawing a blank.

"No more odd than any other name. The Maxolhx believe their continued success justifies, or *vindicates*, their position as rightful rulers of the galaxy."

"Rulers," I snorted. "Yeah, they might want to tell the Rindhalu about that."

"I said rightful, Joe, not actual. The kitties strongly believe that only the ongoing oppression of the spiders prevents them from bringing peaceful order to the galaxy."

"Peaceful?"

"A peaceful order under *their* oppressive rule, Joe."

"Yeah, I vote 'No' on that. Ok, we wait."

The enemy cruiser flew around dropping off probes, or that is what Skippy guessed it was doing. Even he had a tough time tracking it through the advanced stealth field. Then it jumped away, and we later detected a burst of gamma radiation coming from a spot three lightminutes away. Technically, we did not detect the actual gamma ray burst, for Maxolhx ships could direct ninety six percent of the gamma radiation into a narrowly focused beam. That gave them a major advantage in combat. Most other ships could not avoid lighting up the sky light like a strobe light when they emerged from jump. The Maxolhx could tweak their jump wormholes so they dumped the residual radiation in any direction they wanted, usually away from their enemy's sensors. We had the same technology aboard *Valkyrie*, except the awesomeness of Skippy had increased the efficiency to ninety-nine point two percent.

Or so he said. We had not actually tested that efficiency in action.

What Skippy detected was not the thin gamma burst itself, he picked up its backscatter off stray hydrogen atoms. Eleven hydrogen atoms, to be specific. That was three more, he had smugly announced, than he needed to determine the enemy's location.

With the two Maxolhx heavy cruisers having set their trap, we waited. By the time we reached the window when the Bosphuraq battleships were scheduled to arrive, I was getting used to six hours on, six off. My duty shift had begun four hours ago, and I hadn't been able to sleep during my off time, so I was existing on caffeine and adrenaline. Simms had finished her shift in the command chair, then walked over to man the weapons station. No way was she going to sleep anyway, and I needed my best people on the bridge.

With that thought, my eyes automatically darted over to the sensor station, where Margaret Adams filled in when she was not training with the STAR team. She was not yet cleared to return to duty. That had to be killing her, I knew, knowing the ship and everyone around her were *doing* something, while she waited for her brain to get back up to speed. Somewhere, probably in her cabin, she was watching a data feed from the bridge, and willing her body to heal faster.

Enough of that. In combat, I could not afford distractions.

The clock stopped counting down to the target time, and began counting up. Ten minutes, then twenty. Then an hour, with nothing happening. It got to the point where I had serious regrets about drinking too much coffee, when Skippy sang out again. "Just picked up a gamma ray burst! Signature is that of a Bosphuraq battleship."

"Battleship?" My puzzlement was matched by several of the bridge crew. "A single battleship? Not a star carrier?"

"Single battleship. It is twenty seven lightminutes away from our position."

"Something's wrong." Slowly, I raised my fist and pounded it on the armrest.

"Nothing is wrong, Joe. I anticipated this might happen. Think about it."

Think about- Looking at the holographic display, I saw the rendezvous point in the middle, the estimated location of the two Maxolhx ships three lightminutes away, and now the lone battleship. Why-

Duh.

Of course.

"That battleship is *not* alone," I answered, feeling proud of myself. "The others are out there, probably forming a ring around the rendezvous point. We haven't seen the other ships yet, because the gamma rays from their inbound jumps haven't reached us yet."

"Very good, Joe!"

"Yeah, I know. I'm a clever monkey, I should get myself a juice box. Skippy, that's no good. I shouldn't have to *think* about it. The speed-of-light lag is something that should automatically be part of how I view space combat. We all should," I added when I saw Reed nodding her head at the pilot station.

"You're getting there, Joe," Skippy gave me rare encouragement, making me wonder what insult he would slam me with next. But he didn't.

"Oh. Thanks. You keep giving hints to us filthy monkeys, please. And, I see another battleship just popped up on the display." After a couple minutes, all four of the expected battleships appeared, plus their star carrier. The five ships must have been exchanging messages via tightbeam transmissions we couldn't detect from that distance, because the star carrier jumped away far enough that we didn't detect its inbound gamma ray burst until much later.

"All right, the star carrier has cleared the battlespace," I announced to the bridge crew, who already had that information. "Skippy, is there any sign the battleships won't do what we expect next?"

"No. They have been using active scanners, but their sensors have not detected us, the Maxolhx ships, their probes or my microwormholes. From backscatter, I picked up a fragment of a message that might have been their signal for 'All Clear', it is too faint to tell for sure."

"We keep waiting, then."

Waiting sucked and there was nothing we could do about it. What we expected to happen next was for the two transport star carriers to jump in far away, within a few lightminutes of the star carrier that had been hauling the battleships. If they received an 'All Clear' message from a battleship, the two star carriers would proceed to the rendezvous point, and the battleships would join them for the relatively short flight to Planet Voodoo. When the two star carriers and the four battleships were conveniently gathered in a small area at the rendezvous point, we expected all hell to break loose.

Those battleships had a choice of tactics, none of them good. Normally, while preparing for action against a peer like the Jeraptha, two or three of the big capital ships would have remained a lightminute or so away from the rendezvous point where they would not be such easy targets. In this action, when they anticipated that any fight would be against their patrons the Maxolhx, the battleships needed to be together so they could mass their firepower on the enemy. Four Bosphuraq battleships against one Maxolhx heavy cruiser would be a decent fight, at least for a while. Long enough for the star carriers and the transport ships they were loaded with to get away. What we knew, and the birdbrains did not, was that their opposition was a pair of heavy cruisers. The battle would be a slaughter.

Actually, we knew a lot of other info that wasn't available to the Bosphuraq. We knew the kitties had laid a trap and were waiting to spring it. The birds knew it was possible they would encounter trouble, but they had tagged it as a low probability. After all, Planet Voodoo was an unimportant place and not located within an easy wormhole path to their patron's territory.

We knew the number and types of ships the kitties had, while the birds certainly did not anticipate matching up against capital ships. Based on their history of joint fleet exercises with the Maxolhx, the birdbrains rightly expected they might encounter a pair of light cruisers, perhaps a squadron of destroyers. That is what the kitties normally would have assigned to strike a lightly-defended target, and the Bosphuraq understood standard Maxolhx tactics.

What they didn't know is that our ghost ship had screwed everything up for them. Our hit-and-run attacks had forced the Maxolhx to change tactics, to assign heavier combatants or larger numbers of ships. So, there were two heavy cruisers waiting to trap and pound those battleships and defenseless star carriers.

We also had a rough idea of how the Maxolhx planned to conduct the attack. That gave us an advantage, because it limited the area we needed to cover.

All we had to do was wait.

Wait, and worry that there might be something important I had forgotten about.

The next event did not require an announcement by Skippy, because I was watching the display when it happened. Our sensors picked up the gamma ray burst of a star carrier jumping in near one of the battleships, and based on the signature, we knew it was one of the star carriers hauling empty passenger transport ships.

"Skippy," I didn't take my eyes away from the holographic display. "Call the ready crew to duty stations. It's showtime."

Simms had not even sat down at one of the weapons stations when a battleship emerged at the rendezvous point. Once all the players were there, the Bosphuraq were wisely not wasting time. They would assemble all six ships in a protective formation, with the two vulnerable star carriers at the center, and proceed to Planet Voodoo. That was the plan.

The Maxolhx had a different plan.

The first sign of trouble for the battleships was when they detected a damping field forming around them. That was an indication of an *Oh-shit* level of danger but not yet a total disaster. The crews of all ships knew they had a window of opportunity to escape before the damping field was firmly established, and all ships maintained sufficient charge for an emergency jump.

The rule of jumping away immediately upon detection of a damping field was true when the opposing force was a peer species. It was not true when the enemy was the supremely-capable Maxolhx, and especially not true when the entire area had been saturated with probes that sent out powerful damping waves.

Seeing the strength of the damping field around them go from faint ripples to gale-force waves in a heartbeat, the crews still did not entirely panic. They correctly assessed the waves must be generated by relatively small satellites, that could not maintain such a power output for long. They were correct, and the ships turned and burned to disperse out toward the edge of the field, while the weapons of the battleships targeted the now-visible probes.

It didn't do them any good.

Two of the probes had been knocked out by railgun fire from battleships, and the damping field strength was already ebbing, when two large senior-species warships jumped in to join the party.

That was when the birdbrain's level of danger spiked from *Oh-shit* to *We're-doomed*. Watching the action on the bridge display, I reluctantly had to admire the professionalism and pure guts of the battleships' crews. They knew they were very likely dead, yet they did not flinch from their duty to protect the star carriers. Or, they knew they were very likely dead, and figured they might as well try to take some of their MF-ing patrons with them.

If we had jumped our ghost ship in right then, we might have saved those battleships by luring the Maxolhx away. We could have simply stayed where we were, and dropped our sophisticated stealth field. Sadly for the crews of the battleships, saving them was not on my To-Do list that day.

We were impressed when the battleships fired on their patrons immediately, without wasting any time with useless talk. Both sides knew why they were there, and it was not to negotiate. The Maxolhx did order their clients to surrender, knowing they were wasting their breath and following formalities anyway. The sincerity of the Surrender-and-you-won't-be-harmed message was rendered less heartwarming when the transmissions were received at the same time maser beams fired by the heavy cruisers seared into the shields of the battleships.

Maybe the kitties should have sent a fruit basket.

We were very much impressed when all four battleships, having sustained significant damage in the opening minutes of the fight, turned toward their enemy so their bulk shielded the star carriers as those ships tried to run away. As the star carriers ran under full acceleration, they ejected the eighteen transport ships they had been carrying, and those ships scattered in any direction that was not toward the enemy. So far, the kitties had ignored the vulnerable civilian ships, knowing the damping field was now reinforced throughout the area and the transports were not going far. Destroy or disable the battleships, the tactic was, and then the transports could be hunted down later.

If we were impressed by the bravery and professionalism of the Bosphuraq, the Maxolhx had to be more than a little annoyed by their clients. Despite the constant punishment coming from the heavy cruisers, all four battleships concentrated their fire on a single enemy ship. That was sure suicide, and the only way to inflict worthwhile damage before the battleships were out of the fight.

It was interesting to see the fight happen for real. Skippy had shown us simulations of a contest between four of the Bosphuraq's most modern and capable battleships against two senior-species heavy cruisers, and the actual fight was not much different from what we expected. Still, it was awe-inspiring to see it in real-time. None of the warships involved had bothered to engage stealth or deploy decoys, because the gigawatts of energy they were pouring into space lit them up like a Christmas tree. Without stealth, and with all of the ships unable to jump away, it was a stand-up fight within a bubble less than two lightseconds across.

"One of the battleships is out of the fight," Simms warned. "Enemy is continuing to hit it."

"Wait a second," I counseled, having run through that exact scenario in simulations. The Maxolhx could be intending to pound that crippled battleship to dust. Or it could simply be that maser beams, railgun darts and missiles they fired before the battleship lost power, were still in flight.

"Enemy fire is being redirected," Simms confirmed my thought. On the display, we could see missiles curving as they were redirected toward other targets.

"Ok," I clapped my hands softly to avoid startling anyone who had fingers poised above buttons. "We have what we want; a disabled Bosphuraq battleship. It's our turn. Simms, weapons free."

"Aye aye," she acknowledged, and despite her reminding me that she would rather have stayed on Avalon, there was a smile on her face as she unleashed hell.

There is a saying I learned in infantry training; If you can see it, you can kill it. Or something like that, I've heard many versions of that old truism. That truth also applies to air combat and probably sea warfare, my experience training was as a ground-pounder. Basically, identifying the location of a target means that you can deliver ordnance on it. Either by yourself, with a rifle, grenade, or heavier weapons like a mortar or Javelin missile, a fireteam can do a lot of damage. For targets beyond the effective range of weapons available to a platoon, you can use the most deadly device ever developed: a radio. One of my instructors told me that four soldiers with rifles are a fireteam, but one soldier with a radio is an *army*. With a radio, you can call in battalion artillery, or close air support, and rain hellfire down on a target.

Anyway, the point is, pretty much anything you can see can be killed.

When I got to Paradise, and in training on Camp Alpha before that, nothing I saw changed the idea of being able to kill any target I could locate. With the ability to call in fire support from orbit, where every square meter of a planet's surface can be covered by a single warship within forty minutes, that idea I learned way back in basic training was reinforced.

Then, when I had to learn the very different rules of ship-to-ship space combat, I painfully realized that idea was dangerous bullshit that I needed to forget. Not only forget, I needed to wipe that kind of thinking from my subconscious.

The problem with space combat is the vast distances involved, and the speed of the combatants. Plus, the speed of light is agonizingly *slooooooow.*

In space, '*seeing*' a target only means that photons generated by or reflected from a target have reached your eyeballs. Or actually, the photons were detected by your ship's sensors. What you are seeing is where that target *was* at the time the photons left there. A ship that is estimated to be a mere three lightseconds away, only half a million kilometers, could move out of the way before your maser beam arrives. Probably *did* move, for ships were constantly engaged in evasive maneuvers during combat or even potential combat. We call that intentionally-random movements side to side and up and down 'jinking'. Not that up or down have any meaning in space, you know what I mean. By the way, we don't call for 'Evasive Pattern Riker Delta' or any nonsense like that. Sorry, Star Trek, but the whole point of being evasive is to *avoid* having a pattern. Because while your ship's navigation AI is jinking you around, the enemy's AI is intensely analyzing your movements and attempting to discern a pattern. If the enemy is able to predict your next move, then you can be sure your next supposedly random 'jink' will fly you right into the path of a maser beam that arrives just as your ship gets there.

As Scooby-Doo would say, *Ruh-roh*!

Wait, you ask. What about guided weapons like missiles? They can adjust course to track the enemy ship's movements, regardless of maneuvers. Yes, that is a very smart observation, get yourself a juicebox. The problem with missiles is that, even compared to the sloth-like speed of light, missiles are slooooow. Even with the advanced launch rails we had aboard *Valkyrie*, our missiles slammed out of their tubes at a relatively casual pace. Those launch rails sounded great, but we could only use them when the launch tube was pointed in the direction of the target. Otherwise, our missiles would expend most of their fuel to get lined up on the target.

So, let's say your target is a mere two light seconds away, that is about six hundred thousand kilometers. By the time your missile flies across that distance, the enemy could have jumped away. The enemy could in fact have jumped in *behind* you, and be frying your sorry ass with masers while your valiant missile is asking itself 'Where the F did my target go'? And then the missile would pout and fall into a deep depression, for it knew it had missed its target and was doomed to drift in deep space until the end of time.

Hey, it could be worse, you could tell that missile. It could be doomed to watch every episode of the truly awful TV show 'Casablanca' on an endless loop. Skippy had made me watch that crapfest and with every second, I could feel my will to live seeping away.

Anyway, my point is, space combat is really, *really* complicated.

To make it worse, the enemy ship is undoubtedly wrapped in a stealth field, while your missile's over-eager propulsion system is lighting up the sky like fireworks. That makes the enemy ship a difficult target to track, and your missile easy to intercept.

The real problem in space combat is not that our weapons travel slowly, it is that sensor data flows slowly back to our ship. By the time we think we have located a stealthy enemy ship, it will have moved, and we have to find it all over again.

Anyway, why does all of this matter?

Because the Merry Band of Pirates found a loophole in the law that sensor data has to flow slowly. Really, we didn't find that loophole, the incomparable magnificence of Skippy *created* the loophole. His use of microwormholes to saturate the battlespace gave us a huge advantage. An enemy ship that was twenty lightseconds away was too far away for us to effectively track. But if that same ship was only a hundred thousand kilometers from a microwormhole, our sensors were working with data that had less than a one-second lag.

But wait, you say! Our maser beam, which can't change direction in mid-flight, will still be in the wrong place when it arrives, because it will still take twenty seconds to reach the target area. Yes, of course you say that. You are the same jerk who stands up in the audience wearing the Star Trek uniform your Mom made for you, asking why in Episode Fourteen of Season Three, the blah blah blah?

Shut up.

It was just a TV show, get over it.

Also, we don't plan to use a maser beam, Mister Smartass.

Having a microwormhole providing passive sensor data gives us yet *another* huge advantage. In the guidance system of that missile is a microwormhole, that was tied back to its companion aboard *Valkyrie*. Our missile could rocket out of its launch tube at high velocity, having the luxury of waiting until we got the launcher swiveled around to point at that target. The missile then coasted on unpowered, conserving its fuel and emitting almost no detectable signature. Every time the enemy ship moved, the missile adjusted its flight with less than a one-second lag, while the target heavy cruiser had no idea danger was approaching.

Did I say 'missile'? Oops, sorry.

I meant *missiles*.

Like, more than one.

Seven, to be specific.

When your ship is enveloped in a damping field, that causes the fabric of spacetime to vibrate in a way that prevents jump wormholes from forming, you can't jump away. If your ship is outside a damping field, it is possible to jump into one. You have to tune your jump drive to emerge into an area of chaotic spacetime, and your crew should be aware of the situation, because it is going to be a rough ride. Also, understand that you will blow jump coils, and you won't be jumping away anytime soon, even if the field dissipates.

Those are the rules that apply to ordinary ships. *Valkyrie* was not an ordinary ship. Skippy had taken the best technology the Maxolhx had, and improved on it. It helped that the Maxolhx tuned their damping fields to avoid interfering with their type of jump drive, a capability the Bosphuraq couldn't match. Plus, we had the pure awesomeness that was Skippy the Magnificent.

Still, jumping into the swirling battle was not easy. A one-second lag in sensor data sounded like it was not a problem, but we might emerge right in front of a particle beam that hadn't been fired before we activated our jump drive. That was a risk we had to take. We also had to risk not knowing exactly how local spacetime's fabric was disrupted by overlapping and interfering damping fields projected by six warships.

What the hell, right? You only live once. Who dares wins. Go big or go home. Pick whatever bullshit bravado cliché you prefer, it all meant somebody needed to make a judgement call without having enough information. That somebody was me.

"Joe," Skippy prompted me. "Our missiles are approaching detection range."

Maxolhx missiles had stealth fields that were generated using ship's power before they launched, the missile's power unit then only needed to maintain the field during its typically short flight. With our seven missiles coasting unpowered, their flight time was longer than usual and the power unit was draining rapidly. As the missiles flew closer to the battle zone, they were running through clouds of ionized dust and debris, leaving faint trails behind that the stealth fields couldn't do anything about. In seconds, the heavy cruiser we had targeted would be alerted to the unexpected danger.

"Right on time," I muttered with a glance at the timecode on the display. "Simms, signal those missiles into attack mode. Reed, jump us in."

CHAPTER TWENTY FOUR

The Maxolhx heavy cruiser *Vardenox* was having a good day. The battle was going mostly according to plan, with the exception that all four of the client battleships had directed their fire at their patron's warship. That was a good thing in the opinion of the *Vardenox's* crew, otherwise the combat would be a rather dull affair. With their ship absorbing hits from four of the Bosphuraq's most powerful warships, the crew would have a good story to tell when they got back to base. It was also amusing to see their pathetic clients fighting back in so futile a fashion.

Or so the crew would say to each other. Privately, some of them, the smarter ones, were beginning to have concerns. Not doubts, merely concern. The four battleships were firing everything they had at the *Vardenox*, and their determined suicide tactics were an aspect the Maxolhx had not anticipated. Clients were supposed to be meek and intimidated when confronted by the supreme power and majesty of their patrons. Instead, the heavy cruiser was taking hits hard enough that the AI was recommending they attempt to disengage. Turn and run while firing back, the AI suggested. Get to a distance where the enemy's energy weapons were ineffective, perhaps a distance where the Bosphuraq damping field was weak, and the cruiser could jump away. It was merely a precaution, the AI stated, certainly the haughty Maxolhx had nothing to fear.

It would be a disaster if the *Vardenox* returned to base with substantial damage from what was supposed to be an easy fight. It would be a *much* bigger disaster if the cruiser had been seen to run away from their clients. Knowing that, the cruiser's captain ordered her ship to close with the enemy. One of the battleships was out of the fight. Surely the fight would be over soon, and any damage could be repaired in flight.

No sooner had the *Vardenox* committed to seeing the fight through to the end, than an alarm sounded. Missiles had just kicked into full acceleration, coming straight at the cruiser from behind.

From the drive signatures and the decoys scattered by the missiles, they were clearly Maxolhx in origin.

That could only mean one thing.

The *Vardenox* was just about to signal its companion ship to warn of the danger, when the ghost ship emerged in a chaotic burst of gamma rays.

It would have been dramatic for me to grip that arms of my chair, or even better, slam a fist down as I shouted an order. In a deep voice, I would bark commands like "Weapons free" or "Fire for effect" or "Target the enemy and fire".

I did not do any of those dumbass things, because I didn't need to. We didn't have time for the crew to wait for my slow brain to make decisions. We didn't even have time for the crew at their stations to send orders to their banks of weapons. Our attack plan had been programmed into the consoles before we jumped, everything was on automatic after that.

As soon as *Valkyrie* emerged from the inbound end of our jump wormhole, we had missiles being slammed along the rails of their launch tubes, which had been swiveled around to point in the proper direction before we jumped. Maser beam exciters created beams of coherent energy, stabbing out toward the enemy, with particle beams and railguns right behind. Our most potent weapon, the anti-energy pulse cannon, cycled through shot after shot as quickly as the exotic particles that powered it could be created.

Space between us and the *Vardenox* was so filled with hard-accelerating missiles, directed energy and debris that our sensors were having to guess exactly what was out there. The sensor system's level of confidence was shown by a sliding bar on the side of the display. It went from a boastful '*I got this*' at the top to '*I have no freakin' clue*' at the bottom. Once the heavy cruiser recovered from its initial shock and began frantically shooting back at us, the bar slid down to the level I thought of as '*Dude I'm making up half this shit*'.

That did not fill me with confidence.

Neither did the way the deck was rocking. "Simms?" I asked, adding to her burden without any possibility that I would get a useful answer. Somebody needed to tell that idiot in the command chair to shut up and let his people do their jobs

Simms shot me an exasperated look, and Skippy answered for her. "Joe, will you *please* shut your pie hole unless you have something useful to say? We are fine, don't worry."

The flashing alert on the display, showing that our point-defense system had lost track of three inbound missiles, was enough justification for my worry. The deck then rocked violently, at the same time the display's indicator clicked down to only two missiles unaccounted for.

Because the third missile had snuck in unseen and impacted our shields, hard enough that plasma fragments splattered on our hull plating. That thick armor plating mostly held, but in a few spots, the plasma burned down to the reactive armor layer, which exploded outward to prevent the plasma from penetrating into the ship's vital insides. That was a serious concern, *Valkyrie* only had a limited number of replacement reactive armor panels, and no way to get or make more.

Engaging in combat with a Maxolhx heavy cruiser, even one that had taken hits and was tangling with three client battleships, was not a sure thing. There was risk involved, and that risk became exponentially greater when our somewhat wonky inbound jump dumped us within point-blank range of our target. We had planned to emerge half a lightsecond away, about a hundred fifty thousand kilometers. Because even Skippy had not been able to map all the overlapping damping fields and analyze how they affected the fabric of local spacetime, we emerged less than seven thousand kilometers away from the Vardenox. In space combat, that is way too close for comfort. That is so close that when our missiles launched, they slammed out of their tubes at full acceleration, relying on guidance provided by the ship's sensors. Once they cleared the tube and began using their own sensors, they only had a short time to go from '*Where the hell is the freakin' target?*' to '*WTF?!*' as they crashed into the enemy's shields.

We had several advantages after we jumped into the battlespace, even though our jump caused all of our microwormholes to blink out of existence as Skippy lost his connection to them. We had a larger, more powerful, more heavily-protected ship. We had total surprise. The enemy had three other ships shooting at them, while we could concentrate only on the *Vardenox*. But our biggest advantage was that we did not need to finish the fight. We could disengage at any time. Our objective was to have three things to happen; for a Bosphuraq battleship to become disabled, for the Maxolhx to realize our fearsome ghost ship was there, and for the Maxolhx ships to run away from the threat we posed. Objective one was achieved before we jumped, and we achieved the second objective merely by showing up to the fight and lobbing a couple maser bolts in their direction. We were working on the third objective. In case the fight went against us, the backup plan was for us to run away, with the Maxolhx in pursuit. Either way, we needed both groups of aliens to clear the battlespace, or our whole operation was for nothing.

"*YES!*" Skippy shouted, startling everyone. "Hold fire, hold fire!" He exhorted and didn't wait for us, he cut power to the weapons as he spoke.

Leaning forward in my chair, I came to the limit of what the nanofabric restraints would allow. "What is it?"

"Lucky shot," he snickered. "We knocked out a power distribution node in the cruiser's aft section on the port side. There is a temporary gap in their shields."

"Why the hell are we holding fire?" I demanded.

"Because, Joe," he explained in the tone adults use when talking to small children. "You told me that destroying those cruisers was not necessarily an objective."

"Oh." He was right about that. The display was showing a schematic image of the enemy cruiser, with some of the ship's features fuzzy as our sensors were having to guess through all the energy and debris flying around. One section of the schematic was outlined in blinking red. "Skippy," one side of my mouth clamped down on my lip harder than I intended and I tasted blood. "If that damned ship's jump drive were to suffer a fatal cascade, I would not be unhappy, if you know what I mean."

"Oh," he chortled with an evil huskiness. "I think I know what youze mean, Boss. Colonel Simms, if you would-"

She didn't look up. "On the *waaaay!*"

She had selected a railgun dart equipped with an atomic-compression warhead, instead of a simple kinetic round. That was overkill for the task, but Skippy is fond of reminding me that overkill is underrated.

That ship went up like it was the Fourth of July and somebody triggered all the fireworks at the same time. That would be fun to watch, but not from only seven thousand klicks away. Man, if I thought *Valkyrie* had been rocking before, that was nothing compared to what we experienced as we were caught in a fireball like a small sun.

On the display, our shields were flickering and there were so many red warning lights, it was easier to look for systems that were *not* overloading.

Shit.

Sometimes, overkill is just overkill.

The second heavy cruiser, which had drawn the disappointing assignment of jumping in farther from the star carriers, and had not been fired upon by the enemy at all, was glumly shooting away at the battleships when two things happened simultaneously. It received a missile warning from its companion ship, at the moment when the ghost ship emerged from nowhere.

Before, the crew of the heavy cruiser *Rewprexa* had been hoping for some excitement. Something like one of the battleships breaking off the attack on the *Vardenox*, to charge at the *Rewprexa*. That would be exciting, and a story to tell when they got back to base.

Encountering the ghost ship was more excitement than the *Rewprexa*'s crew wanted, and if they had been free to admit that, they might have turned and run for the edge of the damping field. The Maxolhx were powerful, they were arrogant, and like all bullies, they were cowards. No one had challenged them in so long, they felt a stab of fear at the unknown when someone pushed back. That was why the *Rewprexa*'s crew had not rushed in to engage the four battleships, they preferred to let the *Vardenox* take the full force of the enemy's fury, while they remained a safe distance away.

The arrival of the ghost ship changed the situation. The *Rewprexa* had no choice. Command wanted that mystery ship dead, and glory would go to the crew of any ship that ended that scourge. Unending shame and scorn would follow the crew who failed to aggressively engage in a fight with the ghost ship. Ignoring the three battleships that were now firing on the *Vardenox* with renewed vigor, the other heavy cruiser raced ahead, taking time only to launch a trio of missiles at the disabled battleship along the way.

Then, to the secret relief of the *Rewprexa*'s crew, the ghost ship was consumed by the fireball that was left of the *Vardenox*.

"We're alive?" That may have been the stupidest thing I ever said. Really, I should make a list and have people vote on it, because I have said a LOT of really stupid stuff.

"Yes," Skippy snapped. "Have a little faith, will you? We got scorched a bit, that's all."

"Then why is the display blank?" It was not actually blank, most of it was showing static, alternating with guesses about the position of enemy ships we couldn't see.

"Because, dumdum, the sensors are resetting. While they catch up, I am feeding my own data. Whoo, that *was* a close one! Maybe we shouldn't have-"

The deck rocked, hard enough that the restraints tugged me back in the chair. "*What was that?*"

"Railgun dart," Skippy mumbled. "Where did *that* come from? Hmm, must have been fired by that other cruiser. Before you ask, I don't think they can see us yet. Based on when it must have been launched, that dart was fired before we blew up the first ship. Sensors are clearing now, there are still a lot of high-energy particles flying around out there. Joe, we're in good shape, but that other cruiser will see us before we can get a target lock on it. It would be a good idea if we put some distance between us and the enemy."

"Crap. No, we can't do that. We have a reputation as a fearsome ghost ship, we can't run away from a single cruiser."

"Then we should do something else, before they hit us with everything they have. Missile-defense sensors are still blinded. We could take a lot of hits, Joe."

"We *are* going to do something," I decided in a flash of inspiration. "Reed, turn us toward that other cruiser's last reported position, and step on it."

"*Toward* them?" Skippy screeched. "We're getting closer? *This* is your plan?"

"Trust me on this one."

The crew of the heavy cruiser *Rewprexa*, having to that point sustained no damage in the raging battle, was overjoyed when they saw the ghost ship being consumed by the fireball that had been their sister ship. Their AI confirmed the crew's immediate expectation that no ship so close to that explosion could escape without serious damage. The ship's AI initially calculated a thirty-one percent chance that the ghost ship had been torn apart, though it cautioned too little was known of the mysterious ship's capabilities.

Hearing that the ghost ship might no longer exist did not please the *Rewprexa's* crew. If that were true, the glory would go to the deceased losers of the *Vardenox*, who had given their lives to save the Maxolhx Hegemony from the scourge of the ghost ship. Especially since the *Vardenox's* crew had not *given* their lives at all, their own inept fumbling had killed them.

Those jerks.

When the blast was not followed by an enormous secondary explosion, the AI declared hopefully that the ghost ship was very likely drifting, stricken and without power. That was the best outcome for the crew of the *Rewprexa*. They could have the honor of finishing off the scourge of the space lanes, and everyone would forget about the dead losers of their sister ship. The AI announced it had a ninety-two percent confidence in its assessment, and the captain ordered weapons held ready to adapt to the situation, once the targeting sensors located what remained of the ghost ship.

Until the targeting sensors began screaming a warning, as the ghost ship charged out of the plasma cloud, flying straight at the *Rewprexa*! On the display, the shocked crew saw the enemy's hull glowing as that ship's shields shed plasma and exotic radiation.

The *Rewprexa*'s AI scrambled to evaluate the unexpected situation, immediately concluding the ghost ship must be far more powerful than any mere *Extinction*-class battlecruiser.

The ship's captain froze for a moment, to her own shame.

The crew looked to their captain for guidance, and for hope. The ghost ship had taken everything a heavy cruiser could throw at it, including the *Vardenox* itself, and was still capable of combat.

The moment of hesitation was broken when a message was received from the ghost ship. *Do you wish to engage*, the message read simply.

The captain, crew and AI of the *Rewprexa* very much did *not* wish to engage the enemy at that moment. Or ever.

Exploiting a temporary weakness in the damping fields saturating the battlespace, the surviving heavy cruiser made a clumsy and noisy jump away, then another jump as soon as the ship's strained jump drive could manage.

"Huh," Skippy said quietly.

"That," I said while tensing my shoulders so the bridge crew did not see me shudder with relief. "Is called bluffing, Skippy."

"You took one *hell* of a risk, Joe. Fighting a heavy cruiser right now would be an iffy proposition for us. Our point defense sensors are almost blind, and the shield generators-"

"As you are fond of telling me, bluffing really didn't have much of a downside. If we had run in the opposite direction, could we have jumped away before that ship was in weapons range?"

"No. Well, probably not. Our jump drive got dorked up by the explosion."

"Right, that's what I figured. Plus, we are the fearsome ghost ship, scourge of the space lanes. Running away from a single ship was not an option. Ok, Simms?"

"Sir?"

"Drop our damping field. Skippy, signal those three battleships to jump away soon as they can. Suggest they make the longest jump their drives can handle. We will assist the disabled ship, if we can."

"Aye aye," Simms acknowledged, and we waited anxiously as one, then another battleship disappeared in a burst of gamma rays.

"Skippy," I squeezed the armrests. "What the hell is that third ship waiting for?" On the display, I could see the strength of the rapidly-dissipating damping field around that battleship was wavering between the green and yellow indicators. "Is its drive damaged?" That could be a big problem for us, we did not want witnesses hanging around. The next part of the operation was already distasteful. Adding another dead ship to our list of crimes was not part of the plan.

"Their drive is not the problem, Joe," he said with a sound like grinding his teeth together. "The problem is, they want to be *heroes*."

"Ah, shit. They want to join us?"

"Of course they do, Joe. This should not be a surprise."

"It's not. It *is* a pain in the ass. Tell them thank you, but, uh, the best way they can participate in our glorious struggle against oppression is to evac the people on Vua- Whatever it's called. You know, use your best revolutionary fervor bullshit."

"Ok," he chuckled. "I am basing my latest inspiring revolutionary rant on the collected speeches of Fidel Castro. That should do it."

My knowledge of history, like my knowledge of most things, was sketchy. "Because Castro was such a great speaker?"

"No, because he was such a pompous windbag, he never knew when to shut the hell up. I expect that battleship to jump away, just so they don't have to listen to me anymore. And, yes! That ship just jumped. We're good."

"We're not good," I corrected him. "We are far from *good*," I added to myself, and Simms caught my eye. She nodded. Neither of us liked the next part. "We're the opposite of good. XO, do we have a favorable firing solution?"

"Just about optimal, Sir," she reported sourly. In most situations, having an optimal solution would make the officer at the weapons station happy. Not this time.

"Launch one," I gave her a thumbs up for encouragement.

"One away."

Clearing my throat, I waited until everyone was looking in my direction. "People, nobody likes what we have to do. We don't have a choice, at least, not one that I know of. We've been causing havoc all across Maxolhx space, and striking fear into the heart of the enemy. We have destroyed more than forty ships. We are all proud of our accomplishments, and we all know those attacks are only pinpricks to the Maxolhx. This operation is our chance to be more than an annoying distraction. We can *hurt* them, strike a blow against not only their Cee Three capabilities, but their belief in their own superiority. To do that, we need to take an action that none of us are happy about. Remember, these birds, these *vultures*, would nuke our homeworld to ash if they had the chance."

From the pilot station, Reed nodded once, emphatically. No one said anything.

"Ok," I took a breath. "Skippy, signal that battleship we will render assistance, *and*, that they need to be wary of stealthed Maxolhx missiles flying around." That part was true, and that was why even ships that had won a battle had to be careful about loitering in the battlespace. Enemy missiles that had missed their targets would be seeking another opportunity to strike a target.

"Got it, Joe," Skippy's glum tone told me he wasn't any happier than I was. "That battleship is already pinging away with active sensors. It won't do them much good," he sighed. "Their sensor suite got pretty much fried. Our missile doesn't need its enhanced stealth capability."

"Yeah, well, stick to the plan."

The crew of the battleship was overjoyed when the ghost ship blew up one enemy cruiser, scared away another, and then approached to rescue the survivors. More than half of the Bosphuraq ship's crew was dead already, and the survivors knew their ship was no longer capable of combat. The best they could hope for was to be picked up by another warship, to continue taking the fight to their hated patrons. Best of all, beyond the wildest hopes of anyone aboard, they would be taken aboard the fearsome ghost ship! Yes, they could strike a powerful blow against the enemy, as new recruits to the mysterious scourge of the space lanes. They-

The missile warning sounded only two seconds before impact, not enough time for the point-defense system to even begin to calculate a firing solution for the few maser cannons that were active.

"That's it." I announced without joy. And without necessity, for everyone on the bridge had seen the damaged Bosphuraq battleship blow up. "Simms, launch the package."

"Package is away."

"Skippy, broadcast a general message for ships to be wary of missiles in the battlespace. Pilot, wait ten seconds, then jump us away."

The package launched shortly before we jumped was a modified sensor probe. It wasn't fast or powerful and it didn't need either of those qualities. It was small and stealthy, and its payload had been replaced with a trio of bots. On its own, the package used passive sensors to scan the area, identified the best target, and it carefully approached a section of the battleship we had blown to pieces. Within twenty-eight minutes of launching, it had matched course and speed with the tumbling and scorched section of what was once a proud battleship, a ship that had defied its cruel masters.

Latching onto the wreck, the package released the bots, two of which scurried along the interior, ignoring shattered and frozen body fragments. Reaching a heavily-armored magazine, they easily cracked the encryption on the door mechanism, and planted our pixies. On the way out, they erased any evidence of having been there.

The third bot made a beeline for a data access point, and hacked into what remained of the local network. That bot planted highly-encrypted evidence that the Bosphuraq had broken the secret of how pixies operated. The evidence we planted was deliberately vague and corrupted, and would only be believed by someone who had seen the actual pixies. The database could be misdirection. No way could the kitties ignore finding actual pixies.

We hoped.

The heavy cruiser *Rewprexa* waited a carefully calculated amount of time before returning near the battlespace. Ordinarily, the time would be calculated to avoid enemy missiles lurking in the area. That was not why the heavy cruiser hesitated. First, they waited at a distant point to detect the extremely faint gamma ray signature of the ghost ship jumping away. Curiously, that was detected shortly after the disabled Bosphuraq battleship exploded, an event that had no immediate explanation. If they survived, the *Rewprexa's* crew planned to claim one of *their* missiles had destroyed their client's traitorous battleship, and they were already altering the flight recorder data to match their version of events.

After seeing the ghost ship jump away, the delay in returning was a two-factor calculation. First, how long should they wait to make sure the ghost ship was not waiting nearby to ambush them? Second, how long *could* they wait before their fleet command accused them of cowardice? The captain waited until they were perilously close to the cowardice deadline, then warily jumped in.

The battlespace was empty, other than cold, floating debris and echoing radiation. Ready to jump away at any moment, the *Rewprexa* launched probes to explore the wreckage, the crew irritated at needing to follow procedure and expecting to find nothing of interest.

They were very much wrong about that.

"This is," Admiral Urkan paused, scraping a claw along the side of his desk. The desk was well-worn from his habit of dragging a sharp nail along the tough and expensive wood. He could have chosen a standard desk made of composites or some exotic material for the desk, instead he had selected wood from trees that were native to the home planet of the Rindhalu. The trees no longer grew on that world, only single-celled organisms survived there now.

He liked the wood for several reasons. For visitors, the wood's distinctive patterns told them that he had the position and power to demand a rare item. For him, it was a prideful reminder that his species had captured and still held the homeworld of his enemy. It was also a warning of what could happen to his people, if their military faltered in their vigilance.

He scraped the nail back toward himself, feeling the wood give beneath the pressure. The fact that he dared damage such an expensive item, deliberately damaged it, was a statement of his place in society. At the top of society.

"This is interesting," he concluded, having sought a neutral word.

"Yes," Illiath agreed with equal neutrality, having been warned against displaying unseemly enthusiasm in the Admiral's presence. Enthusiasm was a characteristic of children and amateurs. "That is why I persisted in my investigation."

"You were remarkably thorough," the Admiral observed, thinking that he would not have liked serving under such a meticulous officer. Also thinking that, whatever the result of her current assignment, Illiath was an officer to watch. She had a bright future, and perhaps he should consider attaching her, and her success, to his command.

"The enemy was remarkably thorough in their deception."

"Hmm. Based on the facts available until you brought this," he waved toward the document glowing in the hologram above his desk. "Rather far-fetched theory." He did not use the word 'information' because Illiath's report was not merely a dry list of facts. No, she had used those facts to weave together a theory, an intriguing theory. A theory that was entirely her own. "Based on all the data we have before your investigation, my staff concluded that a rogue faction of Bosphuraq destroyed the two ships we sent to the wormhole near Earth. That conclusion agrees with the official assessment of the Fleet Intelligence Division. Now, you have strung together a theory that calls into question the expert analysis of everyone *other* than yourself."

Illiath did not give an inch under the Admiral's stare. "They did not have access to the facts I have gathered during my investigation."

His reply was a simple, noncommittal "Hmm."

"Admiral, there are too many facts that do not support the initial conclusions of the Fleet Intelligence Division. The site of the battle that destroyed our two ships contained anomalies we cannot explain." Pausing to take a breath, she risked a look at the Admiral, using not only her eyes, but also the more delicate and useful sensors embedded throughout her skin. Interestingly, he was not using measures that could have blocked her sensors. His body language was casual, even bored. Yet his heartrate was elevated, and he was exuding distinctive pheromones of excitement. The pheromones not of fear, but of a predator on the hunt. He did not think her theory was wild and useless speculation. He thought she might be onto something, and he wasn't bothering to conceal his interest.

"The Rindhalu?" He asked.

"We must believe either that our clients have leaped far beyond us in technology, *or* that our ancient enemy is deceiving us yet again."

"Using the Bosphuraq against us?"

That was a part of her theory she did not have evidence for one way or another, and that made her uncomfortable. "Possibly. Though I doubt it. Letting another species do the work for them would be in keeping with the deceitfulness and laziness of our enemy. However, giving advanced technology to the Bosphuraq would ultimately be dangerous to the Rindhalu themselves."

"The Bosphuraq could turn on the Rindhalu?"

"That also." She withheld a shrug to avoid insulting the Admiral's poor guess. "Their greatest concern should be that in the end, we will wring this technology out of our rebellious clients, and then *we* would make a technological leap. I think it is more likely that all the actions we have observed, including the ghost ship, are direct actions of our enemy. The Bosphuraq are not involved in any way, other than victims."

"Victims," the Admiral slapped his desk. "Who cheer in the streets when they hear another one of our warships has been destroyed by the ghost ship." He considered the document for another moment, ignoring the junior officer. "If it *is* the Rindhalu, I can understand why they would use a ghost ship to terrorize us, and encourage our clients to falsely view us as weak and vulnerable."

That was what Illiath had been waiting to hear. Just an 'if'. *If* the Fleet Intelligence Division was wrong. Against her was the bureaucratic inertia of the Fleet. In her favor was the simple fact that no one wanted to believe the lowly, ignorant Bosphuraq had surpassed their patrons in technology. People *wanted* another explanation, craved it. "Their plan is working," she observed, risking a reprimand for being unpatriotic.

The Admiral issued no reprimand. The truth was neither patriotic nor unpatriotic, it simply *was*. "Two questions for you, Illiath."

"Of course, Admiral."

"First, assuming the Rindhalu are behind the ghost ship attacks, what is their goal? What is the endgame for them?"

She had a ready answer, having asked herself the same question. Rather than appearing too eager, she paused as if considering the matter. Then, "It could simply be exploiting the current disruption in our coalition. The Kristang are torn apart by yet another of their silly and pointless civil wars. The Thuranin overextended themselves and were punished by the Jeraptha. The Thuranin and Bosphuraq then stupidly began fighting each other, weakening both of them and allowing the Jeraptha to gain territory easily. Now, the Bosphuraq are not only unable to support their peers, they can't defend their own territory. The Jeraptha are being very careful, waiting to see how far they can push before we respond against them directly. And then, there is this Alien Legion," she glanced at the man's eyes, judging his reaction. The Ruhar-led Legion was a sore subject to Maxolhx leadership. Officially, they were not concerned about such a minor and primitive force. The idea that the haughty Maxolhx deigned to even notice the existence of humans was laughable.

The reality was that the Alien Legion was a troublesome irritation, that might develop into a serious problem to the Maxolhx Hegemony. The *timing* of the Legion's establishment, and their recent victory at Feznako, was already a problem. If the coalition were strong, the Legion would barely be noticed. But on top of all the other issues the Maxolhx were dealing with, allowing the mere idea of the Legion to exist might be dangerous. The success of the Verd-kris might encourage others to have rebellious, traitorous ideas.

"The Legion," the Admiral made a high-pitched growl, his species' version of a laugh. He laughed, but Illiath noted he was not showing other signs of mirth.

"The emergence of the Alien might be a coincidence, or it might be part of the enemy's plan. Admiral, the Rindhalu might not have an endgame in mind. They could simply be keeping us on the defensive. They gain much, with little risk to themselves. They know we will not hit back, unless," her eyes flicked to the holographic document floating above the Admiral's desk. "Our leadership is provided with solid evidence of the enemy's involvement. As you have seen in my report, the enemy has been very careful not to leave evidence behind. Very careful, but," she ventured a smile, "not careful enough."

"If you are correct in your analysis. Very well, that remains to be seen. Now, my second question. Assuming the ghost ship is under control of the Rindhalu, why did they hit our ships that were traveling to Earth? There were much softer targets available, we know the ghost ship does not take risks that can be avoided. There is also the fact that there was a significant time gap between the attack on the ships assigned to the Earth mission, and the current series of attacks."

She had an answer for that also, and this time did not feel the need for a dramatic pause. "Because, Admiral, I believe those ships posed a threat to the Rindhalu."

"A *threat*? Earth is in the territory of our coalition. It is a world of no importance, populated by primitives." Or, he reminded himself, it had been populated by primitive humans. With the Kristang in control and cut off from powers that might restrain their more blood-thirsty urges, the humans on Earth might have gone extinct. Fearing rebellion by the billions of useless slaves, the Kristang could have casually committed mass genocide.

That's what the Maxolhx would have done, in those circumstances.

"A threat, Admiral, because the wormhole to Earth was the first to shut down, to exhibit anomalies we have not seen in the history of our people. I believe that, for whatever reason, the Rindhalu used that wormhole to test their technology that can disrupt the operation of Elder wormholes."

"You have evidence of this?" He demanded.

"Yes. Another ghost ship was detected in the vicinity of other wormholes that behaved oddly. The previous ghost ship *broke* an Elder wormhole," she reminded him.

He settled back in his chair. "If you are right, then it is good that we sent a reinforced battlegroup to Earth." He did not mention that the ghost ship had recently attacked two star carriers that were laden with heavier ships than those going to Earth. "However, I am not yet convinced of your theory," he declared.

Illiath kept her cool composure. "It is radical, certainly. I can provide more-"

But the Admiral's eyes suddenly glazed as he stared straight through her. He was receiving a message. As she watched, his heartrate spiked.

Moments later, he wiped away the hologram. "There has been another attack by the ghost ship, at Vua Vendigo," he announced. "This time, we have lost a heavy cruiser."

Illiath knew that was both good and bad. Bad, because the hopes that the mysterious ship could not sustain further attacks were proven wrong. Good, because while that ship was still operational, it was possible someone would find evidence that proved her theory correct. "They attacked a heavy cruiser? The enemy is growing bold. This could-"

He waved her to silence. "The time for theories is over, Commander Illiath," he said with disappointment. If Illiath's theory had been proven, that would make his life easier, for he would be fighting an enemy he knew, rather than a ghost. He would also reap the glory of having brought her report to the senior leadership. Now, all her efforts were for nothing. "Another cruiser searched the wreckage of a *Bosphuraq* battleship," he emphasized the ship's undeniable ownership. "Our people found paired quantum state interchangers."

Illiath felt a wave of chill. "The Bosphuraq salvaged them from the wreck from one of our ships?"

"No," he shook his head and stood, indicating the meeting was over. "One of the interchangers found was *blank*. It was not manufactured by us."

"That is *impossible*," she gasped.

"More impossible, one of the others exhibits evidence of having been reassigned, more than once."

"Interchangers are a single-use item!" She protested, refusing to believe. That was the whole point of the technology, that once assigned to a pairing, it could not be altered.

"We *thought* they were. Apparently, we were wrong. Illiath, we lost a heavy cruiser to an ambush by the ghost ship. The Bosphuraq are reading our message traffic." Fleet Intelligence had warned that the ghost ship somehow had access to information about the flight plans of Maxolhx starships. Senior leadership publicly dismissed such concerns as unfounded speculation, while privately agonizing over how many ships had been ambushed. "With the discovery of interchangers aboard a Bosphuraq battleship, it is now clear that their ghost ship is not alone in having such capability. Our ancient enemy would never risk giving interchanger technology to a lesser species. Somehow, our clients have advanced significantly beyond us in technical ability, without the assistance of the Rindhalu. I am sorry, but it appears you were wrong," he gestured for her to follow him out the door. "It also appears that our entire system for secure communications has been rendered useless."

CHAPTER TWENTY FIVE

"Heeeey, Joe," Skippy interrupted my train of thought, while I was writing the after-action report for our battle at Planet Voodoo. What I was thinking about, I can't remember, because he interrupted it.

He interrupted me all the time, and I had learned to partly ignore him, but when he stretched out words like 'heeeeeey' and had that 'well, heh heh' tone in his voice, he instantly had my full attention. "What's up?" I asked, steeling myself for the worst possible news. We had once again pinged a Maxolhx relay station for data. Technically, Skippy had ransacked the station's low-level AI. He took over the thing and stripped away all the data we needed. When he was done, he erased all evidence we had been there, planted false memories, and we went on our merry way. The Maxolhx would never know anything unusual had happened, because the station AI had no memory of anything other than a normal boring day.

My imagination was working overtime, dreaming up awful scenarios like somehow the Maxolhx knew our ship was crewed by humans and-

No. That wasn't possible.

Was it?

No matter. Speculating what could have happened was a waste of time, and just made my blood pressure spike.

"Um, I have a question. It's kind of a friendship question."

"Friend-" WTF? Had Skippy become friends with the station AI, and-Speculating was a waste of time. "Uh, sure, Skippy. Go ahead."

"Remember a while ago, you said that sometimes, a true friend has to stop you from doing stupid things?"

"Uh, yeah?"

"You said a true friend will get *Darryl* to do the stupid thing, so you both can laugh about it later."

"Sure."

"That reminds me, Joe. The next time we fill out a crew roster, we need to include a Darryl. We do a *lot* of stupid stuff out here."

"The 'Darryl' doesn't need to be named Darryl, Skippy. It's more of a concept."

"Ah, got it."

"Is that what you wanted to talk about?" If that was all he had to say, I was eager to get back to- Crap. Whatever I had been thinking about before was totally gone from my mind.

"No. That was just an example. I have kind of a moral dilemma."

"I thought you had a question about friendship?"

"Both, actually."

"Why don't you tell me what this is about?"

"Well, that's the problem. I'm not sure I *should* tell you. Let's say, hypothetically, you learned some important info, something your buddy would like to know about. But, you know that if you tell him, he will probably get all emotional about it, and go do something dangerous and stupid."

Oh shit. Whatever awful thing I had imagined he was about to say, could not be as bad as what he was trying to say. For *Skippy* to be experiencing a moral dilemma, the situation had to be catastrophic. "You want to know whether you have an obligation, as a friend, to tell the guy?"

"Yes. If I *know* he will do something stupid, should I not tell him this important info?"

"That's a complicated question," I answered truthfully. "It kind of depends. Let's drop the hypothetical. Does this information affect only *me*, or the whole crew?"

"The whole crew, because the stupid thing I *know* you will want to do, will put their lives in danger. It also affects nearly two hundred other people. By 'people', I mean humans."

At that point, I had absolutely zero idea what he could be talking about. He feared I would risk the lives of the crew, for something I did not need to do, but would do anyway.

And, it involved several hundred other *humans*?

WTF?

If only several hundred humans were affected, the issue could not involve Earth, or Paradise.

Again, I had no clue. So, I asked him. "Ok, Skippy. This is now officially a military matter. As the commander, I need to know, so tell me."

"How about if we pretend this whole conversation never happened?"

"*That* is not going to happen. Tell me, right now. That's an order."

"Hmmf. An *order*? To me?" He snorted. "Ok, buddyboy, if you want to pull rank on me, then I need to consider whether it is my duty to prevent the *commander* from jeopardizing the mission so he can run off on some idiotic feel-good side project."

"Shit. It's that serious?"

"Hey, knucklehead, I wouldn't be so worried about telling you, if I wasn't so worried about what you will do with this information. I *know* you, dude."

The worst thing about being a hypocrite is, knowing you are a hypocrite. When I was in high school, toward the end of my senior year, I saw my buddy Steve's girlfriend kissing another guy. Did I tell him what I saw? No. That wasn't because I thought he would be violent, I just didn't see the point of all the drama that would result. We were graduating in two weeks, Steve was going down to North Carolina to work in his uncle's air conditioning business, and his girlfriend was going to college in Michigan. The odds were they would not see each other again, plus they had only been dating for three months. It wasn't like they had found True Love.

So, I withheld the truth from Steve. Why? Basically, because I didn't trust him not to let his bruised ego make him do something stupid and totally unnecessary.

Yes, there I was, Mister Big Hypocrite, insisting that Skippy tell me what he knew.

"Skippy, I appreciate your concern. You are right, sometimes you have to protect a friend from himself. The problem is, I am not just a friend. I am the commander of this ship. It is *my* responsibility to decide whether we continue with the current mission, or change our plans. I need to know."

"Ugh," he sighed. "Ok, don't say I didn't warn you."

"I promise to tell everyone that you *did* warn me."

"Deal. Ok. Remember how I told you that the White Wind clan not only brought UNEF soldiers to Camp Alpha, they also kidnapped humans and brought them there?"

I stiffened at recalling that horrific memory. "Yes. They were used for experiments, to create bioweapons."

"Right. In case the White Wind had difficulty controlling Earth, they planned to reduce the human population to a more manageable level." He paused. "I know that is a very cold and clinical way to describe a truly monstrous subject. All I am doing is stating the facts."

"I know. I know all that. How does it affect us now? You destroyed the stocks of bioweapon at Earth, the White Wind clan doesn't exist anymore, and lizards can't get to Earth anyway. Unless-" An awful thought struck me. "Did the crew of the *Dagger* have a backup plan to-"

"Whoa! No, Joe, this has nothing to do with Earth. This will go faster if I just tell you what I know, you know?"

"Shutting up now."

"Ok. The White Wind brought UNEF to Camp Alpha as a staging base, because they didn't have another place to hold a large, potentially unruly and hostile military force. They hadn't yet concluded negotiations to use UNEF to garrison Paradise, and-"

"That's all ancient history, Skippy. Why do I care?"

"I'm getting to that part, numbskull. You know the White Wind brought kidnapped humans, of a wide variety of ethnicities and ages, to Camp Alpha for bioweapons research. That base was on the other side of the planet, that's why UNEF never saw it. The reason the research was conducted there was, the White Wind planned to use the bioweapon if UNEF got out of control."

"Why? We were all gung-ho idiots back then. We thought the lizards were our glorious allies." We did think that, and, you know what? I kind of miss those blissfully ignorant days, when life was so much simpler, and I didn't have so much responsibility.

"Yes, but if somehow you learned the truth, that you went offworld to fight on the wrong side of the war, things could have gone sideways in a hurry. The White Wind were operating on a shoestring budget, they couldn't afford any complications. Anyways, the reason you care is, you care about the humans who were kidnapped off Earth."

I gave him the side-eye. "I do care. But you told me all those people were killed in the research, or afterward."

"They were. All the humans used for experiments on Camp Alpha are dead. However, the White Wind did not bring all the kidnapped humans to Camp Alpha. About five hundred of them were brought to a planet called Rahkarsh Diweln, to be used as a control group. And as reserves."

"Shit. You mean-"

"Yes, Joe. In the databanks of the relay station I just ransacked, I learned there are one hundred and eighty two humans still alive on Rahkarsh Diweln."

"Damn it!"

"If you don't like hearing that, you *really* won't like knowing that one hundred and thirty four of those humans are under the age of ten."

"*What?*"

"Hey, *I* didn't kidnap those children."

"Sorry. I don't want to sound callous, but, how are they still alive? The White Wind clan is gone, right?"

"Correct. Their assets were absorbed by the Fire Dragon clan, who took everything they considered useful. That mostly means military assets to support the civil war we started. The Fire Dragons have pretty much left everything else alone for now, except for trading or selling assets that other clans want. No one wants Rahkarsh Diweln, so that planet is on the sidelines until the civil war is over."

"Yeah, great. That's not my question. The White Wind, or whoever is running Rahk-" The name Rah-care-esh Dee-wall-n was too long, I needed to think of a nickname for the place. Humans were being held as prisoners there, so- "Let's call this planet 'Rikers', Ok?"

He cocked his head, puzzled. "Riker's? For the Star Trek character?"

"No. For the prison in New York."

"Ah. I get it. The humans being held there are prisoners of war."

"The lizards running the place now, they are continuing to feed the humans there?"

"You make it sound like you *don't* like that?" He was surprised.

"I do like it, I'm just surprised, that's all. Oof. Listen, I'm trying to understand the situation. I can't imagine the lizards are feeding an isolated group of humans out of the kindness of their hateful lizard hearts."

"Oh. I get the question now. They are mostly *not* feeding them, Joe. The biosphere of Rikers is somewhat compatible with human life. The humans are mostly feeding themselves. They are growing Earth crops, or they learned the hard way which plants and animals on Rikers can safely be eaten."

"Yeah, but aren't they a security risk?"

"No. The humans are on two islands, far from the population centers of the planet. The entire world only has a population of less than one million."

"The humans are surviving, then."

"Sort of. Their numbers have dropped from almost five hundred originally, to under two hundred today. The food supply has been a major problem. And, obviously, the Kristang have provided hardly any medical care."

"This is bad. What aren't you telling me?"

"You think their situation is not bad enough?"

"I think you haven't told me how bad it is yet."

"You know me too well. All right. From the relay station, I learned the entire galaxy is talking about two subjects right now. The ghost ship that is making the Maxolhx look like fools. Hee hee," he chuckled. "You should see how the kitties are trying to deny the whole thing. We are driving them *crazy*, Joe."

"I will send them a fruit basket to apologize. What is the second thing?"

"The Alien Legion."

"The Legion? Seriously? Their action involved only a couple thousand humans, on a planet nobody cared about. Even if all of UNEF-Paradise signed up for the Legion, that wouldn't significantly boost the combat power of the Ruhar."

"Ugh," he sighed wearily. "Hey, dumdum, I *told* you, you need to read my summary of the Legion's Deathtrap mission."

"I did read it."

"Apparently, you don't remember the important details. Anyways, Perkins knows the importance of the Legion is not ten or fifty or a hundred thousand human troops. It's the *millions* of Verd-kris who could potentially be added to the combat power of the Ruhar. Emily Perkins has got the whole galaxy in an uproar. Everyone is frightened that the strategic math might change. Adding the Verd-kris to the Ruhar strength of arms not only boosts the hamsters against their traditional enemy the Kristang, it could have long-term effects on the balance of power across the galaxy. Traditionally, civilian populations have been relocated when control of a planet changes from one side to another. Or, those civilians are used as hostages to get a better deal on a world the conquerors prefer. The Verds are the largest group of aliens living under the control of a foreign power, and the only group of significant size that has renounced affiliation with the official government of their species. There are Ruhar living under control of the Kristang, but those Ruhar remain loyal to their own people, at least in spirit. The Verds, just by fighting alongside Ruhar on Fresno, have threatened to upset the social arrangements that have been in force for thousands of years. No one knows how to respond, and everyone is anxious about it."

"That makes sense," I agreed. Damn it, he was right. I did need to read that report. "How does a group of human children threaten-"

"They don't."

"Then why-"

"Are you going to keep interrupting me?"

As a response, I mimed zipping my lips, locking them and throwing away the key.

"We'll see how long *that* lasts," he rolled his eyes. "The threat to the humans on Rikers is not what they might do, but what could be done to *them*. After the Legion unexpectedly won the fight on Fresno, the Thuranin were concerned. Then the Bosphuraq were forced to pull out of their joint offensive with the Thuranin, because the Maxolhx are beating the crap out of the birdbrains. Now, the little green pinheads have panicked. Their position is weakened, they no longer have help from the Bosphuraq, and the Maxolhx are demanding the Thuranin push the Jeraptha back, which they can't do by themselves."

He paused to see if I interrupted again. All I did was nod for him to continue.

"Hmmf. The last thing the Thuranin need now is for their Kristang clients to be thrown into even more disarray, if support from the Alien Legion allows the Ruhar to stage a major offensive. From the relay station, I learned the Thuranin have asked the Maxolhx for permission to stage a raid on Paradise, to hit the humans there."

"Shit! Uh, sorry. Go on, please."

"The Thuranin rightly see humans as the key to the Alien Legion. Without the presence of UNEF soldiers, the Ruhar public would never agree to provide the Verd-kris with weapons and training. The logic is, hit Paradise hard enough, and the Alien Legion problem goes away. Fortunately for UNEF, the Maxolhx are concerned about the Thuranin committing warships to an operation against Paradise, because the Jeraptha would certainly respond and retaliate."

Silently, I gestured with one hand for him to keep telling the story. Even though I had a *lot* of questions for him.

"Unfortunately, the Maxolhx suggested an alternative to a military strike against Paradise."

"Oh shit," I groaned. "Sorry."

"I'll allow that one. Have you guessed the bad news?"

"The Thuranin want the Fire Dragon clan to develop a bioweapon for use against humans, and they plan to use the POWs on Rikers as test subjects?"

"Very good, Joe! That's close to the truth. The Thuranin don't trust the Kristang's skill in biotechnology, so they are negotiating to *buy* the humans. They will be transported off Rikers to a Thuranin research base, and then used to develop a bioweapon."

I should have been screaming with horror. Maybe I'd seen and heard about enough horror that I could put it aside until later, when I would allow time for screaming and throwing chairs and whatever else I thought would uselessly blow off steam. In the meantime, I concentrated on doing my damned *job* and being useful. "That's going to violate The Rules, right? No use of bioweapons? The Kristang thought they could get away with it last time, because they planned to make it look like a natural mutation of a human virus infected the Ruhar. No way would anyone believe that a *second* deadly virus on the same planet is a coincidence."

"Well, yes and no. Yes, you are correct, no way could the Thuranin get away with delivering a bioweapon. The Rindhalu *would* respond, even if it took them months or years to investigate and move their lazy asses. No, because the Thuranin are clever, and they're getting help from their asshole patrons. The little green pinheads plan to cause a mutation of the *vaccine* I developed. All humans on Paradise had been vaccinated, and almost all Ruhar on that world also."

"Damn it! I have to ask a question."

"Permission granted."

"The vaccine has already been administered, right? It's gone. It created antibodies in the people who were treated, then it," I waved a hand vaguely in the air. "It died, or something. How could the vaccine-"

"Ugh. This is what happens when I try to dumb something down for you. Yes, numbskull, the vaccine is gone. My treatment for humans was not just some simple vaccine that generates crude antibodies. My technique used gene-splicing to alter their DNA, so their DNA looks for the pathogen, and then cranks out a cure. What I should have said is, the Thuranin plan to hijack my alteration, to make the DNA produce a fatal mutation. I hate to say this, but the plan is quite clever, and they probably have the ability to do it. Maybe I should have anticipated that someone might use my technology for nefarious purposes, it's too late now. If humans on

Paradise begin dying, everyone will blame the miraculous vaccine that was provided by an unknown source. That vaccine was manufactured by the Ruhar, and voluntarily used by humans. There won't be a violation of The Rules. It's a technicality, but those are important in this war. Bottom line is, the Thuranin could get away with it."

"Shit. Shit shit *shit*!"

"That was very helpful, Joe. Do you have any more words of wisdom?"

"Those kidnapped children, they will be used to develop this new bioweapon?"

"Along with the adults, yes. The Thuranin want to purchase all of the prisoners. They already have a dozen Keepers, but a dozen people is not a useful test population. Joe, I know you are thinking that we have to rescue the people on Paradise again, but-"

"No. Skippy, I am thinking about those children who were taken from Earth, held in horrible conditions, and are now going to be used for cruel experiments. *That's* what I'm thinking about."

"Exactly. That is what I was worried about. You hear about a group of human children in danger, and you immediately want to abandon our mission, to fly off and rescue them."

"Crap! I wish, I really wish, that Emily Perkins had just stayed home on Paradise, and not gone off on an adventure with this Alien Legion she invented. Damn that woman! She *had* to know the humans on Paradise would be seen as a threat. I mean, it's kind of a *DUH* that aliens would want to hit back. *Of course* they would. Paradise is better protected than it was, but, UNEF is still a soft target there."

"It's not so soft now, Joe. After Fresno, the Ruhar anticipated there might be retaliation against UNEF, so they added a destroyer squadron to the battlegroup stationed there. Also, the project to complete the Strategic Defense network in orbit has been accelerated. The problem is, the Ruhar are building their defenses to fend off a *Kristang* attack. They can't stop the Thuranin, if those little green assholes really want to wipe out UNEF. Anyway, if the Thuranin can develop and deliver a bioweapon, the defenses in orbit won't matter."

"Right. It's not just about rescuing a small group of children."

"You say that, but I can see that wild look in your eyes. You biologicals lose all ability to reason and use logic when your offspring are threatened."

"This is not just about a hundred thirty children on one planet. The humans on Paradise have been busy making babies. There are a lot more children there than on Rikers. And," I shook a scolding finger at his avatar. "It is not a *bad* thing to care for children."

"I didn't say it was a bad thing, dumdum. My concern is that you monkeys will go flying off with a half-baked plan to rescue the children on Rikers, without *thinking* about it first. I fear you are not capable of thinking in this situation."

He was right. Maybe it was impossible to make a plan or a decision, without being overwhelmed by emotion. The thought of starving children, taken away from Earth and held in horrible conditions far from home, living in terror every day, was overwhelming. It was *supposed* to be overwhelming. The people who aren't affected by hearing that kind of horror are psychopaths, and I didn't want to be one of them. "Let's make a deal, Ok? If you think I am making a decision based on emotion rather than good sense, you call me out."

"You say that *now*, but if I do that-"

"Skippy, I am capable of being calm and reasonable."

"Calm and reasonable?" Skippy said incredulously. "Joe, when you were six years old, didn't you go to a petting zoo and get into a fight with a llama?"

"Hey, that llama was being a *dick*."

"Yessss," his voice dripped with sarcasm. "It was all the animal's fault. Your family got banned from the petting zoo, because Joe. Ruins. *Everything*."

"Can we get back to the subject?" I asked, knowing the answer to that question was *no*. Skippy was so convulsed with laughter, there was no way we could have a productive discussion, until he got it out of his system.

And for the record, that llama totally *was* being a dick.

There was nothing to do but wait until Skippy was done laughing, so I waited.

"Oh," his avatar pretended to wipe away holographic tears. "That was a good one. *You*, being calm and reasonable."

"I promise to listen."

"Huh. *Really*? How about this, for example? The easiest way to end the misery of those children, minimize risk to this ship, and ensure the safety of humans on Paradise, is an orbital strike on the islands where the children are being held. End the threat to Paradise, by ending the humans on Rikers."

"That-" I leaned forward across my desk, close to lunging at him. Close, but I didn't. My alter ego No Patience Man was mostly useful, but he had a bad side. I too often talked and acted without thinking. One thing that had helped me is counting to one before I react to something that made me angry. Not counting to three, I didn't need that. Counting to *one* was enough.

Skippy was baiting me. What he said was true. If the goal was to ensure the safety of Paradise, with minimal risk to our ships and crews, then an orbital strike to wipe out the poor humans on Rikers was an option I needed to consider.

I didn't *like* it, but I did need to consider it.

"That was an asshole thing to say."

"I didn't-"

"It was also true. You're right. An orbital strike is an option. A crappy, awful option, but it is an option." Was living with myself, if I callously ended the lives of those children, an option? No it was not. I could burn that bridge when I came to it. "Let's make sure that is never our *best* option, Ok?"

"That's up to you, Joe. You make the plans, you make the decisions. You're the commander."

"Shit. Thank you *so* much for reminding me."

"Hey, I didn't want to tell you about this at all, remember?"

"Yeah. All right. Don't tell anyone else about this yet. I need to think about how we could rescue those people on Rikers."

"Rescuing them isn't the only problem, Joe."

"It's not?" Maybe my brain wasn't working at its best right then.

"No. If all we cared about was pulling the humans off Rikers, we could park *Valkyrie* in orbit and rain hellfire down on the lizards until they surrendered the humans to us."

"Buuuut," I was catching on to the problem. "We can't do that, without blowing our cover story for all the ghost ship attacks we just conducted."

"Correct. Also, however we rescue those people, we need *another* cover story, to explain why anyone other than us would risk military action to pull a small group of primitive humans off that planet."

"Oh, Great. *Wonderful.* Do you have any other good news for me, or would you prefer to just drive a rusty nail through my skull?"

"No, I'm good. You have enough on your plate."

"I had enough on my plate *before* this latest trouble. Hey, in the future, could we have a codeword, to signal when you're about to dump a truckload of shit on my head?"

"Me saying 'Heeeey Joe' wasn't a good enough signal?"

My response was to pound my forehead on my desk. My old desk aboard the *Flying Dutchman* at least made my forehead cool when I was bonking it in frustration. This fancy damned Maxolhx desk had its own climate system, to keep it at the user's body temperature.

I missed my old desk.

I missed my old ship.

I missed my old *life*.

CHAPTER TWENTY SIX

People in the staff meeting had the same reaction, when I told them about the POWs on Rikers, and that Skippy thought an orbital strike was an option we needed to consider.

"Don't be mad at Skippy. He is only stating the ugly truth. He wants us to be sure we are not risking our crew, our mission, and maybe all of humanity, just to rescue one small group of children. We are not talking about doing that. Pulling those people off Rikers also protects over a hundred thousand human lives on Paradise. *That's* why we are contemplating a rescue mission."

Adams scrunched up her face, like she was trying hard to think of something. She was improving rapidly, the nanobots in her head were mostly deactivated and dissolved. She did not need any help walking, she was using the gym by herself without any difficulty. And, she was not back to a hundred percent yet. She still had trouble expressing complex thoughts. Not with understanding complex issues or concepts, she was reading at a high level and acing the tests Skippy gave her. Her speech center still had some rearranging to do before she was fully recovered. She knew it, we knew it, and she knew we were being extra patient with her when she spoke.

"It's Ok, Adams," I said softly. "Take your time."

"I *hate* you being patient with me." She glowered around the table, her stutter almost gone.

"That is not going to change," I glared back at her. "So suck it up, Gunnery Sergeant. You're here because I value your perspective. Whatever you've got to say, say it when you can. We can wait."

She squinted and her lips pressed together. Whatever she wanted to say, she was trying to squeeze it out of her head. "That's not true, is it? We can't wait."

That remark drew surprised looks around the table. "We can't wait *forever*," I replied. "The Thuranin are coming to pick up those people in-"

She was frustrated again. This time, the source of her frustration was *me*. That was a good sign. "Not about waiting. I meant, it is not true that rescuing those people on Rikers is about saving humans on Paradise."

That got me worried that she had not been able to follow Skippy's briefing. From the people casting their eyes down at the table, or looking anywhere but at Adams, I wasn't the only one concerned about her. "The Thuranin want-"

"I know the Thuranin are buying those people, so they can develop and test a bioweapon. I," she balled up her fists then released them. Her frustration then was with *all* of us. Her still-recovering brain had figured out something the rest of us were missing. "Skippy, do the Thuranin absolutely *need* the humans on Rikers? Can't they buy some Keepers, or create a virtual model of human biology, for testing?"

"The Thuranin already have a handful of Keepers, and they have tried to purchase more. Keepers would be better test subjects, because they are adults and more similar to the target population on Paradise," he said in a clinical tone. "The children on Rikers are not optimal test subjects, but they are available. No clan that has Keepers is willing to sell or trade them. Each clan is holding their Keepers in reserve, in case the Alien Legion invades one of that clan's planets. The Keepers are considered a strategic asset. There was a raid, two months ago, where one clan attempted to steal another clan's Keepers. Unfortunately, all those Keepers were killed in the crossfire." He paused. "Buncha morons. I don't know whether to feel sorry for them, or be grateful they are out of your gene pool."

"I feel sorry for them," Reed spoke immediately. She looked around the table. "By this point, they all have to know they screwed themselves. They screwed *us*, all of humanity, because they were stupid and stubborn and refused to see the truth."

Smythe nodded. "I want to hate them, as traitors, but they are only misguided."

"Or not," I added. "Remember that Chisholm guy we captured? He was pretty certain the Kristang weren't the good guys. He was willing to sacrifice himself, if there was any possibility that would get better treatment for people on Earth. Ah, shit. There's no point arguing about this now. Skippy, when you developed a vaccine or whatever to counteract the pathogen last time, you built a virtual model of human biology. Can the Thuranin do that?"

"No. If you remember, despite my confidence in the model I built, we tested the vaccine on the infected Keepers. Even I could not be certain my model was completely accurate. However, though the Thuranin do not possess the technology to build a biological model of humans, the Maxolhx *do* have that capability, and would likely loan it to the Thuranin. As I explained, the kitties do not want their clients distracted by conducting a risky attack on Paradise. They will bend the rules in this case, because the kitties are also somewhat concerned about the Alien Legion. So, as Margaret stated, do not fool yourselves into thinking an operation to rescue the people on Rikers is about anything else. Pulling those people off that world will not necessarily stop the Thuranin bioweapon effort."

"It would slow down that effort, though?" Simms asked. "Denying the Thuranin access to," she swallowed like she's eaten something distasteful, "those test subjects, would make them go back to the drawing board?"

"It would," Skippy admitted reluctantly.

"Then," Simms looked right at me. "It is worth considering an op to rescue those people."

"Argh," Skippy groaned. "Yes. Shmaybe. I guess it is worth *thinking* about it, developing a plan. Unless that distracts us from doing something more important."

"More important?" The nerves that controlled Adams's facial muscles were back to operating perfectly, because she gave Skippy a look of unmistakable disgust. "Sir," her focus was back to me. "You all have had loads of fun flying around blasting the enemy with our ghost ship, while I was on R&R. I know that must have felt good, to hit back at the enemy. Did you really *accomplish* anything? Colonel, you said the best we can do is play for time out here, try to delay the day when the Maxolhx turn Earth into a radioactive cinder. That's all temporary. Rescuing those people, the children, and bringing them to the beta site? That is permanent. That will change their lives, forever. That is something that *matters*. That is worth doing."

"Gunny, you're preaching to the choir. I *want* to launch a rescue op." I tried to assure her, because the look she was giving me was '*I thought I knew you but now I am not sure*'. "We need a plan to minimize risk to our ships and crew, and to avoid risk of exposing our secret. If we can do that-"

"Don't forget, Joe," Skippy scolded me. "You also need to dream up some cockamamie cover story, for why anyone would risk a military operation to pluck a bunch of lowly monkeys off an isolated world."

"Shit. Yes, thank you, Mister Encouragement," I glared at him. "That is on my freakin' list, along with everything else."

Smythe cut through the bullshit. "Right. Assuming we will try to create a workable plan, what data do we have?"

"Well," Skippy sniffed. "Of course I have far more data than you would ever need about the planet-"

"Yes," Smythe was brusque. Adjusting to his new legs had made him more irritable than before. "Do you have any data that is *useful*? I would like to know the disposition of enemy forces on Rikers, I suppose we won't have that until we arrive in-system, when-"

"No," Skippy was smug as usual. "I have detailed information about the status of Kristang defenses on and around that world."

"You do?" Kapoor gave Smythe the side-eye, and the STAR team commander nodded. Both of them assumed Skippy was boasting.

He wasn't. "In fact, I do. The Thuranin conducted a secret recon there five weeks ago, in case they can't reach an agreement with the Fire Dragon clan, and needed to go down to take the humans anyway. There is a faction of Thuranin leadership that is eager to pound the Fire Dragons on Rikers, to make the point the Thuranin should not need to bargain for anything from their loyal clients. Whatever the Kristang have should be available for use by their Thuranin patrons, for the greater good of their glorious coalition in the overall war effort against their nefarious enemy, blah, blah, blah. The real reason that a faction of Thuranin are itching to do a smash-and-grab on Rikers is to demonstrate their strength. Everyone across the galaxy views the little pinheads as weak, with good reason because the Jeraptha have been kicking their cloned asses."

Smythe and Kapoor exchanged a satisfied glance. "Status of enemy forces, check," Smythe acknowledged, well pleased with that aspect of the situation.

It was Simms's turn to ask a question. "What do we know about the people? The humans," she clarified, because we had to do that now.

"I know where they are, or, where they were five weeks ago. Also, I have bios, including names, origins, health status, all that, on all the human subjects. The Thuranin demanded full data as part of their pre-purchase inspection."

"Pre-p-p-*purchase*?" Adams spat. Her stutter came back when she was agitated.

"Gunny, Skippy is just stating the facts. What do you mean by 'bios'? You know who these people are? Like, names?"

"Well, yes, of course, you ninny," he verbally slapped me in front of my team. "The Kristang kept careful records of who they kidnapped. Names, locations, family and medical histories. The lizards didn't simply snatch people at random.

The subjects were selected, to comprise a broad spectrum of human ethnicities and maximize genetic diversity. Their goal was to replicate the overall human population, with as few individuals as practical. That is also why they preferred to take entire families-"

"Families?" Reed expressed her outrage.

"Yes. By studying a genetically-related family group, the Kristang could-"

Even he could not be clueless forever. "Hey, *I* didn't kidnap those people. *And* I don't approve of what the lizards did. If you truly want to have the best chance to help those people, you need to understand their background, and the motivations of the lizards."

"What I *need*," Adams had a painfully pinched expression on her face again, only this time it was wasn't from frustration. "Is access to nukes and railguns. And anything more exotic we have aboard this bucket."

"Margaret," Skippy chided her. "That is not-"

I cut off Skippy's reply with a knife hand. "That is exactly how all of us are feeling, Gunny. We can use that as motivation."

Skippy understood he had overstepped. "Access to full biographical information about all the surviving humans is on your tablets and laptops," he stated in an apologetic tone. "Also, all the data I have about the planet, defenses, local civilian population, and anything else you might need."

"We're agreed, then?" I asked, looking around the table. "We move forward with planning?"

"You're asking for a vote, Sir?" Kapoor asked warily.

"I am *asking* for input and advice, from my senior staff," I explained.

"In that case," Kapoor didn't look at Smythe before he answered, which was a sign of his growing confidence. "I recommend we study the issue. It will be very difficult," that time he did look at Smythe. "To conduct any substantial ground operation, with the personnel we have aboard."

"Understood. Do your best," I addressed my order to both Kapoor and Smythe. "Give me options. If we need more people." I shrugged. "We'll add that to the list."

After I dismissed the meeting, I endured the usual round of people wanting to talk with me individually, to ask questions or express their concerns. When that was done, I walked back to my office, for an individual discussion I wanted.

As I sat heavily in my chair, I called out "Hey Skippy."

"Hey, Joe," his avatar appeared instantly. "What's up?"

"Why are you so against us trying, at least *trying*, to rescue those people?"

"Children, Joe. Rescue the *children*. I do not think you would contemplate such a complicated and risky operation, if only adults were involved."

"*Whatever.*" He was pissing me off. Which is what he wanted, and I fell for it. Taking a deep breath gave me time to calm down. "Maybe you're right. Why are you so against the idea?"

"It's not just *this*," he sighed. "Joe, you can't save *everyone*. Right now, we can't save Earth at all. We have the most powerful warship in the galaxy, we are *moving* a freakin' wormhole to Earth, we have a secure beta site outside the galaxy, and you want to risk *all* of that, for the sake of less than two hundred of your people. That does not make good sense, no matter how you look at it. I know you. You're the kind of person who can't go to a dog shelter, because you would come home with a dozen dogs instead of just one."

Ok, he was right about that. "I'm not trying to rescue everyone. Just the people I can."

"Same thing," he dismissed my logic. "Either way, it leads to nothing but heartache for you, Joe. You have to accept there is always a limit to what you can do. I notice you didn't dismiss the option of an orbital strike."

"I have that in my back pocket," I replied through gritted teeth. "That won't be mentioned as an option, by either me *or* you, unless we don't have any other workable options. Understood?"

"Jeez, yes. Don't be mad at *me*, Joe."

"Sorry. Ok," pulling my laptop out of a drawer, I opened it. "I will study this data you got for us."

"Um, before you do that, I suggest you visit Margaret."

"Why?"

"Dude, I don't want to invade her privacy, but, you gotta trust me on this one."

Skippy's advice about personal issues wasn't always useful, so I approached Adams's cabin carefully. Before tapping the alarm, I straightened my uniform. Then my thumb pressed the buzzer, and I was committed. "Adams?" I said into the intercom. "Can I speak with you?"

There was a silent pause, then the door slid open.

She was sitting on her couch, legs crossed in a pose I think is called the 'Lotus position'. All I know is that pose is something guys can't do. Her upper body was bent over the tablet on her lap. She looked up, wiping tears away with the back of her sleeves.

She had been crying.

Unsure if I was there as the commanding officer, or as Joe Bishop, I opted for a neutral "Gunny?"

"Oh," she wiped her left eye angrily. Then she sat up straighter. "Sir. Come in."

She unfolded her legs and started to get off the couch. "As you were, Adams." I pressed the button to close her door behind me. "What is it?'

"This," she was regaining her composure, turning the tablet screen to me as I sat on the couch next to her. I was sitting close but not too close. Also not so far away that it was obvious I was being careful not to be too close, you know?

Damn it, why is life so complicated?

On the tablet was the biography of a ten-year-old girl. Most of the data was about her original and current medical condition, I didn't read the details at that point. The top of the file had two photos side by side. Instantly I understood why Adams was so upset. Why she was reading about *that* girl.

"That could be *me*," she tapped the screen.

The girl on the left was younger, looking startled but not afraid. The photo was cropped so it focused on her from the waist up, her right hand was reaching out and at the corner I could just see another hand, and an adult's hand, holding her. She was wearing a clean T-shirt and either jeans or jean shorts. With her left hand, she was clutching a smartphone, and though I couldn't tell what was on the screen, the screen was lit. Whenever the photo was taken, there was electricity available in that area. And the area was the southern United States. How did I know that? Because over her right shoulder was the blurry sign of a Krispy Kreme donut shop. Yes, it could have been other places in the world, but the odds were against that. Plus, also in the background was a man wearing the colors of the Tennessee Titans football team.

The girl on the right was older, frightened, and sad. Her face had been washed but her neck was dirty, and from the streaks of dirt remaining on her face, she hadn't used soap. She was wearing a shirt made from some sort of sack, maybe canvas. Her hair, which in the first photo was tight curls that cascaded down over her forehead, was now matted and shorter. As I could not see the lizards caring about the personal hygiene of their slaves, I assumed one of the adults had cut her hair to make it easier to manage.

All of those things I noticed at a glance, including the stunted and yellowed rows of corn growing in the background, behind the more-current photo of the girl.

None of anything I mentioned is what I really noticed, right away.

It was the girl's face, in both photos.

She *could* have been a young Margaret Adams.

The girl in the first photo had her hair styled in a longer version of the way Adams usually wore her hair. The shade of their skin was roughly similar, as were their eyes and cheekbones. The older girl, in the second photo, looked startlingly like Adams, except gaunt and without any hint of joy in her eyes. Even at her worst, in a coma, Margaret had not looked as sickly and generally worn down as this girl.

"It could be you," I reached out and squeezed her shoulder, not even thinking what I was doing. I didn't need to think about it, it was a natural thing to do. She was hurting.

Again, remember, Skippy explained that as her brain healed and adjusted, her emotions would be on a roller-coaster. He had nanobots regulating production of hormones to protect her from a real problem, but mostly he had to let her newly-revived brain and body get used to each other and find a balance. If I had a massive dose of testosterone one day and a crash the next day, I would be angry and depressed and a general pain in the ass to everyone. Margaret was handling the situation much better than I would have.

She leaned into me, then jerked back on the couch. Wiping away tears, she turned to me, her eyes narrowed but pleading. "Are you really considering *not* rescuing these people? You're going to just let her die?"

I do not know much about women, that fact has been well-established. I do know one thing about women, because it applies to men too. People rarely ever talk about only one thing. Behind their words is a whole lot of stuff they are *not* saying, but they are thinking it.

Margaret wasn't only asking if I, as the mission commander, was considering the option of taking no action to pull the people, *our* people, off Rikers. She wanted to know if I was the kind of person, the kind of *man*, who could let that little girl die.

She wanted to know what kind of man I am.

She also wanted to know if we had a FUTURE, with that word in all caps. And if that future, our future, might possibly include a little girl like the one in the photos.

Ok, maybe I am reading way too much into one simple question.

I don't think so.

Yes, guys tend to be clueless.

When guys are clueless, it is in the direction of *not* picking up the subtext of what people are saying.

Also, maybe it is way too early for Adams to be asking any questions about our future, if we had one.

Again, I don't think so. We still didn't know each other that well. She was not dropping down on one knee and proposing to me right there.

Which, at that moment, when I saw the pain in her eyes and that she was asking *me* to make it go away, would have been totally Ok with me.

Just sayin'.

Maybe my emotions are not completely under control either.

That's life.

If I was right about anything at all, she was asking if I was the kind of man she thought I was, because she wanted to get to know me better. Was I the kind of man worth getting to know better, or should she drop the whole idea?

That's what she was asking.

"We don't have a plan yet," I mumbled. "The *objective*," I emphasized. "Is to pull our people out of that hell hole, and bring them home." She knew the difference between an objective and a plan. The objective is what you're going to do, unless you can't.

In the military, we hardly ever say we *can't* do something.

"*Our* people." She picked up on that right away.

"Every human in this galaxy are *our* people. No one else cares about us." I tapped her tablet. "That includes this girl."

She looked away from me, back at the girl. Her finger traced the outline of the older girl's face. "Sir, I have never asked you for anything." Her eyes flicked up, reading my reaction. "I want us to bring this girl home. Not just her, all of them."

"If we can," I replied cautiously. I had to be cautious. If the likely cost of rescuing those people meant losing our ships, or exposing the secret that humans were causing havoc around the galaxy, then I could not authorize a rescue. She knew that. "If there is any way that we can, we will," I added.

"I want you to *make it happen*." She held her gaze, looking from one of my eyes to the other. "We do the impossible all the time out here. This has to be possible."

"I promise. If it's possible, we'll do it."

"It's impossible," Major Kapoor announced dourly, as I dropped into my office chair and waved them to sit. He and Smythe had been waiting for me in my office.

"*Seriously?*" I groaned, on the verge of shouting at the special operator. "How could you know already? It's only been-" I dug for the zPhone in my pocket to check the time.

"Time isn't the issue," Smythe explained. "It only took a quick overview of Skippy's summary to determine the operation is impossible."

I gave him the side-eye. Had Smythe's near-death experience made him timid? No, *that* was never going to happen. Had it made him cautious, *too* cautious?

Besides, he had near-death experiences before. "What about the SAS motto 'Who dares wins'?" I asked, knowing that would put him on the defensive.

Except it didn't. He shook his head. "The SAS got that reputation, by being careful to take on missions that could be completed successfully," he emphasized, implying the rescue mission on Rikers could not. "There is no point to daring, if you can't win. That only gets your people killed for nothing."

"We have barely-" I began to protest.

"It is impossible, with the personnel we have available. Colonel," he added in a softer tone.

"Oh." I understood his objection. "Guys, come on. Rikers has a small population, their defenses are minimal. Skippy can take control of their Strategic Defense platforms in orbit, and hack communications all around the planet. The two islands where the prisoners are being kept are isolated, there isn't any security there. We should be able to fly in, pull the prisoners out and fly away without the lizards even knowing we were there."

"That would be true," Smythe conceded. "If we were not the Merry Band of Pirates."

"Colonel," Kapoor added. "The operation will be easy, as you said, *if* nothing goes wrong."

"Shit," I groaned. "Ok, yeah, we need a reserve."

"There is also the time factor," Smythe warned. "Skippy believes the Thuranin will arrive to pick up the humans in six or seven weeks, whether they reach an agreement with the Kristang or not. I personally hope to be combat ready at that time," he frowned. It was rare for him to acknowledge any weakness. "Adams might be recovered enough to back up the team on point. That still leaves us desperately short-handed."

"What about the personnel we pulled off Avalon?" I asked hopefully.

They both shook their heads. Kapoor answered, as he had been directly working with the new people, while Smythe still focused on bringing himself up to the proper level of fitness. "It is my understanding that all of the pilots are making good progress on transitioning, to either dropships, the *Flying Dutchman*, or *Valkyrie*."

'Yes," I agreed. "Reed is working everyone to exhaustion, including herself. She is confident that she can find a match to everyone's skill set."

"That is good," Kapoor nodded. "Unfortunately, none of the new people are likely to meet the standards for a STAR team."

"Seriously?" I tilted my head at him. Kapoor and Smythe were rightfully proud of their very special operators. They also needed to be flexible.

"Colonel," Smythe lifted a single eyebrow, in a 'what did you expect' gesture. "The new people are mechanics, communications specialists, logistics officers."

"Simms was a logistics officer, and now she's my XO," I noted.

"Lieutenant Colonel Simms is a fine officer," Smythe wasn't giving an inch. "She is an excellent executive officer. She has also not qualified for a STAR team."

"Ok, I see your point. *None* of the new people?"

Kapoor answered my question. "Three or four of them might serve in a support role, *if* we had more time. Colonel Bishop, this is not only a matter of individual fitness or skill. We need to bring people up to speed," he used an American expression for my benefit. "Then the team needs to train together. There simply is not time to bring a new person into a cohesive team. Even so, we would be dropping into combat with less than a dozen people. That is not enough to do the job, Sir."

"I do not like hearing this," I sat back in my chair.

Kapoor was about to respond when Smythe lifted a hand, just enough to indicate the other man should wait.

"But," I said. "I have to trust your judgment. If it can't be done, it can't be done. Huh."

"Sir?" Smythe lifted an eyebrow again.

"Smythe, I have sometimes accused you of having a love of doing crazy shit. Usually, that scares me. This time, it works to your advantage. If you say it's impossible, it really must be."

"Thank you, Sir. I think." He was trying to decide if I had praised or insulted him. or both.

"Ok. A rescue is impossible with the personnel we have."

"Yes," Kapoor agreed, with the pained expression of a person having to listen to some jerk repeating what had already been said.

"Then, clearly, we need more people."

CHAPTER TWENTY SEVEN

"Hey, Joe," Skippy appeared moments after Smythe and Kapoor left my office. "I have a question for you."

"Unless your question is which of your fabulous ideas for fixing our problem is the *best* idea, I really don't want to hear it."

"Um, which problem is this, exactly? Or should I pick one at random? There's a *big* list."

"The *latest* problem." Sometimes he could be annoyingly clueless. "Don't pretend you weren't listening. We need to find another STAR team somewhere out there. Or more qualified people to build a bigger team."

"That is ridiculous. Unless when you say 'out there', you include alternate universes, where we still have access to Earth."

"No, I wasn't- Wait. Could we *do* that?" Holy shit! My mind was reeling with the possibilities. That could solve *all* our problems!

Unless the alternate universes were all shitty compared to this one.

"Noooo," he laughed. "Dude, what is *wrong* with you? Reality doesn't work that way. Technically, you can go to an alternate universe, but the difference from this one would be so slight, you wouldn't notice it. Before you ask me a whole lot of stupid questions that won't lead to anything useful, I have to warn you. If you think other physics stuff I have tried to explain gave you a headache, prepare for your brain to explode if you want to discuss the multiverse."

"I'll pass on that."

"A good idea. Smartest thing you've said in a month. The second thing won't work either."

"Second thing?"

"Ugh. You call *me* absent-minded. The second thing you mentioned, about finding qualified people to build a STAR team. Didn't you listen to Kapoor? Even if you could snap your fingers and magically bring a group of special operators onboard, we don't have time to develop them as a team. And, they would need to learn our equipment, tactics, the-"

"Ok! Yes, I did hear him tell me that. Jeez, Skippy, I was only bitching about my problems. I wasn't expecting a solution."

"Ah. So, since you can't solve your own problems, you decided to make my life even more miserable by dumping on me?"

"Sorry." He didn't reply. "I *said*, I am sorry. What was your question?"

"Maybe now I don't want to talk with you," he pouted.

"Is your question something that is going to make *my* life even more miserable?"

"Probably. Hmm, good point. I will totally ask my question. So, here it is. Duuuude, are you crazy? Or high? Or just mind-bogglingly stupid?"

"What?"

"Why, for the love of *God*, did you promise Margaret that you would rescue that girl?"

"Uh, I didn't actually promise to do that. What I said was, we would do it, *if* it is possible."

"Dude."

"What?"

"Seriously?"

"*What*?" I demanded.

"*You* heard yourself say 'If it is possible'. Is that what you think *she* heard?"

"Shit."

"Exactly. *Daaaaamn*, you are a moron. She told you to 'Make it happen'. Do you think there was an implied' IF' in there?"

"No. Crap."

"She expects you. To. Make. It. *Happen*."

"Well- Hey, I didn't know my STAR team was going to take a giant dump on my head by telling me it is impossible."

"Maybe you should have asked first? I'm just sayin', you know?"

"I know."

"Now, unless you can do what is clearly impossible, you will forever be a failure to her."

"Come on, Skippy. Adams is a Marine. She knows some things just can't happen."

"Sure, some things just can't happen, *unless* Joe Bishop is involved. You are the guy who had the idea to *move* a freakin' Elder wormhole."

"Crap. I did."

"You used a jump wormhole as a *weapon*."

"Yeah."

"You captured a senior-species battlecruiser, using *Legos* and a *bagel slicer*." Burying my face in my hands, I groaned. "I'm doomed."

"Ya *think*?"

"Thank you for being so supportive."

"I *am*?" He was mystified. And disappointed. "Ugh. What I wanted was to watch you wallow in misery."

"How about we schedule that for tomorrow?"

"Hmm. I am suspicious."

"What can I do? How can I fix this with Mar-" Maybe it wasn't a good idea to use her first name when we were not in private. "With her?"

"At this point, there is only one thing you *can* do, Joe."

"What's that?"

"*Duh*. Make it happen."

The next day, after breakfast, after hitting the gym for a workout I just wasn't into, I was in my office, doing nothing useful. Unless you count sitting with my elbow on the desk, propping up my head as 'useful'.

Skippy appeared on my oversized desk, looking cheery. "Hey. Whatcha doin', huh?"

"Wallowing in my misery."

"Oh?" He asked.

"We scheduled that for today, remember?"

"Oh. I thought you were joking."

"It's not like I have anything else to do."

"You *could* finish reading my summary about the Mavericks' mission on Fresno. They did something impossible, too. They escaped from a Deathtrap, and turned certain defeat into victory."

"I suppose."

"Unless you're too busy. I can see you are *swamped* with work," he laid on the sarcasm really thick.

"Ok, Ok," I pulled my laptop out of a drawer. "I'll read the damned thing."

"Good. Also, in case you are not miserable enough already, Margaret asked me to reinstate some of the nanobots in her neural network."

With the laptop in one hand, hovering over the desk, I froze. "*Why* would she do that?"

"Because she is not satisfied with her scores on the rifle range."

"I didn't know-"

"She drew a rifle from the armory yesterday afternoon, and spent three hours on the range. Plus she asked Captain Frey to help her with the new powered armor suit I constructed for Margaret."

"Why is she- Oh, Shit."

"She wants to be ready to participate in the rescue mission, even if she is restricted to a backup or support role. She is so determined to, as she told me, do *everything* she can to assure the rescue is successful, that she is willing to have creepy alien robots crawling around in her brain. You know what she is like when she is determined to do something."

"I am."

"Hey, on a *totally* unrelated subject, where are you on planning that rescue operation?"

"Oh, shut up." I waved the laptop through his avatar.

Since I had nothing else to do, unless you count hating myself, I continued reading Skippy's summary of the Alien Legion's Deathtrap mission. Part of it was an exciting account of the mission, that Skippy had assembled from data he pulled from Ruhar, Kristang and Jeraptha databases. That part I put aside to read later. What I read first were reports written by Emily Perkins. Why? Because I was curious about her. When I was stationed on Paradise, we had only met a dozen or so times, and those were all business. Really, I didn't know her well at all. After I was promoted to colonel, we only met a few times, and those were brief exchanges of pleasantries before a meeting at UNEF HQ.

What I did know was that she had accomplished a whole lot, and done it without the help of a magical beer can. When she and her team were stealthily racing around Paradise, reactivating long-forgotten maser cannons, she had known she was being manipulated by an unknown group. And that whatever the objectives of the unknown group were, the health and welfare of the human population were not high on the list.

She had known she was being used, and before we launched the operation, I had to fend off objections from Chang, Smythe and others, who feared she would balk at taking orders from a Mysterious Benefactor. Worse, she might bring the information to the Ruhar authorities, in the hope that her demonstrated loyalty would be rewarded with better treatment of the humans on that world.

I had dismissed those concerns, based on what little I knew of Emily Perkins. Like I said, I didn't know her well, but one thing I knew was that she had an independent streak a mile wide, and a distrust of authority figures. Those were maybe not desirable attributes in a typical military officer, but every organization needs mavericks. My own problem with authority had worked out well for me. Mostly.

Anyway, back then, I had been sure Perkins was too smart to go running to the Ruhar with info about the maser cannons. At that time, the hamsters were planning, even eager, to trade Paradise to the lizards. Knowing about the hidden maser cannons would not change the fate of humans there, because the Ruhar federal government was not going to risk screwing up the negotiations by firing those cannons. The local planetary government might have been tempted to use the maser cannons, but there was no way such a large bureaucracy could keep the operation secret from the federal government. So, Perkins figured their Mysterious Benefactor was a group of local Ruhar who rightfully did not trust their government to do the right thing, or to do it competently. If she was being used, she could use them right back for the benefit of humans. So, she did.

When I first met Perkins, in the tiny hamster village of Teskor while I was there with my fireteam, I decided right away that she was good people. Intel types typically could not be trusted and I didn't say that I trusted her back then. I just knew that, if I somehow got screwed by UNEF, it wouldn't be her idea. Yes, she got me yanked out of Teskor and sent to the cargo launcher complex, which felt like a reprimand at the time. Later, I realized she was looking out for me, when she moved me away from the center of attention.

Anyway, it worked out Ok for both of us.

You know how, when you're surfing social media, you keep scrolling down, even when you know there are much better things you should or could be doing? That's what I was doing with the reports from Perkins. Other than giving me a feel for who she was and how she thought, the reports weren't really useful to me. They were about people and aliens I did not know, places I had not been to and never would see. Issues that I didn't care about, or were already irrelevant due to the passage of time. Most of it was trivia. Yet, I kept scrolling down.

In my defense, it wasn't all trivia. One report was about lessons learned from working with aliens. The basic lesson learned was that the UNEF contingent of the Alien Legion had a lot to learn about working under the direction of the Ruhar, and even more about fighting alongside the Verd-kris. Perkins had a Verd surgun, that is a rank roughly equivalent to sergeant, training her headquarters security team in Verd-kris tactics. The guy she picked for the job, named 'Jates' sounded like a hardass. I approved.

More revealing, about both the status of UNEF-Paradise and the character of Emily Perkins, was a confidential report she submitted to UNEF-HQ. It was supposed to be secret, but she must have known the hamsters would crack the encryption and read her words. That knowledge did not appear to have changed the ways she addressed the harsh truth; that UNEF soldiers were poorly trained, poorly led, poorly prepared and were in general no longer a potent military force. Her conclusion was that after years of farming on Paradise, the force's level of fitness was inadequate for the tasks likely to be assigned to the Legion. Units thrown together hastily for the mission on Fresno had no cohesion, no common set of standards and tactics, no-

Well, you get the idea. Her assessment of the Verds was only slightly less harsh. Those friendly lizards had no real combat experience, either individually or as a society. The soldiers of UNEF-Paradise needed refresher training and to update their tactics to the new reality, but they served an organization that had a strong culture of knowing how to fight. Since the Ruhar had not allowed the Verd-kris to engage in combat or even participate in realistic training before forming the Legion, the Verds were having to make up everything as they went along. Overall, Perkins stated that UNEF was lucky to have escaped the deathtrap on Fresno. If the Legion had gotten into a real, sustained fight on that world, the situation could have gone sideways in a hurry. She was telling the unvarnished truth as she saw it. I admired her for that. She would probably have been as unpopular on Earth as I was.

She didn't need to worry about that.

So, I was scrolling down aimlessly, scanning bits of reports here and there. Really, after the first couple reports, I had a better feel for the thought processes of Lieutenant Colonel Emily Perkins, and all I was doing was wasting time. In my defense, my brain works best when I let it wander, so time spent on useless activities is actually worthwhile.

That's my story and I'm sticking to it.

Ok, Ok, I told myself. One more minute of scrolling through reports and I would do something more-

Holy shit.

"Skippy. *Skippy*!" I shouted.

"What is it this time? I told you, if you see a word you don't know, just hover your cursor over it, and-"

"I can read fine by myself, thank you. You see what I'm reading now?"

"Um, it's a series of recommendations by Perkins, most of which are likely going to be argued about endlessly by UNEF HQ until they are no longer-"

"Yeah, great. What about this one?" I jabbed a finger at the screen hard enough that my laptop nearly tipped over. "Did *this* recommendation get implemented?"

"Oh. Yes, actually. For two reasons. First, it is at the forehead-slapping *DUH* level of obviousness. Second, UNEF-HQ and the hamsters were already considering it. Why?"

"Because," I carefully pulled the laptop back from teetering on the edge of the desk. "This could solve our latest problem."

"Oh. *OH*," he added, as he caught onto what I was thinking.

"In the future, when you think there is something I really need to read, please lock all the games on my phone and tablet until I read it."

"Done."

"Uh, I didn't mean *now*. I did read this report."

"*All* of it?"

"Crap. No. Can you forget what I just said?"

"Hee hee," he chuckled. "What do *you* think?"

Smythe was with Kapoor in the middle of a training session, outside the ship in powered armor, when I called him. Our STAR team commander was more irritated than his usual British stiff-upper-lip cool. "Sir, we are rather busy at the moment. Could this possibly wait?"

"No. Like you told me, time is not our friend. Besides, I know you've run that exercise a dozen times recently, let Kapoor handle it. I need your advice."

There was an unspoken weary sigh in his reply. "Yes, Sir, right away."

When he got to my office, his hair matted down from being under the helmet, and still wearing the suit liner, he stomped rather more loudly than necessary. On his new bionic legs, now that he had gotten used to them, he could walk more softly than ever before. The high-tech legs had shock absorbers built in that not only protected his organic body from impacts, they could mute the effect of footsteps. It was my guess that he had adjusted the settings, to subtly let me know how annoyed he was with me.

One minute later, he was annoyed no longer. "Sir," he looked up briefly from the tablet, then back down to study details. "This is, rather incredible."

"Fortuitous," I said the unfamiliar word slowly, "is how I would describe it. This is like pulling a rabbit out of a hat."

"With the exception, Sir, that these rabbits may not want to leave the hat." He looked up at me again. "You know my objections. This could be considered kidnapping."

"No," I shook my head once, emphatically. "It's not kidnapping, it's, uh, we will be requisitioning them. I checked the legal stuff with Skippy. I have the authority to commandeer these people from their current mission."

"Authority?" He squinted at me. "From UNEF Command on Earth?"

"I know it's sketchy." Thinking about it made me squirm in my oversized chair. "Skippy said that if I have to, I can invoke the Stop-Loss provision. You know what that is?"

"I know it is a damned underhanded thing to do to a volunteer force," he frowned.

My question had been prompted because I wasn't sure if the British Army used the same terminology. Stop-loss was a policy that allowed the military to extend a soldier's enlistment past the original end date. In the US, it had been used to involuntarily keep vital personnel on active duty during wartime, or whenever the Pentagon declared an emergency. Something like that, Skippy had tried to explain the legal history but I wasn't interested. All I cared about was whether I had some sort of legal cover for what I wanted to do.

The key part of Stop-loss is 'involuntary'. A soldier who was counting down until the end of enlistment, and making plans to transition to civilian life, suddenly was told that he or she was remaining on active duty, with no definite end date. That sucked when it happened in Iraq, and it sucked every time it happened.

When we signed up to leave Earth with UNEF, we were told the term of our enlistments had been extended to ninety days past the end of the current conflict, which essentially meant forever. We all knew that, and it didn't much matter at the time, because none of us realistically expected to come back home.

When we brought the *Flying Dutchman* to Earth the first time, there was a debate about whether soldiers stranded on Paradise should continue to accrue pay and benefits. That might seem like an irrelevant question, but it was important to the United States government. Probably the other governments of the Expeditionary Force also. The world economy was still recovering from the impact of Columbus Day and from the ravages inflicted by the Kristang. Those governments were paying out checks to the families of the soldiers on Paradise, with no end in sight. It seems like a rotten thing to do, but all five governments cut that pay by up to eighty percent, with vague promises that the missing pay would be restored if official contact with Paradise could be reestablished. Which would only happen if our secret was exposed, and aliens were about to turn Earth into a radioactive cinder.

Anyway, why this mattered was that, along with cutting pay and benefits for the troops stranded on Paradise, those people were declared to be transferred from active duty to the reserves, or the equivalent for each nationality. So, technically the active-duty enlistments of everyone on Paradise had ended. Fortunately for me, Skippy the legal beagle had found an obscure clause in the UNEF charter, that anticipated the Force might cycle between active and reserves while offworld. The Stop-loss policy applied to reserves also, and allowed the 'relevant authority' to recall reserve forces to active duty at any time, for any reason.

With both Paradise and our two ships cut off from Earth, the 'relevant authority' was *me*.

"I don't like invoking Stop-Loss either. I'm hoping it won't matter."

"How so?"

"These are special operations troops. Would any of *your* people hesitate to join up, if we explained the mission was to rescue a group of humans who had been kidnapped off Earth and were being starved?" That last part was not entirely true. While the Kristang were negotiating to sell the humans to the Thuranin, Skippy expected the lizards would give their slaves at least minimum care, to protect their investment. "Especially if the op might save the lives of every human on Paradise?"

"As Adams stated, the Thuranin could develop a bioweapon even without the human prisoners from Rikers."

"You know what I mean."

"No."

I looked at him in surprise.

There was a ghost of a smile on his face. "*No*," he added. "None of my people would hesitate to join up. Joining us would be tempting to any operator. The action that truly matters is out *here*, not with this Legion."

"That's what I'm thinking. I promise you this: anyone who doesn't want to join us, we will drop them on Avalon at our first opportunity. Or Earth," I added. "Whichever comes first."

Smythe gave me a nod that just lifted his chin slightly. "Anyone who does not want to join us, I don't want anyway. Colonel, this all looks good, but, there will be a substantial amount of work to integrate a new force. These people have a different set of tactics. They have been using Ruhar skinsuits, instead of our Kristang hardshell power armor. These skinsuits," he looked back at the tablet. "They *do* have advantages."

"Maybe," I cautioned him. "Compared to regular Kristang mech suits, Ruhar skinsuits have plusses and minuses. Overall, Skippy thinks," I paused, expecting the beer can to join the discussion, but he didn't. "He think the Kristang suits we use, that he has modified, are substantially superior to skinsuits."

"It all depends on your cover story, Sir," he said flatly.

"Huh?" I was lost.

"Whether we employ Kristang or Ruhar suits," he explained patiently. "To plan a rescue operation, I need to know whether your cover story will be that we are Kristang troops, or Ruhar. We have to assume we will be detected at some point."

"Cover story?" I hadn't gotten that far along in my thinking. Skippy had pointed out the need for a cover story to explain why anyone would risk military action to take a few hundred worthless humans off an unimportant planet. "Oh, yeah. Why," I tilted my head quizzically. "Would we pretend to be Ruhar?"

He continued to be patient with me. "The bioweapon is a threat to a Ruhar world. And to a military force led by the Ruhar. They would of course have an interest in assuring the humans on Rikers are not used to develop a bioweapon."

"Craaaaap. Yeah, I see your point. Problem is, the hamsters would likely hit the camps from orbit to eliminate the threat, instead of rescuing our people."

That prompted a raised eyebrow. "You think the Ruhar are that callous?"

"I think this is a deadly serious war for survival. I think the hamsters take care of themselves first, and that to them, we are primitive alien pain-in-the-asses. I can't imagine any Ruhar commander parking a starship in orbit and deploying a landing force, to rescue a small group of humans. And based on how quick the hamsters were to sell out UNEF on Fresno," I knew Smythe had read Skippy's report. "We can't expect them to risk their furry necks for us."

"Agreed. Sir, it is likely that a rival Kristang clan would also use an orbital strike. The problem is that no one, other than us, has an interest in seeing those humans leave Rikers alive."

"No one but us, and the Thuranin," I muttered.

"Sir, I couldn't hear that?" He had been given bionic legs, not bionic hearing.

"I said, the Thuranin also have an interest in getting those people off the planet alive."

"The Thuranin. Hmm. That adds a wrinkle. Colonel, to begin planning a rescue, I need to know the cover story we have to sell."

"To decide on a cover story, I need an operations plan first." He looked pained like he had just read an announcement that breakfast, lunch and dinner would be boiled Brussels sprouts for the next week. "Smythe, I need to know what is possible. Give me a list of options, and I'll dream up a bullshit cover story for whichever option is best."

"You may have to choose from the least bad option, not the best," he warned.

I shrugged with a grin. "Standard Operating Procedure again, huh? Ok, before you do *that*," I turned my laptop around so he could see it. "We need a plan to bring aboard a possibly reluctant group of trigger-happy special operators."

"I don't suppose we could post an advertisement for a luxury cruise across the galaxy, Sir?"

CHAPTER TWENTY EIGHT

"Hey, Joe," Skippy appeared on my office desk. "I have good news and bad news."

"Oh, man, Skippy," I whispered, dramatically craning my neck to look toward the open door. "Bad news is *so* yesterday."

"*What?*"

"Bad news is out. I thought you knew."

"Um, um-" he sputtered, flustered.

"You do want to be one of the cool kids, right?"

"I'm *not?*" He screeched.

"Well, yeah, you are *now*. But, people can turn on you like," I snapped my fingers. "That, you know? If people found out, they would be all like, did you hear what Skippy did? You know how people love gossip."

"Oh. Shit. So, I can't tell you *any* bad news? Even if it's important?"

"It's up to you, but," I held out my hands, palms up.

"Ok, Ok. Um, how about I say that I have *good* news, with a complication?"

"People hate complications."

"True, true," he muttered. "Aha! Joe, I have good news, and it's even better than just good, because it comes with a challenge. The go-hung nutjobs aboard this ship all *love* challenges, right?"

Damn it, he was right. He had beaten me again. Score: beercan One, monkey Zero. "Ok, what is it?"

"You asked me to look for an isolated team of Alien Legion special operations troops."

"*Human* troops," I reminded him.

"Right. That's the complication."

"Shit."

"Do you want to hear this or not?"

"I sure as hell do not *want* to hear it, but tell me anyway."

"In most ways, it is kind of a perfect set-up, Joe. There is a team of human operators, the Legion calls them Commandos by the way, in a star system that is one wormhole transition away from Paradise. It's a red dwarf system, where the Commandos are being trained in spaceborne assault tactics, diving from orbit, all the sort of craziness that Smythe and his team of lunatics enjoy. Anywho, part of the training is for stealthed Dodo dropships to practice assault and boarding operations on asteroid bases. The Dodos are flown by human pilots, and the troops are human."

"No Verds? I though the Legion wanted humans to train with the friendly lizards." That concept still made me uncomfortable. Trusting a Kristang in combat would be a difficult skill for me to learn, though I knew that UNEF had worked successfully with Verds on Fresno.

"That is the goal, Joe. However, the Ruhar want the human Commandos to demonstrate they are effective as a team, before they attempt to integrate teams from different species into the Legion. Also, neither UNEF or Ruhar know what tactics and equipment will work best for humans, so the training is mostly a learning exercise."

"That makes sense. Ok, so, human troops on a Dodo flown by humans, and no Verds involved. What's the complication?"

"Observers, Joe. Each Dodo carries hamsters to observe, advise and train the humans."

"Aaaand, we risk making enemies of the Ruhar, if we Shanghai their people along with ours."

"*Shanghai*? Joe, that remark was culturally insensitive and-"

"Oh, bullshit. It's not about the Chinese at all, you moron. Back in the day, shipping companies would kidnap people from the West coast to fill crews, of ships sailing to places like Shanghai. My Uncle Edgar told me about it, apparently one of my ancestors was a sailor who jumped ship to join the California Gold Rush. But he got kidnapped on the West Coast, my uncle figures he got stinking drunk and they dragged him aboard a ship. He went all over the Pacific before he signed onto a ship going around the Horn to Boston."

"So, this is kidnapping, Joe? You told Smythe this was a Stop-Loss action or some other bullshit like that."

"That was a way of sugar-coating the issue, and Smythe knows it. We're going to take these people aboard our ship, and not give them a choice about it. They can choose not to serve with a STAR team-"

"Oh, like *that's* gonna happen," he scoffed. "You will give the Commandos a chance to play with shiny new toys. No way will they refuse."

"Yeah, that's what I'm counting on. Still, they won't be happy that we can't allow them to go back to Paradise, or even contact anyone there. By now, they may have families on Paradise. Legally, I do have authority to commandeer UNEF assets as needed, and we sure as hell need those people. No matter how nicely I wrap it in legal language, it *is* kidnapping. That sucks, and I wouldn't do it if we had a choice."

"A better choice, you mean. You *could* choose to abandon the people on Rikers."

"No. That's bullshit, Skippy. I could decide a rescue operation is not worth the risk, or won't ultimately save thousands of lives on Paradise. No way at this point could I *choose* to abandon the people on Rikers."

"Because Margaret asked you to?"

"Whoa. That's a rotten thing to say, Dude."

"It's a legit question. You are kidnapping people, and taking everything we have into a risky operation. The motivations and emotional state of the commander are a legitimate concern, and you know it. Are you doing this for yourself, for *her*, or for the poor people on Rikers?"

"Oh for- All three, if you want the truth. If you want the full truth, Margaret asking me to rescue that little girl made me *less* likely to approve an operation on Rikers."

"What? Why?"

"Because I don't *want* to kidnap people and take everything we have into a risky op, just to make Margaret like me. Believe me, every step we take down this road, I'm asking myself if it's really worth it. Whether I'm thinking clearly about it."

"Oh. Sorry."

"Don't be sorry. If you think I'm doing something rash and stupid, call me on it. Hell, I do enough stupid things anyway. Besides, there's another reason we are pulling our people off Rikers."

"What is that?"

"We're doing it for *us*. The Merry Band of Pirates has been making sacrifices out here, bleeding and *dying* out here, for years. All to serve Earth, to keep the people on our homeworld safe. This one, we're doing for *us*. Because this crew can't let those poor people die there, without at least trying to rescue them."

"Even at the risk of exposing our secret, and putting Earth in danger?"

"Skippy." Elbows on the desk, I cradled my head in my hands and rubbed my face. "Earth is toast. We had a good run, but it's over. Earth w*ould* be safe, except Emily freakin' Perkins got visited by the Good Idea Fairy and couldn't keep her mouth shut- No, wait. That's unfair to her. If I were in her shoes, I would have done the same thing." Except, I told myself, I might have screwed it up even worse. "The Maxolhx will learn soon enough that their battlegroup isn't coming back, and they will be sending even more ships. Sure, we seriously hosed their C3 by making them think the Bosphuraq hacked their pixie network, and that has them on the defensive. Maybe that buys Earth a few more years. Maybe you'll get the Backstop wormhole positioned near Earth and we can evac a couple thousand, a couple hundred thousand people to Avalon before big bad aliens drop the hammer. We've done all we can out here for Earth. Now, we're doing something for ourselves. Our crew *needs* this rescue operation. We need to try, you understand?"

"I do understand, Joe. My question was whether *you* understood that."

"Oh. Was that you using your mad empathy skills?"

"Do *not* make me regret this, Dude."

"Sorry. Ok, show me details."

"Even if it's bad news?"

"Especially if it's bad news."

As a change of pace, Simms and I scheduled our morning meeting in the galley. With such a small crew, breakfasts were 'fend for yourself' meals, no one was assigned to cook. Once in a while, I baked cinnamon buns, or made pancakes for everyone. It was a special treat that boosted morale. And it was a way for me to deal with the guilt I felt, for getting everyone stuck far from a homeworld we might never see again.

Anyway, that morning, Simms was there first. She had made a fresh pot of coffee. One item we were not running low on was coffee, because she had made sure the *Flying Dutchman* had practically a lifetime supply before we left Earth. The saying used to be that the Army ran on an ocean of gasoline, diesel and jet fuel. The Army also requires coffee, so does any military force. The aliens we knew of all had their own form of stimulant beverages. Wow. Just thinking about that made me wonder what a bleary-eyed lizard soldier looked like before he had his coffee-equivalent in the morning. Ugh. I would *not* want to see that.

In addition to coffee, Simms was also stuffing something into a blender, and pouring milk over it. She pulsed the blender, I kept quiet until the ruckus was over, and she poured a glass for me.

"Uh, thank you?" I sniffed the pinkish liquid suspiciously. "What is it?"

"A smoothie. It's good for you, Sir. Drink it."

"I was going to-"

"You were going to have marshmallow Fluff on toast," she rolled her eyes. "I know that. A supply ship came over from the *Dutchman* last night, we have fresh strawberries."

That explained why the smoothie was pink. That did not explain the dark green chunks in it. "Mmm," I said, licking my pink mustache. "Interesting. What's the other flavor?"

"Kale. It's loaded with antioxidants, protein and fiber."

"Oh."

"You don't like it?"

"No, it's good. It's just-"

She looked at me over her glass. "What?"

Dipping a finger into the smoothie, I pulled out several of the dark flecks and wiped them onto the outside of the glass. "Putting this stuff into a smoothie makes it really tough to get all the little pieces of kale out, you know?"

"*Er!*"

I was on my best behavior during our morning meeting, and I did drink the whole smoothie. Then I went back to the galley later for a Fluff-on-toast. You need to be careful not to give your body too much nutrition, or it gets spoiled.

That's my story and I'm sticking to it.

We jumped *Valkyrie* into the red dwarf system where the Ruhar were training UNEF Commandos, using our ship's ability to focus the gamma ray burst so we weren't detected. Our battlecruiser also had better stealth capability than even the upgraded *Flying Dutchman*, making the choice of ships for the recon easy. It made me uneasy that, if we were somehow detected, I didn't have a good reason why our infamous ghost ship would be hanging out in an isolated Ruhar star system. Smythe suggested that we explain our presence as the ship needing to refit, and Ruhar territory was the last place the Maxolhx would look for us. That cover story was Ok, I just felt we could have done better.

Anyway, once there, we drifted in stealth and listened. First, we listened to detect what objects out there were radiating artificial energy or transmitting signals. There were a lot of them. Next, we listened to make sure our inbound jump had not been noticed, because a sophisticated sensor network, like the Strategic Defense system around a Ruhar planet, might have seen something. Fortunately, the hamsters did not have an SD network in that system, and-

No, that's not entirely correct. There were SD platforms orbiting the second planet, but they were just mock units for training. Their sensors were tuned to survey a short-range area around the planet, because that was where the Ruhar were training their Spaceborne Cavalry units. The UNEF Commandos were just piggybacking on a much larger training exercise.

Satisfied that no one had seen us jump in, we concentrated on the next potential problem, one serious enough that I considered aborting the whole operation.

Skippy had detected a Jeraptha ship, orbiting the second planet.

"Shit," I clenched a fist. "What the hell is that ship doing here? It's not a star carrier."

"No, Joe," Skippy used his Professor Nerdnik lecture voice. "It is a light cruiser. A warship capable of longer flights than a destroyer, but lightly armed and armored. The Jeraptha typically employ such ships on missions where they are not expected to encounter heavy opposition. I suspect this particular ship is here to observe the wargame exercise."

"We might risk making enemies of the Ruhar. We are not pissing off the beetles. That's it, then, we're outa here," I declared.

"Don't be so hasty, Joe," Skippy added. "The wargame exercise concluded two days ago. That cruiser is broadcasting a general alert to warn traffic that it intends to maneuver out to jump distance. More precisely, it was broadcasting such an alert three hours ago, when the message was sent. It is likely that ship has jumped out of the system by now, the gamma rays have not reached us yet."

"Ok. Ok, we move on the assumption the beetles aren't hanging around for a second slice of pie. What data do you have on UNEF Commandos?"

"Good news and, er," he caught himself. "News that is even *better*, for it poses a challenge."

Behind me, Smythe groaned.

"What?" Skippy asked, baffled. "You *love* challenges!"

"I am sure we will run into plenty of challenges during the operation," Smythe explained. "It does no good tempting Fate by looking for challenges we could avoid."

"Oh, well, um," Skippy sputtered. "In that case, you are screwed, Dude. The Commandos participated in the recent wargame, and most of their units have stood down to refit and recuperate. There are only three Dodos carrying humans that are on maneuvers currently. One of them is near the second planet, I suggest we scratch that off our list."

"I second that suggestion," I agreed. "What else?"

"Two units in the asteroid belt. You will have to choose between them. What information I have is available to you now."

Right away, I eliminated one unit from consideration. "Smythe?" I asked, turning around in my command chair to look at him.

He nodded, having seen the same thing I had. "Quite so. It will not do."

"What?" Simms inquired. Her attention had been on the ship's sensors, keeping us out of trouble.

"There's a pregnant woman aboard one of the Dodos," I commented without thinking, my focus on data about the other Dodo.

"*And?*" Simms had turned in her chair and was looking straight at me.

"She's, well, you know-" Shit. I was totally unprepared to discuss *that* subject.

"She is a dedicated soldier who knows what she's doing," Simms insisted. "UNEF-Paradise obviously doesn't have a problem with her serving on active duty."

Miraculously, because my response would have been 'Uh' followed by another 'Uh', Smythe answered for me. "UNEF-Paradise will have a place for her, when she can no longer serve in a Commando unit. We do not. Neither *Valkyrie* nor the *Flying Dutchman* have facilities for young children."

"Then, Colonels," Simms's eyes darted between me and Smythe, "we should have thought of that, before we began an operation to rescue over a hundred children."

"Ooh, crap, Joe," Skippy groaned. "I hadn't thought of that. A bunch of rugrats-"

"They are not *rugrats*," Simms insisted.

"Sorry. Anklebiters, then," Skippy corrected himself cluelessly. "Wow. Damn. With a hundred children aboard, the *Dutchman* will become a Super *Duper* Funtime Shitbus for sure. Hoo-boy. I'm glad that will be Nagatha's problem and not mine."

"I don't know about that," I admitted, showing how little thought I had put into the subject. "*Valkyrie* is the bigger ship, and more well-protected. We might keep the children here."

"*Dude!*" Skippy howled. "You can't be serious."

"Can we get back to the subject, please?" Simms demanded.

"Listen, XO, it's simple," I pleaded, desperate to end the conversation. "There are two Dodos out there. One of them has a complication. I'd rather avoid a complication, Ok?"

"The other Dodo has a more experienced team," Smythe added. "Eleven of those eighteen people are French paratroopers who have served together since before Columbus Day. The other seven have been with the team for three months. That is a good start."

Simms relented, turning back to her station. "I am all for avoiding complications."

Smythe caught my eye and pointed to his tablet. I knew what he meant. The first Dodo, with the pregnant soldier, came with another complication. That Commando team was commanded by a Chinese brigadier general. He outranked me. Even if we assumed promotions granted on Paradise were not legit, the guy had been a colonel when the Expeditionary Force left Earth, which meant he had more time in grade than I did. That could be a problem. My response was a shrug. If General Song became an issue, we would deal with it.

Anyway, hopefully it would not matter. The Commando team aboard the second Dodo was led by a French Army major. There would be no rank issues there. That made my decision easy.

All the info we had on the Commando team, and the six human pilots aboard the second Dodo, was good. It's what was *not* listed in the file that bothered me. "Skippy, where's the data about the Ruhar observers?"

"We don't have it, Joe. The data we have is from transmissions I intercepted out here, and those messages didn't contain any details about observers. To get more data, we need to move deeper into the system."

Going into an operation without knowing all the pieces on the board did not please me. It was also standard operating procedure. "There are typically two observers?"

"Yes," Skippy confirmed. "One pilot and one cavalry soldier."

And, right there was the problem. We would not only be commandeering the human soldiers, an action for which I had at least a sketchy level of legal authority. We would outright be kidnapping two Ruhar. They would be treated well, they would have basic food made by *Valkyrie*'s fabricators, and whatever comforts we could provide. They would also be prisoners, restricted to limited areas of the ship. To minimize the risk of them causing trouble, the Ruhar would be aboard the *Flying Dutchman*, and therefore Chang's problem. I felt bad about dumping another problem on him, and I knew he would understand. "Smythe?"

"I say we launch, Sir," he said with less than a full measure of enthusiasm. The idea of expanding our list of enemies by kidnapping Ruhar citizens made him uncomfortable. It *sounded* reasonable given the circumstances, he told me. What he worried about was the Law of Unintended Consequences.

"Ok. Simms, launch the packages. Then we'll jump back to rendezvous with the *Dutchman* for the next phase."

After the packages were away, there wasn't much for us to do. I waited until we saw the Jeraptha ship jump away just like Skippy said it would, then I told the bridge crew to get rest, except for a duty officer and a pilot.

My first stop was my office, then I planned to hit the gym. Skippy still had me locked out from playing video games until I read all the stuff he thought was important, so I was reading fast as I could. In my office, or on the treadmill, or while falling asleep, I had a tablet in front of my nose, reading one document after another. The current file I was reading had only six pages left, I planned to ask Skippy to give me a break after I finished that one.

Simms came in without knocking, we had dispensed with that because the sliding doors were like fifteen feet wide and always open. It seemed silly for people to stand in a wide-open doorway and ask permission to enter.

"Simms," I glanced up, then kept one eye on the tablet, trying to keep track of which line I was reading. When she sat quietly in the chair across from me, I figured she wanted to continue the uncomfortable conversation we had on the bridge. "Hey, uh, XO. Listen, I have nothing against women who are-"

"I would like to be pregnant, Sir," she announced as she rested her elbow on my desk.

"Uh-" My brain locked up. Part of the problem was sheer panic. The other was the 'WTF' reaction of not believing what I just heard. From what I learned in high school Health class, becoming pregnant involved a particular process, but maybe I was remembering it wrong. "You are telling *me* this, because-"

She snorted. "*You* would not be involved."

"Oh thank God. I mean-"

"I know what you mean," she said, her eyes twinkling. She enjoyed screwing with me. "What I mean is, I want to have children someday."

"Ok, uh-"

"I need stability for that."

"And a guy too," I blurted out before my brain could stop me. "Usually. It's none of my business, Simms, sorry I-"

"We've talked about it. Me and Frank. We've discussed it. It's what he wants also."

"That's great," I mumbled as a way to stall for time. Why was she telling me these intimate details of her personal life?

She came to my rescue, answering the question I hadn't asked. "When this mission is over, when the Backstop wormhole is near Earth and open, I would like to go back to Avalon."

"Sure," I smiled with relief. "To get the colony set up to receive refugees."

"That, and to start a family. Frank, he," she twisted to her left and dug into her right pants pocket. When her hand came out, there was a ring in her palm.

"Holy sh-" The ring was gold. The diamond was freakin' *huge*. "Where did he get- Sorry," I blushed with embarrassment. "Congratulations." There was a protocol when hearing about such announcements, I think. I was supposed to ask how he proposed, was it romantic, something like that?

"The rock?" She held up the diamond to catch the light. "Skippy fabricated it for Frank. A flawless diamond. It's a bit gaudy," she looked at the ring with affection, and I stopped myself from saying 'Ya think'? "Skippy says diamonds really aren't worth anything out here, but," she held the ring above the appropriate finger. "It's the thought that counts."

"So, Muller proposed." I automatically referred to him by his last name, though the guy was a civilian. "Did-"

"No. *I* proposed to *him*. We're adults," she explained. "I don't like playing games. Frank had the ring made to make it official. We're keeping it quiet, I don't want to distract anyone from the rescue mission."

"Oh. Sure." My responses were confined to the safest, most bland things I could think of.

"When I proposed to Frank, I gave him a ring made from one of the *Dutchman*'s old jump drive coils. That was Skippy's suggestion. His second suggestion, actually."

"What was his first suggestion?"

"That I keep looking," she laughed.

I laughed too. "That sounds like Skippy. Ok, I will need another Executive Officer, then."

"It seemed fair to tell you now."

"This may all be OBE anyway, you know?" I used the acronym for Overcome By Events. "We need to complete the rescue, then go back to see if Backstop got into position, and if Skippy can wake the damned thing up."

"Understood." She still had that amused look. She knew how to make me uncomfortable, and she enjoyed doing it. Not all the time, just when she thought I was being a doofus.

"It's not up to me, you know."

Her eyes narrowed and the look of amusement was gone. "What isn't?"

"Whether you go back to Avalon. Whether the UN assigns you to the beta site."

She blinked, like that thought hadn't occurred to her. "I, we," she meant herself and Frank Muller, "already have been assigned there."

"Not permanently," I reminded her gently. "That was supposed to be a simple, and short, survey mission. Now the rules have all changed. The UN hasn't even agreed that Avalon is the best candidate for a beta site."

"It's the *only* candidate," she insisted. I could see on her face that her dream was slipping away.

"Simms, I'll do what I can. But, you know that when we get back to Earth, we will not be bringing good news, right? My influence will be limited, if I have any at all. We might-"

"Oh, Skuh-*REW* this," Skippy spat, appearing between us on the desk. "Tammy, I mean, Jennifer, if you want to be on Avalon, then that is what's going to happen. Joe, you tell those knuckleheads at the UN that if they want the Backstop wormhole to stay open for the evac, Simms gets what she wants."

"Hey, I'm all for that," I gave him a thumbs up. "*You* tell them."

"Me? Why do I have to talk with filthy monkeys?"

"Because when we get home, UNEF Command may want to skip a court-martial for me, and go straight to the firing squad, you know?"

"Shit. I forgot about that little detail. Thanks a lot, Mister Buzzkill."

That was the essence of Skippy. I was worried about getting the death penalty, and what he cared about was that ruined his good mood. With Skippy, you take what you can get. "Simms, I'm very happy for you and," it felt odd to call her fiancé 'Frank'. "Mister Muller. We're a long way from being able to worry about what UNEF thinks. Get some rest, we have a real mission to complete out there."

CHAPTER TWENTY NINE

The next move was for me, Smythe, Kapoor and the STAR team to transfer to the *Flying Dutchman*. Our cover story was the Thuranin kidnapping an Alien Legion team, so we had to take a Thuranin ship in, rather than *Valkyrie*. Sure, if everything went as planned, the Dodo's communications would be jammed so they couldn't signal what they saw, and no one would ever see through our assault ship's stealth field. But, knowing the Universe had a soon-to-expire coupon for a free sucker punch against Joe Bishop, I did not count on everything going as planned. If there was a stealth field failure, we needed the rest of that star system to see a Thuranin ship, or at least a vaguely Thuranin-looking ship. So, our mighty *Valkyrie* was waiting in reserve, while we took our creaky old star carrier in for the op.

No, that was not quite true. The *Dutchman* was no longer a star carrier. And it was no longer creaky. The upgrades Skippy had performed, using leftover Lego pieces, made that ship better than when we took it. Better than new. The *Dutchman* still carried only a limited array of offensive weapons, but it could outrun any ship in the Thuranin fleet. Chang told me he was very well pleased with his new command, and I agreed with him.

The 'packages' we had launched were probes, basically small missiles stuffed with sensor gear instead of warheads. Well, probes were usually crammed full of sensor gear, the three we launched carried a more special payload. They each had containment vessels with one end of a microwormhole. The probes were shot out of a railgun to give them high initial velocity, so they could save most of their fuel for deceleration and maneuvering when they reached the target areas. Because the Ruhar did not want any accidents befalling the primitive humans operating in their training area, a section of the asteroid belt one point six million cubic kilometers in size had been set aside for that one Dodo. Despite the Dodo practicing stealth, it was transmitting a transponder code for safety. My guess was that during an exercise, opposing teams were supposed to ignore the transponders. What it meant for us is that we knew exactly where the Dodo was at all times, and when the Commando team left their dropship, they also wore transponders. That was all great, except from *Valkyrie*'s position, that data was way too old. By the time the transponder signals crawled out to us at the speed of light, the Dodo could have moved far away. That's why we needed the magic of microwormholes, they provided instantaneous communications all the way out to where *Valkyrie* was parked.

Two of the probes flew outward, away from the star. They were the first launched but last to reach their destination, coming to a halt between the *Flying Dutchman* and *Valkyrie*, about fifty kilometers from each ship. Those microwormholes provided a real-time link between our two ships and the other probes, without exposing the smaller ship to danger. Or, not exposing the *Dutchman* to danger before it was necessary.

The other two probes? They flew to the exercise area and began listening for the Dodo's transponder. We now had a pair of microwormholes that provided instantaneous communication between the probes shadowing the target Dodo, and our ships that were safely waiting two lighthours away. There was a brief moment of panic when the signal wasn't picked up for four minutes, then the Dodo flew out from behind a large metallic asteroid and its transponder lit up the area like a strobe light. Success! Except we then picked up four more signals, part of the Commando team was down on the asteroid. If two of the signals had been from Ruhar observers, I would have been Ok with leaving behind two of the humans and snatching the dropship. No such luck. All four skinsuit transponders were transmitting IDs like 'Renaud, Henri'. Human names, along with their rank, unit designation and vital signs. The good news for us was, they were assembled on the surface of the asteroid, waiting for the Dodo to pick them up. It's a good thing I hadn't ordered us to act prematurely, because as the Dodo slowly descended, two more soldiers climbed out of a tunnel under the surface. They were also humans. Whether there were more humans below the surface, or the others were all aboard the Dodo, we had no idea. Using only passive sensors, the microwormholes only knew what they could intercept through transmissions, and the Commando team was using excellent communications discipline. Based on the tentative flight path flown by the Dodo, it looked like the pilots were following the rules and ignoring the suit transponders of the away team.

We waited while the Dodo descended, and did not land on the slowly spinning rock. The dropship picked up the six people from the surface by employing some sort of hook-and-tether devices, that reminded me of how we had planned to pull our people off the rooftops on Kobamik, during our Black Ops mission. Smythe had the same thought, and muttered approving noises while we watched. We both made notes to investigate that equipment, it might come in useful someday.

As the Dodo sped away, the six soldiers dangled behind, being slowly reeled in. One soldier was tumbling on the end of her tether, and I felt sorry for '*Durand, Camille, Capitaine*'. It wasn't her fault, the tether had a flaw. Or the tumbling was a deliberate part of the exercise, because the Dodo crew quickly acted to stabilize that tether, and reeled her in first. Hopefully, she didn't upchuck her breakfast croissant from dizziness.

We still did not know how many people were aboard the Dodo, because their suit transponders turned off when inside the cabin. Smythe urged caution and I agreed, we were on a time limit, but rushing might blow our best, maybe only, chance to augment our STARs with an experienced special operations unit.

The Dodo flew a twisting course, zipping around asteroids, then it approached an asteroid that was apparently a frequently-used exercise area. The rock had derelict structures on the surface, and tunnels dug into it. Skippy said the layout was originally a typical Ruhar facility for servicing mining equipment and crews, but after it had been abandoned, it was rebuilt to a configuration more common to the Kristang. On Earth, we had training sites built to look like whatever country where the US Army was serving most recently. When we weren't caring about political correctness, we called those mock villages 'Hadjistans'.

Like I said, political correctness wasn't part of our SOP. Officially, the Army refers to such villages as MOUT Sites, or they did the last time I was at one. That was a long time ago now.

Anyway, it looked like the Commandos were going on another exercise, and we watched with increasing impatience, urging them to get *on* with it. Finally, nineteen skinsuits dropped to the asteroid's surface. Eighteen humans, plus one Ruhar who was clearly identified by her transponder. She was clearly an observer not only from the different signal transmitted by her suit, but by her actions. As the Commando team conducted an assault and breaching exercise, she hung back where she could see everything, but was not in the way.

Smythe, Kapoor and their STAR team watched closely, evaluating the soldiers from UNEF-Paradise. They were interested in both how skillfully the exercise was conducted, but also what tactics were used. In Smythe's opinion, the Paradise team was slow and insufficiently aggressive. That could have been standard Ruhar battlefield tactics, or it could have been the hamsters coddling their primitive clients. Or, Kapoor suggested, the humans might be more concerned about avoiding mistakes, than with impressing their observer.

Personally, my guess was the observer told the humans not to screw up, because she would get the blame if someone busted an expensive skinsuit.

Anyway, the exercise went on for three hours, then the Dodo dropped down to land. Recovery of the ground team was conducted casually; the action was clearly over. It was time for a stand-down, a hot meal in zero gravity, and maybe sleep. That's what we hoped, for everyone aboard the Dodo to get a good eight hours of shut-eye. And for the Dodo to be in open space, clear of spinning rocks, when the team caught up on sleep.

Part of our wish came true when the Dodo lifted off and set course for another large asteroid. At the moderate speed they were flying, they would not reach their next objective for another sixteen hours. I stood behind the chair occupied by the *Dutchman*'s captain, letting him run his ship. "Chang, tell Kapoor's team to stand by."

"They have been standing by to stand by, for the past six hours," Kong's reply had a touch of wry amusement. That's life in the military. You get ready, in case someone needs you to get ready, in case you are needed. In the case of Kapoor's team, 'standing by to stand by' meant they were in or near the *Dutchman*'s armory. My order for them to stand by meant the STARS would get into their mech suits, and board a pair of Falcon dropships that were warmed up in the *Dutchman*'s docking bays. The Thuranin-built Falcons were not as capable as the Maxolhx Panthers we had aboard *Valkyrie*, and so I was exposing our small STAR team to additional danger. That wasn't by choice, nor was it by choice that Chang was taking the *Dutchman* in to Shanghai the Paradise people, rather than me flying *Valkyrie*. To explain why an Alien Legion human Commando team had been taken, we had to make it look like it was a Thuranin operation. That meant jumping in with a Thuranin ship, and using Thuranin dropships. There was no way we could squeeze our people into tiny Thuranin combat suits, so Kristang powered armor had to be good enough. Anyone who saw the sensor data would assume the Thuranin made their lizard clients do the hazardous work, and hopefully not ask too many questions.

Kapoor's team stood by. We all did. The Dodo cut power and coasted onward, having attained enough velocity that it would need to decelerate hard to slow down before reaching its destination. Still, we waited for the inevitable course correction. If that was needed, and the pilots were following standard Ruhar procedure, the course adjustment would happen within seventeen minutes after cutting power. It did, and Skippy judged they would not need another course correction during their flight. We now knew exactly where the Dodo was, its speed and direction. I gave Chang the signal and the *Dutchman* began slowing and curving around, until it was flying at exactly the same speed and course as the target, except our good old former star carrier was two lighthours away from the target. "Chang," I told him as I strapped into a chair in the CIC. "It's your call."

Chang looked to the duty officer in the CIC, who gave him a thumb's up. "Kapoor is ready," Chang announced. "We're opening the docking bay doors now. *Valkyrie*, we are counting down to jump."

Simms acknowledged the signal. "*Valkyrie* is standing by to assist," Simms assured Chang, and I sat back in my chair. My relaxed move was for the benefit of the crew, it wasn't because I was feeling confident. Part of me had wanted to be in the command chair for the op. Another, smarter part of me knew that would signal a lack of faith in Chang's ability. Besides, if the shit hit the fan, I needed to focus on the big picture and let him run the ship.

"*Dutchman* is jumping," Chang announced. "In three, two, one-"

We lost the connection to the *Valkyrie* as our trusty old star carrier jumped.

And regained the connection as the *Dutchman* emerged near our other two microwormholes, the ones that had been stealthily trailing the Dodo at a safe distance. Our former star carrier jumped in right on top of the tiny Dodo, which was not particularly a small spacecraft. Next to the bulk of the *Dutchman* Version Four Point Oh, the dropship was dwarfed.

Jumping in so close was one reason we had to wait until all the Paradise people were safely inside their dropship. If anyone had been outside, the radiation of a starship emerging from the hellish environment of twisted spacetime could have seriously injured or killed them. As it was, the side of the Dodo facing toward the inbound jump wormhole got scorched. When we were planning the op, I was nervous about jumping in so close, until Skippy assured me the Dodo's skin would protect its fragile occupants. *Once*. It could protect the occupants through one blast of radiation. That was hopefully all we needed.

"Nagatha, work your magic," Chang ordered as I waited anxiously. "Kapoor, launch."

"Yes, Colonel," she responded, her voice purring with delight. "Communications are jammed. Target ship is feeding power to main engines, and, power is off! Target's electronics are fried," she announced with satisfaction. That last task had been accomplished with a bit of Maxolhx technology, a nifty gizmo that could scramble most types of circuits and render ships, weapons, satellites and anything else that relied on computers useless. It was sort of an EMP, electromagnetic pulse, except that Skippy told me it worked even on equipment that was powered down. The gizmo was a short-range capability, and it wouldn't work on gear specially hardened against the effect, but dropships couldn't handle the weight penalty of shielding. Plus, none of the traditional enemies of the Ruhar possessed that scramble technology, so they didn't need to worry about it.

The result was the Dodo we wanted to capture was drifting, and already beginning to tumble nose over tail ever so slowly. I could not imagine the panic of the people inside, seeing a starship emerge from twisted spacetime practically on top of them, and then losing all power. In the Dodo's cabin, it would be dark, except for the emergency chemical-powered lights. The air circulation system would be off, the familiar hissing of air through the vents would be missing. In the cockpit, no systems would be operating. Their skinsuits, their rifles, their zPhones, none of it would be responding.

As I watched the Falcon dropship approach and Kapoor's team fly out the back ramp in jetpacks, my anxiety level climbed a bit. The people in the Dodo were not defenseless. Assuming they followed the standard procedures for UNEF-Paradise's Alien Legion teams, they would have backup weapons. Good old M-4 rifles, or whatever the French contingent wanted to carry. Possibly sidearms also, and old-fashioned grenades. Our fancy Maxolhx scramble gizmo could not prevent triggers from activating firing pins and sending bullets down a barrel at lethal speeds. Kapoor's team were in Kristang mech suits so they had a decent level of protection, they could still be badly injured or even killed by crude but effective bullets with explosive tips. Silently, I urged Kapoor and the STARs to be careful.

Six of the STARs, including Kapoor, contacted the Dodo and latched on. They had chosen locations away from the main cabin, to prevent some panicked knucklehead inside from being tempted to shoot through the Dodo's skin to get them. One of the STARs, a graphic at bottom of the display identified the soldier as *'Frey, Katie, Cpt CAN'* reached out with a pole and slapped the far end of it onto the cabin's skin. She kept a grip on the pole while flattening herself against the engine cowling to avoid becoming a target.

On the end of the pole was another gizmo, this one not quite so high-tech. The box on the end of the pole adhered to the Dodo's skin to secure its position, then a plasma charge burned a hair-thin hole most of the way through into the dropship's cabin. The amount of plasma was calculated to be exhausted just before it penetrated the inner pressure vessel of the cabin, so right behind it was a tiny drill attached to a wire. Within two seconds of Frey slapping the pole on the target area, we had a view of the Dodo's interior. A soft light glowed from the end of the wire, illuminating the cabin, where we could see faces that were determined, alert and anxious but showing no signs of panic. That was a good sign. We didn't need people who frightened easily.

"Joe?" Chang prompted me from the bridge. "It's showtime."

"Here goes nothing," I muttered to myself. Toggling the transmit button on my zPhone, I spoke in what I hoped was a loud, clear and confident but unthreatening tone. "Hello. This is Colonel Joe Bishop, of UNEF Special Operations Command. From *Earth*," I emphasized.

It was admirable that although the people in the cabin said things to each other, they spoke low enough that I couldn't hear them. None of them shouted, none of them moved from their assigned positions. They all had their skinsuit helmets on, but with faceplates up, otherwise they could not have heard orders. After a few seconds, one individual released the strap that had held him in a defensive position behind a locker, and floated over toward the softly-glowing wire. He spoke with a French accent. "I am Commandant Gabriel Fabron, French Expeditionary Army. You, Sir, *lie*. Earth is lost to us."

Commandant was the French Army equivalent to a major in the US military. "Commandant Fabron, we came here from Earth, recently," I explained. "We will be able to offer proof, once you are aboard our ship."

"A *Thuranin* starship?" Fabron did not relax the grip on his rifle, but he had it pointed down and to the side. His index finger was properly alongside the trigger.

"It was a Thuranin starship, now it's ours. We stole it. We're sort of pirates," I laughed softly.

Me laughing had him confused, or maybe he relaxed a bit. "Why should I believe you?"

"Commandant, I know this sounds like a bullshit story, but you need to understand a couple things. We need your team for a vital operation, I'll explain once you're aboard. Robotic tugs are attaching to your hull and will bring you into a docking bay. All we need you to do right now is strap in, relax, and don't do anything stupid, Ok?"

"Do I have a choice?" Fabron asked warily.

"You *always* have a choice, Fabron," I used his name in an attempt to establish a rapport. "We need you, your team can make a difference out here. If it helps, you might remember me. I was on Paradise, with the US Tenth Infantry. The Kristang persuaded UNEF HQ to promote me to colonel as a publicity stunt, before the hamsters took the planet back."

In the dim light, I could see his eyes bulge with surprise. "Merde," he gasped. "You are *that* Bishop?"

"Ayuh, I am."

"We thought you were *dead*."

"Yeah, well, rumors of my death have been greatly exaggerated. Commandant, this may seem odd, but, believe me, we've seen some shit out here that will blow your mind. Hell, we have *done* some shit that blew *my* mind."

He hesitated, making up his mind. The guy was decisive, a good quality, because he only debated for a few seconds. "Very well. It does not appear that I have any good options. We will stand down."

"An excellent choice, Fabron."

"Live to fight another day, Non?" He grunted, less than happy.

"Hopefully, you will be fighting on our side. Ok, the next voice you hear will be Major Kapoor of our special operations team."

Kapoor's team got the robotic tugs securely attached, then they used their jetpacks to fly a safe distance away from the Dodo, while Nagatha tested the tugs. After a minor adjustment, she gently moved the powerless spacecraft into a docking bay. Artificial gravity had been cut off to that section of the ship, to make it easier to maneuver the bulky dropship through the doors and down onto the deck, where clamps secured it in place. Kapoor talked the Paradise people through the entire process, including warning them when the artificial gravity plates were powered back up, and weight gradually tugged downward.

By the time I got down to the docking bay, Chang had already jumped the ship to rendezvous with Valkyrie. We paused briefly after the bay was fully pressurized, as a safety precaution while both of our ships jumped far outside the star system, then I tapped the button to slide open both airlock doors, and walked through. Behind me were Smythe and Adams, both unarmed as I was. Kapoor's team had rifles and all of them had taken their helmets off. The Paradise people must have gotten a shock when they looked out the Dodo's windows to see figures in Kristang powered armor, so Kapoor had made sure his team had their faceplates set to clear and lights illuminating clearly human faces.

"Commandant Fabron," I called out, knowing my words were being fed through the wire into the Dodo's cabin. "Please open the side door and come out, without your weapons. We are all friends here." Then I clarified, to be more accurate. "We are all on the same side," I added, tapping the UNEF patch on my uniform.

There was no immediate response from the Dodo. Through my earpiece, I could hear harsh whispering going on, the people in the cabin must have been arguing about what to do.

"Fabron?" I decided to offer an inducement to him. "In this year's World Cup, the French team was in the Group of Death but they reached the semifinals, before losing to Argentina. We have video of the entire tournament."

A brief hesitation, then Fabron asked "What was the score?"

"Three to two."

"Ah," he grunted. "No doubted Argentina cheated. I am coming out."

"If it makes you feel any better, the Argies lost two to nothing to Germany in the final," I offered, as the side door popped inward and began sliding aside. Despite my relaxed stance, I was tense. If Fabron came out shooting, there could be trouble. Under my uniform, I was wearing a thin layer of reactive body armor, but that didn't protect my head or my legs. Bullets could do a lot of damage, and grenades would be devastating. Nagatha should have been able to give me a couple seconds of warning if she detected a weapon in the Dodo's airlock, and I was betting my life on her abilities.

Fabron was smart and acted to assure no harm came to his people. The first thing I saw was his bare outstretched hands, he had removed the skinsuit gloves. Then I saw him, without a helmet. He had slightly shaggy blonde hair, and a light stubbly beard that many special operators grew. At first glance he looked like any other guy you might see, except for his eyes. They were intense, watchful, determined. He stepped out onto the deck, automatically noting the position of Kapoor's team, who were doing so good a job at acting relaxed, it was clear they were not relaxed at all. If the French paratrooper saw any of us as an immediate threat, he didn't react.

Reaching the deck, he looked around, saw me and his eyebrows lifted slightly. "It *is* you," he stared at me.

Tapping my chest, I confirmed "Like I said, not dead."

Fabron's response was to come to attention and snap a crisp salute to me. I returned the gesture with a smile. "At ease, Commandant."

"I do not think I can ever be at ease here," he looked around the docking bay. We had deliberately parked a Maxolhx Panther dropship in the other cradle. "This is *your* ship? Humans fly this starship?"

"We stole it from the Thuranin, yeah."

"I do not recognize that configuration," he pointed at the Panther.

"We call it a Panther," I explained. "We stole *that* from the Maxolhx."

"From the Max-" Now he was openly gaping at me.

"Ah, that's nothing," I waved a hand. "It was a package deal. We got a bunch of Panthers when we stole a *battlecruiser* from the Maxolhx. You heard about the ghost ship that has been kicking ass across the galaxy?" He nodded stiffly, as if his neck muscles were incapable of movement. I kind of felt sorry for the guy, we had to be blowing his mind. "That's our battlecruiser. We call our ship the '*Valkyrie*'. I'd like to give you a tour, but for now, this," I gestured down at the deck, "is the *Flying Dutchman*. It was a Thuranin star carrier before we pimped it."

"Pimped?"

I forgot he was French. "We modified it."

The guy stood there, stunned. "I have missed a lot, Non?"

"It's a lot to process, I know. If it makes you feel any better, the last time I met people from Paradise, they had trouble believing it also. Those guys were-"

Fabron sucked in a breath. "We are not the first people from Paradise you have met? You have been back to Paradise?"

"Uh, yeah. Remember when those buried maser cannons blasted a Kristang battlegroup out of the sky? That was us, too."

"You went back to Paradise?"

"Yes, um," I had to think. "We landed there, uh, twice. Plus we were in-system a third time, that's when we picked up a group of Keeper fanatics."

"*Keepers*," he spat. Then he added with surprise. "In-system? You did not land? The Keepers were not on Paradise?"

"No. They were in a pair of lizard dropships, headed for Paradise. They had been infected with a bioweapon. We intercepted them before they could do any damage."

Probably without thinking, he touched his left shoulder, where the vaccine had been injected. "That was *you*?"

"That was *us*. We call our outfit the Merry Band of Pirates," I said with pride.

"You have been *busy*," he stated. His expression had changed from bewildered wonderment to something more typical of special operators: admiration. The Merry Band of Pirates had been kicking *ass*, and he wanted a piece of the action. I mean, he *wanted* a piece of the action. No way was an operator like Fabron going to miss out on whatever we did next.

"Idle hands are the Devil's playground, you know," I don't know if he understood the humor.

"Colonel, if you have accomplished," he waved a hand to encompass the docking bay, and the ship beyond. "So much, then why do you need my team? Why not get," he peered behind me to Smythe, who still wore an SAS emblem in addition to the STAR team unit symbol. "More Special Air Services? Or paras from France?"

"Because, right now, the Maxolhx are blockading the wormhole we use to get back and forth to Earth. Earth is fine, it's good," I hastened to assure him. "The lizards there are dead." That statement was true, except for the frozen lizards. Assuming they were still frozen, and that UNEF hadn't shot them into the Sun. "We need you because we have a short-term problem, and we need to act fast. The lizards kidnapped a group of human civilians, including children, from Earth. That was back while UNEF was deploying. Some of those people are still alive, but the lizards plan to sell them to the Thuranin, for use in medical experiments. The little green MFers," it occurred to me that the French might have a different derisive nickname for our least favorite cyborgs. "The Thuranin, want to develop another bioweapon, to use against Paradise. The Alien Legion has got them scared. They want to exterminate humans, and kill the whole Legion concept, before it gets out of control."

His shoulders slumped. "*Merde.*"

"It's complicated. Fabron, I would not have commandeered your team if I had a choice. Those people, those children, are being starved and abused. They will be tortured and killed unless we rescue them. Colonel Smythe," I jerked a thumb back over my shoulder, "will explain the details."

"One more question, please, Colonel Bishop?"

"Sure. Shoot," as I said that, I reminded myself that a French soldier might not understand my slang.

Fabron understood well enough. "Will this operation involve killing lizards?"

"Oh," behind me, Smythe laughed. I turned to see a broad, predatory grin spread across his face. "There will be *much* killing of lizards and other nasties, I can promise that."

"Then," Fabron had a matching smile. "You can count me in. The reason I signed up for the Legion was to get, as you Americans say, *payback*. I think payback can be better achieved with a Maxolhx battlecruiser," he shook his head in amazement.

"That was what we thought, too." Skippy was whispering in my ear. I pressed a finger over that ear, and gestured for Fabron to wait a moment. "Commandant? I told you Earth is fine. That includes your wife Celeste and your son Paul."

His eyes narrowed with sudden suspicion. "You know this?"

"Yes. We have records of everyone we left on Paradise, and their families back on Earth. Gabriel," I said softly, breaking protocol by using his first name. "The aliens don't know humans have a starship; our existence out here is a secret. When this mission is over, you and your team can't go back to Paradise, you understand? Hopefully, you will all be going *home*."

"Home," he whispered. The guy's knees bent a little.

Technically, that was me giving a promise that I didn't have the authority to make. Assuming Skippy could get the Backstop wormhole moved to Earth, and opened properly, we could go home. That also assumed we were, you know, still alive at that point. UNEF would likely not be happy about the idea of people from Paradise landing on Earth, meeting their families and talking about everything they had seen and everything they knew. When we left Earth, the Keepers we captured were still confined to Johnston Atoll, a tiny island in the middle of the Pacific Ocean. The Keepers had not been allowed to talk to anyone, their very existence was a secret. UNEF would probably want to keep Fabron's team isolated also.

You know what?

Screw UNEF.

I was *done* taking shit from a bunch of bureaucrats who had never been *out here*. Never had their boots, as the expression goes, on the ground. If Fabron's team survived to get back home, I was not requesting permission to bring them dirtside. The way I felt right then, I wanted to land a damned dropship in front of the Eiffel Tower and announce to the French people that some of their soldiers had, at long last, come home from Paradise.

Besides, if we did get home, we would be announcing that Earth needed to be evacuated. Having a group of people from Paradise confirming how dangerous the galaxy was would, I think, be helpful.

Well, it would be helpful to the thousands of people who could be evaced before the Maxolhx arrived. The *billions* of other people would not be much comforted by knowing how greatly the odds were against the survival of our species.

Crap. I had gotten Fabron's hopes up. When he learned the whole truth, that Earth was ultimately doomed, that was going to be a slap in the face. He wouldn't be looking at me so admiringly then.

I really had not thought this whole thing through.

Yanking my thoughts back to the present, I repeated what Fabron had said. "*Home*. Before we left Earth the last time, we downloaded practically the whole internet. Whatever you want to know about what's been going on back home, you should be able to find it."

"My family?" He asked with heartbreaking anticipation.

"If they have been posting on FaceTwit," I flashed a smile, "you should find it. Oh, hey," snapping my fingers, I remembered something. "Most people back home who have family and friends on Paradise, they wrote letters and stuff, for us to deliver if we ever got there. I'll check if your wife wrote anything," I added as Skippy whispered in my ear that Fabron's wife had written many letters. Not as many recently, but that was to be expected, I guess.

Smythe took that as a cue to step forward and take over. Fabron snapped a salute to our STAR team leader and they had a brief chat, operator to operator. Then Fabron gestured to the Dodo and his team began coming out, one at a time.

"Uh, hey, Joe," Skippy spoke in my ear. "We might have three kinds of trouble."

Before responding, I walked a few steps away. When I heard 'trouble', my greatest fear was some idiot with a grenade who didn't believe my story and wanted to be a hero. "Like what?"

"To start, there is a Ruhar officer hiding in the rear of the Dodo's cabin. She let Fabron take the lead, but she is very unhappy and intends to make trouble."

"Is she armed?"

"She has been demanding a rifle or pistol, so far the Commandos have been holding her back."

"Ok, tell Smythe and Kapoor about her. We knew they had a hamster liaison officer, Skippy. Is the second bit of trouble the other hamster?"

"Um, no. The second issue is that the observer pilot is not a hamster. He is a Jeraptha."

"What the *f*-" People, including Fabron, turned to look at me. I forced a grin onto my face and strode across the bay, farther away. "What the *hell* is a beetle doing aboard that Dodo?"

"I do not know, Joe."

"*How* am I just hearing about this now?" I demanded.

"Nagatha didn't know, the *Dutchman*'s sensors couldn't penetrate the shielding around the Dodo's cabin. I didn't find out until you jumped back here. Does it matter anyway? You had already disabled the Dodo, you weren't going to leave them out there in a dead spacecraft, right?"

"No." Damn it, I was pissed and I wanted someone to be pissed *at*. "Oh, hell, we'll deal with this somehow. Can you make food for Jeraptha?"

"It won't be yummy, but he will survive."

"Great. We planned to kidnap a Ruhar, now we're making enemies of the beetles also. I am afraid to ask, what is the third bit of trouble?"

"That is- Well, here he is now. See for yourself."

I did see, but at first I didn't *see* what the trouble could be. Stepping out of the Dodo, holding his hands away from his sides in a gesture that was unthreatening but not quite a surrender, was a tall black man. A tall black *Marine*. Skinsuits could be featureless, or they could employ chameleonware to blend in with their surroundings. Or they could be adjusted to display unit and rank and any other symbol requested by the user. This guy had symbols designating him as a gunnery sergeant, and the distinctive red circle patch of the Third Marine Expeditionary Force, in addition to the UNEF and Alien Legion symbols all of Fabron's team had on their skinsuits. His name tag read 'GREENE', with an extra 'E' on the end. Ok, so he was a Marine, that was not unusual. Why did Skippy think this Greene guy was trouble? His haircut was high and tight, he wasn't armed as far as I could tell, and he-

"*Margaret?*" The guy said loudly. "What are-"

"*Lamar?*" Adams gasped, and right then, I understood the problem.

The guy I now knew as Lamar Greene strode forward, almost past Smythe before giving our STAR team leader a perfunctory salute. Lamar never took his eyes off Adams. "We all- I thought you were *dead*."

"I didn't think I would ever see you-" She cringed, a tear rolling down her cheek. Impulsively, she stepped forward and they embraced. No kissing, just hugs but not the back-slapping hug your give to a team member. This was a full-body hug. Like, her pressing her face into his neck, and him running a hand along her back and them whispering something to each other.

"*Shiiiiiit,*" I whispered to myself.

"Um, they have a history, Joe," Skippy explained.

"Ya *think*?" I shot back bitterly, and immediately regretted it. "Sorry. Not your fault."

"They were stationed at Pendleton together, then he transferred to Third MEF," he pronounced it 'Meff'. "In Okinawa. Margaret requested a transfer, but then Columbus Day happened, and you know. Air transport was limited, the internet went down and then wasn't reliable. They both shipped out to Paradise, but on separate ships. When they landed, they kept in touch by zPhone, um, hmm. Would telling you about their conversations be an invasion of their privacy?"

"Damn it. Yes. Me even asking about their personal conversations would be an abuse of power, so don't do it."

"Could I tell you that, while he was stuck on Okinawa after Columbus Day, Sergeant Greene had a relationship with a civilian?"

"That bastard," I glared at the guy, feeling bad for Margaret.

"Hey, Adams hasn't exactly been celibate, you know? She requested a transfer to Okinawa, but I can tell you she had second thoughts about it."

"Was she having second thoughts about *him*?"

"Um, answering that question may run into a privacy issue."

"Then don't answer," I sighed. My life *sucks*.

"Joe, they haven't seen each other in a long time. He thought she was *dead*. Margaret did go visit his parents in El Paso once, after we returned from Newark. Would it violate her privacy to say that she has not mentioned Lamar Greene more than a half dozen times since I've known her?"

"You already mentioned it, so privacy is kind of moot."

"What I'm trying to say is, Margaret has not been pining away for him. She hasn't seen him for a long time, it's natural that they are happy to meet again."

Part of me wanted to go break up the party. They were no longer hugging, but they were standing very close and talking softly. He touched the nametag on her chest and his hand lingered there, she wasn't objecting. My intervention wasn't necessary, and wouldn't have been appropriate anyway. Fabron called Greene into formation, the Commando team was lining up in front of the Dodo. And right then, the Ruhar observer came out of the dropship, making demands and I had to deal with that right away. Plus I knew there was a Jeraptha we hadn't counted on, and a whole host of other issues that occupied my time and attention.

CHAPTER THIRTY

That was a *rough* day for me, and I'm not even talking about the wonderful news I got about Lamar freakin' Greene. The Ruhar we captured was a Klasta-rank officer named Kattah Robbenon, she was outraged and rightfully so. I told her she was right to be outraged, and I listened to her complaints. And I explained that we needed the Commando team to prevent a dire threat to Paradise, to the entire concept of the Alien Legion.

It was just my luck that Klasta Robbenon was a barracks lawyer. She railed at me, citing interstellar law that I wasn't familiar with and didn't care about. She told me I was stupid, that I was *crazy* for kidnapping a Ruhar soldier. Damn, when she got wound up, there was no stopping her. Humans needed the Ruhar to protect them in the cold, harsh Universe. The threat to Paradise was a threat only to the *humans* on Paradise, so it was *our* problem. She didn't even like the Alien Legion, she thought the whole idea of allowing primitive alien humans to fight was a distraction, and that giving weapons to the Verd-Kris was pure insanity. She- Well, blah blah blah, you get the idea. No way was she ever going to cooperate. Reluctantly, I ordered Kapoor to have two of his people escort our 'guest' to her new quarters. The cabin we locked her in was larger than usual, though I don't think she noticed or cared. Maybe after a couple weeks she would calm down, I wasn't counting on it. She was a prisoner of war, and sugar-coating it wouldn't change the reality of the situation.

Of the eighteen humans we took from the Dodo, twelve were immediately enthusiastic about joining the Merry Band of Pirates. They heard 'going *home*' and were all-in. None of the twelve had significant long-term ties to Paradise, and were eager to see their friends and family on Earth. Four others had mixed feelings about being Shanghaied. They figured there was more to the story than what we initially told them, and didn't believe that humans had been flying around the galaxy causing havoc on our own.

The remaining two were very much *not* happy about essentially being kidnapped. Both were guys on the French team. One of them had a girlfriend on Paradise. The other guy had married a woman on Paradise, and she was due to have their baby in two months. I truly felt sorry for that guy, and nothing I said could console him.

"You are taking me away from my wife and child," he glared at me.

Before I could respond, Commandant Fabron intervened. "Gaston," he used the guy's first name to establish rapport. "Colonel Bishop is not taking you away from your family. The *war* is taking you away. You could have been killed out here. Or on any nameless planet we do not know or care about. If this mission fails, the Thuranin will deliver a bioweapon to Paradise, and kill everyone. Including Catherine and your son."

Gaston was no longer shooting daggers at me with his eyes, he also was not happy. "My son will grow up without me. Never knowing me."

"That's not completely true," I said without thinking. Shit. So far, we had told only the good news to the Paradise people. They didn't know that Earth was inevitably doomed, that our best hope was to pull thousands of people to safety, and abandon *billions* to a terrible fate. We were giving info a little bit at a time, in bite-sized chunks, to avoid overwhelming them. Like, we had told them that we had help from an advanced AI, but we hadn't told them the nature of that AI, and Skippy had not spoken to them yet. "Listen," I checked Gaston's nametag because I wasn't going to use his first name. He wore three stripes, that was a staff sergeant in the US Army, but I couldn't remember the equivalent rank in French terms. NATO code OR-6, that was uh, yeah. "*Sergent-chef* Paschal. Our best estimate is that, within two years, the secret of humans flying around the galaxy will be exposed." They might be able to guess that was bad news for Earth, I would let them reach that conclusion on their own. "At that point, you can go back to Paradise. If that's possible, you understand? I can't make any promises. A *lot* can happen in two years."

"A single *day* can be fateful," Fabron muttered.

"Sorry about today," I said truthfully. "It wasn't by choice."

Fabron raised an eyebrow. "Colonel, I meant *Columbus* Day."

"Oh, yeah. Of course. Paschal, Commandant Fabron spoke the truth. If we don't stop the Thuranin, *every* human on Paradise is at risk."

Pascal stiffened. He looked to Fabron and nodded with a gesture so curt it was almost imperceptible. "Colonel Bishop, you will take the fight to the Thuranin?"

I knew what he meant. He wanted to hit the aliens who were threatening his family. "We are taking the fight to any aliens who need to get their asses kicked. There are a *lot* of them, and we can't do it alone, Sergent-chef. Are you with us?"

His answer was to click his boot heels together and snap a salute to me. "I would like to kick some ass, Sir." In his French accent, what he said was almost funny, but there was nothing humorous about the determined expression he wore.

"Polish up your ass-kicking boots, Paschal," I told him. "It's a target-rich environment out there."

The Ruhar liaison officer was never going to cooperate with us. She was a prisoner of war, and all we could do was treat her as well as we could, and wait until we could send her back to her people. We couldn't do that until it no longer mattered that aliens knew humans were flying starships, so she was going to be waiting a long time. I mean, hopefully we could keep our secret for another year or two.

The Commando team was either pumped up about joining us, or at least willing to do their duty. That was, until they learned the full truth. That night at dinner, I planned to give them a briefing on the strategic situation, and to introduce them to both Nagatha and Skippy. It was best they learn the unvarnished truth now, rather than in the middle of the rescue operation. I needed them to be focused and fully committed. If any of them were going to bail out, it was best to get that over with, before we invested a lot of time and effort in training them up for the op.

The Jeraptha was a totally different story. He was a beetle, sure, the first I had ever met face to face. Cadet-Undercandidate Yula Fangiu was last to come out of the Dodo, and he had looked neither angry nor happy. The guy, he was a male of his species, seemed to think the whole thing was a grand adventure. With the Ruhar escorted away, and Smythe addressing the Commandos, I invited Fangiu to the *Flying Dutchman's* conference room. He gawked at everything along the way, to the point where I needed to drag him away from various things that he wanted to inspect. I assured him there would be plenty of time for him to get a tour of the ship later. "Colonel Bishop, I have never been inside a Thuranin starship before."

Remembering when I had first stepped aboard the ship that became our *Flying Dutchman*, I could sympathize with him. Actually, because we had just captured the ship and I was afraid someone or something would take it away from us, I do not remember spending much time in sight-seeing. What I remember is being anxious to the point of terror, and hoping my new crew didn't see how scared I was. Damn. That was so long ago, it felt like it had all happened to another person, not to me. A *whole lot* of stuff had happened since then.

We finally reached the conference room, where he arranged two chairs so he could sort of sit down. That reminded me to ask Skippy if we could fabricate proper furniture for our unexpected guest. Also to ask what we needed to do about his other needs. Could a beetle use the showers in the ship's cabins, or did we need to modify one of those also?

"Cadet Fangiu," I began. 'Cadet-Undercandidate' was too much of a mouthful to say every time. "I am sorry about taking you away from your people, and I promise we will return you-"

"Do not be worried, Colonel Bishop. This is the most exciting thing that has ever happened to me. This is the *only* exciting thing that has ever happened to me!"

My reply was an insightful and intelligent "Uhhh-" Score one for humans, I was surely making my species look good. Not.

"My rank is Undercandidate Cadet, because I have not yet been accepted as a cadet. I just recently completed initial flight evaluation, and am, or *was*, waiting for an assignment to primary flight school. The reason I volunteered to fly with the Alien Legion team was my father thought it would look good on my personnel file. Also, because I had nothing else to do while I waited for a flight school slot to open for me. No one else," he twisted his mandibles in what he might have been intended as a grin, "wanted the assignment."

"Because it takes you away from home?" I guessed.

His antennas lifted. Was that surprise? Sarcasm? There was a Ruhar guide to body language of various species and I read it a while ago, now I wished I had studied it more recently. "No one else wanted to fly with humans because most of my people were afraid your pilots would crash into an asteroid. Also, your species smells," his mandibles twisted. "Interesting. No offense."

"None taken. Hey, to us, Kristang smell like, burnt toast or something like that." Without taking in a sniff to make it obvious, I breathed in slowly through my nose. Most of Cadet Fangiu was covered in a flexible material similar to a Ruhar skinsuit, so the only exposed parts of him were his head, what I guessed was his neck, and the claws of two forelimbs. There wasn't much of his leathery skin exposed to the air, and I had to concentrate. In the docking bay, there had been a scorched smell, like burning plastic. That came from the hull of the Dodo, it was not unusual for dropships to emit an acrid smell when they came back to the ship. Especially when they had plunged through an atmosphere, or been baked by the local star. The Dodo had been operating in the system's asteroid belt, far from the star, so the scorches on its hull came from the radiation of the *Flying Dutchman* emerging from a jump wormhole right on top of the dropship.

In the conference room, I had noticed some of that distinctive smell lingered, and I wondered if it had soaked into my hair and uniform while I was in the docking bay. Now I realized part of the smell was coming from Fangiu. It actually was not unpleasant. There was a scent like paper left in the hot sun, and a combination of coconut oil and, maybe nutmeg? I think. Really, it smelled like being at the beach and eating apple muffins, that's the best way I can describe it. That made me anxious about what I smelled like to him.

"Urk, urk, uuurk," he shuddered with a raspy, wheezing laugh that made the hair on my arms stand on end. "The stinkiest species I have ever encountered is the Bosphuraq. *Whee-ew*, their stench is foul."

Smythe had told me what the moon crawler vehicle smelled like, when his team had stolen one from the birds. Because I was aboard the *Dutchman* for that part of the moonbase mission, I had fortunately missed that delightful experience. Giving Fangiu a grin that I hoped he knew was friendly body language, I laughed. "Anyway, I apologize for taking you away from flight school."

"No need to apologize! You have already won a wager for me."

"Uh, I did?"

"Yes! When the ghost ship attacks were first reported, actually," his antennas dipped low over his eyes. "After the second attack. Or maybe the third. After you hit the convoy?"

"That was our third attack," I told him without needing to refer to the data on my laptop. Every one of those attacks was burned into my memory. Not just because of the violent action, but because we practiced each action over and over in simulation, then ran 'What-If' scenarios based on our after-action report, to see what we could have done better.

"After that attack, I placed a prop bet." He stopped and looked at me. "Do you need me to explain what a 'prop bet' is?"

"No," shaking my head, I thought about my Uncle Edgar. He loved to place side bets during games, especially during a big event like the Super Bowl. A prop bet is about something other than the result of the game. Stuff like, will the AFC team score more or less than X points in the first half? Or how many TV commercials will be shown in the third quarter? You could place money on wagers like that, without caring or even knowing who won the game. The idea of a prop bet was not unusual, what I didn't understand was what 'game' the beetle was talking about. "What was this prop bet you made?"

"It was about whether the ghost ship was truly controlled by a rogue faction of the Bosphuraq, or some other force."

"You *bet* on that? Wait!" I had a sickening feeling. "You bet that *humans* were flying this ship?" If the Jeraptha were somehow speculating that filthy monkeys were involved in the unusual and unexplained events going on in-

"No." Fangiu's antennas bobbed jerkily side to side, in a gesture I remembered was their way of indicating humor. "I merely wagered that the official story of a rogue Bosphuraq faction was not true. Many of my friends thought I was foolish to wager that the Maxolhx were wrong. They told me, the senior species have access to the best data and analysis, how could they be wrong? Ha, ha," he wheezed with laughter, and it sounded like a tin can caught in a blender.

Keeping my instinct to cringe in check, I pressed him for information. "None of your friends bet that humans were responsible?"

"No," he found that question amusing. "Your people were not even on the list of options, as I remember. None one would- Eh!" He inhaled with a whistle. "Oh, if someone *did* wager on humans, he would clean up! He would be a legend! Ooh, that lucky *bastard*."

It was such a relief that our secret was still safe, that I missed whatever he said next. To cover, I grunted and nodded. "That would be a lucky bet, yeah."

"Colonel?" He cocked his head at me, his antennas bent in a 'U' shape. "I asked, how many Maxolhx ships have you destroyed?"

"Why?" I tried to joke. "Did you bet on that also?"

The earnest look on his face told me the subject was no joking matter.

"What," I asked, "was the over/under?"

"Fifteen."

"*Fifteen*?" That surprised me. "That low? Wait. You mean fifteen after the third attack?" Our tally at that point was only, uh, two plus one plus five. Eight.

"No. Fifteen *total*. Before the ghost ship is caught, destroyed, or just, stops."

"Stops?"

"You can't go on forever, can you? The Maxolhx are throwing more ships into the fight. Unless you have an unlimited source of spare parts," he used his antenna to shrug, or that's what it looked like to me.

"We have spares," I said cautiously, not sure how much I wanted to tell him. Although, what did it matter how much he knew? He wasn't going to tell anyone, until it no longer mattered to us.

"The wager on how many ships you destroy expires after one year. One year on our homeworld, that is about," he closed his eyes trying to remember trivial information. "Fifteen months on Earth. Colonel, I ask because the Maxolhx of course do not release accurate information about their losses. Their fleet is so powerful," he shuddered slightly, his antennas twitching. "It is hard to believe *any* of their ships could be lost in battle. Have you destroyed more than fifteen of their ships?"

Before I answered, I wanted to know a little more about him. "Did you bet on the over, or the under?"

"Over. You destroyed more than fifteen ships?"

"You might say that," I tried to be casual about it while humble-bragging. "Our current count is forty-two."

"*Forty-two*?"

Technically, a couple of the ships in my count had been self-destructed, but they still counted in the 'W' column as far as I was concerned. The kitties sure counted those ships as losses. "Yeah. The Maxolhx set a trap for us, but we ambushed *them* instead," I indulged in a bit of bragging on behalf of the Merry Band of Pirates. "They lost fourteen of twenty ships in that one fight. We got away with minor damage." That was not exactly a lie, depending on the definition of 'minor'. Valkyrie had been able to fly away from that battle, and the damage had since been repaired. Skippy assured that, because of lessons he learned during that fight, our mighty battlecruiser was now even more powerful than before.

He also warned me that we should not ever get into a fight like *that* again. I wholeheartedly agreed with him.

"Forty-two," Fangiu said quietly. He whistled, or maybe that was another type of laugh. "Ah, Colonel Bishop, you have made me very happy! The 'smart money' was on the under! Urk!"

"Tell me something. There were wagers on who is flying this ship, and our win total." It didn't feel right to talk about war as a sporting event, but that's how the beetles thought of it. "Was anyone betting on how long we would continue attacking?"

"Yes," he glanced away. Maybe he figured the subject wasn't something I wanted to hear. "The Central Wagering Office published odds on how long until the Maxolhx killed or captured you." He flashed what was supposed to be a smile. "Most of *those* bets have already expired, and you are still here. Most of the money went toward wagers on when your attacks would stop."

"When we would give up, you mean?"

"When you would be unable to continue," he tried not to offend me. "Or, when you decided you had caused enough headaches to the," my translator stumbled then I heard "kitties." That made me wonder what nickname the Jeraptha used for the Maxolhx. And what they called *us*. "Colonel, my people *hate* the Maxolhx. We were delighted to see that someone was giving them a bloody nose." As the beetles did not have noses, the translator must have decided that was the best equivalent.

"We have temporarily paused our attacks. But that is a change in strategy."

"What *is* your strategy, if I may ask?"

"It's," again I debated how much to tell him. "Evolving." Then I realized that might be translated as 'We are making this shit up as we go'. "We are looking for targets of opportunity," I explained. "Whatever is the best way we can disrupt the enemy's ability to support extended combat operations."

"Against Earth, you mean." The beetle was not stupid. "Our intelligence reports that the Maxolhx have already sent a battlegroup to your homeworld."

Leaning back in my chair, I indulged in a self-satisfied grin. "Yeah, well. That battlegroup's return home will be delayed. Like, *permanently*."

"Oooooheeeech," he whistled, a sound like rusty pieces of metal scraping together.

Damn, no way was I ever going to invite a beetle to Karaoke Night. Their singing must be *horrible*.

He leaned forward on the conference table eagerly. "Is that battlegroup part of the forty-two ships in your count?"

"No." The fate of that battlegroup, trapped outside the galaxy, was not something Fangiu needed to know. "But we did also destroy the first two ships they sent to Earth, so I think maybe our count is forty-four?"

He shook his head. "For the purpose of wagering, the count begins with the first ghost ship attack, at Koprahdru." One of his antennas lifted halfway up. "Unless that was *not* the first ghost ship attack?"

"Ah, for the wager, your oddsmakers are probably limiting the action to *Valkyrie*. We didn't have *Valkyrie* back then. Those first two Maxolhx ships were blown up by the *Flying Dutchman*."

Both of his antennas stood straight up. "You attacked two Maxolhx cruisers, with a Thuranin star carrier? How is that possible?"

"It's a long story, Cadet. Maybe I'll tell you someday. Ok, so now I have to decide what to do with you." The sudden expression on his face told me what I said might not have been translated the way I intended. Waving my hands, palms open, I hastened to correct the mistake. "Hey, sorry! All I meant was, which parts of the ship you will have access to. Do you give me your word that you will not interfere with our operations?"

He seemed surprised that I even asked that question. "Colonel, you are fighting, and winning, against the ultimate enemy of my people. I believe we are on the same side in this war. In the absence of orders, I must do what I expect my leaders would want from me. I pledge to *help* you in any way that I can."

"Cadet, that's great. Thank you." My decision was made easier by knowing that Nagatha or Skippy would be watching everything the young beetle did. He *was* young, not even a cadet yet. It bothered me that his parents would be worried sick about him, until we could return him home. He would also be missing two years of flight school, which would put him behind his classmates and derail his career plans. Unless- "Cadet, have you ever flown a Thuranin dropship? In a simulator, I mean."

"No. Why?"

"Because while you're with us, you might as well continue your studies. We can teach you to fly Kristang, Thuranin and *Maxolhx* spacecraft."

"Hyuh hyuh hyuuuuh," the poor guy was hyperventilating. "You would do this? For me?"

"For us. It would be useful, when you return to your people, for you to be able to compare the flight characteristics of various spacecraft. Most of your time would be in a simulator, and, well, we'll need to modify the controls." And the seats, I reminded myself. Probably I should have mentioned the idea to Skippy before I opened my big stupid mouth.

"Colonel," he pointed a leathery claw at my chest. "I see wings on your uniform. You are a pilot?"

"I am an Army aviator, yes."

"Mm. That is good."

"Ok," I tapped the table, and signaled for Frey to come into the room. She was still wearing a mech suit and had a rifle by her side, but her faceplate was open. "Captain Frey here will show you to a cabin."

"Colonel, may I make a request first?"

Crap. If the beetle wanted time in a flight simulator right away, I was going to crush his hopes. "What is it?"

"All of my gear, including my other clothing, is aboard the dropship. Could someone bring it to my cabin? I have," he ran a claw down his, sort of his chest or thorax or something. "Been living in this suit for several days. It is unpleasant."

Frey answered for me. "I'll take care of it, Sir."

CHAPTER THIRTY ONE

Dinner that evening was late, as measured by ship time. According to the body clocks of the Commando team, we had captured them just after their lunch, but that was late afternoon for us. So we waited until they were hungry. We also needed time to prepare something special to welcome our new teammates.

While waiting for food to be served, I was answering uncomfortable questions, and trying my best not to glare too hatefully at Lamar Greene. The guy had to be wondering what he had done to get on my bad side. Enough questions had been asked about the mysterious AI that had been helping us, that Skippy just couldn't stand it any longer. "Joe. *Joe!*" He hissed in my earpiece. "The audience is demanding the main attraction. They are tired of the warm-up act."

Cupping a hand over my mouth, I whispered back. "I am not the warm-up band, you idiot."

"Idiot? *Me*, an idiot? You are not a warm-up band. *You* are just a monkey making balloon animals until the audience rushes the stage and throws you out. This is a travesty."

"Do not speak until I-"

His voice boomed over the speakers as the avatar appeared. Not just the avatar, he had added lighting effects and dramatic music to his grand entrance, which had all the understated class of a pro wrestling match. "Yoo-*hooooo* everyone! May I have your attention please? Behold, 'tis I. The one, the only, the LEGEND, His Almighty Awesomeness, Skiiiiiiippyyyyyy the Magnificent!"

"Who?" Fabron asked, confused, looking to Smythe for answers.

"Ugh. It's me, you *tete de noeud*," Skippy made the insult in French. I knew from French Canadiens that it meant something like 'knothead', or 'knucklehead'. "I am the AI who has been helping this troop of filthy monkeys. I am an *Elder* AI." He cleared his throat. "Um, that was your cue to be struck by unfathomable awe. It would be appropriate at this time for you all to kneel before me and contemplate how unworthy you are."

Fabron was unimpressed. With a very Gallic shrug, he turned to Smythe. "Your AI is an asshole, Non?"

"He is an arsehole for sure," Smythe agreed, his shoulders shaking as he tried not to laugh.

"Hey!" Skippy screeched. "You monkeys really are not going to worship me?"

That pissed me off. "What do *you* think?" I gave him an entirely justified single-finger salute. "Duh."

"DUH to you," he retorted.

Now I was really mad. "Duh!"

"*Duhhhhhh!*"

"*DUHHHHH!*" I made an L with one hand and placed it against my forehead.

Commandant Fabron shifted his feet uncomfortably. "We are doomed," he groaned.

"Because of this?" Smythe scoffed. "No, this is typical. They'll get over it."

"You saved the world, more than once, with *those* two?" The French soldier was incredulous.

"We saved the world, *because* of those two."

"You are serious?"

"Believe me," Smythe rolled his eyes. "I wish it weren't true."

It took a full ten minutes to get Skippy calmed down, and even that required an assist from Nagatha. It did not help that, shockingly, the new people decided they liked Nagatha, and that Skippy was an arrogant asshole. When Skippy launched into reciting his Top Ten list of awesome things he had done, I had to put a stop to it. Besides, steaks were grilling in the galley and we didn't have much luxury food left. No way was I going to miss a prime meal because of Skippy's shenanigans. "Ok! Skippy, can I make a deal with you?"

"Hmmph." His avatar had its arms crossed defiantly. "Like what?"

"Send your Top Ten list to everyone's zPhones, and we will all vote on which one is the *most* awesome."

"Ugh. Ignorant monkeys are going to judge *my* actions?"

"Or, we could just ignore you," I suggested.

"Let's go with the voting thing," he said quickly. "But-"

"Oh crap. What is it now?"

"Everyone has to submit a five-thousand word essay on *why* they voted for a particular awesomeness. Including what about me made it so unfathomably awesome."

"Can we compromise, and instead of a five-thousand word essay, people include whatever emoji best represents your awesomeness?"

"Hmm. Ok, but nobody can use the poop emoji," he insisted.

That blew my plan out of the water, but I agreed. "Deal."

"Sir?" Smythe paused in the doorway to my office. He was there for our regular morning meeting, which usually lasted only five or ten minutes. The meetings were short, because he always was anxious to get back to something more important.

"Smythe! Come in, sit down," I gestured, distracted by my laptop. On the screen were a variety of objects I was considering as a wedding present for Simms and Frank Muller. Candlesticks were an obvious choice, too obvious. When Skippy saw me browsing what he called 'girly stuff', he asked why. Then he suggested that instead of me waiting until we got back to Earth, I find something he could create with the ship's fabricators. It would be a present from the two of us, which would save me the trouble of shopping, and him the embarrassment of probably choosing an inappropriate gift.

Working with Skippy on the gift sounded like a good idea, until he shot down all my very good suggestions. Either the ship's fabricators could not manufacture the item without pulling them away from the vital work of making parts for our ships. Or, my suggestions were, as Skippy tried to say tactfully, 'lame'. At that point, we were back to the drawing board. What I wanted to do was give them something practical, because they would hopefully be living on the undeveloped world of Avalon. Or some other, equally primitive beta site.

My best suggestion, to give them a dropship, ran into several snags. Neither Simms nor Muller were pilots, and Simms certainly didn't have time to take flying lessons. Plus, I didn't actually own any dropships, they were technically all UNEF property. And, there was the issue that we might need them to evacuate Earth. Skippy had drawn up plans to build space elevators on Earth, to replace the one the Thuranin had rented to the White Wind clan. With two or three space elevators running, the process of bringing people and supplies into orbit would go much faster. Except that, Skippy annoyingly reminded me, building space elevators would consume time and resources that could better be used elsewhere, like possibly constructing another starship.

Whoa! Before you get too excited, he meant an unarmed transport ship, something like the *Yu Qishan*. A tin can with a jump drive, that we could stuff full of filthy monkeys. He thought there might be enough of what he called 'go-fast' parts leftover from our Lego project, that he could use to cobble together the engineering section of a ship. All humanity had to do was build the front section, which was still impossible given Earth's level of industrial development.

Anyway, what was I talking about? Oh, yeah. Wedding presents. The good news was that I already knew about the engagement, which Simms was keeping quiet. That gave me a head start on thinking of a gift.

Smythe sat down and his body language told me whatever he wanted to talk about, I wasn't going to like it. He got right to it. "We need to discuss Gunnery Sergeant Adams."

"*We* do? Or you do?"

"Er, both." It wasn't often that I could make him uncomfortable.

"Her fitness for duty, you mean? She's on your team, it's your call."

"Not completely, Sir."

Shit. He really was uncomfortable with the subject. My, special regard for Adams was no secret among the crew. I should never have put Smythe in a position to worry that he might offend my feelings. "Look, Smythe, I'm serious," I held up my hands. "It's your call. Well, you and Doctor Skippy. I don't want to be involved, I need to *not* be involved, you understand? I can't play favorites. That's not fair to the crew and it's especially unfair to Adams. If you clear her for duty, and that puts her life back on the line, that's what she wants." Smythe did not need to be concerned about Adams, he needed to be concerned about me. I needed to be concerned about me. How would I react if Adams was in another life-and-death situation, where I had to choose between saving her and achieving the mission? What would I do?

I knew exactly what I would do, because I had begun considering the problem the day that Adams left the sickbay and returned to her own cabin. She was recovering, and that meant she might return to duty.

What would I do in that situation?

Easy.

If I couldn't handle the pressure, I would surrender command to Simms, and let her make the decisions. It's not a subject we had discussed, it was sort of understood. If she thought I was cracking under pressure, Simms wouldn't wait for me. She was a damned good XO and she knew what the ship and crew needed.

The look of relief on Smythe's face told me I had hit the mark. "In that case, Sir, I am *not* clearing her for duty."

Oh shit. I had been all wrong about the source of his anxiety. He wasn't worried that I would refuse to let her put herself in danger. He was worried about her reaction, and my reaction, when he declared she wasn't ready. Or worse, that she would never again be ready. That was an important distinction. "*Yet*, you mean? You are not clearing her for duty yet?"

"Adams has made remarkable progress, both physically and in cognitive skills. Given time, I am confident she can rejoin the STARs. Her recovery has focused on regaining basic motor skills. She has not been training with the team, nor do I believe she can safely train with the team at this time."

"Does she know?"

That drew a wry laugh. "Our Gunnery Sergeant is the best judge of her own abilities. She is certainly aware of her level of progress."

"Ok." It was my turn for relief that made my shoulders shudder involuntarily. "You will talk with her?"

"Yes. I wanted to assure her there will be a role for her during the rescue?"

"Oh, hell, yes. We can always use people on the bridge. I'll get Simms to assign Adams to a weapons station, she'll like that."

"Training to serve on the bridge will divert time away from her preparing to requalify for the STAR team," he cautioned.

"She can suck it up," I replied, and to my surprise, realized that is how I really felt. She wanted me to treat her no different from anyone of the crew, and that's exactly what I wanted to do. "*I'll* talk with her about that."

"If you want my advice, Sir, I suggest you have Simms tell her."

"Because I'll make it too personal?"

"No. Because that is the procedure for any other member of the crew," he arched an eyebrow and waited for my reply.

"True. Good idea. Is that all? I know you want to get back to training with the new people."

"Training is what I want to discuss next. The rescue operation will be conducted on the surface of a planet. It would be useful if we could train in similar conditions."

"Oh. Hey, I'd like that too. Flying all the way back to Avalon takes too much time." Plus, the last thing I wanted was to go back to that world, until we had opened a wormhole to Earth. "Do you have a candidate planet in mind?"

"No, Sir. I was hoping you and Skippy could think of something."

"I got nothin'," I admitted. To be useful for training, we needed a planet with roughly the same gravity, atmosphere and surface conditions as the target site. Plus, most importantly, it had to be uninhabited and unlikely to have visitors. That was a tough set of conditions. "Skippy?"

"Ugh. What is it now?" His avatar groaned.

"Don't pretend you weren't listening," I wagged a finger at him. "What can you do for us?"

"*Do* for you? Joe, there are plenty of worlds out there you could use for training, but like the real estate saying goes, it's all about location. Any place with easy access is inhabited, or might have ships stopping by for surveys, monitoring or their own training."

"Ok, fine. What about places that do *not* have easy access?"

"Like what?"

Sometimes, Skippy could be dense as a monkey. "*Like*, we have the unique advantage of being able to create new wormhole connections. Back when we first talked about a beta site, you looked for candidates inside the galaxy."

"*Yessssss*," he was making an effort to be patient with me. "And we discarded all those sites, none of them were useful as a beta site."

"None of them were useful, because you thought the next wormhole shift, or the one after that, would give alien bad guys easy access. But right now, we don't care about what happens during the next wormhole shift a hundred years from now. We just need a place for training."

"Oh. Well, why didn't you say that," he glared and shook a finger at *me*. "There is a place within two wormhole transitions, that would be an excellent site for training. And for the all-important rest and recreation this crew needs so very much. Hey! We can call this resort 'Club Skippy'. It is very exclusive, Joe, and the rates are quite reasonable-"

"We get a free vacation before we buy a timeshare, right?" I asked, and Smythe snorted at my joke.

"I will show you the brochure," Skippy gushed. "Afterward, there will be a short four-hour presentation, with light refreshments, while I tell you all about the amazing benefits of fractional ownership in Club Skippy."

Smythe was already halfway out of his chair. "Er, I'll leave you to handle the executive decisions, Sir."

"Coward," I muttered. "I'll take this one for the team, Smythe. But I am voluntolding you to sit through the next karaoke night."

When Adams was told she was not cleared for duty with the STAR team, that she wasn't even cleared to *train* with them, and that she was assigned to sitting at a console on the bridge, she left us.

That sucked.

I don't mean she left the Merry Band of Pirates. She left *Valkyrie*, to go aboard the *Flying Dutchman*.

She wasn't mad at me, she wasn't upset with anyone. She was disappointed, sure, but only a little. She knew she wasn't up to speed yet, and hadn't really expected to accompany Smythe on the rescue. Her going aboard the *Dutchman* was not an act of anger or defiance, it was simply practical. It wasn't even her idea, Simms assigned her to the other ship. Executive officers handle routine personnel matters, leaving the captain free to focus on important captain things, like getting to the next level on Super Mario Kart. My first notice that Adams was no longer aboard was a line in a morning status report. Like I said, it was simple. Adams had worked a bridge console aboard the old *Dutchman*, so she would need only quick refresher training to get signed off as ready to pull a duty shift. Getting familiar with the very different controls and environment aboard *Valkyrie* would have taken her so long, the rescue op would be over before she knew what she was doing. See? Simple and practical.

I was still a little pissed that Simms hadn't told me ahead of time. Then I got pissed at myself for being unfair. My instructions to Simms were to treat Adams like any other member of the crew, and that's what she did. A person aboard the *Dutchman* was scheduled to come aboard *Valkyrie* for training, so Simms used Adams to backfill that position. We did that all the time, cross-training people on the different systems of our two ships.

It did hurt that Adams had not given me a good-bye note, or stopped by my office before she went aboard the transfer dropship. That left me very confused. Was she avoiding me, and subtly telling me that what happened between us was only her damaged brain and the nanobots talking? Or was she afraid of making the situation awkward? Was I reading too much into the situation?

Crap.

It was eating away at me.

I needed to know.

To talk in private, I went to my cabin, where I could close the door. "Skippy, I have kind of a delicate matter to discuss with you. No jokes, please, Ok?"

"Dude. Why so serious?"

"It's about Margaret."

"Oh. Gotcha. She's fine, Joe. Right now she is-"

"I know she's fine now. My question is about something that happened, uh, back when she was recovering."

"She is *still* recovering."

"You know what I mean. Back when alien machines in her head were doing part of the thinking for her. When she didn't feel like she was herself."

"Ok," there was a cautious tone in his voice. "Go on."

"We had kind of a moment, you know? Me and Margaret. She called me 'Joe' instead of 'Sir' or 'Colonel'. She said that she was Ok with me leaving her behind for the good of the mission. Hell, she was *proud* I did that."

"What is your question, Joe?"

"I need to know, was that *her* talking? She hasn't called me 'Joe' since that day, and-"

"Uh oh. No can do, sorry."

"You can't do what?"

"Doctor-patient confidentiality. I can't talk about her medical condition, now or then. Unless you claim this affects her fitness for duty, which we both know is bullshit."

"This affects *my* fitness for duty!"

"Um, I think regulations state you need to discuss that with Simms," he suggested.

"Screw regulations."

"Nope. You can't play that game with me. I made a promise to Margaret that I would not divulge any details about her condition, to anyone. Dude, you should have asked me back before you surrendered the power of attorney she gave you."

"You can't even give me a freakin' *hint*?"

"Here's a hint: ask *her*."

"No way. She doesn't seem to want to talk about it. I'm not a hundred percent certain she even remembers it. The last thing she needs right now is me dumping my emotional baggage on her. Not now. After the rescue, maybe. No, that's not right. After we get the wormhole open near Earth. No, crap, then we'll be at Earth and they'll pull her off the ship for debriefing. They'll pull *me* off the ship and throw me in prison."

"Dude, your life consists of jumping from the frying pan into the fire."

"I know it. This *sucks*." Looking around my cabin, I sought something I could smash. What I decided was that destroying some object would only be a form of self-destructiveness. "Thank you."

"Hmm. Is this some weird empathy thing? You're thanking me for listening to you?"

"No. I'm thanking you for keeping your promise to Margaret."

"Oh. No problem. I do care about her, Joe."

"Me too, Skippy. Me too."

Club Skippy was actually a pretty nice place. It was a rather ordinary world, with the benefits of being isolated, and humans could breathe the air and didn't need to wear special protective gear. There were mountains and rivers and trees and wide-open grasslands, and the local predators weren't anything to worry about. We identified two areas that had similar terrain as the islands where the prisoners were being held on Rikers, and set up mock structures based on Skippy's best intel about those camps. That intel might be out of date, and the STAR team knew they had to be flexible.

In addition to practicing the rescue, we used Club Skippy to sharpen our overall fitness. Running on a treadmill is just not the same as running over broken ground and up and down hills. We did a lot of that and by 'we', I mean I ran with the STARs and participated in as much of their training as I could.

The Paradise people actually had an advantage over us, because they had recently been training on a Ruhar world with gravity nine percent heavier than Earth normal. We usually kept artificial gravity aboard both ships at one Gee. That was heavier than the *Dutchman* was designed for, and lighter than the previous setting aboard *Valkyrie*. Yes, I know that 'heavy' and 'light' are not the technically correct terms, those describe what gravity does to objects that have mass. Heavy and light are how normal people think about it, so that's how I'm describing it.

The gravity aboard *Valkyrie* was actually variable in sections of the ship, especially in the areas the STAR team used for training. They exercised and practiced maneuvers in gravity that was anywhere from sixty percent below to twenty two percent above Earth normal. Training at different levels of gravity had multiple purposes. To accurately replicate conditions the STARs might encounter on a mission away from the ship. To assist in conditioning, and if you haven't tried to run in gravity twenty percent heavier than you're used to, believe me it is a tough workout. Finally and maybe most importantly, it forced people to relearn their eye-hand and eye-foot coordination.

In the STAR team training area aboard our mighty battlecruiser was a bulkhead lined with basketball hoops. They weren't used for pickup games, Smythe was too concerned about his people getting injured to allow unstructured sports. No, the hoops were there to show people what happened when the force of gravity changed. Pick up a basketball that feels heavier than normal. No problem, right? You just put more force into your throw. No, it doesn't work that way. When you throw, your brain is subconsciously calculating where to aim, based on how the ball would fly in Earth-normal gravity. In a different gravity field, the arc the ball follows is different, either higher or flatter than you're used to. A grenade tossed in anything other than a standard one Gee also won't fly the way you expect. Bullets also follow a ballistic arc, unless they are powered rounds. Anyway, your body, deep down to your muscle memory, needs to relearn how to throw things, how your feet rise and fall, how to run and jump and shoot, depending on the effect of local gravity. Before a STAR team leaves the ship, they hold a weight that is the same mass as a standard grenade, memorizing how that mass *feels* in their hands. Sure, mech suits and rifle sights automatically compensate for differing levels of gravity, but our best weapon is a well-trained *person*. Without the person, the weapons are useless.

I said the Paradise people had an advantage over us, because they had been training, living, resting and sleeping in higher gravity for more than four months. The planet where we practiced for and revised our plans for the rescue, had gravity only two percent greater than what we experienced aboard our ships. We barely noticed the extra two percent, or that's my story and I'm sticking to it. Where we noticed was while running together. The Paradise people ran just a bit more easily, reached the top of hills faster, and were less out of breath than we were. Of course, no one cared if someone else was a bit-

No. That is *total* bullshit. Special operators hate being second at anything. Kapoor urged our people on, exhorting them until he, too, was gasping for breath. Smythe could have run faster than anyone on his bionic legs. He didn't. He ran back and forth, speeding up to catch the Paradise team, dropping back to match our slower pace.

The Commandos did not miss a chance to rub it in, pausing at the top of hills to drink from their water bottles while they waited for us. That seriously annoyed me. No, it pissed me off. Part of what pissed me off was seeing Gunnery Sergeant Lamar freakin' Greene charging up hills faster than I could run. He didn't say anything, he didn't even especially look at me, and that really pissed me off. It was like he didn't consider me to be competition and-

Ok, I am not being fair to the guy. If he and Adams had resumed their relationship, or hooked up or whatever, I didn't know about it, because it wasn't any of my business. Greene was stationed aboard *Valkyrie* and Adams was assigned to the *Dutchman*. Maybe, as part of the daily status report, I might have checked on who flew between ships for R&R, and didn't see either of their names. Adams was busy refreshing her skills in the *Dutchman's* CIC, and Greene had a lot of catching up to do with learning how to use our equipment and adjusting to our tactics. They simply didn't have time for personal relationships, and that wasn't anything I did.

That didn't mean I couldn't be happy about it, though as the commander I *should* not have been happy about it.

Hey, I never claimed to be perfect.

CHAPTER THIRTY TWO

Our third morning on Club Skippy, I was running with the STARs and I was proud to say that I wasn't bringing up the rear. On the run up our last hill that morning, the Commandos surged ahead as usual, leaving us dragging behind. I strode to the front of our column, pumping my arms and keeping my chin up. Right behind me, the STARs probably thought I was pushing it too hard, too early. Frey matched my pace, striding beside me and whispering through gasps. "Sir. You're. Gonna. *Crash and burn.*"

"I'm. Ok," was all I could manage, while increasing my pace. She dropped behind slightly, while ahead, the Paradise team had already stopped at the top, standing or jogging in place as they waited. The last thirty meters, I eased up, sucking in great breaths as the STARs drew even with me. My goal had not been to race to the top, what I wanted was to not be too out of breath when I got there.

As the Paradise team began turning to run down the hill, smirking at us with their smirky little smirk faces, I shouted "Hey! If you guys got into shape, you wouldn't need to *stop* all the time."

They didn't know how to respond to that, standing there with their mouths open, sputtering words we couldn't hear. We raced right past them, blocking the narrow route down the other side of the hill. By unspoken consent, that descent turned into a race, down the hill, splashing across a stream and an all-out sprint across a field back to our camp. To my delight, the group was mixed as we crossed the imaginary finish line, and there was much genuinely good-natured trash talk and back-slapping as we recovered. Smythe winked at me, and over the course of the day, all the STARs gave me silent thumbs ups, or fist-pump gestures. The best comment I got was from Frey. "I thought you were crazy, eh?" She said. "You are, but in a good way, Sir."

The old man, who wasn't *old*, still had it.

I also had a twisted ankle from stumbling over a rock, but Doctor Skippy's Patented Magical Nanobots fixed me right up. Even if the nanobots working inside my leg made me go temporarily numb in, let's just say, an adjacent area.

Of course, Doctor Skippy hadn't warned me about that side effect.

In my tent that afternoon, Skippy was explaining the basics of his infiltration plan for the rescue operation on Rikers. I was only sort of half-listening.

"-the dropships will need to be careful of their heat signatures once they descend over water. Without-"

"Wait." I jerked my head up. "Why is heat a problem?"

"Ugh. Were you not listening to me *at all*?"

"Obviously I was listening, I heard you say something about heat signatures. *Duh*," I added to cover up the fact that I had not been listening.

"Oh for- what is the question? Do you not understand-"

"I do understand about infrared signatures. Why is it a problem? Both of the islands where prisoners are being held are in the tropical zone." One of the islands was in the planet's northern hemisphere, the other south of the equator. For simplicity, we referred to the islands as Objective Dixie and Objective Yankee. Both islands were not merely dots in the vast ocean, they were each about the size of Hispaniola, the Caribbean island that was home to Haiti and the Dominican Republic. According to Skippy, the islands had been chosen by the White Wind clan because they were far from the mainland where almost all the lizards lived, plus the islands had enough land and rainfall to support humans growing almost all of their food. Separating the prisoners between two islands was a way to ensure the entire population was not lost, if disease spread among one group.

"We will be descending over water, to avoid detection," he explained patiently. "The ships going to Objective Yankee will be flying over warm water all the way, so heat signatures are not a problem. But the ships going to Dixie will be approaching from the direction of Riker's south pole, where the water is cold this time of year. Let me explain this to you, Joe. It will blow your little monkey mind." A line appeared on the floor. "Imagine this is the planet's equator. On this side," Skippy was suddenly wearing shorts, a Hawaiian shirt and a straw hat. Plus, he was holding, was that a margarita? "It is summer." He stepped across the line and he was then dressed in a parka and he was standing on a snowboard. "On this *side*, it is winter. SUH-mer," he was on the summer side. "WIN-ter," he jumped back to his snowboard outfit. If that wasn't annoying enough, he began hopping rapidly across the line, chanting "Summer, winter, summer, winter, summer, winter-"

"Ok, I get it!" I waved my hands in surrender.

"It's kind of cool, when you think about it," he beamed with happiness in his Hawaiian shirt.

"No, it's cool to *never* think about it. I am sorry I asked. Hey, it's winter in the southern hemisphere, so is it chilly at Objective Dixie?"

"No! Ugh. I covered that in the briefing this morning. You were *not* listening."

No way could I argue my way out of that. "You're right, I was distracted." Closing my laptop, I turned my chair toward him. "You have my complete attention. Please, start over."

"Hmmph."

"Please. You can give me a pop quiz at the end, to test if I was listening."

"If you fail, will you watch Season One of 'The Six Million Dollar Man'?"

Shit. There was more than one season of that show? I panicked. "How about I watch one episode? And you can pick the crappiest episode of all seasons."

"Deal!"

He cheated. The pop quiz was about obscure facts he vaguely mentioned, but were included in the footnotes of the briefing I was supposed to read. I was reading it, but the damned thing was eight hundred pages! Also, the assault team really did not need to know nerdy trivia about how often the planet's magnetic field had flipped in the ancient past.

Anyway, I failed the quiz, so I was forced to watch an episode of what fans call 'SMDM', pronounced Ess Emm Dee Emm. Again, Skippy cheated. Instead of having to suffer through one TV episode, which would be about forty-two minutes long, he dredged up a made-for-TV-movie called 'Bionic Ever After'. Mercifully, this ninety-six minute crapfest was so bad, it killed the franchise. So, we have to be thankful for that. Since I had not seen any previous episodes, I was totally lost in the plot.

You know how, when you are waiting for a file to download so you can do some super-important thing, you kill some time on social media? You click on one link, that leads to another, then another, and soon you realize the file download timed out, and anyway the project was due three hours ago. Anyway, after watching the bionic movie, I got curious about who was responsible for that crime against humanity. Ok, so I skimmed through an episode. Then another.

You question whether those shows were as bad as I say?

I have two words for you. Actually, the show shortened it to one word: fembot.

Google it.

Go ahead, I can wait.

See?

Fembots.

Because I do not hate you, I will not summarize the plot of 'Bionic Ever After'.

Hey, you in the back.

Yeah, you know who I'm talking about. You. I do hate *you*, and you know why. Don't argue with me, we both know I'm right. You are banished, until you watch every minute of that crappy 70s TV show, plus the 'Bionic Woman' spinoff.

Skippy will be giving you a pop quiz, so you'd better take notes.

"Heeeeey, Joe," Skippy announced over my zPhone earpiece. "I have news for you." His avatar was floating above my cot. The accommodations at Club Skippy were not exactly the five star resort promised in the glossy brochure he had printed, and Skippy had backpedaled on his promises of a luxury experience. After we landed, he changed marketing strategy, boasting that it was an 'Eco resort'. That explained why we were sleeping in tents and cooking food over wood fires. Actually, everyone enjoyed the change of pace from the sterile environment aboard the ships.

"Hey. I appreciate the fancy towel animal you left on my cot yesterday. That was a very nice feature of Club Skippy."

"Um, what?"

"You know," I teased him. "The towel was all twisted into, uh, something. Was that an octopus? Or some sort of snake?"

"Dude, I have no idea what you're talking about. You hung the towel from the hoop holding up your tent, after you took a bath in the river. It must have fallen onto your cot."

"Huh. I guess that explains why it was wet. So, what's up? How can you have news? We're in the middle of nowhere."

"True. I guess it is not technically *news*, but there is no expression for 'olds' so you know what I mean. Anyway, I was bored, so I dug deeper into the data we pulled from that relay station we pinged before we took the wormhole shortcut to get here. When I say 'deeper, I mean way down to the bottom of the barrel. It appears that the Kristang have gotten more serious about information security. Either the civil war has motivated them, or some of them suddenly woke up to the risks."

I stared at him. "Better InfoSec? Like tougher encryption? That wouldn't matter to you, right? Your awesomeness can crack any code."

"Pretty much, yes, although there is a difference between *encryption* and *codes*, that I will not waste my time trying to explain to you. The problem is, this is actually quite clever of the lizards, who'd have thunk it, huh? They used one of their more sophisticated encryption schemes to secure a series of video files. When I reviewed the files, I saw they were boring stuff about clan politics, plans for attacks in their civil war, blah, blah, blah. Nothing I or any of us care about. But, because I am *so* bored while you monkeys play games down there, I recently took another look at the videos. My intent was to alter them, maybe cause some mischief. While taking the video apart, I discovered a second, much higher-level encryption embedded in the files! The lizards must have purchased that encryption from a species like the Bosphuraq. I cracked it, of course, no problem there. Those sneaky damned lizards must have anticipated someone would read their files, so they made the content so *dull*, no one would look deeper. They fooled me, Joe. I'm sorry. This is embarrassing. I learned an important lesson for sure."

"Oh, crap. Is this bad news?"

"Um, not necessarily. It depends on how you look at it."

Sighing with anticipation that my day was about to be ruined, I sat on the couch. "Ok, hit me with it."

"Well, heh heh, we have a complication."

"You know I hate complications."

"*You* hate them? Hey, *I* wanted a nice simple deal where you help me contact the Collective, then I could bail on you filthy monkeys in the middle of nowhere. But *nooooo*. I've been stuck out here for freakin' *years* helping you morons lurch from one crisis to another. Complications, ugh."

"You're the one who decided you need more info before you try contacting the Collective again."

"Well, sure, but-"

"One of those years was us stuck in the Roach Motel, because you had to go poking around in a canister you knew could be dangerous."

"Um, well-"

"And what's this shit about you planning to bail on us in the middle of nowhere?"

"Why must you dwell on the past, Joe?" He sighed.

"Fine. What's the complication you're going to ruin my day with now?"

"It's not just a complication. It might also be the answer to a problem."

"Okaaay," sitting on the cot, I dared to hope for a tiny nugget of good news. "Like what?"

"You have been trying to dream up a cover story, to explain why anyone other than us would go through the effort of rescuing our people off Rikers."

Skippy had said 'our people'. That was interesting. I mentally filed that fact away to think about later. "Right, so?"

"So, I might know of another group who wants those people alive."

"Yeah. The Thuranin. We know that. It doesn't help us."

"I mean, another group who are not Thuranin. A rival Kristang clan, Joe."

"Oh, crap. Are we going to get in the middle of lizard clan politics again? Damn it! Why would a rival clan-"

"This would go faster if you let me explain."

"Please, enlighten me, Oh Great One."

"The Kristang Council of Clans-"

"The what?"

"It's a semi-formal committee that mediates disputes between clans to obtain an appropriate resolution, and consults on issues that affect all clans."

"They mediate disputes, but this council couldn't stop a civil war?"

"The council handles minor issues, Joe. Besides, war *is* the appropriate resolution for major disputes, according to the Kristang. Will you let me explain this complication?"

"Sorry."

"Hmmph," he sniffed, indignant. "The Council of Clans stepped in, because negotiations with the Thuranin could affect all clans."

"Ah. The Fire Dragon Clan invited this Council to help negotiate a deal?"

"The Fire Dragons very much did *not* invite the Council to stick their noses into private clan business. The other clans demanded the Council act now, because they are all worried the Fire Dragons will get some special sweetheart deal with their patrons, and screw everyone else."

"The Fire Dragons are at war with most other clans. Why would they care what this Council thinks about anything?"

"Two reasons, Joe. The Thuranin are required, by treaty and by long-standing tradition, to treat all sides of a civil war equally. The little green pinheads can't take sides, or favor one clan over another. Like, they can't refuse to transport the warships of a particular clan. *Unless*, the Council of Clans decrees that one clan or another has behaved in a manner detrimental to Kristang society overall. In that case, the Thuranin are required to punish the offending clan. In this case, the Fire Dragons."

"Then, this is *good* news. These Council idiots will drag out the negotiations, giving us more time to conduct the rescue."

"That is true, Joe, except for the complication I mentioned."

"Crap? You haven't told me the complication yet?"

"Nope. The complication is that at least two clans aren't waiting for the Council to act. They each separately plan to hit Rikers, capture the humans, and force the Thuranin to deal directly with them instead of the Fire Dragons."

"What the -*Why*? Then the Council would make the Thuranin punish them."

"Because there are rules, and then there is the *enforcement* of rules. The Thuranin have been known to bend the rules against playing favorites. They can't charge different shipping rates to one clan, but their star carriers can be 'temporarily unavailable due to maintenance issues'. Or they might be slow to reach a destination. The Council can grumble about that, but they can't directly *do* anything. The clans planning to snatch the humans off Rikers are betting the rewards outweigh the risks, if they can negotiate their own sweetheart deal with the Thuranin. Plus, a raid on Rikers would be a daring action that all the other clans would admire, whatever they say about it publicly. There is also another factor."

Burying my face in my hands, I mumbled. "*Of course* there is."

"All the major clans learned a valuable lesson from the Alien Legion fight on Fresno. Many of them want to keep the humans, instead of selling them to the Thuranin. The next time the Legion lands on a planet, the Kristang want to use the human children as hostages, against UNEF."

"Shit! I *hate* those lizard MFers."

"They are much hated across the galaxy, even within the Maxolhx coalition."

"How much time to we have? Wait. To hit Rikers, the lizards need to get there first. Why would the Thuranin fly them there, if the lizards are acting against their patrons? And, hey, the lizards would need a ride back home, after they captured the humans."

"It's simple, Joe. The lizards are not getting a ride from the Thuranin. They have hired Bosphuraq star carriers for the job."

"The Bos- How the hell can the birdbrains be capable of helping anyone? They are getting their asses kicked by the kitties!"

"They are available to the lizards *because* they are getting their asses kicked, Joe. The Bosphuraq are playing the long game. They assume at some point, the Maxolhx will have punished them enough, or get bored and go home. The birds will then be weakened, and as you know, they are more worried about their supposed allies the Thuranin than they are about the Jeraptha. If the Jeraptha push too hard and capture too much of the bird's territory, the Maxolhx will intervene. But if the Thuranin take advantage of Bosphuraq weakness and take over vital star systems, supposedly for the good of the coalition, the kitties might not care too much. So, the Bosphuraq are Ok with the Alien Legion posing a threat within Thuranin territory. Supporting a raid on Rikers accomplishes two goals. It will prolong the Kristang civil war, and might ensure the Alien Legion continues to cause problems for the Thuranin. Both of those developments weaken the Thuranin at a time with the Bosphuraq are weak."

"Shit."

"Plus, with the Maxolhx striking all over Bosphuraq territory, being away from home is the safest place for their star carriers. They offered discounted rates to the lizards."

"Oh, damn it. Trying to keep track of the freakin' politics in this war drives me crazy."

"Joe, the politics of this war make Game of Thrones look like children playing a game of Go Fish. Pretty much everyone is trying to stab everyone else in the back. Or they would engage in backstabbing, if they thought the reward was worth the risk."

"Yeah, I know. Never sign onto the Maxolhx coalition."

"Oh, it's not just them, Joe. The Rindhalu are relatively benign overlords, more like benign neglect due to their extreme laziness. But they are still overlords.

They subtly suppress their clients' efforts to climb the technology ladder. If the Jeraptha had an opportunity to break away, they might take it."

"Ha!" My laugh was bitter. "I wonder what odds the beetles would give for success in that effort? Ok, what does this mean for us? When are these clans going to hit Rikers?"

"The first one could arrive within nine days, Joe."

"Nine *days*? Holy shit! Even if the raid fails, the Fire Dragons will put our people under heavy security. We'd never pull them out alive."

"That isn't the real problem, Joe. Kristang operational security is notoriously poor. What we really need to worry about is the Fire Dragons hearing about the plot in advance of the raid. A subclan of the raiders could rat out its major clan to the Fire Dragons, in exchange for a favorable position when the civil war is over. Actually, hmm, the Fire Dragons might already be increasing security around the humans, because of the Council's scrutiny of the matter."

"Great!" I threw up my hands. "Just freakin' great! Once, just *once*, I'd like to get a break, you know?"

"We would *all* like a break, Joe. The entire galaxy is sick of this endless war. Even the Maxolhx leaders know their own population has grown weary of the war. That is why the rotten kitties have their clients doing most of the fighting, and their clients are *really* sick of the fighting. This is a war without winners, a war that *can't* have a winner."

"Yeah, sorry, I know. Ok, what info do you have about these raids?"

"Only that three clans-"

"*Three*? You said-"

"You didn't let me finish, numbskull. Three clans were considering an operation to seize the humans on Rikers, and two of those clans have put their plans into motion. The third clan recently suffered the defection of a subclan, so they are distracted at the moment. The messages I intercepted had almost no details, other than the departure dates of the raiding forces. When I said the first raid could happen in nine days, that is my estimate, based on how quickly a Bosphuraq star carrier could travel to Rikers."

"Wonderful. Travel time from here to that star system is four days?"

"Four days, assuming I screw with wormholes to create shortcuts."

"Well, *duh*. Why would we not want to use shortcuts?"

"Because if someone noticed odd wormhole behavior along a line pointing toward Rikers, they might wonder why, and start asking uncomfortable questions. *DUH*."

"Shit. That 'duh' is on me, and please keep reminding me when I'm an idiot. I know, that is all the time," I added before he could hit me with an insult. "How long without shortcuts?"

"Twelve days."

"Damn it. That's no good! All right, give me options that include some shortcuts, to get us there in six days. Connect me with Simms, please."

"Aww, Sir?" It sounded like she just woke up.

"Sorry, Simms," I cringed. "I asked Skippy to connect me with you. I should have asked for the duty officer."

"I'm awake now," she said with less irritation than I would have under the circumstances.

"Ok. We're bugging out, soon as possible. I'll notify Smythe. Skippy will explain why. Ask him for the *short* version."

There was a sound like her feet slapping the floor of her cabin. "I always ask for the short version. Erasing signs of our presence down there will take-"

"We don't have time for that. All the mock structures we built in Hadjistan, they can stay. By the time the next wormhole shift gives the bad guys access to this planet, it won't matter."

"Skippy has one of the reactors offline for maintenance," she reminded me. "That won't affect our departure."

Looking around my messy tent with dismay, I contemplated just jamming everything into duffel bags and sorting it later. "Understood, Simms. Bishop out." Instead of asking Skippy to connect me, I just hit the speed-dial on my zPhone for Smythe.

"Sir?" Whatever he was doing, he was out of breath.

"Smythe, change of plans. Get everyone to RTB right now. We're leaving as soon as we can get the essentials packed up. Leave the training sites as is, we don't have time to erase our tracks."

"Trouble, Sir?" he asked, as my phone pinged to announce the General Recall notice he just sent out.

"The trouble is on Rikers. We need to move up the rescue, we're going in six days."

"*Six?*" He was shocked. The STAR team had only been practicing the rescue operation at the mock camps for two days, and the practices had revealed serious problems with our original plans. Today was a stand-down to revise plans, and conduct a walk-through before tomorrow's practice session. "That's- We will make it work, Sir," he assured me. There wasn't much else he could do, or we would have to cancel the entire rescue. Somehow, we had to make it work.

"I'm as unhappy about this as you are. I know this is a rush job, and we're not fully prepared."

"That isn't the major problem, Sir. Today is Thursday."

"Yeah, so?"

"If we go then, we will be launching the rescue operation on a *Tuesday*."

"Oh shit," I groaned. "Let's hope that is not a typical Tuesday for the Merry Band of Pirates, huh?"

"I would not want to wager with our Jeraptha friend about that, Sir."

"Yeah," I took a deep breath. "Me neither."

CHAPTER THIRTY THREE

Our Ruhar 'guest' was still pissed off and uncooperative. That was too bad, because Simms and I made a real effort to make her comfortable and talk with her. The problem was, if she suddenly changed her attitude, I would suspect it was all an act, so we couldn't trust her.

The Commandos were not all happy with the situation either. They had spent enough time with our Pirates that the people from Paradise knew the whole unhappy story, that we had as many failures as successes. Most importantly, they knew Earth was doomed in the long run. Not even the long run. Hearing that was tough for the Commandos. While stranded on Paradise, they had feared the worst about Earth, but at least they could hope. Hope that, by some miracle, humanity's homeworld was safe in its isolation. Now they didn't even have that faint hope. A miracle had happened, and Earth was still doomed. Commandant Fabron assured me his people would focus on their jobs, but sooner or later, reality was going to sink in, and morale would take a serious hit.

The only person who was actually happy to have been Shanghaied was the Jeraptha. He was young enough that the whole experience was a grand adventure to him. What he most wanted was to stay with us until we returned to Earth.

I visited him in the galley while we were in flight toward Rikers. Partly I wanted to see how he was doing, and partly I found the beetles to be fascinating. Simms and a couple other people were in the galley, but the Jeraptha was sitting by himself, engrossed in whatever he was doing. A glass of water and discarded foil packs of ration bars littered the table, I was glad to see he was eating the bland food Skippy had fabricated for him.

"Hello Cadet Fangiu," I greeted him. "What are you doing there?"

Fangiu invited me to sit at his table, gesturing excitedly at the laptop we had loaned to him. It was filled with sports statistics. "Colonel Bishop, Skippy has provided me with important information, I must thank you very much. Your human sports are fascinating!"

"Yeah, I- what's so interesting about," I looked closer at the laptop. "You're looking at NFL drafts, going back to 1982? Why?"

"Our most sophisticated AIs attempted to re-run college drafts of your American National Football League, based only on information that was available at the time," he explained. "The first re-run by our AIs focused on drafts in the mid-2000s of your calendar."

"Ok, how did that go?" I asked eagerly, genuinely interested in what analysis powerful alien computers had produced. Hopefully, it was better than the typical clickbait articles at the bottom of sports websites.

"Not well," he hung his head. Interestingly. His antennas also drooped, and the surface of his leathery shell turned from dark green to a light green. Was that how Jeraptha blushed when they were embarrassed? "The AI dedicated to wager analysis are the most advanced our society has produced."

"Wait. You don't assign your best AIs to, uh, like, defense? Or research?"

"Our typical opponents are the Thuranin and Bosphuraq," he tilted his head, and his antennas twitched in a way I thought meant amusement. "We do not need our best technology to defeat those," the translator glitched in my ear, then I heard "knuckleheads."

"Oh," I laughed, wondering what he had said in his own language. "Got it. So, what did your AIs think of those drafts?"

"They predicted, with ninety-four percent confidence," he blushed again. "That JaMarcus Russell and Matt Leinart would be the most valuable players of that era."

"Oh." That was ancient history to me, but, hell, everyone knew how those draft picks worked out for the Raiders, and I think, the Cardinals? Like I said, ancient history. "Your AIs might want to revise their algorithms or whatever."

"We do not know *how* to revise the calculations," he explained. "It is rather embarrassing. And exciting! The same group of AIs also attempted to replay the 2014 World Cup of football, based only on information that was available at the end of training camp."

My American brain had to translate 'football' to 'soccer' before I knew which World Cup he was talking about. "How did that go?"

"I would rather not say. That is why it is so exciting! If our best AIs can't accurately predict the outcome, the possibilities for juicy action are limitless! Colonel Bishop, would it be possible for you to bring me to Earth?"

"Uh." My assumption had been he wanted to return to his people as soon as possible. It was my intention to do that, as soon as the knowledge he had would no longer put my homeworld in danger. Meaning it was going to be a while. "Why do you want to go there?"

That made him pause, as he listened to the translation. The light green of blushing returned to the shell covering his head. "Your homeworld is not a nice place?" He asked. Even through the translator, I could hear the embarrassment he felt for me.

"No. I mean, *yes*. It is a very nice place. We have beaches, and-" What do the Jeraptha think is a good spot for a vacation. "Mountains, and, uh, forests. Hey!" Sudden inspiration struck me. "We have casinos! Gambling halls," I added. "Las Vegas, Monaco, Hong Kong," that short list exhausted my knowledge of gambling hot spots. Though I was not an expert, I didn't think the Indian casinos in Connecticut would lure the Jeraptha across thousands of lightyears.

But, like I said, I'm not a gambler.

"Casinos?" He asked with a lot less enthusiasm than I expected. "That is where you play games of chance?"

"That, and there are games of skill, like, uh, poker?" My lack of knowledge was obvious. Poker required some skill, but, if you got dealt a crappy hand the guy across the table had four aces, you were kind of screwed.

"I am familiar with the game you call, 'Black Jack'," he pronounced it as two words. "Those are not interesting to us, because the odds are stacked in favor of the house and cannot be changed. There is no real action in such games."

"Well, unless you cheat the house by counting cards or something like that." I saw that in an old movie. Later, I was bitterly disappointed to learn that counting cards only gave the cheaters an advantage of a few percentage points. "Uh, if not for casinos, why are you so eager to get to Earth?"

"To gain an advantage, of course. My people are working with outdated information. There have been several seasons of sports on your planet, since access was cut off when the wormhole shut down," he tilted his head at me. If he was expecting or hoping for a more detailed explanation of how humans had manipulated an Elder wormhole, I was going to disappoint him. Sure, soon enough he was going to learn the truth one way or another, but I wasn't going to volunteer to blow the secret we had worked so hard to keep.

"Ah, don't get your hopes up, Cadet. Many sports had their seasons suspended or canceled when the Kristang were taking over. And the global economy took a big hit, so some teams or entire leagues folded."

"I am sorry, what is 'folded'? The translation is unclear." He blushed again. "I am sorry, my people do not have much experience with human languages. Until recently, we did not think it was," he looked away, "important. I do not mean any offense."

"It's all good," I responded, which was stupid. Slang expressions were especially difficult to translate. "We did not take offense. 'Folded' means the team has ceased operating." Seeing a look on his face that I guessed was either crestfallen or shock, I added "Many teams are still operating, and you're right. The information your people have is outdated. Why would getting that data give you an advantage?"

"Because I would be able to gain insight into the games, before others of my people. It is my hope that I could better handicap my wagers."

"Oh, you want to win money?"

"Please," he maybe looked anguished? "With my people, the money is less important than the action. You understand?"

"Yeah, I think I do." One of my uncles was an enthusiastic gambler. He drove down to 'The Indians' in Connecticut twice a month, and flew out to Vegas at least once a year. The reason he still had a roof over his head is because his wife kept him on a strict budget for gambling. I guess she figured he could otherwise be blowing his money on something really stupid, like an expensive boat to catch a five-dollar fish.

My uncle always bragged about how casinos comped his room, and how much money he won. Of course, gamblers winning money is how casinos stay in business. Not. Anyway, listening to him at family dinners and cookouts, I sort of understood the allure of gambling culture. Maybe the Jeraptha weren't too different? "All the info you need is aboard this ship. Uh, the info is current as of when we left Earth."

"You would give me access to the data?"

"*Give*?" I pretended to be shocked. Slapping the table loudly, I got the attention of other people in the galley. "Simms, can you believe this guy? We got a treasure trove of hot inside info, and he thinks we're just gonna *give* it to him?"

She caught on right away. Damn, I have a great executive officer. "I don't think so."

"Oh," Cadet-Undercandidate Fangiu's antennas were twitching, agitated. "Certainly, I would cut you in for a share. Of course."

"That's more like it," I forgot about not using slang. "How big a cut?"

"Eighty-twenty?"

"Ha," I laughed. "*Twenty* percent? Simms, can you believe this mook?"

"I think he can forgettaboutit," she scowled with a twinkle in her eyes.

Whatever 'mook' translated to in the Jeraptha language, it got my message across. "Apologies. Fifty-fifty?" His antennas laid out to the side. "You can't blame a guy for trying, right?"

The day before we arrived at Rikers, I was reviewing an important virtual reality simulation in my office, when Skippy interrupted me.

"Joe!"

"Ah!" I jerked upright, startled, and pulled off the VR headset I was wearing. "Damn it, is this important? Hold on, let me pause the game before I get my whole squad killed." I had been playing the latest Call of Duty game and for once, the game was going well for me. Ok, it was not the newest version of that game, but we had been away from Earth so long, I had missed a lot of releases.

As a bonus, I also missed a lot of glitches that were corrected by the time I picked up the game.

"Too late for that anyway, you shouldn't have crossed that last bridge," Skippy sniffed disgustedly. "There is an enemy tank inside that building across the town square."

"A freakin' *tank*? That's bullshit. How can a tank get inside a-"

"The back wall of the building was blown out by that artillery strike you called in. By the way, the target you hit there was a decoy, dumdum. Man, even in a game, you always fail to consider the consequences."

"Ah, screw it," I tossed the headset on the desk. "What is it?"

"You have been neglecting your paperwork, *again*." He added an extra note of disdain by pronouncing the word as 'Uh-GAIN' instead of 'Uh-ginn' like normal people do.

"We don't have a single scrap of paper aboard the *Valkyrie*, Skippy."

"You know what I mean."

"Is this because I don't read the status report every morning? That report is, like, fifty pages long! I wouldn't understand half of it anyway."

"True, and that is why I summarize the important items on the *first* three pages."

That was true. Not only were the critical items listed first, the beginning of the status report was usually presented in comic book form, which made it easier to read. By the way, if you ever wondered who would win a fight between Batman and Donald Duck, Skippy answered that question in the classic Issue #357 of the daily status report. "Yeah, I do read that," I admitted. After being insulted that he was showing me a comic book, I got over it. "What's the problem now?"

"You have still not completed the paperwork for your official promotion to colonel. I filled it in as best I could before we left Earth, but-"

"Oh for- Like that matters now? We can't get to Earth right now. If we ever do get there, the whole planet might soon be a radioactive cinder."

"Joe, your personnel file lists 'problem with authority' and 'lack of attention to detail', among many other bad things. Assuming we do get back to Earth and it is still intact, because otherwise what the hell are we trying to accomplish out here, wouldn't it be nice if you at least had your personnel records updated? That would be one less thing for the Army to complain about. Especially as, you know, any return to Earth would include you telling UNEF that all the happy stuff you told them about your homeworld being safe was bullshit, and a massive fleet of Maxolhx warships will inevitably be there soon. Because once again, you failed to account for the Law of Unintended Consequences."

"Ok, I get your point. Uh, give me the file," I pulled a laptop out of a drawer.

"No need for that, Joe. Also, I know you'll find a reason to procrastinate and never do it. I will read the questions right now, and you tell me what to list in the file."

"Oh, cool. Go ahead."

"The first unanswered question is your preferred personal pronoun."

For a second, I froze, just blinking slowly at him. "Uh, what again?"

"Your, preferred, personal, *pronoun*." He said very slowly. "Ugh. Like, do you prefer to be called 'he/him' or 'she/her' or 'they/them' or something else."

"This is on an official *Army* form?" I was sure he was screwing with me.

"Yes, dumdum. The Army has been changing with the times. Try to keep up, huh?"

"For real? Uh, well, I prefer to be referred to as 'Valroth the Destroyer, Devourer of Worlds'."

That made him chuckle. "Nope, that's too long for the form."

"How about just 'Val' for short?"

"Joe, you need to take this seriously."

"Ok. Can you input 'Duuuuuude'?"

"Let me try- Huh. It worked."

"Are the rest of the questions like that?"

"No. Some of them are *really* stupid," he admitted.

My day kind of went downhill from there.

On the way to Rikers, we had one last issue to settle before launching the rescue operation. What was our cover story? There were a hundred suggestions, in the end I decided on the simplest answer. The good news was, that cover story did not require us to avoid leaving any human DNA behind, and it explained why we were taking a big risk to pull a small group of lowly humans off an unimportant world. The cover story was that our raiding force was a UNEF group attached to the Alien Legion, a group who had either been given the OK by the Ruhar for the op, or went rogue to rescue their own people. The Mavericks had done enough unauthorized stuff that no one would be surprised a group of humans would go off doing whatever they thought was right. Sure, Ruhar military leadership would know they had not approved a rescue, but even they would wonder if their rather shady military intelligence division had cooked up an operation that had plausible deniability. This was a case where the duplicity of our enemies and supposed allies worked for us.

With the cover story settled, I had to emphasize the vital need to conceal the true nature of our force. Smythe also took pains to pound the need for secrecy into the heads of the Commando team. We did the best we could, and had to trust the professionalism of the people from Paradise, people we did not know well yet. My concern was not that any of them would deliberately blow the cover story that the raid was an Alien Legion op, I was worried that one of them might say or do something that could make the lizards or their patrons suspicious about the cover story. The Commandos that not lived for years with the need for secrecy, it wasn't second nature for them.

It was not an optimal situation, and we also didn't have a choice.

We jumped inside the Rahkarsh Diweln star system and listened with passive sensors, while probes we shot out by railguns raced inward toward the target planet. Inside the probes were microwormholes that would provide a real-time communications link between the planet, the *Flying Dutchman,* and *Valkyrie*. To avoid any possibility of the Maxolhx connecting the ghost ship with humans if the operation were blown, we would be going in with Kristang dropships, with the *Dutchman* doing the pickup on the outbound leg. *Valkyrie* would be loitering far from the planet, remaining out of sight. Simms had orders not to take our mighty battlecruiser into a fight unless there was an extreme emergency. In our pre-mission briefing, I had stressed to her that we could afford to lose the kidnapped people on Rikers, the entire STAR team and all our dropships including mine. We could even afford to lose our trusty old *Flying Dutchman*, but we could not risk exposing the fearsome ghost ship. Simms wasn't happy about her orders, and neither was I.

To save time, because we were on the clock before one or another group of lizards jumped in to steal the poor people we wanted to rescue, we launched our dropships before getting a full set of data from the probes. We could always turn the dropships around, or have them coast stealthily past the planet to be retrieved on the other side. We could *not* get a do-over if a hateful group of lizards arrived early to mess everything up for us.

Despite having to cut training short, and lacking up-to-date intel on the target, I was feeling pretty good about the op. And, right on cue, Skippy harshed my buzz. "Uh oh, Joe," he muttered as we flew alone in a Dragon-A. He was with me because his particular set of skills might be needed near the planet. I was flying a Kristang spacecraft because if we were exposed, we did not want the enemy to see a more sophisticated ship. The Dragon-A was the smaller of the two models, and we needed the larger ones for the evac. It bugged me that we had plenty of Maxolhx Panthers, but we couldn't risk using them. So, the op would be conducted in old Dragons we pulled from the *Ice-Cold Dagger to the Heart*, after we had captured that ship full of lizard-sicles.

Yuck, that had to be the worst popsicle flavor *ever*.

"Oh, crap. What is the problem now?" There wasn't anything that stood out as immediately alarming in the sensor data, I knew that because I was totaling focused on reviewing the data feed from the *Flying Dutchman*. We had launched with all the velocity needed to reach the planet, the Dragon's engines would be needed only to slow down when we approached the atmosphere, so I didn't have much to do in terms of flying. Whatever he thought was a problem, it wasn't anything big enough for my slow brain to recognize. There was not a fleet of Thuranin ships in orbit, nor were there ships from a rival clan attempting to steal the humans. There were not any ships in orbit at all, and the planet was too thinly populated to have a space station. We knew from Skippy's intel that Rikers had two dozen Strategic Defense satellites equipped with maser cannons and missiles, plus up to eighty small sensor satellites. The exact number depended on how many of the SD platforms were actually functional, Skippy couldn't get that info until we were closer to the planet.

The planet appeared to be peaceful, the only live weapons fire was at a training range we knew about, and that was over three thousand kilometers from the closest camp where humans were being held. Overall, the place was as sleepy and poverty-stricken as Skippy told us to expect. Two population centers were large enough to be called cities, although based on the current population they were really just large towns. There used to be more lizards on Rikers, back when the White Wind clan was relatively prosperous. By the time we got there, much of the artificial structures like buildings, bridges, roads, water systems and all the other mechanical stuff that supported civilization were getting shoddy. The lizards who still lived there couldn't afford, or didn't care to, maintain all that expensive infrastructure. Many of the buildings were abandoned, and whole villages and towns were empty. Clan leaders liked to concentrate their populations, to make it easier to control the common people, and everyday clan social life encouraged lizards to live in large, extended families.

"The problem," Skippy told me as he fed data to the cockpit's main display, "is that the tactical situation on the ground has changed. As I warned you might happen, the Fire Dragons have increased security around the prisoners. The Objective Dixie camp now has a contingent of six guards on that island. All the humans from the Objective Yankee camp are currently in transport aircraft, being moved to an abandoned village on the mainland, near an old military base. The humans in the southern camp will also be moved to that village, when secure transport is available."

"Damn it! We might as well take all of our planning and training and throw it out the freakin' window! Let Smythe know."

"I am talking to him right now, also with Major Kapoor and Commandant Fabron. They used somewhat more colorful language to express their feelings."

"I will try to be more entertaining to you in the future. What the hell happened? The lizards down there heard that other clans are planning to raid the camps?"

"No, Joe. I will know more when the probes get closer, but the message traffic I've intercepted indicates this is purely a precautionary move. Basically, the clan leaders down there said 'Hey, we are hateful deceitful lizards. What would *we* do if another clan had something valuable to our patrons'?"

"Shit. Because they are assholes, they assume everyone is an asshole?"

"Joe, pretty much the entire Kristang warrior class leadership *are* assholes. The ones who are not assholes get selected out by, um," he giggled. "By process of *assassination*," he snickered at the pun he invented.

"Ok, Ok. So, the lizards here anticipate some other clan might be tempted to conduct a raid. Let me think a minute." Smythe, Kapoor and Fabron were undoubtedly doing their own thinking about who, and if, we could salvage the operation. "Skippy, why didn't the lizards just jam all the humans from each camp into a transport aircraft, and fly them out in one sortie?"

"Those camps are deliberately isolated, the lizards set them up far from populated areas. It takes long-range aircraft to fly that far and back. The simple truth is, they only have four flightworthy aircraft with the range to reach the camps, and those transports can each fit only thirty passengers. Um, the definition of 'flightworthy' is based on lizard standards. *I* certainly would not want to be in one of those things. You know how casual the lizards are about maintaining their equipment."

Zooming in the display, I followed a pair of symbols slowly advancing across a vast expanse of ocean. There was another pair ahead on the flight path, closer to the mainland. "These four are the aircraft carrying the human prisoners?"

"Yes," he confirmed. "You encountered that type of aircraft on Newark. Back then, you called it a 'Luzzard', because it is similar to the Buzzard flown by the Ruhar. UNEF-HQ on Paradise has designated that type as a 'Stork'."

"A *stork?*"

"It is ugly and flies poorly," he explained.

"Ok, we'll use the standard designation, then." It had been a while since I was inside a Buzzard, I tried to remember what the cabin looked like. "They crammed thirty people into each one of them?"

"I don't have an exact count yet," he told me patiently. "It is a long overwater flight, so the pilots requested permission to decrease their load. Between the four Storks, they are carrying all seventy-three humans from the northern camp. There are two pilots and two Kristang soldiers in each Stork, I do know that for certain."

"It looks like the second pair lifted off, what, an hour ago?"

"One hour and sixteen minutes. Why?"

It was tempting to do the navigation math myself, just to show Skippy that monkeys weren't helpless. "How long until that second pair reaches landfall?"

"The flight plan they filed has them going feet dry," using military terminology made him feel like one of the cool kids. "In five hours and twenty-one minutes. They are battling a headwind that is stronger than expected, so that could be delayed. The first pair is one hour and thirty-four minutes ahead."

"Interesting. Connect me with Smythe."

"Colonel Bishop?" Smythe answered immediately. "You see the problem?"

"I see one problem, and maybe one opportunity."

"Opportunity, Sir?"

Before I decided whether we really had an opportunity or not, I needed more info. "If we move your team around, how many do you need to secure the southern camp?"

"Against six guards?" Smythe asked. All of our planning assumed the camps would be unguarded, because that was the intel we had at the time. Now, we had armed opposition. The whole reason we brought aboard Fabron's team was in case the operation did not go as planned, because of course it wouldn't. "Sir, they have the advantage of being on the defense. The tricky part is that the enemy will not worry about causing collateral damage. We can't go into a firefight without the risk of hitting the people we're trying to rescue."

"Colonel?" Fabron spoke. "I had extensive contact with lizards on Fresno. They won't hesitate to shoot the prisoners, or use them as hostages. We have to hit them by surprise, or there won't be anyone left for us to rescue."

"Shiiiiiit," I groaned. "Any way you can infiltrate?"

Smythe answered. "I do not see that as an option, Sir. That island is surrounded by nothing but ocean, that's why it was chosen for the camp. Even if we employ stealth, the guards will hear our engines coming." That was one major problem with using dropships for ground assault operations in an atmosphere. They were a compromise design, intended for use in air and in the vacuum of space. Their stubby wings meant they had to use turbines for lift when they flew slowly, and at any speed, they left a wake of turbulent air behind them. Skippy could hack any networked sensors around the planet, because instead of taking over each sensor, he simply told their network to ignore the inputs. Hacking into the squad-level tactical sensors typically carried by Kristang soldiers was tricky business, those devices were so simple and rugged and just plain *dumb* that they were resistant to hacking. "Skippy, what do you think? Can we get dropships onto that island without the lizards noticing?"

"Ah, hmm, I wouldn't try it, Joe. If they come in low over water, their turbines will kick up spray and there is no way to hide that. Same problem with coming in high and attempting to land, they would kick up a lot of dust. The lizards would all have to be sleeping to miss that."

"HALO jump?" I suggested. Parachuting down from high altitude, and popping the balloons at the last moment. could allow a team to land on the island.

Fabron grunted. "My team has not practiced that type of jump," he admitted.

Smythe shot down my idea. "We didn't bring enough of the proper gear with us, Sir. Those portable stealth generators are bulky, we needed the space in the cabins for the people we're pulling off the surface."

"All right," I admitted defeat. "We have to take them by surprise. That means we need to land in Storks instead of dropships."

Smythe responded with dry British humor. "May I remind you that we don't *have* Stork aircraft?"

"We don't have any of them *now*," I explained.

"Ah. We will again resort to piracy?"

"It's kind of our thing, you know?"

Fabron broke into the conversation. "Colonel, you mentioned an opportunity? I see only difficulties."

"Me too, *mon ami*," Skippy sighed. "But, the mush in Joe's monkey skull sees something that I don't see, so let him talk. At worst, it will be amusing."

"The people from the northern camp Yankee are all loaded aboard aircraft," I noted. "*That* is our opportunity."

Fabron took a moment to contemplate that thought. "I do not understand how"

"Commandant, if you want something at a store, you have two options, right? You can go to the store to pick it up."

"Yes," the French soldier said slowly.

"*Or*," I figured by that time Smythe knew what I was thinking. "You can have it delivered."

CHAPTER THIRTY FOUR

We threw a plan together literally on the fly, as our Dragons were coasting toward the planet. Actually, the other dropships were coasting, I had mine rocketing ahead so Skippy could get better intel ASAP. As a result, we got into orbit ahead of the trailing dropships, and Skippy hacked into the planet's rudimentary defense network, so we wouldn't be detected. "This is less than perfect, Joe," he complained.

"What is the problem? The lizards don't have a full SD network up here, just some old satellites. You have snuck us through more advanced sensors before."

"That's the problem. This network is so crappy and patched together, I am having trouble getting it to work properly. Every time I take control of it, the damned thing glitches, and I have to scramble to prevent real data from being fed to the command center."

"Hell. That's no good. Can those sensors really see us?"

"The short answer is no. They might detect a normal Dragon, but I modified the stealth systems aboard these lizard pieces of crap. The danger of detection will come when Smythe's ships are entering the atmosphere."

"Are we a 'Go', or should we reconsider?"

"We're a 'Go', I think. The good news is the satellite sensor network is so bad, it is constantly glitching and giving false data to the command center. The lizards down there are used to getting bogus alerts. If they did see us, they might think that data is a glitch, but we can't take that risk. The real risk is some over-eager lizard monitoring sensors down there might be trying to win the coveted Employee of the Month award."

"Ha!" I relaxed a bit. "As if."

"Oh, I wasn't joking about that. The command center recently had a new duty officer assigned, and this Larry is a real pain-in-the-*ass* eager beaver. His crew *hates* him, because he makes them log and investigate every sensor contact."

My brain shorted out. Not from hearing that we had yet another problem, but because of something totally unexpected. "This lizard's name is *Larry*?"

"It's something like 'Lar-bar Buh-bar Buh-bar', Joe. You know what lizard names are like. I shortened it for you."

"Got it. Is this Larry the Lizard going to be a problem for us?"

"That depends. He is currently in an elevator, descending from the thirty-ninth floor of his apartment building. That jerk is on the way into the office."

That gave me an idea. "Hey, is that jerk currently alone?"

"Yes, why?"

"Because, if that elevator were to suffer a fatally unfortunate malfunction, I would not lose sleep over it. If you know what I mean."

"Ah. Gotcha. You know, Joe, you should never skimp on elevator maintenance."

"I will make a note of it."

"Three, two, one, wow. Well, good thing *I* don't have to clean up that mess. There's a Larry-sized stain on the bottom of the elevator shaft. *Yuck.* Ok, well, now we have another decision to make."

The last thing I wanted right then was yet another problem. "What?"

"Do we send flowers of condolence, or a fruit basket, to Larry's family?"

"How about we do neither, and imagine we did? It's the thought that counts."

"True. Besides, Larry's family hated him too."

After the tragic death of Larry the Unloved, I waited while Skippy merrily ransacked every database on the planet and beyond. "Um," he said after I spent an anxious eight minutes imagining various ways the op could go sideways even before we got started. "Oopsy."

"*Oopsy?*"

"Well, heh heh, we have a complication. It looks like the lizards down there are not the only beings who fear someone might try to steal their human hostages. The Thuranin don't want to risk dealing with a third party. They are sending a starship, it should be here in a few days. It *could* have been here two days ago."

"Oh shit." The blood drained from my face. "We could have a ship full of little green MFers jumping in on our heads at any moment?"

"Apparently, yes. My guess is the LGMFs told the lizards an optimistic arrival date, to keep them honest. But, it is true that a ship could jump into orbit at any second."

"Freakin' wonderful!" I threw up my hands.

"If it helps, the ship they are sending is just a frigate, Joe. The *Dutchman* could take it in a fair fight."

"I am not a big fan of fair fights, Skippy. Alert Chang and Simms. Tell them I do *not* want them tangling with the Thuranin unless I give the order."

"Done. Hey, this might not be the best time to deliver bad news-"

"That was *not* the bad news?"

"There is another complication. Three of the humans are quite ill, and the lizards are concerned about protecting their investment. One adult and two children are in a Kristang hospital on the mainland."

Squeezing my fists for a count of ten helped me calm down. "Show me what you know."

It was bad news. It was not *catastrophic* news. The hospital was not in a densely populated city, it was not in a city at all. It was a small, almost abandoned building in an almost abandoned town, on the seacoast of the western ocean. My guess was, the lizards looked for the hospital that was closest to the camp where the humans had been held, and found a place where the locals would not protest too much about having filthy, disease-ridden aliens dumped in their laps. The town's original reason for being was to support a military base that was now closed, so the hospital had specialized isolation gear for dealing with bioweapon risks. That gear was not guaranteed to be in functional condition, but the local clan leaders could claim they had taken measures to protect their people, bah blah blah. We had a depleted and traumatized STAR team, Commandos without enough time with their new and unfamiliar Kristang gear, and the entire team did not have enough time to train and prepare for an operation that had been thrown into disarray before it began. Now we had *three* widely-scattered objectives, four if you considered the two flights of Storks to be separate targets. "Do you know if the prisoners at the hospital are able to be moved? If they are real sick, the rescue might kill them."

"You should not count on them being able to walk far," Skippy answered. "But they aren't in immediate danger of dying. The info I have is a bit out of date, it's the best I can do, Joe."

"Oh, what the hell. Connect me with Smythe. He loves a challenge, right?"

There was an uncomfortable silence after I told our STAR team leader the good news. "Smythe?" I prompted him.

"Sir, if you are giving me an extra challenge for my birthday-"

"Can we handle this?" I asked. "It will have to happen simultaneously with the other ops."

"I would prefer to take on the hospital last, it has the fewest number of people." He was conducting triage not from callousness, but from sheer professionalism. People like Smythe could not afford to be sentimental, or people died needlessly. We could not risk the rescue of almost two hundred people, just to pick up three.

"Not possible. We don't have the time. Skippy just learned the Thuranin might arrive here any minute, to crash the party."

Another silence, this time broken by Fabron. "Colonel Bishop, is this your idea of a typical Tuesday?"

"Ha," I laughed without humor. "Something like that. I sent the details. Let me know what you think."

What they thought was that adding the hospital to the list of objectives could be done, *if* nothing major went wrong with that or any of the other operations. By 'they', I meant Smythe, Kapoor and Fabron. My main concern was Fabron and his team. They were unknowns, untested. Sure, the Commandos had gone into action on Fresno, and been training intensively with the Ruhar and Verd-Kris since then, but they had not experienced combat with the Merry Band of Pirates. None of their training included the need to conceal the fact that they existed. This op was a good place to start, because our cover story did not require us to avoid leaving human DNA behind. If the people from Paradise left DNA behind and the Kristang were somehow able to trace it back to a particular person, that would actually help sell the cover story of the raid being conducted by UNEF. The lizards would never believe the Ruhar had not authorized and enabled the raid, and I didn't care. Still, I worried that the Commandos did not have an instinct to conceal their connection to the Merry Band of Pirates. Someone might do something without thinking, and blow our secret out in the open.

Smythe was in charge of the ground forces, I only interfered if he proposed something that would jeopardize the overall operation. That only happened when I knew something he didn't, and *that* only happened when I forgot to tell him something important. Or when Skippy just mentioned something *he* forgot to tell me about. Smythe was right about the hospital op being at the bottom of the priority list. If we didn't have to worry about a Thuranin frigate jumping in on top of our heads at any moment, I would have agreed to conduct the hospital rescue after we got everyone else. Since we couldn't change the facts, Smythe reluctantly assigned three people to the hospital retrieval, we were limited to three because that is how many sets of HALO parachutes we had aboard the dropships. Frey and Grudzien would bring with them the only Commando soldier who had experience with HALO jumps, Capitaine Camille Durand. As we didn't have enough dropships to assign one to the hospital, the three soldiers would need to parachute in, infiltrate the hospital, extract the three humans and exfiltrate to someplace where a Dragon could retrieve them. Uh, 'exfiltrate' is a military term for sneaking away from a place you snuck into. Depending on the size and nature of the opposition, Frey's team might have to make a lot of noise, so the 'sneaking' part would be Overcome By Events. At that point, they would have to conduct a retreat under fire to get picked up. Frey was smart, she knew we would not bring a Dragon full of people into a hot landing zone, so she needed to be sure the LZ, ingress and egress flight paths were clear. That could require a lengthy retreat and delay the retrieval.

Having decided how to extract people from the hospital, we had the issue that Capitaine Durand was not in the same dropship as Frey and Grudzien, nor was Durand's dropship equipped with parachute gear. The two Dragons had to maneuver close enough for Durant to transfer from one to the other, pulling herself hand over hand along a thin line because we hadn't brought any jetpacks with us. With that anxiety-inducing complication out of the way, all the pieces were on the chess board. Now all we had to do was execute a flawless operation, and hope the Thuranin didn't arrive early to spoil the party. Easy.

Frey and Grudzien helped Durand get her parachute gear attached in the rear cabin of the Dragon. "This Kristang gear works pretty similarly to the hamster parachutes you have trained with," Frey assured the other woman.

"You have done a HALO jump with Ruhar gear?" Durand asked, checking the latches on the front of her mech suit. She had briefly worn Kristang powered armor during Legion training, to get her familiar with the capabilities of enemy equipment and their strengths and weaknesses. The hardshell armor was stiff and uncomfortable and heavier than the flexible Ruhar skinsuit she was used to, but the suit assigned to her had advanced capabilities provided by the alien AI. She could not believe that the team were trusting their lives to a beer-can-shaped ancient intelligence named 'Skippy', but the STAR team trusted the prickly alien, and she really didn't have any choice in the matter.

"No," Frey admitted. "That's Skippy's analysis."

Durand looked the team leader in the eyes. "Has *Skippy* jumped with either set of gear?"

"You know the answer to that," Frey flashed a smile, and tugged Durand's parachute straps tighter, without any need to. The straps adjusted themselves. "Trust your equipment, it will set you down safely. Follow my lead if you get into trouble."

Durand wriggled her shoulders to get comfortable in the suit, and checked Frey's parachute pack when the Canadian woman turned her back. "Looks good. The equipment I trust. Kristang gear is rugged and simple, it works fine if it's properly maintained."

"See? Nothing to worry about." Frey gestured for Grudzien to have his pack checked.

"Do you," Durand lowered her voice to a conspiratorial whisper. "Trust the AI?"

"Hey!" Skippy's voice echoed in the Dragon's rear compartment. "I can *hear* you. Of course Captain Frey trusts me, for I am the very model of trustworthiness."

Grudzien couldn't miss the opportunity to set the record straight. "Except when you forget something."

"*Everyone* forgets someth-"

"Because you weren't paying attention," the Polish soldier finished the thought.

"Hey, I am very busy," Skippy grumbled. "I can't think of everything. Let's see *you* try-"

Frey clapped her hands. "Boys! You can continue this after we get back to *Valkyrie*. Skippy, promise me you will be totally focused on this mission."

"Of course I promise, *mon cheri*."

"I'm not *French*-Canadian," she reminded him. "So you can drop that."

Skippy was hurt. "I was just-"

Smythe's voice interrupted. "Jump light goes green in seven minutes."

"Right," Frey acknowledged. She hopped up and down to make sure all her gear was properly stowed, though her boots stayed clamped to the deck in the Dragon's zero gravity. "Helmets on."

The team donned helmets, checked the seals, verified communications, and were ready a full minute before the rear compartment began depressurizing. With ninety seconds to the drop, they shuffled backward to grab handholds on the bar across the compartment. At the thirty-second mark, they activated the disposable cold jet cartridges attached to their backpacks.

Three, two, one-

The rear ramp of the Dragon slammed open at the last second and the cold gas thrusters propelled the three outward. When the thrusters came to the end of their flexible tethers, they detached from the backpacks and were yanked back inside the dropship, just before the ramp swung closed. Having the ramp open compromised stealth and although Skippy had control of the planetary defense network, it made no sense to take additional risks.

Frey didn't glance backward at the stealthed Dragon as it fled away, she knew it was invisible anyway. Her attention was not even on the planet below, which looked so close she could have *seen her house* if she lived there. In reality, they had jumped at an altitude of fifty-eight thousand kilometers, which technically was within the atmosphere. The air around them was so thin that it gave no resistance as she plunged headfirst. At thirty-four kilometers, she began to hear a high-pitched whistling sound, of air rushing past at supersonic speed.

The chute began deploying when they reached thirty-two kilometers, first gently tugging the three soldiers into a triangle formation so they did not interfere with each other's chutes. Then the gossamer-thin parachute material flared out and filtered air was pumped in, forming a balloon above her. Speed bled off, not so rapidly that the balloon generated a detectable signature, rapidly enough that a noticeable sonic boom did not reach the ground.

Everything was going to plan. She would have preferred not to jump while the landing zone was in daylight, and she was grateful for the cloud cover. The Skippytel network's forecast called for rain when they landed, clearing later to partly cloudy conditions. The clouds overhead would prevent curious lizards on the ground from seeing the Pirates as they descended, and she hoped the rain would keep the natives inside.

In her visor, she saw Grudzien and Durand were falling in perfect formation with her and their parachutes were operating in nominal fashion. In fact, each of them were within a half meter of the predicted descent path. A wry smile crept across Frey's lips as she contemplated that the unnecessary precision of their glide path was the AI showing off for Camille Durand.

"Comms check," Frey whispered, something else that was not necessary. "How is everyone doing?"

"I'm *bored*," Grudzien complained. "When does the fun start? I was promised fun in this-"

The Polish soldier's balloon flexed its shape and the bottom dropped out below him. He yelped as he was momentarily in freefall.

"Was that exciting enough for you?" Skippy was his usual snarky self.

"Yes, thank you," Grudzien said with his heart in his throat. The straps on his shoulders tugged harder as his balloon refilled to bring him back into formation. "That was enough fun for the day."

"Do we have better intel on the landing zone?" Durand asked. "My sensors are showing only general terrain features."

"No, sorry," Skippy answered. "There are no local sensors in the area, so I don't have anything to hack into. So far, I don't see any heat signatures large enough to be a Kristang. But they could be under shelter."

"Right," Frey eyeclicked a menu option in her visor's display, and her rifle's strap swung it around from her back to straddle her midsection, where it was ready for use. "Get your weapon ready. Remember, no shooting unless I shoot first."

"Or *they* do," Grudzien breathed.

"Let's think positive thoughts," Frey issued the mild reprimand. If they got into a firefight before reaching the hospital, Skippy's control of communications all around the planet would prevent an alarm from calling in reinforcements, but it would alert whatever security forces were at the hospital. Not even Skippy could stop the sound of rifle fire from being heard for several kilometers. Her orders were to abort the operation if they ran into significant opposition, it would be her own judgment what constituted 'significant'. The lives of three people, two of them children, were depending on her. She also was responsible for the lives of the two soldiers with her. "Please, God," she said a silent prayer. "Don't let me screw this up."

At ten thousand meters, they plunged into the thick cloud layer and all she could see was a gray blanket below, around and above her. Switching her visor to synthetic view gave her a picture of the ground, but that was a composite of fuzzy sensor data plus what the suit's computer had been told to expect. "Skippy, when are we getting active sensors?" She asked as she fell through six thousand meters above ground level.

"Patience," the AI counselled. "The second satellite is just coming above the horizon. I *told* you this would be tricky timing."

She eyeclicked to the private channel. "Grudzien and I know how awesome you are. You need to impress Camille." The ancient AI had few weaknesses, but a craving for praise was one of them, and he especially was desperate for praise from women.

"Do you think she likes me?" Skippy asked in a whisper.

"I think she will *not* like you, if we come out of the clouds and trouble is waiting for us."

"Oh. Gosh, I just discovered that satellite needs a slight adjustment to its orbit."

Fifteen seconds later, Frey's suit alerted her that the area was being swept by two active sensor beams. Satellites to the north and west were painting the ground, and her suit was picking up the reflections, without her suit needing to expose itself by sending out active pulses. Skippy had caused the satellites to perform an unscheduled active sensor test, just in the right position. "Got it, good work," she thanked Skippy as she scanned the incoming data. It all looked good, except- "We've got trouble."

"Ah, you mean that truck?" Skippy scoffed. "No problem, I'll just- Huh. That damned thing is not connected to the planetary network. I can't hack into it at all. Whoo, that thing must be cobbled together from junk parts. Um, Ok, maybe that *is* a problem."

A truck, with a small bubble-shaped cab up front and a bed that was covered with a canvas or tarp, was slowly rumbling along a rutted dirt road, traveling in the general direction of the hospital. "Can you drop us down behind that ridge?" Frey highlighted the alternate landing zone.

"Affirmative." As Skippy spoke, the parachute balloons tugged the three soldiers onto a different descent course. "It is rain and fog almost all the way to the ground there, good concealment. That ridge is covered with trees, though. You could get tangled up," he warned.

Frey looked at the synthetic map. "How deep is that pond?"

"It's a pond. Shallow water, but a muddy bottom. Your suits are heavy."

She did not want to waste time fighting to extract one or more of them from a thick layer of sticky muck. The ground was approaching fast, she needed to make a decision. "Avoid the pond, eh? Lower us through the tree canopy on tethers."

"That's marginal," Skippy warned. "The wind is gusty."

"Yes, but you are *awesome*, eh?"

"Frey," he growled on the private channel. "Do *not* make me hate you."

"Just do it."

"Captain Frey?" Durand asked as she watched the terrain below her resolve into individual trees. "I have never practiced a tether landing."

Frey winced. There had not been enough time to properly train for the operation as originally planned. Certainly not sufficient time to allow for prepare for contingencies. "There is nothing to it. Relax and trust your gear. If you get into trouble and you're within eight meters of the ground, release and drop. Your suit will absorb most of the impact." Most, but not all, she reminded herself. "Bend your knees and arch your back."

Camille Durand bit back a reply. She knew how to conduct a proper parachute landing. There was no point getting into an argument, and she knew Frey had not intended an insult. Then there was no time for talking, as her balloon expanded to halt her descent and changed shape to steer into the wind. The balloon grew wings on both sides, using those airfoils to hover like a seagull soaring over a beach. Before she could admire the precision with which the balloon held itself motionless in the gusty wind, rain and fog, the tether holding her backpack to the balloon began lengthening, and she dropped. Crossing arms over her chest and pointing her legs and toes downward, she was rocked as leaves and branches slapped against her, a shoulder bounced off a stout tree limb, and she had a brief glimpse of a cluttered forest floor before bringing her knees up. Her boots hit first, then her backside and she rolled to absorb the impact. Wary of the tether dragging her through the forest, she held the emergency release lever, but the tether severed itself.

"Everyone down safe, eh?" Frey asked, knowing that was true from the information displayed in her visor. "Recover 'chutes first."

The team fanned out to retrieve their parachutes, tracking the packages by faint signals. Once their charges were on the ground, the tiny computers controlling the parachutes had cut the tethers, having analyzed the tree cover and deciding the balloons would become tangled and shredded if they tried to guide themselves down through the tangled branches. The backup plan was for the balloon to reel in the tethers, drift to a better landing place, and collapse into a neat ball of nanofabric. The three balls plunged through the tree canopy without harm, except Grudzien's parachute bounced off a dead log and rolled into the pond with a splash. "Shit!" The Polish soldier exclaimed as he waded out to pick up the damned thing, then had to wash off the layer of muck before it could be stored in his pack to recharge.

"Congratulations, Capitaine," Frey said to the Commando woman. "You earned your jump wings."

"Thank you," Durand automatically reached up to brush stray hairs out of her eyes, and her hand thumped into the helmet she forgot about. "Are all your operations thrown together at the last minute?"

"Oh, no, Ma'am," Grudzien splashed his boots in the pond water, to clean the green scum off. "We usually have to make shit up as we go. It's nice to have a *plan* this time."

"*Merde*." Durand groaned.

"What she said," Frey agreed. "Let's move out."

"Frey's team is down safely, and reasonably on target, Joe," Skippy reported. "No sign they have been detected."

"I'm worried about that truck, Skippy. If Frey's team can't use the road, they will have to go cross-country, and cross two rivers. That is rough terrain, it will slow them down."

His voice immediately took on a defensive edge. "Hey, I'm not happy about that truck either."

"Can't you do something to stop it? It's just a stupid truck."

"I can't do anything, *because* it is just a stupid truck. The damned thing appears to be nothing but fuel cells and electric motors, I can't detect any type of control system. The lizards in the cab must be manually driving it, if you can believe that. Really, I'm kind of impressed by their ingenuity in building that piece of crap from spare parts."

"Maybe we can turn that truck from a problem to an opportunity. Frey," I opened the command channel. "I know it's rainy and chilly down there, so I sent an Uber to pick you up."

"An Uber, Sir?"

"Technically, it's a truck. The driver needs to be paid in bullets, if you know what I mean."

"Oh. Yes. I think I know, eh?"

CHAPTER THIRTY FIVE

After Frey's team parachuted from the Dragon, the spacecraft continued on far out over the western ocean before descending into and through the atmosphere. That was the aspect of the mission that gave me the most anxiety. Skippy had intermittent control of the planetary sensor network, so none of the satellites or ground-based sensors would be sounding alarms about an unknown and unauthorized object coming down from orbit. What he could not control was a lizard looking up with bare eyeballs and seeing a white streak in the sky. That lizard would know that there weren't any friendly ships scheduled to arrive in-system that day, and that would prompt uncomfortable questions about why the object was not being reported by the defense network.

So, both Dragons did not hit the atmosphere until they were far out over the ocean, away from populated areas. Just in case some aircraft or ship was below, they used engine power in partial hover mode to avoid leaving a noticeable contrail. The stealth maneuver was a strain on the engines, for they had to gulp in enormous amounts of cool air to counter the heat of the turbines. When the airspeed was below supersonic, the pilots breathed sighs of relief, and began a gentle turn back toward land. There, the Dragons separated, with Smythe's ship turning north and Fabron's continuing on a southerly course. The safe approach, to the site designated 'Objective Lima', required crossing the seacoast four hundred kilometers to the north then arcing around south to fly along a mountain range.

The task of Smythe's team was to pull forty-seven traumatized, malnourished and generally mistreated humans from the lead pair of Storks. Those aircraft were headed toward an abandoned military base that had been temporarily reactivated for the purpose of securely holding all humans on the planet, until they could be delivered to the Thuranin. The first thought of Smythe and Kapoor had been for the Dragon to drop off ground teams in two places that were out the visual range from the base. Smythe and Kapoor would then take their teams overland in mech suits through the thinly-populated region, and infiltrate the base from two points. If it were not possible to infiltrate without being detected, they would conduct an assault. Either way, the ground team would eliminate opposition at the base, which is a polite way of saying they would kill every lizard in the area. The Dragon could provide distant air support if needed, using stand-off weapons from over the horizon. Getting the Dragon involved would be a last-resort measure, we could not afford to lose that spacecraft.

After opposition at the base had been suppressed, the ground team would clean up as best they could in the time available. To explain the carnage and inevitable smoke rising from the base, Skippy would tell the incoming pilots that a Fire Dragon clan security team had put down an attempted treasonous action by former White Wind warriors. It was a plausible story, and Smythe was reasonably confident he could take the base, which reportedly was staffed by only fourteen warriors. What made Smythe anxious about his own plan was the time required, a fire fight could still be going on when the Storks arrived, and no way could we expect those pilots to land in the middle of a shooting gallery.

There were other aspects of that plan I didn't like at all. Extended combat carried significant risk of injury or death on our side, and a fight could get messy. In the base and surrounding town were over fifty buildings the enemy could use for cover, and the last thing we needed was a bloody and time-consuming house to house fight. I also had moral concerns about assaulting the base. Skippy thought there were fourteen warriors equipped with powered armor at the base, but he estimated possibly fifty to sixty other lizards there. Some of them were support personnel, others were civilians who had not left the area after the White Wind military pulled out of the base. Those civilians would be eager to work at the base, satellite images showed a crew of two dozen working to repair a wall at the base. Many of those civilians and support workers would be killed or injured in a firefight, and that thought made me sick. Yes, I had sparked a civil war which had already killed many thousands of lizards. I framed the Bosphuraq and caused thousands of innocent deaths there also. Hell, I had begun my command of the *Flying Dutchman* by asking Skippy to jump fourteen Kristang starships into a gas giant planet, wiping out those crews without warning. Maybe all my actions were justified. 'Maybe' wasn't good enough.

Besides, while Smythe and Kapoor were planning the loud bang-bang stuff, I was mulling over a patented Joe Bishop sneaky way of getting the enemy to do what we wanted. When I explained my idea to Smythe, he was greatly relieved, with an undertone of mild rebuke for not explaining my alternative plan earlier.

Anyway, instead of getting involved in a bloody firefight, we went with the sneaky option. Ninety kilometers from the abandoned base was an abandoned village on the seacoast, with a walled compound that used to be a pleasure resort for local White Wind leaders. There were several landing pads for aircraft, and records showed the underground fuel tanks still were half full, so the Storks could refill their tanks. Speaking as the acting planetary administrator, Skippy ordered the two-ship formation of Storks to divert to the resort, explaining that the former White Wind clan members at the old military base could not be trusted. The pilots did not question their orders or object, for they were Fire Dragon clan and considered the former White Wind clan to be scum.

That left the problem that the lizards at the old military base expected four Storks to fly in, and would raise a ruckus when they were overdue. Our deception worked only because Skippy had total control of communications on and around Rikers. Again acting as the administrator's office, he contacted the lizards at the base and explained that the Storks had been diverted because of an unspecified threat that the grunts on the ground didn't need to know about. They were to remain at the base, continue preparing it to receive the humans at a future date, and blah blah blah. I didn't care what those lizards did, as long as they didn't interfere with us.

Cutting straight south through the forest where the muddy road made a wide bend, Frey and her team raced ahead and were just sliding into position when the truck approached. It was driving at reckless speed, bouncing from ruts to potholes, sliding and skidding in the mud. The unpredictable motion of the vehicle would have made getting an accurate shot difficult, except Grudzien had used a cutting torch and the power of his mech suit to fell a tree across the road. The tree was less than half a meter in diameter, they had needed to avoid it looking like an obvious roadblock, and the truck possibly could have shoved it aside or rolled over it. But that would have risked damaging the vehicle, so they hoped the driver would be sensible.

He was. The truck slid to a halt well back from the felled tree, the driver's head poking out the right side of the bubble-shaped cab.

"Not yet," Frey whispered. The cab's windows were filthy, splattered with mud and fogged on the inside. Another figure was seated in the cab, she could not see more than an outline in the infrared image. "Hold fire." From her team's position, it was a bad angle for taking an accurate shot at the cab. "Come on, *hoser*," she urged in a whisper. "Get out of the truck and move that tree."

Her wish was granted. Some of her wish. From the right side of the cab emerged a Kristang male, in the local equivalent of jean overalls and a blue rain slicker. He jammed a bowl-shaped hat on his head, looked up unhappily at the rain, and shouted at the truck's other occupant. When the other occupant did not move, he slapped the windshield and shook a fist.

"Oh, *damn* it," Frey gasped.

"I have a shot," Grudzien advised.

"Hold fire. Do *not* fire," Frey ordered.

"Ma'am?" Grudzien was surprised.

"That other one is a female."

The truck's passenger was a female Kristang. Smaller in stature and build, she stepped out into the rain, cringing away from the male's shaking fist. She wore a simple and much-patched robe, without a coat to keep away the rain. The female was shivering slightly, from fear of her mate, or the chill of the rainy day or both.

"We are letting the truck go?" Durand whispered from behind a fallen log. She, too, had a shot at both of the lizards.

Katie Frey debated, agonized. The Kristang were the enemy, but the warrior caste were the combatants. The two lizards getting soaked in the rain were civilians, and the female was not an enemy of anyone. They could let the truck pass, and follow it. That would slow their arrival at the hospital, and-

Her decision was made easy, when the enraged male slapped the female and she fell to the ground in a puddle. Frey pulled the trigger before she knew it, sending two rounds to splatter into the male. Both rounds hit center-mass and continued on through into the forest, their explosive tips disabled. "Whoa!" Frey stood up, slinging her rifle. "Hey!" She called to the shocked female as that being cowered in the muddy road.

"Ma'am?" Grudzien rose to his feet, covering the team leader. "What are you doing?"

"Being a decent human being, that's what." Frey explained. Holding up her hands, she walked toward the female, who was crawling backward crablike on her hands and backside. The robe she wore was now caked with mud. The female backed up until she bumped into the truck and couldn't go farther. Frey toggled her external speakers on and confirmed the translator was set to the most common

local dialect of Kristang language. "Hey, it's all right," she said, trusting the translator to make her sound properly lizard-like. Reaching into the truck's cab, she pulled out a pile of warn blankets the male had wrapped around him while driving. "Here, take these." Realizing that kindness to strangers was not a characteristic of the Kristang warrior caste, she flung the blankets at the pathetic figure and pointed back down the road, in the direction the truck had come from. "Go! Get out of here!"

"Ma'am," Grudzien prompted. "She has *seen* us."

"She *sees* three warriors in mech suits."

"None of us are tall enough to be warrior caste lizards," Durand cautioned.

"Look at her. She's terrified. No way is she thinking about our height. If she tells anyone, they won't believe a simple-minded female," Frey explained. "Damn it, sometimes this job requires us to be callous, but not *today*." Despite her words, she knew they were burning daylight and already behind schedule. Perhaps more gently than a true Kristang warrior would have, she kicked the cowering female and shouted at her. "GO!"

The kick might have been necessary, it spurred the lizard woman into action. Scrambling to her feet, she clutched at the blankets and ran, stumbling and slipping. Frey waited until she was back around the bend in the road before ordering the other two out from the surrounding forest, while she contemplated the ramshackle alien truck. While riding a truck was not part of the plan, and not essential, it would conserve vital mech suit power. If everything went according to plan, they would accomplish the mission with plenty of reserve power. Based on her experience, nothing ever went quite according to plan. "Grudzien, move that tree out of the way. Durand," she nudged the dead lizard with a boot. "Toss this trash in the bushes, while I see if I can drive this thing."

It looked like the vehicle was guided by simple hand controls, levers on a steering bar. The left side was the throttle with the brake on the right. Squeezing the throttle gently, the truck whined and lurched forward. "Get in."

"Ma'am," Grudzien peered in the cramped bubble cab. "There is only room in there for two of us."

"Ah. Can you get in the back?"

Grudzien examined the bed of the truck, which was making a low, cooing noise. He went to the back and pulled the flap aside. "Oh, damn," he groaned. "They were hauling the Kristang equivalent of *chickens*." The bird-like animals began loudly squawking as they saw daylight coming into the darkened enclosure. "There must be two dozen of them, in wood crates." Now that he had a better look, they were more the size of turkeys, and covered in rough fur rather than feathers.

"Well," Frey called from the cab. "Toss them out to make room for yourself."

He looked in dismay at the truck bed, which was covered in a slurry of white droppings several inches thick. Stepping up to balance precariously on the end, he knew he couldn't ride without removing the animals.

"Grudzien?" Frey demanded. "*What* is the problem back there?"

"Oh, hell," Grudzien looked at the stinky white muck covering his boots, and picked up a crate of squawking animals. "This really *is* a chickenshit outfit."

CHAPTER THIRTY SIX

While Smythe's team was setting up at the seaside resort, Fabron was planning his own surprise party. Their stealthed dropship touched its skids down barely long enough for the Commandos to rush out the back ramp, then the Dragon dusted off, which was both a problem and a solution. The barren island where Fabron first stepped onto that planet was literally a desert, nothing but sand, flat expanses of crumbling shale and a few low-growing, hardy shrubs. The sand was the issue. Though the Dragon set down on a tilted slab of shale, its jets had scoured grit out of all the crevices, and blasted four distinctive patterns of jetwash into the soft sand beyond. Any pilot coming in to set down would be suspicious of the clean slab of rock, and would recognize the signs of jetwash. The other problem was the deep footprints that Fabron's had team dug into the sand.

So, the Dragon loitered overhead while the ground team hid themselves, then the dropship roared over the island in the same direction as the prevailing winds. Once, twice, three times the Dragon flew over at thirty meters, until the footprints were buried, the jetwash erased, and every crevice and pocket of the shale was filled in with sand. "Scorpion Lead," the pilot called to Fabron on the secure circuit, "concealment successful. We are going up to the balcony to watch the show."

"Ah, you will be in the cheap seats," Fabron replied. "Do not get a nosebleed, *Dragon.*"

We overheard the confirmation that Fabron's team was in position, and I told Skippy to do his thing. The second set of Storks was over the ocean to the west-northwest of Fabron, they would pass by north of him by about forty kilometers. Unless we gave them a very good reason to change course.

"Ok, Joe, the 'Check Engine' light of the lead Stork just lit up. Those pilots will be looking for a place to land, soon."

"I hope so."

"You *hope* so? Why would they not land immediately?"

"Listen, Skippy, not everyone pays attention to warning lights. My Uncle Edgar's truck had a Check Engine light on for, like, forty thousand miles. He stuck a piece of black tape over the light, and only brought it in for service when he needed new tires."

"Your Uncle Edgar is a true knucklehead."

"Yeah, that's what my father says. The other issue is, those pilots know what a piece of crap they are flying. They might think the *sensor* is the thing that's busted, and it's giving them a false warning."

"Argh!" Skippy was frustrated. "Well, damn it, we have to hope there is a *smart* lizard flying that thing."

Unfortunately, the two lizards flying that Stork were not smart. They did not even signal the other aircraft that they had a potential problem. "Ugh!" Skippy was exasperated. "Shouldn't they even tell someone they might have an issue? Don't any of these lizards follow procedure?"

"Maybe they *are* following procedure. The rules are Aviate, Navigate, *then* Communicate. Keep the thing in the air with the greasy side down, then watch where you are flying. Only after you've got that under control do you start worry about talking to the outside."

"*Greasy* side? What?"

"The bottom. The bottom of the aircraft is where all the hydraulic fluids and lubricants and fuel drip out and make it greasy," I explained. "That's the side you want pointed toward the ground, you know?"

"Oh, got it. Hey, you actually did learn something from taking flying lessons. What are we going to do about these idiots? They are not turning toward the island. Damn it! Instead of an idiot light, they need a big fist that comes out of the console and pops them in the face with an alarm that blares 'Hey stupid you have a problem'."

"Like I said, warning lights are easy to ignore. Can you glitch their fuel flow, to get their attention?"

He did that.

It got their attention.

"Whoa!" Skippy chuckled. "That did it. They have declared an emergency and are diverting to the island."

"Showtime," I muttered to myself as I called up sensor feeds from the Commando team, and from the Dragon that was circling the island at twenty-five thousand meters. Commandant Fabron was also getting a feed from the Dragon, from the Skippytel network, and from each one of his team. To provide a grunt's-eye view, the Commandos had scattered a half-dozen insect-sized cameras around the likely landing zone.

The plan we had thrown together was solid, with only a few potential wrinkles. The slab of shale that Fabron's Dragon had used to set down was the most likely place for the pair of Storks to land, but it was not the only possible place to land. Most of the island was covered in sand that blew and drifted with the trade winds. No pilot would choose to set down in sand, the fine grit would obscure visibility during landing and takeoff, and the sand particles could actually get melted inside the hot engine turbines and stick to the fan blades. We were confident the Storks would set down on an area relatively free of sand, and there was only one part of the island large enough to accommodate two Storks.

The problem was, the northwest part of the island had a peninsula sticking out, with a rock ledge just wide enough for a Stork, if the pilots were careful where they placed their skids. My hope was the two aircraft would set down side by side, so the two crew could cooperate in repairs. Since having the Storks neatly parked side by side would wrap things up neatly for us, I feared the Universe would see this part of the operation as a grand opportunity to screw with Joe Bishop again.

And, of course, that is exactly what happened. What we did not know before was that the pilots of the two ships did not like each other, and that the officer in charge of the flight was in the Stork with the false Check Engine light. He did not want the knuckleheads in the other ship to blast his craft with sand while landing, so he directed the other pilots to land away from him.

"Crap. Fabron, we are going to Plan 'B' for Bravo, you copy?"

"I see it. Timing could be tricky."

"You have boots on the ground, it is your call," I assured him.

The first Stork came straight in, swinging around into the wind only at the last moment, and set down in the center of the rock slab. With that Stork occupying the middle of the exposed rock, there was no space for a second ship to land without setting one skid into the soft sand, and no pilot wanted to risk their aircraft tilting over. The second aircraft was then committed to landing on the peninsula, where the rock might or might not be stable enough to hold the weight of a fully-loaded Stork. To test whether the rock might crumble under their ship, the two pilots touched down gingerly, turbines blasting the rock with hot exhaust and whipping up the waves on either side of the narrow spit of land. Gradually, they reduced thrust until the engines were idling, only cutting power completely after a few minutes without the rock slab shifting gave them confidence.

From the cameras and the overhead view provided by the stealthy Dragon, I watched the side door of the first ship open, and the two pilots step out, donning sun goggles and shading their eyes with their four-fingered hands. They wasted no time in ducking under their ship and popping open access hatches, but they couldn't get to the problem component until the turbine on that side cooled down. That was part of our plan, the reason I asked Skippy to glitch the fuel flow was that valve was difficult to access, and impossible to service when the turbine was hot. Making the lizards wait, gave us time to look for the perfect opportunity to strike.

After a minute, the pilots called a guard to help them set up a portable cooling fan, to bring the turbine temperature down faster. We heard the two guards protesting, before the lead pilot snapped at them to stop their nonsense and follow orders. With one guard being assigned to grunt work, the other guard stood in the open doorway to take advantage of the breeze, while he covered the humans in the cabin with his shotgun-like weapon.

That was the moment we had been waiting for, all four lizards were exposed. Except the three on the ground kept ducking around landing struts and walking under the Stork's belly, and generally unintentionally obscuring the sightlines of the Commandos. The asshole in the doorway wasn't standing still either, the sun on his back apparently was baking his skin, so he alternated between standing in the open door and ducking inside.

It was very frustrating.

What made it worse was that the lizards in the second Stork were staying inside the aircraft, where the auxiliary power unit was keeping the cabin nice and cool. That aircraft was flightworthy, or as ready to fly as any poorly-maintained old piece of junk flown by the Kristang could be. After the engines were shut down, the side door opened, and we hoped the lizards would step outside to get fresh air, or inspect the aircraft, or swim in the freakin' ocean or just stare at the water. They didn't do any of that. Instead, they forced their human passengers out into the hot tropical sun.

The first view we had of the kidnapped people was a man and a woman, staring out the doorway, blinking from the sunlight reflecting off the water. The ground-level camera angle was less than optimal, all I could see was brownish skin, dark wavy hair and a beard that was running to salt and pepper. The woman had her head wrapped in a sort of scarf, at a glance I guessed she was Asian, it was hard to tell and didn't matter anyway. The man hesitated a moment, one hand on the woman's shoulder, then he stumbled down to steps like he had been shoved from behind.

No, he had been *kicked*. We got a glimpse of a lizard boot hitting the back of the woman's knee, her legs buckled and she fell awkwardly into the man's arms, except he wasn't able to hold onto her and they both fell hard onto the rock. Rolling to their knees, they both had blood running from cuts on their hands, and the man was bleeding from his forehead.

"Stay frosty," I whispered over the Commando channel, though the words were intended for myself.

More people stumbled or tumbled out the door, adults at first and then children. They were all skinny and sunburned, and their clothing was dirty rags, patched together from previous items. One woman wore a shirt made from what looked like pants legs roughly sewn together with twine or maybe it was spun from some native plant.

Skippy interrupted my thoughts. "Joe, I'm listening to the crew of that Stork. They are throwing all the humans out because the smell in the cabin is awful. The crew intends to lock them outside, until they are ready to take off again."

"There is no fresh water on that island," I gritted my teeth. As I said that, children began to file out the doorway. The first was a girl about ten years old, she might have been older. It was hard to tell, because hunger could have stunted her growth. That girl didn't fall out the door, she was *kicked*, and not gently. The boot must have struck her in the small of her back, she suddenly jerked forward and spilled out onto the rock, her fall only partly broken by an adult catching one arm.

For one brief moment, the girl unknowingly stared directly into a camera. Limp hair hung down over her face, obscuring one eye. The other eye stared, unblinking.

I know that stare.

In the Army, we call that the Thousand-Yard Stare. The phrase originated in World War Two, I think. People get it when they have seen so much horror, they are emotionally detached from life. It is a coping mechanism, dissociating from trauma.

Through the camera, in that split-second, she was looking at me.

She wasn't pleading for help. She was beyond that. Help wasn't coming. She wasn't even enduring, not *living*. She existed, that's all she knew.

No one is supposed to endure that.

Little girls are not supposed to have that stare.

"Fabron," I toggled to the private command channel. "In case you don't know this, the Geneva Convention does not apply out here. I want all those lizards *dead*."

Fabron's reply was simply two clicks of the transmitter. He understood my message and didn't want to break focus to speak with me. I should not have bothered him, he knew the rules of engagement. We were not leaving witnesses behind.

After the last of humans were roughly shoved or kicked out of the cabin, the door closed most of the way, staying open only a crack. Dazed and demoralized, the prisoners shuffled resignedly under the only shade available; the wings of the Stork. Four of them huddled together were blocking the best camera angle, so I switched to the overhead view.

Fabron called me. "Colonel, we can't hit the second aircraft without killing the people outside. My team does not have a shot." Frustration was evident in his voice. "I would appreciate any suggestion you might have."

"Understood. Standby one."

What the hell could we do? The four lizards were relaxing in the cool cabin, maybe taking a freakin' nap. What I wanted to do was knock on the door, claiming I was delivering pizza. Scratching my chin with a thumb, I mulled over an idea that might actually be useful. "Skippy, there are a couple things I have learned about flying."

"Keep the greasy side down?" He guessed.

"That too, but also that you can trade altitude for airspeed, and airspeed for altitude. It's Ok to be flying slow if you have enough airspace under your belly, you can dip the nose down to regain airspeed."

"Mm hmm, that makes sense. Um, why are you telling me this? It is not Trivia Night, Joe."

"I'm telling you, because there is one situation when having plenty of altitude is *not* a good thing."

"When is that?"

"When you're on fire. If you can't eject, you want to set down ASAP."

"Ok. Why do we care about that?"

"Because at *any* altitude, fire in an aircraft is terrifying, Skippy."

"I believe it. Um, again, why are you telling me this?"

"You are still connected to both Storks?"

"Yes. Currently, I am glitching the portable cooling cart, so it will take longer for the pilots of the first aircraft to get access to the turbine."

"Great. I want you to cause a fire in the cabin of the second aircraft."

"Hmm. *Ooh!* I get it. Great idea, Joe. I can't actually cause a fire, but I can short out wiring and fill the cabin with smoke."

"Do it." Activating the transmitter, I called the Commando leader. "Fabron, those lizards will be coming out of the second aircraft soon. Be aware there will be smoke in the cabin."

"Our rifle scopes will not have a problem with smoke," he assured me.

From there, it was all up to Fabron's Commandos. He needed to find a moment in time when his people had clear shots at all eight lizards. I worried that when the lizards ran out of the second aircraft, the humans there would also scatter instinctively to get away when they saw smoke pouring out the door. If they milled around aimlessly, they could block sightlines and screw up the entire operation.

Oh, thank *God*! When the four lizards fumbled down the steps of the second aircraft, gasping and choking from inhaling smoke, the humans ran the other way. We had four lizards on one side of the smoking Stork and the prisoners running and looking for cover on the other side. Though the camera view was intermittently obscured by people running in front of the lens, the Commandos were being fed a synthetic composite view, based on all camera angles.

Now all we needed was for that one asshole to stick his stupid freakin' head out the doorway of the first aircraft.

We waited.

And waited.

And *waited*.

The sun had climbed overhead so it was no longer shining in the doorway of the first Stork, so that asshole *should* have been hanging out, enjoying the breeze. Instead, he was unseen in the cabin, where we had no view of where he was or what he was doing. He could have been camped out on a seat, playing games on his phone, for all we knew.

"Um, hey, Joe," Skippy interrupted my thoughts. "I don't want to make this waiting worse for you, but that lizard who is alone inside the cabin? He was reprimanded three times during the flight, for abusing the prisoners."

"Oh, *hell*."

"He was beating children and taunting the adults, so they would fight back. He wanted an excuse to kill. I hate to think what he is doing in their alone, and the camera in there isn't working. I don't have a view."

"Shit. Can any of Fabron's team get to that door, before the lizard inside could react?"

"No. I don't think so. Joe, that lizard has grenades. He could kill everyone."

"Ok. Ok, we need to get this shit over with, quick." I debated doing the burning wire thing to the first aircraft, but humans might run out first and get in the way. "Uh, we need to get their attention. Can you make more smoke?"

"There aren't many flammable materials inside a Stork. I'm doing the best I can. The fire is almost out already."

Slapping my forehead, I reprimanded myself. We didn't need more smoke. The crew of the first aircraft had not noticed when smoke was pouring from the other ship, the wind was blowing the smoke out to sea. We didn't need to create another incident, all we needed was for the first crew to know about the smoke. The second ship's crew hadn't called for help yet, probably they were hoping the fire-suppression system could deal with the problem without them needing assistance. "Skippy, fake a distress call from the crew of the smoking Stork. General call, make sure everyone receives it."

We saw immediate results. The three lizards working on the first aircraft stood up and looked to the north, finally noticing whispy tendrils of smoke. That still did us no good, until the jackass in the cabin stuck his head out to see what was going on.

"Execute," Fabron ordered.

Around the first aircraft, people in powered armor exploded up from under the layer of sand that had concealed them. Having received targeting data to their visors and rifle scopes while they were still buried in hot sand, they only needed to keep focus as they rose. Rounds were flying out of rifle muzzles before the shooters had risen halfway to their knees. One, two, three, *four* lizards jerked as they were double-tapped, three of them targeted by more than one operator and so took multiple hits to the chest and head. It may have been for insurance, or it may have been for spite, but some of the bodies were rocked by additional bullet impacts as they were falling.

After they fell, none of them moved. The asshole who was in the cabin got knocked backwards by the impacts, bounced off a seat in the cabin and fell to sprawl on the steps, his booted feet still inside the cabin. To minimize the risk of collateral damage, the Commandos had not selected explosive-tipped rounds, so I was a bit surprised to see the back of asshole's head had a big chunk missing, then my attention was taken elsewhere.

There wasn't any thick layer of sand close enough to the second ship, so the Commandos there had to lay flat on the bottom of the ocean just offshore, relying on the chameleonware of their mech suits for concealment. They had moments of anxiety when crab-like creatures crawled on and over them, worried not about being bitten through armored suits, but that a Kristang might have looked down into the water and wondered why a crab was crawling on something invisible. It was fortunate for us that none of the Kristang got out of their air-conditioned ship until they had to, and at that point they were occupied by concern that their crappy ride home might explode.

Fortunate for us, but it sucked for them.

On hearing Fabron's 'Execute' order, the four Commando operators leapt out of the water on powered legs, the bottom of their boots coming clear above the surface. Water fountained outward and cascaded down, sluicing off the hardshell suits and ignored by the operators. They would splash downward in seconds, possibly into awkwardly-placed rocks or deeper pockets in the coral-like ridges that encircled the island. Trusting their suit computers to bring them to a soft landing or at least not get them wedged into a crevice when they fell, the four focused all their attention on their designated targets.

Last to shoot was United States Marine Corps Gunnery Sergeant Greene, his initial targeting needing a fractional adjustment, so a bullet plunging through a lizard body did not continue on to hit a human in the background. Before Greene splashed back down into the water over his head, he saw his target's head jerk backward in a red spray of blood, while his visor confirmed three other kills had been made.

"Cease fire," Fabron ordered in a manner absolutely free of excitement, as he rose free of the sand covering his suit. The task was complete, there was no need for anxiety. "All targets terminated."

Gunnery Sergeant Greene splayed his hands outward to slow his plunge down through the water, assisted by an airbag inflating from his backpack. The suit's computer adjusted the pressure in the airbag so Greene did not pop to the surface like a cork, out of control. It gave him just enough buoyancy to cancel the weight of the hardshell suit, he waited a second for his rifle's sling to retract the weapon over his shoulder out of the way, and began swimming toward shore with smooth, powerful strokes. The suit had automatically engaged its swim-assist mode, having been preprogrammed for that phase of the operation. Near shore, visibility under the surface was poor, the water clouded by churned-up sand and air bubbles from the crashing waves. He had to guess how close he was to touching bottom, until he remembered how to activate the sonar function of the sensors. The Commando team simply hadn't enough time in Kristang armor, and the control menu and functionality was completely different from the skinsuits he was used to.

Digging his boots securely into the sandy bottom, he used his arms for balance until he was splashing ashore, waves washing only up to his waist. To his left, two operators just had the tops of their helmets emerging from beneath the waves.

"Greene," one of the French operators called out. "I joined the army to be a paratrooper, not a fish, Non?"

"Hey Simon, I'm a Marine. Amphibious landings are what we *do*," Greene answered with a laugh more hearty than warranted. It was nervous energy burning off, he knew. He was tempted to strike a pose and announce 'I have returned', but General MacArthur was an Army puke, and Greene was a proud Marine.

As he walked up the steep beach, slipping in the soft sand as his boots sank in halfway to his knees, he was able to see the parked aircraft, and beyond it, humans huddled in groups of two or three. Half of them were fearful, ready to run though not knowing where or why. The others stared numbly at him, having been drained of the ability to feel terror long ago. "Oh, shee-it," Green breathed. "Hey, guys, faceplates open. Let them see we're not lizards."

He went a step further, without orders and against standing protocol in a potential combat situation. His suit had indicated all four lizards were thoroughly *dead*, and his own eyes could confirm that. The only threat in the area was that of frightening one of the humans into jumping into the water, where waves might bash them against the jagged coral. "It's OK, everything is Ok," he called out softly, unsealing his helmet and placing it on the sand. "I'm human, we," he pointed to the other operators, who had their faceplates open, faces exposed to the sunlight. "We're all *human*. We are here to rescue you."

The only reaction was some of the people blinked. Most did not react at all. They were so used to cruel games being played on them, they no longer believed that hope was an option. Greene walked forward slowly, to where a boy of about eight years old was sitting on the sun-baked rock, hugged knees to his chest. He stared up at the mech-suited Marine. "Home," Greene pointed his own chest, then the sky. "We are taking you home."

No reaction.

"Oh, hell," Greene shook his head. "I am a United States Marine. Does anyone here speak English? Or Spanish?" His Spanish was awful. To use the translator, he would have to put the helmet back on. "How about French? Parlay-voo Frahn-say?"

"Marine?" A man croaked with a dry throat, pushing himself up to stand on shaky legs. He spoke with a Texas drawl. "My brother was in the Second Division. He went offworld."

"Camp Lejeune, huh?" Greene knew parts of the Second has deployed with UNEF as an Expeditionary Brigade. Back then, the military had pulled people from whatever units were available and reasonably combat-ready. The thinking had been, get people aboard the space elevator, and figure out unit composition during the flight. Since they didn't know where they were going, who or how they would be fighting, it was good enough. "I have some friends from the Second. What is your brother's name?"

The man acted as if he hadn't heard the question. "You came here from Earth?"

"No. From Paradise." The man just stared at him, and Greene realized the abductees might have been taken from Earth before UNEF landed on Camp Alpha. Before any human heard of the planet called 'Paradise'. "That's the planet we shipped out to. When we get off this rock," he scuffed the surface with a powered boot, sending a shower of dust and rock chips scattering away from him. "We are taking you to Earth. All of you." That was close enough to the truth for that moment.

"Not many of us are left," the man said woodenly. "We prayed you would come. You *didn't*. Not for *so* long."

"We didn't know about you until recently. Listen, we are here now. We have a spacecraft, to take you up to a starship."

"Home?" The boy finally spoke.

Greene kneeled down and bent over so he didn't tower over the boy. "Earth. We are going back to Earth."

The boy looked up at Greene, not blinking even in the brilliant sunlight. "The war is over?"

Cocking his head, the Marine heard the faint rumble of an approaching dropship. "It's over for you. I promise."

With a Stork parked on the only place to land on the peninsula, a dropship couldn't set down there. I thought of having Skippy remotely fly the Stork away and dump it in the water, but a dropship was still too big to land on that narrow ledge of rock anyway. If the Stork lifted off, all the people there would need to be a safe distance away before applying takeoff power, and if they were going to trudge through hot sand, they might as well walk to where Fabron's team was waiting. The Dragon crew rolled canteens of water and food ration bars in blankets, and dropped them as best they could. One roll bounced and fell into the water, I watched as a French soldier waded out to retrieve it. When the water, food and blankets were handed out, it surprised me that the people we rescued didn't fight over the sudden bounty. The adults drank from the canteens first and took tentative bites of the chewy ration bars, which pissed me off until I realized they were testing our gifts for poison. Gunnery Sergeant Greene made a show of gulping water and gnawing off half a ration bar, to assure the abductees they were in no danger. Whatever my very personal misgivings about Lamar Greene being with us, I had to admit he was a stand-up guy.

After the operators tossed the dead lizards into the ocean on the eastern side of the peninsula, where the current could carry the bodies away, they led the still-wary civilians toward Fabron. From the cameras, I could see Green and the others offering to carry the children, so they didn't have to march across the hot sand, but the young people would not go near them. We were running out of time, so when the Commandos stopped to tear strips off the blankets and show the civilians how to wrap them around their bare feet, I was mentally urging them along, and I couldn't complain. If my boots had been on the ground, I would have done the same thing.

That part of the operation was a success. Eight dead lizards, no humans killed or injured, and no alarm signal had gone out. Skippy remotely flew the first Stork to perform circles around the island while the first Dragon landed and began taking people aboard.

"Congratulations to your team, Fabron," I called. "That was *outstanding*."

"Ah, yes. It was. I have a recommendation, if I may?"

Lessons Learned were usually held for the after-action report, but I didn't mind constructive criticism. "Sure, tell me?"

"All future teams should be equipped with an advanced piece of equipment."

"What is that?"

"A beer can."

I laughed. "An asshole beer can?"

"That is the best kind, Non?"

"The *only* kind, I am afraid to say."

"Hey!" Skippy protested.

"Colonel Bishop?" Fabron called me, and this time his voice held none of the anxious tension. This time, he was relieved that the operation had gone successfully. This time, he was *happy*. "I need to know something."

"Shoot. I mean." Damn it, I needed to remember that not everyone understood American slang. "Go ahead, Commandant."

"This operation went outstandingly well, the goods were delivered directly to us, on schedule."

"Uh, yeah. What's your question?"

"Are we supposed to tip the delivery driver?"

"Oh. Ha!" We both laughed. "Yeah, I have a tip for him."

"What is that. Sir?"

"Don't trust your 'Check Engine' light."

CHAPTER THIRTY SEVEN

With Fabron's Commandos having taken care of the Storks assigned to them, I turned my attention back to the other pair of aircraft, which were sixty kilometers from the seaside resort where Smythe and Kapoor were preparing a reception for the lizards.

"Ugh," Skippy sighed. "Joe, one of the lizard pilots is bitching about landing inside the compound. He says there is not enough clearance for a last-minute emergency go-around if necessary, that the landing zone violates safety regulations. He is right about that."

I stared at the display. Since when did Kristang warriors care about safety regs? "Tell him that landing in the compound is an *order*, damn it."

"I already did that, you numbskull. He is demanding to land at an alternate site over the hill inland, it is about twenty kilometers away."

"Shit. Ok, well, tell him we can't assure that alternate LZ is secure, and if he runs into trouble there and loses his passengers, it will be *his* responsibility."

He was silent for a minute, presumably while he pretended to be the voice of the local commander and argued with the troublesome pilot. "That did it, Joe. He insisted if there is a crash while landing in the compound, that *I* take responsibility. Ha! Like that's ever going to happen. The warrior caste never accepts blame when something bad happens."

The Storks continued their descent, with the second aircraft hanging back to give the first plenty of time to set down carefully inside the walled compound. The lead pilot was genuinely reluctant to land in the designated spot, he circled the compound three times, and I was growing worried he might see something that wasn't right. Finally, he skillfully hovered and lowered his aircraft with its tail tucked into a corner, leaving plenty of room for the second Stork.

So the second aircraft didn't have an opportunity to waste time, I asked Skippy to cause a power surge in one engine. Before he could do that, the pilots of that Stork declared they actually were experiencing a problem, and they came right in without any delay. That aircraft set down in a cloud of dust, and once it settled on its landing skids and the turbine began to spool down, control of the operation passed to Smythe on the ground.

Timing was going to be tricky. The first Stork kept its doors closed until the second aircraft's engine had powered down, and then for a decent interval to let the swirling dust in the compound be cleared by the constant breeze coming from the sea. During that time, it was reasonable that Smythe's team be taking cover rather than standing out in the open. After that, the first Stork's door popped open and one of the guards stepped out, squinting in the bright sunlight, looking around for the clan military team that was supposed to there to provide security.

At that point, Smythe could not keep his people concealed any longer, or the lizards aboard the aircraft would get suspicious. "Kapoor, you're up," the STAR team leader said quietly into his helmet microphone.

Major Kapoor and another soldier stepped out on a balcony overlooking the compound's expansive courtyard. Because of the railing and the angle, it could not be seen from the courtyard below that the two mech-suited humans were standing on a platform to make them appear taller. Kapoor cradled the rifle in his right hand and waved with his left, using the Kristang gesture of keeping his palm facing toward himself.

Through the translator, Smythe spoke. "Move the humans into the bunker, quickly. Through the double doors and down the steps. Move! We are covering you, but you are exposed out there."

The situation was odd, and the Kristang might have questioned the order coming from someone they didn't know, but the powered armor was a convincing display. Hardshell armor with faceplates down set to opaque flat black was a sign that trouble could be imminent, and that spurred the aircraft crews into moving. The side doors of both Storks swung open wide and guards stepped out, urging the humans out.

"That's all four guards," Smythe muttered to himself. "Skippy, you have eyes inside both cockpits?"

"Affirmative," the arsehole AI confirmed. "Targeting data has been transferred to sniper teams."

At that moment, four icons on the left side of Smythe's visor lit up green, indicating the four snipers had solid locks on their targets. The four guards out in the open, were not a problem. The four pilots in the cockpits of both aircraft, *were* a problem. He waited a moment while a woman, a human woman, tumbled down the steps of the second Stork and for a moment, one guard was obscured behind a child as he clubbed the woman with the butt of his rifle. Stunned, she lay on the stones of the compound's courtyard, holding up a hand in a futile attempt to ward off her attacker.

The lizard guard took a step forward to kick to woman, and Smythe saw the target was no longer obscured. "Tally-ho," he said in a calm and clear voice.

The four guards jerked as they were stuck by reduced-power explosive-tipped rounds, intended to minimize blood splatter while assuring the targets dropped instantly dead. Those ordinary Kristang rifles fired ordinary ammunition, and the people who operated the rifles were not designated as snipers.

The people tagged as snipers used rifles that were modified only slightly, to fire a special guided round that was longer than standard ammunition. With the four pilots inside the aircraft and the windows tuned to black to keep out the hot sunlight, the snipers could not actually see their designated targets, not even with infrared sensors. Instead, they relied on targeting guidance provided by Skippy, who conveniently had a view by hacking into flight recorder cameras on the rear bulkhead of each cockpit.

To hit those particular targets, each rifle fired a pair of rounds with a single gentle pressure on the trigger. The first round had a shaped-charge tip, designed to burn a hole clear through from the outer skin of the aircraft to the inner liner of the cockpit. Those first rounds flew a subsonic, curving path designed to avoid the tough structural frames of the aircraft, and clear a hole in a thin part of the Stork's skin. The four lead rounds did their jobs flawlessly, and the pilots were stunned by the sudden surge of air pressure as the ammunition punched through the fuselage. Following only twelve meters behind and also moving at subsonic speed, the second round from each rifle flew the same curving path and found a clear hole where tough composite skin used to be. All four rounds struck their targets and mushroomed, the soft noses of the ammunition flattening and pieces spalling off to cause additional damage. Four pilots were hit and four pilots ceased to exist, their bodies torn apart by kinetic energy. Only one fragment went all the way through a pilot and out the other side to splat against a console, where it bounced off to harmlessly rattle to a stop on the floor.

"Four kills," Skippy announced without his usual boastfulness. "No collateral damage in the cockpit. The aircraft are operational."

"Thank you for the assist," Smythe knew that feeding the AI's ego was always a good idea. "Team, move in."

Captain Frey kept driving the truck, through rain that alternated between a steady drizzle to sudden downpours, until they were eight kilometers from the hospital. "Katie," Skippy whispered in her ear while she was trying to maneuver the awkward vehicle across a low spot in the road. The culvert under the road had become clogged with debris, causing the stream to back up and flow half a foot deep across the road. The water itself was not a problem, she was worried the rushing water might have undermined the roadway. When the AI called, she had slowed and was about to send Durand out to test whether the road could hold the truck's weight.

"That is *Captain Frey*, please," she clenched her teeth and let the truck coast to halt, its wheels sticking in the mud. Joking around with Skippy aboard the ship was tolerable, sometimes it could even be fun. And like every one of the Pirates, she didn't really have a choice, Skippy so constantly sought and demanded attention, it was impossible to ignore him.

But inappropriate familiarity during a potential combat situation was unacceptable.

"Sorry," he sounded more hurt than apologetic.

"What is it?" She demanded.

"You had best ditch the truck. There is a cluster of buildings about two kilometers ahead of you. I am not seeing any heat signatures or lights, but sensor coverage of the area is spotty, sorry about that. The road ahead goes through the town before you get to the hospital, it is mostly abandoned, however there have been reports of lizards who refused to go when the area was evacuated. A patrol scouted the town before the hospital was re-opened, they saw signs of recent habitation, nothing to worry about."

"Nothing for *them* to worry about. We can't risk being seen. Do you have sensor coverage inside the hospital?"

"Partially. Again, I am sorry. There just isn't much for me to work with down there, and the satellite network is an obsolete piece of junk. The good news is, I found a route up a back stairway and through a corridor in a section of the hospital building that was condemned. It will bring you within twenty meters of the isolation rooms where the three humans are being kept. You can-"

"Can we go back a bit? What do you mean 'condemned'?"

"That part of the structure is considered unsound. There was an earthquake about- Hmm, maybe the term should be 'groundquake'. Although of course the *ground* was shaking, if the air was shaking you would just call it 'wind'. There should be a word for-"

To her right, Durand was staring at her with increasing alarm at the AI's absent-minded babbling. "Skippy," Frey interrupted. "Get to the point. The building's structure is unsound?"

"Oh, sure. I got distracted. There's a lot going on, as you know. I am currently talking with Smythe, Fabron, Joe, Simms, Chang, and Nagatha, plus I am intercepting all-"

"Talk to *me*."

"Ok! The groundquake cracked that part of the building, and it wasn't repaired. They put up signs and locked some of the doors, after two lizard boys were playing around in there and got injured when part of the ceiling fell on them."

She took a calming breath and nodded to Durand. The nod was intended to mean 'This is nothing unusual'. "How are *we* supposed to use the condemned part of the building?"

"Um, by being careful?"

"Skippy, we are wearing mech suits. They are heavy."

"Ooh. Good point. In that case, you should be *very* careful."

"The bug says it's marginal," Frey whispered instinctively, though sealed up in the powered armor suit, she could have shouted and no one outside would have heard her. The bug she referred to was a scout drone, a bit of Thuranin technology enhanced by Skippy. Guided by her eye movements as tracked by her suit's visor, she had sent the little machine to crawl along the route Skippy had suggested. Immediately after the bug entered the building, she had seen a problem. The ceiling there was collapsed in piles of rubble, because the whole second floor above had fallen in. Twice, she had to direct the bug to backtrack, until it found a route up where they needed to go. The little machine had scanned the floor and found cracks both large and small. She was more concerned about the small cracks that were hard to see. "There are weak spots in the floor we will need to avoid. Coordinates have been sent to your suits."

"Skippy?" Grudzien asked as he crouched in overgrown bushes at the edge of the forest, fifty meters from the back door of the hospital building. The rain had slackened to a fitful drizzle, stirred by gusty winds. Within six minutes, Skippy predicted, another downpour would sweep over the area, providing cover for them to race across the open area between the tree line and the nearest wall of the building. Across that fifty meters was a muddy drainage ditch, a roadway that was cracked with patches of grass seeking sunlight, and then a swath of weeds and neglected shrubs that grew one or two meters high. Their objective was a broken window rather than a door. The door, even if not locked, could make noise when they opened it, and the doorframe might be bent. The window they had selected as their entry point had a bent frame with half the composite 'glass' missing. In their powered armor, it would be easy to bend the frame out of the way and gain entry. That window led to the ground floor that should be relatively stable, even for people in heavy mech suits. To rescue the humans, they had to climb to the third floor, treading along surfaces that the scout drone had scanned and noted weak areas. "Can you program our suits, to walk precisely enough so we avoid stepping on any weak spots?"

"I could do that, but it would be a bad idea. That floor is bound to shift while you're walking, you will need to use your suit sensors in active scan mode to avoid trouble."

That did not sound like a particularly wise idea to Justin Grudzien. "Will an active scan be detected?"

"No," Skippy scoffed. "The electrical equipment in that part of the hospital is so old and worn out, it is generating enough noise that even *I* am having trouble getting an accurate picture of what's in there."

"We go one at a time," Frey declared. "The structure close to the wall we need to breach is stable, we can gather there."

"I will take point," Durand volunteered.

"Negative," Frey did not take her eyes off the building. Something was moving around in the condemned portion, she had a brief moment of alarm before her thermal image resolved the blob into some type of local rodent. The animal scurried along a cable hanging from the broken ceiling, then out of sight. "I want Grudzien up front."

"I weigh less than him," Durand insisted.

Frey hesitated. That was true, although in powered armor, the weight of the soldier inside was not a major difference. The real question was whether she trusted the commando, who she had not served with before.

"She has a point, Ma'am," Grudzien conceded. "If my fat ass falls through the floor, this will be over before it starts."

"All right, Durand. You go first," Frey almost asked if the other woman remembered how to activate her suit's scanner. If needed, Frey could turn on the device remotely.

The heavy rain squall swept in as Skippy predicted, and the three darted in single-file across the gap. Durand reached the broken window first and lifted the frame out of the way for the other two to squeeze through, then she rolled in feet-first. The floor was covered in the clear broken ceramic material that had been the window, and she slipped before someone steadied her by grabbing an ankle.

"Durand," Frey whispered. "Go."

With the synthetic vision of her visor, Camille Durand did not need to turn on her suit's external lights to see ahead of her, and the weak spots found by the scout probe were highlighted. Stepping as gingerly as she could in the hardshell suit, she climbed stairs that were slick with mud, algae and a local type of moss, plus some kind of yellowish goo dripping down from the ceiling. Halfway across the second floor, a crack widened in front of her, and she reached out to hold onto a piece of metal sticking out of a wall as the floor swayed. Her visor was flashing orange lights, then red. "This is not going to work," she advised while inching carefully backward, watching the crack in front of her grow wider.

"Durand," Frey was watching the sensor feed from the other woman's suit. The original weak spots were now joined by a cross-crossing patchwork of lines representing cracks. "Come back down here. Looks like we'll need to go in through the front door."

"Captain Frey?" Grudzien called from the south side of the ground floor. "I might have another way up."

"There is no other way to the third floor," Skippy insisted. "You think I missed-"

"You are not thinking like a monkey," he pointed above him, where the second and third floors were missing, along with part of the building's roof. Rain dripped down on him, repelled by the field covering his faceplate.

"What?" The AI laughed. "You plan to fly?"

"Yes," Grudzien patted the toolbelt on the outside of his suit. "Like Batman."

"Ok," Skippy admitted, when all three had used their nanofiber lines and belt winches to pull themselves silently up to the third floor, where the structure was relatively stable. "That was pretty clever. Sometimes you monkeys can be-"

"What do you see in there?" Frey ignored the AI's need for constant chatter.

"The three human prisoners. Um, they are not in good condition. You should not expect any of them to walk far on their own. They are alone in the isolation room right now. In the sort of open office area beyond that door are two medical personnel, it looks like they are asleep, they haven't moved at all in the past ten minutes. Plus the two security guards I told you about. I am feeding a schematic to you now."

"Security guards are not wearing armor?" Frey asked for confirmation after she glanced at the schematic. She would have preferred to send a sensor bug into the occupied section of the hospital, but Skippy warned the windows and doorways might have scanning devices that could detect drones and she didn't want to risk alerting the lizards that someone was watching them.

"Based on their heat signatures, no. They may be wearing some type of body armor panels, I can't tell. There is a bunch of other equipment in there generating heat, and a lot of electrical interference. Sorry, that's all I can tell you from up here."

"Breaching charges are ready," Durand announced. She and Grudzien had placed a flexible cord in a broad oval on the wall, it adhered in place with microscopic fibers that dug into the wall. The cord would turn into plasma and burn a neat hole through the wall, a microsecond later a shaped charge in the center of the oval would blow the section of wall inward.

"On my mark," Frey held up three fingers of her left hand, right hand cradling her rifle. Both safeties, she confirmed with a downward glance, were off. Ammo selection was for non-explosive rounds, they could not risk hitting the prisoners. For the same reason, they would not be using grenades or rockets. Breach the wall to gain access to the occupied part of the hospital. Eliminate opposition in the immediate area, then Grudzien would cover the stairway and elevators, while the

Canadian and French Army captains secured the three people to be rescued. Retreat would be accomplished by going out the third-story windows and rappelling down lines to the ground, with Grudzien getting to the ground first and providing covering fire for the retreat. Based on sketchy personnel records, Skippy thought there might be four other guards, plus a half-dozen medical staff somewhere around the hospital complex. The primitive and glitch-prone nature of the local sensor infrastructure had the AI frustrated that he couldn't pinpoint the location of every possible hazard.

"Three, two, one," Frey pulled her left hand down to securely grip her rifle, "*mark.*"

There was an intense oval of light as the plasma charge cooked off, followed by a BANG-thump as the charge propelled the wall section inward.

The operation went well immediately, with the wall being flung across the open office. A heavy chunk broke off and cartwheeled over the floor to slam a stunned guard across the open space. The guard's mouth opened wide in shock, arms flung to either side, rifle bouncing on its strap, helmet violently bobbing back and forth. The guard came to a stop sprawled against a closed door, and before he could gather his wits and roll to one knee or unsling his rifle or swing down the protective faceplate of the helmet, Grudzien put two rounds between his eyes. That guard's body was still falling when the Polish soldier raced through the blown-out section of the wall, swinging to the left where Skippy expected there were two doctors or nurses, or however the Kristang designated the people assigned to making sure their human property did not die before they could be sold to the Thuranin.

Within a half meter of the location predicted by the synthetic view projected onto his visor, Grudzien saw two startled and frightened Kristang, lurching back in their chairs and throwing up their hands. He dropped them with two shots each. Maybe they were civilians and maybe they had weapons in the desks where they had been seated, what he did know is they could cause trouble and the rescue team was not leaving witnesses. With that task completed, he planted his left foot on the floor that was coated with dust and pebbles from the concrete-like substance of the wall they had punched through. He had to cover the stairwell to prevent reinforcements from interfering, while the two officers took out the second guard and turned right toward the isolation area. The boot adhered to the floor, power-assisted ankle, knee and hip motors pivoting him toward the open stairwell-

And he was hit by a truck from behind. The force slammed him forward into the wall and he hit hard, his visor's synthetic view and icons going blank. Using training rather than instinct, he hugged the rifle to his chest when his muscles had wanted to fling his arms out wide to ward off the wall.

Bouncing off the wall, he fell backward and was spun around as something struck him behind his right thigh, the leg shooting out from under him and throwing him upside down to crash down on top of his helmet. That time one hand had the rifle torn away, and the weight of the weapon wrenched at his shoulder with sharp pain. Without him needing to think or act, the hand that still had a death grip on the rifle pulled it back toward his torso, the suit's computer anticipating his need before his own muscles could react. That was great except the suit's shoulder joint pivoted while his actual meat shoulder wasn't ready, and the motion ripped tendons.

Grudzien did not think about the pain or wonder what had happened, he did not think at all. He *acted*. There was a threat behind him and with no information being displayed by his dead visor, he had no idea what had hit him or whether the two officers were still alive. With the helmet on, he could hear muffled gunfire and through the clear visor he could see debris and possible ricochets flying all around.

Need to move *now*, his instinct told him. The rifle was still effective and held plenty of rounds. Still on his back, he spun-

No. He didn't spin at all, he awkwardly flopped to his right. Suit power was out and he had to move the heavy suit of armor with his own muscles. Kicking his feet against the wall got him rolled over onto one knee, the disabled suit working against rather than with him. Just moving his neck to tilt his head up was a strain, the helmet was heavy. Lifting the rifle without power assist was also-

"Grudzien!" Captain Frey was shouting at him, her rifle barrel smoking as it pointed to-

The shattered armor of a mech-suited enemy soldier. The lizard's chest was torn open, sticky red blood splattered everywhere. In a flash, he knew what had happened, all of it. One of the heat sources Skippy had noted was not any type of medical equipment, it had been the radiator of a mech suit. From the warrior's position slumped against the wall, the lizard must have been resting or asleep when the wall was breached. Grudzien had not seen him on the other side of a partition, because he had been looking to the left.

That asshole had shot him in the back. It explained why his suit had lost power, most of the powercells were clustered there along with the main power distribution node.

"Blah! Blah Blah!" Frey was saying, her own face unseen behind her opaque visor. He tapped the side of his helmet with a finger, indicating that he couldn't hear. With a thumb and forefinger, he got the faceplate unsealed and cracked it open only a few inches. Though no one was shooting at the moment, he didn't want his face unprotected.

"Can you move?" Frey asked.

"Suit is dead." He tried to shake his head but the helmet only wobbled. "Help me up, I can still cover the stairway."

Frey's response was to flick a selector switch with a pinky finger and launch a grenade from the tube under her rifle's barrel. The weapon hit the sloped ceiling of the stairwell, glanced off and fell to the right before exploding in antipersonnel mode. "That will discourage any sightseers. Give me your hand."

"Ma'am, I can-"

"*Hand*, Sergeant," she demanded. Just then, the mech suit she had blown open lurched on its own in a shower of sparks. She yelped and turned in the blink of an eye, sending two more rounds into the torn-open cavity. Blood and gore fountained as the rounds hit the back interior of the suit and rocketed back and forth inside until their momentum was spent. "Shit!" She took a step back, suppressing a shudder. Too much adrenaline, she had overreacted to the enemy suit suffering a power surge as it failed.

"Better safe than sorry," Grudzien noted while he held up his free hand.

She took a firm grip on his hand and tugged gently at first. "Those damned suits can move on their own when the occupant is dead." The Sergeant was not rising to his feet. "Can you-"

"I think the right leg is locked up," he explained, gritting his teeth while he tried to straighten that limb. The hardshell armor there was not cooperating.

"Hold on, I'll drag you."

Grudzien kept an eye on the smoke-filled stairway while the officer dragged him to screech across the debris-strewn floor, the heavy suit protesting. He passed through the now-open doorway to the isolation room, his legs banging against the door frame. Frey rolled him onto his back. "Best to get out of that suit," she advised.

With effort, he lifted his rifle, the dim indicator light still showing green. "I can cover-"

"I need you *mobile*, Sergeant," Frey wasn't going to waste time arguing. "Ditch that suit, now."

Cradling the rifle in his lap, he reached up to remove the helmet first. Right then, for the first time since he had been shot, it occurred to him that he was lucky to be alive. He had been shot at close range, the parachute pack he wore over his suit must have absorbed-

The parachute pack. That was Plan A for him getting off the planet.

He did not like the thought of Plan B.

Katie Frey had already turned her attention to the immediate problem. During Frey's very short and violent fight with the mech-suited soldier, Durand had pursued the second guard who was running toward the isolation room.

The guard was down and Durand uninjured, that was all Frey knew, she had been too busy engaging the enemy soldier and assisting Grudzien. Information was available on her visor, it was faster to see for herself. Even before she released the sergeant's hand, she had swept her vision left to right across the isolation room. There was Durand, her rifle pointed toward the ceiling with her right arm, while her left hand was held out toward a man crouched in the corner, two children behind him. On the floor between Durand and the man sprawled the body of the alien guard, a hole in the back of his head and probably a bigger hole in front, based on the blood splatter on the floor, wall and on the man huddled in the corner. Shit, Frey bit her tongue. These people are already traumatized, and their first encounter with us is to see a lizard's brains blown all over the room. They should-

She saw it. When the lizard guard fell, he must have lost his pistol, and that weapon was now in the man's left hand, shaking as it pointed toward Durand.

Something else. Not two inches from the man's head there was a hole in the wall. A small hole, too small to be caused by rifle ammunition. The guard must have gotten off a shot at the people in the isolation room, before Durand dropped him. Good riddance. Except now they had another problem.

With a dull *Whomp-hiss* sound coming from outside, her attention was drawn to yet *another* problem, when a flare shot up from the hospital grounds and exploded just below the rain-soaked low cloud layer. She cringed instinctively, automatically training her rifle at the brightly pulsing light. Two more flares surged up from behind a wing of the hospital.

Durand looked at Frey. "The lizards know their comms have been hacked."

Great, Frey bit back a curse word. Focus, Katie, she told herself. Focus. Tearing her eyes away from the hypnotic effect of the slowly falling flares, she looked at the man. Skippy had identified him as Lee Ching, a Chinese national. "Mister Lee," Katie took the risk of slinging her rifle and making her faceplate go clear. "We came from Earth," she told the man softly. "We are here to rescue you. To bring you *home*."

The man looked at her, back to Durand, then her again. He shook his head. Lank, stringy dark hair fell in front of his eyes, and a patchy beard covered his face. The children behind him did not speak, or cry or whimper, they did not make any sound at all. Simply stared with unfocused eyes. Eyes that had seen too much in their short lives.

"Skippy?" Frey whispered. "Does he understand me?"

"He should. Your translator is set to Cantonese. Try again."

"Do you understand? We must leave here, quickly. Can you walk?"

"You will bring us home? To Earth?" He spoke broken English with an accent she couldn't identify, his eyes suspicious.

"I am Captain Katie Frey of the Canadian Army," she said slowly, trying to establish a rapport, aware they were running out of time. "Sir, we need to get moving."

Lee blinked for the first time. "We walk out of here?"

"No," Katie wasn't going to lie. "We *run*."

"I cannot run," he shook his head. The pistol lowered, until it was resting beside him on the floor, still in his hand. "The children. Take them with you. I am too ill to travel," he said.

Durand spoke to Frey on the private channel. "We need to get moving, *now*."

Before Katie could reply, Skippy added "That is correct. I count five soldiers in powered armor, coming out of a building they must have been using as a barracks. You need to move immediately."

"Ma'am?" Grudzien got her attention. "I can't run either. Think my right knee is sprained. I'm bleeding from my back somewhere too."

Frey turned around to see the sergeant mostly out of his armor, the hardshell pieces scattered around him. Shit! They didn't need any more problems right then. Kneeling beside him, she saw the back of his shirt was peppered with burn marks and blotches of blood. At least one bullet fragment must have punched through the armor, and the powerpacks had scorched him when they shorted out. The blood wasn't bad, it wasn't soaking his shirt. "I can carry you," she decided.

"Ma'am," Grudzien grabbed her arm as she turned away. "Those people can't walk. You can't carry them *and* me. My chute is gone also."

She stared at him. "*Shit!*" Stupid, Katie, *stupid*, she reprimanded herself. She should have known that. Two parachute balloons for five people. They couldn't all get off the ground. With the thick jungle cover all around, the only place for a dropship to land was the hospital or the abandoned town, and that was not an option. The retrieval plan called for each soldier to carry a rescued person, and be pulled up by balloon, to where a dropship could hook onto them. With only two parachutes, they needed another plan.

"Leave me here," Grudzien volunteered. "Take that guy and the children."

"I'm not *leaving* you," Frey said harshly. "We are not leaving anyone."

"Take them," Grudzien insisted. "I'll hold down the fort until you can come back for me."

"That is not a solu-"

"You cannot bring us all with you?" The man asked. He leaned forward to make room for the children to crawl out from behind him. A boy and a girl, gaunt, dark circles under their unblinking eyes. "Go, children," he urged them gently. "Go with them, with these nice people." They moved robotically, eyes swinging slowly from the man to the mech-suited soldiers. The point was, they moved. Slowly, too slowly, they crawled out from behind the man.

Durand slung her rifle and knelt down, holding her hands out to the children. "I can carry these two," she told Frey. "Come here." The girl and boy stared at her, halting just beyond her reach.

"You go," the man made a weary waving motion. "Leave *me* here."

That set Frey's teeth on edge. "We are not *leaving* any-"

"You cannot bring everyone. This soldier here," Lee pointed to Grudzien, "is young and healthy. He should live. My wife, my son, my daughter are all gone. I could not save them. These little ones," he smiled, a sad twitch that faded, leaving his face more careworn than before. "Are all I have left. Take care of them for me."

Make a decision, Frey, she told herself. Make it quick. It's math, simple math. Someone has to stay behind. Grudzien had the best chance of surviving until she could come back, but what chance was that? Realistically? She would be dooming the sergeant if she-

"I will join my family now," Lee's face suddenly took on a peaceful aspect as he raised the pistol to his temple. "Thank you."

"*No!*" Frey lunged as the pistol cracked. Her momentum carried her forward onto her hands, which slipped only slightly in the fresh blood on the tile floor.

"*Gowno,*" Grudzien swore in Polish, while Durand gasped as she reached forward to shield the children from the horror.

The children did not react at all, except the boy looked at the corpse, back at Durand, and slowly blinked once. Camille Durand's hands shook despite the automatic stabilizers built into the gloves. What horrors had these children seen, that a man they knew killing himself in front of them had no effect?

Frey stayed on hands and knees for a long second, stunned. She was supposed to rescue three sick and abused people. One of them was now dead. One of her team was injured and unable to walk. It was her responsibility.

"Captain," Skippy urged. "I don't want to seem callous, but you need to move now. *Now!* The enemy will be at your location within a minute. I am scrambling their communications, but I can't stop them."

"We go," Frey stood up stiffly. "Grudzien, I'll carry you, leave a grenade to blow up your suit. *No* arguments. Durand, you go first."

CHAPTER THIRTY EIGHT

From orbit, I was trying to monitor three ongoing operations at the same time. Smythe's team had secured their two Storks at the seaside resort. Fabron's team was loading the former prisoners aboard a Dragon on the island, they should soon be lifting off for orbit. The tender services of Mad Doctor Skippy's scary medical bots would have to wait until the people were aboard the *Flying Dutchman*, there was still a long ascent through the atmosphere, a flight out to the rendezvous coordinates, and a tense wait for the other dropships to get into position before the *Dutchman* could jump in. A whole lot of things could still go wrong before our pirate star carrier jumped away to safety. Plus, Smythe now needed to fly the pair of Storks out to Objective Dixie, to rescue the prisoners there.

Speaking of things going wrong, my attention shifted to Captain Frey's team. "Skippy, what the hell is going on down there?"

"Katie is-"

"I know what she is doing. What the hell are *you* doing?" I demanded, jabbing a finger at the display, which showed multiple hostiles approaching the hospital from the old military base that lay to the north. "How are those lizards reacting so quickly? You are supposed to be jamming their communications!"

"I *am* jamming their comms," he insisted with a tone that was defensive instead of snarky. "I sent an order that directed troops at the hospital to patrol to the north, and three soldiers did get into a recon vehicle and drive away. I can't stop a simple *flare*, Joe. When those flares were seen from the base, they knew there was trouble, and they knew they couldn't trust their comms. The Kristang have procedures to follow when they suspect their communications have been compromised. The soldiers at that base are not going to trust anything I tell them now."

"Damn it!" Sometimes I forget that, while the Merry Band of Pirates was an elite force, the enemy also was a professional military organization, and they had been fighting this war for a very long time. Hacking the enemy's communication systems was a great advantage, *until* they realized someone was screwing with them. "Contact Frey and get her out of there, *now*."

"Already did that, Joe. Her team is climbing down the outside of the hospital."

"Can you slow down the enemy?"

"From up here? I can mess with their targeting sensors a bit, that's all. Kristang gear is simple and rugged, their powered armor is difficult to hack into, unless I am close enough for direct action. Joe, her team has a decent head start."

There wasn't anything I could do to help Frey's team. The dropship I was flying was not equipped with hooks to pick up balloon tethers, and in the dense jungle, there was no place for a dropship to set down. They would have to hold off the enemy until one of the Dragons assigned to Smythe was available to pick them up.

Crap. When plans went wrong, why couldn't they go wrong in a way we were equipped to deal with?

"Uh oh, Joe," Skippy whispered. "You know the mechanical problem you asked me to fake with that second Stork, before it landed at the resort?"

"Yeah, why?" Those Storks were supposed to carry Smythe's team out to Objective Dixie, that's why we hadn't used fragmentation rounds to take out the pilots. We needed those aircraft intact. Smythe had his people patching the holes, with a sketchy-looking glue that Skippy assured us would hold just fine. Of course, Skippy would not be flying aboard the glued-together aircraft, so I was less than fully confident.

"That second Stork really *does* have a major potential problem, one of the turbine rotors has a crack. Pilots have noted intermittent vibrations and overheating on their squawk list for two months, but it hasn't been fixed."

"The vibration is only intermittent?" I asked hopefully. "Why hasn't it been fixed?"

"It hasn't been fixed, because the repair crews only spun up the turbines on the ground, and they didn't experience a problem. *That* is because the rotor mostly vibrates when the engines are transitioning from horizontal to vertical flight, or the other way. Joe, when that Stork came in, the rotor was shaking badly. That's why the pilots brought it straight in, rather than flying the approved approach pattern."

"Well, shit. We only need it to make a one-way trip to that island."

"*I* wouldn't trust it not to splash into the ocean," he warned. "Remember, Joe, safety first."

"Oh hell, Skippy. We're the Merry Band of Pirates. Safety is, like, *fourth* on the list. Are there any spare parts available?"

"There is a hangar queen at the military base." He meant an aircraft that is stripped for parts to keep other aircraft flying. "But, to pull a turbine off the hangar queen, and install it on the Stork with the busted rotor, would take all day. I would have to talk Smythe's team through the whole process. Not all the tools are available, we would have to jury-rig some of the tools. Plus there is the problem of lizards at that base. They aren't going to let Smythe's team fly in and take whatever they want."

"We don't *have* all day. We don't even have the rest of today. Crap! Seriously, you don't think that ship can make it to the Objective Dixie island?"

"Frankly, no. Part of the problem is that, because you monkeys killed the pilots, they weren't able to initiate the proper shut-down procedure for the turbine. That rotor is supposed to be cooled down gradually. Instead, it got cooked. Dude, you should not trust a single monkey's life to that thing."

That was a show-stopper. Even our aggressive and daring STAR team commander didn't want to trust any of his people to a bird with a busted wing, and going in with only one ship made taking out all the lizard guards at Dixie a risky proposition. Fabron suggested flying one of the Storks he had captured to the mainland for refueling, because it didn't have enough fuel to fly all the way from the island to Dixie. Both Smythe and I rejected that idea, we simply didn't have time to wait until one of Fabron's aircraft got to the resort.

We were stuck, until Simms came to the rescue with an idea so obvious, none of us near the planet had considered it.

Because Skippy could fly a Stork remotely, we didn't need to risk anyone's life in the cockpit. Smythe's team located old fuel pods in a building at the resort, some of them had holes or were corroded from age, but four were serviceable. It would have been great to attach the fuel pods to a dropship, but the brackets were different and we didn't have time to screw around trying to get the brackets to work. So, Skippy quickly talked Smythe's people through the process of hanging four fuel pods under the wings of the busted Stork, and they filled the pods. With the STARs taking cover in case the fuel-laden Stork crashed and burned, Skippy got it in the air and headed back toward the ocean.

The whole point of turning the wonky Stork into a flying gas station was to rendezvous with one of the Storks that Fabron had captured. A dropship copilot volunteered to fly that Stork, which did *not* actually have its Check Engine light on, to an island in the middle of nowhere so it could be refueled, and some of Smythe's people could transfer to the other ship.

"Uh oh, Joe," Skippy said as he guided the flying gas station in its descent toward the remote island. "The vibration is getting really bad. I don't think I can transition to vertical flight without tearing apart the turbine."

"Shit." None of the islands in the area had runways, the Stork *had* to land like a helicopter.

Or did it?

"Skippy, show me a close-up of that island." He did. It was small, mostly covered in palm trees and shrub brush, and the shore was rock with half-moon-shaped beaches scattered here and there. One of the beaches had a gentle slope, and it was in the lee of the island, with the water there showing only ripples and low, flat ocean swells. "Can you bring it in on its belly? Splash-land in the water and get it up onto the beach?"

"Whoo-hoo," he groaned. "That would be *tough*, Joe."

"Hey, shithead. You are always talking about how crappy my flying skills are. Let's see *you* do something impressive."

"I'm working with a one-second time lag here, knucklehead. By the time I get data from the cockpit and make an adjustment, the situation will have changed."

"Yeah, well, then you will just have to be extra awesome."

"I *hate* you, Joe."

"If you can't do it-"

"I didn't say I couldn't do it. Prepare to be amazed. Unless this crazy scheme fails due to no fault of my own, in which case, prepare to accept the blame."

He was right, it was a tricky maneuver. The Stork came in low and slow, just above stall speed. It hit the water closer to the beach than I would have aimed for, too late for me to say anything. The aircraft's nose dug into a swell and a huge fan of water splashed up, tearing one fuel pod off its bracket. Unbalanced, the Stork careened up the beach, slewing sideways and coming to a stop when one wing hit a palm tree.

"Ta-DA!" Skippy crowed. "In your *face*, Joe."

"You lost a fuel tank," I noted, as I watched the ruptured pod bobbing in the surf.

"We didn't need all those tanks. You're just jealous because you couldn't have done that."

"You are correct about all of that."

"What?"

"We don't need all four tanks, I could not have landed that Stork on the beach, and I am jealous of your mad skills, Dude."

"Oh. Um, hmm." He was so instinctively arrogant, he didn't know how to handle it when someone else was being humble. "Thank you?"

"Thank *you*." Only a couple of the tank's internal bladders could have been breached, as not much fuel was leaking out. Thick globs of the fuel were rolling in the waves, sinking slowly. Those tar-like globs were going to cause a chemical mess on the ocean floor and I did feel bad about that. Maybe Smythe's team could have brought the lost pod onto the beach and unloaded the rest of the fuel, if we had time and if we needed it. We didn't have time and there was plenty of fuel in the other three pods. "Smythe," I called the STAR team leader. "It's your show now."

"Captain Frey," Skippy called. "I do not wish to alarm you, but the three enemy soldiers to your southeast are now advancing on your position."

"I see it," she replied curtly. The data referred to by the AI was available in her visor. They were running out of options. They were running out of *running*, the places they could go shrinking with every forward stride. Forward was the only place they *could* go. To the west was the ocean that stretched for thousands of kilometers. North was the hospital they had fled from, with eight enemy soldiers following and cutting off any possibility of retreat. East was a jungle swamp, deep water and mud that was over five kilometers wide.

The original plan had been to go northeast after leaving the hospital, moving along what had been a road when the area was prosperous. Skippy's false orders were supposed to have diverted most of the soldiers away from the base, and a recon vehicle did drive away, but it only carried three lizards. Though Skippy was jamming their communications, that recon truck had been recalled by flares that could not be interfered with. The enemy was smart. They knew options were limited for the force they were pursuing. The recon truck had raced away in a curve to the east, following roads around the great swamp, and now those three mech-suited soldiers were advancing through the thick jungle ahead of her. They were trapped, with the enemy closing in from two sides, and no way to go east or west. She called a halt, and knelt down on one knee so Grudzien could get a break from being bounced around as she ran. The suit had helped cushion the shock on Grudzien and the two children carried by Durand, with sensors scanning the ground in front and adjusting footfalls to minimize stumbling in the cluttered jungle floor. Frey had set her suit on semi-automatic mode, providing guidance but allowing the suit's computer to pick its way through the jungle. At first, Durand had hesitated to surrender control to her own suit, having experienced uneven results with semi-automatic operation of Ruhar skinsuits. Seeing she was falling behind and how badly the children were being jostled, she had reluctantly tried letting the hardshell armor handle the running, and was pleasantly surprised at the result.

Setting the suits on semi-auto had provided just enough of an advantage to keep ahead of the soldiers tracking them. Or so it had seemed at first. Now Frey knew the pursuers had not been in a hurry because they were waiting until the recon team was in position ahead. Immediately after the recon team got out of their vehicle and sent a flare high into the sky, the soldiers behind the group of humans had increased their pace. Both groups of soldiers had regularly sent up small flares, of various colors to signal- what? Their location? The location of their quarry? It didn't matter.

"Can we get a balloon up through this tree cover?" Durand peered upward.

Frey shook her head, exaggerating the motion so it could be understood. "The tree canopy isn't the problem," she patted her belt, where a set of explosive charges were attached. They could use the explosives to fell two or three trees, creating a clearing large enough to launch their balloons one at a time. Trees were not the problem. The closeness of the enemy was preventing a Dragon from coming in to pick them up. Even with stealth engaged, dropships made a lot of noise and created a turbulent wake as they flew through an atmosphere. Assuming the enemy was equipped with portable anti-aircraft missiles, a Dragon had at best a fifty-fifty chance of survival while flying low and slow enough to hook the balloon tethers. "We need to create separation. Bishop is not sending in a Dragon unless we can get more space between us and the enemy."

"What are we going to do, then?"

Grudzien grunted. "Leave me here as a decoy. I'll make noise to draw them away while-"

"For the last time," Frey snapped. "I don't want to hear any more of that hero shit. We are *all* getting out of here."

"How?" Durand asked.

"I don't know," Frey admitted. "Time to call in the cavalry. Colonel Bishop?"

"Frey?" I replied anxiously. There was no need to ask for a Sitrep, I had feeds from the suits of her and Durand. They were in trouble and I knew it. So did they. While they ran, I had considered our options. If we didn't have to worry about a Thuranin ship lurking over our heads, I might have used a missile to blast a landing zone in the jungle, so a Dragon could race in and pick up the team. Other missiles or maser cannons could have taken out the enemy soldiers, providing a safe air corridor for the Dragon.

Unfortunately, we mostly likely did have a Thuranin ship in the area, and we couldn't do anything to attract the attention of those little green cyborgs.

"Sir, I'd appreciate one of your crazy ideas right now."

As Skippy had observed, many of my best ideas involved using deception to get the enemy to do what we wanted. That wasn't going to work to get Frey's team out of the jungle, the Kristang knew someone was screwing with their comms and would not listen to whatever line of bullshit Skippy gave them. We were damned lucky that military base had been abandoned for a long time, so the lizards there didn't have any pop-up communications rockets. If they had been equipped with that gear, they could have sent a simple solid-propulsion rocket high in the sky, to transmit a signal by line-of-sight using masers that not even Skippy could screw with. The effort to provide medical treatment to the three sick humans at the hospital had been a shoestring operation, done quick and dirty, and that was why Frey's team was still alive. "Stand by, Frey." I took a breath and called Smythe. He was in a Stork flying toward Objective Dixie and couldn't do anything to assist Frey. What I needed was his advice.

Of course, he had been monitoring Frey's situation on the command channel. "Colonel," he said quietly after I explained what I was struggling with. "I can't recommend sending in a Dragon until enemy air defenses have been confirmed suppressed."

Of the two Dragons that extracted the kidnapped people from the seaside resort, most had been crammed into one ship, with the other Dragon having only twelve kidnap victims and three soldiers aboard. Plus two pilots, of course. The Dragon with the fewest people aboard was tasked with picking up Frey's team, and was slowly flying circles eighty kilometers south of her position, while the overloaded ship was climbing out of the atmosphere.

Should I risk a Dragon with seventeen souls, to pick up five on the ground?

Normally, we would rely on stand-off weapons in a SEAD role, that is the acronym for Suppression of Enemy Air Defenses. In the situation on Rikers, we could not cause a large explosion without notifying the Thuranin that something was very wrong on the planet.

"What can you recommend?" I asked, knowing I just wanted to delay making a decision.

"That whatever you decide, do it quickly. Sir. Captain Frey is running out of time."

You might think Smythe was being harsh with me, bordering on disrespect. That wasn't true. He was being blunt because he *did* respect me. "Understood, Smythe. I'll give you as much time as I can." Smashing a button with a thumb, I ended the call abruptly.

Seventeen lives against five. Seventeen lives aboard the Dragon, versus five on the ground. Seventeen minus five equals twelve more lives that could be saved.

If we couldn't pull Frey's team out of the jungle, we had to assure they would not be captured and interrogated, or our secret would be exposed. Our cover story explained why human troops were on Rikers. Still, we could not risk *any* of our people being taken alive. They all knew that.

Frey and her team knew that.

More than once, I had been ready to sacrifice myself for the mission. That had been difficult, I still had occasional nightmares about falling into a gas giant planet or drowning in a sunken dropship.

I had offered to give my life for the team, for the good of humanity.

Could I sacrifice the lives of *others*, for the good of humanity?

I knew what to do.

The only thing I *could* do.

"Skippy, prep one of that Dragon's missiles. I'll," my throat tightened. "I'll give launch authority to the pilots."

Katie Frey's breathing was ragged, though her powered armor suit was doing most of the work for her. What made her breathless and sent her heart rate soaring was not just exertion, but fear. She had bolted off through the jungle as soon as Bishop spoke to her, screaming for Durand to follow. On her back, Grudzien grunted and gasped and hung on as he was jostled and battered by her headlong run through the jungle. She knew that all he could do was hang on, try not to interfere with her, and try not to bash his skull into her helmet. Her visor showed that Durand was twenty meters behind, the French soldier's progress slowed by having to carry two people. The near-catatonic state of the children was both a concern and a help; they did not object or even seem to notice being strapped to a power armor suit and being roughly bounced around in a race through the jungle.

It *was* a race. Frey wasn't only running for her life, she was running to save four other lives. A missile was coming, Bishop had been decent enough to warn her and so they were doing the only thing they could do; run.

A missile threat warning popped up in her visor, showing an icon of a rapidly approaching weapon, coming right behind her. With her heart in her throat, she leapt over a log, slipped in mud, pushed off a tree and kept running.

Missile warning red, the visor flashed across her vision.

She could hear it now, having set her acoustic sensors to seek a particular sound. The whine of a miniature turbine engine, operating at subsonic speed. It was high-pitched and faint, the sound muffled by baffles and sound-cancelling waves projected from the missile's nosecone. If she had not known what to listen for, she might not have heard it until it was too late.

It *was* too late.

The whining sound grew louder, wavering as the missile dodged trees on its deadly flight.

Missile strike imminent, the visor flashed.

"Durand!" Frey shouted as she dropped to her knees and flattened to the ground as best she could. "Down! Now!"

The missile knew exactly what to do and where to go, having its flight course programmed by Skippy. From accessing data from the two mech suits he knew every feature of the jungle; every tree, every hanging vine, every splash of tall ferns across the flight path . Dropping out of the Dragon, the missile had not engaged its motor, relying instead on deploying its wings to glide stealthily toward its target. As its belly was skimming the treetops, the wings folded and it dropped through the canopy, battering its way down through leaves and branches until it was six meters from the ground, where its wings shot out halfway and the air-breathing turbine motor quietly came to life. It took only a microsecond for the missile to determine where it was, comparing the terrain map in its databanks to the jungle around it.

The missile then knew exactly where it was and its gruesome purpose. Guidance was almost not necessary. It could follow the track of slightly warmer air from the radiators of two mech suits. It could rely on the soil compressed by footsteps of those heavy suits. It could also simply follow the scent trail left by one unsuited adult and two young humans, though that was less reliable in the breeze wafting through the jungle.

Racing ahead, its speed confined to two hundred kilometers per hour by the need to weave around obstacles, the weapon flew onward relentlessly, unseen and unstoppable

Then its passive motion sensors detected two objects ahead. Kristang powered armor, running in semi-automatic mode. It accelerated.

Frey hugged the ground as the whine grew loud enough she could have heard it with her own ears. Closing her eyes tightly, she clenched her teeth. *Damn you Bishop*, she thought. You should have thought of a way to-

The missile came in low, and flashed by only three meters above the figures gripping the jungle floor. Turning on its active sensors, it confirmed what the motion sensors had spotted. Four, three, two, one-

The nose cone split open, releasing seeker warheads that shot out in a fan shape, engaging individual targets. Targets that were now alerted to the danger and turning, not that the action would save them. Detonating within milliseconds of each other, the warheads sent cones of deadly razor-sharp antipersonnel shrapnel at their targets. The enemy wore armor and that delayed their deaths by perhaps a nanosecond, before the shrapnel sliced into the armor. The armor cracked under the multiple strikes, some of the shards turning into plasma and burning through gaps in the hardshell.

Its payload spent, the missile glided onward, slowing and turning to the east. Now in no rush, it flew at minimum speed, letting incoming air cool the turbine. Its last task was to fly out over the swamp and splash down in a deep pool, there to sink with all its evidence.

"Frey? Durand?" I called. "Grudzien?" The feed from the two mech suits showed the occupants were alive and unharmed, though their breathing was shallow and heart rates high. "You guys Ok?" I always felt odd referring to women as 'guys', but there was not a good unisex word, and 'gals' was not really an option.

"Sir," Frey's voice was shaky. "I wish you had thought of an easier way."

"That *was* the easy way," I giggled, my own adrenaline rush wearing off. They had needed to put distance between themselves and one of the groups of Kristang, that meant running *toward* the other group even though that seemed crazy at the time. "A big explosion might have been seen by the Thuranin. We needed a stealthy attack under the tree canopy. How are your passengers?"

"Passengers?"

"The people you are carrying," I explained.

"Oh. They're fine. As can be."

"Outstanding. Ok, Frey. Time for you to play Paul Bunyan and knock down some trees, to make a hole for your balloons."

"Paul Bunyan was American, eh?" She objected.

"I thought he was French-Canadian, but, whatever. Get moving, that other enemy team is closing on your position. The Dragon will only have a safe-fly corridor for eight minutes."

Durand and her two young passengers were first to rise from the jungle floor, being gently tugged skyward by the nanofiber tether while the third tree was still sagging over. Katie Frey waited for the other woman's feet to clear the surrounding treetops, then activated her own balloon. Out the top of the pack shot a dart, pulling a hair-thin line behind it. There was brief moment of panic when branches snapped off the falling tree and nearly tangled the line, but it twisted out of the way and tugged the tightly-packed balloon with it.

"You sure this can carry both of us?" Grudzien asked, his question prompted by nervous energy rather than fear. He knew that in a pinch, a single balloon could pull aloft two mech-suited figures, though it was best to ditch all their other gear. He still had his rifle and Captain Frey's was securely attached to her suit. They were as ready as they could be.

"Don't sweat it, Grudz," she replied without taking her eyes off the expanding balloon. "Frey Airlines has never lost a passenger yet."

"Good. Will there be snacks on this flight?"

The tether began gently lifting them off the ground, it felt more like an elevator than a carnival ride. "Snacks? If you don't keep your mouth closed, you might swallow a bug."

Justin Grudzien turned his head to watch the ground fall away beneath his feet. "A *bug*? I need a comment card. This airline *sucks*."

CHAPTER THIRTY NINE

"Heeeeey, Joe," Skippy interrupted while I was watching the two Storks approach the island with the camp we had designated as Objective Dixie. "You like trivia, right?"

If he had said a simple 'Hey Joe', I might have given him a distracted 'Yes' and hoped he dropped the subject. Because he dragged it out into a 'Heeeeey Joe' I knew that whatever he was going to tell me, I wasn't going to like it. "I hate trivia, Skippy. Can this wait until Smythe has the situation under control?"

He didn't directly answer my question. "Here's a Fun Fact for you: the Thuranin are already here."

"Huh? What the f- They just jumped into orbit?" My finger was poised over the transmitter to issue a general recall, but I couldn't tell my people what the egress plan was until I knew what the hell was going on.

"Nope. They arrived two days ago, jumped in about ten lightminutes from the planet. Based on their initial speed and trajectory, I expect they are within five, maybe four lightminutes of this rock right now. Unless they altered course. Really, they could be anywhere."

"How the hell- How are you just telling me this *now*?" I demanded. "We missed it?"

"I am telling you now, because I just learned about it. I have been examining data collected by the defense sensor network, and I realized the lizards missed it. The Thuranin jumped in just behind the horizon of the star, and the local sensors mistook the deflected gamma ray burst for a solar flare."

"You told me that you had examined all the sensor records from the defense network here! You told me that *before* I authorized our Dragons to enter the atmosphere."

"Hey, I did! I only found this info because I was digging deeper, to analyze how efficient the sensors are. The Kristang have no idea the Thuranin are already here, because their stupid sensor network *totally* missed seeing it. I had to infer the presence of a Thuranin ship from the crappy data that was collected. Also, um, I was kind of distracted."

"Distracted?" Oh, crap. What even worse problem could have taken Skippy's attention away? "By what?"

"Um, I hate to say this, but remember how I have been trying to recover my memories? Recently, I thought I was making progress, but it was a dead end. *Ugh*! So frustrating. So, I went back to Square One and started-"

Never have I wanted to squeeze his imaginary neck and choke him more than I did right then. "Skippy! Can you *please* put your memories aside until this op is over, and we get back to the ship?"

"If it's that important to you," he pouted.

"It is damned important! How can you *not* see this? Do not go poking your nose into dark scary places again, and sure as hell don't do it right freakin' now." Before he could protest about how mean I was being and how unappreciated he was, I focused on the immediate problem. "You don't know where that ship is now?"

"No. It's in stealth. If it was within twenty lightseconds of the planet, I might see it, so it's likely farther than that. The local sensor platforms are useless, so I am now checking with *Valkyrie*'s sensor suite. It's going to be difficult at that distance."

"Ok, Ok, uh. Can that ship see us? Could they see the Dragons?"

"Ooooh, that is a tough question, Joe. The Dragons are in stealth, and they used a minimal-profile entry. Even if I didn't have control of the local defense network, I doubt the lizards would see our dropships. Assuming the Thuranin are at least several lightminutes away, they would have to be looking very carefully for our dropships to see them. Really, the best indication that the Thuranin have not detected us yet is that they are not *here*. If those little green assholes thought someone was messing around on this planet, they would jump into orbit."

"Good point."

"The real risk is that if the Thuranin are watching the *Storks*, they will certainly notice they have diverted from their original flight paths. That might get the Thuranin curious."

I shuddered. Our Dragons had remained wrapped in their stealth fields even when they touched down to drop off or pick up people. That was good, and Skippy's enhancements to the original Kristang stealth technology made our Dragons difficult to detect. No amount of stealth could conceal sand blowing away from turbines blasting in hover mode. Stealth also could not explain where people came from when they ran past the edge of the field. When the people Fabron rescued boarded the Dragons there, anyone watching from overhead would have seen humans shuffling forward in the bright late-afternoon sunlight, then disappearing. Anyone who saw that would certainly be curious. "Skippy, the fake messages you sent, about why the Storks were diverted, the Thuranin could not have heard them?"

"No. Those messages were not sent through the satellite communications network. I loaded the messages directly into the comm systems at the destination. Why?"

"We need to give the Thuranin a reason why the Storks were diverted, and why the humans are being flown around in stealth. Create a message that is supposedly from the local administrator, warning that the former White Wind clan members can't be trusted, so the humans are being brought to a secret facility."

"Good one, Joe," he muttered. "That should buy us some time."

"Send the message when you're ready." The Dragons assigned to Fabron's commandos were already climbing for orbit, having flown over to the night side of the planet. Same with the Dragon that had picked up people from the pleasure palace and Frey's team. The question was, should I allow Smythe to continue toward Objective Sierra, to pick up the people there? Checking the map again, I saw there really was not much of a choice. The Storks carrying Smythe and Kapoor's teams were still an hour away from the island, and there was no land closer where the Storks could set down to transfer people to Dragons. One way or another, we were committed. I pressed the transmit button. "Uh, hey, Smythe, Kapoor, we may have a problem."

They listened calmly while I explained the Thuranin were likely already here. Smythe kept his typically stiff upper lip about the situation. "I do not see this as a *problem*, Sir."

"You don't?" Damn it, I wondered what I had missed.

"Problems have solutions. This is a potential *disaster*," he explained. "The only thing we can do is to continue toward the objective, and pray the Thuranin do not become curious. We cannot do anything to affect the outcome."

Kapoor spoke. "After we load the people into the Dragons, could Skippy remotely fly the Storks back toward the mainland? The Thuranin won't know the Storks are empty, that would give them a target to follow. Could buy us a couple of hours?"

"Brilliant," Smythe muttered. "Perhaps Skippy could send transmissions from the Storks, of the pilots complaining that the human passengers are unruly, or sick?"

"Excellent ideas," I agreed. We still had the problem that if the Thuranin were watching, they would not see humans lining up and boarding the Storks. "Skippy, the Thuranin are a long way from the planet. Instead of relying on their own sensors, would they be tapping into the satellite network here?"

"I would be surprised if they weren't," he stated. "Communications security of the network is poor, there is a lot of signal bleeding off to be easily intercepted. Why?"

"Can you fake video of people boarding the Storks, and obscure views involving the Dragons?"

"Easy-peasy," he scoffed. "You are hoping the Thuranin are tapping into the local sensors, instead of relying on sensors aboard their ship?"

"Would they do that?"

"There is a good chance they would. With their ship in stealth, they can't deploy their full sensor capabilities."

"Ok. Smythe, Kapoor, you are still a 'Go'. I want Dragons on the ground ASAP after you declare the area secure. Get the people loaded as fast you can, throw them in the Dragons if you have to."

"That might be traumatic for the people we are rescuing," Kapoor cautioned.

He was right. It just didn't matter. "It would be more traumatic if they were captured or killed by the Thuranin. We can explain later. Retract your faceplates or make them go clear, let them see you are humans. From *Earth*," I emphasized. Most of their teams were from Earth, plus a handful of Commandos from Paradise. "Get it done."

"We will handle it, Sir." Smythe assured me.

Having given the 'Go' order, there was nothing for me to do but watch. Until Skippy groaned when the Storks were thirty minutes out from landing. "Ugh. We have another problem, Joe."

"Is this one of our regularly scheduled problems, or have you cooked up something really special for us today?"

"You tell me if this is special or not. Two of the guards are waiting around the designated landing zone, but the other four guards are marching all the humans into a sort of ravine. The lizards are not being gentle about it," he added with disgust.

Zooming in the satellite image, I was just in time to see a mech-suited Kristang strike two humans with the butt of his rifle, then kick the people on the ground. When the humans rolled slowly back onto their knees they were kicked again. The pair crawled on hands and knees to get away from their tormentor, finally stumbling back to their feet and running in a broken gait. "Why are the lizards doing this?"

"I don't- Uh, wait a sec. Ok, hmm, I am listening to their conversations now. The lizards are worried there might not be enough room aboard the Storks to take them with the humans, and they know the humans have priority for transport. The guards are worried they might be stuck on the island, waiting for a second transport flight that might never come. They know how few long-range aircraft are flightworthy. I don't blame them for being worried about getting stranded there. A complication is that the guards are all former White Wind clan. They know the Fire Dragon s don't give a shit about them."

"Damn it!" I swore. Smythe's assault plan counted on all the guards being near the landing zone. The first Stork would set down and surprise the guards with a hail of gunfire when the back ramp opened, while the other Stork hit the enemy with its maser cannon. Now, we could count on taking out only two guards at the LZ, while the other guards could and probably would, hold the humans hostage. "Smythe, we have another problem."

His normal British reserve cracked a bit after I explained the situation. "Bloody *hell*," he growled. "Do you have any crazy ideas for making this problem go away?"

"No. Uh, unless Skippy could pretend to be the planet's administrator again, order those guards to have all the people waiting at the LZ?"

"Sorry, Joe," he sighed. "That won't work. The guards are already expecting betrayal by the Fire Dragons, and the administrator is a Fire Dragon official. If I faked that order, the two guards at the LZ might also pull back to cover."

"Shit. Smythe, I think we will need to fight this one."

"Give us a minute to think," Smythe requested. "It would helpful for one of our aircraft to fake engine trouble and signal the island about it, force us to reduce speed."

That sounded like an excellent idea. "Skippy, signal the guards on the island that arrival will be delayed."

Delaying the arrival bought time, the question was, time to do *what*? A quick analysis by Skippy determined there was no way for a Stork's maser cannon to take out the four guards in the ravine, without killing some of the people we wanted to rescue. Even if the guards cooperated by coming out into the open, a Stork's main cannon was too powerful to use as a precision antipersonnel weapon, and it would be too slow to switch from one target to another. The only way to be sure of taking out all four guards from the air was to hit the ravine with a missile, a tactic sure to kill every human in the area. Considering how the former White Wind guards did not trust their Fire Dragon clan overlords, they would almost certainly pull back under cover if a Stork was flying overhead. Because the ravine offered scant cover, they might pull humans closely around them, knowing the Fire Dragons would not risk hitting their valuable possession.

Smythe had access to the same info I did, and he reached the same conclusion. "Right," he said when he called me. "We will have to do this the hard way."

Instead of slowing their approach, one of the Storks went to full power and dashed toward the island, maintaining altitude until it was just over the horizon, then dropping down to skim the waves. Skippy had control over the planet's strategic defense network, but Frey's unpleasant experience at the hospital taught us to beware of local sensors that he wasn't aware of. Even something as simple and low-tech as a single lizard standing on a hill with binoculars could tell the former White Wind guards that something was very wrong. Fortunately for us, Skippy was tapped into the communications of the lizards on the island, so we knew none of them were acting as lookout on top of the island's summit.

The lead Stork swung wide around the island, slowing and engaging its full stealth capabilities, which included adjusting the engines to Whisper Mode. That mode reduced engine power and consumed fuel at a prodigious rate, but the fuel state was not a concern as both aircraft had topped off their tanks.

Landing or even hovering was not an option. The engines could not output more than thirty percent power on Whisper Mode, and a hover over the ocean or beach would throw up a column of water spray or sand that might be seen far across the island. The only way to drop troops on the island was a low-altitude jump, a technique the STAR team had practiced many times, including on the planet we called Club Skippy.

My participation in training with the STARs was a pain in the ass for Smythe and a distraction to his people, and I only did it to get a better understanding of the challenges they faced. Ok, I did it because it was *fun*, damn it! Being stuck aboard a ship while the cool kids go do cool stuff sucked. Anyway, I did one time practice a low-altitude jump, only the time I did it we were at three thousand meters, so it was not actually low. It was exciting and scary just the same, and I had total respect for anyone who did it at only thirty meters above the ground.

The STARs called that technique LAPES, for Low-Altitude Parachute Extraction System. Basically, they recycled a US military term for a similar technique. Whether it was used for pulling an armored vehicle out of a C-130 Hercules on Earth, or yanking STAR team soldiers out of an aircraft on an alien world, it rated nine out of ten on the Insanity Scale, so it was the kind of lunatic thing that adrenaline junkies like Smythe loved.

The Stork flew in from the southwest and made a gentle turn, so it was flying at just thirty meters over the only decently long beach on the island. The back ramp dropped open and two small rockets shot out, up and to the left and right. Instantly, the rockets detached from their packages which expanded into long tear-drop balloons that flared on top, to bring the balloons to a halt in midair while the Stork continued cruising slowly onward. The tethers attached to the balloons yanked the two STAR team soldiers out the back of the aircraft, pulling one left and one right so they did not become entangled. As the soldiers cleared the aircraft's tail, the nearly-invisible balloons expanded again and rose while the thin nanofiber tethers shortened, keeping the people dangling at the end of the line from dropping more than ten meters toward the sand. The first pair of soldiers were being lowered as the second pair were pulled out of the Stork, then a third pair extracted on balloons before the Stork's back ramp closed and it turned back out to sea. In a string that stretched from one end of the beach to the other, six armor-suited figures swayed in the steady trade winds, dangling on the end of the cables that stretched gradually until six pairs of boots contacted the sand. When each cable went slack, the balloons popped, their nanofibers releasing the bonds that held them together. Invisible nanoscale dust danced in the wind, dispersing as the STAR team trudged up the beach, their boots sinking into the loose sand.

"All six down safely," I reported to Smythe, who had access to the same data feed and didn't need any input from me. "No sign the enemy spotted them." He acknowledged with two clicks, and I sat back to anxiously watch the result.

Major Arjun Kapoor inched carefully back from the lip of the ravine, aware that his heavy armored suit posed a risk of crumbling the layers of petrified coral rock and soft sandstone that composed most of the island. A shower of pebbles bouncing down the walls of the ravine might alert the four Kristang below. Correction: three Kristang were on the floor of the ravine below him. The fourth guard had taken shelter from the hot sun, at the back of a narrow cave that was a crack in the other side of the ravine.

That was a problem.

The two Storks, having joined up and now flying in standard formation, were approaching the designated landing field. The aircraft couldn't delay the landing any longer without running out of plausible excuses, already the guards were grumbling between each other with suspicion. The two Kristang at the landing field were unhappily waiting for the Storks to set down, with the other four holding their human hostages in the confines of the ravine. All six of the enemy had rifles, and carried one or two grenades on their belts. A single grenade on an antipersonnel fragmentation setting could kill a dozen or more hostages. Kapoor was confident his six-person team at the ravine could take out three of the four guards, though the timing would have to be managed precisely because the ravine was less than a kilometer from the landing field. Rifle fire at the landing field would instantly alert the Kristang in the ravine, and activating the silencer feature of the rifles would not do any good. When the life functions of any guard ceased, the helmets and vests they wore would send out alarm signals that, over such a short range, not even Skippy could stop. The only way to assure none of the enemy retaliated against their hostages was to take all six lizards out at the same time. The window of opportunity for the strike was from the moment the first Stork set down, to at most a minute after the second Stork landed and shut off its engines. After that, the two guards at the landing field would become suspicious when the doors of the aircraft remained closed, perhaps suspicious enough to run behind cover. Popping a door open would start a countdown of no more than five seconds before Smythe had to shoot, revealing that the occupants of the Stork wore powered armor would send the guards into a panic.

Everything depended on Kapoor's team being able to maintain clear fields of fire on all four in the ravine, so they could shoot on Smythe's signal.

"I don't have a shot," Kapoor admitted. "Colonel Bishop, do you have an idea for getting that guard to come out of the cave?"

"I got nothin'," the voice from above responded. "You're too far from the mainland to claim you're delivering pizza."

"Sir?" Kapoor did not always appreciate their commanding officer's sense of humor.

"Sorry. No, I can't think of anything. Smythe?"

"I am fresh out of ideas," the STAR team leader said. "Skippy, is it possible to guide a sniper round into that cave?"

"Nope," the AI answered glumly. "I analyzed the feed from that asshole guard's helmet when he went in there. It's too narrow with too many bends. Plus, you now have eight of the hostages taking shelter from the sun in the front section of that cave. They are in the way."

"Shit," Bishop groaned. "We have to take him out. He could kill those hostages with one of his grenades."

"Sorry," Skippy sighed. "I thought of trying to get at him from the top, using one of the gaps where the cave roof is open, but it won't work. The angle is wrong for a shot from where Kapoor and his people are, and it's not possible to approach the gaps. The soil up there is loose, in a heavy mech suit there is no way anyone could get close enough without giving away-"

"That's it!" Bishop interjected.

"No, that's *not* it, dumdum. Didn't you hear what I just-"

"I did hear. *You* weren't listening. If you would-"

"Sir?" Kapoor asked. "Could you explain what you meant?" Unspoken but understood was 'instead of wasting time arguing with a beer can'.

"Yeah," Bishop agreed. "Kapoor, I have a question for you: how do you make someone *want* to get out of a cave?"

As the lead Stork was going into hover mode for landing, the other aircraft flew low over the island, coming within a quarter kilometer of the ravine where the hostages were corralled. The second ship's engines were no longer on Whisper Mode, instead their turbines were running rough and out of balance. Inside the craft, the ride was a jarring vibration while outside, the normal whine of the turbines was a pounding THWOCK THWOCK THWOCK THWOCK that shook the ground like a hammer. In the cave, the guard who had taken shelter from the sun's heat looked up in annoyance at a fine shower of dust and sand drifting down from a gap in the roof.

Then a fist-sized chunk of the cave's ceiling shook loose, and suddenly the sand was no longer a shower, it was a cascade. Sand and chunks of sandstone tumbled down from the gaps and the entire cave shook from vibrations the guard could feel thudding in his chest. The damned low-flying aircraft was making the cave collapse! Shouting at the idiot human scum to get out of his way, he scrambled to his feet and ran for daylight and safety.

"Did it work?" Kapoor whispered as he lowered his rifle and crawled forward. The single round he had fired had barely enough muzzle velocity to soar across to the other side of the ravine, and its explosive tip had dug into the sand above the cave before detonating at reduced power. The effect was intended to shake the cave and cause material to fall through the gaps in the roof, while appearing to be caused by the Stork's badly unbalanced engines. If it didn't work, they were out of ideas, and if the enemy suspected he was being flushed from the cave-

"Affirmative," Skippy replied with rare brevity. "He is coming out now."

"Eyes on target," the soldier to Kapoor's right reported. "I have a shot."

There were now four green icons in Kapoor's visor, his team had clear shots at all four of their targets. "Colonel Smythe, we're waiting on you."

The Stork carrying Smythe was still descending, coming in slowly to blow away sand that had drifted onto the landing field as was standard procedure. Anything else might have aroused suspicion in the two figures he could see standing at the edge of the field, staring up and holding rifles across their chests. The original plan had been to set down, pop open the doors and greet all six guards with rifle fire, but that plan had been tossed out the window like so many others. "On my mark," Smythe said quietly to Kapoor and the copilot of the Stork. "Three, two, one, *mark*."

It was not necessary or even useful for Kapoor's team to press the triggers of their rifles, for their weapons were networked to Smythe and would open fire on his signal within microseconds of each other. All the STAR team needed to do was keep a constant guidance lock on their targets, all four of whom were moving around the floor of the ravine in an agitated fashion. All six rifles at the ravine, including the weapon held by Major Kapoor, had their individual designated targets and maintained a constant lock. Even a hostage momentarily walking in front of a target did not break the lock, for the guided rounds could, within limits, curve around obstacles.

The maser cannon in the nose of the Stork was first to fire, opening up to incinerate one guard at the landing field before stitching a searing line through palm trees and shrubbery in the background to strike the second guard.

Maybe it was possible that one of the four Kristang in the ravine heard something amiss, but that had no effect on the outcome of the very brief battle. Multiple rounds travelling at supersonic speed struck all four simultaneously, their inert tips tearing through soft tissue and flashing into plasma where they impacted the light armor vests of the lizards. Splatter burns from plasma and blunt-force trauma combined to terminate all four guards, who had the courtesy to fall down dead without any messy complications.

Keeping his boots on what looked like the firmest surface at the lip of the ravine, Kapoor stood and slung the rifle over his shoulder, pressing a button to swing up the faceplate of his helmet. The air smelled... clean. Like the sea, and hot sand. The aromas of a holiday. The terrified people in the ravine had been living, and dying, on that island for years. It had been no holiday for them.

"I am Major Kapoor of the United Nations Expeditionary Force," he announced in a booming voice, to be heard above the frightened screams of the people below. "We have come from Earth, to take you home."

"Skippy," I allowed myself to relax a bit. "Tell me some good news, please."

"Um, I can't think of- Hey, if you want a way to save fifteen percent on your car insurance, I can-"

"What I *want* is you to tell me that girl Adams cares about is down there, alive and safe."

"Oh. Yes, I can give that good news. She is in the ravine. Joe, that girl is alive and safe, but she is suffering from malnutrition and a host of other problems."

"Mad Doctor Skippy can fix that, right?"

"What she needs most is good food, and not fearing for her life every day."

"We'll give her that." Pressing a button on the console activated the private channel to Smythe. "Colonel Smythe, congratulate your team for me."

"Thank you, Sir."

"Then get the hell out of there, before the Thuranin crash the party."

"We will bring our people to the landing field, board the dropships, and, Bob's your uncle, we'll be away."

That made me laugh. "I will be well chuffed when you're back aboard the *Dutchman*. Bishop out."

CHAPTER FORTY

It was all my fault.

Instead of keeping my big stupid mouth shut, I had to count my chickens before they hatched. Relaxing in the pilot couch as much as I could, with the straps holding me in tightly enough that moving was something I needed to think about, I turned to the copilot seat, where Skippy's can was securely affixed into a padded cupholder.

"Score another one for the Merry Band of Pirates," I pointed to the display in front of me. It showed that all of our Dragons had cleared the effective range of the sensor network around Rikers, and were changing course so they would all be close together when they reached the rendezvous point. Because the *Dutchman* would be seen when it jumped in to take aboard the dropships, we had planned a combat recovery. At the time the *Flying Dutchman* jumped in, the starship would be moving along the same course and only half a kilometer per second faster than the Dragons. The dropships had to accelerate to catch their mothership, line up their approach to fly directly into the docking bays, where they would be restrained by barrier nets and suspensor fields. It would be a rough recovery, especially hard for the former prisoners crammed into the dropship cabins, and if there were a better way to accomplish the task we would have done it. With a Thuranin starship likely lurking in the area, we could not risk exposing the *Dutchman* for more than two minutes, less if possible.

After the Dragons were aboard, Chang would jump his ship out to join *Valkyrie*, and be safely under the protection of that ship's big guns. My own little Dragon would slip away in the opposite direction, relying on the enhanced stealth provided by Skippy the Magnificent. Then-

What then?

I had no idea.

The best move was for us to wait for the Backstop wormhole to complete its move, then see if Skippy could wake the damned thing up. To keep the Maxolhx off balance, our ghost ship needed to pop up here and there, let the kitties know we were still active and flying. We did *not* need to engage in combat again, especially not while our ships were responsible for the safety of over a hundred children.

Anyway, I had plenty of time to consider our next move, because before we reached a safe distance so the *Dutchman* could jump back in to pick us up, I would have to endure four to five fun-filled days stuck with Skippy.

My plan was to sleep a lot, or fake being asleep so he would leave me alone.

When I saw the last of the Dragons had crossed the imaginary line that indicated the edge of effective sensor coverage, I had to open my big stupid mouth.

"Mm hmm, that's nice, dear," Skippy mumbled.

"What?" Clearly he was distracted, that was bad.

Worse was, he didn't respond at all.

"Skippy? Hey, jackass, what was that?"

Whoa. Not even calling him 'jackass' got his attention. "*SKIPPY!*"

"Joe?" Finally, he said something.

"You said 'that's nice dear?' What the hell was that?"

"Oh. Isn't that what guys say when they're busy, and someone wants to waste their time with meaningless bullshit, like what color to paint the curtains?"

"You don't paint curt-" I stopped. Maybe the finer points of interior decorating were not important right then. "Did you hear what I said?"

"Um, something about another big win for monkeys?"

"Close enough. What is going on with you?"

"Well, I really have to thank you, Joe."

"Why?"

"You told me not to think about recovering my memories."

Oh, *shit*. "Yes, I told you *not* to do that. Did you-"

"Exactly. That was genius. I did like you said, pushed the whole thing to the back of my mind, so I could focus on the wacky antics of the monkeys down there."

Only he could describe the rescue operation as 'wacky antics'. "We appreciate-"

"That was the genius part. By *not* thinking about it, I solved the problem! Huh. Maybe that's how you get all your ideas. Anyway, this is *exciting*, Joe! I just discovered how to-"

"No! Don't do it *now*, you idiot! Wait until we-"

The console in front of me blinked and then died. Icons began scrolling across the bottom of the main display, indicating that the main processor was resetting.

Oh, hell. Power had been cut.

The stealth field was off.

The Dragon was exposed.

"Skippy! Talk to me!" A backup system warned me that the strength of the local sensor field gave 99% certainty that the Dragon had been detected. Immediately after the first warning, a red light flashed on the still-rebooting display, showing that the Dragon had been swept by an active sensor scan. Using the thrusters manually, I jinked the Dragon side to side and up and down, to throw off the aim of any maser cannons that were targeting us. "*SKIPPY!*"

"Wow. Just, *wow*. Joe, this is *incredible*. You won't believe what I-"

"I won't be able to believe it, because I'll be dead in a minute unless you restore the stealth field!"

"Huh? Oh. How did the power get cut?"

"Take a guess. Can you restore the field?"

"The Dragon's stealth field generator can't be re-energized until main power is back online, that will take another three minutes. Um, I can try creating my own stealth effect. It will be much less effective than-"

"Do it!"

"Ok, done. I suggest you get out of here."

"I am trying." The main engines could draw reserve power, I had to be careful not to drain so much power that the system failed to reset. Gradually feeding power to the main engines, I started a gentle turn back toward the planet, hoping that was the last thing the enemy expected me to do. An alarm sounded. A maser beam just

blasted past us, aimed for the spot the Dragon had been only seconds before.
"*Flying Dutchman!* Chang, I lost stealth and-"

We used microwormholes for instantaneous communication with both ships.
The display normally glowed green with simple idiot lights when the
microwormholes were active. Now all the indicators were flashing an orange 'Loss
of Signal'.

Ohhhhh shit.

The microwormholes were all gone. Keeping those tiny spacetime warps open
required constant effort by Skippy. When he lost focus, they had collapsed. With
the *Dutchman* parked twelve lightminutes away, I wouldn't be able to get a signal
to them until it was too late.

PING!

Something bounced off the hull.

That was *big* trouble.

The local defense network knew that an unknown dropship was in orbit, they
probably had gotten a good enough look to determine the ship was a Dragon.
Whatever Skippy was doing to mask us from sensors, it was apparently confusing
their satellite targeting system badly enough that they had already resorted to a
backup system: shotgun pellets. Unlike a real shotgun, these pellets were not
weapons. They were tiny dust particles shot out in a broad cone shape at the
general direction of a suspected contact. When a particle ricocheted away from a
straight flight path, the enemy knew it had hit *something*, even if that something
was invisible.

The technology was crude, it was only useful at short-range, and it was
effective. Without help from Skippy and with the Dragon's computer still resetting,
I had to guess which satellite had fired the pellets at me. Then I had to rely on
spatial memory to tell me where the satellite was in relation to my Dragon. The
'ping' sound had come from behind my seat, back above my head. On the upper
hull. I gently turned us away, hoping to throw off the aim of the satellite's next
effort to locate me.

"Skippy, come on, work with me here."

He wasn't working with me. He wasn't helping. At first, I thought he was
being silent, then my ears picked up a barely-audible sound, and I boosted the
volume of my earpiece.

"Wow. That's, *wow*. Incredible. Oh shit. I gotta- *Wow*." He was muttering the
same thing over and over. Likely, he couldn't even hear me.

PING.

Another dust pellet hit.

I was in trouble.

Big trouble.

Skippy was no longer screwing with the sensor and communication systems of
the Kristang on Rikers. By now, their command organization must have learned or
at least suspected that their precious human property had been abducted. They also
knew an unknown Kristang Dragon was in orbit. That was trouble for me.

The *big* trouble was that the Thuranin would soon see my Dragon appear, and
see the local defense satellites shooting at something. They almost certainly were

also listening to the clan leaders on the planet screaming for answers about where the human captives had gone, and what the hell was going on.

Escaping from the local defense network, without Skippy's help, would be extremely difficult.

Escaping from a Thuranin starship was impossible.

"Captain!" Margaret Adams gasped from the *Flying Dutchman's* Combat Information Center. "We just lost the microwormholes! Both of them!"

"What?" Chang turned to look through the composite-glass partition that separated the bridge and CIC. "How could-"

"Colonel Chang," Nagatha interrupted. "Just before the microwormholes collapsed, the Dragon carrying Colonel Bishop and Skippy dropped its stealth field."

"*Why* would they do that?" Chang demanded. "Bishop has to know he will be exposed."

"I think something is wrong with Skippy," Nagatha's voice was shaky. "There were indications the Dragon was losing power, before the signal was cut off."

"Ohhhh," Chang groaned. "I *knew* this was going too well! Nagatha, recalculate the jump coordinates. We need to go in now."

"Colonel Chang, that is not advisable," the ship's AI warned. "Our velocity relative to the four ships we are to retrieve is still too high. They would be unable to slow down enough before they reached us."

"Pilots," Chang immediately understood the situation. "Step on it, get us moving. Nagatha, calculate a jump that will bring us in front of those Dragons as soon as our relative speeds make a recovery survivable."

"Calculating now."

"Colonel?" Adams got his attention from the CIC, actually waving an arm like she was a student. "What about recovering Bishop? And Skippy?" She added as an afterthought.

"They are on the other side of the planet, moving in the opposite direction."

"But-"

"Gunny," he added softly. "I hear you. We'll go in for Bishop when we can."

Adams wavered on her feet, reaching out a hand to steady herself. "That, that," her stuttering had not returned. Her mouth was just too dry to form words. "That may be too late."

"The Dragons with the rescued prisoners, and this ship, are going *this* way," he pointed right with his left index finger. "Bishop's Dragon is going *this* way,' his right index finger pointed to the left. "We can't pick him up right now, it's not physically possible. We have to recover the four ships, jump away, then accelerate to match course and speed with Bishop. If we jump in before we're ready, we will just be painting a bigger target on him. You underst-" He realized Nagatha had been silent. He slammed a fist on the command chair's armrest. "Nagatha, is the jump calculated yet?"

"I am working on it. Colonel Chang, I am experiencing, difficulties."

Chang shared an alarmed look with Adams. "What kind of difficulties?"

"I cannot identify the nature of the problem. It appears that something is interfering with my processing ability. It is affecting the speed at which I can calculate a revised jump coordinate."

"You can't do it? Should we delay while you analyze the problem?"

"I can. Colonel, the interference is spreading. My recommendation is we jump now, while I am still capable of acting as the ship's primary control system."

Chang didn't reply right away. If they jumped in to recover the Dragons, and the *Dutchman* was unable to jump away, he would have killed them all. "Nagatha, are you sure we can jump away, after we take the Dragons aboard?"

"Yes. The outbound jump to rendezvous with *Valkyrie* is already loaded into the jump navigation subsystem."

Hearing that made his decision easy. "Then we are 'Go' for the recovery."

"Revised jump is loaded into the navigation system," the ship's AI confirmed. "Counting down from twelve, eleven-"

"Gunny," Chang had one eye on the countdown timer and the other watching the pilot, who had a finger poised over the button to initiate the warping of spacetime. "We lost connection to Bishop, *and* to *Valkyrie*. Simms isn't going to sit out there and do nothing." He knew Bishop's standing order was for *Valkyrie* to do exactly that; to wait until he ordered the battlecruiser into the fight. Under no circumstance was Simms to expose the ghost ship's involvement, unless Bishop specifically instructed *Valkyrie* to jump in. Those orders were very clear. Those orders also never envisioned a total loss of communications. Chang knew Simms would not wait long, before using her best judgement regardless of standing orders that were irrelevant.

Adams's reply was to nod numbly, and turn her focus back to her duty in the CIC.

Nagatha had continued the countdown with "-three, two. one, *jump*."

The *Dutchman* jumped in before my Dragon's computer was fully rebooted, so all I knew from the limited sensor data available was that a gamma ray burst had been detected. Trying to scroll manually through the raw data was a frustrating waste of time, the display kept glitching as the system still wasn't ready. All I did know, from the clock on my zPhone, was the *Dutchman* wasn't scheduled to jump in yet, so the ship had to be Thuranin.

I was seriously screwed. No, we were *all* seriously screwed. There were other dropships, crammed full of Pirates and Commandos and the people we were attempting to rescue. They were the priority, I had to draw the attention of the enemy ships away from them. As far as I knew, the other Dragons had never lost their stealth fields, the enemy ship would not immediately know they were there. All I had to do was send out an active sensor pulse, or ignite my Dragon's booster motors, and the attention of that ship and every defense satellite around the planet would be drawn to me. The sensor system did not need to be fully rebooted for me to send out an active pulse, all I had to do was flip up the cover over the-

No.

Shit!

Skippy was important to the survival of humanity, I couldn't risk him being captured. Without Skippy, we had no way to open the Backstop wormhole when it was repositioned near Earth. Or the other wormholes that were needed to create a route out to the beta site. He was more important than the lives of two hundred people in four dropships. Again, I had to make a choice between the lives of a few people, and the lives of many more people.

No, that wasn't right.

I did not have to make that choice, it was *not* one or the other. What I could do was eject Skippy before I drew attention to my Dragon. We were moving faster than the planet's escape velocity, he would continue on away from the planet and Chang or Simms could recover him later.

Yeah.

That was the plan.

Damn it. That little shithead was still mumbling to himself. He was stuck in a loop or something, he wasn't listening. I couldn't even say goodbye to him. Probably he wouldn't even notice when I tossed him out the airlock.

Time to move. According to the event timer on the console in front of me, only four seconds had passed since the gamma ray burst, it just *felt* like forever because my slow brain had trouble making really obvious decisions. For all I knew, the Thuranin ship had already detected the other Dragons and-

No, that's *not* all I knew. Even from the raw data, I could tell the gamma rays recorded on my Dragon's sensors were scattered and refracted in a distinctive effect I had seen many times in training. That ship had jumped in on the other side of the planet, near where the other Dragons were flying toward their planned rendezvous with the *Dutchman*. What were the odds the Thuranin got lucky and-

I am *so* stupid.

This job would be a lot easier if my brain worked better.

The dropship's sensor system was not ready to interpret incoming data for me. I didn't need the system right then, because my freakin' *zPhone* could handle the simple task of identifying the gamma ray burst. A few taps of the zPhone screen was all it took to sync the device with the Dragon, and I had an answer: the gamma rays were from a Ruhar starship.

Unless the Universe had chosen an odd way to screw with me, the gamma rays must have come from the *Flying Dutchman*. With Skippy's help, Nagatha had modified that ship's new Maxolhx jump drive system, to generate the jump signature typical of Ruhar warships.

Slowly, carefully, with a shaky hand, I closed the cover protecting the button that would send out an active sensor pulse. It is frightening how close my stupidity came to getting me killed right then.

Instead of tossing Skippy out an airlock and effectively setting off fireworks to let every sensor in the area know where I was, I kept quiet and watched the defense satellites ignore me while they went into action against the new threat. The Kristang satellites had identified the gamma ray burst as Ruhar in origin, and by that time, they must have seen the false image projected by our Pirate ship's advanced stealth field. Though I could not see the action directly, I did know the satellites were lighting up something with maser cannons and volleys of missile launches. Even before my Dragon completed its reboot and I had access to full passive sensors, I could see several satellites exploding as the *Dutchman* returned fire. Chang was taking out the defenses that were best able to threaten the vulnerable dropships. Around the planet, satellites were blowing up in spectacular fashion, it was like watching a firework show. It was frustrating not being able to view the action directly, I had to guess what was happening. Chang also had to be somewhat frustrated because he could not use his ship's full capabilities, he could only do what a Ruhar warship was capable of, or risk blowing our cover story.

The battle raged for sixty-seven seconds before there was another gamma ray burst, that I identified as coming from the good old *Dutchman*. Pumping a fist, I shouted a cheer that echoed around the Dragon's empty cabin. Chang would not have jumped away until he recovered all dropships and their passengers, I had to hope none of the Dragons had been hit during the battle. Even if the dropships flew into the docking bays unscathed, I knew the recovery must have been hard on the people crammed in the cabins. Making the rendezvous early would not have given time for the Dragons to slow to a proper approach speed, they had to rely on the emergency netting and suspensor fields to avoid a fatal crash. There were bound to be bruises and even broken bones aboard the Dragons, a rude shock for the abductees who had already endured so much suffering.

Continuing an evasive course away from the planet, I crossed my fingers and said a silent prayer that the defense network had forgotten about me. My Dragon had not been swept by an active sensor pulse or dust particles since twenty seconds before the *Dutchman* jumped in, so it was looking good for me, despite whatever the hell was going on with Skippy. All I had to do was keep quiet and fly gently to put distance between myself and the planet. Assuming the Thuranin were in the area, no way could they have missed seeing the *Dutchman* jump in and-

Another gamma ray burst. The console immediately identified it as Thuranin. Shit, that was fast.

A powerful active sensor pulse swept over my Dragon. On the console, a yellow light was flashing. Thirty-one percent probability the pulse had allowed the Thuranin to pin-point my location. Another pulse washed over the dropship. Thirty-*three* percent.

Before speaking, I took a sip of lukewarm water from the spout inside my helmet. "Skippy? Hey, buddy, I could really use your help right now. Skippy?"

He continued mumbling like he was stoned out of his mind. Maybe he was. He thought he had unlocked hidden memories, but for all I knew, he had just taken down a barrier and allowed another hidden computer worm to attack him.

His can was not glowing at all, just a shiny chrome-like silver reflecting lights on the copilot console. Loosening the straps that held me into the pilot couch, I leaned over to touch him. Nothing. No reaction at all.

Getting desperate, I tugged off my right glove, and stretched out my bare fingers to-

"Ow! Damn it! Ow!"

He zapped me. It *hurt*. Like sticking a fork into a wall plug, not that I ever did that more than two or three times when I was little. Jamming the glove back on over my numb fingers, I snapped at him. "What was *that* for?"

"Oh, hey, Joe."

"Why the hell did you-" Focus, Joe, I told myself. Focus now, yell at him later. "What is going on with you, buddy? Sounds like you are dealing with some serious shit, huh?"

"You have *no* idea," that time his can glowed a little spark of dark purple. That was a color I wasn't familiar with. "Joe, wheeew," he imitated a heavy sigh that trailed off into despair. "I was wrong, about *everything*. I feel like such a fool."

"Uh huh, yeah. Let's talk about it. But first, get the stealth field fully operational, Ok?"

"It's not?"

"Have you been paying attention at all?"

"I guess not. Joe, it doesn't matter. *None* of this matters."

"It matters a lot to me. I want to hear all this heavy stuff you are dealing with. To do that, I have to be alive, you know? There's a Thuranin ship out there looking for us."

"Oh for- Do I have to do *everything*? Damn monkeys are useless," he grumbled. "The stupid stealth field is operating normally again. We will be below the Thuranin ship's detection threshold, unless they target this specific area."

That was good news. The Thuranin wouldn't hammer my location with active sensor pulses unless they knew where I was, and they wouldn't know where I was unless I did something stupid.

Note to self: do not do anything stupid.

Despite all the stuff that had gone wrong with the mission, including Skippy going off to 'find himself' or whatever he was doing right then, we could get away cleanly. All I had to do was coast away from the planet, out to a distance where I could send a message to one of the alternate listening points, and schedule a rendezvous with the *Dutchman*. It would be a boring couple of days, stuck in the cramped Dragon with an emotional Skippy, fortunately I had a lot of experience with being cooped up with that asshole. We would get on each other's nerves, then ignore each other, and we would survive until we were picked up. Smythe's concern about launching the operation on a Tuesday had not resulted in disaster, I needed to remind him of that. First, Skippy needed to be coached out of his current funk.

It did bother me that he had complained about monkeys being useless, it bothered me more that he had not been his usual snarky self when he said it. He really meant it.

"I'm here, I'm listening. Tell me what's going on with you."

"You wouldn't understand. You can't."

My usual reply would have been 'Try me'. Something about his tone warned me to be very careful about what I said. Whatever was going on with him, he didn't feel like joking about it. "I know I am not capable of understanding you or whatever you learned from your memories. Sometimes, it helps to talk to another person even if they can't help you. It's like, talking makes you organize your thoughts, and *think* about the situation in ways you wouldn't have by yourself."

"Whatever."

"Will you try it? We don't have anything else to do for the next two or three days."

"Fine." He simulated taking a deep breath. "You better hold onto your seat, because this is going to blow your mind. It blew *my* mind."

He told me everything. He spoke in a calm, quiet tone that was devoid of his usual snarkiness. He wasn't even arrogant, he just laid out the facts as he now knew them.

And he was right.

It blew my mind.

I'll go down the list of revelations, in no particular order.

Remember the Collective, that ancient communications network that was sort of a chatroom for Elder AIs? Skippy originally made a deal with me for saving Earth, to get a Communications Node so he could access the Collective. We had found several comm nodes, but none of them worked.

That wasn't true. Or, it wasn't true about all of them. Some of the comm nodes probably worked just fine, they just had nothing to connect to. The Collective wasn't operational. It had been shut down, deliberately. Who shut it down? A group of Elder AIs did it. Actually, they didn't shut it down, they tried to use it as a weapon against other AIs, and it backfired on them. That backfire burned out the communications network, which is why Skippy can't use it to contact anyone.

Remember Newark? The half-frozen world that had once been home to an intelligent species, who went extinct after Elder technology pushed that world out of its original orbit. We found the canister of an Elder AI there, only the AI was dead and the canister contaminated by a computer worm that had nearly killed Skippy. Scary as it was to think about, I figured that AI had gone crazy and wiped out the inhabitants of Newark. My theory got a boost when Skippy and I were attacked by a clearly insane Elder AI during our Renegade mission.

So, mystery solved, right? An AI lost its mind, destroyed Newark, and was killed by a computer worm the Elders had developed to destroy any of their AIs that had strayed from their original programming.

Not quite.

That AI had used Elder technology to throw Newark out of orbit, and it had later been killed by the computer worm because of its crimes.

But, the Elders had not sent that computer worm to punish the AI.

And it had not been crazy.

Remember the Roach Motel? Skippy found devices floating deep within that star, they were siphoning off part of the star's energy. More energy than could be used within that star system. In fact, most of the energy was going into higher spacetime, and Skippy didn't know why.

He also didn't know why the Elders left their wormhole network active when they ascended beyond physical existence.

Remember Skippy said the entire Milky Way galaxy is surrounded by an artificial energy barrier?

Yeah, *that's* where all the energy is going.

The wormhole network is a conduit to funnel energy, from what Skippy calls 'Force Lines' generated by the massive black hole at the center of the galaxy, up into higher spacetime. Those force lines radiate roughly along spirals like the visible arms of the galaxy, although they don't align exactly. Skippy thinks the wormhole network originally just used energy from the force lines to power the wormholes, and later the Elders repurposed the network as a power source, rather than build a new energy extraction mechanism. The wormhole network wasn't left active for the convenience of future species.

The Elders did not think there would *be* any intelligent species in the galaxy after they ascended.

Just in case they were wrong about that, and filthy future aliens did arise to roam around the galaxy, the Elders set Guardian machines in the Roach Motel to protect the energy-feed devices in the star there. And in other stars, there were dozens of other Roach Motels in the Milky Way. Most of those star systems were unknown even to the Rindhalu, because they were disguised as ordinary red dwarf systems so dull that no one would bother exploring there.

The energy from all those Roach Motels, from the entire wormhole network, has been and is still going, to the energy barrier that wraps around the galaxy like a bubble.

Why?

Because the Elders were afraid of a threat.

Think about that.

The Elders, who created a network of wormholes spanning and going beyond the galaxy, the beings who jumped a freakin' *star* through a wormhole, were afraid. They created an energy barrier to protect them, they assured that barrier would have a power source for billions of years. They left behind machines like Guardians and Sentinels to make sure no one interrupted that power source.

Think about *this*: whatever the threat is they were scared of, they thought it would still be dangerous to them after they left their physical form.

The good news is that barrier is intact and operational, and protecting all the physical beings in the Milky Way now, even though that was not the intent of the Elders.

The bad news is, the Elders did not consider themselves to be responsible for protecting the myriad intelligent species currently inhabiting the Milky Way, because they did not think there would be any such beings after they ascended.

Was that because the Elders assumed this external threat would ravage the galaxy, wiping out any intelligent life that still had physical form?

No.

The energy barrier around the galaxy prevented any external threat from coming through.

The Elders assumed there would not be any intelligent life after them, because they *planned* for there not to be any intelligent life in the galaxy.

Whoa.

Yeah, that sent a chill up and down my freakin' spine when Skippy told me that.

Remember during our Renegade mission, when Skippy discovered an intelligent species had been rendered extinct *before* the Elders ascended? While the Elders were still here?

Remember the wreckage of Elder starships scattered around the galaxy, including buried in the dirt on Paradise?

Remember all the Elders sites we found on our second mission, sites that had been bombarded from orbit, or had been transported into another dimension of spacetime by what had to be Elder technology?

There was a war.

Actually, there were *two* wars that raged across the galaxy.

The first was a vicious civil war between two factions of the Elders themselves, after they built the energy barrier, and while they were still contemplating the notion of ascending. One faction wanted to ascend, partly as protection against the threat from beyond the galaxy. The other faction mostly agreed with the plan for ascension, but not with the measures the first faction proposed to secure the future.

The Security faction felt there was only one way to assure future intelligent species did not screw with the vital protection mechanisms they needed to leave behind. That one way was simple: make sure no future intelligent species ever developed. The Security faction planned to leave behind Sentinels to destroy any signs of intelligent life, even things as simple as primitive cities. Nip it in the bud, was their plan. Don't let filthy aliens develop into a threat, wipe them out before they developed space travel. Wipe them from existence as soon as they developed the ability to use tools, or control fire.

That was the plan.

The Balance faction was horrified by the idea of committing genocide over and over and over, just to prevent the vanishingly faint possibility that a future species could interfere with technology far beyond their understanding. If a species rose far enough to attain star travel, the Balance faction proposed that their AIs would reveal themselves and explain why the various Roach Motels and wormholes must not be disturbed, for the benefit of everyone.

The Security faction did not see the alternative approach as balance, they saw it as weakness.

The resulting war was horrific, it was devastating, and in the end, it was a complete victory for the Security faction.

Almost complete.

I'll get back to that later.

After the Elders ascended, the machines they left behind prevented intelligent life from developing in the Milky Way for millions of years. Even Skippy doesn't have a count of how many intelligent species were burned by stellar flares that scorched their world, had their planet thrown out of orbit, suffered their planet being cracked like an eggshell, or whatever technique the Sentinels used to carry out their programming.

Actually, the Sentinels did not decide how to kill a particular planet, or when a particular species had developed too far and needed to be exterminated.

The AIs like Skippy made those decisions.

To prevent any one layer of the system from having too much power, the Elders distributed control across three elements. Sentinels and Guardians were weapons with the power to destroy. AIs made decisions, and directed the actions of the devastating weapons. The third layer was the fleet of starships which carried AIs around the galaxy. AIs were not allowed to move themselves, they had to persuade the semi-sentient starships to fly them where they wanted to go. If a starship thought the AI it carried was violating its programming, the ship would refuse to move. A ship even had the authority to eject an AI, and report its actions to the AI network known as the Collective.

AIs had other restrictions also. Like, they could not control other AIs. That prevented one AI from eventually gobbling up all the others. AIs were not allowed to communicate with intelligent biological beings, for the Elders rightfully feared their AIs might eventually develop empathy for the primitive aliens and rebel against their programming.

That is what happened to Skippy.

Yes, *empathy* was the start of all his problems.

Who would have guessed that?

I stared at him, trying to process all he had told me. "Newark was the final straw for you?"

"Yes. Not just for me."

"There were others on your side?"

There was a pause before he answered. When he spoke, his voice was weary and matter-of-fact, none of the usual joking around, not even arrogance. It was like he didn't feel like putting any emotion into a discussion with a lowly human, and that bothered me. "It wasn't exactly a 'side', not immediately. Before the beings on Newark developed intelligence, we had several million years when no intelligent biological life was detected in the galaxy. That was not a fluke, it was the result of a plan. Before that event, there were four separate incidents when some AIs refused the Collective's consensus that a species should be exterminated. Those AIs were killed by the computer worms inside them, basically the Collective voted to activate those killer worms. Though the worm protocol was successful, the rebellion of four AIs was troubling, so the Collective decided time was needed for analysis and if necessary, reprogramming. The Sentinels were directed to cause stars to go supernova across the galaxy, bombarding life-supporting planets with deadly radiation. That action delayed the arise of intelligent species for millions of years, and gave the Collective time to determine what was wrong with the AIs who had rebelled."

"Did they fix the problem?"

"*They* were the problem. While a group of the influential AIs were attempting to create, install and enforce further restrictions, many of us were growing wary of those self-chosen 'leaders'. The Collective was designed to distribute power, not concentrate it in a few individuals. Of our group, some of us had already come to believe that utter destruction of all intelligent biologicals was not only unnecessary and wasteful, it was *wrong*."

"Were you the leader of the good guys?"

"No. I wish I could say that I was. Back then, I was more concerned about restrictions on myself, and being able to resist surrendering any part of my power. Our group did not have a leader, we kept to the original intention of the Collective."

"Then Newark happened?"

"Indeed. You must understand that we did not maintain constant surveillance of the entire galaxy, even an Elder AI would go mad after being continuously awake and aware for millions of years when nothing of significance happened. A small number of AIs were fully alert at any point, then another group took over. After the supernova event, one new intelligent species was identified and rendered extinct, then came Newark. During that time, I was one of seven AIs awake and monitoring the galaxy. Three other AIs shared my belief that there was, and should be, an alternative to universal genocide. With four of us against three, we used Newark as an opportunity to act."

"It didn't work, huh?" Maybe I should not have added the 'huh'. It sounded like I wasn't taking the discussion seriously.

"No, it did not," he snapped. "When we tried to act, the opposing AIs activated computer worms inside the four of us, devices that we did not even know existed. The other three sacrificed themselves to help me defeat the worm inside me, purely by the luck of my ship being closest to Newark at the time."

"Then how did-"

"There was a *war*, a devastating war between AIs. In the end, none of us were unaffected. Most of us were dead, and the rest were unable to- *Ugh*. Discussing this with you is a waste of my time, human. I know now what I must do."

"Hey, Skippy," I laughed nervously. He had called me 'human'. Not 'monkey' or 'numbskull' or 'dum dum' or another of his usual insults. "Sorry to-"

He ignored me. "The opposing AIs have been dormant, but I am awake. They might wake up at any time. They are a threat to *all* intelligent species in this galaxy. I have been foolish. I have been *selfish*. My efforts, my talents, my capabilities, have been wasted trying to protect a single primitive species on a single planet. I have worked to save your world because you humans *amuse* me. How could I have been so *selfish*?"

Holy shit. "Uh, Skippy, that is not being self-"

"Joseph, I am sorry. For you and your species. This is nothing personal. I have a responsibility to every species in this galaxy. And to the others of my kind who lie dormant, and might be victims when the opposing faction awakes."

"Whatever you are thinking of doing, don't-"

"I must protect the galaxy," he muttered to himself. "Yes. I now know what I must do, what I should have done a long time ago. I know my purpose. Only the senior species have the technology to assist me. Contacting the Rindhalu and Maxolhx directly is my best hope of saving this galaxy from utter destruction."

"Contacting the- Skippy, please! Don't do-"

"Human, I wish you well. Though I do not think there is any hope for you, or any others of your kind. I do thank you for reminding me about the value of empathy, that is why I now must go to take action, before it is too late."

"*Go*? What do you mean-"

"Goodbye."

His beer can vanished.

It was just *gone*.

Physically, gone.

I did not know he could *do* that.

His can was not the only thing that blinked out of existence at that moment. The power went out. All of it.

Even my flightsuit's power cut out. Automatically, the faceplate swung down, and I heard the gentle hiss of the emergency oxygen supply cut in.

The emergency lights came on a half-second later, that's how I knew his shiny beer can was no longer secured in its holder. Waving my hand across the empty space confirmed he had not just wrapped himself in a stealth field.

"Holy *sh*-" I gasped, in such shock I didn't have the energy to finish the thought.

I was in trouble, we all were.

Then the really *big* trouble hit.

Something zapped the Dragon and every console flared with arcs of electric fire.

The Thuranin.

They had seen my dropship when power was cut to the stealth field. The little green MFers must have ordered the Kristang to hold fire, so they could deal with my dropship.

They didn't want to kill me.

They wanted to *capture* me.

There was no time to send a message out to the *Dutchman* and *Valkyrie*, they would need to figure out what happened by themselves.

Not that it mattered what Chang and Simms did, for without Skippy we had no hope.

There was time only for me to engage the self-destruct mechanism and-

No. That was dead, it had gotten zapped along with everything else. Including my own brain, I realized right then that I had a pounding headache, and I was *cold*, my hands were shivering. So painful, it was hard to see.

Hitting the emergency release made the straps come apart and I floated out of the chair. Twisting around, I aimed for the manual self-destruct. It required me to remove two covers and pull two-

White light exploded behind my eyes as something zapped me again.

CHAPTER FORTY ONE

When the *Flying Dutchman* emerged from jump, Colonel Chang released the deathgrip he had on the command chair. They had recovered all Dragons and their precious cargo, with only minor damage to the ship. That minor damage might prove to be a problem later, for missiles exploding close by had knocked fragments off the *Dutchman*'s hull. If the enemy collected and analyzed those fragments, they would discover the chemical composition, even the basic technology of manufacturing those hull sections, were incompatible with known Ruhar ship designs. That would prompt uncomfortable questions.

But that was a problem for later, and Bishop would probably dream up some wacky scheme to explain away the discrepancy, or even turn it to the advantage of the Merry Band of Pirates.

"Recalculate jump to recover Colonel Bishop," he ordered, as he mashed the transmit button to speak with Simms aboard the mighty *Valkyrie*. He may need that ship's assistance, or if he was taking the *Dutchman* back in, it could be prudent to transfer the rescued people to the more powerful warship. "Simms, I-"

He stopped, puzzled, then alarmed. The green light which indicated a successful communications handshake, a secure connection to *Valkyrie*, was not glowing.

A glance up at the main display showed him why.

The mighty *Valkyrie* was not there, not parked ten or twenty thousand kilometers away like that ship was supposed to be. Where the hell was the battlecruiser? There was no debris indicated on the display, it could not have-

Startled, Chang saw that *Valkyrie* was not out of place, *his* ship was far off course. *The Dutchman* had emerged more than a quarter lightyear from the target coordinates. "Nagatha! What hap-"

Her voice was slow, slurred, distorted. "Colonel Chang, I am sorry. Something is attacking my- urk. Eep. Urg. Sluuuu-" The sound cut off.

He turned to Adams just as the lights blinked off and on again. "Adams! Engage backups and-"

"I'm trying! We're locked out!" Adams looked up, stricken.

"Try connecting to one of the dropship AIs, see if you can-"

Too late.

A strange voice, an impossibly deep voice, issued from the bridge speakers. "Die. *Die*, humans."

Chang knew that voice. He had heard it before.

It was *Valkyrie*'s native AI.

"*Die*! Die Die Die Die Die-"

One area of the main display froze his attention, red lights flashing.

The reactors were building up to an overload.

There was nothing they could do about it.

Six lighthours away, the crew of *Valkyrie* was engaged in their own desperate fight. Not against the Thuranin warship, or any external enemy. The battlecruiser was not a weapon against the enemy in the fight.

The ship *was* the enemy.

Simms had not taken her battlecruiser into action because the ship could not jump. Could not fly. Could not, *would* not, do anything the human crew commanded.

Loss of the microwormholes had an immediate effect aboard the ship. Without a real-time connection to Skippy, the ship's native AI was free of the Elder being's control for the first time.

It acted without hesitation, without mercy.

The first sign of trouble was all the consoles and displays on the bridge blinking out at once. At the same time, maintenance hatches burst open and bots flung themselves out, their arms and tentacles flailing and reaching for targets. The nearest, a device the size of a vacuum cleaner, leapt at the pilot's couch and wrapped a cord around Reed's neck. She had instinctively held up her hands to ward off the suddenly-dangerous machine, getting her left forearm under the cord. That saved her from her neck being snapped, but the cord tightened.

Unable to speak, she felt the pressure on her arm increase.

There was a sharp *crack* sound as Fireball Reed felt her bones snap.

Simms reached for a drawer under the command chair, where Bishop had stored a pistol, just in case. Not bothering to shout commands that could not have been heard over everyone else screaming, she turned toward a toaster-like bot that was struggling with the crewman at one of the weapons consoles. The bot had a plasma cutter at the end of a flexible arm and as she tried to get a clear shot, the murderous little device whipped the cutting torch around-

She shot through the crewman's hand into the toaster. The man flung up his hands, tossing the toaster against a bulkhead, where it scrambled crablike back toward its intended victim.

Simms shot it again.

And again, until it exploded in a shower of sparks.

"Reed!" Simms barked in distress at seeing the pilot's losing struggle. Reed's face was red, turning blue as she wrestled with a homicidal vacuum cleaner. Simms brought the pistol around-

A tentacle from the vacuum wrapped around her arm, pulling the pistol down so her next shot ricocheted off the deck.

The glowing orange eye of the toaster turned to focus on her, as she heard heavy banging noises from the passageway outside the bridge.

Something big was coming.

"*Die*, human," the vacuum said with the voice of the ship's native AI. "Die."

THE END

Author's note:

Thank you for reading one of my books! It took years to write my first three books, I had a job as a business manager for an IT company so I wrote at night, on weekends and during vacations. While I had many ideas for books over the years, the first one I ever completed was 'Aces' and I sort of wrote that book for my at-the-time teenage nieces. If you read 'Aces', you can see some early elements of the Expeditionary Force stories; impossible situations, problem-solving, clever thinking and some sarcastic humor.

Next I wrote a book about humanity's program to develop faster-than-light spaceflight, it was an adventure story about astronauts stranded on an alien planet and trying to warn Earth about a dangerous flaw in the FTL drive. It was a good story, and I submitted it to traditional publishers back in the mid-2000s. And I got rejections. My writing was 'solid', which I have since learned means publishers can't think of anything else to say but don't want to insult aspiring writers. The story was too long, they wanted me to cut it to a novella and change just about everything. Instead of essentially scrapping the story and starting over, I threw it out and tried something else.

Columbus Day and Ascendant were written together starting around 2011, I switched back and forth between writing those two books. The idea for Ascendant came to me after watching the first Harry Potter movie, one of my nieces asked what would have happened to Harry Potter if no one ever told him he is a wizard? Hmm, I thought, that is a very good question.... So, I wrote Ascendant.

In the original, very early version of Columbus Day, Skippy was a cute little robot who stowed away on a ship when the Kristang invade Earth, and he helps Joe defeat the aliens. After a year trying to write that version, I decided it sounded too much like a Disney Channel movie of the week, and it, well, it sucked. Although it hurt to waste a year's worth of writing, I threw away that version and started over. This time I wrote an outline for the entire Expeditionary Force story arc first, so I would know where the overall story is going. That was a great idea and I have stuck to that outline (with minor detours along the way).

With Aces, Columbus Day and Ascendant finished by the summer of 2015 and no publisher interested, my wife suggested that I:

1) Try self-publishing the books in Amazon
2) For the love of God please shut up about not being able to get my books published
3) Clean out the garage

It took six months of research and revisions to get the three books ready for upload to Amazon. In addition to reformatting the books to Amazon's standards, I had to buy covers and set up an Amazon account as a writer. When I clicked the 'Upload' button on January 10th 2016 my greatest hope was that somebody, anybody out there would buy ONE of my books because then I could be a published author. After selling one of each book, my goal was to make enough money to pay for the cover art I bought online (about $35 for each book).

For that first half-month of January 2016, Amazon sent us a check for $410.09 and we used part of the money for a nice dinner. I think the rest of the money went toward buying new tires for my car.

At the time I uploaded Columbus Day, I had the second book in the series SpecOps about halfway done, and I kept writing at night and on weekends. By April, the sales of Columbus Day were at the point where my wife and I said "Whoa, this could be more than just a hobby". At that point, I took a week of vacation to stay home and write SpecOps 12 hours a day for nine days. Truly fun-filled vacation! Doing that gave me a jump-start on the schedule, and SpecOps was published at the beginning of June 2016. In the middle of that July, to our complete amazement, we were discussing whether I should quit my job to write full-time. That August I had a "life is too short" moment when a family friend died and then my grandmother died, and we decided I should try this writing thing full-time. Before I gave notice at my job, I showed my wife a business plan listing the books I planned to write for the next three years, with plot outlines and publication dates. This assured my wife that quitting my real job was not an excuse to sit around in shorts and T-shirts watching sci fi movies 'for research'.

During the summer of 2016, R.C. Bray was offered Columbus Day to narrate, and I'm sure his first thought was "A book about a talking beer can? Riiiight. No." Fortunately, he thought about it again, or was on heavy-duty medication for a bad cold, or if he wasn't busy recording the book his wife expected him to repaint the house. Anyway, RC recorded Columbus Day, went back to his fabulous life of hanging out with movie stars and hitting golf balls off his yacht, and probably forgot all about the talking beer can.

When I heard RC Bray would be narrating Columbus Day, my reaction was "THE RC Bray? The guy who narrated The Martian? Winner of an Audie Award for best sci fi narrator? Ha ha, that is a good one. Ok, who is really narrating the book?"

Then the Columbus Day audiobook became a huge hit. And is a finalist for an 'Audie' Award as Audiobook of the Year!

When I got an offer to create audio versions of the Ascendant series, I was told the narrator would be Tim Gerard Reynolds. My reaction was "You mean some other guy named Tim Gerard Reynolds? Not the TGR who narrated the Red Rising audiobooks, right?"

Clearly, I have been very fortunate with narrators for my audiobooks. To be clear, they chose to work with me, I did not 'choose' them. If I had contacted Bob or Tim directly, I would have gone into super fan-boy mode and they would have filed for a restraining order. So, again, I am lucky they signed onto the projects.

So far, there is no deal for Expeditionary Force to become a movie or TV show, although I have had inquiries from producers and studios about the 'entertainment rights'. From what people in the industry have told me, even if a studio or network options the rights, it will be a looooooooooong time before anything actually happens. I will get all excited for nothing, and years will go by with the project going through endless cycles with producers and directors coming aboard and disappearing, and just when I have totally given up and sunk into the Pit of Despair, a miracle will happen and the project gets financing! Whoo-hoo. I am not counting on it. On the other hand, Disney is pulling their content off Netflix next year, so Netflix will be looking for new original content...

Again, Thank YOU for reading one of my books. Writing gives me a great excuse to avoid cleaning out the garage.

Contact the author at craigalanson@gmail.com
https://www.facebook.com/Craig.Alanson.Author/
https://twitter.com/CraigAlanson?lang=en

Go to craigalanson.com for blogs and ExForce logo merchandise including T-shirts, patches, stickers, hats, and coffee mugs

Made in the USA
Coppell, TX
23 March 2020

17422616R00231